THUNDEROUS APPLAUSE FOR
TO DIE IN BABYLON:

"The descriptions of flying and battles are engrossing
. . . Livingston has some interesting political insights
about Desert Storm."

—*Library Journal*

"Livingston moves his characters around with considerable skill . . . The depiction of war carries the sound
of real experience . . . The combat scenes have an
easy authority . . . Nobody will put the book away
half-read."

—*Air & Space*

"Vivid descriptions of the sound of war."

—*Orlando Sentinel*

"The author's technical know-how and ability to weave
a pattern combining all the elements needed for sus-
pense make this good reading . . . Recommended."

—*Association of Jewish Libraries Newsletter*

"Dramatic . . . There's action to spare here."

—*Anniston Star*

"A cut above the usual military thriller . . . Livingston
has taken the time to sort out the politics, giving proper
weight to the large, problematic role of television in this
odd war, and his characters are fleshed out far more
completely than fans of the genre have come to expect.
Well done."

—*Kirkus Reviews*

BOOKS BY HAROLD LIVINGSTON

THE COASTS OF THE EARTH
THE DETROITERS
THE CLIMACTICON
RIDE A TIGER
TOUCH THE SKY
TO DIE IN BABYLON

TO DIE IN BABYLON

HAROLD LIVINGSTON

ST. MARTIN'S PAPERBACKS

TO DIE IN BABYLON

Copyright © 1995 by Harold Livingston.

Library of Congress Catalog Card Number: 93-24165

ISBN: 0-312-95315-1

Printed in the United States of America

St. Martin's Press hardcover edition / October 1993
St. Martin's Paperbacks edition / June 1995

10 9 8 7 6 5 4 3 2 1

To the memory of our daughter,
Myra, who taught us
the real meaning of class and style

Who carried the great war from Macedon
Into the Soudan's realm, and thunder'd on
To die at thirty-five in Babylon.

MATTHEW ARNOLD

PART ONE
SHIELD

ONE

The second rocket-propelled grenade, which followed the first by no more than three seconds, landed in the road. The concussion blew him into a runoff ditch at the roadside, where he lay on his back in stagnant water, wondering why he felt no pain from the shard of metal that had torn into his leg. He had actually heard the bone snap.

A moment before, just as he downshifted to ease the jeep up the gentle incline, he had heard the all-too-familiar cork-popping sound of an RPG being fired. Without an instant's hesitation, or thought, he had literally dived out of the moving vehicle. He hit the ground on all fours, scrambled to his feet, and began running. He did not know where he was going, only that he had to get away. He had to save his life. But even then, even through the fog of black fear, he knew he had panicked. He had run away.

That first round impacted squarely on the jeep's hood. Driverless on the incline, the jeep had rolled backward directly into the grenade's downward trajectory. A five-gallon jerrican of gasoline strapped to the front bumper exploded in a burst of red and orange flame. Like a clap of thunder, the main fuel tank exploded. Bits and pieces of the jeep and of the two marines seated in it were hurled into the air and across the road into the village. Metallic fragments sliced through the village's bamboo-walled huts and hurtled on into the jungle, severing the limbs of trees. The shredded rem-

nants of the two marines fell with less ferocity, although
one large chunk of a man's torso thudded into a tree
trunk in a splash of red blood and pink body tissue.

Now, on his back in the ditch, Nicholas Harmon
opened his mouth to scream, but no sound came. He
tried to throw his arms protectively over his eyes, but his
muscles would not obey his brain. He thought about
praying to God, but since he had always, proudly,
claimed not to believe in God, he knew he did not have
the right to pray to God. He deserved no mercy. God, if
God existed, would not look kindly upon cowards.

He heard the muffled roar of the incoming RPG and
saw it arcing in over the trees behind the village. He
wanted to turn and burrow facedown into the mud of
the ditch but his arms still refused to move. He gazed at
the plume of black smoke from the wrecked jeep and
the red and gray stains on the tree trunk. The grenade
impacted with a thunderous explosion. Immediately, another round was launched. He waited for the detonation.

He heard it and, simultaneously, people screaming.
Children and women. He wondered why he could not
hear Lieutenant Burger's quiet, calm voice, or the sand-
paper-hoarse voice of the grizzled old master gunnery
sergeant, Bill Hardwick. They had been in the jeep with
him.

"Harmon . . . !"

The voice was not Lieutenant Burger's or Bill Hardwick's but was vaguely familiar. Nick waited for the next
explosion and this time found the strength to turn over
on his stomach. He buried his face deep into the wet
ditch. The foul, fetid stench of the water made him gag
and gasp for air. He wondered why he could not feel the
weight of his helmet on his head or the cool metal
grooves of his M-16 magazine. But he knew why: The
helmet and rifle were in the jeep, where he had left
them. No, not left, *abandoned.* If he had remained at
the wheel of the Jeep and continued driving, even only
another few yards, the grenade would have landed behind them. If he had not panicked.

"Harmon . . . !"

They had assigned a patrol to reconnoiter the village of Chu-Bai to investigate reports of VC activity. "They" being Captain Moorehead—Roland A. Moorehead, USMCR—the new company C.O. Both Burger and Hardwick tried to explain to the captain that you simply did not go barreling into villages in this sector. You also, responded the captain, who had been in country less than three days and not yet heard a shot fired in anger, do not question a superior officer's orders. And, speaking, he noticed Nick, just then emerging from the latrine tent.

"Hey, you," he had called out.

"Me, sir?"

"Yes, Marine, you," said the captain, and ordered Nick to drive the jeep.

"Harmon, goddamn you . . . !"

Nick dug his fingers into the mud as another round struck, and then another. His face was soaking wet. His whole body was wet. He rolled over on his back again and stared up at the sky. It was very white, cloudless, and hurt his eyes.

It was not the sky. It was the white plastered ceiling of his hotel room. The whummp-whummp-whummp of the incoming grenades was the sound of someone banging on the door.

"For Christ's sake, Colonel Harmon, open the door!"

Nick lay motionless another instant as the dream slowly fragmented. The dream that really happened and that for twenty-two years had lingered on the fringes of his memory, recurring now and then, always with the same frightening vividness. He rolled off the bed now, rose, and walked to the door. The anxiety of a few seconds ago—of twenty-two years ago—dissipated in the relief of reality.

The glare of the late morning sun on the hotel's snow-blanketed lawn streamed into the room, burning the postcardlike view of the Virginia countryside into Nick's vision. He was momentarily startled. He had expected to hear the shriek of jet engines from the F-16s constantly taking off and landing, and to see the gold dome of a minaret looming up behind the corrugated iron roof of the big 358th Tactical Fighter Wing maintenance hangar. Every morning, for the past three months, when he awakened to the sound of the jets, the minaret tower was the first thing he saw. From his room in the BOQ at Al Kalir.

But this was not Saudi Arabia, this was Washington, D.C. More accurately, Crystal City, just inside the Virginia state line, near the Pentagon. Nick had arrived a day and a half ago and was still in jet lag. He glanced at the neatly folded newspaper on the glass-topped dresser. Yesterday's *Washington Post,* delivered by the room-service waiter last night along with the champagne. Nick studied the date: Monday, December 4, 1990. It was as though he needed to assure himself he was really here, and not in Vietnam in the dream, and not at Al Kalir.

For a moment now he regarded himself in the dresser mirror, his sleep-rumpled thick black hair, his sweat-stained pajama top. Yeah, he told himself, you're beginning to look your age, fella, thirty-nine. But what the hell was so old about thirty-nine? He remembered that at thirty-nine his father had seemed very old. But then, at fifteen, thirty-nine would seem old.

"Harmon . . . !" the indignant voice outside shouted once again.

"Okay, I'm coming," Nick said, and smiled to himself, reaching down to feel his pajama trousers, wondering when he had put them on. He knew he had not been wearing them the last time he said, "I'm coming"—earlier that morning, and uttered under far more pleasurable circumstances. He opened the door.

"You look like shit," Frank Kowalski said. He was a short man, some four inches shorter than Nick, and at least four years younger, although his rapidly receding hairline made him look older, which did not displease Nick.

"You're not looking so bad yourself," Nick said.

Kowalski's nose wrinkled in distaste. "You stink," he

said, and pushed past Nick into the room. "The whole place stinks. Jesus, get some fresh air in here!" He flung open the window. Backing away, he nearly tripped over an empty champagne bottle. He picked up the bottle and examined the label. It was Schramsberg, bred and bottled in the state of California, no competition for Dom Perignon but an acceptable enough wine. "What were you celebrating?"

Nick did not particularly like Frank Kowalski, who supposedly was a Defense Department deputy something-or-other, but who Nick suspected was probably either CIA or NSA. Two days ago, when the MAC C-141 that brought Nick in from Dhahran landed at Andrews, Kowalski was waiting in the terminal, displaying a cardboard sign with the sloppily printed letters COL. N. HARMON.

Condescension had been written all over Kowalski's clean-shaven, rosy-cheeked face; as though by deigning to personally welcome a lowly light colonel he had embarked upon a mission above and beyond the call of duty. Nick immediately recognized him as a Feather Merchant, a civilian with big juice in the military.

Kowalski's words of greeting were, "You're the same Harmon who shot his mouth off about Panama, aren't you?"

"Yeah, I'm the same Harmon who shot his mouth off about Panama," Nick had replied. "I thought I was brought back here to talk about MiGs?"

"The MiG incident is how we refer to it."

"The MiG incident," Nick had repeated. "Guilty, your honor. Okay, so what do you want to know about it?"

But Kowalski said Nick looked too tired for any debriefing or even casual discussion about MiGs. He had driven Nick directly to the Stouffer Hotel in Crystal City, told him to take a day off, sleep, and they'd get together tomorrow. Now Kowalski tossed the empty champagne bottle onto the sofa and said again, "So what were you celebrating?"

"Thanksgiving," Nick said.

"You're a week late."

"Christmas, then." Nick closed the door and padded back to the bed. "I'm a month early."

"How hung over are you?"

"I'll know after I have some coffee," Nick said. He sat on the edge of the bed, groping for the cigarettes on the night table. There were none. He had quit two months, three weeks, and three days ago, one week after arriving in Saudi Arabia. God, but he'd love one now, that first of the day; he could actually feel the smoke roll around deep down inside his chest and the tangy dry flavor of tobacco in his mouth.

"Get dressed," Kowalski said. He picked Nick's rumpled uniform blouse from the back of a chair. He held the blouse up before him a moment, then smoothed it out, running his hands over the silver oak leaves on the epaulets, and the command pilot's wings above the left breast pocket, and the four rows of service ribbons. He folded the blouse neatly, placed it on the bed, and started to sit in the chair. A pair of black silk panties that had been draped over the armrest of the chair fell to the floor. Kowalski picked them up and flipped them to Nick. "In a high-G turn, Colonel Harmon, this underwear must chafe the hell out of you."

"Fuck you, *Mister* Kowalski." Nick fell back against the pillow and crumpled the panties in his hand. He resisted an impulse to rub the soft smooth fabric against his face and inhale the owner's fragrance. She had left the panties as a souvenir, a reminder. Millie, that was her name. A petite little redhead, a Pentagon civilian secretary with a pair of breasts like firm little grapefruit.

Kowalski craned his neck to see into the bathroom. Nick said, "I'm alone." He glanced at his wrist, but his watch was not there. He had removed it and not bothered to put it back on, hours ago, when he joined Millie in the shower. It was on the night table. It seemed too much of an effort to reach for the watch. "What time is it?" he asked.

"Quarter after ten," Kowalski said. "Now get

dressed." He nodded at the wrinkled uniform blouse on the bed. "That the only suit you have?"

"Where are we going?"

"The Pentagon. General Gordon wants to see you."

"I promised Johnny Donovan I'd have lunch with him," Nick said.

"I know. I told him you couldn't make it."

You know, Nick repeated to himself, thinking that it would not surprise him at all if Kowalski knew that Donovan had arranged Nick's seance of the previous evening with the redhead of the grapefruit breasts. Donovan—Lieutenant Colonel Donovan, an Academy classmate of Nick's, now flying a Pentagon desk—said he felt obligated to do something to relieve Nick's jet lag. Therapy, said Johnny, good old-fashioned Therapy.

Nor would it surprise Nick if Kowalski also knew that Nick had won some money playing gin rummy with the two-star who had boarded the MAC C-141 when it stopped for refueling at Frankfurt. The two-star's name was George Koffler, and he was an embarrassingly bad gin player. Even at the friendly stakes of a penny a point, Koffler lost $105 to Nick. As the general agreed, no easy task: You almost had to cheat to lose that much in so modest a game. General Koffler, whose military career stretched back to the Cuban missile crisis, was retiring this year and glad of it. He was a logistician. The problems of transporting an army of some five hundred thousand to the Persian Gulf, and then supplying and maintaining that army had driven him nearly mad. It had started as an interesting challenge but turned into a nightmare—no, a quagmire. Between the theocratic bureaucracy of Saudi Arabia and the ego-fed ambitions of people in the Pentagon, it was like trying to walk in molasses. Nick wasn't so sure that after his visit to the Pentagon he, too, might not look forward to retirement.

But General Koffler's $105 enabled Nick to splurge. He invested $44 of the winnings in awesome New York steaks for himself and the therapeutic redhead. Another $40 went for an excellent Australian Pinot Noir, and the remainder on the domestic champagne.

Sure, Kowalski probably knew about that. Kowalski knew everything. About everybody. And probably about Chu-Bai, too, and that Nick won his Purple Heart lying in a muddy, stinking ditch, trembling with such fear that he had not even been sure which leg was broken.

Nick said, "I have a feeling, Mr. Kowalski, that I am now about to find out what 'when the shit hits the fan' really means."

"I think, Colonel, that you're right," Kowalski said. "Now get dressed. Please. And shave," he added.

2

The bow tie Larry Hill wore today was a black and white polka-dot. All Larry's ties were custom-made, not from choice but because most men's stores no longer carried bow ties. Ronald Reagan had once remarked that Larry Hill and U.S. Senator Paul Simon were the last two men in America who wore bow ties. Proving, said Larry, that the former president was sometimes actually aware of his surroundings.

At sixty-nine, slim and trim, with his full head of only now graying hair, Larry Hill looked and felt twenty years younger. This, despite his hobby, food. He enjoyed referring to himself as Washington, D.C.'s finest amateur chef. Food was more than a hobby, it was closer to an obsession. Indeed, his obsession with food was surpassed only by his obsession with the company he had founded and still supervised, World Cablenews Network, WCN.

Although preferring dinner to lunch, today he had personally planned and cooked lunch in the kitchen of the executive dining room, which was in the penthouse of the seven-story WCN building on Connecticut Avenue. Lunch, today, for a special reason. For two special people, to be more accurate.

He had prepared what he called *Pasta Laurens*, one of his specialties: capellini, tossed with sautéed onions and garlic, chopped bacon, olive oil, and small pieces of broiled turkey breast. He was experimenting today by adding a simple tomato and basil sauce. With a Ruffino Chianti Classico, '87, it was a resounding success. Both of his guests devoured their portions and did not refuse smaller, second helpings.

In deference to one of the guests, the conversation pointedly avoided Iraq and dwelt instead on the only other significant news items of the day: junk bond entrepreneur Michael Milken's ten-year prison sentence and Margaret Thatcher's resignation as prime minister of Great Britain.

At Larry Hill's table, however—if Christine Campbell were present—sometime during dessert or coffee, Larry was sure to entertain his guests with the story of how he and Chris first met.

Today, Larry told the story over coffee. Christine, as usual, sat on his left, and, as usual, at her request, he did not light his usual after-lunch cigar.

". . . well, there she was, this long-legged, gawky, well-scrubbed kid just out of Vassar," Larry said with a pleased smile at Chris, who smiled back accommodatingly. There wasn't a shred of truth to the story. He persisted in telling it—with endless embellishments—because he knew that it enhanced her image as a television personality. It also helped him validate his own relationship with her.

Larry measured a half teaspoon of sugar into his cup, stirred it, tasted it, and continued, "I walked past her into my office, and I hear her—this child whose family owns half of San Francisco and goes all the way back to the Mayflower, and maybe even before—I hear her saying to the receptionist, 'Listen, you little snot, I don't care if it takes a month. I'm sitting right here until I can talk to that arrogant son of a bitch!' "

He smiled at Chris again. This was only the second time he had seen her since her return two weeks ago from a four-month overseas assignment. She wore a different perfume, strong yet subtle, wafting up to him from the open collar of her white, pleated shirt. He could never quite decide if he liked her best in street

clothes—those impeccably tailored suits she favored—
or in an evening gown.

Of course, he would prefer her in a negligee. A black
negligee to contrast with her blond hair, which would be
taken down and flowing over her shoulders. Yes, definitely, and he sat silently a moment, enjoying the reverie
and at the same time realizing that he lusted after a
woman some forty years his junior. In truth, for all the
lust he felt, what he wanted from her was lovemaking.
Good old-fashioned fucking. No frills. That idea excited
him more than a dozen kinky fantasies.

He felt himself actually hardening. Yes, well that was
no special problem, getting it up. Keeping it up, sus-
taining the erection, was the problem. Lusting in my
heart, he thought, an expression borrowed from Jimmy
Carter—just about the only idea of the former president's that Larry deemed worthy of even a vague acknowledgment. He glanced to his right at his other
guest and went on with the story of his first meeting with
Chris Campbell.

". . . so I did an about-face and said to this big-
mouthed kid, 'I'm Larry Hill, and I don't like people
who abuse my associates, nor do I particularly appreciate being called a son of a bitch. Especially an arrogant
one!'" He paused to once again smile at Chris, and she
once again returned the smile.

Larry went on, "She says, '*I* don't like people who are
too egocentric to know when they're being done a
favor!' 'What the hell kind of favor are you doing me?' I
asked. 'Offering you the chance of a lifetime,' she says.
'And what's that?' I asked. 'To hire me,' she says." Larry
shook his head nostalgically. "That was seven and a half
years ago." He swallowed down half the coffee, then
leaned over and kissed Chris on the cheek, and said,
"And the rest is history."

"Ancient history, Larry," Chris said, thinking that by
now she nearly believed the story herself. She had been
a WCN mailroom messenger for six months before she
ever saw Larry Hill. She delivered a package to his
home one evening. His wife was away in Europe. Al-

though often tempted, he never violated his own strict policy of not spitting where you eat. But not in years had a woman excited him as much as this tall blonde full-breasted, full-bodied, twenty-one-year-old.

She turned him down. She was too clever. She, who at age fourteen had lost her virginity on the cold linoleum floor of the kitchen in her uncle's Detroit apartment, did not believe that the bedroom door opened all other doors. Moreover, she planned to be a star reporter, not the guest of honor at the boss's invitation-only matinees. Besides, Larry Hill reminded her too much of the uncle.

She got what she wanted. It took most of those seven and one-half years—the nights of four of these spent obtaining a master's in journalism from American University—a lot of hard work, and considerable luck. Luck meaning being in the right place at the right time—in Chris's case, meaning August 2, in Kuwait City. She just happened to be there that day wrapping up a week-long series on the oil-rich little nation, and artfully dodging the horny advances of one of the Emir's Harvard-educated nephews.

Christine was spared the trouble of further dodging. By the afternoon of August 3, the flag atop the Emir's palace had been replaced by the red, white, and black flag of Iraq, and the horny nephew was in a penthouse suite at a resort hotel in Saudi Arabia, calming his nerves in the gold-fauceted Jacuzzi of the marbled bathroom.

With the help of Entessar al-Azimi, a Kuwaiti woman who free-lanced as a WCN film editor, Chris managed to smuggle out three reels of videotape. WCN broadcast them the very same day. The images of Iraqi tanks rumbling along the wide, tree-lined boulevards of Kuwait City were seen throughout the world.

Over the next three months, on WCN's nightly special, "Gulf Watch," the cool, calm, smoky-hoarse voice of Christine Campbell became as familiar to American television viewers as Walter Cronkite's once was. ". . . this is Chris Campbell in Amman." In Riyadh. In Tel Aviv. In Cairo. And soon, hopefully, in Baghdad.

"Talk about history," Larry Hill was saying now, "our little Christine is about to rewrite it." He was addressing his other guest, a man whose age Chris Campbell had correctly guessed to be between thirty-five and thirty-eight. "When she gets to Baghdad, there won't be a Nielsen or Arbitron meter high enough to register WCN's ratings!"

"I'm sure," said the young man, who sounded like an Englishman and whose Savile Row clothes gave him the appearance of an Englishman, but who was the farthest thing from an Englishman. His name was Adnan Dulaimi. He was a thirty-six-year-old Iraqi diplomat, Oxford educated, with important connections in the Baath Party and reputedly to Saddam Hussein himself. He had been in Washington more than a year, serving as a special assistant to the Iraqi ambassador. He was also an army officer, a major, and a decorated hero of the Iran-Iraq war. Now, with the UN ultimatum demanding an Iraqi withdrawal from Kuwait no later than January 15, he had been recalled to duty. He would be returning home at the end of the week.

Larry Hill had a special purpose in inviting Adnan Dulaimi to this luncheon, and in having him meet Chris Campbell. Of course, almost everything Larry did was for a special purpose. This time, very special.

"Yes, sir," Larry said. "WCN will be the envy of the journalistic world when Chris Campbell begins reporting from Baghdad."

Which might be sooner than anyone expects, Chris thought. The Pentagon was stonewalling the reissue of her press credentials. She wanted to stop off in Saudi Arabia en route to Iraq; she planned to do a feature on the U.S. Army's "women warriors." Well, if DOD didn't come through within two weeks, she'd go on to Iraq and to hell with the U.S. Army. So she'd skip Saudi Arabia. Enough journalists were there, anyway. The beat was in Baghdad. The Iraqis had certainly wasted no time issuing her an entry visa. The Baghdad Beat, she thought. Not a bad title for the show.

What was it a caller on the Larry King show had labeled her? Oh, yes, the Jane Fonda of Desert Shield. All this because she had the honesty to say that she considered the idea of going to war over Kuwait obscene.

A four-letter word, she had said. Oil.

Oil is a three-letter word, Larry King had said.

Not if they're shooting at you over it, Chris had replied. It was this comment that bent some Pentagon noses out of shape.

She knew Larry Hill was talking to her—something about him taking the matter of her press credentials straight to the White House if he had to—but she was watching Adnan Dulaimi and thinking he looked more like Robert Redford than the Sheik of Araby. Their eyes met and, for an intense moment, held. She felt herself redden.

She hardly realized that, as per plan, Larry had excused himself to make a telephone call. After lunch, as per plan, Larry would leave Chris alone with Adnan. "He's on Saddam's good-guy list, he can set up the interview," Larry had said. "And while you're at it, ask him what he thinks about the hostages."

"He'll say they're guests, not hostages," Chris had replied.

Larry's white-streaked, bushy brown eyebrows had risen in an inverted V. "I thought you didn't disapprove of Saddam holding all those people against their will?"

"I said I understood why he was doing it. We've pushed him into a corner. I did not say I approved. You didn't listen carefully to my last broadcast, Larry."

"I was too busy admiring you."

Now, alone with the Iraqi, as per plan, Chris suddenly wondered if he were married. She decided to find out. "Tell me, Major Dulaimi, how does your wife feel about your being here, among the 'enemy,' so to speak?"

"She never mentioned it," he said.

"Oh, I see—"

"—because I have no wife. Not yet."

Chris wondered what "not yet" meant, if anything, and said, "What do you think about President Bush traveling to Syria to meet with Hafez al-Assad?"

"What I think about it, Miss Campbell, is that you
don't give a damn about it." But he said it good-naturedly, almost as though amused. "What you want to
know is how fast can I arrange an interview with Saddam Hussein."

Chris felt herself redden again, this time in anger.
Larry, she thought. The bastard had "neglected" to tell
her that he'd already approached this supposedly influential Iraqi about the interview. Larry enjoyed little
tricks like that.

"How fast *can* you do it?" she asked. To hell with the
niceties.

"It all depends on how interested he is."

"It's important that Americans see and hear Iraq's
point of view," Chris said.

As she spoke, she was thinking, I wonder how they
say "bullshit" in Arabic, because that was the message
in his eyes. And they were large, clear, blue eyes. How
on earth did he get blue eyes? she wondered.

". . . seriously doubt that Americans care, one way
or the other, about Iraq's point of view," he was saying.
"From what I read and have seen—"

"—on WCN, naturally."

The hint of a smile appeared, not on his lips but in his
eyes. Those intriguing blue eyes. "As a matter of fact,
yes, on WCN. But the message I get is that your country
is convinced of Iraq's evil intent. And nothing will
change that impression."

"Not when your ambassador insists that the sole purpose of invading Kuwait was to call attention to the
Palestinian cause," Chris said. "And when Saddam Hussein says that Americans will soon be swimming in their
own blood."

Adnan's face tightened. "Look, Miss Campbell—"

"—Chris."

The tight face betrayed the hint of another smile.
"Chris," he said. "Statements such as that are not rhetoric. He means every word. But to answer your first
question: I believe Mr. Bush's visit to Syria is simply
designed to annoy us. Bush is determined to attack. No

matter what we do, he'll send his planes and tanks into Kuwait."

"Not if you withdraw," Chris said.

Now Adnan did smile, a cold, cynical little smile. "The Americans know we can't do that. Not now. You have made it impossible for us to do it with even a modicum of honor."

"May I quote you on that?"

"I would prefer you didn't. Your face is quite familiar in my country. I think everyone with a television set watches the WCN news. I know that the President does."

"I'm flattered," she said. "I can't wait to meet him."

"I'll keep that in mind," Adnan said.

"Yes, Major, please do."

Chris accompanied Adnan to the lobby. She wished him a pleasant trip back home, said she looked forward to seeing him again in Baghdad, then rode the elevator to her fifth-floor office. It was a corner office, very light and airy, furnished in classic WCN fashion: functional. Which meant a metal desk to support the computer and monitor, a few Dansk chairs, a sofa, a built-in bookcase, and a file cabinet.

The red message light on her telephone was blinking. She sat at the desk and punched in her code number, 425. Larry Hill's recorded voice boomed into her ear. "Chris, honey," he said in his carefully practiced southern drawl. "Come see me before you leave. Important."

She hung up and swiveled her chair around to the window. It had begun snowing. Low-hanging dark clouds obscured the top of the Washington Monument. Weather, she thought, that did not match her mood: She felt marvelous, triumphant. She was certain that the handsome Iraqi would arrange the interview with Saddam Hussein. She felt her stomach flutter as she recalled that moment when they had gazed into each other's eyes.

She got up, gathered her coat and purse from the couch, and strode down the hall to Larry Hill's outer office. It was a suite all unto itself. A huge bronze reproduction of WCN's logo hung pretentiously above the glass-doored entrance: **W C N,** in letters composed of lightning bolts, superimposed over a three-dimensional mercator projection of a world globe. A phalanx of three secretaries occupied desks in the foyer. Larry's private secretary or, as she liked to be called, Executive Assistant, was stationed near the door of his office.

The Executive Assistant, a frowzy lady named Mae, who had been with Larry since Day One, looked up at Chris and said, "Let me buzz him, Chris."

"Don't bother," Chris said. She reached behind Mae's desk and pressed the button that unlocked the big wood-paneled double doors. She entered Larry's office and closed the doors behind her.

Someone once claimed that Larry Hill had modeled his office after Adolf Hitler's cathedrallike quarters in the Reich Chancellery. Larry's was probably bigger and probably as Spartan. No bookshelves. One entire wall contained television monitors. Another wall, behind the enormous horseshoe desk, consisted almost entirely of a window that overlooked downtown Washington. The other two walls, oak-paneled, were barren but for a single framed photograph of WCN's original headquarters, a storefront on K Street near Union Station. The room exuded a certain cold, indifferent competency, a perfect reflection of Larry himself: all business.

Lawrence Grantland Hill had not exactly worked his way up from poverty. In 1942, at age twenty-one, he came into sole possession of the $2,500,000 trust left him by his father, a North Carolina tobacco farmer. In 1947, at age twenty-six, he was flat broke, no simple task when you consider that he did not touch a dime of the money during his two years as an enlisted man in the U.S. Army, 1943 to 1945, working as a reporter on *Stars & Stripes,* stationed first in London and then in Paris.

In 1945, out of the army only a month, he used the $2,500,000 to bankroll a new Minneapolis newspaper, the *Twin Cities World.* Larry Hill had some unique ideas about journalism and news gathering. These ideas included purchasing only the most talented personnel, hence the most expensive. Not to mention establishing bureaus in major U.S. cities, and in Europe as well. The final edition of the *World*, actually a first-class newspaper, was published on Christmas Day, 1949.

In 1950, in Boston, with $50,000 lent him by the forty-eight-year-old widow of a Massachusetts shoe manufacturer with whom he was having an affair, he started a syndicated television news service. ANN, American News Network, a creative and innovative idea, but far ahead of its time: There simply were not enough independent stations—or, for that matter, enough homes with television—to support the service. By 1955, Larry Hill was broke again and, when the widow of the Massachusetts shoe manufacturer discovered him sleeping with her maid, homeless.

It took him twenty years, four different television station jobs, and two marriages and five children, to accumulate sufficient financing for another try at his own business. WCN, World Cablenews Network, came into existence in 1975 in the K Street storefront office. No one at first took the upstart little news service seriously, let alone bought enough advertising to keep it on the air. They took it seriously now.

Now WCN's slogan, "The Sun Never Sets on a WCN Bureau," was a geographical fact, along with billings that would exceed $1 billion this year. B, as in Billion.

Larry, blue-penciling an editorial for the six o'clock news hour, did not glance up at Chris but knew she was there. She sank into a deep leather armchair on the other side of Larry's desk. "Larry . . . ," she said impatiently.

He continued working another few moments, then put the editorial aside and faced her. She sat with her coat folded neatly over her lap. "Damn, I sure like that old coat," he said. It was a camel's hair polo coat, silk-lined and comforter-warm, a gift from Larry two years before. They were in New York, strolling along Madison Avenue, passing Brooks Brothers. Chris had stopped to

admire the coat in the window. Larry said she belonged
in mink. She said she would never wear a coat made of
animals' fur. You'll kill for a story, Larry said, but you
won't wear a fur coat. The next morning the polo coat
was delivered to her hotel.

"How'd you make out with our Iraqi friend?" Larry
continued now.

Chris momentarily considered giving him hell for not
telling her that he'd already spoken to Adnan Dulaimi
about the interview. But she knew Larry. This was what
he wanted, a reaction, preferably an angry one. She
wasn't about to give him the satisfaction.

"I think he's very handsome," she said. "Very sexy."

"He'll swing that interview."

"I'm sure he will," she said. "Was that what you
wanted to see me about?"

Larry pulled a white copy sheet from under a stack of
other papers. "This came in from Tom Layton an hour
ago." Tom Layton was WCN's Baghdad bureau chief.
Larry handed Chris the paper.

WCN INTERCOM
Usually authoritative sources here confirm rumors
of American/Iraqi dogfight over Kuwait. Our
sources here and Riyadh say Iraqi MiG downed by
USAF pilot, N. Harmon—H A R M O N—at
present in U.S. on top secret mission.

"*My* sources say this N. Harmon is the same N. Harmon who nearly got himself cashiered from the air force
for publicly criticizing Mr. Bush's Panamanian caper.
My sources also say that N. Harmon happens to be right
here in town." Larry pointed a pencil at Chris. "Now
suppose you mosey on across the river and talk to your
friend, that colonel in the PIO office. What's his
name . . . ?"

"Donovan," Chris said.

"Go see if you can track down this guy Harmon.
Maybe he'll go on the air with you."

"That's a great idea, Larry. We can build a whole

show around him." Chris flattened the WCN intercom message on the desk in front of her. "He'll thrill the audience with the story of how he shot the enemy out of the sky."

Larry shook his head apologetically. "I'm sorry, Chris. I forgot about your father."

"Forget it," she said. "I'll go and find your"—she glanced at the message—"N. Harmon." She turned and strode from the office. She closed the door quietly behind her.

Larry felt foolish. Chris's father, a navy fighter pilot, had been shot down over Hanoi in 1968. Chris was seven at the time. The Secretary of the Navy sent her mother his gold wings and a folded American flag. The mother gave the wings to Chris, who had them mounted on black velvet and framed.

Larry Hill's moment of remorse lasted only that long. He smiled elatedly. He was envisioning the promos for Christine Campbell's exclusive interview with Saddam Hussein. They would run every half hour, a fifteen-second bite—a montage of some of Chris's previous celebrity interviews—for an entire week before the event. The ratings would go through the roof.

3

The shit that had hit the fan—in less vernacular terms, the MiG incident—had hit it five days before, seven thousand miles from Washington, D.C., at 22,000 feet, on a heading of 352, ten miles southwest of the Kuwaiti border, during what had started out as a routine two-ship BARCAP, barrier combat air patrol. Cruising at a fuel-efficient 250 knots, listening to the hum of the engine and quiet hiss of the air conditioner, Nick Harmon had been thinking that flying this F-16C Fighting Falcon was like directing a great symphony orchestra.

Even after more than 1,600 hours in the F-16, the airplane still awed him. The F-16—the Electric Jet—could, would, and did anything you asked. She carried nearly the same ordnance load as an F-4, but with twice the maneuverability and twice the range. You sat comfortably, tilted back at a 30-degree angle in a cockpit that gave you 360-degree visibility, your right hand wrapped around the side stick control, left hand resting on the throttle quadrant. The ancillary buttons studding the handles of both sticks gave you fingertip control of every combat function from communications to weapons release. At eye level, projected onto the windscreen, the HUD—heads up display—presented a constant stream of real-time operational information: anything and everything you needed to know, from airspeed and altitude to the position of approaching enemy aircraft.

Below and ahead, the desert stretched endlessly. To the right, sparkling in the sun, were the clean blue waters of the Persian Gulf. The highway paralleling the Kuwaiti border resembled a thin pencil line on a map. Down there, snugly dug in under their sand berms, were the T-72 and T-62 tanks of the Republican Guard. Nick had no doubt that those men, the "enemy," shared the Americans' impatience for the war to get started and over with. It was the natural way of things.

His earphones suddenly crackled with the hollow rush of an activated transmitter. "Lead, Two: Do you see it down there?" It was Stovepipe Two, Nick's young wingman, First Lieutenant Ralph Keyes, 5,000 feet above and a mile behind, flying a "Loose Deuce" combat spread formation off Nick's left wing. "On the road, left of the wadi at three o'clock low," Keyes continued. "Looks like tanks."

It was not the first time that Keyes's remarkable 20/10 eyesight spotted something Nick had missed. Sure enough, below, snaking slightly to the right of the seeker head of the Sidewinder missile extending out from Nick's right wingtip, a trail of brown dust churned along the highway. Too fast for tanks. A convoy of trucks and smaller vehicles. "Negative on the tanks, Two," Nick said into the microphone. "Supply stuff, probably."

"Rog, Lead," Keyes replied, his voice in Nick's earphones immediately drowned out by another: "Stovepipe Lead, Sentry Zero-three." Sentry was the call sign for the AWACS E-3A electronics surveillance aircraft controlling the sector. Sentry went on, "Multiple bandits out of Delta Two, your zero two zero, one eight nautical miles, angels seven, climbing, heading one niner zero—"

"Jesus!" Ralph Keyes's voice blotted out Sentry. "I have contact, zero seven at eighteen nautical!"

"Tone it down, Two!" Nick said, managing to filter out the remainder of Sentry's message: Four Iraqi aircraft had taken off from their base at Jalibah in southern Iraq. The bandits were headed south, toward Saudi Arabia.

"Copy you, Sentry," Nick replied, and called to Keyes, "Stovepipe Two, right thirty! Push it up!"

Even as he spoke, Nick was rolling his F-16 thirty degrees right, heading directly into the Iraqis, placing the MiGs well within the head-on kill capabilities of his two AIM-9L Sidewinder missiles. He dropped the nose, increased his airspeed to 480 knots, and leveled out at 17,000 feet.

"They're closing on us!" Keyes said, nearly blocking Sentry's transmission vectoring two F-15s toward the intruding Iraqis. The Iraqis, as they had been doing for weeks now, would taunt Allied BARCAP aircraft by skirting the edges of their own space. A game of Chicken, played with equal gusto by each side, each attempting to provoke the other into a misstep that would obviate the Rules of Engagement and legitimatize a dogfight.

"Sentry, Stovepipe. Can you ID the bandits?" Nick asked, knowing they were probably Sukhoi 25s or MiG-21s, the aircraft based at Jalibah.

"Roger, Stovepipe," Sentry replied. "Probable MiG-21s. They are fourteen miles, climbing. Stovepipe, be advised that you are approaching Iraqi airspace. Recommend you immediately start a left turn."

"Roger, Sentry," Nick said into his microphone, and rolled into a left turn. "Say position on the bandits."

"Stovepipe, bandits are zero six zero at ten, coming to

your six—" The controller's voice tightened. "Stove-pipe, be advised the bandits have received a Redcat!"

Redcat was the Iraqi code for permission to arm weapons. An Arabic-speaking controller, monitoring the Iraqis' transmission aboard an American EC-135, had relayed this information to the AWACS.

"Lead, they're searching!" It was Keyes again.

"I see it," Nick said. His RHAW—radar homing and warning display—was alive with aircraft symbology that indicated the MiGs' radars in a searching mode. Nick's thumb fondled the missile button on the control stick. Pure reflex, as normal as breathing. The result of day after day, month after month, year after year of practice. You knew precisely what to do, how, and when.

And why.

"Lead, I've got an AI lock-on!" Keyes's voice rose in excitement as Nick's own RHAW confirmed an Airborne Intercept tracking by at least one MiG. The bandits were ready to launch missiles.

"I'm on it," Nick said, and reefed the F-16 back around toward the Iraqi border, at the same time uncaging the seeker head on his left Sidewinder. Although he knew all this would end up as just another exercise, they might get lucky. The Iraqis might overreact and keep coming.

No, no such luck. Sentry radioed, "Stovepipe, the bandits are turning east. No cross-border pursuit is authorized. Acknowledge."

"Roger that, Sentry," Nick replied, rolling out just west of the border, abeam the MiGs. His eyes flicked down to the radar map on the MFD screen, the multifunctional display, where three of the four little green blips were swinging east. The fourth appeared to be lagging behind. "We'll parallel them for a bit until we're sure they're disengaging."

"Lead, Two has a tally on the trailer, one o'clock level!" Keyes shouted. "He's turning back into us! Oh, shit, now he's reversing again! They're playing that game again. Shit!"

Nick had to smile at the disappointment in Keyes's

voice. He liked Keyes, a lanky redheaded boy from Iowa, a class of '88 Academy graduate. He had come into the 358th TFW full of piss and vinegar, convinced he was the hottest pilot since Chuck Yeager. They were all like that these days. These days? It had always been like that. You completed undergraduate pilot training, went on to your various upgrades, and when they finally turned you loose in a $20 million fighter, you were sure of your invincibility. But the macho attitude was carefully, if unofficially, inculcated into the cadet. Not much different from taking the child out of his mother's arms and educating him for the benefit of the State.

He radioed the AWACS. "Sentry, Stovepipe. Give me a confirmation on the bandits' turn—" He broke off the transmission. Ralph Keyes's tailpipe had just then belched flame as his F-16, in afterburner now, virtually rocketed away, east toward the withdrawing MiGs. In an instant the airplane was out of sight, one green blip following four other green blips on Nick's MFD screen. Nick recalled little of the next few minutes. He knew only that Keyes, the dumb kid, was chasing the MiGs and was split seconds away from entering Iraqi airspace and he, Nick Harmon, had to somehow stop him.

Nick touched the transmit button on the throttle control stick, then abruptly lifted his finger. He had been about to order Keyes to break off the pursuit; the words had already formed on Nick's lips: Are you crazy, boy? Get your ass back here! What in the name of Christ are you doing?

But Nick knew what the kid was doing, and why. Young Ralph Keyes shared with Nick Harmon—and probably each one of the more than twelve hundred other fighter pilots of Desert Shield—a continual concern: that the Iraqis would withdraw from Kuwait, depriving Ralph Keyes and Nick Harmon and the more than twelve hundred other fighter pilots of the opportunity to fight a war.

No, not depriving them, cheating them. This, after all —fighting, proving themselves better than the enemy— was what they were paid to do. What they had been trained for. What they lived for. Few would ever admit this, but each in his own secret heart knew it was true, a universal truth shared by all fighter pilots. As all this flashed through his consciousness, he heard Keyes shouting, "Bandit, two o'clock level! Break, Nick! Break!"

Nick slammed the throttle into afterburner and pulled the Falcon into a vertical arc toward the sun. Rotating a quarter turn to the right, he saw Keyes belly up in a hard left turn into where he had said the MiG was.

And into Iraqi airspace.

Leaving Nick now no choice but to follow Keyes in and adhere to a prearranged plan of maneuver. In the inviolate protocol of aerial combat, the pilot who first observes the threat and calls a break automatically assumes control of the engagement. He receives immediate and unquestioned obedience. You sort out the details later.

Nick came out of burner at 28,000 feet, rolled inverted, and drifted over the top of a loop. He had a visual on Stovepipe Two, and on the speck 4,000 feet below at his three o'clock position. Quickly, the speck materialized into a southwesterly-bound MiG-21 closing fast with constant bearing and decreasing range.

"Lead's tally," he called to Stovepipe Two. "Bandit is on the nose three miles, closing right to left. Do you have me?" Two audible clicks of Keyes's microphone button confirmed that Stovepipe Two was aware of the situation.

The preplanned, exhaustively practiced—and now perfectly executed—offensive split by the two F-16s had bracketed the MiG, sandwiching him between Nick in the sun above, and Keyes slashing in for a front-quartering kill shot. Instead of running when he had a chance, when Keyes came barreling in after him, the Iraqi had turned to face Keyes. Brave, but foolish.

From his high position, Nick watched a puff of flame and smoke erupt from Stovepipe Two's wing, as Keyes fired a Sidewinder straight into the MiG from two miles out.

"Fox Two!" Keyes called, and turned belly up in a hard right turn. The Sidewinder raced toward the MiG, which continued straight and level without evasive action. The Iraqi was helpless; there was nothing he could do but stay head-on to the missile, presenting it the slimmest—and coldest—target possible, and hoping the Sidewinder would go stupid.

Nick pulled hard down toward the MiG, stroked the afterburner, and brought his radar out of standby. The MiG was below him, at his eleven o'clock position, on a collision course with Keyes's Sidewinder. But it threaded the needle: The Sidewinder smoked past the MiG, missing literally by inches, and detonated harmlessly.

The next thirty seconds were, at once, the most exhilarating and most frightening thirty seconds of Nicholas Harmon's life. He would recall each single second clearly, even to taking the time to make sure that Ralph Keyes was now in the high position. But what he recalled with absolute clarity was the fear. Fear that the Iraqi might somehow evade the trap and somehow outfly and outfight Nick. Fear that he himself had somehow fallen into a trap. Fear that he would fail. He was no stranger to fear, and had always equated it to Chu-Bai. But this fear was different. This fear had a certain quality; this fear contained no shame.

He was thinking all this as he got in behind the MiG, locked on, and prepared to fire the Sidewinder. There was an instant, the instant before he pressed the pickle button, when he considered breaking off, letting the MiG escape. The Iraqi had proved a brave adversary. Moreover, the MiG pilot had almost earned a reprieve; he had watched Keyes's Sidewinder hurtle straight at him, and lucked out. Yes, it would be a noble gesture on Nick's part. But this was no game. This was why the U.S. had come here. This was what it was all about. More important, it was no Panama: These people could shoot back.

Nick pressed the pickle button. The Sidewinder's rocket motor ignited. The missile dropped from its wingtip pylon, wobbled almost imperceptibly and then, accelerating, leveled off. Through the HUD, Nick watched it roar unerringly toward the MiG, which at this distance was only a black dot in the sky.

The dot exploded in a flash of orange that immediately became a white cloud bursting into tendrils of smaller clouds of white trailing downward, dispersing in all directions in ever thinning wisps of yellow and black smoke.

What amazed Nick was that he felt neither elation nor remorse. It was too soon to feel anything; it would hit him later, one way or the other. But this lack of immediate emotion troubled him. He had killed a man; you were supposed to feel something. Particularly when it was not only your first victory, but the first victory to have been scored by either side in this so-called conflict. Yeah, he told himself, they'll give you a medal.

No, he continued to himself. No medal. Maybe some sincere slaps on the back from the troops and side glances of envy from the Big Gears, but no medal. Not for pushing the Rules of Engagement envelope to its limit. He was already preparing his report. He could just see Barney Gallagher's face at this very moment. Barney, Colonel Bernard Gallagher, was the 358th's C.O. The phones on his desk would be jumping as the scope dopes—the controllers in the E-3A AWACS—relayed the news that two 358th F-16s had penetrated Iraqi airspace and knocked down a MiG.

Now, not a half mile ahead and five hundred feet below, Ralph Keyes's F-16 suddenly appeared. Nick dropped down and drew abreast of him. Nick raised two fingers, signaling Keyes to switch to Channel Eleven on their VHF radios, a channel unlikely to be monitored.

"Nice going, kid," Nick said dryly.

"I'm sorry, Nick," Keyes said. "I guess I got a little too eager."

You can say that again, Nick said to himself, thinking how that would look on the mission debriefing report. A little too eager. It belonged to the "unusual circumstances" category.

The flight leader's wingman, 1st Lieutenant Keyes, became a little too eager. Signed, N. Harmon, LTC, USAF.

And the AWACS controllers had seen it all happen. Witnesses to the crime. But hold on, he thought. Wait just one second. The close proximity of the two F-16s and the rapidity of events made it difficult for the scope dopes to identify which airplane was first into Iraq. Nick could say he, Stovepipe Leader, went in first. He, with his rank and tenure, could get away with it. Not Keyes; they'd make an example of the poor kid. His flying days would be over. He'd be lucky if he ended up as Snow Removal Officer at Thule.

Nick said into the microphone, "When we get down, Ralph, I'll handle the debriefing. Do not—I repeat, do not—say word one to anybody. You let me do the talking. Copy?"

"Yeah, but—"

"Just do it!" Nick said. "Now get back on UHF." Nick punched button six and informed Sentry that Stovepipe was departing the area.

All the way back he wondered why he had chosen to take responsibility for the impetuous conduct of a young overzealous subordinate. He could not decide if it was an act of nobility, or defiance.

Barney Gallagher had another word for it. "Dumb!" Barney bellowed. "No, stupid! Just plain stupid!"

"I didn't want to let the bad guys get away with it," Nick said. "It's that simple."

"*You're* simple, Nick! Simpleminded!"

They were in Gallagher's office in the operations building at the base, a one-story structure not unlike a World War II barracks. But it was factory-new, prefabricated, and had been erected in a matter of days. All the buildings at Al Kalir were prefabricated. The base, on the eastern edge of the Saudi Arabian desert, was three hundred and fifty miles west of Kuwait City and seventy-five miles from the Iraqi border. It consisted of a single ten-thousand-foot concrete strip, reinforced steel and concrete revetments for the aircraft, a control tower, several large maintenance hangars, an air-conditioned "tent city" for enlisted personnel, three two-story pre-fabricated BOQ buildings, a number of garages and other support buildings, and a tented mess hall that accommodated both officers and enlisted personnel. Another tent served as an unpretentious officers' club.

The November sun shone dully off the gold minarets of the mosques in the village just beyond the base perimeter. The muffled ringing of incessant telephones blended with the continuous pounding of shoes on the vinyl-tiled floors of the corridor outside the office, and both blended almost musically with the whine of jet engines from airplanes constantly landing and taking off. The clamor was so familiar it was comforting.

". . . this, for sure, is the Mother of All Dumb Moves!" Gallagher was saying. His irritation made his Boston accent even more conspicuous. "What in the name of God were you guys trying to do—start the whole fucking war all by your fucking selves?"

"Come on, Barney, I never expected it to end up like that."

"Yeah, Nick, I read your report—" Gallagher's eyes narrowed—"or should I say, your account of the incident?"

Nick's report, deliberately vague, implied that he had not heard the AWACS no-pursuit order. Keyes, according to the report, had followed Nick into Iraq. Obviously, Barney was not buying. Nick said, "I didn't think the MiG would fight. I thought he'd run for home."

Gallagher reached into the hammered silver humidor on his desk and plucked out a huge cigar. He bit off the tip and spat it into the wastebasket in the well under the desk.

"Bullshit."

Nick knew Barney Gallagher well enough to know

not to argue. Barney had him cold. They had been friends since the Academy. Gallagher, three years ahead of Nick, graduated in '70 and went on to flight school, and then Vietnam. He flew F-4s out of Thailand, finishing up with one hundred and seven sorties and a chestful of ribbons. Two and one half years ago, when he took over the 358th, Gallagher's first task was to upgrade the wing's F-16s to a new night visibility capability system, LANTIRN. As project officer, he brought in the most dependable and competent man he knew, Nick Harmon.

Gallagher lit the cigar and leaned back in his chair. He opened a bottom desk drawer and propped his feet up on the drawer. "I suppose it never occurred to you that not two hundred miles from here a former navy bomber pilot, one George Bush, is celebrating Thanksgiving with his devoted troops?"

"This might remind him why we're here," Nick said.

Gallagher was in no mood for wisecracks. The colonel's normally ruddy face turned even redder. "Keyes didn't follow you in," he said. "It was the other way around."

Nick wondered if Gallagher were guessing or somehow knew the truth. "No, Barney, that's not what—"

"Shut up, Nick! I know better." Gallagher dropped his feet to the floor and swung around to face Nick. "You wouldn't lose control that way. You're too experienced. Why are you fronting for the kid?"

Nick almost welcomed the ear-piercing shriek of an F-16 taking off; it gave him a moment to compose an acceptable answer. The airplane roared past outside. The aluminum-frame walls of the building reverberated with the jet blast, which rattled the windows and the glass in the office door.

"I pressed the Rules of Engagement, Barney. Why can't we let it go at that?"

"That'll look good on your OER . . . especially when the colonel's selection board reviews your records next time around." Gallagher's jaw tightened. "And I don't have to remind you, do I, that you've been passed over once already. Thanks to your big mouth," he added.

"You're full of compliments today, Barney."

"I'm thinking about your career, Nick. This little incident sure won't help."

"Come on, Barney, it's not the crime of the century. I got a little aggressive, so what?"

"You got *very* aggressive." Gallagher tapped his finger on a file folder on the top of a stack of other folders. "You departed your BARCAP orbit, headed straight for the border, and deliberately snookered one of those MiG drivers into pointing his nose at you. You wanted the guy. And you got him."

Nick said nothing; there was nothing to say.

Gallagher said, "You haven't answered my question: Why are you covering for Lieutenant Keyes?"

"Barney, I'm not saying you're right—that it was Keyes, not me, who chased the Iraqis—but if it was him, he did something we all want to do: fight. You, me, every last man in this outfit. We're here to fly, fight, and win."

A disgusted wave of Gallagher's hand silenced Nick. "Spare me the flag-waving, Nick. We know each other too well. Just hope we get a little lucky with this. I mean that the Iraqis don't start screaming. I can't see them doing it, but if they do, the Pentagon will issue an indignant denial and then jump all over CENTCOM, and CENTCOM will be on CENTAF's ass, and CENTAF will be on mine. And I'll be on yours." Gallagher waved his hand again, this time a gesture of dismissal. "Get out of my sight."

"You're a bundle of compassion, Barney."

Gallagher laughed humorlessly. "This is one kill you'll never get credit for. You'll still need five to make ace." He propped his feet up on the desk drawer again. "You're bound and determined to make up for not flying in 'Nam, aren't you?"

"I paid my dues in 'Nam, Barney."

"We all did, Nick."

* * *

If twenty-four years in the military had taught Barney Gallagher anything, it had taught him that nothing ever came easy. Or, putting it a different way, nothing was ever as simple as it seemed. He thought about this for a long time after Nick left, sitting in that same position, leaning back in his chair, feet propped up on the open bottom drawer, dead cigar clenched in his teeth. No, he thought, never take anything for granted. This included the general's star he soon expected to wear.

He sat up and punched the intercom buzzer on the telephone console. "Yes, sir . . . ?" Master Sergeant Joan Carlisi's foghorn voice echoed through the speaker.

"That message that came in a while ago on the computer from CENTAF, Joanie," Gallagher said into the speaker. "The one about Colonel Iverson. Bring it to me."

A moment later Sergeant Carlisi entered. Her voice, as Gallagher had noted from the moment he first met her two and one-half years before, matched her body perfectly. A short, dumpy, graying lady in her late thirties, Carlisi had been in the air force seventeen years. Gallagher considered her the most efficient paper pusher in the service. Administrative NCO to a succession of commanding officers, she had been with the 358th some six years, a kind of fixture.

"Here you are, Colonel." Carlisi placed a sheet of paper neatly on the desk.

"Thank you. Read it, please," Gallagher said, noting that the sergeant's eyes were fixed disapprovingly on the cigar. "It's out," he said, flipping the cigar into the oversized bronze ashtray. He knew she hated the smell of cigars. For that matter, so did his wife. Which reminded him: He hadn't written Helen in two weeks. But what the hell was there to write about? The gourmet food? The night life in Al Kalir? The excitement of war? There was no war, for Christ's sake. But there would be, and soon. Which made him feel bad for what he was about to do.

" '. . . awaiting reply re previous conversations re

Iverson.' Signed—" Carlisi stopped in mid-sentence as
Gallagher reached out and snatched the paper from her.

"Excuse me," he mumbled as he pulled the message
onto his lap. He knew she was glaring at him for his
rudeness. He suppressed an urge to explain that the
droning monotone of her voice had only increased his
own frustration. "Sorry," he mumbled again, concentrating on the preamble of the message.

It was from Tactical Air Command HQ at Langley
Field, Virginia, relayed from Riyadh. From TAC's vice
commander, a three-star named Perry Arbogast. The
"previous conversations re Iverson" could hardly be
called conversations. Directives, more accurately, and
they concerned Gallagher's imminent promotion and
transfer to a staff position at CENTAF in Riyadh. It was
the boss's suggestion, said Arbogast, that Ed Iverson
succeed Gallagher as C.O. of the 358th. Gallagher, who
had planned to recommend Nick Harmon for the job,
knew that when the boss—a four-star general who did
not readily suffer fools, or arguments—"suggested"
something, it was a done deal. Gallagher had asked for
time to think the matter over. What he wanted to think
over was a strategy for convincing the boss that Nick
was the man for the job, not Ed Iverson.

Iverson, a full colonel and currently on staff at the
Tactical Air Command Control Center in Riyadh, was a
competent enough officer. A fine pilot with an acceptable, if mediocre, Vietnam tour. In Gallagher's opinion,
however, Nick Harmon not only was better qualified but
more deserving.

Gallagher stared at the message a long moment,
thinking about Ed Iverson and Nick Harmon. The two
loathed each other. On the other hand, Nick might be
the perfect counterweight for the by-the-book Iverson.
Carlisi cleared her throat discreetly. Gallagher handed
her the message. "File it, and bring me Colonel Harmon's personnel folder."

"Right away, sir," Carlisi said.

Gallagher swung his chair around, facing the window
on the far end of the room. It provided a glimpse of the

taxiway and the runway. An F-16 had just landed, touching down with a chirp of tires and muted whine of idle thrust.

He heard the door open, and Carlisi's footsteps on the vinyl floor. "Put it on the desk, Joanie," he said.

"Yes, sir," she said, and he heard the rustle of papers on the desk as Carlisi arranged the unruly pile of TWXs, E-mail, and other correspondence into two neat stacks. Gallagher waited until he heard the door close behind her before he swiveled his chair around again.

He opened the folder on his lap, wondering why he had even bothered to ask for it. He did not have to read it to know there were indeed comments in the "Other Comments" block of previous performance reports. Ordinarily—unless an officer had committed some horrendous, unforgivable blunder—these observations would not adversely affect his future. In Nick's case, although there were an even dozen notations, dating back to 1974, none was really serious. Collectively, however— especially with the most recent one in Panama—they might give a cautious review board cause to nitpick. Indeed, this had already happened; the board had passed Nick over the first time. And now, with the MiG, you could add a Rules of Engagement violation.

Yeah, Gallagher thought, the guy could damn well have already had his Eagle, and a cinch for a Star, if not for an almost suicidal propensity for speaking his mind. Always, naturally, to the wrong people. But to be fair, all that should be balanced against an otherwise absolutely exemplary record. A first-class pilot whose skill and leadership were universally respected, the flight leader whom you followed without question.

To be fair, Gallagher thought, and where the hell was it written that the air force was fair? Absently, he browsed through the other pages of Nick's folder. The story of the man's life, including a reference to his marriage to that Las Vegas dancer, Joan. No, Jean. That was her name, Jean. Back in 1979, at Nellis, attending Fighter Weapons School, Nick met and married the lady all within three or four weeks. Gallagher had never seen the woman in the flesh but certainly had heard enough about her from mutual friends. A knockout, they said. Nick never talked much about her, only that it hadn't worked out. And then there was that sad business with the child.

Gallagher tossed Nick's OPR folder into the OUT basket. He sat back and fixed his eyes on the clock on the wall above the door. The wing's sergeant major had scavenged the clock from the NCO club at MacDill. The hour and minute hands were shaped like propellers. It reminded Gallagher of windmills.

Windmills, type Mark I, the Don Quixote kind.

Tilting at windmills. An apt description, Gallagher ruefully acknowledged, of what he would be doing if he made an issue about Ed Iverson taking over the 358th instead of Nick Harmon.

Yes, Gallagher told himself, if he thought there was even the remotest chance of changing the boss's mind, all right, then he'd damn well go to bat for Nick. And damn the torpedoes. But there wasn't a chance, and Nick would simply have to wait for Colonel Gallagher to become Brigadier General Gallagher. Then he'd have different cards to play. Then he'd be able to do something for Nick. Then, as a one-star—and once the war started, on the way to more stars—he'd be in position.

Gallagher sat up now and began reading and initialing the daily reports, all the while formulating his speech to Nick Harmon, explaining why Ed Iverson was coming in as C.O. After ten minutes, Gallagher gave up. Nothing sounded right. Everything sounded hollow and trite, and he really did not want to think about it; it made him too uncomfortable.

Three days later, to Barney Gallagher's great relief, the matter appeared to have been taken out of his hands. Nick was back in the colonel's office, listening to Gallagher read a TWX just received from CENTAF in Riyadh.

" '. . . LTC Harmon will proceed ASAP to DCS/ OPS, HQ, USAF, Room 5D267, Pentagon.' " He tossed the paper across the desk to Nick; the edges were ragged where it had been torn carelessly from the printer. "That's the deputy chief of staff for Operations himself, Nick. He wants an in-person report of the incident. So you get a free trip to Washington."

Nick scanned the message. "Yeah, to get my ass chewed out . . . in person." He returned the paper to Gallagher. "Well, maybe it won't be so bad. Gene Gordon's the D.O."

"Your patron saint."

Patron saint was an understatement. Gene Gordon, now a three-star, had been director of admissions at the Academy back in 1969 when Nick, still officially a marine, first applied. The then Colonel Gordon had made it possible for Nick to enter the Academy. And it was Gordon, Nick suspected, who had smoothed things over for him after the Panama faux pas.

But Nick also knew that it would take more than Gene Gordon to get him his colonel's eagle and then his first star. Not with the Panama reprimand stapled to the first page of Nick's Officer Performance Report, and not with some of the egos he had managed to bruise throughout his career. Nick Harmon would win no popularity contests. In Nick Harmon's world, there were only two ways of doing things: the other way—and his way.

What it would take in Nick Harmon's case was a war. Which would commence, on schedule, on or about January 15. Like a football game. Careers would be made and broken. Or, in Nick Harmon's case, resurrected.

"Okay, Colonel, have a nice trip," Gallagher said. "And try not to shoot down any MiGs on the way."

"You're a real comedian, Barney." Nick flipped a mock salute and started to leave. He was at the door when Gallagher called to him.

"Nick, how did it feel?"

"How did what feel?"

"That first taste of blood. When you splashed that raghead. When you saw the Sidewinder split him in two."

"It felt good," Nick said, after a moment.

TWO

Nick Harmon's dislike of Frank Kowalski stemmed not from any particular prejudice toward Feather Merchants, but because of his certainty now that Kowalski was more than the fussy civilian bureaucrat he purported to be. Yesterday, driving in from Andrews, Kowalski had recited from memory the high points of the service career of Nicholas Harmon, SSN 030-14-0627, Lieutenant Colonel, USAF, Air Force Specialty Code 115Q.

Kowalski had it all down pat. From Nick's U.S. Marine service in Vietnam, to his 1973 USAFA graduation, his pilot training at Laughlin AFB, his transition to F-4s, his 1978–79 tour at Nellis AFB, his below-the-zone promotion to major in 1983, his master's degree in business administration from Florida State University. All the way to his present Desert Shield assignment at Al Kalir as deputy operations officer of the 358th TFW. Kowalski also, almost as an aside, mentioned Nick's marriage in 1979 to a Las Vegas showgirl and, four years later, divorce.

The point of most interest to Kowalski, however, apparently was Nick's second tour of duty in 1985 at Nellis, training Israeli pilots to fly the F-16. Nick had developed a close friendship with one of them.

". . . Sharok," Kowalski was saying, consulting a small, spiral-bound notebook. "Major Zvi Sharok, highly placed in the Defense Ministry and highly regarded. He was in on that raid on the Osirak nuclear reactor in '81."

They were seated around a small circular conference table in Lieutenant General Gene Gordon's corner office on the second floor of the Pentagon, Nick, Kowalski, and Gordon. Gordon had listened to Nick's recounting of the MiG incident with what appeared to be vicarious pleasure. He had asked only a few questions, all technical and routine. It was almost as though he was proud of Nick.

"You're slipping," Nick said to Kowalski. "Zvi also shot down eight Syrian MiGs."

"Seven," Kowalski said. "The eighth was destroyed on the ground."

"That puts him only six ahead of you, Nick," Gene Gordon said dryly. "All right, now tell me about this Israeli fellow."

"Tell you what?"

The corners of Gordon's mouth turned abruptly down; his good humor of an instant before seemed to have vanished. It was then, facing Gordon, that Nick realized he had been summoned to the Pentagon not to talk about MiGs, but something entirely different.

"He's a close friend, isn't he, this Major Sharok?" Gordon said.

"Yes, sir, he's a close friend. What's the point?" Nick asked, and answered his own question. "That is the point, isn't it?"

"Let me explain what's happening," Gene Gordon said. He sat back and stretched his long legs far under the table. He was an athletic, craggy-faced man whose thick black hair belied his fifty-six years. Nick thought that he had changed very little since the day they first met twenty-one years before.

Nick's application for the Air Force Academy had been rejected for substandard high school academic grades. Gordon was then the director of admissions and, Nick learned, had recently returned from Southeast Asia with ninety-seven F-105 Thud missions over North Vietnam to his credit. Nick, just back from Vietnam

himself, went to Colorado Springs and waited three
hours in the bitter cold on Gene Gordon's front porch
for the colonel to come home. Three hours after that,
almost in self-defense, Gordon agreed to consider
Nick's application for entrance into the Academy's prep
school. When Nick graduated, twenty-second in his
class, the gold bars on his epaulets were the same gold
bars Gene Gordon had once worn.

". . . we're into a situation that's a little dicey,"
Gordon was saying. "Our embassy in Tel Aviv informs
us that the Israelis are seriously considering a preemptive strike. At Iraq, of course—"

"At Iraq, you *hope*," said Kowalski.

"I doubt like blazes, Mr. Kowalski, they're thinking
about hitting Moscow," Gordon said.

"I was referring to a Jordan overflight, sir," Kowalski
said. "That could really create some problems."

"For sure," said Gordon, and went on to Nick,
"When this business with the MiG came up, Mr. Kowalski reminded me of your Israeli connection." He paused
and glanced again at Kowalski. It made Nick think of
two doctors pondering the best way to inform a patient
of his terminal illness.

Nick said to Kowalski, "You do your homework."

"That's my job," Kowalski said.

"Now that you mention it, what *is* your job?" Nick
asked.

"Mr. Kowalski is with the National Security Council,"
Gordon said. "He is, shall we say, a troubleshooter.
And, Nick, we've got trouble." He fingered a small
white file card next to the telephone on the table. "Your
friend Major Sharok has approached us with a concept
for a joint operation. The object is to destroy a missile
silo complex in western Iraq. It's quite imaginative,
really."

"I'd call it wild," Kowalski said impatiently. "What
happens if the Israelis run into any of our Special Forces
teams in that area?" He noted Nick's surprise. "Yeah,
Colonel, they're in there. At least half a dozen three-

and-four-man SOF units. One of them has been operating inside Iraq for more than a month."

"I'm sure the Israelis have taken all that into consideration," Gordon said.

"Maybe," said Kowalski, and went on to Nick, "What they're proposing is that an Israeli demolition unit, wearing American uniforms, flies in an American transport airplane to a U.S. air base in Saudi Arabia. There, they unload a helicopter—from the same American airplane—and fly the helicopter into Iraq. They blow the missile launchers and get the hell out. They estimate the whole operation to take not more than half a day."

Nick said, "That sounds like something Zvi would dream up."

"What do you think of the plan?" Gordon asked.

"Are you asking my opinion?" Nick said. Even as he spoke, he was wondering what the hell difference *his* opinion could possibly make and, more important, why all this was being confided to a mere light colonel. They were playing some kind of game with him. Even the blithe disclosure of U.S. Special Operations Forces deployed inside Iraq was part of it. All right, then, he'd play along.

He said, "The Israelis will be wearing American uniforms. What makes you so sure the Saudis *won't* know that the 'Americans' aren't Americans?"

"The Israelis' idea is that the transport plane that ferries the helicopter and men into the U.S. base will be a MAC aircraft, flown by an American crew, and its point of origin will supposedly have been Germany," Gordon said. "And that's how it will look on Saudi radar screens. The only way the Saudis would ever suspect that an Israeli commando team used their territory to get back and forth on this mission would be if the people got off the plane singing 'Hatikva.'"

Nick wanted to laugh. Kowalski was not the only one who had done his homework. Gene Gordon, ordinarily, would not have known "Hatikva" from a Mozart sonata. Nick said, "Don't sell the Saudis short. They're a hell of a lot smarter than you think. And what this amounts to is that you're deliberately deceiving them. Lying to them. Making fools of them, really."

Kowalski said, "This is only a proposal, Colonel. We haven't given it our approval."

"Everybody's so damned worried about an Israeli preemptive strike," Nick said. "Wouldn't you call this operation exactly that?"

"If the Israelis wanted to preempt, they'd make downtown Baghdad a parking lot," Gordon said. "I think they're considering this prophylactic, rather than preemptive."

"What happens if you don't approve this . . . prophylaxis?" Nick asked.

"That's what we'd like you to find out," Gordon said.

The very flatness of the general's tone chilled Nick. "Excuse me?" he said. It was all he could think of to say.

"We're thinking of putting you in as air attaché at the embassy in Tel Aviv," Gordon said. "It's a TDY assignment, a few weeks, a month at most."

A month at most, Nick thought, which brought it almost to January 15. He wondered if Gordon was trying to tell him that the Allies would actually hit Iraq on that date.

Kowalski said, "The Israelis know you. They trust you and respect you. Also, it was your friend, Major Sharok, who presented this scheme to—"

"Hold it!" Nick said. He glanced apologetically at Gene Gordon for the sharpness of his tone, then went on to Kowalski, "You're asking me to *spy* on the Israelis? To obtain information on their tactical and strategic plans? And what the hell makes you think the Israelis would confide in me, anyway?" He gave Kowalski no chance to reply as he immediately continued to Gordon. "Sir, I'm sorry, but I have to turn you down on this one."

"We really need that information, Nick," Gordon said. He spoke in a quiet, almost gentle voice. Nick would have preferred the general's steely tone of command, which he had heard on numerous other occasions and resented not hearing now. Gordon was calling in one of several old markers: payback time for past favors.

But then, markers or not, the general did have a point. An Israeli preemptive strike at Iraq could not only trigger an Iraqi response and thereby prematurely push the United States and its allies into action, but might also jeopardize the already uncomfortably fragile coalition. In point of fact, both the Syrians and Egyptians had announced their intention—in the event of an Israeli attack on Iraq—to "review their status within the coalition." The Syrians had even suggested that they might switch sides.

". . . your job will be to keep your eyes and ears open, your mouth shut," Kowalski was saying. "You're to report the gist of any and all conversations and movements, casual or otherwise, that might bear on the probability of an Israeli preemptive strike."

One half of Nick's brain heard and digested this. The other half was rehearsing a flowery speech of rejection. He was a professional, a man dedicated to the defense of his country. He had started as a teenage marine grunt in Vietnam, been wounded in action, gone on to win an appointment to the United States Air Force Academy, and become a top fighter pilot and an officer destined for the Stars.

Nick never did deliver the flowery speech. The grim faces of the two men at the table told him it would have been a waste of words. Nick had a choice: accept the assignment, or be reasonably assured that Lieutenant Colonel Nicholas Harmon would finish his air force career as the oldest living lieutenant colonel in history. Which—after Panama and now the MiG incident—was a distinct possibility anyway.

"You said a few weeks, a month at best," he said to Gene Gordon. "What guarantee do I have that that's all it will be?"

It was Kowalski who replied. "No guarantee, Colonel. You're to report immediately to the ambassador in Tel Aviv."

"Shouldn't I read *The Spy Who Came In from the Cold* first?" Nick asked.

"Not necessary," Kowalski said, poker-faced. "I'll tell you what to do." He smiled thinly. "I'll be over there with you."

2

Johnny Donovan patted his stomach and said, "Don't say it, Nick. That's all I hear from my wife: 'What happened to that Schwarzenegger stomach?'"

"I think she meant Schwarz*kopf*," said Nick. He prodded Donovan's middle. "A little flab, it'll get worse."

"Thanks, pal."

Donovan had come striding into the anteroom from his office the moment his civilian secretary informed him of Nick's arrival. Lieutenant Colonel John Donovan, Deputy Director of Air Force Public Affairs, built like a fireplug, hair perpetually rumpled, looked as Irish as his name. And he was as tough as he looked. In pilot training, rather than eject from a flamed-out T-37, Donovan had elected to ride the airplane down, confident of his ability to make a dead stick landing. He was wrong. They had to nearly scrape him out of the cockpit. It finished his flying career but opened a whole new field: public affairs. He liked his job, and was good at it, and expected to soon make full colonel, which he knew would be his retirement rank. He was satisfied; under the circumstances, and as a nonrated officer, he had done quite well for himself.

Nick had returned to his hotel from the meeting with General Gordon and Frank Kowalski to find a message from Donovan. Could Nick come back to the Pentagon to see him at four that afternoon? Nick was only too glad to comply. He needed someone to talk to. He was being taken off the line to assume some asinine cloak and dagger role. Air attaché in Tel Aviv. Gordon and Kowalski were playing a game with him, all right. Tennis. And he was the ball.

". . . yeah, Norma looks after me pretty good," Donovan was saying. "Too good."

"How is Norma?" Nick asked, relieved that Donovan mentioned his wife's name. Nick had forgotten it. He had served as an usher at their wedding, back at the Academy in 1974.

"She's fine, maybe getting a little thick in the middle, too, thank you. By the way, you made quite a hit with Miss Morgan. . . . Millie," Donovan added, noting Nick's bemused frown. He lowered his voice so the secretary would not hear. "Last night . . . ?"

"Oh, Jesus!" Nick said.

" 'Oh, Jesus!' is right," Donovan said. "That's why I was sorry you couldn't keep our lunch date. I was hoping for a blow-by-blow report."

"A little audio voyeurism?"

"Call it vicarious pleasure."

"That's what it was, then," said Nick. "Blow-by-blow."

Donovan laughed. "We take good care of our boys in the trenches. How about dinner tonight?"

"I won't have time," Nick said. "I want to get out of here by seven."

"That's right. Gordon told me to fix you up with a ride to L.A. A little detour on your way back to the war."

"What war?" Nick asked.

"The one I understand you almost started the other day."

"Oh, that war," said Nick. "Yeah, I'm spending a few days in Los Angeles before I report back." General Gordon had arranged a three-day delay en route for Nick so he might visit his father in Santa Monica. Nick hadn't seen Bob Harmon in nearly a year.

"Barbara, cut a set of travel orders for Colonel Harmon to proceed to Los Angeles on official business," Donovan said to his secretary, a graying, middle-aged lady whom Nick thought must have been a beauty in her earlier years. "Sign my name, by order of General Frobisher. There you are, done," he said to Nick. He wrapped an arm around Nick's shoulder and guided him into the private office. "I asked you to come over here at this time because there's someone who's very anxious to meet you."

Donovan started to open the office door, then abruptly closed it and faced Nick. "By the way, I got an early Christmas card from Elaine Mason. Her unit was activated. She's up in Fort Ord, getting ready to ship out for the Gulf. She's now a major, if you please."

"That's great," said Nick.

"You don't hear from her anymore, I take it?"

"Not since she got married, no."

"Nice lady," Donovan said. "I always liked her."

Me, too, Nick thought, as Donovan opened the office door and gestured Nick in. Seated in a leather armchair opposite Donovan's desk, her legs folded with the hem of her gray flannel skirt falling primly below her knee, was a young, good-looking blonde. Even seated, Nick could see she was tall; a glance at those perfect legs told him that. She seemed vaguely familiar. For a moment he wondered where he had seen her. Her name came to him an instant before Donovan spoke.

"Okay, Chris, as promised: the famous Colonel Harmon," Donovan said. He sat at his desk and motioned Nick into a chair beside Chris. "Nick, this is Christine Campbell."

Her eyes swept appraisingly over Nick's face and on his four rows of service ribbons. "Bronze Star, Air Medal, Purple Heart," she said, impressed. She pointed at a yellow, red, and green striped ribbon. "Vietnam. That where you got the Purple Heart?"

"That's where I got it," Nick said, and for at least the hundredth time in the past twenty-two years asked himself why he continued to wear the damn ribbon. In his case, it was almost a badge of disgrace. "The 'famous' Colonel Harmon?" he continued quickly, changing the subject. " 'The famous Christine Campbell,' I can understand. But what am *I* supposed to be famous for?"

Donovan replied for Nick. "Some rumor about a MiG," he said. He rolled his eyes in mock dismay.

"Which says volumes for our so-called classified information. I even heard the salad girl at the cafeteria talking about it."

Chris said, "I don't suppose it's occurred to you, Johnny, that DOD *wants* the 'rumor' to be made public? A little bit of saber rattling, shall we say?" Nick liked the sound of her voice, low and throaty. It sounded even better in person than on television. More interesting, more character.

"Yes, Chris, that has indeed occurred to me," Donovan said. "But just so there'll be no misunderstanding, I am officially notifying you that the individual involved is under strict orders not to discuss the 'rumor' with any members of the media."

"Is the individual involved"—she looked solemnly at Nick—"is he allowed to confirm or deny the 'rumor'?"

"How the hell can you confirm or deny a rumor?" Donovan said. "And the answer is no, anyway. Okay, Chris, I produced him for you. Now what?"

"Now I'd like to buy him a drink," she said, and to Nick, "if you're available, Colonel."

"If he's not, he'll make himself available," Donovan said. "Right, Nick?"

"Right," said Nick, thinking it was the understatement of the year. "I'm available."

No, the understatement of the century, he thought, fifteen minutes later, seated opposite her in a banquette in the dimly lighted cocktail lounge of the Crowne Royal Hotel.

". . . did some research on you," she was saying. "You certainly are no paragon of discretion."

"Panama, you mean?"

"I've heard the story from three different sources," she said. "And they're all basically the same. So it must be true."

"It's usually referred to as Harmon's Disease," he said dryly. "Also known as foot-in-the-mouth illness." Which, he thought but did not say, was a potentially terminal ailment. It had happened at the MacDill officers' club upon his return from a Panama sortie. He couldn't even blame it on one drink too many; he hadn't even had one drink. He had walked into the club foyer and nearly collided with a two-star he once worked for at Wright-Patterson.

The two-star had innocently asked how the mission went. Nick replied, Mission? Since when is clobbering a PDF barracks in downtown Panama City a mission? When the two-star's eyebrows narrowed disapprovingly, instead of backing away, Nick plowed ahead. I wish to Jesus Christ, he said, that somebody could explain to me why we're making a full-goddamn-fledged war out of what should be no more than a battle drill with live ammunition!

The image of that wooden building, the living quarters of some thirty Panamanian soldiers, disintegrating under the impact of three perfectly placed five hundred pound HE bombs was still fresh in Nick's memory. In his night vision glasses, the structure had been there one instant, then simply vanished. Vaporized. Talk about elephants squashing ants.

And then he compounded the felony by saying to the two-star, Next thing you know, we'll send in a couple of B-2s. Makes sense, doesn't it, sir? A half billion dollar bomber hitting a target that's probably worth at least a couple of thousand dollars. It sure makes sense to me, General.

The next thing Nick knew, his "intemperate" remarks earned him a letter of reprimand direct from CGSOCOM, Commanding General, U.S. Southern Command. The letter somehow fell into the hands of a nationally syndicated, antiadministration newspaper columnist. The whole affair—whose existence the parties concerned denied, claiming they had been grossly misquoted—quickly blew over, but the damage was done.

Harmon's Disease.

"Look, the Panama fiasco was a case of shooting myself in the foot," Nick said. "And I happened to be dead wrong, way out of line."

"Desert Shield," said Chris. "Tell me about Desert

Shield. You're the first GI I've talked to who's been over there."

"Hot during the day, cold at night," said Nick, thinking about the music from the film *Out of Africa*, which his impulsive young wingman, Ralph Keyes, claimed to be an aphrodisiac miracle. According to Keyes, it never failed. As a token of gratitude, Keyes had presented Nick with his personal cassette of the movie's sound track. Nick brought the cassette to Washington and played it on the Sony tape deck built into the hotel room's television receiver. With the redheaded secretary of the previous evening the result, true to Keyes's prediction, was nothing short of miraculous.

". . . does that mean you don't *want* to tell me anything, or you've been ordered not to?" Chris was saying.

"It means I don't think I should," Nick said, deciding that *Out of Africa* was not for this lady.

He forced himself to concentrate on her words. She was telling him about her father, a navy lieutenant commander, shot down over Vietnam. ". . . he flew off the *Forrestal*," she said.

"Do you remember him at all?"

"Some childhood images, but I'm sure they're more my wistful imagination than anything else. We have his photos, though, so at least I know what he looked like." She faced him directly. "I know about your daughter. I'm so sorry."

He smiled appreciatively; it was the polite thing to do. Donovan, he thought. Donovan must have filled her in on Nick's failed marriage and about the child. He said, "Do you have children?" What the hell, television star or not, if she could get personal, so could he.

"No," she said. "And no husbands, either. Not yet, thank you." She tapped a fingernail against Nick's almost empty glass, then signaled the waitress. "Let's let WCN buy you another drink."

"Sure, you think you'll get me drunk, and I'll talk about the MiG," he said.

"The hell with the MiG," she said. "I just want you to level with me about Desert Shield. All off the record.

I'm curious to know, in your opinion, how many GIs really know why they're there?"

"Excuse me?" The question startled him.

"How many GIs really know why they're in the Gulf?"

"They all do," he said. "They all know why they're there. They're professionals."

"So why are they there?"

"What do you mean, 'Why are they there?' I just told you: They're professionals."

Her voice hardened. She enunciated each word, as though addressing a stubborn child. "Do they know why they are there?"

He had heard that question before, and in those same accusatory tones. He had seen it before. Twenty-two years ago, home from Vietnam in his Marine uniform— and on crutches—hobbling around the campus of Santa Monica High School. Everyone had asked him if he knew why he was in Vietnam. He finally had wised up to it and began answering, Sure, I know why—to kill babies!

Now he almost gave the same answer to Chris Campbell, but at the last instant changed his mind and said instead, "Did your father know why *he* was there?"

He felt no remorse at the flash of pain in her eyes. She deserved it. She said, "He thought he did."

"He 'thought'?"

"He thought he was there so the Big, Bad, slant-eyed Commies wouldn't come marching down Pennsylvania Avenue."

"How do you know that's what he thought?"

"His letters," she said. "I've read his letters to my mother. He died, really believing that's what he was dying for."

"So did a lot of others," Nick said.

"No, and that's the pity of it," she said. "Those others died without the slightest notion of why. Somebody told them to do it, so they did."

"Then try to feel good that at least your father died for what he believed in," Nick said.

For a moment he feared she might weep. But her eyes remained dry and angry. The waitress came over just then. Nick finished his drink and handed her the empty glass. "Beefeater on the rocks," the waitress said. "How about you, miss?" She hovered over Chris, sure that she had seen her on TV but not quite able to place her. "Another Stoly and tonic?"

"Nothing for me, thank you." Chris dismissed the waitress with a polite smile and said to Nick, "I'm not much of a drinker." She sounded nearly friendly now. "Can you tell me what the GIs think is the reason they've been sent to Saudi Arabia?"

No, lady, Nick thought, you don't get away with it so easy. He said, "Why don't you tell me what *you* think we're there for?"

She answered immediately, almost eagerly. "To begin with, it's not to liberate Kuwait. It's to throw the Iraqis out, which is not the same as liberating the country. Liberating it would mean getting rid of the overfed, overpaid, and oversexed handful of desert sheiks that own the place. But we don't want to do that because those same sheiks own the oil, and we need the oil."

The waitress brought Nick's drink. He tasted it. The gin was not cold enough yet. He had an eerie feeling that he was watching a movie: Before his very eyes, the lovely seductive blonde princess was turning into an angry wrinkled old hag.

". . . the same with the Saudis," she was saying. "You don't believe for one minute, do you, that we're really worried about evil old Saddam Hussein violating the integrity of our great democratic ally, Saudi Arabia? It's the same four-letter word, Colonel, o-i-l!"

"Nobody said it wasn't," Nick said.

The wrinkled old hag's mouth tightened. "And that's all right with you, Colonel? To kill our soldiers so that the Emir of Kuwait and the King of Saudi Arabia can sell us more oil, so that they can keep sitting on toilets with solid gold flush handles, buying Rolls-Royces, and trying to break the bank at Monte Carlo?"

The waitress came over again. She fussed about, wiping the table, arranging the little cocktail napkins; she was still trying to identify Chris. This time Chris did not wait for the waitress to leave. She said to Nick, "I have a theory—" She glanced icily at the waitress. The girl blushed and walked hurriedly away.

"I think we've developed a whole new class in this country," Chris continued to Nick. "A warrior class, whose prime function is to root out and destroy anyone and anything that threatens whatever at the time happens to be conveniently referred to as our national interests."

Jesus Holy Christ, Nick thought, what have I gotten myself into? I have heard about the so-called antiwar faction, but never dreamed I would actually encounter it. And in the person of a celebrity, who is too good-looking a woman and should be too smart to be wasting her time on such bullshit.

". . . not so long ago, you'd have been calling me a fascist," he heard himself saying, wondering why he bothered to dignify such drivel. Why he felt it necessary to defend himself.

"And you'd be calling me a communist," she said.

No, he thought, I'd be calling you Stupid. But he knew she was not stupid, far from it, which saddened him. He wanted to explain to her that now that the Cold War was over, America had inherited the job of Global Peacekeeper. If you had to knock a few heads together to keep the peace, then that's what it took. But he knew it would be a waste of breath. With these people it always was. What truly saddened him was that she did not understand—more important, not respect—why her father had so readily and willingly sacrificed his life.

He finished the drink and excused himself, declining her offer of a lift back to the Stouffer. He wanted to walk. He needed the exercise. What he did not say was that he also needed the fresh air. He walked the short distance back to his hotel, feeling foolish now for the sexual fantasy that had enveloped him at his first sight of Christine Campbell. An old story—a bad habit—

those first-sight sexual fantasies. That was how it had started with Jean.

Jean.

The auburn-haired goddess, she who could have made Nick Harmon's life so complete. That first instant he saw her, he truly believed he had found the woman of his dreams.

His nightmares, as it turned out.

3

Chris was glad—no, relieved—that Nick had not accepted her offer of a ride. She, too, needed fresh air and now, driving away from the Crowne Royal Hotel, was getting plenty. Despite the forty-five-degree temperature, the sun was warm enough to lower the top of her white 1967 Mustang convertible. Larry Hill wanted her to drive a newer car—a 560 Mercedes or BMW; WCN would foot the bill—but she loved the Mustang, which she had bought from a junkyard four years ago and spent $18,000 restoring to mint condition.

She drove through Crystal City, crossed the bridge and headed north on the parkway. The early evening traffic was surprisingly light, enabling her to push the Mustang past 65. She would have enjoyed 85 more, even 90 or 95. Once, on this same road, the first week she had the car, she had watched the needle edge past 100. It was almost sensual. She loved driving fast. Of course, so far this year it resulted in no fewer than four tickets, but she had lucked out each time. The PRESS placard on the right-hand sun visor was magic. The fact that the parkway police recognized her did not hurt, either. Yes, driving at high speed was an expression of perfection that demanded total concentration and total control. Control was the key. As long as you had control, you were in control. The world was yours.

Although Chris reached Baltimore in forty minutes, it was after six and dark by the time she edged through the downtown area and pulled up outside a duplex row house on Morton Avenue. Some children, blacks and

Hispanics, bundled against the cold, played on the side-walk. Chris brushed past them and climbed the porch stairs. She tapped the knuckles of her gloved hand on the glassed front door of 261. She knew the doorbell was not working; it had not worked for years.

Chris tapped harder on the glass. After a moment, a woman opened the door. She was tall, nearly as tall as Chris, with dull, unkempt brown hair streaked with yellowish gray. She wore a shabby housecoat and tattered felt slippers. In the harsh light from the naked bulb of the porchlight, the deep-wrinkled haggard face of the woman gave her the appearance of an elderly person. She was not yet fifty.

"Come on in, Christine," said the woman, whose name was Beverly Adams.

Chris sighed resignedly. "You're drunk, Ma."

"Don't be silly," Beverly Adams said, but with a little shrug, as though what the hell difference did it make, and who cared? "Come on in."

Chris stepped carefully into the darkened living room. Behind her, Beverly closed the front door and switched on the hall light. It illuminated the living room enough to see a few magazines spread neatly on the coffee table, and the sofa pillows fluffed pristinely. Chris doubted there was a speck of dust on the furniture. It could have been the house she was born in, which was also a row house, but in Philadelphia. Chris and her mother had moved from that house twenty-two years ago, not long after Beverly's common-law husband—Chris's father—went to Canada.

"I was in the kitchen," Beverly said, stepping past Chris and leading the way from the living room, through a swinging door, into the kitchen. Like the living room, the kitchen was immaculate, neat as a magazine ad. Although there was no sign of food being cooked or in preparation, the table was set with a single plate, folded paper napkin, and silverware. On one side of the plate was a small plastic container of orange juice and a half-empty bottle of Kamchatka Vodka.

"I got your check, thanks," Beverly said. She sat at

the table and poured some vodka into a water tumbler, then poured some orange juice into the water tumbler. "Can I fix you some coffee?" she asked.

"I'm only staying a minute," Chris said.

"What's the occasion?" Beverly drank some of the screwdriver, then placed the glass on the table and added more juice. "You were here less than a month ago. Usually, it's at least six weeks between visits. Sure, the time before that was back around Labor Day. You must need something, Christine. Money, I bet." She winked to show she was only kidding.

"I had a meeting with the PBS people in Baltimore," Chris said. "They want me to do a special. About Kuwait," she added, at her mother's blank look.

"That's nice."

Chris glanced around the incongruously tidy room. It looked exactly as it had at her last visit, and the visit before that. In concert with Beverly Adams's personal slovenliness, you would have expected dirty dishes piled high in the sink, the stove littered with food-encrusted pots and pans. It was as though Beverly used neatness as a kind of final, desperate attempt to compensate for the liquor. For the empty life.

"I'm going overseas again," Chris said. "I'll leave enough money with Mr. Licari." Philip Licari was an Annapolis attorney Chris retained to handle her mother's expenses. He doled Beverly a $600 monthly allowance and paid miscellaneous bills. There was no rent; Chris owned the building. Licari was one of the few people who knew of the existence of Beverly Adams, and that she was Christine Campbell's mother.

Licari knew little else about Chris, mainly because there was no reason for him to know more. Certainly, he did not know that Chris had changed her last name to Campbell out of pure whimsy, inspired by a supermarket display of canned chicken noodle soup. She made this decision the day after she graduated junior high school, which was the same day she ran away from home, Detroit, where she had lived the previous six years. Certainly, the attorney did not know—nor, again,

was there any reason for him to know—that Chris's uncle, her mother's brother, with whom she and her
mother were living, had celebrated his niece's graduation by drinking a pint of Christian Brothers brandy,
which he chased down with three cans of Labatt's Finest
Canadian Ale. All within one hour.

And then raped her.

He pinned her down on the kitchen floor with one
hand on her chest, while he unzipped his trousers with
the other hand. Chris at first fought him, but when he
threatened to hit her with his fist, which she knew was
no empty threat, she submitted. She lay on the floor,
spread her legs as he instructed, and felt him plunge
into her.

She had closed her eyes against the pain. She would
never forget the sour, rancid-alcohol odor of his breath
in her face, or his animal grunts of pleasure, or his
hoarse scream of satisfaction when he exploded inside
her and she thought that she herself might burst open.

No, the attorney knew nothing of that nor, to be sure,
that Michael Houvnanian, Chris's father, had been
killed in 1968 in an automobile accident in Toronto,
Canada, where he had gone to evade being drafted for
naval service in Vietnam.

". . . have plenty of money, honey," Beverly was saying. "You're real good to me. You're a real good daughter, loyal and loving." She swirled orange juice in the
container, then poured it into the glass. "Why'd you say
you were in town? I forgot. Oh, yeah, some kind of
meeting."

Some kind of meeting, Chris thought, which of course
was untrue, although a reasonable excuse for the real
reason. The real reason, Chris had been aware of from
the moment she had driven away from the Crowne
Royal Hotel. No, from the moment she had first seen
the air force colonel, that Nazi, and looked him in the
eye and told him about her "navy pilot" father.

She had come here as though to punish herself for
her dishonesty. To visit, as it were, the scene of the
crime. There was even a photograph of her father in

Beverly's bedroom. Chris refused to look at it. She hated him for his cowardice and for the danger, even in death—especially in death—he posed to the life she had built.

The "Vassar girl" whose family owned half of San Francisco, whose father was a Vietnam hero. So logical a story that not even Larry Hill ever questioned it; he had no reason to, nor any reason to doubt the authenticity of the mounted and framed gold wings Chris had purchased from a military supply house catalog. But that son of a bitch of a Nazi, the air force colonel—and she had momentarily forgotten his name—he seemed to sense the falsity. Something in his eyes told her. Or was it her own guilt?

". . . Sure you won't have any coffee, hon?" Beverly was saying.

"No, Ma, thanks," Chris said. She rose and looked down at Beverly. "I have to run."

Beverly reached up and touched the sleeve of Chris's coat. "What a pretty coat," she said. "Broadcloth, isn't it?"

"No, Ma, camel's hair."

"Camel's hair." Beverly stroked the fabric again. "Is it real?"

"Yes, Mother," Chris said. "It's real."

THREE

Nothing had changed. The same heavy traffic, the same shrill clamor of automobile horns and choking odor of diesel fumes and gasoline. The same sun, breaking through the morning clouds to warm the air and brighten the day. The same fishing boats moving up and down the river and under the bridges. At every other street corner or intersection, the same gigantic portraits and posters of Saddam Hussein.

On Sadik Street, less than two blocks from the Saddam Art Center and the fashionable shops and restaurants of Haifa Street, old men in ankle-length white cotton shirts, *galabiyyas,* sat cross-legged on the pavement in front of the tea houses. They smoked hookah pipes and hawked their wares: fresh herbs, spices, winter produce, bread, fruit juices. Women dressed in black *abayahs* that covered every inch of bare skin but for one eye trudged through narrow cobblestone alleys. Barefooted children darted in and out among the stalls and under the overhanging balconies of ancient houses whose sagging walls all seemed to lean against each other.

But this was Baghdad's charm. From the broad tree-lined boulevards of a modern cosmopolitan city where Dior-frocked women strolled along sparkling new mosaic-tiled sidewalks, you could turn a corner and be ten centuries back in time. Back in the Old City, which looked as it did seven hundred years before, after being rebuilt on the very ashes of the city that had been sacked and burned to the ground by Mongol invaders.

In truth, Adnan had not expected any great changes. Yes, the President's palace was now studded with anti-aircraft guns, including two batteries atop the triumphal arch at the palace's main gate, and the people endured daily mandatory air raid drills, and food and fuel were rationed. But for all that, and after four months of the most severe economic sanctions ever imposed upon any nation, the city functioned normally. Moreover, for early December, the weather was unseasonably warm, almost like summer.

The fine weather bothered Adnan. It made him jumpy and uneasy because it seemed some kind of ill omen. Ordinarily, such welcome weather would have been considered just the opposite, a good omen. These were hardly ordinary times.

On the other hand, ordinary weather would have been too chilly for the car's top to be down. The car, a 1983 ocean-blue Chrysler Le Baron convertible, had been stored on blocks in a friend's garage the entire time Adnan was in Washington. The car handled as well as the day he had driven it, brand-new, from the Mansur Street dealer's showroom.

A day to remember. He had just been discharged from the military hospital in Basra. A month's leave for recuperation and relaxation, a reward—as the citation read—for having distinguished himself as a true patriot and loyal member of the Baath Party. Translated, this meant that he had saved the life of one of the President's distant cousins, a battalion commander who panicked under Iranian artillery fire during the second battle for Khorramshahr. Adnan had assumed command of the unit in the absence of the C.O., the President's cousin, who was later found hiding in a toolshed near the railway station.

The car was a personal gift from the President to Adnan, an expression of appreciation for Adnan's omission of certain salient facts in his written report of battle that day. The President's cousin was relieved of command

and transferred to a tank group on the Turkish border. Adnan heard later that the man conducted himself irreproachably in a skirmish with a Kurdish guerrilla group, although his uncharacteristic bravery this time cost him his life.

"Yes, and I'll bet a thousand dinars to a dollar that the poor son of a bitch was shot in the back of the head by a political officer," Adnan said aloud. "At the direct order of his cousin, the President."

"I beg your pardon?" the girl seated beside him asked. She had to shout to be heard over the whistle of the wind. Adnan was driving fast on the smooth asphalt ramp to the 14th of July Bridge.

Adnan smiled self-consciously. "I was thinking out loud," he said. He rubbed the palm of his hand over the wood-grained plastic of the steering wheel. "About how I got the car."

The girl, who was young—twenty-two—and quite attractive with the long black hair and flawless dark complexion and deep black eyes of her Assyrian forebears, had heard this story before. The President was famous for that, for heaping lavish gifts upon those who served him faithfully. The President, they said, knew everything that went on within the army. Lieutenant Adnan Dulaimi had spared the President considerable embarrassment. Saddam never forgets. The thirty-day leave, the car, and later, Adnan's promotion to captain and then major and his choice assignment to Washington exemplified the President's gratitude.

"Darling, please slow down," the girl said as Adnan steered the car onto the bridge.

The bridge was not crowded. A double-decked bus, two produce trucks, and several taxis sped past in the opposite direction. Adnan cut in behind a canvas-tarpaulined army truck and followed the lumbering vehicle across the bridge. The policeman in the traffic kiosk at the foot of the bridge on Haifa Street drew himself up to full attention and saluted the Chrysler. More accurately, he saluted the driver's scarlet-and-white dress uniform. The policeman, an army veteran, recognized the driver as an officer of the Republican Guard.

Adnan returned the salute, swung left on Haifa Street, and found himself in bumper-to-bumper traffic. Even with the strict new gasoline rationing—which did not, of course, affect Republican Guard officers—automobiles clogged the streets. The girl jabbed her elbow into Adnan's ribs.

"Thank you for slowing down," she said facetiously. Her name was Hana Badran. She was a third-year medical student in the college of medicine at the university, daughter of a prominent Iraqi political figure and, for nearly a year now, Adnan Dulaimi's fiancée.

They had known each other since childhood. Adnan's father had been the Badran family's longtime gardener, chauffeur, and handyman. As a tenth birthday gift, Jamal Badran, Hana's father, presented Adnan with a new suit. The boy seemed displeased with the gift and—to his father's embarrassment but at Jamal's insistence—explained that he would have preferred a soldier's uniform. He was determined to become an officer and perform heroic deeds. As a sixteenth birthday gift, Adnan received an appointment to the military college. It required just one telephone call from Jamal Badran to his friend, Sadoun Nasir, then the Assistant Director General of the Baath Party.

". . . he should have done it months ago," Hana was saying. "No, he should never have done it at all!"

"Well, let's just be thankful he changed his mind," Adnan said. They were discussing the President's decision that morning to release all foreigners.

"Yes," Hana said. "As you say, keeping all those people as hostages, or 'guests' as he called them, was a foolish business to start with."

Adnan glanced quickly at her. "I never said it was foolish. When have you ever heard me refer to our revered leader as foolish?"

"Oh, no more than a dozen times."

"Please, darling: two or three times, perhaps, *not* a

dozen!" He reached over and clasped her hand. "You look very beautiful in that dress."

"You said that before."

"I must mean it, then."

She did look exceptionally beautiful in the dress, a white shawl-collared double-breasted coatdress. It blended perfectly with the white nylons and black patent leather pumps she had bought only yesterday at the new boutique, Flamant, in Mansur not far from where she and her father lived. She smiled to herself, thinking of Delal, one of her third-year classmates at the medical college. Delal, Hana's age and quite pretty in her own right, always wore the traditional black *chador* and continually scolded Hana for what Delal termed "disrespect of Islam." But Delal's face was uncovered, an inconsistency coolly explained away by Delal as her concession to the twentieth century.

Hana was suddenly aware that Adnan had resumed speeding. The road in both directions had opened up. Traffic now was mainly army vehicles, jeeps, and huge brown-canvas-topped trucks that roared past in clouds of dust.

"Please, I want to see my brother graduate, not end up in the medical center's emergency ward," she said. "And suppose he's not at the club? What do we do then?"

"We'll go back to the academy and hope he shows up."

Hana nodded tightly. Her brother, Amir, younger by one year, was graduating today from the military college after four grueling years of training. He had already received an assignment to the Republican Guard, personally requested by Saddam Hussein himself.

Until six years ago their father had been one of Iraq's foremost cardiologists. An ardent advocate of Palestinian rights, Jamal Badran had decided to devote his remaining active years to that cause. He now occupied a position as special consultant to the Foreign Ministry on Palestinian affairs, a job that demanded every minute of his time. He traveled widely and had formed important contacts throughout the Arab world and in Europe and America.

Jamal Badran was determined to find a solution to the present crisis or, as described by the Ministry of Information, "the events of last August." To that end, he had arranged a meeting in the next few weeks with a high American emissary, a man he trusted implicitly and who shared his belief that a war would be disastrous for both sides and must be averted at all costs. They would meet in Algiers.

Jamal had hoped Amir would follow Hana into medicine, but the younger boy idolized Adnan Dulaimi and had every intention of emulating him. Hana convinced her father not to push Amir into something he did not want to do. And Adnan was certainly an acceptable role model. More than "acceptable," for Adnan would soon be Jamal Badran's son-in-law, which as recently as a generation ago was unthinkable. The son of a gardener marrying above his class. But the new Iraq was a classless society. For all his eccentricities and rashness, Saddam Hussein had accomplished that. Give the devil his due.

Hana was thinking all this as Adnan turned off Abi Nwaas Street onto the rickety wood bridge to Al Khanazir Island. He drove across the bridge and pulled up at the gate of the Waziria Sporting Club. Ahmed, the wizened old gatekeeper—he had been there since Hana's earliest memory—saluted Adnan, then broke into a pleased smile. For Ahmed, too, Adnan represented the new Iraq.

"Major Dulaimi, sir. So good to see you," Ahmed said. He nodded respectfully at Hana. "And Miss Badran. No, excuse me, *Doctor* Badran—" "Not yet, Ahmed,' Hana said. "A year from now, hopefully. Until then, I'm still plain 'Miss.' Is my brother here?"

"I believe he's on the court."

Ahmed raised the barrier and saluted once more. Adnan drove through the gate and followed the curving eucalyptus-tree-lined avenue to the clubhouse, a low, rambling building patterned after an English manor house. Forty years ago the Waziria Club was an exclusive British officers' club whose amenities had included a nine-hole golf course, a half-mile racetrack, stables for fifty horses, and a grassed exercise and grazing area.

The club had fallen into gradual disrepair, and in 1958 when General al-Karim Qasim overthrew the monarchy, it was finally closed. Ten years later, when the Baath Party came to power, a group of high army officers and wealthy civilians reopened the premises. Over the years the facilities had been restored and the clubhouse faithfully reconstructed, all but the racetrack, which was replaced by a complex of tennis courts and the largest swimming pool in Iraq. The club's dining room, with its French chef, served some of the finest food in Baghdad.

Jamal Badran had held a family membership in the club since its 1968 reopening. His wife, deceased now some twelve years, had won the women's golf championship six consecutive years. Jamal's two children, Hana and Amir, each had twice won the junior golf title. Since commencing medical school, Hana found little time to play golf, and Amir had abandoned the game in favor of tennis and to concentrate on his hobby, painting abstract art.

Amir and another young man, Khalid Sadoon, their arms laden with rackets, sweaters, and towels, were just walking off the center court when Hana and Adnan drove up. Amir was a lanky, dark-haired boy, endowed with the firm facial features of his father and the deep, probing but gentle brown eyes of his mother. He and Khalid were engrossed in conversation.

"Amir . . . !" Hana shouted.

Amir waved to her, and spoke again to Khalid, obviously inviting him to say hello to Hana and Adnan. But Khalid shook his head, no, waved to Hana, and left. As Amir trotted over to the car, Adnan said wryly to Hana, "I don't think Khalid is very fond of me."

"He's jealous," Hana said, not displeased. Khalid, several years older than Amir, was a doctor, a radiologist, and made no secret of his warm feeling for Hana.

Or, likewise, his distress at her forthcoming marriage to Adnan.

"I cleaned his clock," Amir said, jerking his head toward Khalid. "Six-love, six-two, six-one. And last year he was the bloody club champion! Oh, did I tell you?" He grasped Hana's arm. "They'll be showing six of my paintings at Galerie Fontan! Hello, Adnan."

"Have you any bloody idea of the time?" Adnan asked.

"Ten-thirty . . . ? Eleven?"

"Twelve, you damn fool!" Adnan said. "The passing-out parade starts in half an hour!"

Amir closed his eyes in dismay. "My uniform—" he started to say.

"We brought it," Hana said. She reached behind her into the backseat of the car. She held up the sleeve of a scarlet formal dress tunic that, with trousers, shoes, and the other accoutrements, was folded neatly on the seat.

"Get in the car, idiot!" Adnan said.

Amir tossed his tennis equipment into the backseat and vaulted in after it. They drove out of the club, waving good-bye to the old gatekeeper, who saluted them and turned away, only to whirl around, peering in astonishment at Amir in the backseat, stripping off his clothes.

Most of the fifteen-minute drive from the island and across town to the Academy was consumed with Hana scolding Amir for his utter disregard for time. No, excuse me, disregard for anything. And anybody. The most important day of his life, and he forgets himself playing tennis!

Amir mumbled excuses and continued the awkward task of struggling into his uniform in the confined space of the backseat of a fast-moving automobile. But by the time they reached the Academy he was fully dressed, choke collar tightened, purple beret tilted at a properly rakish angle.

Adnan braked to a stop under the entry gate portico. The sentry came to full attention and saluted crisply.

Adnan returned the salute, then indicated Amir in the backseat.

"Lieutenant Amir Badran," Adnan said.

The sentry, an acne-scarred teenager, saluted Amir and gestured Adnan to proceed. The car had moved ahead only a few yards when Amir pounded Adnan's shoulder.

"Adnan, stop! Stop, dammit!"

Adnan jammed on the brakes. Amir scrambled from the car and strode back to the sentry. He drew himself up to rigid attention and saluted the bemused sentry. Without another word, he about-faced, raced back to the car, leaped in, and motioned Adnan to drive on.

"My first salute," Amir explained. "I have to return it, don't I?"

Jamal Badran was the third in a distinguished line of physicians. His father had served for three years as special medical consultant to General Sir William Fitzgibbon, the British military governor of Iraq. His grandfather had been personal physician to the Turkish caliph of Baghdad when Iraq was part of the Ottoman Empire.

The Badrans were no Bedouin tribesmen; they traced their lineage back to Syrian merchants and tradesmen who settled in Iraq three hundred years before. Although Jamal had lost much of his family's land holdings in the revolution of 1958, he regained a substantial portion of those losses with the Baathist ascension to power. In truth, he had no special need or desire for a great fortune. He lived comfortably, enjoying his new role as diplomat—no, he more than enjoyed it, he was passionately devoted to it. His children were clearly on their way to a respectable adulthood. What more did a man of fifty-six need for happiness?

Well, of course, a good woman. This was Jamal Badran's sole regret, the loss of his wife, Irène, a Frenchwoman he had met and married in 1963, during his second year of internship at the Institut Pasteur in Paris. Not at all a religious man, Jamal was nevertheless grateful to God for at least giving him those fifteen years of happiness with Irène. She had walked off the golf course one afternoon, complaining of a mild stomachache. Two weeks later she was dead. Pancreatic cancer, the most insidious of all cancers.

"Come back to us, Jamal."

Jamal smiled self-consciously. "I'm sorry, Hassan, what were you saying?" He was speaking to the man seated beside him in the reviewing stand, Hassan Marwaan. Hassan, a major general, chief surgeon of the Iraqi Army medical corps, was gaining weight. His uniform bulged in all the wrong places. Jamal, himself a colonel in the medical corps reserve, had known Hassan Marwaan since both were young residents at Shuhada Hospital. They had been friends and colleagues that long.

"I was saying," Hassan Marwaan said, "that you have a fine boy, and you have a good reason to be proud of him."

Hassan's eyes were fixed on Amir, in the third and last row of new officers, who were all standing at attention in the center of the court. The commandant of cadets, a young major general, stood on a dais calling the names of each man. Each stepped forward, saluted, and accepted the ribbon-tied commendation presented by the commandant. Then a handshake, another salute, and the newly commissioned second lieutenant returned to the formation.

". . . and that daughter of yours," Hassan continued, "she's grown into a real beauty."

"And grown more independent as well," Jamal said, nodding indulgently, gazing at Hana, who sat with Adnan in the temporary grandstand on the parade ground. Her white dress stood out against the darker colors of the clothes of the civilians and scarlet tunics of the military in the crowded grandstand. "I suppose she really is a new breed. What is it they call them? Feminists?"

"It's the new Iraq, Jamal."

"I only hope to God, there'll be an Iraq, period,"

Jamal said. "If this man does not soon come to his senses—"

"Jamal, please." Hassan glanced worriedly around. They were in the midst of more than one hundred spectators, mostly army officers and their wives. No one had overheard; they were all too engrossed in the ceremony.

Jamal knew Hassan shared his disapproval of the government's current policies. It was like riding in an engineerless, runaway express train, hurtling downhill toward a demolished bridge. But Hassan, like everyone else highly placed in the party, feared to speak freely.

Which made Jamal ponder the wisdom of his journey next week to Algiers, the "unofficial" meeting with the Americans to explore a means of ending the crisis. The meeting had been quietly encouraged by the Foreign Ministry, desperate to extricate the nation from the situation "he" had created.

"He," Jamal thought, and smiled grimly to himself: even when thinking about the President, you referred to him as "he," as though uttering the name might be considered a form of disloyalty.

So preoccupied with these thoughts was Jamal, he nearly missed Amir's presentation. Hassan Marwaan nudged him sharply in the ribs. "Jamal! Look alive, for God's sake. It's Amir."

Jamal, overwhelmed with pride, watched his son step up to the rostrum for the diploma and handshake. The remainder of the ceremony passed in a blur. The sun flashed off the brass instruments and glossily shined boots of the musicians of the 22nd Division's band as they marched past the reviewing stand, led by their busby-hatted drum major. Behind them, as one, came the entire corps of cadets and the new officers. Overhead, a squadron of jet fighters appeared, each plane emitting a stream of colored smoke: red, green, white, and black for the colors of the flag.

The jets screamed past overhead and in an instant were only thin dark specks in the bright sky. The roar of their engines was loud in the distance. It made Jamal wonder if perhaps this time the President's words might be more than mere rhetoric. Perhaps the Americans would indeed end up swimming in their own blood.

Two gigantic tents had been erected on the quadrangle for the reception following the ceremony. All the new officers and their families milled about, exchanging congratulations, sampling the meager offering of hors d'oeuvres, and making much too frequent trips to the bar. Someone did in fact remark that while the UN sanctions had created a serious food shortage, there was no shortage of alcohol. There was more beer—Japanese and German—than Adnan ever recalled seeing.

"We're some Islamic people," he said, gesturing at the queue at the bar. He was talking to Amir, who had just come from the bar with a bottle of Kirin beer in one hand and a tumbler of Scotch in the other. Amir handed him the Scotch.

"That's why we're not a second-rate power like the rest of the Arabs," Amir said. "We Iraqis, dear Major Dulaimi, are civilized."

Adnan drank some of the Scotch. It burned his throat. In America he had discovered the joys of iced whiskey. Now that, he thought, was truly civilized. "Your father wants us to join him," he said to Amir.

Amir followed Adnan's gaze across the tent. Near the entrance, Hana and Jamal stood chatting with Hassan Marwaan and his wife, a stout middle-aged lady in a conspicuously expensive tailored suit of French design. They had just been joined by a white-haired Soviet admiral, the commander of a small cadre of Russian naval advisors.

Hassan introduced Adnan and Amir to the admiral, whose name was Spugarin. Spugarin raised a champagne glass. "To Lieutenant Badran."

"To Iraq," Amir said. He brought the beer bottle to his lips, only to immediately lower it at Jamal's admonishing glance. "To Iraq," he repeated.

Admiral Spugarin seconded that toast, then excused himself and walked off. Jamal waited until the admiral was out of earshot. "We might also drink to communication," he said.

"Communication?" Hassan said. "I suppose you mean your attempt to open some kind of back channel with the Americans? To initiate . . . what did you call it? An exchange?"

"Of ideas," Jamal said. "A dialogue."

"And that's the purpose of this pilgrimage of yours to Algiers next week?"

"Hassan, in five weeks, five weeks from today in fact, the UN ultimatum expires. . . ." Jamal paused. He knew Hassan wanted to goad him into a debate, hoping to discourage the trip. Hassan believed the Americans would consider the meeting a sign of Iraqi weakness. Jamal smiled indulgently. "Yes, Hassan, that is the purpose. Oh, by the way, you might do me a favor: I want Adnan to accompany me. As my aide, you might say. I'm sure you can arrange it."

"I'm in the medical corps, Jamal, not the Defense Ministry."

Jamal smiled again. "A phone call from you to your brother-in-law, the deputy defense minister, will do it."

"It's my idea, General," Adnan said. "I don't think he should be traveling without some . . . support."

"Support?" Hassan said. "That's another word for bodyguard, isn't it? Who does he need protection from —the Americans?"

"Just make the phone call, Hassan," Jamal said.

"A phone call," Hassan said. "The whole damn world works on phone calls." He turned to his wife as though expecting her to agree. But she was engaged in conversation with another fashionably dressed woman, the wife of the Soviet admiral.

"A phone call," Hassan repeated, this time addressing Hana. "Is there no way you can convince your father to return to his medical practice and stop meddling in politics?"

"He's not meddling, Uncle Hassan," Hana said. Hassan's attitude annoyed her. Hassan annoyed her, period. He always had. She remembered him from childhood, continually discouraging her father from activities outside his direct realm. "He's trying to prevent needless bloodshed."

Amir slammed his beer bottle down on the seat of a folding chair. "That kind of bloodshed is *not* needless, Hana! It is very much needed. It is necessary! It's the only way we'll maintain our honor!"

Jamal said to Hassan, "There you are, Hassan, the 'new Iraq.' "

"I happen to agree with him," Hassan said.

"And you?" Jamal said to Adnan. "Do you also agree?"

"Agree we should fight?" Adnan asked. He had anticipated the question and prepared an answer, one he did not for an instant believe. "It will never come to that. The Americans aren't stupid. Neither are we. All the oil in Kuwait isn't worth a single drop of American blood or Iraqi blood. I guarantee you that this issue will be resolved, long before the fifteenth of January, and in an amicable manner."

"The Americans don't want peace!" Amir said.

"Perhaps not," said Jamal. "But we owe it to ourselves to find out. I mean, really find out, one way or the other. To do that, we have to show ourselves as serious. We must stop behaving like Arab shopkeepers haggling with tourists in the bazaar."

Hassan glanced past Jamal's shoulder at Amir. Amir shrugged helplessly, a message that it was useless to try to reason with Jamal. Hassan said to Hana, "How long have I known your father? Thirty years?" He faced Jamal and continued to Hana, "He hasn't lost a shred of that damned idealism."

Hana said, "*Realism,* Uncle Hassan. Our 'new Iraq' will not be built by bleeding it to death on the battlefield."

"Nor, dear sister, will it be built by expressing weakness to our enemies," Amir said.

"No, 'dear brother,' it's *you* who is the idealist," Hana said. She slipped her arm through Jamal's and faced Hassan. "And all the rest of you."

She said something else, but her words were drowned out by a loud rumbling that shook the ground under their feet. Everyone rushed from the tents. T-72 tanks were just then rolling across the quadrangle. Ten rows, five tanks abreast. Behind the tanks came APCs, also in rows of five, each vehicle fully manned with helmeted soldiers gripping AK-47 automatic rifles. The procession seemed endless.

2

For Elaine Mason, it was what she called his "impregnability" that had finished her with Nick Harmon. He had placed an armored shell around his emotions. No ordinary woman could pierce that armor, not even Elaine Mason, who certainly was no ordinary woman. To begin with, she was a major in the U.S. Army. True, a reservist, not regular army, but a field grade officer nevertheless and now on active duty.

She was thirty-four years old, five feet eight inches tall, and weighed a symmetrically distributed 130 pounds. Her angular face and wide-set brown eyes were framed, halo-like, by brown hair fashioned in a feather cut. By any standards, a good-looking woman. She also had an IQ of 137 and a Michigan State University master's degree in psychology, neither of which bore the slightest relation to her chosen profession, which was flying helicopters.

She loved flying helicopters.

She loved the army.

It was in the genes. She was an army brat, born in a U.S. Army hospital in Germany, where her father served as a master sergeant and senior NCO with an 8th Air Cav regiment. By the time she turned fifteen, she had lived on army posts in five different countries and attended twice as many schools.

At seventeen she was ready for college. West Point, naturally, but the Academy's minimum entry age was eighteen. A year was too long to wait. She accepted an ROTC scholarship to Michigan State and remained there through the master's degree. Psychology, however, held less interest than flying helicopters. It had started as a lark, a challenge really, that quickly turned into an obsession. And when a Seattle radio station offered her a job as a helicopter traffic reporter, the obsession became a career.

And three years ago, in 1987, a marriage.

A very nice man, nineteen years her senior, a former confirmed bachelor, an orthopedic surgeon with a prosperous Bellevue practice. She had been his patient—a broken leg in a skiing accident—and, one week after he removed the cast, flew off with him to Jamaica, where they were married. An ideal marriage. He was busy, she was busy, and each respected and was tolerant of the other. Equally important, they understood each other. He even understood her delight and excitement last August at being recalled to active duty with her reserve army aviation unit.

She loved the army.

She did not love Nicholas Harmon. More accurately, no longer loved him. They had met on a rainy morning six years ago at MacDill when she brought her Black Hawk in for an emergency landing. Nick, then a major and squadron operations officer, came racing out in a staff car—his face frozen in horror realizing that the pilot was a woman (and a reservist, which only compounded the crime)—demanding to know why in the name of Jesus Christ she had dumped that clumsy piece of machinery on the VIP ramp right in front of the tower? Didn't she speak English? Hadn't she been instructed to land in the transient aircraft area?

Yes, Major, I speak English, she had replied. And I did not, as instructed, land in the transient aircraft area because the ramp was closer and I was afraid that before I could reach the transient aircraft area, I and my clumsy piece of machinery would be splashed all over the countryside. Does that answer your question, sir?

The classic beginning of a classic romance. With classic characters: he, recently divorced; she, young, single, intelligent, attractive. She was a first lieutenant then,

serving her annual two weeks' reservist tour of active
duty.

After that, they saw each other as much as possible,
sometimes as often as every four or five weeks. It went
on for two years, fun and games—and marvelous sex—
but the word "love" never once crossed his lips. And he
knew that she was in love with him. Finally, she told him
that she wanted—no, *needed*—more from the relationship than a dozen pleasant weekends per year. He, said
Nick, had been under the impression that they both
were eminently satisfied with the status quo. He knew
he was, Nick said. That's fine, Nick, she said, but I'm not
and unless we change the status quo, it's all over. Kaput.
Finito. And, when he did not argue the point, it was.

She still remembered her resentment and sense of
rejection when, a year later, she informed him of her
impending marriage. She had half expected him to protest, to ask her to wait until they could discuss it. Speak
now or forever hold your peace. So what was his reaction to her news? He congratulated her.

Hey, that's great, he had said. Congratulations!

Congratulations, your ass, you son of a bitch, she was
thinking now, standing on the observation platform on
the roof of the Monterey Peninsula Airport, watching
the USAir turboprop taxi up to the flood-lighted terminal. She had been standing here in the windy, chilly
drizzle nearly twenty minutes, waiting for his flight to
arrive, wondering why she had agreed to meet him in
the first place. But he sounded so down on the phone
when he called from Vegas, she didn't have the heart to
say no. Not that she was so big-hearted, at least not
concerning Nick Harmon, but they did go back a long
way. A lot of water over the dam.

On the phone he had explained that Johnny Donovan
told him that she was up there at Fort Ord with a
UH-60 supply and support squadron. Well, since he just
happened to be coming to California that evening,
maybe they could get together.

I'm shipping out for the Gulf next week, she had replied. And I can't think of a single reason why we should get together, Nick. Can you?

I'd like to see you, he had said. Isn't that reason enough?

No, not nearly reason enough, she thought now, watching him shift his small leather B-4 bag from one hand to another to enable him to assist a fat, elderly lady down the narrow three-step ramp built into the door of the USAir Beech 1900. He hadn't changed a bit. Same husky frame, same confident, almost cocky stride, same habit of adjusting his cap squarely on his head whenever he started walking. She wondered if his hair was graying. Hers was, a few dismaying strands.

She had honestly intended making him wait in the terminal five or ten minutes—let him think that maybe she wouldn't meet him after all—but she hurried down the marble stairway to the terminal. She stood, arms folded, near the USAir ticket counter, and nodded hello.

My God, but he looked good. The bastard! She wanted to make some clever crack about him using the same aftershave lotion, but it would have been an acknowledgment that she was thinking about him. One thing pleased her, at least: She knew she looked good. She could see it in his eyes. She wished she had worn civilian clothes, with heels. He always said she had legs that could conquer the world.

". . . you look great," he was saying, grasping her hand and squeezing it gently. She had expected him to try to kiss her, whereupon she would turn away and offer him only her cheek. She should have known better.

"The rewards of good, clean living," she said. "You don't look so bad yourself."

"That's what a couple of days away from the desert does for you," he said. "No more Saudi sand in your powdered eggs. Well, you'll find out soon enough. Where are they sending you?"

"Dhahran."

"Dhahran isn't so bad. It's a real airbase with real

food. Speaking of food, I hope you'll let me take you to dinner."

"Nick, I sure as hell didn't drive all the way down here in the rain just to hear you tell me how good I look. You're damn right I'll let you take me to dinner." Which, again, raised the question of why exactly she was here, meeting him.

Curiosity, she told herself, nothing more, nothing less. Moreover, and to her relief, she did not feel any of the old hormones stirring. Was that the origin of the curiosity, hormones? And suppose there had been a stirring, what then?

She was thinking all this as they drove in her '89 Caddy Fleetwood into Carmel—she was taking him to a restaurant she liked, Chez O'Shea, an old-fashioned steak and chop house—as she chatted away about how she hated having the car driven back to Seattle by some stranger, but that was the only way to get it home after she left for the Gulf.

". . . naturally, I couldn't ask my husband to come down here for it," she was saying. "He's much too busy." There, she had reminded Mister Lieutenant Colonel Nicholas Harmon that she was married, and very much so, thank you.

"How does he feel about you going off to war?" Nick asked. They were already in Carmel, proceeding slowly along Ocean Avenue. It had begun raining harder. The glare of the Caddy's headlights bounced off the rain-slicked rear window of a station wagon in front of them.

Elaine did not immediately reply; she had just remembered that when they first met, six years ago at MacDill, it was the same kind of weather. "How does my husband feel about me being recalled?" she said. "He understands."

Nick said nothing. He listened to the rhythmic beat of the car's windshield wipers. The sound actually relaxed him, the first time he had relaxed in three hours, since leaving Las Vegas.

"He understands," Elaine said.

"He sounds like a nice guy."

"He is," she said. "And one hell of a fine doctor."

"You must be happy."

"I'm very happy."

"I'm glad."

"I'm glad that you're glad," she said, and cut the wheel sharply to edge in close to the red taillights of a car pulling away from a parking place near the restaurant. She slid into the spot and snapped the gear selector into PARK, switched off the ignition, and turned to him. "All right, Nick, now tell me the real reason for this charming little reunion?"

"I told you: I was heading this way, and knew you were here, and . . ." he shrugged.

"And you wanted to see if my eyes were still brown? No, you were curious about my hair: Did I still wear it the same way? Come on, Nick, cut the crap."

He said nothing for a moment; he listened to the rain drumming hollowly on the car roof. Then, "I saw Jean in Vegas."

Elaine nodded tightly, knowingly. "You saw Jean in Vegas," she repeated.

"It was a mistake."

"A mistake," she repeated in that same cold, flat tone. "You saw her, and you just had to tell me all about it. Cry on my shoulder a little, is that it, Nick?"

"Something like that, probably."

"Probably. Well, Nick, I don't want to hear about it." Elaine opened the car door. "I heard it all, a hundred years ago." She stepped out into the wet street and hurried into the restaurant. She did not wait for Nick to accompany her or even glance back at him. It was as though she really did not care what he did.

He sat alone in the car now, gazing at the opaque reflection of automobile headlights on the wet road surface, pondering the true answer to Elaine's question: why had he come here? But the answer he gave *was* true, disarmingly so. He had seen and talked with Jean.

Jean, the former Mrs. Nicholas Harmon.

The former mother of his former child.

Nick, en route to Los Angeles, had hitched a ride

from Washington to Nellis with a TAC courier. With two
hours to kill before his flight left Las Vegas for L.A., he
stopped at the Desert Inn for a drink. It was early afternoon, a few minutes after three. The only customers at
the bar were two men drinking beer and playing the
video poker games built into the bar surface. Nick ordered a Beefeater on the rocks. A man and a woman
moved over to a table directly behind him.

The woman, in her late thirties, garishly dressed although not unattractive, was a friend of Jean's. She recognized Nick immediately. After commenting on his
silver oak leaves—he was a captain when she had last
seen him—she said she talked with Jean only yesterday.
Jean was doing fine.

Nick asked the woman if she happened to have Jean's
phone number. Next he knew, he was in the lobby at a
pay phone. What the hell, he had told himself, he was
here, why not say hello? Sure, why not? It was only
decent. For all her problems and the misery she caused
him, she had been an important part of his life.

After five rings he almost hung up; in truth, relieved.
But then the answering machine clicked on. "Hi, if this
is Fred, at two o'clock, I'll be in the Rainbow Bar at the
Flamingo." The Flamingo was only a mile or so down
the Strip, and on the way to the airport.

Jean was there, alone, nervously twirling ice in a half-
filled bucket glass. Vodka-tonic, he assumed, her daytime beverage of choice. She wore a low-cut, short-
skirted, sheer black dress and black fishnet stockings
and gold high-heeled pumps. Across her shoulders was
slung a beaver coat, the same beaver he had given her
on her twenty-sixth birthday, eleven years ago. Even
from a distance, Nick saw that the heavy makeup did
not conceal the little network of wrinkles under her eyes
and around her mouth. Her long red hair, coiffed in a
tight chignoned backsweep, shone dully in the reflection
of the neon beer signs above the bar.

She had just finished her drink and slid the empty
glass toward the bartender when she looked up and saw
Nick. She seemed not to recognize him, which amused

him: She was nearsighted but too vain to wear glasses in public. Then her eyes softened. She half smiled.

He said, "I eavesdropped on your message to Fred."

She got off the bar stool and walked over to him. She tapped the face of her wristwatch. "He's an hour late. A good indication I've been stood up, wouldn't you say? Never trust an airplane driver. I should know, eh, Nick?"

"Somebody from Nellis?"

"A civilian, an airline pilot. I met him last winter in Tahoe. He's a fun guy," she said. "You're looking good. How long has it been? Two years? Three?"

"Five," he said. "You're looking pretty good your-self."

"I'm thirty-seven, Nick, and I look every year of it," she said. "What brought you to town?"

"I'm passing through," he said, and explained that he was on his way to visit his father reporting back to duty in Saudi Arabia.

"What time's your plane?" she asked.

"Four-forty."

"Catch a later one," she said. "Have a drink with me."

Almost as a reflex, his eyes swept disapprovingly over her dress. "I don't think I can. . . ."

"Oh, yes, I remember how you like your ladies sedate and tailored. My God, you are such a snob!" But she spoke good-naturedly and had already slipped her arms into the coat sleeves and closed the coat tightly. "Is that better?" she said. "Now I'm not so flashy." She tucked her arm into his, and in the same breath said, "Come on, have a drink."

It was not all that unpleasant. They chatted, innocu-ously at first, mostly about the Gulf crisis and his career. It was as though each carefully avoided their common past and, in Jean's case, the present.

In addition to the beer he ordered, Nick had had only that single gin at the Desert Inn, which left him three vodka-tonics behind Jean. If the liquor affected her, she did not show it. Not until Nick placed a twenty-dollar bill on the bar and rose to leave.

"Nick, I'm so lonely. I'm so alone. . . ." She grasped his hand. "Come on home with me. I have a nice little place and it's not far from the airport. There's a one A.M. flight you can make."

"Jean, why are you doing this?"

She smiled wanly. "You were in love with me once."

"Once," he said.

The smile froze. She withdrew her hand from his. "You bastard," she said, her voice rising with each word. "You rotten son of a bitch!" A man nearby glanced irritably at her. The bartender, washing glasses, pretended not to hear. Nick looked around, embarrassed.

"You're drunk," he said to her.

"Big deal," she said.

"Nothing ever changes, does it?"

"That's your fault."

My fault, he thought. That again. She was reminding him that she had started drinking only after the child died. Until then, her only desire in life was to please him, Nick. Nick, her Lord and Master. Nick wanted her to be educated, so she signed up for night classes at UNLV. Remember, Nick? Remember the basic accounting course I was taking that night? Where the hell were you, Nick? You were at a poker game at the club. The Wing Commander personally invited you to play, and you couldn't turn him down. You were bucking for major. So I had to hire a baby-sitter, Nick. A baby-sitter. Because you were bucking for major.

You remember the baby-sitter, don't you, Nick?

Yes, he remembered the baby-sitter. He even remembered her name, Nicolene. A wave of nausea enveloped him. He felt hot and cold all at once. His stomach began rolling. Bile choked his throat. Without a word he left the bar and hurried into the lobby and to the men's room.

It had all started in 1979, Nick's first tour at Nellis. One night Nick and three other pilots were comped to dinner and a show at the Tropicana. One of the dancers in the show, the *Folies Bergère,* was Jean Stratton. Nick could not keep his eyes from her. The six weeks that followed were the fulfillment of all Nick's dreams of the woman of his dreams. On the final day of the sixth week, Jean informed him that she was pregnant.

On the second day of the seventh week, Nick and Jean were married in the Little Chapel of the West on the Las Vegas Strip. They honeymooned in a suite at Caesar's Palace—courtesy of a friend of a friend of Nick's commanding officer—and then set up house-keeping in a Capehart bungalow on the base.

Later that same year, Nick was transferred to Langley Field. There, in the maternity ward of the base hospital, the baby was born. A girl, also named Jean. The child was not a month old when her mother began urging Nick to leave the service. The airlines and aircraft companies were sorely in need of experienced personnel. Good salaries provided more of life's good things.

Nick tried to explain that, for him, the air force was the best of all life's good things. He loved the air force; the air force was his life. He was a lifer. He intended to one day wear at least two stars, hopefully more. Hopefully, all the way to four. And in practical terms, no civilian aviation enterprise could match the challenges and opportunities offered by the military. But then, of course, how could Jean be expected to appreciate that? How could she be expected to understand the sense of achievement at being entrusted with the safekeeping of a multimillion dollar piece of machinery that could propel you through the air at twice the speed of sound? Or the utter ecstasy of operating that piece of machinery?

Well, she could not and did not understand, but was as tenacious in working toward her goal as Nick. To that end, to her credit, when Nick returned to Nellis as an Aggressor Pilot in the Red Flag program, Jean enrolled in night classes in hotel management at the University of Nevada, Las Vegas. She truly enjoyed the course and the prospects of a gratifying future. She was happy, and so was Nick. Little Jean was a miniature replica of her mother. A beauty.

And then, one freezing winter evening, it all ended.

Jean was at school. Nick was playing poker. Jean had hired a sixteen-year-old girl to baby-sit. The girl, who accepted the job only on condition that her seventeen-year-old boyfriend be allowed to keep her company, defrosted a pizza for herself and the boy, and shared some with Little Jean. Little Jean loved pizza, especially with green and red peppers and chunks of salami.

The pizza came wrapped in a large plastic bag. The baby-sitter left the bag on Little Jean's bed. Little Jean, planning to frighten the baby-sitter, placed the bag over her own head. Within seconds she was thrashing for breath. She knocked over a chair and the radio from her night table, neither of which was heard by the baby-sitter or her boyfriend, although they were less than ten feet away in the living room. Their ecstatic grunts and groans drowned out all other sounds.

Jean fell into a deep depression. It was understandable. But she needed pills to sleep, and pills to keep awake, and pills for energy. To stimulate her appetite. To repress her appetite. She dropped out of school, spending her evenings now at the casinos with some of her old friends. She would arrive home late at night or sometimes not at all. She began wearing garish clothes, for which she ran up horrendous bills at department stores. Once, at Neiman Marcus, she was accused of shoplifting; it cost Nick $1,500 for the store to drop the charges. When she and Nick talked, which was seldom, it invariably ended in recrimination. If he had listened to her and left the air force, what happened would not have happened. His fault, his responsibility.

She refused help. She could handle it. She knew what she was doing. Not a day passed when she did not berate Nick. He tolerated it for more than a year. Finally, when he was transferred to MacDill, he asked her for a divorce. She agreed, which did not surprise him, and demanded no alimony, which did surprise him.

Her last words to him were, "And just think how lucky you are, Nick, you're not stuck with any child support." He had never in his life struck a woman, and did not then, although he came dangerously close. He borrowed $10,000 from his father and $5,000 from the base credit union, and gave her the $15,000 in a lump sum. It made him feel better.

Nick remained in the Flamingo men's room until the nausea subsided and his stomach had settled. He ran cold water over his face and combed his hair. He remembered studying his face in the mirror. He had no color. Death Row complexion, he remembered thinking, and returned to the bar. Jean still sat there, but not alone. She was in a bantering conversation with a bespectacled middle-aged man, wearing casual but expensive sports clothes. The man, whose carefully blowdried hair was too black and too heavy to be his own, nursed a highball. They were not conversing, they were negotiating.

Obviously interested in whatever the proposition was, the man motioned the bartender to serve Jean another drink. At that moment, Jean noticed Nick. Nick read the message in her eyes: You don't like what I'm doing, that's your problem! Get lost! He strode past her, out of the hotel, and into a taxi.

At the airport, on the moving walkway, Nick passed a row of USAir gates. One gate read MONTEREY. The flight was scheduled for departure in ten minutes. Nick's Delta flight to Los Angeles would not take off for another hour. He had no real desire to see his father. He knew the visit would include at least one caustic reminder that Bob Harmon had correctly appraised the woman Nick married, and that it was Nick's good fortune to be rid of her.

Nick gazed at the USAir MONTEREY sign another moment. Fort Ord was near Monterey. Elaine Mason was stationed at Fort Ord. He wheeled around to the nearest telephone, called Fort Ord, and spoke to Elaine. With only one aviation battalion on the base, she was easy to find.

Once, a hundred years ago as Elaine liked to say, she had provided him the shoulder to cry on. More, to be

sure, than a shoulder, much more. But he had met
Elaine too soon after the divorce. Jean had burned him
out, squeezed him dry emotionally. He had nothing
more to offer, emotionally.

At the time.

In truth, he was afraid. He could not bring himself to
trust another woman, not after Jean. He did not want to
expose himself to a repetition of the pain and frustration and bitterness of that experience. As much as he
desired and needed someone else—at the time, Elaine
—he refused to take the risk.

A hundred years ago, as she said, he was an emotional cripple. And now, a hundred years later, nothing
much seemed to have changed. So meeting her tonight
was another mistake, another in a long series of mistakes. But she certainly did look good, he thought, joining her now at a secluded table in a quiet corner of
Chez O'Shea.

"I ordered a drink for you," she said. "Gin on the
rocks, right?"

"You remember," he said.

"I remember everything, Nick," she said. "Everything."

"Is that a compliment?"

In reply, as the bar boy served their drinks, the corners of her mouth turned down ever so slightly. "All
right, so you want to tell me about your little seance
with Jean. So tell me."

"You said you didn't want to hear it."

"I changed my mind."

"So did I," he said. "You're right: I'd be crying on
your shoulder. The hell with it." He signaled the waiter.
"Let's eat."

" 'Crying on my shoulder' is the wrong phrase," she
said. " 'Pouring your heart out' is what I should have
said, because that, Nick, you can do. Crying is what you
won't do. No, what you *can't* do. And that's a shame,
because I'm sure it would make you feel better."

"That's right, you're a psychologist," he said. "I forgot."

"Don't knock it, Nick. That advice would cost you a hundred bucks somewhere else."

"It's the same advice you gave me a long time ago."

"Yes, and you didn't follow it then, and you won't now," she said, as the waiter presented the menus. "They specialize in lamb here." She tapped a fingernail on the menu. "And it won't cost you a hundred, only thirty-five."

They ordered a double rack of lamb, medium rare, and a bottle of '85 Jordan Cabernet, which he knew would probably set him back another $35, but which he recalled was her favorite. They ate and drank and talked. He told her about the MiG, and his new but hopefully brief assignment in Israel. And about the incredible U.S. military buildup, and the probability of war, and what it was like in the desert, and what she could expect. Sand, he said, plus horrible weather. Daytime heat and night cold. And more sand. Although, as he had already noted, Dhahran was not bad duty.

Throughout dinner, his memory continually drifted back to their relationship. She had come into his life at the wrong time. She had demanded a commitment when he was unprepared—no, unable—to offer any. And he did not fault her for moving on. He understood. Yes, he thought wryly, as they finished coffee, everybody understands. Her husband included.

"So you're happy?" he asked.

"Very," she said.

"I don't believe you."

"You don't *want* to believe me."

"You're trying too hard to convince me."

"You ran into your ex-wife, and it brought back all kinds of bad memories. So, just as you did . . . a hundred years ago . . . you raced on up to me. Maybe I'd make it all better again. Like I did the last time. What is it that famous baseball player used to say, 'It's déjà vu all over again.' " She shook her head solemnly. "It's too late, Nick. You're too late."

He felt like a fool; no, worse, like a child being reprimanded. Well, goddammit, he was behaving like a child.

Racing, as she so correctly described it, up here to see her. For what? Because he felt lonely and alone? Because he wanted to be with someone who might understand? Understand what? She was right, it was too late.

Elaine drove him back to the airport in time for the last flight to San Francisco. From there he would fly straight to Washington. She dropped him at the terminal entrance. He got out of the car and spoke to her through the open window. "Maybe we'll run into each other in Saudi Arabia," he said.

"Take care of yourself, Nick."

"You, too."

"Good-bye, Nick. Good luck."

He stood on the sidewalk and watched the Caddy's taillights recede in the distance. After a moment, he adjusted his cap, slung the B-4 bag over his shoulder, and went into the terminal. Only after he purchased his ticket and was walking to the gate did it occur to him that they had parted without a good-bye kiss. They had not even shaken hands.

Elaine was listed in the telephone book under her maiden name, Mason. Her paychecks were issued in that name, and her automobile registration and driver's license. She voted as Elaine Mason and had a dozen different department store accounts in that name, as well as two Visa cards and one American Express card. Otherwise, she was known as Mrs. Marc Oldenfeld.

Mr. Oldenfeld—Marc Oldenfeld, M.D.—had no objection; indeed, literally, he never gave it a second thought. If Elaine wanted it that way, fine with Marc. He doted on her. She was, as he enjoyed telling his colleagues, his whole life. Not in all his fifty-three years had he known the happiness of the past three.

On her part, Elaine was equally happy. She had everything a woman could possibly want from a man. Love, respect, freedom, financial security. This was why it would be so difficult for her to tell him she was leaving him.

She closed her eyes an instant against the glare of the

early afternoon sun on the glass facade of the airport
terminal. She smiled to herself and, aloud, said, "You
should be doing this for money, you idiot. You're running a goddamn regular airport shuttle!"

She had just swung the Caddy into the airport's metered parking area. The same parking lot—and probably
the same meter—she had used not eighteen hours earlier. When she came here to meet Nick Harmon. The
other man in her life.

The previous evening, immediately after taking Nick
to the airport, Elaine had phoned her husband and
asked him to come to Monterey. For the car, she said;
to drive the car back to Seattle. She couldn't stand the
thought of a stranger driving it, which was what she had
told Nick, and was true. She honestly had not intended
to ask Marc to do it. After seeing Nick, she changed her
mind.

Seeing Nick evoked memories of old times, good
times, and made her realize she was not getting any
younger and not getting what she wanted from life.

But what the hell did she want?

Well, if she did not know what she wanted, at least
she knew what she did not want.

Children.

In that, too, Marc was understanding and cooperative. Yes, he would like a family. But if Elaine did not
share the desire, perfectly okay with him. So what was
wrong? What was missing?

Romance? Excitement? Adventure? Love? Sex?

One or all of the above, she thought, steering into a
parking space whose meter still had nearly thirty minutes. A small but gratifying victory. She cranked two
quarters into the meter, enough for thirty more minutes.
The United flight from Seattle was late, so Elaine occupied herself wandering about the busy terminal and
browsing in the airport gift shop. She was in uniform
and now and then a man—usually a civilian—would
glance at her, appraisingly at first and then, noting her
silver aviator's wings, with genuine respect. She enjoyed

the attention, and why not? Ask not what you can do for
your country.

Something about a soldier.

There was a song with that title. As a child, she remembered her mother standing at the kitchen sink,
washing dishes, humming the tune. "Something about a
Soldier." Something about a lot of soldiers, plural,
Elaine thought, peering at a huge pile of newspapers
stacked just outside the gift shop entrance. The banner
headline of the *San Francisco Chronicle* read:

CONGRESS TO DEBATE JAN 15 DEADLINE
FOR IRAQ ATTACK

Five weeks away, which meant she would be in on it.
If it happened, which seemed to be an ever-increasing
probability. Five hundred thousand Americans were in
Saudi Arabia, and more on the way. For sure, they had
not been sent there to sit waiting indefinitely in the desert.

Something about a soldier.

Yes, that was what Elaine wanted, the army. She had
always wanted the army and should have and could have
made it her career. She should have gone into the regular army fresh out of college. But better late than never,
which was what Nick Harmon's visit had made clear to
her. The mere sight of him had served, finally, to resolve
her indecision. That was her reason for asking Marc to
come to Monterey. To break the news to him in person,
face to face. Driving the car back was a good excuse.

A crowd of people was descending the stairway from
the gate area now. Marc's flight. She hurried up the
stairs toward the gates. She had started through the
metal detector when she saw him. She stepped back
behind the X-ray machine and watched him approach.
A tall, sandy haired man with a neatly trimmed mustache. Very handsome, very distinguished. And those
lovely, delicate hands. Surgeon's hands. Those fingers
that stroked her body so gently. He enjoyed doing it.
She would lie on her stomach, naked, while he ran his

fingers up and down the length of her body. Ankles to neck, stopping caressingly here, and there, and there. One hand would slide under, first, one breast, kneading the nipple until it hardened, then move on to the other breast. She could actually feel her body tingling.

"Hi," he said, and all at once she was in his arms, her cheek brushing against the rough tweed of his jacket, which exuded a faint aroma of tobacco and aftershave lotion and his own masculine odor.

"Hi," she said, and stepped back and removed his pipe from his jacket breast pocket. She aimed the pipe stem toward his mouth and placed it between his teeth.

"You look marvelous," he said. He removed the pipe from his mouth and dropped it back into the jacket pocket. "But you always look marvelous."

"That's what you tell all of your female patients," she said. "Where's your luggage?"

He tugged the strap of the leather tote bag slung over his shoulder. "This is it," he said. "I thought I'd stay over tonight, and then get started early in the morning. I rescheduled three surgeries for day after tomorrow."

She was relieved. Since he was staying the night, she had until then to decide how to tell him. She had feared that he might want to return to Seattle immediately; she would have had to tell him right there and then at the airport. She had slept poorly, running the imaginary conversation over and over in her mind.

Oh, by the way, Marc, I'm leaving you.

I realize that, he would say. And he would smile indulgently and add, You're going off to war.

No, I mean *leaving* you.

". . . what's wrong?" he was saying. He had stopped abruptly and was staring at her. Walking, he had placed an arm around her shoulder. To her, lost in her reverie, the touch of his hand was like an electric shock. She had shuddered involuntarily.

My God, what had she done? The look of bewilderment in his eyes, his face wrinkled in disbelief. She grasped his hand. "You startled me," she said.

"So it seems."

"I'm edgy today. I'm sorry."

"Is today the day?"

They resumed walking. She tried to make a joke of it, put him at ease. "For my PMS, you mean, or the day we ship out? It's neither. They'll give us a twenty-four-hour notice before we go. The end of the week, I figure."

"Well, you'll phone me. Just say something like, well, how about 'Just wondering if the dog's okay.' Yeah, that'll work."

Elaine laughed. "Darling, for this war we don't need code words. In fact, we *want* the Iraqis to know we're coming. I'll call and say, 'Marc, we're taking off for the Gulf tonight. Be sure and feed the dog.' How is he, by the way?"

"Hamlet is fine," Marc said. "But he misses you. We both do." Hamlet was their two-hundred-pound, three-year-old Harlequin Great Dane. A gift, as a twenty-pound, six-week-old puppy, from a grateful patient of Marc's, a breeder. Elaine jogged with Hamlet every afternoon, three miles around the lake.

Elaine knew that in her absence Hamlet always crawled into bed beside Marc. She wanted to say something witty about that. But it wouldn't work, not with what she had to tell him.

Darling, I'm leaving you.

It was at the motel, several hours later, that she decided to tell him. By now she had composed and rejected no fewer than a dozen scenarios. A dozen different ways of saying it. She had even seriously considered mentioning Nick Harmon's visit of the previous evening. An old friend—a friend in the most intimate meaning of the word—had, in a perverse way, helped finalize her decision. This old friend, a fighter pilot, represented everything Elaine wanted. Not him per se, but his life, his career.

They had just finished making love. She had promised herself to tell him before they went to bed. But then she decided to at least give him some pleasure. The last meal before the firing squad. Yes, of course, at least let him have that much. She felt like a whore, grunting and groaning, writhing, with no sensation other than him inside her, her brain whirling with guilt. And then, like a whore, she had turned away from him when he tried to kiss her at the moment of his orgasm.

Oh, God, she was so ashamed. Immediately, she drew his mouth down to hers. "You didn't come," he said quietly, a gentle accusation.

"Yes I did," she lied. "It was a small one."

"Sure," he said, and smiled understandingly. He rolled off her and lay on his back, wrapping his arm around her and holding her close. "Christ, how I love you," he said.

It was then she knew she could not tell him. Later, when she returned from the Gulf. Yes, later, it would be so much better, so much easier. Why hurt him now, needlessly? No point to it.

". . . have you any idea when you'll be leaving?" he was saying.

"Leaving? What do you mean, leaving?"

"Shipping out," he said.

He had switched on the bedtable lamp. It was a small, narrow-shaded lamp that illuminated only the immediate area and projected a circle of light up onto the ceiling. For some reason it reminded her of rooms she had shared with Nick Harmon. She had had that feeling sometimes with Nick, that feeling of being a whore. In truth, with Nick, she had relished every minute of it. When they made love it was wild, totally uninhibited, no holds barred. Everything went. Around The World In Forty Minutes—stopping at every important port.

"Hello?" Marc said.

She looked at him, bemused. After a moment, his words registered. "When am I shipping out?" she said. "I told you: probably at the end of the week."

She realized why she was thinking of Nick. Association. She had seen him only a few hours before. Poor Nick. He seemed so lost, so forlorn. And she had treated him badly, almost cruelly. Revenge. That was probably why she had not told Nick about leaving her husband. Nor that she had been offered—and already accepted—a slot, in rank, in the regular army.

To be sure, Marc also knew nothing of this. Of course, joining the regular army and leaving him—ending the marriage—was all one and the same. She never should have married Marc Oldenfeld. Or, for that matter, anyone else.

". . . Are you hungry?" he was asking. He cupped her chin and kissed her. "I'm starved."

"So am I," she said. She returned the kiss. "Let's get a huge meal and a bottle of the most expensive wine they have."

He remained in bed, lazily watching her slip into the beige knit shirtdress and black-and-white Chesterfield pumps she had brought along. She knew he liked that ensemble.

"What is it they say about 'those who sit and wait . . .'?"

"What's that, darling?"

"You know, 'They also serve, those who sit and wait.' Something about women whose men go off to war." He swung his legs over the edge of the bed and sat up. "That's me, isn't it?"

She looked at him. Now, she thought, now is the time to tell him. Get it over with. Tell him.

"Good-bye Broadway, hello France," he said.

"Good-bye Seattle, hello Saudi Arabia," she said.

"I love you," he said.

She stepped over to him and threw her arms around him. " 'Those who sit and wait,' " she said. She pressed his face to her breasts. "I'll be home sooner than you think. Before you know it. Yes, before you know it."

3

Through the southwest window of the young consular official's office, Chris could see the top of the brown concrete tower that jutted high up out of the UPM complex. Although UPM—the King Fahd University of Petroleum and Minerals—was located a half mile from the

U.S. Consulate, the gleaming geometric glass of its twenty-first-century design dominated the landscape. But then utter, total newness described most of the architecture not only here in Dhahran, but throughout Saudi Arabia.

Oil, Chris thought, in her mind superimposing those three magic letters over the raised bronze letters on the nameplate on the young man's desk, JOSEPH A. HADLEY III. She wondered what the "A" stood for. Asshole, she thought. He certainly acted like one. A typical eastern preppie, Brooks Brothers seersucker suit, blue Oxford button-down shirt, regimental tie, cordovan loafers. To be fair, if not for his oversized glasses with their tortoise-shell frame and his intent and so obviously practiced studious expression, he might have been handsome.

". . . you've embarrassed us terribly, Miss Campbell," he was saying.

Chris noticed his eyes now for the first time. Blue-green that did not match the close-cropped black hair. "You'll forgive me, Mr. Hadley, but I think your so-called embarrassment is all in the eye of the beholder." She stifled an impulse to giggle. The poor little fellow was so serious about the whole stupid episode.

"That's precisely the point," said Joseph Hadley. "It's because it is in *his* eye, the beholder's, that it's all so embarrassing. And why I'm taking the heat."

"You're taking the heat?" Chris asked. "You, personally?"

"The embassy is."

"And you want me to issue an apology?"

"In writing," said Hadley. "To His Majesty, personally."

"To His Majesty, personally," Chris repeated.

"Those are my instructions."

"Those are your instructions," Chris repeated.

Had young Joseph A. Hadley known Chris better, he might have been more sensitive to her mocking tone and realized that it always presaged a burst of temper. But he had seen her only on television, and she had

been in Saudi Arabia only a day, and in Dhahran less
than three hours. She had flown directly from the States
to Riyadh, hoping to see and talk with General
Schwarzkopf. But twelve hours after arriving in Riyadh,
she was on a USAF plane to Dhahran, two hundred
miles south to do a story on American servicewomen.

It was Johnny Donovan's idea, and a good one. He
had introduced Chris to a friend, an army helicopter
pilot, a woman reservist en route to her new duty station
in Dhahran. Donovan arranged for Chris and the helicopter pilot, Major Elaine Mason, to fly on the same
Pan Am charter flight from Washington. Chris planned
to spend no more than a week in Saudi Arabia before
returning to Amman, and then on to Baghdad.

During the long flight, Chris and Elaine Mason had
chatted for hours on end about the myriad problems
encountered by women in the service. From leaving a
husband at home, as in Elaine's case, to a shortage of
tampons in the theater of operations. It all ended up to
one hell of a human interest feature. If CENTCOM
censors cleared the story.

Which now, after what had happened in Riyadh,
might not be easy. Christine Campbell, as young Mr.
Hadley took such delight in explaining, was on the State
Department's shit list, thereby automatically earning
her a place on CENTCOM's list. However, an apology
from Chris might help placate the injured parties.

The apology to which Hadley referred was for WCN's
"Gulf Watch" program of the previous day, December
16. Chris's first broadcast from Saudi Arabia, from Riyadh. Talk about being in the right place at the right
time.

Chris had checked into the Hyatt Regency, hoping to
sleep off her jet lag. She was awakened a few hours later
by a commotion outside. She looked out her room window and could hardly believe what she saw. Within ten
minutes she was dressed, and out on the King Abdul
Aziz Street with a full camera crew.

A line of cars, horns blowing, extended for blocks
along the street. It reminded Chris of a victory rally

after a football game. The motorcade, composed mainly of late-model Mercedes, BMWs, and Cadillacs, proceeded slowly and triumphantly past the golden-domed minaret of the King Saud mosque and the twelve-story aluminum-facaded Oil Ministry.

The drivers of the cars, women—all clad in their flowing black *abayahs*—were the wives of prominent Saudi businessmen and government officials. Someone had convinced these women that now was the time to protest. Now, with five hundred thousand Americans in the country, now was the time to defy the law prohibiting women from driving a car.

Men rushed from buildings and lined the sidewalk watching, shocked, as the women drove past. If the women were naked, the onlookers could not have been more offended. Chris and Jerry Skaff, her Aussie cameraman, filmed more than twenty minutes of the event.

No, not an event, a revolution.

Chris also managed brief interviews with some of the women. The tape was transmitted directly to Washington and ran, unedited, on that morning's "Gulf Watch." Chris's narration emphasized the consequences of the women's protest: Each woman who had participated in the motorcade would be punished. At present, all were locked up in their own homes.

Within an hour of the broadcast, just as Chris had finally gotten back to sleep, she was awakened by Al Bartlett, WCN's Riyadh Bureau chief. He had just spoken with Larry Hill in Washington. The Saudis were outraged at WCN's airing of the women's "revolution." A stern protest had been lodged with the U.S. State Department and with U.S. Central Command in Riyadh. Larry would try to smooth things over. In the meantime, he recommended that Chris get the hell out of Riyadh, fast. Al Bartlett finagled her a seat on an air force MAC flight to Dhahran leaving in forty minutes. She had hardly finished signing the register at the Dhahran International Hotel, when Mr. Joseph A. Hadley III summoned her to his office at the consulate.

"An apology, in writing?" Chris repeated now.

"Those are your instructions? Well, please let me tell you what you can do with your instructions—"

"—your remarks were inappropriate, Miss Campbell," Hadley said. "You have to admit that."

"What remarks?"

" 'Finally, the women of Saudi Arabia speak out,' " Hadley said, paraphrasing Chris's commentary on the women drivers. " 'Women, who have traditionally been regarded as second-class citizens, are at long last demanding their basic rights as human beings!' My God, didn't you give any thought to the implications of such statements?"

"Are you suggesting that what I said was untrue?"

"I am suggesting that it was ill-advised."

"Ill-advised?" Chris fairly spat the word. "Those women are treated like chattel! And just look at what's happened to them: confined to their homes for an undetermined period. House arrest, for Christ's sake!"

"We are guests in this country," Hadley said. "We have no right to criticize the culture and customs of its people. They are entirely within their rights to demand an apology."

"These people we've come over here to save, you mean?" Chris said. "These people we're prepared to spill blood for? So they can perpetuate their feudal society? Do you realize that Saudi women aren't allowed to own property or even keep a bank account? My God, they can only visit the Riyadh Zoo at specified hours, the *zoo!* And you"—she pointed a finger at Hadley— "you sit there and pompously tell me that my remarks are ill-advised? And you want a written apology, no less!" She rose and glared down at him. She was so angry that she forgot how tired she was, and that she had slept no more than three hours of the past thirty-six.

"Unless you apologize, the Saudi government will cancel your visa," Hadley said. "Moreover, the military authority will revoke your press credentials."

Chris wanted to laugh. She felt giddy. It had just occurred to her that not only did she need sleep, she was ravenously hungry. A steak, she thought, smothered in sautéed onions and mushrooms. With a side of *Pasta Laurens.* Poor Larry, he had probably heard from George Bush himself about Chris's tape.

". . . forty-eight hours to leave the country," Hadley, who had risen to face Chris, was saying.

"Excuse me?" She had heard him clearly but did not believe it.

"I said that unless you change your mind, you have forty-eight hours to leave. Voluntarily, that is. They'll make it quite unpleasant for you if they have to deport you."

Chris really didn't care. Forty-eight hours was more than ample time. Twenty-four of it to get over the jet lag and have a good night's sleep—and the onion-and-mushroom-smothered steak—and then the meeting with Major Elaine Mason.

She smiled politely at Hadley. On second thought, he wasn't so handsome. He had bad skin and little tufts of hair emerging like toothbrushes from his nostrils. Still smiling, she said, "Mr. Hadley, if I weren't a lady, I would tell you to go and fuck yourself."

As it happened, not even a dozen written apologies would have saved Chris from being asked to leave Saudi Arabia. In diplomatic language, accelerated transit. In English, kicked out.

At first, the incident in Riyadh that had resulted in the fast trip here to Dhahran seemed a stroke of luck. It provided Chris an opportunity to flesh out her story about American servicewomen, personified in Elaine Mason. If, that is, Chris could talk Elaine into a three- or four-minute on-camera appearance. They would do it at the airport, filming Elaine in or near her helicopter.

To that end, then, the day after her encounter with Mr. Hadley—after a decent night's sleep—she made a lunch date with Elaine. They were to meet at Al Shular, an air-conditioned mall in downtown Dhahran. Chris was a few minutes early. She wanted to look around the city. The Filipino taxi driver who dropped her off a block from the mall tried to sell her a fifth of what he called "real California wine."

". . . made in your own cellar," Chris said.

The driver grinned and lowered the price from twenty dollars to ten. Chris thanked him, but passed. She walked toward the mall. She could not help admiring the city. High-rise office buildings fronting broad, tree-lined boulevards. Hospitals, schools, parks, playgrounds. A steel and concrete oasis in the middle of a desert.

All built on a sea of oil.

Traffic was brisk. Civilian automobiles, from the usual white or black Mercedes sedans favored by wealthy Saudis to shiny new Hondas and Toyotas, taxis, small and large trucks, and a continuous stream of U.S. military vehicles. U.S. servicemen crowded the sidewalk, along with western-garbed Saudi businessmen and other Saudis in traditional robes, and extraordinary numbers of Asians, Indians, Sri Lankans, and Filipinos. Almost all the women wore the black *abayahs*. The women, and many of the men, all stared curiously, almost indignantly at Chris as she strolled along in her white wool slacks and charcoal-gray corduroy blazer and borrowed U.S. Army boonie hat.

Western women were allowed to wear slacks and some manner of head cover. By special permission—dispensation, if you will—granted by His Imperial Majesty himself, Fahd Ibn Abdel Aziz, Sheik of all Sheiks, protector of the nation and of its faith, and, to be sure, of his loyal subjects' morals. Truly generous of His Majesty, Chris thought, magnanimous.

Chris arrived at the mall, a replica of any American shopping arcade: Sony camcorders to Gucci luggage, pizza parlors and other fast-food establishments, including a Med Mac, the Saudi version of McDonald's. The mall bustled with people. Business was good, thanks to Desert Shield and, therefore, Saddam Hussein.

Elaine was waiting for Chris outside the Med Mac. Chris did not recognize her at first. Elaine wore an *abayah*. Chris could not help laughing. "My God, you look like some Saudi prince's concubine-of-the-month!"

Elaine nodded glumly. "CENTCOM orders," she said, and quoted the order: " 'In deference to the wishes of the host country, female service personnel when off base and not on duty will wear clothing in keeping with local custom.' "

It was at that instant Chris felt a sharp pain in the small of her back. She whirled around. A thin, scraggly-bearded man confronted her. His long white robe was spotted with food stains. Gripped in his hand, like a saber, was a long bamboo cane.

He was a Mutawa, a public morals policeman, and dedicated to his job. He had spotted Chris on the street outside the arcade and followed her inside like a hyena stalking his prey. In Arabic he said now, "You are insulting our people!" He prodded the cane hard into Chris's ribs.

"Keep your filthy hands off her!" Elaine said. She seized the tip of the cane, wrested it out of the Mutawa's grasp, and shoved him backward with it. The Mutawa fell back against the plate-glass display window of the adjoining electronics shop.

"I'm an American, you son of a bitch!" Elaine said. She pulled the top hem of the *abayah* down enough to reveal the jacket of her desert BDU and the bronze oak leaves of a major on the jacket collar tabs. "I'm an American!" she said again. And as though for additional proof, she raised the skirt of the *abayah* for the Mutawa to see her canvas and leather GI jungle boots. She hurled the cane to the ground at his feet. "I'm in the United States Army!"

The man picked up the cane. He said something in Arabic, and with a disdainful glance at Chris, stalked off. A crowd had gathered, a few GIs and some Saudi civilians, all men. One, a clean-shaven young man, said in heavily accented English, "He said he is going to notify the military police. I hope they arrest both of you." He wagged an admonishing finger in Chris's face. "You, I know. I have seen you on TV."

Chris had already opened her mouth to respond, but Elaine pulled her away and literally pushed her out of the arcade. "Let's get the hell out of here—far and fast," Elaine said. "We have standing orders not to argue with those characters."

They started out but did not get far. Three burly U.S. Army MPs raced into the mall. The ranking MP, a staff sergeant, saluted Elaine and said, "Begging your pardon, ma'am, but I'll have to ask you to return to base." He nodded grimly behind him. The Mutawa, cane slung under his arm, stood just inside the arcade entrance.

"Sorry about this, Major," said another MP, a buck sergeant. He lowered his voice. "We're supposed to take immediate action any time one of those ragheads finds something to complain about. We told him we'd make an official report—"

"—official report about what?" Elaine asked.

The staff sergeant could not repress a grin. He jerked his head toward the Mutawa. "He says you assaulted him."

Elaine and Chris looked at each other. Elaine said to the staff sergeant, "I never assaulted him, Sergeant. I tried to push him through a window, that's all."

"Yes, ma'am," the staff sergeant said with a straight face. "Like I said, we're supposed to make a report. Between you and me, though, all we'll do is drop you back at the base."

Chris and Elaine made arrangements to meet later, and Elaine left with the MPs. The scraggly-bearded Mutawa had moved to the sidewalk outside the mall. Chris went over to him. She enjoyed looking down at him.

"You're an ugly little bastard, do you know that?" she said, and walked off.

Later that day, Chris filmed a two-minute segment with Elaine. They staged it at the airport, Elaine seated in the cockpit of her UH-60, the sounds of jets loud in the background. An innocuous piece, Chris presenting Elaine as a typical U.S. Army female, devoted to her work, her associates, and her country. Yes, it was a little tough getting used to Saudi Arabia, but they were managing. Yes, everyone looked forward to getting the job done and getting home. The tape was submitted to the U.S. military censor, approved, and went out on the satellite that same evening.

Chris returned to the hotel immediately after the filming. Waiting for her in the lobby was Joseph A. Hadley III. One glimpse of his smug face, and Chris knew why he was there. The Mutawa had had the last laugh.

That same evening Chris was on a Saudia 737, en route back to Riyadh where, according to Mr. Hadley, someone from the U.S. Embassy would meet her. Someone did meet her. A pleasant-enough woman who could have been anyone's maiden aunt, who informed Chris that her CENTCOM press credentials were revoked and that the Saudi Arabian government had declared her persona non grata.

Not two hours later, Chris sat in the first-class section of another Saudia airplane, an L-1011, headed for Damascus. Chris had no special reason for going to Damascus, but that particular flight was the first available transportation out of Saudi Arabia. They were that anxious for her to leave.

It was not an especially long flight, under three hours, but Chris used the time well. She wrote the opening segment of next Sunday's "Gulf Watch Review," WCN's hour-long weekly summation of the week's Desert Shield events. Chris's report included an in-depth account of her expulsion from Saudi Arabia and her editorial comments on the lowly status of women in that nation. She also mentioned the CENTCOM directive that forced American servicewomen to subject themselves to the same degrading treatment, citing her personal witness to Major Elaine Mason's experience with the Mutawa in the Dhahran shopping mall. A replay of Elaine's two-minute segment was integrated into this larger report.

In Chris's words, ". . . a sad day when the most powerful nation on earth rushes to save an ally and blithely instructs its soldiers to adhere to the cruel and archaic customs of the ally's feudal society."

As Larry Hill said, defending the piece, it was good

journalism. It was also good business. That week's "Gulf Watch Review" won its time spot with a thirty-two share, five points better than CBS's "Sixty Minutes." WCN's stock, which had opened Monday morning on the NYSE at $7.25, closed at $10.50. By the end of the week it was selling for $12. If the war started on January 15, on schedule, the stock would probably double.

Larry, whose personal profit that week amounted to slightly less than $3 million, was tempted to send Chris a version of the famous William Randolph Hearst cable: "You provide the pictures, I'll provide the war."

The only problem was that he had lost contact with her. He knew she had left Damascus and arrived in Amman and set out for Baghdad. But that was days ago, and she had not yet arrived in Baghdad. He had no idea where she was.

FOUR

The monochromed LED display of the calendar clock on the brigadier general's desk read 22 December. "December," of course, in Hebrew, which Nick Harmon thought did not alter the fact that only two shopping days remained before Christmas, nor that few people in Israel celebrated that holiday. Nor, for that matter, was Christmas widely celebrated in Japan, where the general's calendar clock had been manufactured.

For Nick, Christmas in Tel Aviv posed no problem. For all it meant to him, he could just as well be in Tehran, or Toronto, or Teterboro, New Jersey. Christmas was a day created by merchants to stimulate sales. On a par with Mother's and Father's days. He smiled to himself, remembering an old New York subway ad for bread, "You don't have to be Jewish to like Levy's." You didn't have to be Jewish not to like Christmas, either.

By slightly averting his head he could look out the window and see the Mediterranean. Although he could not see the beach, he knew it swarmed with people on this warm sunny Saturday afternoon. Shabbat, they called it, Hebrew for Sabbath. It had been crowded hours earlier when he'd eaten breakfast on the beachfront terrace of his hotel, the Dan.

"Colonel?"

The brigadier general's voice startled Nick. He glanced away from the window and faced the BG. "Sir?"

"Are you still with us?"

"Yes, sir, I'm sorry." Nick strained to recall the general's words, delivered in fast, impatient, guttural English. Nick had not really been paying attention, which made the BG's speech even more difficult to follow.

"What was her name, Nick?" Zvi Sharok asked. Zvi's English was flawless, nearly accentless. "The one you were thinking about just now."

"Nobody you know, Zvi," Nick said, as everyone laughed accommodatingly. He looked at Zvi with a half grin, his eyes drawn to the Israeli Air Force pilot's wings gleaming silver against the blue of his tunic. Zvi was thirty-three, six years younger than Nick, and probably a hundred years more experienced. Not only did Zvi have those seven Syrian MiGs to his credit, he had flown wingman to the leader in the 1981 raid on the Iraqi nuclear reactor.

"Please go on, General, I'm listening," Nick continued to the BG, whose name was Avi Posner and who resembled a young college professor more than a decorated paratrooper general and director of the Israeli counterpart of the National Security Agency.

They were in Posner's office on the third floor of the main building in the Defense Ministry compound, which was located south of the city, in the suburb of Hakiriya. Nick, Frank Kowalski, Zvi Sharok, and a middle-aged man from the U.S. Embassy, Harry Fleet, sat in wood-backed folding chairs in a semicircle around Posner's desk.

Avi Posner said, "I was mentioning the three so-called test missiles fired by the Iraqis yesterday. These are long range, improved versions of the Soviet R-17 model, which NATO calls the SS-1C, or Scud B, capable of carrying a nuclear warhead. These are the weapons that pose the greatest threat to Israel, and the ones we therefore must take out." He nodded at Kowalski. "I understand that you brought us an answer to our proposal?"

"Yes, sir, I did," Kowalski said. He looked at Nick, as though expecting Nick to deliver the message. Nick had no intention of obliging. Let Kowalski do his own dirty work. Kowalski started speaking, then stopped; he wanted to reconsider what he had to say.

Nick tightened the thread of a loose gold cuff button on his gray flannel blazer. He was wearing the blazer and black worsted slacks, the only civilian clothes he had, at Kowalski's instructions. In uniform, Kowalski said, Nick would be too conspicuous. The Israeli government preferred not to call attention to the presence of U.S. military personnel.

Kowalski cleared his throat quietly now. "The reply from Washington, General, is no. The United States will not participate in a joint military operation with Israel." He cleared his throat again. "In a word, sir, the operation is considered unsound," Kowalski said.

"Unsound," Posner repeated quietly. "We wish to eliminate a threat to our safety and security, and the United States considers this 'unsound'?"

The man from the U.S. Embassy, Harry Fleet, ostensibly a protocol official but whom everyone in the room knew was CIA, spoke up. "Unsound, General, only from a tactical standpoint—"

"—a political standpoint, you mean, don't you?" Posner said. He touched a button on a black plastic console on his desk. Immediately, on the opaque sheet of glass covering the wall at the far end of the room, a map materialized. A detailed, small-scale projection of the area from the western edge of Iraq, westward across Jordan, to Israel.

Posner rose and walked to the wall. With his finger, he circled a spot on the map just inside Iraq. "The village of Shab al-Bir," he said. "A village in name only. The occupants are Iraqi army regulars and technicians. There may be some women, we don't know. The 'village' consists of buildings that conceal twelve concrete launching bays, storage area for twenty-four missiles—with a separate storage facility for the warheads—fuel tanks, workshops, everything. Even an electrical power station.

"Our intelligence reports—confirmed, incidentally, by American reconnaissance satellite data—indicate that the missiles stored at this location have been modified to carry chemical warheads. The distance from here"— he ran his finger from the spot on the map, across Jordan, to Israel—"to Tel Aviv is four hundred and twenty-two kilometers." He returned to his desk, sat, and touched the button on the console. The map vanished. "Now kindly tell me what is 'political' about that?"

Fleet said, "General, we are well aware of your situation. Believe me, sir, we've thought of little else these past weeks. We ask you to consider *our* situation. We're dealing with a coalition that can come apart if someone breathes too hard."

"Your situation, Mr. Fleet, is one of which we are equally well aware," Posner said. "But that will not help Israeli children choking to death on Iraqi nitrogen gas."

Kowalski's face tightened with annoyance, and Fleet sighed impatiently. In his mind, the dramatics notwithstanding, Nick applauded Posner. As Nick learned long ago, Israelis did not waste time on subtlety. When they had a point to make, they made it.

Fleet said, "I'm sorry, General, but that's the decision."

"And yet you still expect us to 'cooperate'?" Posner asked. "To stand by and do nothing, as Mr. Hussein announces to the world his intention to incinerate Israel?"

"We expect you to consider the broader aspects of the . . . the situation," Fleet said.

Posner said, "Frankly, my friend, among those broader aspects is the possibility that Saddam may be correct in suggesting that the United States will give up after suffering ten thousand casualties. Where will that leave us?"

"I can assure you here and now, General, that the United States has no intention of giving up," Fleet said.

"I shall inform the prime minister of your assurance," Posner said. "I am sure he will find it very comforting."

"President Bush himself has given the prime minister that assurance," Fleet said.

Despite his bland expression, for a moment it seemed

Posner might laugh in Fleet's face. He said, "I hope your government understands that if conditions demand it, Israel will take whatever measures are deemed necessary for its self-defense."

Fleet said, "Sir, are you suggesting that if the United States chooses not to go along with you on this Shab al-Bir operation, you will do it on your own?"

Zvi said, "I don't think the general's statement requires any elaboration."

"May I be blunt, sir?" Kowalski leaned toward Posner. "I believe that your intention is to provoke an Iraqi response. Either against Israel or against the Allied forces in Saudi Arabia."

Posner's face remained expressionless. "What leads you to that conclusion, Mr. Kowalski?"

Kowalski clearly welcomed the question. "An Iraqi response serves Israel's purpose. It provides Israel an excuse to enter the war, thereby precluding any possibility of an Iraqi withdrawal, which is the last thing Israel wants. If Iraq leaves Kuwait, there will be no war. A war would be disastrous for Iraq, but a godsend to Israel: It eliminates, or at least minimizes, the Iraqi threat to Israel."

"Is that your personal opinion, Mr. Kowalski, or does it reflect the view of your government?" Posner asked. Before Kowalski could reply, Posner waved his hand dismissingly. "It's of no matter." He rose abruptly. Everyone rose with him. "Thank you for coming, gentlemen." He turned to Nick. "It was a pleasure to meet you, Colonel. I hope you enjoy your stay with us."

"Not if first impressions count, Avi," Zvi said. He strode to the door and opened it for the others. They filed past, Nick bringing up the rear and thinking, Only in Israel. Only here could a lowly major address a general by his first name, let alone smartmouth him. And get away with it.

Zvi walked them to the compound's main gate. A high cinderblock fence topped with concertina wire encircled the entire complex, some dozen buildings housing various branches of the Israeli Defense Forces. A blue-bereted, Uzi-armed sentry came to attention, while another raised the candy-striped barrier. Kowalski and Fleet walked into the courtyard where the embassy Chevrolet was parked. Zvi gestured Nick to lag behind a moment.

"Your colleagues certainly aren't worried about making friends," Zvi said mildly.

"I didn't hear anybody dispute their . . . thesis," Nick said.

"Which thesis are you talking about? They had at least a half dozen."

"The one that says Israel's greatest fear is that Saddam will withdraw. Ergo, there's no war. Ergo, Israel will do its damnedest to start the thing."

"How can you dispute logic?"

"So when does the attack start?"

Zvi said, "What are you doing for dinner?"

Nick laughed. "That tells me there'll be no preemptive strike tonight. It just so happens I'm free."

"I'll pick you up at two."

"Much too early," Nick said. "I like to have a drink before dinner, and I don't like to drink before seven. Well, six-thirty. Six, at the earliest."

"We're going to Jerusalem," Zvi said. "I know a place that makes the finest *gnocci* this side of Rome. And my father is joining us. He doesn't like to drink before seven, either," he added.

Tel Aviv to Jerusalem, normally a forty-minute drive, took more than an hour. The highway was clogged with military traffic. Israel was on high alert. Jerusalem itself bustled with uniformed soldiers. The twilight sky was bright with contrails, and now and then the staccato boom of a jet cracking the sound barrier.

Strangely—or perhaps not so strangely—the meeting at the Defense Ministry was never mentioned. It was as though Zvi knew that Nick realized the Israelis would launch a preemptive attack, and that any discussion was a waste of time. Nick did tell Zvi about the MiG, and they reviewed the incident detail by detail. They also brought each other up to date on their personal lives: Zvi was still a bachelor, still enjoying it, although he had met a girl he thought might change his mind.

"She's terrific," he said.

"They all are," Nick said. "Until you marry them."

Abruptly, Zvi dropped the subject. "One of the reasons I wanted to pick you up earlier was to take you to Yad Vashem."

"I've been there," Nick said. "The second day I got here. The ambassador insisted on it."

"What did you think of the place?"

Nick really did not know how to answer, or answer intelligently. Yad Vashem, the Holocaust museum, was so overwhelming it had literally struck him dumb. No, made him feel ignorant, ashamed of his ignorance. He had never realized the scope of the Holocaust. Worse, perhaps, he had always taken Israel for granted. As though it had always existed. After all, their military prowess was the stuff of textbooks, their air force second only to the USAF—and some people in the USAF itself might dispute that claim.

Now he replied to Zvi's question. "I couldn't believe what I saw at Yad Vashem. What did I think of it? I don't know how the hell to answer that."

"Nobody else does, either," Zvi said.

Not until Zvi pulled his battered Saab coupe up in front of the restaurant on Ben Yehuda Street, was Yad Vashem mentioned again. Zvi got out of the car, studied the street signs for no parking warnings, then came around to join Nick. They started into the restaurant. Nick stopped. In the dark he faced Zvi.

Nick said, "I think your reason for wanting me to see Yad Vashem was to make me understand what Israel is, *why* it is, and why it needs to defend itself. You insult me, Zvi: I knew all that, anyway. I didn't have to go to Yad Vashem for a lesson."

"I wish your colleague, Mr. Kowalski, felt the same."

"Kowalski is a horse's ass," Nick said.

"He's also a Jew-hater," Zvi said.

"The fact that he believes Israel is doing whatever it

can to make sure there's a war—that a war is in its best interests—doesn't make him a Jew-hater."

Zvi said nothing. He opened the restaurant door. Immediately, he closed it and turned again to Nick. "For more than a year now, Kowalski not only has been pushing the U.S. government to pressure Israel into signing a nuclear nonproliferation pact, but to dismantle the weapons as well. He knows damn well and good that our nukes are all that has prevented Saddam Hussein from taking a shot at us, never mind keeping Syria quiet. If he had his way, the sanctions would be applied against Israel, not Iraq. To me, Nick, that's a Jew-hater."

"No, Zvi, that's doing what he's paid to do. He's carrying out American foreign policy. He believes it's a proper policy. Just as you believe Israel's policy is proper."

The flowing script of the neon sign that hung in the curtained plate-glass window of the restaurant, Antonioni, cast an orange glow over Zvi's grim face. "Speaking of policy," he said, "I happen to know why you were sent here, your specific assignment. I also know it was Kowalski's idea. Is that what you call a proper policy?"

Nick did not know whether to be angry or to laugh. Laugh, he decided, because it was funny. But he could not laugh, mainly because the joke was on him. What Zvi had told him, after all, was that whatever Nick learned of Israel's plans would be what the Israelis wanted him to learn. What the Israelis *allowed* him to learn.

Zvi said, "Don't look so shocked, Nick." He smiled. "You're playing with the big kids now."

Dinner was quite pleasant. The food was, as Zvi had promised, excellent. Nick had a veal chop, grilled with a sprinkle of garlic and rosemary, a perfect match for a marvelously dry South African cabernet. The evening passed so quickly and so congenially that Nick hardly realized that it was past midnight by the time they were on the highway, headed back to Tel Aviv. Nick had instantly liked Zvi's father, Dani. At fifty-three, Dani

Sharok looked forty. He was not a tall man, but very wiry and muscular. His red hair, which Zvi had not inherited, was thinning with frightening rapidity, so he compensated for it with a close-trimmed beard.

Dani Sharok was a Sabra, a native-born Israeli. An attorney, he was famous—or, depending upon your point of view and nationality, infamous—for espousing unpopular causes and clients, and a decorated hero of three Israeli-Arab wars. He and Zvi enjoyed an easy relationship, more like brother and brother than father and son. They respected each other.

Respect, Nick had thought enviously, the ingredient missing in his relationship with Bob Harmon. Now, in the car, driving along the dark, busy highway, Nick thought of it again when Zvi remarked that Nick had impressed Dani.

"How do you know?" Nick asked.

"He listened to you," Zvi said. "He never listens to people who don't know what they're talking about. He refuses to waste his time."

Nick was not so sure about Dani's "listening." Dani had dominated the conversation. And talk about being impressed: It was Nick who had been impressed. He could see why Dani Sharok was considered a brilliant attorney. Dani possessed a talent for getting straight to the heart of the matter.

They had been discussing the possibility of the present Gulf crisis creating an atmosphere that might improve chances for peace between Israel and its Arab neighbors. Dani had asked rhetorically, "How do you make peace with people who insist no peace is possible until every inch of the territories conquered in '67 has been returned? Israel is the only country in history whose enemies demand she return land *they* lost attacking *her!*

"And if that isn't enough," he had continued, "now we have Mr. Bush and Mr. Baker claiming that the West Bank settlements are obstructions to peace. 'Obstructions to peace,' can you believe this?" Dani had paused a moment, then answered his own question. "The obstructions to peace, my friend, are forty years of Arabs making war against Israel. The obstructions to peace are Syrian missiles and Iraqi chemical and biological weapons. And forty years, too, of economic warfare. You cannot buy a Japanese car in this country, do you know that? The Japanese will not sell their products in Israel for fear of a Saudi oil cut-off. There are European companies—and American firms, too—who refuse to open branch offices here. The economic assistance we need from America could be cut in half if the Americans had the guts to tell the Arabs to go to hell."

"Which never will happen," Zvi had said.

"Of course not," Dani had said, and then pointed a finger at Nick. "And do you know who one of the prime offenders is? Kuwait! This great 'freedom-loving' society you've set out to save. The Kuwaitis will do absolutely no business with anyone doing business with us. And they talk of Israeli intransigence!

"And do you realize what absurdities we are sometimes forced into?" Dani went on. "You recall the man who sold British newspapers the story of Israel's nuclear weapons, the so-called top secret information? Israeli agents tracked him down in Italy and brought him back. Well, suppose I tell you that all that was a charade? Deliberately orchestrated, to remind the world that we do have the bomb. To survive, we must play such a game."

Nick had thought, And this is the same man who criticizes his government's harsh treatment of Palestinians. What was it Churchill said? Oh, yes, a riddle wrapped in a puzzle inside an enigma. A perfect description of Israel and Israelis.

Now Nick watched the Saab's headlights cut through the night, briefly illuminating the white Star of David on the turret of a burned-out tank on the roadside. The tank, a relic of the 1948 War of Independence, had been in that same spot since the day it was destroyed. A monument, a reminder.

"You talk about fathers, and listening," Nick said, really thinking aloud, still thinking of Zvi's relationship with Dani. "*I* should have been doing the listening when my father told me I was making a mistake getting married."

Zvi said nothing, discreetly concentrating on the road. He knew of Nick's failed marriage, although not the gruesome details, and certainly not the problems it had created between Nick and his father. Not that there weren't problems to begin with. But Nick considered Bob Harmon the last person to offer advice on marriage. Bob had left his wife of twenty years, Nick's mother, for another woman. Nick took no sides: They were adults and knew what they were doing. Nick's mother lived in Hawaii now, owner and manager of a prosperous flower shop. Happily remarried, she once confessed to Nick that every day of the twenty years with his father was a day of hell.

So when Bob Harmon met Jean and told Nick he was making a mistake—to Bob, Jean's pregnancy made no difference; there were ways of handling that—Nick in turn told Bob to mind his own business. Nick later apologized, and Bob graciously accepted, but the relationship never really improved.

The simple truth of the matter was that Nick disliked the man, a cruel truth he had never fully learned to live with. Even now, thinking about his father, Nick felt a twinge of guilt for not visiting him in California last week.

Bob Harmon would have enjoyed hearing about the MiG. A successful realtor, in World War II he had flown twenty-five missions as a B-24 radio operator-gunner. His proudest moment came when he watched Nick receive his diploma at the Air Force Academy. He had embraced his son, and with tears in his eyes, said, "You've done what I couldn't, kid. You did it for me."

Yeah, Nick thought now, remembering, and I even wonder sometimes, Dad, if it was for you that I married Jean. Out of spite, after you advised me not to. A little job of nose-cutting. It happened again when his father urged Nick not to lose Elaine Mason. Bob said Elaine was the girl Nick should have married in the first place.

So don't be a goddamn fool, he said, marry her if that's what she wants. Nick, of course, ignored that advice as well. More nose cutting? It was not impossible. Anything was possible. Even coming to terms with spying on your friends.

He said to Zvi, "How did you know about my mission here?"

"I didn't," said Zvi. In the half light of the instrument panel Nick saw the glimmer of a smug smile.

"You bastard," Nick said. "You just guessed it, and then I confirmed it by not denying it."

"Come on, Nick, why on earth would a man of your experience and tenure be pulled off a line unit for a shit job?" The smile faded. "Not to mention guilt-by-association."

"Kowalski?"

"As they say in Yiddish, *Vuden?* Who else?"

"Yeah," Nick said. "Who else?"

"Don't worry about it, Colonel. Just play it straight, and none of us will get into trouble."

Nick knew what "play it straight" meant. He was to act like Dumb Charlie and allow himself to be used by both sides. Now, for sure, it was a tennis game. And, for sure, he was the ball.

2

Only now, as the truck approached the Kuwaiti border, with Iraqi tanks parked every hundred yards along the roadside, did Chris begin to feel fear. All the way from Abadan, squeezed between the driver and his fat wife in the sweltering closeness of the truck cab, she had been more troubled by the man's body odor and the woman's rancid breath. She could not decide which was worse, that, or the clouds of brown road dust swirling through the truck cab's open windows, or the suffocating black *abayah* the driver insisted she wear.

She had tried not to dwell on the recklessness—no, the utter absurdity—of this trip. Never mind the problem of getting into Kuwait, getting *out* might prove even more perilous. But no way would she have passed up the opportunity. It could be the beat of a lifetime, the story of the decade.

Inside Kuwait with Christine Campbell.

Entessar al-Azimi, who helped Chris smuggle out the videotapes of the first Iraqi occupation troops, had sent Chris a gift. A hand-painted silk scarf that was waiting when, en route to Baghdad, Chris arrived in Amman two days ago. The note had been written on the protective tissue paper tucked inside the scarf's silk folds.

Chris—The world must be told what is happening here, and about the Resistance movement. We are still able to watch television from Amman. Do you remember the birthday party?

Back in July, in Kuwait City, Entessar had invited Chris to dinner at her apartment on the corniche. A surprise party for Chris, for her twenty-eighth birthday. "Still able to watch television from Amman" meant WCN satellite broadcasts and that Entessar knew, from the promos, that Chris was going to Baghdad via Amman. "The birthday party" meant that Entessar still lived in the corniche apartment. Entessar was asking Chris to somehow make contact, so that the world might know the truth about the rape of Kuwait.

The truth.

Chris had found the rumors of Iraqi brutality hard to believe. Most of the reports came from outside the country, from those heroic sheiks who had scrambled into their limousines and scurried across the border into Saudi Arabia at the first sight of Iraqi tanks. But Entessar's note proved that something terrible was happening in Kuwait.

The instant Chris read the note, she knew what she had to do. And what not to do, which was to ask Larry Hill if he preferred the Kuwait story over the Saddam Hussein interview. Larry would have to choose between the two, because after the telecast of "Inside Kuwait with Christine Campbell," Christine Campbell—and quite likely WCN itself—would be persona non grata in Iraq.

So she notified Larry that she was briefly delaying her trip to Baghdad, that she was on to a story more sensational then a dozen Saddam Hussein interviews. Rather than phone or fax Larry, she sent him a telex, knowing that by the time he received the wire he would be unable to reach her.

She canceled her booking on a Jordanian Airlines flight to Baghdad and instead flew to Tehran. For $2,000 cash, American, she obtained a Kuwaiti passport and, to match her newly dyed black hair, a Palestinian name. From Tehran, with the assistance of WCN bureau staffers, she went to Abadan in southern Iran. For $1,200 cash, American, she engaged the man named Ibrahim to take her into Kuwait.

Ibrahim—with his dark scraggly beard and huge hawklike nose, the classic figure of the fierce desert sheik—traveled back and forth from Kuwait twice weekly. He delivered Iranian fruit and produce to Iraqi troops, paid for by VCRs, telephones, TV sets, refrigerators, automobile tires, canned goods, and whatever else the Iraqis were systematically looting from Kuwait. Although he occasionally encountered difficulty returning to Iran with his cargo, Ibrahim was a world-class entrepreneur and an expert in the art of compromise, and never failed to eke out a profit.

He jabbed Chris with his elbow and pointed at the line of cars and trucks at the customs shed. Rifle-toting Iraqi soldiers inspected each vehicle and its occupants' papers.

"They know me and will ask no questions," Ibrahim said in his guttural pidgin English. He did not for a moment believe Chris's story of returning to Kuwait to search for her husband. Nor had he informed her that, should the border guards question Chris's purpose for entering the country, he would identify her as a Palestinian-born Kuwaiti he was delivering to an army brothel.

But then, on her part, Chris had not informed

Ibrahim that her luggage included items that, if found, might cause him serious trouble. The luggage, a battered wicker valise, contained a Sony EVO 9100 camcorder, a dozen blank cassettes, and a dozen spare batteries. The valise was strapped to the cab roof with several other suitcases.

Ibrahim knew what he was doing, and who he was dealing with, and who and how much to bribe. A half hour after reaching the Iraq-Kuwait border, they were on the six-lane highway into Kuwait City. Ahead, outlined against the sky, were the Kuwait Towers. The three towers, of varying heights, resembled giant needles jutting high out of the ground. The tallest tower was girdled by two huge metal globes, both painted gold, one globe larger than the other. The smaller globe, which was above the larger one, revolved around the tower and housed a restaurant. The larger globe, below, held millions of gallons of drinking water from Kuwait's desalination plants. A similar metal globe, also golden and filled with drinking water, encircled the second, shorter tower. The third tower, the smallest, had no globes; it contained batteries of searchlights that at night illuminated the other towers.

Chris recalled the towers from her previous visit, and the broad tree-lined boulevard, Arabian Gulf Road. The towers appeared intact, not the boulevard. The pavement was torn up and gouged by tank treads. Empty holes in the ground were all that remained of the handsome metal light standards that once had lined the avenue. Several high-rise buildings along the roadway were completely gutted. The facade of every building on either side of Arabian Gulf Road was pockmarked from shellfire, and most of the windows were boarded up. Burned-out automobiles and trucks littered the roadside, the median, and the highway itself. The untrimmed grass of the median was ankle high, cluttered with empty cans, plastic bags, Styrofoam food cartons, cardboard boxes, bottles, newspapers, magazines, and other debris that scuttled back and forth in the wind.

Closer into the city, Iraqi tanks were positioned at

every intersection. The tank crews lolled about outside the vehicles, smoking, eating, playing cards, chatting. The streets were empty of traffic except for Iraqi army jeeps and trucks and, occasionally, a staff car. The staff cars all seemed to be new Mercedes, BMWs, and Cadillacs, all bearing Kuwaiti license plates.

At Jahra Gate, Ibrahim drove past an Iraqi tank, continued on another hundred feet, then pulled over and parked. Using the front seat as a step, he reached up to the roof and slid Chris's valise out from the pile of luggage. He handed the valise down to her and nodded at an apartment building across the street. Every window of the lower three floors was boarded with plywood or cardboard. Half of the metal marquee of the entrance had been shot away.

"This is the place?" he asked.

"No," Chris lied, "but it's close enough." She did not want him to know her exact destination. "I'll meet you at this same spot in two days?"

Ibrahim tapped the face of his wristwatch, a Rolex. "Twelve o'clock in the afternoon," he said. "Two days from today."

Entessar al-Azimi's parents, both now deceased, had moved to Kuwait in 1967 when Entessar, their only child, was seven. Entessar's father, a professor of humanities at the American University in Beirut, had accepted a similar but higher-paying position at Kuwait University. Life was good, so good that Entessar's father encouraged his brother, a physician, to settle in Kuwait with his wife and two children.

Entessar graduated from Kuwait University in 1982 as an English major. A job at the Kuwaiti *Times,* the English-language newspaper, led to the news desk at Kuwaiti Television and then to film editing. In 1986 during the heaviest fighting of the Iran-Iraq War, Larry Hill sent WCN's roving Middle Eastern correspondent, Tom Layton, to Baghdad to open a permanent bureau. Tom also opened a Kuwait office as a kind of neutral observation post. He hired Entessar as a part-time film editor.

Entessar was thirty, unmarried, and not especially attractive. She was nearly six feet tall and so thin that in the western dresses she favored she looked malnourished, which she was not, but which had probably saved her life, or at least her virginity. Iraqi soldiers, when drunk and scouring various neighborhoods for booty and women, ignored her.

This offered other benefits as well, for it allowed Entessar to move about in relative freedom. Although there was no question of working—the Iraqis had removed every piece of equipment down to the paper clips from WCN's Kuwait City office—she was able to purchase food from the few markets and stalls still open. More important it enabled her to carry on her Resistance activities.

With a typewriter and an old Xerox machine salvaged from the WCN supply room, Entessar published a weekly newsletter. Printed on what little paper was available—the backs of old bills sometimes—the newsletter contained personal announcements, coded instructions to various Resistance people, and information ranging from water purification procedures to directions for constructing a pipe bomb.

Entessar's aunt and physician uncle were unaware of her Resistance work. When their own residence was bombed out they had moved into Entessar's small apartment, along with two middle-aged female cousins, and an elderly couple, former friends of her father's. Somehow, in the cramped space—with toilets that did not flush, and lights that did not light, and stoves with no gas—everyone got along with each other. Of course, it helped that they could keep themselves busy—when the electricity was on—watching taped movies or satellite television. The Iraqis had visited this building only once and, carelessly, overlooked the satellite dish on the roof.

Entessar had introduced Chris as a former college classmate, a Frenchwoman trapped in the invasion and dependent upon the charity of friends. Entessar thought it was madness for Chris herself to come to Kuwait. Entessar had expected Chris to send someone else, a Kuwaiti or a Palestinian. But she was enormously impressed with Chris's coolness. "In your position," Entessar told Chris, "I would be shaking in my boots."

"Don't let the facade fool you," Chris said. "I'm scared as hell." And crazy, she thought. Insane, absolutely out of her head to have come here. No, not crazy, suicidal. Which was the same thing, she thought, as she probably would discover tomorrow when they drove around the city taking pictures.

The camera would be concealed in an ambulance Entessar's uncle had arranged to borrow from Al-Sabah Hospital. Entessar had no choice but to take the doctor into her confidence, and by now it made little difference anyway. Chris's very presence had effectively compromised Entessar.

Amateur hour in Kuwait.

But the world would see those pictures of the torn-up streets, the shattered power stations, the wrecked desalination plants, the windowless hospitals. The public parks whose very trees had been torn from the ground, the devastated waterfront. The world would see it, if Chris succeeded, first, in getting the pictures and, second, getting them out. And third, getting herself out.

They were on the terrace of Entessar's fifth floor apartment, gazing out at the blackness of the city. They had just finished dinner—a surprisingly ample meal of roast chicken and fried potatoes—and had come out here to talk privately. Entessar's aunt and uncle, the two cousins, and the elderly couple were in the living room watching television. Of all things, WCN.

". . . and, hopefully, tomorrow I'll also have made contact for you with Ali Hamadan," Entessar continued.

"But will he let us film him?"

Entessar laughed. " 'Us,' " she said. "I'm your crew. Cameraman, soundman, gopher. Yes, he'll let us film him. He may not want his face shown, but he'll talk. And he has some stories to tell, believe me!"

Ali Hamadan, not his real name, was already a legend. A twenty-nine-year-old captain of the Kuwaiti National Guard, he had fought the Iraqis from the beginning. He had organized a resistance group that regularly and recklessly harassed the Iraqis. A price of $35,000 had been put on his head.

Talk about ratings, Chris thought, remembering Larry Hill's remark to the handsome young Iraqi, Adnan whatever-his-name-was. Chris Campbell's exclusive interview with Saddam Hussein, said Larry, would blow the dials right off the Nielsen or Arbitron meters. Well, they'd have to invent a whole new ratings system for Chris Campbell's pictures of occupied Kuwait and her interview with the leader of the Kuwaiti Resistance!

Chris did not sleep well that night. Bad enough being awakened every twenty minutes, hearing footsteps outside—or vehicles, which could only be Iraqi—waiting for Iraqi soldiers to burst into the apartment. But how the hell could anyone sleep curled up in a living room lounge chair, shivering with the cold, listening to the rattlelike snoring of the elderly woman three feet away on the couch?

All twenty-six apartments in the building were overcrowded: relatives, friends, friends of friends, forced out of their own homes, either from lack of water or electricity, or from simple fear. Everyone knew what everyone else was doing. Who had food, firewood, salt, a bar of soap. Entessar's next-door neighbors, a Palestinian couple born and educated in Kuwait, owned three very fashionable jewelry stores whose display cases and shelves were now absolutely bare. The Iraqis had stripped even the black velvet padding from the shelves.

Five other Palestinians had moved in with the jewelers. Because of their nationality—and despite the Kuwaiti origins of the jewelers—all the occupants of apartment 5E were viewed with suspicion. Daily, you heard stories of Palestinians betraying Kuwaitis or committing other perfidious acts.

One of the Palestinians in 5E, a woman formerly a maid in the home of a Kuwaiti family, had passed Chris on the stairs. Chris's *abayah*, although partially covering her face, could not conceal her blue eyes and fair skin.

Early the next morning, this same Palestinian woman knocked on Entessar's door and asked to borrow some tea. "I'm sorry, I don't have any," Entessar said.

"I saw your friend drinking tea," the woman said.

"What friend?" Entessar said.

"The one who came here yesterday afternoon," the woman said. She spoke the hard, rolling Arabic dialect of Gaza. It told Entessar that the woman's entire life until coming to Kuwait was spent in the filth and degradation of a refugee camp. Entessar also knew, now, that the woman had seen enough of Chris to recognize her as no Arab. The tea was payment for the woman's silence.

"Yes," said Entessar. "Come to think of it, I do have tea."

The following morning, from the moment curfew ended, Chris and Entessar toured the city in the ambulance. Entessar drove while Chris, from a window in the rear of the vehicle, operated the camera and narrated the film.

". . . there really isn't much for me to say," Chris said into the microphone. "These pictures speak for themselves. Block after block of ransacked storefronts, burned-out automobiles, empty business buildings. Private homes stripped bare down to the toilet seats. Museums, schools, hospitals. This so-called invasion is little more than programmed robbery. Looting on a gigantic, organized scale. Even the seats from the athletic stadium have been taken. Describing life in this city as having come to a complete standstill is, if anything, a gross understatement. Nothing works anymore. I cannot, of course, tell you how I'm filming this, or with whose help—except that it is with a member of the Kuwaiti Resistance, of which I will soon have more to say."

No one, soldiers or MPs, paid the slightest attention to the ambulance, let alone stopped it for questioning. Both women were almost giddy with success, Chris especially. She grew bolder and more confident and once asked Entessar to stop at a roadblock and engage the Iraqi sentries in casual conversation. Chris would film and record the scene.

"No, no, my dear," Entessar said. She wrapped her fingers gently around Chris's. "Let's not go completely crazy."

Finally, toward noon, Chris stopped. She had used up all but two cassettes and three batteries; she needed these for the Ali Hamadan interview. Entessar dropped Chris and the camcorder and cassettes at the apartment, then drove the ambulance back to the hospital. She parked it at the emergency entrance with the keys in the ignition, then returned home on foot.

Not even another visit from the Palestinian woman— this time demanding sugar, which Entessar provided— blunted Entessar's sense of satisfaction. She and Chris had made fools of the Iraqis. If Entessar was pleased, Chris was euphoric. Even the obvious difficulty of leaving Kuwait seemed suddenly not so formidable. She eagerly awaited her meeting with Ali Hamadan.

Everything worked out, even to the electricity being on for several extra hours. Now there was at least minimal lighting to film Ali Hamadan. He was on time, waiting for Entessar and Chris in the basement of the apartment building, in a small storeroom sometimes used to temporarily shelter Resistance members. The room contained a bed, a night table, a camp stove, blankets, even a radio.

A hero of the Resistance movement and a leader, Ali Hamadan looked the part. Chris thought he bore a slight resemblance to Adnan whatever-his-name-was, who resembled Robert Redford. In fact, Ali Hamadan was even better-looking. He reminded Chris of a man she had once briefly lived with and had actually considered marrying, a well-known screenwriter. It never worked out, for a hundred different reasons, all of them women.

Although Ali Hamadan spoke an acceptable English,

Chris decided that for absolute clarity Entessar would translate.

CHRIS:	The outside world has heard stories of the brutality of the Iraqi occupation. Can you document these reports?
ALI:	Visit one of our hospitals. See the children who have been tortured in front of their parents.
CHRIS:	How effective is your Resistance movement?
ALI:	There is a reward for my capture, a very large one. Does that answer the question?
CHRIS:	Are you receiving outside assistance?
ALI:	None, I regret to say. And I also regret to say that we have repeatedly asked for help. Our pleas have thus far fallen on deaf ears.
CHRIS:	You have the opportunity now to address the whole world. What is it you would like to tell them?
ALI:	Send us guns and ammunition —and more body bags *(smiles)* for the Iraqis.
CHRIS:	What are your hopes for the future?
ALI *(another smile):*	More dead Iraqis. *(Serious.)* The struggle is more than driving the Iraqis out. It is for a free and democratic Kuwait.

Chris used her two cassettes, asking questions she had prepared, recording his answers but hardly hearing them. She was way off in an imaginary place of her own, in an imaginary bed. With Ali Hamadan.

His very presence—the white linen shirt, the leather jacket, the denim trousers, the cowboy boots, the .45 strapped to his waist, even his odor—exuded sex. Hearing her own voice, and Entessar's off-camera translations, and Ali Hamadan's excitingly lyrical voice replying, she smiled to herself. The ideal way to do this, she thought, would be for him to service both women. She wondered if Entessar had ever had a man. No, not likely. Kuwaiti men demanded virgins for brides. Chris had heard of Arab girls spilling tomato juice over the bridal bed sheets as proof of purity.

Chris did not know how long the interview lasted, only that all at once it was over. Ali Hamadan had gone, and Chris was watching Entessar label the cassettes with a grease pencil and pack them carefully into the valise with the other cassettes and the camera.

"He's an exciting man, isn't he?" Chris said.

"Exciting?" Entessar said. "In what way?"

Oh, come on now, Chris told her in her mind, as if you don't know what I'm talking about. Stop playing with me, girl. The single light bulb in the lamp on the bedtable flickered. Chris thought the electricity was going off. But the bulb glowed steadily again.

Entessar said, "Yes, I suppose he is exciting at that. You found him so, is that it?"

"Didn't you?" Chris said. "Don't you?"

Even in the mottled dim light of the lampshade, Entessar's face was flushed. Chris wanted to laugh: They had probably been thinking the same thoughts. Sharing the same man.

"I never really thought about it," Entessar said.

"Not even a little?" Chris asked, teasing.

"I have no interest in him," Entessar said, after a moment. She was gazing directly at Chris. "I have no interest in him . . . that way."

Chris had never noticed Entessar's eyes, deep black,

very alive, very alert. The eyes seemed to soften the hard-boned lines of her face. Entessar started to speak again, and at that instant, with no warning, the light bulb went dead.

In the dark, Chris still felt Entessar's gaze. Chris said, "Why don't you turn on the flashlight?"

Entessar said nothing.

"The light, Entessar," Chris said. "Let there be light."

The room remained dark another moment, and then Entessar switched on her penlight and placed it on the bed. The penlight's thin shaft of light illuminated only a portion of the blanket and the wall near the bed. As Chris reached out for the penlight, her hand touched Entessar's. Entessar grasped Chris's hand and pulled Chris down on the bed beside her.

"Entessar . . . ," Chris said, and then felt the fingertips of Entessar's free hand brush her lips, and the same hand gently forcing her backward so that her head rested on the pillow. The shadowed light from the penlight's beam was entirely obscured by the frizzy silhouette of Entessar's hair as she lowered her face toward Chris's.

Chris felt the soft caress of Entessar's lips on hers and Entessar's hand on her breast, fondling the nipple through the cloth of Chris's *abayah*. She felt the hem of the garment being lifted, and Entessar's other hand sliding up along her leg, around the knee and on the inside of her thigh, then making a circle with her fingertip on the mound, and then down again. Entessar gently spread Chris's legs and cupped the vaginal lips in the palm of her hand. And then, slowly, softly, steadily, began massaging.

What amazed Chris then, and later, was that one part of her wanted to push the woman away in revulsion but was prevented by the other part, the curious, intrigued, interested part. Entessar's mouth pressed down harder, forcing Chris's mouth open just enough to accommodate Entessar's tongue. Entessar's hand never stopped moving, and Chris heard a moaning sound, louder and louder. The voice sounded strange, until she realized it was her own voice, and suddenly she wanted to cry out. She had just then told herself that she had made an astounding discovery. She had discovered why Entessar was unmarried.

Now Chris felt the whole lower part of the *abayah* being pulled up around her waist, and her pantyhose being pulled down, and she dreamily wondered if perhaps she shouldn't remove her shoes, and all this while imagining herself shouting for Entessar to stop, for she knew that at any instant she would feel Entessar's tongue flicking in and out of her. The revulsed part of her—the part that wanted it all stopped—was too weak to resist the curious, interested part, which had already noted that while this was not as pleasurable as being with a man, the indescribable pleasure of him sliding back and forth inside you, this had a pleasure all its own.

A different pleasure, one she desperately wanted to reach its peak and at the same time hoped would never stop. Yes, this was so different. This would bring her to the very top, and remain there, until finally she could not hold back and would explode.

It stopped. Everything stopped. The warmth of Entessar's mouth was gone. The cry Chris heard was not her own, it was Entessar's. And not a cry of rapture, but a gasp of fear. Entessar had heard an urgent knocking on the door and had rolled off the bed, and now, standing, she called out in Arabic, "Who is it?"

A child's voice answered in Arabic.

Entessar unlatched the door. A young boy entered. He could have been no more than ten. He wore a shabby coat sizes too large, and a torn wool knit cap. His preadolescent voice was shrill with fear. He and Entessar spoke briefly, tersely. Then the boy hurried away.

Entessar closed the door and said to Chris, "Ali Hamadan sent him. The Iraqis have arrested a man who knew Ali was here tonight. Ali thinks the man might give them this address!"

Chris sat up in bed and for an instant wondered why her feet felt shackled. Then, mortified, she realized that her pantyhose were still crumpled around her ankles. She fumbled for the pantyhose and pulled them on. She turned away from Entessar as she stood up and adjusted the pantyhose and smoothed the *abayah* down over her waist. In the half light of the penlight that had fallen to the floor, she saw Entessar slide the valise from under the bed.

"If the Iraqis come here, the whole building will be searched," Entessar said. "Stay in this room until I return. Do you understand?"

The fear in Chris's stomach had swelled up into her throat. She had to force herself to speak. "Until you return? Where are you going?"

Entessar hefted the valise. "To hide this."

"But why do you want me to stay?"

"You'll be safer staying here than going with me."

"But they'll question me."

"You'll show them your papers and pray to God they believe you are an American married to a Kuwaiti Palestinian. But if they find this. . . ." She hefted the valise again.

"Where are you taking it?" Chris asked.

"I have a place."

"Then I'll go with you."

"Chris, if I'm caught, and you're with me . . ." Entessar shook her head helplessly.

"The tapes, Entessar," Chris said. The words had spilled from her mouth before she could stop them. "If you're caught, what happens to the tapes?"

Entessar seemed to smile. "I'll try not to be caught." She moved to leave. Chris grasped her arm.

"I didn't mean that the way it sounded," Chris said. "I didn't mean that the tapes were more important than you."

"I know," Entessar said quietly. In the dark the two women peered at each other. Chris waited for Entessar to say something about what had happened between them. She expected Entessar to say, I'm sorry, Chris, I couldn't help myself. It's okay, Entessar, Chris answered her in her mind. Don't worry about it, no harm done. A better reply would be the truth: I have to think about this awhile, Entessar, because to tell you the truth, I'm a little confused. No, *very* confused.

Entessar said, "Remember, Chris, do not leave this room." She opened the door, glanced out and, without another word, left.

Chris stood frozen. She did not know how long she stood there, staring at the door, listening for men's voices, vehicles, the heavy sound of boots, and not hearing a sound. It was as though she were watching a video being rewound. Everything moving backward. The entire scene, back to the moment Entessar had grasped her hand. But all that vanished now as she felt her face grow hot and her temples throb, and now not with passion but with shame. What had happened confused her so much that it diluted even the fear of being found by the Iraqis.

She had committed no crime, for God's sake. She had allowed herself to be seduced by a woman. Was that so terrible? As a matter of fact, she damn well might do it again. No, of course, she would not do it again, never, not even with Entessar. Especially not with Entessar. Their relationship would be awkward now, but that could be dealt with.

And those tapes. My God, the biggest story of her life. But Entessar would keep them safe. She could rely on Entessar. It would all work out. Chris could see the faxed message from Larry Hill, his elated words of congratulations.

All night, too nervous for sleep, Chris waited for the police to burst into the room. They never came. Not until shortly after dawn did she finally begin to doze off. She awoke with a start, fell asleep again, the sort of twilight sleep where you are really half awake. In this twilight sleep she imagined hearing the screech of an automobile's tires, the slamming of the automobile's doors, and the sound of the automobile driving away.

And then she heard the scream.

It sounded inhuman, a howl of anguish, the cry of a mortally wounded animal. But it came from a woman.

The woman screamed again, and then again, and once more. Now there were other voices, male and female, shouting excitedly in Arabic.

Instinctively, Chris knew no soldiers were outside. She left the room and hurried up the basement stairs to the lobby. She started across the lobby floor and then saw a crowd of people outside, most of them still in nightclothes. The people were clustered around an object in the center of the courtyard.

The screams were coming from Entessar's aunt. She was staring at the object, wringing her hands in grief. Her husband stood beside her, his eyes also fixed on the object. He seemed in a trance. One of the onlookers, the Palestinian woman living in 5E, turned away and rushed back into the building. She saw Chris in the lobby and stopped. For a moment she stared at Chris, her eyes cold with hate, then she continued on toward the stairway. Chris hardly noticed. Chris's attention was riveted outside, in the courtyard.

The valise.

Open, the valise lay near the dry fountain in the center of the courtyard, filled with pieces of charred, half-melted plastic material Chris recognized as cassette casings. The only sign of the film was a sprinkling of crinkled black ash. Chris's first thought was that the Iraqis had burned the tapes, but she immediately realized that Entessar had destroyed them, not the Iraqis. Had the Iraqis viewed the tapes, they would have known of Chris's existence. By now, she would certainly have been arrested. No, Entessar had kept the tapes out of Iraqi hands.

Chris's ears rang with her own words, her fatuous question to Ali Hamadan: "Can you document the reports of Iraqi brutality?"

She walked into the courtyard and pushed through the crowd. Lying on her back near the waterless fountain, naked, in an almost Christ-like position, was Entessar. Her open eyes stared lifelessly. Her mouth was twisted grotesquely, as though frozen in the midst of a scream. Her entire body was blotched with dark purple bruises and dried blood. Much of the blood appeared to have congealed over the nipples of each breast. But there were no nipples, they had been hacked off.

The blood had seeped down to Entessar's belly and onto her groin, where it coagulated in thin black layers between her thighs. The clotted blood nearly concealed a circular piece of glass protruding from Entessar's body.

The last sight Chris saw before she fainted was the physician uncle removing a wine bottle from Entessar's vagina, and shards of broken glass falling out with it. The bottle had been inserted whole into Entessar and then crushed while inside her. Entessar's stomach bore the clear outline of heelprints. They had stomped on her and kicked her to smash the glass.

Chris's last thought before she fainted was that despite the unspeakable torture, Entessar had obviously not betrayed her. Otherwise, obviously, Chris might have suffered the same fate. Entessar had saved Chris's life.

Inside Kuwait with Christine Campbell.

A week later, on January 3, Chris arrived in Baghdad. She had flown in from Tehran, a ninety-minute flight, almost every minute of it spent thinking about Kuwait. More accurately, about Entessar, and Entessar having saved Chris's life. Never especially religious, even to the point of questioning the existence of a Supreme Being, Chris now wondered if there were not some higher purpose in all that had happened to her in Kuwait. The ease with which she had entered and departed the country. The loss of the tapes. Entessar.

There was no answer, certainly none of a divine nature. It was all coincidence and luck. Good luck for Chris, bad luck for Entessar. She was in Entessar's debt. She would dedicate the Saddam Hussein interview to Entessar. And the book. The book Chris would write of her experiences: *Inside Kuwait with Christine Campbell.*

The airport customs officers did not inspect her luggage or open her laptop computer. No one even seemed to notice that her black hair did not match the fair hair

of her passport photo. She had prepared a truthful reply
for that question: She simply had not had time to see a
beautician. Her first order of business at the Al-Rashid
Hotel, she would explain, was a visit to the beauty salon.

The only question asked of her was how long she
planned to stay in Iraq.

"Until the war is over," she said.

The officers laughed. They all thought it quite witty.

3

Of his six canvases on exhibition at Galerie Fontan,
Amir favored the one entitled *Glory*. So, apparently, did
the attractive young girl. She had been admiring it for
several minutes now. All three canvases in the gallery
display window were Amir's, with *Glory* occupying the
center position. An entirely abstract work, *Glory* was a
collage of somber colors in a pinwheel, converging into
a small gold circle like a sunburst.

From his vantage point in the doorway of the shuttered Air France ticket office on Saadun Street, Amir
had a clear view of the art gallery diagonally across the
boulevard. Only two days of his furlough remained before he reported to his unit in Basra on January 6. Each
afternoon of the previous five days of the furlough, he
had come here to see how many people stopped to look
into the window. This was the first time anyone had
shown more than a passing interest.

The girl, a petite brunette wearing an expensive
leather jacket and a tailored denim skirt, started walking away. No! Amir shouted to her in his mind. Wait!
He hurried across the street, darting around a bus that
had just rumbled to a stop. The girl was nowhere in
sight.

"Shit!" he said aloud, and then saw her. She was inside the gallery, talking to the manager, Nadhim Kazzar,
he of the shiny bald head and parchment face. Nadhim
stepped to the window and lifted *Glory* out and held it
for the girl to see in the sunlight.

Amir straightened his uniform blouse and adjusted

his beret and entered the gallery. He closed the door loudly behind him. Nadhim, precisely as Amir had hoped, glanced up and said, "Would you believe? Here is the artist himself!"

Amir nodded politely. The girl pointed a red-lacquered fingernail at the painting. "Would you mind interpreting this for me?"

"Allow me to introduce Lieutenant Badran," Nadhim said. "I've been showing his work all week. I think he'll become quite popular."

"With *this?*" the girl said. The corners of her mouth turned down in distaste as she pointed to the painting again.

"You don't like it?" Amir said, all the charming and clever banter he had been rehearsing suddenly forgotten.

"I might if I understood it," she said.

"It depicts the glory of battle," he said.

"In war, you mean?"

"Of course."

"The glory of war," she said. "And would you please tell me what is so glorious about war?"

"A just war is glorious," he said.

"No war is glorious," the girl said.

A man and a woman came into the gallery. Nadhim, obviously relieved at the interruption, deposited *Glory* into Amir's hands and left to greet the customers. Amir propped the canvas on the floor against the display shelf and stepped back to study it.

"This sunburst at the center symbolizes the culmination of the battle, the victory. That's what I should have called it, *Victory.*"

The girl sighed. She had deep dark eyes that at the moment were cold with exasperation. "What did the man say your name was?" she asked.

"Badran, Amir Badran." He deliberately did not ask for her name. To hell with her. From the corner of his eye he saw Nadhim escort the customers into a locked room at the rear of the gallery where antique jewelry

was kept. "I'm sorry you don't like the painting," he
said.

"I never said I didn't like it. I don't care for the subject."

"I have some others on exhibit," Amir said. Maybe
she wasn't such a bitch after all. He replaced *Glory* in
the window and lifted out a different canvas, another
abstract collage, this one sprightlier and more buoyant.
"I call this *Spring*," he said.

"Better," she said. "I like it."

"It's for sale," he said.

"I don't like it *that* much," she said. But she said it
with a friendly smile, which encouraged him to show her
his four other canvases. She studied each, from different
angles, different lighting. "You're quite talented," she
said, when they finished and had returned to the front
of the gallery. She tapped her finger on the aluminum
easel supporting *Glory*. "But I wish you weren't so interested in the glory of battle."

"It's part of the human experience," he said. "It's part
of our own Babylonian heritage."

"You've never been in a battle," she said. "You're too
young. The war ended more than two years ago. You
weren't in it."

"I'll be in the one that we're about to have."

"What makes you so sure we'll have war?"

"We'll have one, believe me."

"And you can't wait to get in it, can you?"

"That's my job," he said. "I'm a professional soldier."

"So, I'm right—you can't wait to get into it."

"The truth? No, I can't wait. Every day I pray they'll
attack us."

"Or that we'll attack them."

"Yes. Why not? Look what they're trying to do to us.
Look what they've already done! People are going hungry because of these stupid sanctions!"

"There are other ways to solve those problems."

"Not with honor," he said. He felt foolish discussing
this subject with a woman, but she was obviously educated, culturally his equal and probably socially as well.

It saddened him that she did not understand what was at stake. The whole damn future of Iraq.

He went on, "Forty years ago we were a British colony. Today we're the most powerful country in the Arab world. We have our own science and technology. The Yankee imperialists and their Zionist stooges can't stand that. So they try to crush us. But they won't. Nothing will ever crush us! Ever!"

The girl shook her head sadly. "You're a contradiction. A soldier—and a sensitive artist."

"That's what my sister says," he said, and slapped his hand to his forehead. "My sister! I'm supposed to meet her for lunch!" He glanced at his watch. "I'm a half hour late already!" He smiled at the girl. "And it's your fault."

She smiled back. "Perhaps I'll buy one of the paintings to make it up to you."

He could hardly believe his ears. His first sale! He looked at his watch again. Hana hated to be kept waiting. She'd call him thoughtless, spoiled, selfish, every name in the book. Every one of which, he thought, described him perfectly.

"Talk to Nadhim about it," he said, moving to leave. He was halfway out the door when he shouted, "You're a lady of impeccable taste!"

He ran across the square to the taxi queue. He told the driver to take him to Al Khanazir Island, fast. The taxi was already past the Central Bus Station and turning onto Jumhuriya Bridge when Amir realized that he never asked the girl her name.

Hana wasn't annoyed. Amir hadn't been on time for an appointment since the day he was born. He was a day late even for that. Besides, sitting on the club patio in the warm winter sun, as she waited for him, helped her relax. She was worried about her father and about Adnan. She looked at the big clock above the arched patio entrance and then at her wristwatch.

1:45.

If their plane was on time, they would have already

departed Tunis and be halfway to Algiers. They had
flown to Amman, where they were to transfer to an
Egyptair flight for Cairo, and then on to Tunis and Algiers.

What especially disturbed Hana was Adnan's insistence on accompanying Jamal. For a little extra "security." The implications were obvious. And terrifying.
Even more so in that Jamal had not objected to Adnan's
presence. Never in Hana's memory, in the literally dozens of missions abroad undertaken by Jamal, had he
ever acknowledged the need for security. Let alone accepted it.

Thank God for Adnan. She closed her eyes and
leaned back and let the sun beat down on her face. She
had last seen him early that morning, hours ago, when
he stopped at the house to pick up Jamal for the trip to
the airport. So handsome in civilian clothes, so distinguished. And that hint of gray in the temples and side-
burns of his thick sandy hair.

". . . must be dreaming of something very naughty,"
said a familiar voice.

She opened her eyes. Amir stood grinning down at
her. He raised his hands in mock self-defense. "Don't
say it. I'm thirty minutes late—"

"—forty," she corrected him, tapping her watch.
"Yes, so what else is new?"

He almost answered that by telling her of the marvelous girl he had just met. He did not, because he would
have had to admit that he became so engrossed in his
own pompous patriotic speech-making he neglected to
learn her name.

"I'm starved," he said, sitting and snapping his fingers
for a waiter and opening the leather-bound menu.
"What's good today?"

"They have *quozi*," Hana said. "It's not on the menu,
but I saw it being served." *Quozi*, barbecued lamb steak,
was one of Amir's favorites.

Amir returned the menu to the waiter and said that if
they were serving *quozi*, that was what he wanted. While
Hana studied the menu and finally decided on grilled

masgoug, a Tigris fish, Amir glanced lazily around the patio. Nearly every table was occupied, and waiters rushed back and forth balancing plates heaped with food. He cringed inwardly, recalling his own words to the girl at the gallery: *"People are going hungry because of these stupid sanctions!"* My God, he was glad she could not see him now. She would call him a hypocrite.

He had mentioned hunger to the girl only to make the point, he told himself now. Sure, sometimes you had to exaggerate slightly to get through to people. Nothing hypocritical about it. And the fact of the matter was that the Americans and their stooges were damn well succeeding with their economic boycott: spare parts, for example, everything from automobile tires to electric light bulbs. But nobody was going hungry, which was only further proof of Iraq's self-sufficiency.

He said to Hana, "The stories we hear about the Yankee imperialists squeezing us to death economically are all coming from them, from their goddamn coalition. Propaganda, pure and simple. Zionist propaganda, I'm telling you!"

"If it was propaganda, Father wouldn't be going to Algiers to talk to the Americans," Hana said. "Nor would Adnan."

"Our father is naive," Amir said. "I love him dearly but he lives in a dream world. A 'peaceful solution,' he says. Do you know what that means, darling sister?" Amir paused abruptly; he had just realized that for the second time in the past hour he was involved in a political discussion with a woman. But then Hana was no ordinary woman, and proof of that was her engagement to Adnan. It made Amir feel good just to know that his sister had been chosen by a man like Adnan Dulaimi.

". . . peaceful solution means exactly that," Hana was saying. "No war."

"On the contrary, it means no peace," Amir said. "There can never be peace as long as the Zionists occupy Palestine."

"Do you know what you sound like?" Hana had leaned across the table and placed her hand over Amir's lips. She sat back. "You sound like Radio Baghdad. What rubbish, Amir!"

"I hope Adnan never hears you say that."

"He's heard it from me. More than once, believe me." Hana looked at her watch. "They should be landing in Algiers in an hour or so. Oh, speaking of Adnan: He tells me you're thinking of applying for a transfer to a Commando unit?"

"I haven't done it yet. I'm only thinking about it."

"Are you mad, Amir? Or just stupid?"

Amir's face tightened, but before he could reply Hana raised a silencing hand. "I withdraw my remark," she said. "I apologize."

Amir could not help laughing. "You just don't want another lecture from me."

"That is correct, darling brother, I want to eat lunch in peace," Hana said, and thought, Peace, a word that seemed to have vanished from the world's vocabulary. But it reminded her of her father's mission. She glanced at her watch again, and again at the patio clock. "They'll be landing in Algiers soon."

Amir said nothing. The waiter had just arrived with their lunch. The *quozi* looked overdone. He started to complain, then decided he was too hungry to wait for another serving. He cut into the meat. It was pink on the inside, just as he liked it. He sliced off a neat square and tasted it. It was delicious.

Hana's calculations were incorrect. Egyptair Flight 655 had left Cairo an hour behind schedule. The 737-200 made up some time, but only now—indeed, at that very moment—was on the ground at Tunis, taxiing toward the terminal.

Since the airplane was not crowded, Adnan and Jamal sat in the rear, where they could stretch out and nap. They talked more than napped, most of it a continuation of the discussion—more accurately, debate—regarding what Adnan privately termed "Jamal's Folly."

". . . and, Jamal, I repeat: The Americans are not

serious about peace," Adnan was saying. "I know them. They want Saddam out."

"Is that so terrible an idea?" Jamal asked blandly.

"That is not the point," Adnan replied with equal blandness. He had no intention of indulging Jamal on *that* subject. "The Americans have realized from the start that sanctions won't do it for them. They've only agreed to this so-called back-channel communication with you as a means of lulling their own Congress and placating the UN."

Jamal said nothing for a moment. He was peering out the window at the terminal, a large building, three stories high, glass-fronted and pristinely new. Nearby, towering ostentatiously over all the airport buildings was a hotel, also new. Each room had a small outside balcony.

A ramp attendant directed the airplane into a parking position facing the terminal. Two other attendants wheeled a portable stairway toward the airplane. Jamal turned to Adnan and said, "And now *I* repeat: What can we lose by trying?"

Adnan said, "Jamal, your whole strategy is based on convincing—*trying to convince*—the Americans that both they and Saddam have miscalculated. That the solution is to find some honorable way of—"

"—saving face," Jamal said.

"—some honorable way of extricating us," Adnan continued. "And what you propose is that Saddam will agree to make peace with Israel. Which would then finesse Syria, Jordan, and Saudi Arabia into doing likewise. Pipe dreams, Jamal! Absolutely impossible, and you know it. But for the sake of argument, how would you persuade him to even consider it, and on what terms?"

"If I can obtain an American commitment to delay their attack on that basis, then I think I can deal with him."

"But, Jamal, *why* would he want to make peace with Israel?" Adnan paused, distracted by a flash of white through the airplane window. It was a bed sheet, aired by a chambermaid from the balcony of one of the rooms in the hotel. "What would it gain him?"

"To begin with, it would be a monumental achievement and certainly earn him a respectable place in history," Jamal said. "Not only as the creator of a modern, prosperous Iraq, but as the man who brought peace and honor to the entire region. Look, Adnan, it's time I'm after. Every day without war, every hour, is a chance for the parties to cool off. To consider the consequences."

"It won't happen, Jamal. The Americans are determined to smash us."

Just then the stewardess's voice boomed over the cabin PA system. "Please remain seated until the captain has turned off the Fasten Seatbelt sign. We will be here in Tunis for approximately forty minutes. Those passengers continuing on to Algiers, please report to the aircraft no later than ten minutes before departure."

She repeated her message in French and English, and by then the airplane had come to a full stop. The passengers began assembling in the aisle, waiting impatiently for the door to be opened.

The passengers were not the only people waiting impatiently. On the balcony of a tenth-floor room of the airport hotel, a man studied the Egyptair 737 through binoculars. A young man, not yet thirty, wearing a heavy blue wool V-neck sweater over his open-collared white dress shirt, baggy white trousers, and white tennis shoes. Of slight frame, almost deceptively frail, he might have been considered handsome if not for the very tiny, yet conspicuous criss-cross marks like a ridge of x's on the left side of his nose. The x's, running the entire length of the nose, were scars from some forty stitches acquired in a long-ago automobile accident. His Egyptian passport identified him as Salih Najdat, born in Alexandria. The name was as false as the passport.

Behind him on the carpeted floor of the hotel room, concealed under a blanket, was a shoulder-fired, Soviet-manufactured SA-7 Strela missile launcher. It was an old-fashioned, fairly obsolescent weapon, but could be broken down into components small enough to be packed into a large suitcase, which was exactly how it had been transported into the hotel.

Salih Najdat lowered the binoculars. He stepped back into the room and pulled the blanket off the Strela. The launcher, now assembled and loaded with an 80mm high-explosive heat-seeking missile, resembled a small bazooka. Salih placed the flat of his hand on the Strela's trigger guard. The metal was cool on his fingers. He could feel the rapid pounding of his pulse through his fingertips.

"I've been thinking about the other passengers," he said to another man in the room. "Forty-three of them."

Tall and husky, with angular features and a thick, drooping black mustache, this other man looked older than Salih. Actually, he was several years younger. "What would you have me do?" he asked. "Warn them?"

"But *forty-three* people!" Salih said.

The tall man draped the blanket over the Strela again. He picked up the weapon and said, "When the plane takes off, it will leave the runway approximately there." He pointed to a yellow marker, 6, three quarters of the way from the end of the runway. "We hit it then."

"I'd almost rather go aboard the plane and kill the son of a bitch right there!"

"We have our orders," said the tall man, whose name according to his Libyan passport was Badir Kayali. He carried the Strela out to the balcony. Still cradling the Strela, he gazed out at the runway. From a distance, in Badir's arms, the blanket-covered weapon might have been an infant in swaddling clothes.

An airport policeman had that impression also. Bicycling past the hotel, he had noticed the two men on a tenth-floor balcony. One man held an infant in his arms. As the policeman watched, the man hoisted the infant up onto his shoulder where it teetered precariously. The other man grasped the rear of the blanket, turning it slightly, enough to provide the policeman a full-profile view of the "infant."

Even before the men lowered the Strela back onto

the balcony floor, the policeman was radioing for assistance. Within two minutes, six other policemen armed with automatic weapons cordoned off the area. Six were racing up to the tenth floor.

In the Egyptair 737, Jamal and Adnan, the last passengers to deplane, moved through the aisle toward the door. Jamal ran his fingers over the beard stubble on his chin.

"I might as well shave," he said to Adnan. "I'll get my bag." He started past Adnan, back to the rear.

"I'll take a shave, too," Adnan said. "Stay here, I'll get both bags." He hurried down the aisle to their seats.

Jamal, at the door, stepped out onto the stairway platform. It was a chilly gray day, the sun hidden behind a heavy overcast. But the cool air was refreshing. Jamal took a deep breath. He was tired from the long flight. He looked forward to a good night's sleep in Algiers before the meeting.

From the tenth-floor balcony, Salih and Badir saw the distinguished-looking man standing on the stairway platform. They did not need binoculars to recognize Jamal. "There he is, that piece of disloyal scum," Badir said quietly.

Salih had turned away, attracted by activity on the ground directly below. "Badir!" he cried, and pointed at the hotel entrance. Policemen were rushing into the building.

Badir instantly realized what was happening. "We hit the plane now!" he said. In a single, smooth, swift motion, he whipped the blanket off the Strela, picked it up, placed the barrel on his shoulder, and partially depressed the trigger, which armed the missile.

In the airplane, Adnan retrieved Jamal's tote bag from the overhead bin, and his own attaché case. He opened the attaché case, removed his shaving kit—which was atop his service pistol, a 9mm Tariq—and closed the case. He left it on the seat and started up the aisle again. He stopped. He returned to the seat, opened the case, and withdrew the pistol. It was foolish, if not downright careless, leaving a loaded gun in an unattended cabin. He slipped the gun into his waistband and started up the aisle again.

He was fifty feet from the door when the missile hit. One instant he was striding up the aisle, admiring a stewardess who had just emerged, smiling, from the flight deck. The look of a satisfied woman, he thought, amused at the thought and idly wondering what—more accurately, *who*—had provided the satisfaction.

The next instant, the stewardess vanished. It was like a magician's assistant disappearing in a puff of smoke. Simultaneously, there was a blinding flash of white light and an explosion. Adnan felt himself being hurled backward. It was all very slow and blurry but quite deliberate, as though walking underwater. He knew he had opened his mouth to cry out in pain but felt no pain, only a dull pressure in his lower spine and buttocks, which he realized came from the armrest of an aisle seat that had halted the backward thrust of his body. He was pleased at the clarity with which he perceived all this and intrigued with the sensation of observing his own behavior from afar.

He heard distant screams. A woman's voice. The stewardess. No, she was dead. Must be another stewardess. More screams. Women. Yes, some passengers must have returned to the plane. Some women. Now the entire front of the cabin where he had last seen the stewardess was a mass of flames. The heat billowed down the aisle. It reminded Adnan of desert heat, when you stepped out of an air-conditioned airplane or automobile and felt as though you were walking into a blast furnace.

He gripped the back of the seat in front of him and pulled himself to his feet. "Jamal!" he shouted, and heard the hollow echo of his voice. "Jamal!" The screams from the front were louder than his voice. He walked slowly forward. The heat was even more oppressive, and now the cabin was filled with thick white smoke.

Adnan knew he was choking and also knew he had tripped over something in the aisle. The tip of his shoe sunk into a soft object. He looked down through the smoke. It was a woman. Crumpled in a fetal heap, blocking the aisle. Adnan stepped over the body and moved deeper into the smoke. Now everything seemed to be revolving around him, faster and faster. Yes, if he could lie down and rest a moment. Yes, rest, it would relieve the dizziness and nausea.

No, he could not rest. He had to find Jamal. He had to get him off the plane. That was his job. To protect Jamal. All right, then he would do his job. But, my God, it would be so nice to just sit down and close his eyes.

". . . here! Over here!" Someone, a man, called in Arabic. The voice came from the side, near the windows. "Can't you see me, dammit?"

No, you fool, Adnan imagined himself replying, I cannot see you. The smoke is too thick. But then he felt his arm being grasped and pulled toward the voice, and then all at once the smoke cleared and he was outside the airplane, on the wing at the emergency exit. One of the pilots had dragged him from the burning airplane. The spinning stopped. He could breathe. But everything was turning white before his eyes. He heard the crackle of the flames amidst the wail of ambulance sirens and the clamor of excited voices. The last sound he remembered before the whiteness totally enveloped him was his own voice, a mumbled question: "Where is Dr. Badran? Is Dr. Badran all right?" But even as his lips formed the question, he knew the answer. Jamal had been in the front of the airplane, which was where the bomb exploded.

A half hour later, fully recovered, Adnan learned that it was not a bomb, but a missile, and had impacted in the cabin doorway, disintegrating everything and everyone within a twenty-foot radius. Three crew members and twelve passengers killed, five others injured, one critically, a nine-year-old boy.

Jamal's body, what remained of it, was found on the ramp twenty-five feet away, wedged into the lower compartment of a baggage cart.

Salih Najdat and Badir Kayali had surrendered without resistance. They were still at the airport, in the same tenth-floor hotel room. The civilian police captain in charge told Adnan that the killers had thus far revealed little but would soon be taken into town, where he himself would conduct the investigation. He offered no excuses for what Adnan called the appalling lack of security, but promised that the true identity of the killers would be established, and that they would be dealt with most harshly.

"They'll talk, believe me," said the captain.

"I'd like to see them," Adnan said.

"What in heaven's name for?"

"I want to know why they did it," Adnan said.

The captain, a hard-faced, middle-aged veteran realized Adnan was still in shock. He laughed humorlessly. "They did it for their oppressed Palestinian brethren. But, all right, see them if you wish." He ordered an airport policeman to escort Adnan to the tenth floor.

Several uniformed policemen loitered outside the room and in the corridor. Two more uniformed policemen were inside the room, and a man in civilian clothes. The plainclothesman was talking to Salih and Badir. The two, hands manacled behind them, sat backwards on aluminum bridge chairs.

The plainclothesman beckoned Adnan to come around to confront the prisoners. Adnan hardly saw the black and blue bruises on their faces, and the dried blood around their mouths. He saw only the smoke-filled airplane cabin and the flames. And the body of the woman on the cabin floor. And the white flash of light where Jamal had been standing.

"This man is an Iraqi officer," the plainclothesman said to Salih and Badir. "He wants to know why you committed this horrible crime."

"The attack was not directed against Iraq," Badir said quietly.

"At who, then?" Adnan asked.

"At our enemies," Salih said.

"Who are your enemies?"

"Those who prevent us from having our homeland."

The plainclothesman said disgustedly, "Round and round. The same thing over and over."

"What's your name?" Adnan asked Badir.

"My name is of no importance," Badir said.

Badir continued speaking, but Adnan was not listening. Salih had just then moved his head. The movement gave Adnan a view of Salih in profile, the strip of tiny *x*'s on the side of the nose. It was a face he had seen before.

". . . and as far as the innocent people we killed," Badir was saying, "innocent people are killed and injured in all wars!"

"Your name?" Adnan said to Salih.

"My name is the name on my passport," said Salih.

The plainclothesman said to Adnan, "A waste of time, sir, as you can see."

Adnan was staring at Salih, trying to remember, trying to concentrate. Whenever the correct picture started to appear, it was instantly erased by images of the burning airplane. That face, those scars. Had it been in Washington? At Khorramshahr? The hospital after Khorramshahr? Why was he focusing on Khorramshahr? Wait, there were some Iranian POWs in the hospital. Iranian?

Yes, these two animals could easily be Iranian. Their accent, the hard consonants and rolling contractions, marked them as from the Gulf region.

Badir's voice penetrated Adnan's consciousness, ". . . we'll be released before the day is out."

Released.

Adnan remembered. It was like an electric shock. For a moment he felt faint, but his rage gave him strength. A rage such as he had never known, or known he was capable of. He motioned the plainclothesman to the balcony so they would not be overheard.

"Let me talk to them alone."

The plainclothesman, a dour, clean-shaven man who looked as though nothing shocked or surprised him, regarded Adnan narrowly. "What the hell for?"

"I think I know a way to get the truth."

"So do we."

"Don't give me that crap," Adnan said. "You'll keep them a few days or a week, and then their friends will hijack a plane or threaten to bomb a school—and kill some more innocent people—unless you release them. And you'll do it. Come on, let me try. You have nothing to lose."

The plainclothesman studied Adnan another skeptical moment, then shrugged. "Five minutes," he said. He waved everyone out of the room. Adnan accompanied him to the door, closed it, and started back toward the men.

It was Badir who sensed something unusual. He tried to twist his head around toward Adnan. He had time enough to see the Tariq in Adnan's hand and the muzzle flash as the gun was fired. The bullet ripped into his ear and blew away the entire top of his skull. Salih heard the sound of the gunshot that killed Badir and felt the warm wetness of Badir's blood splattering into his face, and the shreds of Badir's flesh and splintered bone.

That was all Salih felt or heard. The bullet that killed him was fired a split-instant later and entered the back of his head two inches above the neck, on a downward angle that severed the carotid artery and smashed the windpipe and emerged from his chest like a blossoming red flower. For all that, Salih's face was unmarked, although his mouth was open, almost as though in protest. His eyes, open, stared unseeingly. The network of crisscross scars on the side of his nose bulged out like angry blue veins.

Adnan had remembered where he saw those scars, and why the word "release" had triggered his memory. In Baghdad, not long after recovering from the Khorramshahr wound and returning to duty, one of his sergeant majors was arrested in a brawl at a waterfront nightclub. The sergeant major was taken to the central police station and held there until released in Adnan's custody.

It was in that same police station Adnan had seen the man with the scarred nose. Adnan did not know the man's real name, nor was there any reason for him to know. But Adnan did know that the man calling himself Salih Najdat, the man he had just killed, was an Iraqi, and an al-Amm agent.

Iraqi secret police.

Jamal had been murdered by his own people, either as a message to dissenters or to prevent him from meeting the American emissary. Or perhaps both. Whatever the motive, since Jamal's mission was government sanctioned, al-Amm would never have dared undertake an assassination on its own. Someone within the government had ordered it.

And only one person possessed enough power to do so.

And Adnan knew the convolutions of that person's logic. The man believed his own rhetoric: The Americans would drown in a sea of their own blood. The man had convinced himself that the Americans also believed this and therefore would not attack. Conversely, for Iraq to seek peace was a sign of abject weakness, a clear invitation for the Americans to attack.

All this occurred to Adnan in the few seconds between the time he fired the two shots and the time the policemen burst into the room. The pistol in Adnan's hand, a string of smoke curling from the barrel, was still leveled at Salih's head.

"God help us!" a uniformed policeman said. The plainclothesman said nothing. He looked at the dead men, then at Adnan, then at the men, and back at Adnan.

"They tried to escape," Adnan said.

FIVE

Chris's cameraman, Ramon Sandoval, had earned a well-deserved reputation for photographing his subjects in environments that projected dramatic images of time and place. With a subject as photogenic as Christine Campbell, and an environment as newsworthy as Baghdad, the Cuban-born Sandoval was already composing his Peabody Award acceptance speech. Not to mention a Dupont and probably a Sigma Delta Chi.

Now, on the roof of the Al-Rashid Hotel, camera rolling, Sandoval backed slowly away until he had Chris impeccably framed. Behind her were the varicolored bulbs strung along the suspension cables of the Jumhuriya Bridge and the shimmering reflection on the river of headlights from the vehicles rumbling across the bridge's four lanes.

Muhmad, the Pakistani soundman holding the mike boom above Chris's head, adjusted the "blimp," the muffler encasing the microphone. He wanted a slight sound of rushing wind on the track, and the hollow echo of vehicular traffic. The sounds would blend nicely with shots of Chris, her blonde hair ruffling gently in the wind. On Sandoval's monitor, across the bottom of the frame, a white-lettered card read: BAGHAD, IRAQ—WCN, LIVE.

". . . but to answer your question, Don," Chris was saying into the camera, "No, I have heard no official reaction regarding the breakdown of the Baker-Aziz talks in Geneva. The newspapers are critical, but nothing from the government."

On the monitor, the lantern-jawed face of WCN's Washington anchor, Don Blakely, filled the screen. "What about the man-in-the-street, Chris? Have you garnered any reaction from the, well, the ordinary people?"

"I talked to a few people in the hotel, Don. The people who work here. They're disappointed."

On the monitor, the screen split now. To the left, Chris on the Baghdad rooftop; to the right, Don Blakely at his Washington desk. Chris continued, "But I think everybody's waiting to see what the next two days bring, when the U.S. Senate votes whether or not to uphold the UN ultimatum—"

"—Chris, excuse me." The monitor cut to a full shot of Blakely listening intently to his earphone. He nodded. "Chris, I know it's four in the morning there, and you've haven't had much sleep, but can you stand by a few minutes? We're going to switch over to Helen Fairchild, WCN's State Department correspondent."

According to the most recent estimate, a worldwide audience of no less than one hundred million was tuned to WCN's continual war news program, "Gulf Watch." In addition to Chris's Baghdad segment, the early evening edition included reports from WCN correspondents in London, Bonn, Tel Aviv, Amman, and Riyadh.

This was Chris's tenth broadcast from Baghdad, and she had arrived here only a week earlier. She had left Kuwait the same way she entered, clad in a black *abayah,* in Ibrahim's truck. It was almost too easy. The Iraqi border guards had waved them on into Iraq and then Iran, never once stopping the truck for inspection.

No matter how much Chris tried to blot it from her memory, the picture of Entessar lying naked in the courtyard remained like some holographic image. It erased even the guilty memory of their interlude in the room. Only when she finally reached Tehran and boarded the plane for Baghdad, did the image begin to fade. She knew it would never completely leave her. She did not want it to.

From Tehran, Chris had had several telephone conversations with Larry Hill. He gave her hell for her "disappearance" last week. Not a single word from her for more than six days, making him sick with worry. Chris said she would fill him in on everything later. Too delicate a subject for open telephone lines, but a story that would electrify the whole world. Larry did not press for details; he was more concerned with the impending war, a story unfolding so fast and in so many places that no one could keep up with it.

No one except WCN.

One of the one hundred million viewers of Chris Campbell's live satellite report from Baghdad was a modestly overweight, balding, salt-and-pepper-bearded fifty-five-year-old man. He was watching the program in his opulent study on the first floor of the royal palace in Amman, Jordan. An early riser, he regularly watched WCN satellite news programs, although seldom, as now, before dawn.

He had been up since two that morning, awakened by Major General Abdul Hamid, reporting the presence of a large formation of Israeli aircraft in Jordanian airspace. The aircraft were proceeding eastward. Eastward, toward Iraq. Hamid did not request permission to launch Jordanian interceptors. He did not want to embarrass the king, who he knew had received a personal message from Yitzhak Shamir: a blunt warning that any interference with an Israeli overflight would be dealt with most severely.

King Hussein ordered Hamid to inform Iraqi air defense of the approaching aircraft. Then he dressed and went down to his study to review the matter with several other aides. There was no indication of increased Allied aerial activity in Saudi Arabia, and the Iraqis still had five days to comply with the UN ultimatum. The only question, then, was whether the Israelis were acting unilaterally. After a brief discussion, Hussein had dismissed the men and, alone, considered his options.

He had none.

His air force was no match for the Israelis, nor could he ask the Americans or the Saudis for help. By siding with Iraq he had made Jordan a pariah nation. He could only sit, watch, and wait. And wonder what the Israelis were up to.

So now, shortly after four, the king awaited Hamid's return. He sat at his desk, gazing out the leaded window at the dark predawn sky and listening, but not hearing a word, to Chris Campbell's voice from the giant television screen built into the wall at the opposite end of the room. Hussein swiveled his chair around as the door opened. Hamid entered.

The general's youthful face was haggard. He needed a shave. His khaki uniform blouse was rumpled and stained with tobacco ash. He sat, unasked, in the single leather armchair in front of the desk.

"Even through the jamming—which I must say is extraordinarily effective—we've determined that there are eight aircraft," Hamid said. "From their speed and altitude they appear to be transports."

"Paratroopers?"

"We can't tell. But they're turning south."

"South? They're not going into Iraq?"

"It does not appear so, sir."

"If they're turning south, they're still here in Jordan," Hussein said. He leaned forward and switched off the television. On the screen, the image of Christine Campbell on the Baghdad hotel rooftop faded into a ghostly shadow, then vanished altogether. "What could they be up to?"

"It might be a probe," Hamid said. "To test our defenses. To see if we actually would challenge them." Hamid instantly regretted the words; they echoed the king's hollow promise to defend Jordanian airspace.

King Hussein was not offended. He was a realist, a practical man, a survivor. He had aligned his nation with Iraq, an act of pure pragmatism, mandated by the region's very geography. Had Jordan remained neutral, Saddam Hussein would have used this as a pretense to invade—ostensibly to "protect" Jordan's Palestinian population—thereby triggering an immediate Israeli response. Precisely what Saddam desired, for he believed it would shatter the Allied coalition.

The king said, "Well, if it is a probe, then why give them the satisfaction of a response?" He smiled wearily. "Why even waste the fuel?"

"If that is your decision, sir," Hamid said.

"Eight of them," the king said quietly, really thinking aloud. "Turning south. Could they be, say, seven fighters accompanying a tanker? Their F-15s have that capability, you know."

"Anything is possible, sir."

"Turning south, with no apparent intention of penetrating Iraq," the king repeated. "Keep me informed."

"Yes, sir." Hamid rose to leave.

"Yes, Abdul, I think that for the time being at least we'll just wait to see what happens. It might be best for us to just turn the other cheek."

For his part, Hamid thought it best not to remind the king that "turn the other cheek" was a biblical aphorism coined by a man who had been born a Jew.

2

King Hussein's suggestion of seven fighters accompanying a tanker was not that far from the mark. The Israeli formation consisted not of eight aircraft, but nine. Their collective presence, combined with electronic jamming, quite effectively masked the radar signature of this ninth airplane, which was a transport, a C-130.

The main element did indeed include a tanker and seven F-15 fighters, and had indeed swung south and now, remaining within Jordanian airspace, was orbiting the area immediately west of the Iraqi border. The tanker and the seven F-15s had made the turn at a predetermined position where Iraqi and Jordanian radar did not overlap. This narrow gap in the radar coverage allowed the ninth aircraft, the C-130, to slip undetected away from the main formation and drop down to one hundred and fifty feet above the desert. At that altitude, below radar, the transport continued eastward into Iraq. Its destination was a small complex of concrete and cinderblock buildings fifty-three miles inside Iraq, the village of Shab al-Bir.

The transport carried ninety-seven men of an elite Israeli commando demolition team, and four jeeps mounted with 87mm recoilless rifles. The company was divided into two units, one to seize and secure the launch bays and the general area, the other to set and detonate the charges. The operation had been rehearsed nightly for the past two weeks at a site in the Negev where a replica of the village had been constructed, and where the terrain was similar to Shab al-Bir.

Colonel Binyamin Sklar, forty-three, commanded the company. Twice within the past year, Sklar had led similar missions, most recently the successful "neutralization" of a Syrian telecommunications station ten miles from the center of Beirut. Ben Sklar deserved his reputation as the man for the tough jobs.

He was thinking about this, and how much he disliked the overall commander, Avi Posner. Avi might be a brilliant planner, but it was Ben Sklar who executed the brilliant plans. He hated Avi's arrogance and his aloofness, and worst of all, the fact that Avi, five years younger than Sklar, outranked him.

You are jealous, you son of a bitch, he scolded himself, gazing past the pilot's shoulder, at the blackness of the desert. He was standing on the flight deck of the C-130, his face tinged an eerie green in the fluorescent glow of the instrument panel. The pilot had summoned him from the cabin when the fighter escort swung away and the transport, descending, entered Iraqi airspace.

"Fifteen minutes from destination, Benny," the pilot said.

"Okay, I'll go back and get them ready," Sklar said.

"Prepare them for a rough landing," the pilot said,

wondering himself how rough it would be. The C-130 was to put down on a section of desert supposedly flat and hard-packed. The area had been exhaustively mapped and surveyed both from the air and by on-site intelligence teams.

Sklar patted the pilot's shoulder and left the flight deck. He started down the ladder into the darkened cabin, nodding at two men seated in jump seats at the rear of the flight deck. Sklar resented their presence. Although neither of the two was a commando, their safety was Sklar's responsibility.

The presence of one of the pair was legitimate. He was an Israeli Air Force major, charged with coordinating aerial operations. The other man not only had no business here, he was not even an Israeli. He was an American, a USAF lieutenant colonel, officially an observer. Unofficially, in Colonel Sklar's opinion, the American was crazy. Several others, including the American himself, shared that opinion.

"Everything okay?" Sklar shouted.

Zvi Sharok made an "A-okay" circle with his thumb and forefinger.

"You look like Laurel and Hardy in those combat suits!" Sklar said. "Ten minutes!"

Sklar descended the ladder, and Zvi said to Nick Harmon, "I suppose we do look silly in these things." He rapped his knuckles on the top of Nick's steel helmet.

Silly, Nick thought, was not the word for it: sitting in this airplane, wearing desert-camouflaged fatigues, combat boots, steel helmet, clutching an Uzi he hardly knew how to load, let alone use.

For two days now—and certainly for most of the past hour, since taking off from the airbase outside Haifa—he had been analyzing his reason for being here. In truth, it required no analysis. It was not that complicated. The reason had lain—festered, more accurately —deep within him for twenty-two years.

Two days ago Frank Kowalski had burst into Nick's office at the embassy with an urgent E-mail from Washington. The Pentagon wanted confirmation of hard intelligence reports suggesting the imminence of an Israeli preemptive strike into Iraq. This, said Kowalski, was where Nick earned his pay. Nick was to learn when, how, and where.

Nick confronted Zvi Sharok. Nick expected a denial, which he could then in all honesty relay to Kowalski. It did not quite work out that way. Zvi said he would disclose the plan, but only on Nick's word of honor not to reveal it.

Nick agreed. So Zvi explained that the Israeli government, convinced that war was inevitable and that Israel would be attacked, had decided to eliminate the most immediate threat: the Iraqi missiles from the fixed launchers at Shab al-Bir.

And also eliminate any possibility of peace, Nick had remarked. Zvi's reply was a joking invitation for Nick to come along as an "observer." Nick said thanks but no thanks. Hours later that same day, Nick phoned Zvi to say that he'd changed his mind and would like to join the party. Zvi said Nick was crazy. Nick concurred.

Nick was crazy only in the sense that he had begun to believe he was preordained to go on this mission. Payment for a debt incurred twenty-two years before at a place called Chu-Bai. He was convinced that only by reliving Chu-Bai, and this time not as a coward, could he ever purge himself of that shameful burden.

Childish? Irrational? Unrealistic? Yes, all of those, but even now, listening to the drone of the airplane's engines, which seemed to be echoing back into his ears those same words, he knew it was the only answer, the only solution. The only way to redeem himself.

"There it is," Zvi said quietly. He pointed ahead through the windscreen. Pinpoints of light danced on the horizon, Shab al-Bir.

The copilot twisted around and shouted in English to Zvi. "Do you believe this? The place is lit up like Dizengoff Square! You might think they're trying to help us find it!"

Zvi said, "Yeah, that's what I'm afraid of!" But he said to Nick, "If they knew we were coming, a couple of night fighters would have already blown us out of the sky. No, we're in good shape. They're sitting there, fat and happy."

Shab al-Bir was completedly surrounded by a cyclone fence topped with razor wire. Within the enclosure, at the west side and at the east side, were two minarets. Both minarets functioned as sentry towers. The launching bays were dispersed among the village buildings, concealed under flat sliding roofs. The garrison consisted of some fifty technicians and two companies of GHC Commando Brigade troops. Israeli intelligence had not detected the presence of any women or children. It made Colonel Sklar's "no prisoners" instructions easier to carry out.

"Get ready!" the pilot called out in Hebrew.

The drone of the engines reduced to a whisper. Nick felt the bottom drop out as the C-130's forward speed abruptly slowed and her nose rose in a near stall configuration. The pilot, on full flaps, was literally mushing the big airplane in.

"Okay, Nick, here we go!" Zvi said. He tightened his seat belt. In the dark he grinned crookedly. "I'm still wondering how I'll explain this to your people if you're killed!"

"You'll think of something," Nick said. He tightened his own belt and laid the Uzi across his lap. He listened to the hushed whir of the engines as the airplane hurtled silently on, downward into the blackness. It was like being in a glider flown by some bug-eyed extraterrestrial, which was what the pilot resembled with the night-vision goggles strapped around his eyes.

The airplane flared out, wheels feeling for the sand, touching, settling with a gentle jar, then rolling bumpily across the desert, slower, slower, and then, suddenly, stopping. The only sound was the quiet moan of the windmilling propellers, and the louder, metallic grind of the rear ramp opening. And the rumble of jeep engines.

"Welcome to Iraq!" Zvi said. He was already on his feet, moving. "Let's go, soldier!"

Let's go soldier, Nick thought. Go where? To hell,

probably. He unstrapped and followed Zvi down the ladder. The C-130 cabin was alive with jeeps moving down the ramp to the desert, and charcoal-blackened-faced commandos scrambling out after them.

One squad fanned out around the airplane to form a security perimeter, while the jeeps drove off carrying the heavy weapons and the explosives. The main assault force set off on foot over the sand at a double-time pace. One hundred yards from the fence, sharpshooters with silencer-equipped Browning .303 rifles quickly disposed of the sentries in the tower. The gunshots sounded like someone snapping his fingers. An advance team crept to the fence and proceeded to cut a passageway through the wire.

Somewhere within the compound a dog barked, then another dog, and yet another. A man's angry voice drifted across the desert. The dogs stopped barking. Colonel Sklar surveyed the area through night-vision binoculars, then spoke quietly into his transceiver. The commandos moved to the fence and began pouring through the opening into the village. The gate was opened for the jeeps.

Zvi accompanied Sklar's unit but Nick, at the colonel's specific instructions, went in with the squad assigned to hold and secure the general area. An English-speaking sergeant, surely the oldest man in the company—older than Sklar—commanded the squad. And resented Nick's presence even more than Sklar.

"Keep your bloody head down, Yank, and don't lose sight of me!" the sergeant whispered to Nick. He slung his grenade-launcher Galil rifle over his shoulder, and staying close to the walls of the houses, walked rapidly along a deserted street. A dozen men followed in single file.

Nick brought up the rear. The squad had not advanced five yards when gunfire—the zipperlike sound of an Uzi—came from the far end of the village. From the barracks area. Immediately, other Uzis began firing. The fusillade continued for a full thirty seconds. Then, like a radio abruptly turned off, the gunfire stopped. A moment of utter silence was followed by a man's shrill cry of pain, another man screaming a curse in Arabic. More gunshots. Silence.

The sergeant shone his flashlight on his watch. A shot rang out. Flashlight clattering in one direction, rifle in another, the sergeant fell face down into the dirt street. Another shot was fired. The bullet tore into the street in a geyser of dust. Immediately, a commando swiveled his Galil around and upward toward the minaret behind them. He launched a grenade. The parapet of the tower exploded in a ball of orange flame.

A corporal stepped forward and issued quiet, crisp orders in Hebrew. Two men knelt beside the sergeant, while another spoke into a transceiver. The sergeant was dragged into a doorway. The men removed his jacket and pillowed it under his head. Nick knew the sergeant was dead. The way he had toppled, like a tree crashing onto the forest floor. Nick had seen it before, on patrol in Vietnam when he first went up country, not long before Chu-Bai.

Now the corporal gestured Nick and the others to continue forward. They had proceeded less than ten feet when every light in the village went out. The unit assigned to knocking out the power station had done its job. The firing resumed, heavier caliber now, and more intense. Now the night sky was bright with arcing tracers. Nick moved on, staying in the shadows of the buildings. The windows of the houses contained no glass, the doorways no doors; every house on the street was an empty concrete shell.

Ahead, he heard voices calling in Hebrew, and at the same time suddenly realized that he was alone. The others had gone on without him. Probably, he thought, because they considered him safer back here, at the edge of the village. The heavy gunfire came from the west, from the barracks area, where Sklar's detachment was "neutralizing" the garrison. No prisoners.

Nick was calm, not at all frightened, which both pleased and surprised him. He even smiled to himself, thinking about Kowalski learning of the raid and, correctly, accusing Nick of deliberately not informing him. The shit would really hit the fan. Nick was sure that Kowalski's job in Israel was to discourage the Israelis from hitting Iraq. Never send a boy on a man's errand.

A starshell briefly illuminated the area. The desolate street was remarkably clean, not a trace of debris. The flare of light vanished, followed instantly by the rapid chug-chug-chug of a heavy machine gun. Iraqi.

Okay, Nick told himself. You've had your fun, now turn around and get the hell out of here before somebody mistakes you for a soldier. In his mind, he saw himself doing a complete one-eighty, a turn that would point him at the fence, and then out. From there, straight ahead, he would find the airplane.

But no, that would be Chu-Bai all over again. Running away. He had come here for a purpose, to prove something. To prove that he was not a coward. Staying here—not scurrying back to the airplane—would be acceptable proof. But he knew better. He knew that no matter what he did, or did not do, he could never redeem Chu-Bai. He would just have to live with it.

He moved forward, then stopped as the gunfire also momentarily stopped. The brief silence was punctuated by more voices urgently shouting back and forth in Hebrew. Nick did not understand a single word but sensed a certain triumphal tone in the voices.

The gunfire resumed. Nick gripped the Uzi in both hands and began jogging along the street. He reached an intersection and stopped, his eyes fixed on the sky, the strobelike flashes of light from the gunfire. The gunfire was louder. Abruptly, again, everything fell silent and dark. And then, in the distance, the sound of an automobile, and another. Nick flattened himself against a wall as the vehicles came closer. Two Israeli jeeps raced past Nick and careened around the corner.

Nick hurried to the top of the street. He stepped around the corner. It was like a Hollywood movie set. The harsh white light of battery-powered halogen lamps illuminated the entire length of the street, which was strewn with the bodies of Iraqi soldiers and the still-smoldering wrecks of automobiles and jeeps. In the middle of the street was a two-story wood-framed building, the barracks. Every window had been blown out. Part of the roof was burning, flames gutted the interior. The entrance was clogged with bodies, some in uniform, more in their sleeping garments, the white cotton *galabiyyas*. They had been cut down as they reached the doorway, attempting to escape the grenades and flames.

The two jeeps had stopped in front of the building, where Colonel Sklar, Zvi, and several other commandos stood talking. Nearby, an Israeli medic was bandaging the leg of a commando and three other injured commandos were being helped into the first jeep. Two jacket-covered bodies had been placed into the other jeep.

Zvi saw Nick and walked over to him. Even in the winter cold of the desert, Zvi's face glistened with sweat. "The launchers should be almost mined by now." He looked at his watch. "Five more minutes, and we're out of here." He pointed at the jeep with the dead commandos. "I didn't think we'd take such heavy casualties," he said. "Three dead, five wounded."

"I think the Iraqis had it a little worse."

"Yes," said Zvi, "that's a shame, isn't it?"

They were almost out of the village when it happened. The jeeps had gone on ahead to the airplane. Sklar led the first element through the gate and into the desert. Zvi and Nick were in the second element, some two dozen commandos. As they passed the minaret, Zvi stopped.

"I heard something rustling around in there," he whispered to Nick, and called in Hebrew to the men a few feet away. Uzi leveled, Zvi stepped into the minaret doorway. Nick started in after him. A commando brushed Nick aside, pushed past Zvi, and entered the minaret. He swept his flashlight around the ground floor. A blurred object vaulted past the commando's legs and scurried out into the darkness. A cat.

The commando laughed harshly. "I guess we did

leave a survivor," he said in Hebrew, and moved to rejoin his men.

As they quick-marched toward the gate, someone at
the head of the column trained a flashlight on the
ground. Nick followed the beam of light, which suddenly
revealed three Iraqi soldiers lying dead in the street.
Another sat propped rigidly in a doorway, his mouth
open, his arms spread in an almost supplicating manner.
A rifle lay a few inches from his right hand.

They were already past the dead soldiers when Nick
heard the metal-on-metal click of a rifle bolt. He swung
the Uzi around and fired in the direction of the sound.
It was too late. The Iraqi—the one propped in the doorway—had fired simultaneously. The bullet hit Zvi in the
small of his back. The impact spun him around so that
for an instant, still on his feet, he faced Nick. He opened
his mouth as though to cry out but did not utter a
sound. His eyes were bright with surprise, and then, like
a door closing, the brightness faded. He fell forward
into Nick's arms. Nick held him a moment and then
lowered him gently to the ground.

As a commando knelt to examine Zvi, Nick turned to
the Iraqi. Two Israelis hovered over him, flashlights on
his face. He was young, eighteen or nineteen. The entire
front of his *galabiyya* was splotched red, the fabric
ripped away by bullets that had torn open his stomach.
The exposed intestines, spilling from the cavity, glistened a dull pink in the light of the flashlights.

Nick leveled the Uzi at him and fired. A burst of five
rounds. One of the commandos pushed the gun barrel
away. "He's dead," the commando said quietly in Hebrew. "You killed him the first time."

"I know," Nick said in English. He had understood
every word.

The twelve concrete launching bays exploded, one after another, in a series of blinding white flashes and
thunderous detonations that rocked the desert floor
with a shock wave that was felt ten miles away. The
minaret towers and flat-roofed buildings of the village

were outlined against the horizon in a sheet of orange flame. The whole village was consumed in flames that colored the sky with a reddish glow.

Nick watched it from the C-130's flight deck window. The airplane, flying west, hugging the desert, had taken off only moments before. They had been on the ground a total of one hour and twelve minutes, ample time for the Iraqis to scramble fighters. But none were evident, which indicated how quickly and thoroughly Colonel Sklar's men had silenced Shab al-Bir's communications. In a few minutes the C-130 would rendezvous with the waiting F-15s, who would then escort the transport back across Jordan and home.

Nick went down to the cabin. The commandos were all very quiet, almost subdued. Near the ramp at the rear, a white prayer shawl draped over his head and shoulders, a bearded young commando chanted the Kaddish, the Hebrew prayer for the dead. The four blanket-covered bodies lay side by side in a neat row.

The soldier's deep singsong voice blended in with the soft drone of the engines. Listening, watching the soldier's head bob back and forth with the prayer, Nick suddenly thought of the two Iraqis he had killed: the MiG pilot and, now, the young soldier at Shab al-Bir. They had come to mind because it suddenly occurred to him that not once, with either death, had he felt the slightest remorse.

Nor, he told himself, should I feel remorse. We are engaged in a war. In truth, then, it is all justified. In truth, he thought. Whatever that meant, and whatever truth was. He wiped his fingers against the sides of his trousers to scrape away the dirt that had crusted on his hands. After a moment he realized it was Zvi's dried blood.

3

Adnan left his office at the Defense Ministry earlier than usual. Major General Hassan Marwaan had phoned to ask if Adnan might find time to see him that day. Hassan apologized for any inconvenience. With only three days remaining before the UN ultimatum expired, he realized how busy Adnan must be. But Hassan wanted to discuss a matter of utmost importance. And, because of its sensitivity, in private. Adnan suggested his apartment.

Hassan said to expect him between three and four. It was nearly four now. Adnan decided to wait only another thirty minutes. He had promised to meet Hana at the club at five. He had not seen her for several days. The rush of events had taken up all his time.

He stepped out onto the terrace, which provided the flat's most attractive feature: the view. The river flowing south like an undulating blue and green snake. The fishing boats plowing back and forth under the bridges. The bizarre contrast of the new glass and granite high-rise buildings and broad avenues of the central city with the mosques and minarets and cobblestone streets of the old city.

Adnan's apartment building was a sixty-year-old villa completely refurbished into six modern flats, two to each floor. Adnan lived on the top floor. The building was in the Zahra section, on the Rusafeh side, an area that had undergone extensive redevelopment. Not as fashionable as the new areas in Mansur, but with a charm and grace totally alien to Mansur.

Jamal Badran had urged Adnan to take the apartment and lent him the money to purchase it. Before building his house in Mansur, Jamal had lived in Rusafeh, not far from Adnan's apartment. Jamal had often said that if given the choice, he would move back to Rusafeh.

Poor Jamal. They had honored him with a state funeral attended by Saddam himself. The president personally extended his condolences to Hana and Amir and shook Adnan's hand, and, in a private aside, congratulated Adnan for so deftly dispensing justice. The President said he regretted that he, Saddam Hussein, had been denied the privilege of dealing with the assassins. They would not have enjoyed the kindness of a quick bullet. Those hard cold eyes had looked right through Adnan, as though inviting him to challenge the statement. As though daring him to identify Jamal's murderers as Saddam's own al-Amm agents.

Adnan had not told Hana or Amir the truth, nor did he intend to. They believed Jamal's killers were Palestinians, misguided fanatics convinced that Jamal sought peace at Palestinian expense. In their abject grief, Hana and Amir did not question such flawed logic. But they eventually would. Adnan did not want to even think about how to deal with that.

The only person to whom Adnan revealed the truth was Jamal's lifelong friend, Hassan Marwaan. Hassan deserved to know. More important, Adnan knew he could trust Hassan. He also knew that Jamal's assassination was what Hassan wished to discuss. Hassan had said it concerned their late mutual friend.

The phone rang. Adnan hurried into the living room to answer. It was not Hassan, it was a man from the Ministry of Information. Adnan had spoken to the minister about installing an INMARSAT line—a direct satellite telephone—into the Al-Rashid Hotel for the WCN correspondent, Christine Campbell. The man from the ministry wanted to know why the American woman warranted such special attention.

"I explained all that to the minister," Adnan said. "Why must I repeat it?"

"Because I am the person who will sign the order," said the man, whose name Adnan had already forgotten.

This interminable bureaucracy, Adnan thought, the monster that fed on itself. If you wanted anything done, you had to pretend the person with whom you were dealing was important. At least this one was near the top. The exercise might not have to be repeated.

Adnan said, "Christine Campbell is the voice of WCN. Tomorrow, the United States Senate votes whether or not to authorize military means to force us out of Kuwait. Miss Campbell can provide the American public with the truth about what is really happening here. By cooperating with her, as I made clear to the minister, we not only will have made a friend, we will have found a sympathetic voice."

The conversation continued briefly. The man from the ministry promised to approve the request as soon as he confirmed it with the minister. The moment Adnan put the phone down, he started dialing the Al-Rashid to tell Chris he had arranged the INMARSAT for her. He dialed the first three numbers, then hung up. His own words to the man from the ministry echoed mockingly in his ears.

The truth about what is happening here.

No one knew anymore what was true and what was not, although Adnan did know one small truth: He knew why he was helping Chris obtain the direct telephone connection. Not from any desire for "truth," but desire. Desire, period. The moment he saw her, a week before—the day after her arrival in Baghdad—he had felt that same surge of excitement he remembered from their first meeting weeks ago in Washington.

Desire.

She had visited him at the ministry, reminding him of his promise to arrange the interview with Saddam Hussein. To *try* to arrange it, he corrected her. But yes, he would do what he could. She said she would be most grateful and added that since she was seeking favors, perhaps he could do something about the direct telephone line. He promised to look into that, too.

Desire.

He could not help comparing Chris to Hana. Night and day. Black and white. As different as the worlds they came from. He loved Hana, and would marry her and cherish her. But he did not feel the driving need—as he felt with Chris—to immerse himself in her. He wanted to make love to Chris. He wanted to remove her clothes garment by garment and kiss her lips, her chin, her throat, her breasts, her belly, her thighs. He wanted to possess every part of her, to feel her body clamped to his, to taste her fragrance.

This same thought that made his heart pound and

himself hard, also filled him with guilt. Hana, besieged with grief, needed him now more than ever, his support, his loyalty, his love. He was insulting her with these fantasies of sleeping with another woman. He was insulting himself.

At four, on the minute, Hassan Marwaan arrived. The general, wearing civilian clothes, accepted a glass of fruit juice and a Havana cigar, a posthumous gift from Jamal: When Hana went through her father's things, she found five boxes of *Fior de Rafael Gonzales*. She gave them to Adnan.

"Yes, Jamal was very fond of this leaf," Hassan said, after he had lit and drawn carefully on the cigar. "By the way, I've heard stories of an Israeli raid," he continued, almost as though anxious to change the subject, as though Jamal was too painful a subject. "Do you know anything about it?"

"They attacked one of our missile sites," Adnan said. "They wiped out the whole bloody place, and everyone in it."

"The story I heard had it just the opposite," Hassan said. "We wiped them out."

"The Israelis haven't announced it, and I'm sure they won't," Adnan said. "I'm surprised the Revolutionary Council hasn't issued a communiqué proclaiming Iraq's 'great victory.' And a stern warning to the Allies that this is what they may expect from an attack."

"You sound bitter," Hassan said.

Adnan said nothing for a moment. They were on the terrace, seated in comfortable patio chairs. It was warm for January, quite pleasant. Traffic on the closest bridge, the Aimma, was surprisingly light for the time of day. But then the government's new, "state-of-siege" fuel rationing had just gone into effect.

"I am," Adnan said finally. "I am bitter."

"That's what I want to talk about. Look, Adnan, there are rumors of—" Hassan seemed suddenly unsure whether or not to go on. "Rumors of, well, shall we say, discontent?"

Adnan said nothing. In his mind he saw himself shak-

ing Saddam Hussein's hand and Saddam's mouth uttering the hypocritical words of congratulation.

". . . have you heard these rumors?"

"No," said Adnan, which was true.

"Yes, well, my sources tell me this, ah . . . discontent . . . exists on a fairly high level. Within the Revolutionary Council itself, I hear."

Adnan said nothing.

"Have you learned anything more about Jamal's killers?" Hassan continued. "Do you know for a fact they
were al-Amm?"

"No, not for a fact."

"But you are fairly certain?"

"Yes," he said. "No. No, I am not certain. I'm not
certain of anything. Not anymore."

Hassan settled the cigar in a large cut-glass ashtray on
the floor at his feet. He leaned forward, his face inches
from Adnan's. "Suppose, on the fifteenth, the Americans really do attack—"

"—oh, they will."

"What are our chances?"

"To win?" Adnan said, thinking that Hassan could not
possibly be so naive. "Little, and none."

"Then why is he doing this?"

"Ask him, not me," Adnan said, but then immediately
answered the question. "He believes his own rhetoric. I
think he also believes the Americans are bluffing."

"You're not the only one with that opinion, Adnan."

Adnan said nothing. Get to the point, Hassan, he was
thinking. The point. But Adnan knew what the point
was, and even before he heard Hassan's next words, he
felt his stomach quickening with fear.

". . . been approached by certain individuals," Hassan was saying. "They think the situation might still be
saved."

"The 'situation,'" Adnan said. "It wasn't so long ago,
General, that you were preaching an entirely different
sermon. I vividly recall your comment that even if it
meant war with the United States, Iraq's honor must be
maintained."

"If you're asking me why I changed my mind, the answer is one word: reality," Hassan said. "With a capital R."

"Reality," Adnan repeated. His own voice sounded strange in his ears. He envisioned himself rising to his feet, facing Hassan Marwaan, ordering him out of his home. No, not ordering, asking him politely. Instead, he heard himself saying, "How do 'they' plan to save the situation?"

"Are you interested?" Hassan asked.

The other person inside Adnan, the rational one, seized control of the irrational one. The rational one rose and looked down at Hassan. "General, this conversation never took place."

Hassan sat a moment, his eyes fixed grimly on Adnan. Adnan glanced at his watch. "I'm late for an appointment," he said.

Hassan remained seated another moment, then rose. "Yes, I also am late."

Adnan said, "Please, sir, be careful."

"Thank you for seeing me," Hassan said.

"Thank you for coming," Adnan said.

SIX

It was easy to see why Zvi Sharok had boasted of his mother's beauty. One of the most beautiful women in all Israel, he had said, although at the moment she was understandably not so beautiful. The blue-green eyes rimmed red from weeping, the smooth coppery-skinned face now so deathly pale.

Nick really had no desire to meet her, but she insisted. She wanted to talk to him, to hear from Nick's own lips what happened. So Nick told her, and when he described how Zvi had died in his arms, he watched the tears well in those lovely blue-green eyes and almost wept himself.

Exhausted as he had been, Nick's first act upon returning from Shab al-Bir was to telephone Dani with the news. To Nick's dismay, Shoshanna answered the phone.

May I speak with Mr. Sharok, Nick had said.

Is it important? Shoshanna had asked, and added that Dani was sleeping late this morning.

Yes, ma'am, it is important.

Then may I ask who is calling?

Colonel Harmon.

Zvi's friend?

Yes, ma'am.

She knew. Nick heard her quietly calling Dani, and telling him that he had better take this call. She spoke in English, as though out of respect for Nick. Her voice was remarkably steady and calm. Later she confessed to Nick that all her life, first with Dani, and then with Zvi, she had been preparing herself for that phone call. Every Israeli woman did.

The voice was still steady and calm now. "You were very kind to tell me the truth, Nick. I knew Colonel Sklar was trying to keep it from us. Good old Ben, he wanted to spare us any further pain." She turned to Dani. "Well, so now I know. I feel better, honestly."

They were in Antonioni's, the Jerusalem restaurant where only a few weeks before Nick had first met Dani. They had finished dinner and were on their second cup of coffee. It was the day after Zvi's funeral, Thursday, January 10. Although Nick attended the funeral, at the military cemetery in Haifa, he had not been introduced to Shoshanna.

". . . and I don't have to be reminded that I am not the only mother who lost her son," Shoshanna continued. She clasped Dani's hand and smiled wanly at Nick. "I'm not attempting to play the role of the classic Israeli woman, so brave and undaunted even in the face of the worst tragedy, but I honestly am relieved to know how it happened."

"I can understand that," Nick said. It was an automatic response, and untrue. He did not understand how she could be relieved. Yes, he would want to know how his son was killed, but he doubted any feeling of relief. Unless of course the relief came from knowing the boy did not suffer.

The boy, Nick thought. In his case, the girl. His daughter. He had felt no relief learning the details of her death. Anger, hate, bitterness, not relief.

". . . I'm sure you know that Zvi thought the world of you," Shoshanna Sharok was saying. "He spoke of you constantly, of how helpful you were to him in America. He said you were a fine pilot."

A fine pilot. The understated but ultimate compliment. The height of peer acknowledgment. "He was a better one," Nick said, and thought, For all the goddamn good it did him, dead and buried now. On the other hand, Zvi had helped plan and execute an operation that might save thousands of lives. No Israeli would ever be killed or injured from missiles fired from Shab al-Bir. Sure, Nick thought, they'll write that on his tombstone.

The philosopher philosophizing, he thought, watching Dani fold a wad of shekel notes into the waiter's hand. ". . . hope you'll come and see us again, Nick," Shoshanna was saying.

"Of course he will," Dani said.

"Absolutely," Nick said. He rose to help Shoshanna push her chair away from the table. She got up and faced him.

"Well, good luck," Shoshanna said. She shook Nick's hand, then impulsively leaned up and kissed his cheek. The tears brimmed her eyes again. She turned abruptly and walked from the restaurant.

"She'll be all right," Dani said to Nick.

"Will *you* be?" Nick asked.

Dani said nothing a moment. Then he smiled sadly. "Probably not," he said.

They walked to Nick's embassy Chevy. Nick got into the car and closed the door. He had already started the engine when Dani leaned in through the open window.

"Nick, this is a small country and there aren't many secrets." Dani paused, obviously pondering the best way to say it. Then, "Zvi told me that this man you work with, the one with the Polish name—"

"—Kowalski?"

"Kowalski, yes. Zvi said that the government considers this person to be unfriendly to Israel. I have my own sources, Nick, and I've been told that he—Kowalski— has recommended to Washington that they obtain a firm agreement from us, a commitment, that any preemptive action will not be undertaken without tacit American approval. Permission, I think, is a better word."

Nick wanted to laugh. "Dani, can you see the Israeli Air Force—or Army, or Navy—asking anybody's permission for anything?"

"That's not the point. What I am trying to tell you, Nick, is that your friend Kowalski—"

"—he's no friend of mine, Dani."

"He's making a nuisance of himself. There are people here who won't tolerate it."

Nick switched off the ignition. "What does that mean?"

The corners of Dani's red mustache seemed to bristle. "What the hell do you think it means?"

"Okay, I'll tell him," Nick said, after a moment.

"Better than that, Nick," said Dani. "Don't walk down the street with him." Dani tapped Nick affectionately on the cheek, turned, and left.

Nick sat another moment, thinking, then started the engine again and drove off. Fifteen miles from Tel Aviv, a motorcycle cop flagged him down and gave him two tickets. One for speeding—the policeman had clocked him at eighty-five—and one for not wearing a seat belt. Nick had been so preoccupied thinking about Kowalski and about what he would say to Kowalski, he hadn't realized he was traveling so fast, let alone with no seat belt. Nick felt so rattled he did not even try to claim diplomatic immunity. Thank you, Frank Kowalski. For nothing.

He called the Dan Hotel on the car phone. Kowalski was in the cocktail lounge. Nick told him to stay there until he arrived. He did not exceed the sixty-five miles per hour limit the rest of the way and, seat belt tightly fastened, reached the hotel shortly after ten.

Kowalski sat at the very end of the crowded bar, nursing a beer and watching the dancers slither around the matchbook-sized dance floor. He was with Nadia, who seemed to be his regular girlfriend. Nadia was a Soviet émigré, a big woman, half a head taller than Kowalski. He liked them big, Kowalski had told Nick, which was really all he had ever said about Nadia.

Kowalski got off the bar stool and walked over to Nick. This was the first time they had seen each other since Nick returned from Shab al-Bir. But Nick had already heard that as he predicted, Kowalski was furious with him, not for participating in the raid, but for not alerting Kowalski beforehand.

Nick said, "Let's go outside where we can talk."

"Outside?" Kowalski's face tightened in an indignant scowl. "It's freezing out there."

"In the lobby, then," Nick said. He had been about to suggest his room, or Kowalski's, but after Dani Sharok's warning, it would not surprise Nick, now, if the rooms were bugged. Nothing, he thought, would surprise him anymore.

Ignoring Nadia completely, Kowalski followed Nick out of the bar and into the lobby. They sat at a little tea table in a shopping arcade in the center of the lobby. All the shops were closed—it was Friday night, Shabbat—and only a few people strolled about.

Nick wasted no words. He told Kowalski what he had heard: that Kowalski might be in jeopardy. Kowalski laughed. "That's typical," he said. "They break the rules and then get pissed off when you slap their wrists."

"Break what rules?" Nick asked. "Whose rules?"

"Now look, Colonel, I'm sorry about Sharok, I honest to God am, and about the others who were killed, but these people were told not to embark upon any offensive action without United States approval. We disapproved of this operation. But they went ahead and did it, and in the process may have inflicted Christ knows how much damage to the coalition!"

Nick had no reply for that; he could only shake his head in bewilderment. He tapped his breast pocket, feeling for cigarettes, knowing he had none, wishing he had not quit smoking. He needed a cigarette. He needed something, a drink.

". . . and that brings up the little matter of *your* involvement in the operation," Kowalski was saying. "Of all the fucking dumb stunts I ever heard of! Didn't you ever stop to think of the ramifications? Suppose you were captured, for Christ's sake?"

Nick wanted to laugh in his face. "Where the hell are your brains, Kowalski? I'm telling you that they're out for your ass, and you're lecturing me on ramifications."

"Don't worry about my ass, Colonel. Just do your job."

"My job?" Nick said. "My job as a spy, you mean?"

Now Nick did laugh. "My job, Kowalski, is a joke. As a matter of fact, it always was." And, with considerable pleasure, Nick went on to inform Kowalski that the Israelis had always been aware of the precise nature of Nick's assignment.

Kowalski's face never changed expression. Nick might have been reciting F-16 performance figures. When Nick finished, Kowalski said, "And you, Harmon, you went right along with them. You let them use us like that? Whose side are you on, anyway?"

Not on yours, that's for sure, Nick thought, and said, "Using *you*, Kowalski, not me. I knew from the beginning, and I told you, that it wouldn't work. The Israelis were playing this game before you were born. And they're playing you, you asshole, like a piano!"

"You don't have a clue about what's going on here," Kowalski said. " 'Playing' is the correct description, by the way, so you understand that much at least." Kowalski's voice hardened. "The Israelis are playing us—that means the U.S., you and me and the half million poor slobs freezing their balls off in the desert—they're playing us for suckers. They've been doing it for forty years, and they'll do it for forty more unless we find the guts to stop them—"

Nick silenced him with a disgusted wave of his hand. "It's not the Israelis who are charging us a buck and a half a gallon for gasoline, and it wasn't the Israelis who asked us to come charging out here to save their skins. Or is that the thing I don't understand about what's going on here? I mean, is it something else? Something on some grand scale that I'm not privy to?"

"I'm beginning to think that what you're not privy to, Colonel, is what the policy of the United States is all about."

"*Your* policy, you mean," Nick said. "Your personal policy. Frank Kowalski's policy."

"If you had told me about the raid," Kowalski said quietly, "I could have stopped it. Believe me, I could have had George Bush himself call up and order them to cancel it. I could have saved some lives. Your friend,

Major Sharok, would still be alive. But no, you wanted
to show everybody what a big brave hero you are. You
figured it would all be some kind of lark. You're the
asshole, Harmon, not me."

Nick rose abruptly. The thought of continuing the
conversation sickened him. But what really disturbed
him was the ring of unwitting truth in Kowalski's words.
Nick, not the Israelis, was the user. He had used the
Israelis, with the raid as an excuse, for his own self-
serving reasons.

Kowalski read Nick's mind. "You don't like to hear
that, do you?"

"Is that it, Kowalski?" Nick asked. "Or do you have
something else to say?"

"Hey, you're the one with something to say. You
wanted to talk to me, remember?"

"Yeah, I remember," Nick said. He turned and
started away. He was beyond the shuttered gift shop
when he heard footsteps on the marble floor behind
him.

". . . forgot to tell you," Kowalski said as he caught
up with Nick. Nick stopped and looked down at him; he
knew it made Kowalski uncomfortable. Kowalski went
on, "I requested that you be relieved of duty as air attaché. I wouldn't be surprised if your transfer orders
haven't already come in."

"Why the act of mercy?"

"No act of mercy, Colonel. You're of no further use
to me here."

Use, Nick thought, that word again. Everybody was
using everybody. He said, "Transferring me where?"

Kowalski shrugged. "Cleveland, Ohio, for all I care.
Phone your friend, Gene Gordon. Maybe he'll get you
sent back to your squadron. By the way, it might interest
you to know that your Israeli friends are planning another operation. A bigger and better one."

Kowalski paused. A little more game-playing, Nick
knew. Kowalski was either waiting for Nick to ask
"what," or attempting to learn if Nick was already aware

of the operation and had once again deliberately withheld the information. Nick said nothing.

"They'll be hitting that big Iraqi air defense radar installation at Rutba," Kowalski said. "They'll go in over Jordan again, so it'll look like a repeat of the Shab al-Bir operation—"

"—come on, Kowalski, somebody's yanking your chain. The Israelis know they'd never get away with that again."

"I said it'll *look* like another Shab al-Bir," Kowalski said. He smiled in spite of himself. "Talk about *chutzpah*. This time they'll actually land inside Jordan. They'll roll across the border in jeeps—who'd ever be expecting *that*?—do the job and get the hell out. Back to Jordan, into the C-130s, and home."

The very audacity of the idea dazzled Nick. But that, he thought, was why it just might work. No, why it *would* work. He wished Zvi Sharok were around to see it. Now Nick could not control his curiosity. "Do you mind telling me how you discovered all this?"

"Their air attaché in Washington presented the plan to Gordon this morning. They had to tell us about this one. I guess they don't want to risk their people accidentally running into some of our SOF units. As a matter of fact, there's a small team operating in the Rutba area right now. Yeah, Harmon, your Israeli friends are doing their damnedest to make sure there's a war."

"All right, so what is it you want me to do?"

"They haven't given us any dates. It's vital we know."

"The Israelis will let you know in time, don't worry."

"I want the information now, Colonel," Kowalski said. "Now."

"And you expect me to get it for you?"

"In one word, yes."

"You just finished telling me that I was of no further use to you."

"You're disloyal, Harmon, that's why you're no longer useful. But I know how badly you want to get out of here, and I know that *you* know that I can withdraw the request for your transfer as fast as I asked for it. So please address yourself to this final assignment."

Nick said, "First, there's no possible way I can get that information. Secondly, even if I could"—he nodded, pleased with himself—"I wouldn't."

Nick did not wait for Kowalski's response. He walked away. He knew Kowalski had no intention of canceling Nick's transfer. To Kowalski, and to whatever his agenda in Israel was, Nick was a hindrance.

Nick wasted no time. Within an hour he had followed Kowalski's wisecracked suggestion to phone Gene Gordon. Gordon, in Washington, made a few telephone calls of his own and at eleven the following morning, Tel Aviv time, Nick received orders returning him to duty with the 358th TFW at Al Kalir, Saudi Arabia.

He was cleaning out the pitifully few items in his desk when he was summoned into the code room for a Washington call on the secure line. It was Gordon again. The general wanted to speak with Kowalski, who was not available, so he asked Nick to relay a message.

". . . tell him that we've studied his recommendation carefully and decided that since Shab al-Bir went so well, we'd be foolish to argue with success. He's to back off."

Nick said, "Yes, sir, I'll tell him."

"Take care of yourself, Nick," Gordon said, and hung up.

Nick stood a moment holding the dead phone to his ear. Washington had studied Kowalski's recommendation, obviously a negative assessment of the new Israeli operation, and Kowalski was to back off.

Meaning that Kowalski was to make no attempt to discourage the Israelis or otherwise obstruct the action. Clearly, no one in Washington—at least no one of importance—felt concern over possible Arab reaction. So much for Frank Kowalski's foreign policy.

Nick had no sooner stepped out of the code room than he nearly collided with Kowalski. "You'd better make that call to George Bush," Nick said, and relayed Gordon's message.

Kowalski listened impassively. When Nick finished, Kowalski did not immediately reply. He gazed at a miniskirted redhead emerging from an office at the far end of the corridor. The redhead, the press attaché's secretary, carried a bundle of magazines and newspapers into another office. For a moment, Nick almost expected Kowalski to comment on the return of miniskirts.

Kowalski said, " 'Don't argue with success,' is that what Gordon said?"

"That's what he said."

"He doesn't know what the hell he's doing. None of them do. The whole thing will start unraveling."

"Probably." Nick hadn't the slightest notion of what Kowalski was talking about. Nor did he care. What struck him most about the conversation, he later recalled, was Kowalski's ash-white face. It reminded him of an underexposed photograph.

When Nick checked out of the hotel the next morning, he left a note for Kowalski: "From now on, look both ways when you cross the street." He had dated the note January 15. With the fifteenth uppermost in Nick's mind—the day the UN ultimatum would expire—he had absentmindedly written that date. The correct date was January 12. The ultimatum had three more days to run.

2

It was impossible to reason with Amir. For more than an hour now he had stalked about the house in a blind rage, smashing his fist into walls, shouting at Hana and Adnan, smoking cigarette after cigarette. He was wearing civilian clothes, jeans and a white knit sports shirt. The pocket of the shirt bore a charred hole from a live cigarette ash.

Hana was tired of babying Amir. She was bored with his mindless temper. And it was getting late, she was due at the hospital in less than a half hour for the nightly triage course. All third- and fourth-year medical students were receiving accelerated training in emergency procedures.

"Damn you, Amir, listen to what Adnan says!" she said.

"I don't give a damn what Adnan says!" Amir said.

"Thank you for the vote of confidence," Adnan said mildly.

"The Americans killed my father," Amir said. "They, and the Israelis. And you sit there and tell me not to volunteer for the Special Forces, where I can at least avenge him! What the hell kind of man are you, anyway?"

They were in the living room of the Badrans' Mansur home, a two-story stucco house that Jamal had built in 1969, when this section of Mansur was still a fairly undeveloped tract. Now it consisted of blocks of expensive homes, all elegantly landscaped, some with swimming pools. Every street was divided by a grass median and lined with lovely sycamore trees. The area reeked of wealth and power.

Adnan had just come from a meeting at nearby Al-Mutana, the small airport in the center of the city. Driving back, realizing he would be early for the daily five o'clock staff conference at the Defense Ministry, he had stopped off to see Hana. And walked into the house in the midst of Amir's tantrum.

Five minutes before Adnan's arrival, Amir had informed Hana of his applicaton for transfer to the 8th Special Forces Brigade, an elite commando unit now stationed in Kuwait. The Pathfinders, as they were called. Assigned the most difficult and dangerous tasks, from intelligence to infiltration, the 8th SFB during the Iran-Iraq War suffered horrendous losses. At Khorramshahr, Adnan remembered, an entire Pathfinder battalion had been wiped out.

"Now listen to me, you fool," Adnan said to Amir. "The Special Forces are no more than a goddamn suicide battalion. Not to mention a bunch of glory-seeking, neurotic killers. Bad enough you're in the Guard, but at least you'll be with professionals!"

"Sure, professionals who lock themselves up in bunkers, behind three lines of tanks!" Amir said. "Not for me, thank you."

"Speaking of professionals," Adnan said. "What the hell are you doing in Baghdad, anyway? Why aren't you with your regiment?"

Amir laughed harshly. "My furlough was extended. 'Grieve Leave.' There was a death in the family, remember? I don't have to report until tomorrow."

"I'm sorry," said Adnan. He felt foolish. But then he had been behaving absentmindedly for two days now, ever since the conversation with Hassan Marwaan.

Hana, listening, shook her head in frustration. "I don't know why we're arguing. There'll be no war. The Americans are bluffing."

The Americans are bluffing, Adnan thought. Hassan Marwaan's exact words, quoting Saddam: Saddam thinks the Americans are bluffing. Everyone thinks they're bluffing, Adnan thought. Everyone but me, and them.

"We'll know soon enough," Adnan said.

"They won't do it," Amir said. "They'll keep us sweating for awhile to see if we lose our nerve."

"There's still a chance the Russians can do something," Adnan said.

"The Russians are full of shit," Amir said. "Do you notice how fast they're pulling their advisors out of here?"

"Not all of them," Adnan said. "They've left some navy people."

"Sure," said Amir. "To advise us how to run the submarines we don't have."

"Yes, Amir, you know everything," Hana said acidly. She stepped to an end table and turned on a lamp. The room had darkened with the setting sun. She switched on another lamp and looked at her watch. "Are you giving me a ride to the hospital?" she asked Adnan.

"Of course," he said. He waited until Hana had left the room for her coat, then said to Amir, "Let's talk about this Special Forces business."

"There's nothing to talk about," said Amir. "It's done." He lit a fresh cigarette from the half-smoked butt of the old one and flipped the butt into a nearly empty glass of pomegranate juice. It made a soft hiss, like a dying man's final sigh.

On the drive into town, Hana repeated her belief that the Americans were bluffing. Adnan said, "They're not bluffing. They're quite determined."

"Then you think there will be war?"

"Unless we submit, yes."

"Which you said doesn't appear likely."

"No, not likely," Adnan said.

They were just then driving past Zawra Park. Although it was too dark to see the zoo section in the center of the huge park, Hana wondered what would become of the animals. But then no harm came to them during the war with Iran. Except for some Iranian rockets that had landed near the Army Canal, Baghdad suffered relatively little damage. It would be the same this time.

She said, "One of the surgeons at the Medical Center —he retired years ago but they called him back—got his degree from the Faculté de Médicine in Paris. He says that Baghdad this past month reminds him of Paris in the late summer of 1939. That same sense of impending disaster, he said, and the people with an 'eat, drink, and be merry' mentality."

"That's interesting," Adnan said absently. He swung in behind a red double-decker bus as they approached the busy intersection at Dimesho Square near the Central Bus Station.

Hana said, "Can you do something about this insane notion of Amir's? This commando thing? I mean, block it. You know everyone in the ministry. One of your friends, perhaps."

He glanced at her; she reminded him of a little girl pleading for a favor. "Amir would never forgive me," he said.

"Adnan, I've just lost my father. Amir is all I have now."

Adnan glanced at her again. The taillights of the bus in front of them cast a wavy pattern of red lines across her face. "By the time he's finished training, the war will be over. If there is a war," he added.

"Speak to someone, Adnan."

"I don't know if I can," he said, but knew he could. He knew a major in the 8th Special Forces Brigade, Gamal Othman. Gamal had just received a field assignment as C.O. of his own commando battalion. In 1988, Adnan and Gamal were classmates at the year-long course at Al Bakr University for Higher Military Studies. And Gamal, as it happened, was in town for a few days. Adnan saw him at the ministry only that morning. Gamal had ribbed Adnan about Adnan's staff assignment. Gamal said that he never realized Adnan was so determined to make general; after all, what safer or surer way to get there than a headquarters desk job?

". . . will you, Adnan?" Hana was saying. "Please?"

"I'll try."

"What does that mean?"

"It means I'll try," he said, which was untrue, because he had no intention of interfering with Amir's decision. He had no right to.

"Thank you," she said. She leaned up and kissed his cheek. "And for that, I'll let you take me to dinner. Nine? Will you pick me up at nine? Or should I meet you somewhere?"

"I can't, Hana, I have an appointment," Adnan said, which was not untrue, although it was an appointment that made him feel even more guilty for lying to her about trying to help Amir. "But perhaps you'd like to join us?"

" 'Us'?"

"I'm meeting a . . . an American journalist." He had almost said, "a man," and wondered why in the hell he felt compelled to lie about *that.* "This woman who's on WCN," he continued. "Christine Campbell. You've seen her, I'm sure."

"Yes, I think so," Hana said. "Rather pretty, isn't she?"

"Nothing special," Adnan said. "She seems to understand the Iraqi point of view more than the other journalists. I think she can be quite helpful . . . from a propaganda standpoint."

"Propaganda? Since when are you a propagandist?"

"Since I met this woman in Washington."

"Oh, you've known her before?"

Adnan had just steered into the hospital driveway. He pulled up at the ambulance entrance. "I met her only once, at a luncheon," he said. He cupped Hana's chin playfully. "And you, you're jealous."

He expected an indignant denial. Instead, she said, "Yes, I am jealous." She smiled and kissed him. "Very jealous."

"Then you'd better come along and chaperon me."

"No thank you." She kissed him again, opened the car door, and slid out. "Have a good time," she said, and closed the door. She hurried into the building. Adnan sat a moment, thinking, then drove off.

He was surprised to find the ministry as quiet as though today were a holiday, until he remembered that this was indeed the case. A half holiday, decreed by the President to symbolize the army's self-confidence. To that end, the staff meeting had been canceled. Madness, Adnan thought, total madness. In Washington, as the 15th drew near, the Pentagon undoubtedly was bustling with activity, and Schwarzkopf's headquarters in Riyadh as well.

But here in Baghdad, just another ordinary day.

Paris, 1939.

Even Baghdad Radio was subdued. Not even a "the Americans will drown in a sea of their own blood" pronouncement. Or any variation of the same theme. For a confused instant, Adnan wondered if something had happened. If those "discontented officers" mentioned by Hassan Marwaan had made their move. No, the building would have been surrounded by tanks. People would have been racing grimly all over the place. The

very thought of it chilled him. They were mad, all of
them.

3

QUESTION: What is the population of Baghdad?
ANSWER: Eight million. Four million people, four million portraits of Saddam Hussein.

The normality of the city angered Chris. The crowded
hotel lounges and the blare of automobile horns and the
bright street lights and attractive store display windows.
It reminded her, ironically, of Kuwait City and its de-
bris-strewn streets, the charred hulks of automobiles,
the burned-out buildings. It was hard to believe that all
these pleasant people in this lively city so full of ancient
charm were the same people who had ravaged Kuwait.

The same people who murdered Entessar al-Azimi.

One of whom—if not literally, then at least symboli-
cally—was Major Adnan Dulaimi, now seated opposite
her at a tiny vinyl-topped circular table in a Nidhal
Street nightclub, The Fontana. It was like being on the
set of some American movie of the 1940s. The dimly
lighted room with tables arranged in a semicircle
around a spotlighted stage and bandstand. The tux-
edoed orchestra playing vintage dance numbers. Even a
vocalist in a black evening gown studded with sequins
that glittered silvery under the spotlight.

Adnan had suggested the nightclub as an example of
the "new Baghdad." He had picked Chris up at the hotel, taken her to dinner at the restaurant atop the Baghdad Tower, then escorted her on foot around the Old
City. They strolled the narrow streets, browsed in the
bazaars, watched the old men smoking their hookah
pipes, and even stopped in a café for a cup of thick
sweet tea.

He took great pride in his city, which he said was once
the richest city in the world, and had endowed civiliza-
tion with great advances in medicine and mathematics.
But centuries of foreign occupation and exploitation
had followed. As recently as forty years ago, the streets

were unpaved and covered with animal dung. But Bagh-dad, and Iraq, had been resurrected. For all Saddam Hussein's faults, said Adnan, the man had transformed Iraq from an archaic agricultural society to a powerful industrialized nation.

Chris was not all that impressed. She had been wit-ness to some of the results of Saddam's "faults." As the evening wore on, she brooded more and more about this. Adnan asked what was troubling her. Something he said? At first she evaded the question, thanking him once again for the satellite telephone line and for the fascinating tour of the city.

It was when they were dancing she decided she could trust him. No, she *had* to trust him. She had to resolve her personal confusion about him. He held the key to her success. She had decided long ago that if the Sad-dam Hussein interview required sleeping with Major Adnan Dulaimi, then for the sake of journalism and her career, she would do it.

Correction: She would *enjoy* doing it.

She stopped abruptly in the middle of the dance num-ber now and returned to the table. "You asked what was bothering me, so I'm going to tell you," she said. "Last week, I was in Kuwait."

He said nothing; he sensed what was coming.

"I saw some terrible things there."

She was baiting him, he thought. But why? Was she testing him, for God's sake? He said, "Don't believe everything you read."

"Major Dulaimi, I said I *saw* it. With my own eyes. I won't tell you how I got in and out of the country, but I was there. And I saw what your soldiers are doing to those poor people."

On the shadowed stage the vocalist stepped to the microphone and began singing in French. The music and words were familiar. Adnan had heard the song time and again on the radio and, he remembered, one exciting night on television in a Montreal hotel room. Now he could not recall the title of the song. Or the name of the Montreal lady.

"Why are you pretending not to know what's happening in Kuwait?" Chris asked.

"I am not pretending anything," he said. "I'm sure there have been incidents—"

"—what I saw was not an incident," she said, and then told him about Entessar. He listened carefully. When she finished, he offered her a cigarette and immediately mumbled an apology for forgetting that she did not smoke. He lit one for himself.

"Look, I don't doubt for an instant there's been a great deal of destruction in Kuwait," he said. "Ours was an invading army. Invading armies are not exactly showered with welcoming flowers. But as for Iraqi soldiers being responsible for the brutal execution of your friend, I can't accept that. For that matter, you don't even know if they were Iraqis."

"Who, then?"

He almost said it might have been al-Amm, the secret police. But he was too ashamed to admit that such an organization existed, or that some of its orders came directly from the presidential palace. And he would certainly never admit having recently been witness to an operation carried out by this organization.

He said, "It could have been any one of a dozen different renegade factions. They're all fighting with each other, all those so-called Resistance groups."

"They were Iraqis."

"Chris, I'm telling you that our people are too well disciplined for that." He had been unable to keep the exasperation from his voice. "I didn't mean to shout. I'm sorry."

Chris acknowledged the apology with a cold nod. He fought an impulse to say something as banal as "You're beautiful when you're angry." But she was beautiful, and her anger excited him. She excited him, period.

For all that, by the time he drove her back to the Al-Rashid Hotel, his excitement had abated. Since the moment he had thought of the al-Amm—and the one person who could have ordered Jamal Badran's murder or at least approved the plan—he had thought of little else. That, and Hassan Marwaan's circle of discontented officers.

He walked her to the hotel entrance. "I'll say good night here," he said.

She seemed disappointed. "Oh, yes, well thank you for a lovely evening."

"We'll do it again, soon." He smiled. "And without the arguing."

"Absolutely."

They shook hands, and he left. He drove away, still feeling the soft, almost inviting grip of her gloved hand. For one impulsive instant he considered turning around and going back. He would phone her from the lobby with some witty remark. But he could think of no witty remarks. All he could think about was her description of her Kuwaiti friend's murder, and Jamal Badran's murder, which were not unrelated, because both were the work of the same person.

And the only remarks that came into his mind were Hassan Marwaan's: *"There are rumors of . . . of, well, shall we say, discontent?"*

Discontent.

Spelled in any language, c-o-u-p.

Or, more accurately, treason.

He returned to the ministry. He wanted to try to catch up on what seemed to be weeks of paperwork. The building was as quiet as when he had left it, but when he got off the elevator on the fifth floor, the first person he saw was Gamal Othman. Gamal, his friend, the 8th Special Forces Brigade's new battalion commander. The man who could do something about Amir's transfer application. Gamal was just emerging from the lavatory.

Adnan waved his hand around the silent corridor. "What the hell is going on here?" he asked. "Are we expecting an attack, or aren't we?"

Gamal, a short, solidly built man whose high forehead and long chin betrayed his Kurdish ancestry, said, *"You're* asking *me?* You're supposed to be the bright young officer in Plans and Operations." He grinned sourly. "I think the lack of activity in this building is called indifference."

"Arrogance is a better word," Adnan said, and then heard himself saying, "Gamal, I need a favor."

"Anything but money and my wife," Gamal said. He grinned again. "No, I take that back: anything but money."

Footsteps echoed in the corridor. A sergeant, arms laden with file folders, walked toward them. The sergeant nodded respectfully to the officers and hurried past. He went into an office at the far end.

Adnan said to Gamal, "Amir Badran—he's a brand-new second lieutenant—put in for a transfer to your outfit."

Gamal immediately recognized the name. "Sure, I saw the papers this morning."

"Don't process them."

Gamal peered at Adnan, bemused. Then he snapped his fingers. "That's right: You're engaged to his sister!"

"Gamal, I've seen your people in action. I was at Khorramshahr, remember? And I've seen the casualty projections for Kuwait: *five thousand* KIAs! Give the kid a break."

Gamal glanced nervously around the corridor and at the closed office doors. "My God, if anybody ever heard this conversation!"

"You can do it, Gamal."

"He'll be going into a new brigade," Gamal said. "It's still only on paper. We haven't even formed a cadre yet. He'll probably never see action."

"Do it for me, Gamal."

Gamal studied Adnan a tense moment. Then he relaxed. "I'll see what I can do."

Adnan gripped Gamal's elbow affectionately. "I'll remember you in my will."

"Sure," said Gamal, and turned abruptly and walked away. It was as though he did not want to be seen with Adnan. Adnan did not blame him.

SEVEN

The crowd went into a frenzy of cheering, screaming, and applauding as the straw effigy of George Bush burst into flames. The effigy, garbed in a shabby Uncle Sam costume, swung by the neck from a tree limb. The fire quickly consumed the red white and blue striped trousers and ate away at the grease-penciled words sloppily printed on the cardboard placard around the effigy's neck: NO BLOOD FOR OIL!

The demonstrators surged forward but were restrained by a circle of uniformed policemen. Two scraggly-bearded young men wearing faded army camouflage jackets broke through the barricade and started dashing across the park. One carried a burning Israeli flag. A mounted policeman galloped after them. Just as the policeman caught up with the two young men, they hurled the flag to the ground and trampled on it. The policeman seized the collar of one and dragged him back to the barricade. The policeman's horse, whose breath in the freezing air resembled twin gusts of white steam, brushed against a girl holding a printed sign that read VOTE NO FOR WAR! The U.S. Congress, tomorrow, would vote on whether or not to authorize the use of force against Iraq.

"Very nice, Larry," the assistant press secretary said wryly. "I'm sure your cameras won't miss a minute of this delightful exhibition."

Larry Hill and the assistant press secretary were observing the demonstration from a ground-floor office in the White House. "You talk as though WCN is the only outfit here," Larry said. He was standing at the window that faced Lafayette Park. "Every goddamn station in town is doing this one."

"And the networks," said the assistant press secretary, a youthful bespectacled man of thirty-five whose name was Charles Donnelly.

"It's news," Larry said. He turned from the window and walked back to his chair in front of Donnelly's desk.

"That's what you said ten minutes ago," Donnelly said.

Larry sighed. Ten minutes ago they had watched WCN's taped television report of a similar demonstration the previous day from Baghdad. Larry could still hear Chris Campbell's cool voice describing the event.

". . . no, Don, this really appears to me to be spontaneous," Chris had said, responding to a question from the Washington anchor, Don Blakely. Blakely had suggested that the mob chanting anti-America and anti-Zionist slogans might be a carefully staged Iraqi propaganda effort.

Donnelly had summoned Larry to the press office immediately after seeing the WCN program. Everyone, said Donnelly, was disturbed at such "biased" news reporting. Everyone, Larry knew, meant the president himself.

Larry reminded Donnelly that never before had American reporters been allowed to file news reports from an enemy capital. Chris—and all correspondents in Baghdad—worked as objectively as possible under the supervision of their "Minders," the Ministry of Information censors who scrutinized every word and nuance.

"It's news," Donnelly repeated acidly now.

"I'm sorry to tell you, Charlie, but that's precisely what it is," Larry said. "News."

"Sure, just like the other day, that ten-second bite of some man-in-the-street telling your interviewer that he knew of two people who could offer expert advice on how to avoid military service—the vice president of the United States, and the secretary of defense."

The tone of genuine offense in Charlie Donnelly's voice amused Larry. "I'll say one thing for you, Charlie: You're a loyal subject."

" 'Loyal subject' is a term I don't think you should be bandying around, Larry."

"And 'free press' is one you shouldn't bandy with, either, Charlie."

"Yeah, I know. That was the excuse you used for running that special—six minutes of it—showing Saddam Hussein patting the head of the little English kid he was holding as hostage."

"All the networks ran it. So did 'Nightline.' "

"Come on, Larry, the Iraqis didn't give 'all the networks' a direct satellite link, and ABC almost has to use a pay station. The Iraqis aren't being so nice to WCN because you're so objective."

Larry said nothing for a moment. He wondered what Donnelly would say if he knew that the Iraqis had installed WCN's satellite phone directly into Chris's room. Larry *did* know what Donnelly would say: a payoff for WCN's "biased reporting." Some payoff, Larry thought dryly. WCN was doing the paying. A cool $18,000 per month for the wire and satellite relay from Amman to Washington.

A roar of protest from the crowd in the park reverberated through the room. Larry got up and stepped to the window again. A police van had just arrived. Officers were scrambling out to form a second barricade.

"I wouldn't call this a popular war," Larry said, really thinking aloud.

"There's no war yet," Donnelly said. "And there might not be one if Perez de Cuellar can pound some sense into Saddam's head." He was referring to the forthcoming "eleventh-hour" meeting between UN Secretary-General Perez de Cuellar and Saddam Hussein.

"How do you plan on handling the Israeli thing?" Larry asked.

"*Which* Israeli thing? There's a new one every day, for Christ's sake!"

"Tarik Aziz, quoting Saddam directly, said that if there's war, Israel will definitely be attacked."

"The Iraqis are dumb, Larry, but not that dumb."

Larry glanced at the television screen on the console across the room and wanted to laugh. Donnelly had turned the audio off but the neatly bearded face of CNN's Pentagon correspondent, Wolf Blitzer, filled the screen. Donnelly's chicken-shit way of illustrating the administration's annoyance with WCN.

Donnelly continued talking. Larry was not listening. He was thinking about Chris's interview with Saddam Hussein, tentatively scheduled for sometime within the next two weeks. Larry could actually see the horrified expression on Charlie Donnelly's cherubic face when that world exclusive went on the air.

Which brought to mind the man who had arranged it for Chris, the Iraqi army major, whose name Larry could never remember. The man who had also arranged the satellite phone line. Arranged. Arranging, Larry thought, wondering if "arranging" was a euphemism for "fucking." Sure, the bitch was fucking him, she had to be. How else would she have gotten all those favors?

Jealousy, Larry told himself. You are a jealous old man. But he wondered if it was not so much jealousy, as envy. But then he was not sure of the difference. If there was a difference.

". . . so will you do that, Larry?" Donnelly was saying. "Will you ask your people to try to be more objective? Please?"

"More objective," Larry repeated, gazing out at the park another moment. The crowd seemed smaller and less raucous. He returned to the desk but did not sit. He stood behind the chair and looked at Donnelly. "Charlie, you didn't drag me over here just to see George Bush burned in effigy, and not for a lecture about objectivity, either. What's on your mind?"

"We're worried about tomorrow's vote," Donnelly said, after a moment. "We're not worried about the

House, but we think the Senate will be close. We'd like a clear mandate."

"Bush has a seventy-six percent popularity rating. What more of a mandate do you want?"

"A fair shake, Larry, that's what we want."

"What does that mean?"

"It means tone down all this pro-Iraq reporting."

"No, Charlie, that's not what it means. It means wave the flag and bang the drum. What you want are pictures of Iraqis looting Kuwait and torturing women and children. You want a blank check, for Christ's sake! Well, son, you don't need it. You'll get your war, believe me. The only way it won't happen is if Saddam all of a sudden gets smart and backs off. But he won't. We've not only pushed him into a corner, we've pissed all over him. And you know what? He still thinks we're bluffing. No, my people will keep on reporting the news as they see it. If that ain't objective enough for you, then you better start pleading national security."

"It might come to that," Donnelly said.

"It also might come to me doing a little feature number about what this war is really all about," Larry said. "Which is not jobs, as Mr. Baker suggested—I still can't believe he was stupid enough to let that come out of his mouth, not even as a joke. And I don't think it's about oil, either."

Larry paused, waiting for Donnelly to comment. Donnelly would not give him the satisfaction. Larry went on, "What it's about, Charlie, is that we have to smash the Iraqi war machine that *we* built. We, the United States of America, through our greed and misguided policies."

Donnelly's face remained impassive. "I won't even dignify that kind of fantasy," he said. "My only interest is to see that WCN reports the news with objectivity. Objectivity, Larry. It's a simple enough request."

Larry said nothing for a moment. Another flurry of chanting and catcalls drifted in from the park. Larry said, "You'd think those kids would be too cold to keep on protesting like that. Last I looked, the thermometer read twenty-two, and dropping. See you around, Charlie." He flipped Donnelly a mock salute and started leaving.

"Larry, don't say I didn't warn you."

Larry, now at the door, stopped. It would take all of three phone calls, and this little pisspot in the $1,500 Henry Morton cashmere jacket and $250 Barzani loafers would be out of a job. But why waste the energy? This one was no different from a hundred others sitting in a hundred other government offices. Where the hell did they find them? They thought they had power but hardly understood the meaning of the word, let alone how to use it.

He felt tired suddenly, and old. "Yeah, Charlie, you warned me," he said, and left.

Outside, driving away, he noticed that only a few people remained in the park and that most of the police vehicles and the two mounted policemen were gone. Although the burned effigy of George Bush no longer hung from the tree, and the charred remnants of the Israeli flag had been cleaned away, some cardboard placards lay strewn about the snow-covered grass. On one placard a black heel print had obliterated the word NO from the slogan, so that it now read VOTE FOR WAR!

2

Immediately following word of Javier Perez de Cuellar's failure to convince Saddam to withdraw from Kuwait, Chris went on the air with another man-in-the-street interview. She spoke with a housewife, a seventeen-year-old college student, and a taxi driver. All three expressed bitter disappointment at the U.S. Congressional vote authorizing force, and their determination to fight for Iraq's honor. The housewife said she had lost one son in the war with Iran but was fully prepared, and proud, to offer her remaining child. The cause, she said, was just. God would protect the innocent and punish the wicked.

"By 'wicked,' you refer to the Americans?" Chris had asked.

"The Americans, and all others who threaten us," the woman replied. "You will not defeat Iraq!"

The interviews were strictly monitored by Chris's "Minder," a jovial, billiard-ball bald man of forty named Salim al-Sadr, who also functioned as translator. Unlike many Minders, Salim al-Sadr was a professional, supervisor of Baghdad Radio's English programming. He spoke and understood the language well.

Chris tried to explain this to Larry Hill in an early morning telephone conversation. Larry had just finished viewing the unedited tape of Chris's discussion with the Baghdad housewife. "Are you sure the lady wasn't Saddam Hussein's sister?" Larry had remarked, and relayed the gist of his meeting with Charlie Donnelly. Larry had already spoken to Tom Layton, WCN's Baghdad bureau chief, about "objectivity." Tom promised to keep a closer eye, and ear, on the situation.

Tom Layton was a consummate professional, a newsman's newsman. At fifty-one, he was considered the dean of Middle East television journalists, having spent twenty-six years in the area, first with CBS and then NBC. For all that, he had never attained the status he believed he deserved: the recognition accorded a Walter Cronkite or Ted Koppel. He thought it would happen in 1973 when he covered the Yom Kippur War for NBC, and might have happened, had the war not ended so abruptly. The network offered him a position in their New York newsroom as a weekend anchor and backup for John Chancellor.

He turned it down, perfectly aware that it meant his job as well. In truth, he was relieved; now he could write a long-planned book: *Arabs, Jews, and the World*. He moved to Beirut to concentrate full time on the book. He worked hard but was continually distracted: the casinos and night life proved irresistible, as did a young Lebanese girl he eventually married. He had already abandoned the book when, in 1974, Lebanon erupted into full civil war. Larry Hill persuaded Tom to open a WCN bureau in Beirut.

The Laytons remained in Beirut another eighteen

months, then moved to Damascus. There, in 1981, they were divorced. His wife, sixteen years his junior, had fallen in love with a man her own age, a Swiss chemical engineer to whom she was now happily married.

He was thinking about this in the bar of the Al-Rashid Hotel, the Scheherazade Room, as he ordered the first martini of the evening. Ordinarily, it took at least three martinis to evoke those old memories but this time the presence of Chris did it. She reminded him of his former wife. In truth, any resemblance between Tom's ex-wife and Chris lay solely in Tom's mind. More accurately, in his own self-esteem.

They had both screwed him.

Chris had screwed him, albeit unwittingly, simply by being Christine Campbell. Baghdad had been Tom Layton's exclusive beat and, with a shooting war imminent, his ticket to the big breakthrough. Until Chris's arrival. Now he had to share it with her.

She had just entered the busy room, nodded hello to various newspeople, and started to sit at a vacant table. Tom beckoned her to join him.

"Alone?" he asked.

"I'm meeting someone."

"Well, sit down and have a drink with me until he gets here. I want to talk to you, anyway."

Chris sat beside him. "How do you know it's a 'he'?"

"Your eyes," he said. "They have that tiger-stalking-his-prey look. *Her* prey, excuse me."

"What did you want to talk to me about, Tom?"

"Objectivity," he said.

Chris smiled demurely. "Define the word for me, please."

"I'm only relaying a message from the boss."

"Message received," she said. "Next case."

"Well, since we're discussing objectivity—" Tom stopped to wave at a tall, bearded, big-bellied man walking past. Fred Shickfeld, an ITN correspondent, famous for having downed six bottles of beer without once pausing for breath. Tom said to Chris, "I saw Leila coming out of Freddie's room." He laughed quietly. "She sure didn't look like she'd been cleaning the windows."

Leila was the Al-Rashid's eighth- and ninth-floor English-speaking chambermaid, who might be found working at any hour, day or night. On the far side of thirty and at least that many pounds overweight, Leila was no ordinary chambermaid. She was employed by the Mukhabarat, Iraqi security police. This notwithstanding, Leila's housekeeping services were continually requested by an inordinate number of male guests. Those services apparently included what reputedly was the finest blow job in all Baghdad.

Chris said, "Now don't tell me Leila hasn't done *your* room, Tom."

"You really want to know?"

"No, Tom, I really don't."

"Okay, so have a drink anyway."

She ordered a Coke—the all-purpose name for any cola beverage in the Middle East, which almost always was Pepsi—and watched Tom Layton's eyes narrow with surprise. She answered the unasked question.

"No, Tom, I'm not a drunk. I'm not AA. I just don't feel like drinking right now."

"Honey, that's strictly your business."

"Well, thanks," she said. "Now what was it you started to say about objectivity?"

"This Iraqi friend of yours—"

"—that, Tom, *is* strictly my business."

"Wrong, Chris. It's *our* business, WCN's." He waved his hand around the room. "Every goddamn newsperson here is talking about it."

"Just because they've seen us together a few times?" Chris gave him no chance to reply. "Oh, wait a second, that's not what's bugging you, Mr. Layton; you couldn't care less about my sex life—"

"—I wouldn't say that," he said lightly, trying to make a joke of it.

Chris said nothing a moment. My sex life, she was thinking, which had certainly been foremost in her mind only yesterday when Adnan drove her around on a brief "eye-opening tour," as he called it. Seeing some of Baghdad's more affluent suburbs might prove to her that Iraq was not the backward third-world nation of Western propaganda.

Included in the "tour" was his fiancée's home in Mansur, a small estate that could have been in Bel-Air or Grosse Pointe. Adnan said he loved that house. His father had worked there as a gardener, and Adnan had practically been brought up in it. Chris was more interested in the fiancée. No, curious. Curious to see the girl Adnan supposedly loved and planned to marry.

She said to Tom now, "You're just pissed off because my 'Iraqi friend' is helping me get the stories you'd like to have. It's making you look bad with Larry, isn't it?"

"The stories you're getting are the stories the Iraqis want you to get," Tom said calmly. "Pretty soon, if you're not careful, they'll be calling you Baghdad Betty."

"That's quite possible," Chris said and, knowing it was like plunging a rusty knife into his stomach, went on, "Especially after my exclusive interview with Saddam Hussein."

The barman just then served Chris's Pepsi and Tom's second martini. Chris drank half the Pepsi and clicked the glass against Tom's martini glass, and continued, "But then who cares what people call us? We're doing our job, aren't we? That's what Larry Hill pays us for, isn't it?"

"He's not paying us to be a mouthpiece for the Iraqi Ministry of Information," Tom said. "Hey, speak of the devil—" Tom nodded toward the double-doored entrance. An Iraqi officer had just walked into the room, Adnan.

"He may be a devil, but he's *our* devil," Chris said, and thought, No, not *our* devil, mine. *My* devil. She got off the bar stool. "If there's a war, Tom, you know the Iraqis will kick all the journalists out. All of them but me, Tom." She patted his cheek. "I've got connections."

* * *

Adnan had promised to meet Chris at the hotel after attending the daily Plans and Operations staff meeting. He was delayed, as he explained, because of a surprise visitor at the meeting.

Saddam Hussein himself.

Chris resisted an urge to remind Adnan that Saddam had not yet fixed a specific date for the interview. Instead, she said, "What's his reaction to the U.S. vote?"

"On the record? Or off?"

"Start with on."

They were seated in a banquette in a dimly lit corner of the room. Adnan was drinking Scotch over ice, and Chris another "Coke." He drank down half the Scotch and nodded slowly, almost solemnly. "On the record, the reaction is defiance, anger, indignation—the Mother of All Battles is about to begin. Off the record—well, at least the way I read it—he believes the close vote indicates a definite reluctance on the part of the Americans to go forward with this insanity."

"What do *you* believe?"

"What do I believe?" Adnan said, feeling foolish for repeating the question, the same question that was asked of him only an hour before. And he felt the same shame of an hour before, when Saddam had asked him the question. After all, as the president pointed out, Major Dulaimi had lived in America, and keen observer and shrewd analyst that he was, Major Dulaimi should provide excellent insight into American intentions.

"I believe the Americans will attack," Adnan said to Chris now. "And it will come not too long after the ultimatum expires. They might give us a week of grace, perhaps two weeks but no longer. Too much is invested now—materially, psychologically, and politically—for them to simply sit and wait. And they know the sanctions won't work, or if they do work, it will take years before we really feel it here."

"But Saddam doesn't agree with you?" Chris said.

Adnan could not bring himself to tell her the truth, which was that he had never given Saddam any reason not to agree. He had told Saddam what he knew Saddam wanted to hear: The Americans were bluffing.

And may God have mercy on your soul, you cowardly bastard, he told himself now, recalling the meeting and the cold, viselike grip of Saddam's hand when he shook Adnan's, and Adnan looking at Saddam and seeing, instead, Jamal Badran. More accurately, that final instant of Jamal's life. The blinding burst of light from the missile's detonation. The screams of the passengers. And Adnan was shaking the hand of the man who very likely had issued the orders for all that horror.

Very likely, Adnan thought, and for the hundredth time in the past hundred hours pondered Saddam's reason for issuing the orders. If, indeed, it was Saddam. *If?* Now he was giving Saddam the benefit of the doubt. Yes, he thought, because it allowed him, Adnan, to rationalize his own cowardice: that inability, out of fear, to speak candidly to Saddam.

"Saddam pays little attention to my opinions," Adnan said to Chris. "So whether or not he agrees with me makes no difference." This at least was true and made Adnan feel less cowardly. Saddam availed himself of a regiment of trusted advisors and intelligence experts and foreign affairs geniuses. They, too, lacked the courage to convey the truth to him.

"The President is no fool," Adnan went on. "Nor is he so self-deluded that he believes the Americans and their allies can be defeated. But he does believe that the Americans really have no stomach for battle, and that they have great respect for the Iraqi army and air force. Accordingly, to his thinking, no attack."

"May I quote that as coming from a source who requested anonymity?" Chris said.

"You may not quote it at all," Adnan said. "Are you free for dinner?"

Chris appreciated the abrupt, and obvious, change of subject. "Where's your fiancée this evening?"

"She's at school."

"I'd like to meet her sometime."

"You will."

Just then Chris noticed Tom Layton walking toward the men's room. For an instant she feared he might detour over to them. But he only winked at Chris and continued on his way. That son of a bitch, she thought, and said to Adnan, "Would it amuse you to know that people are talking about us?"

"In what way?"

"I think it might be called collaboration," she said. "No, fraternization."

"Are we fraternizing?"

Chris wanted to say, No, but I wouldn't mind. She said, "We're friends. I'm afraid to some of these people that's the same thing."

"Speaking of friends: Do you remember that lunch we had in Washington? Your boss made his special spaghetti. . . . ?"

"*Pasta Laurens*," said Chris. "Yes, of course, it's one of my favorites."

"I have a friend who owns a restaurant in Alwiyah. He's from Genoa. He makes a spaghetti I think you'll find every bit as delicious as your *Pasta Laurens*."

"I'll have to try it, then," she said. "Won't I?"

3

Nick was genuinely surprised to see Ralph Keyes still at Al Kalir, let alone still in the 358th. After the MiG incident, he'd assumed Barney Gallagher would have shipped Keyes off to another wing. But there he was in the briefing tent, one of seventy-nine pilots listening intently to the wing Flying Safety Officer, Major Joe Fallbrook, review safety procedures—more accurately, violations thereof—of the previous week's operations.

Gallagher believed that the close call with the MiG had definitely improved Keyes's overall performance. An unforgettable lesson, said Gallagher: once burned, twice learned. Moreover, Keyes's ability was never in question, only his judgment. Most important, now with the balloon about to go up, the 358th needed every warm body it could find.

Earlier that morning when Gallagher had looked up from a six-inch-high stack of paper and seen Nick in the office doorway, the colonel's usually dour face brightened.

"You sure didn't waste any time getting here."

"I figured you could use some help," Nick said. As they shook hands, Gallagher's expression of pleasure faded. He seemed suddenly uncertain, almost ill at ease.

"I didn't expect you back this soon."

"You don't sound too happy about it."

"Matter of fact, I didn't expect to be here myself. They're giving me a star, I'm told."

"Hey, congratulations!" Nick clicked his heels and offered the colonel a stiff salute in mock-Prussian style. He sat down. "When's it supposed to happen?"

"Momentarily," Gallagher said. "I'm being moved over to CENTAF to run Planning and Training. Hey, what are you talking about, I'm not happy to see you? Of course, I'm happy! You took me by surprise, that's all. Good having you back, kid."

Gallagher had blurted this all out in a continuous, breathless series of sentences. Nick suddenly realized why the C.O. was so uneasy.

"Barney, you're being very careful to avoid telling me who's replacing you."

"That's the thing, Nick," Gallagher said. "I don't know who. They haven't told me; I don't think they've decided yet themselves."

Nick was disappointed. He had expected Gallagher to say he'd recommended Nick. But perhaps Gallagher had done exactly that and preferred to say nothing until CENTAF endorsed the recommendation. All right, Nick wouldn't push the point, not yet anyway.

He said, "When do I go to work?"

Gallagher, clearly relieved at the change of subject, had immediately picked up the phone and dialed Tracy Hart, wing Ops Officer. He told Tracy to put Colonel Harmon into the two-seater F-16B and get him requalified. Now.

During the requalifying flight—which was routine but

to Nick a distinct pleasure—Tracy Hart updated Nick
on Desert Shield. Back in November when Nick went
off on his TDY assignment, the list of targets had
amounted to eighty-three. Today, January 13, the list
consisted of no fewer than three hundred—from the nuclear facility at Mosul to every known missile launch site
in the western part of the country and to the central
railway station in downtown Baghdad.

Strike Packages would consist of four F-4 Wild
Weasels, twelve F-16s, and four F-15s. Navy A-6s and
RAF Tornadoes would join the F-16s in the attack,
along with F-111s for ECM jamming. Iraqi interceptors
would be engaged by the F-15s and, if necessary, the
F-16s. AWACS would monitor the entire operation and
direct any and all aerial encounters.

As Gallagher commented in his closing remarks to
the assembled pilots at the morning briefing, ". . . nobody'll go on unemployment on this gig. We're mount-
ing the biggest air offensive since Vietnam. No, bigger.
Bigger than War Two."

Listening, Nick thought that comparing Desert Shield
to World War II, or even Vietnam, was like comparing
it to Custer's last stand. A single F-16 with full ordnance
load and ECM systems accomplished the work of an
entire squadron of World War II B-17s. Laser-guided
bombs dropped from an airplane as far as twenty miles
away followed a beam straight to the target. The
two-thousand-pound GBU-15s were steered to their
destinations by television cameras in the bomb's nose.
Tomahawk missiles, pinpoint targets programmed into
their guidance systems, would be fired from battleships
anchored in the Persian Gulf and in the Red Sea. The
technological inventory, from radar-evading Stealth
F-117A fighters to tank-killing A-10s, was awesome.

Star Wars.

Along with some old-fashioned but tried and true
performance from the BUFFs, Big Ugly Fat Fuckers,
the ancient B-52s, flying all the way and back, from
bases in the U.S. and in Diego Garcia.

Nick, studying the rapt, eager faces of the pilots, wondered what they were thinking. Were their hearts pounding? Stomachs fluttering? Bladders straining? Yes, of course, despite the facades of nonchalance and cool professional interest. Nick could read each man's mind: How will I behave under fire? Will I conduct myself like the overeducated, exquisitely trained, skilled technician I am? Or will I panic and bring disgrace upon myself and my unit?

Dear God, please don't let me fuck up.

Ralph Keyes insisted on buying Nick a drink. The young lieutenant was anxious to again express his gratitude for Nick's help in the MiG incident. They were at the club, a huge tent with plastic-plank flooring, a few dozen wood picnic tables and plastic chairs, a bar composed of several tables placed end-to-end, a cassette and CD player, and a twenty-three-inch television set.

The tent was noisy with rock music from the tape player, and the chatter and laughter of off-duty pilots. The clamor muffled the occasional scream of jet engines and the constant, hoarse grind of the turbine generators outside the tent that provided power for the lights and air-conditioning/heating units.

"You can buy me a drink, but forget the gratitude," Nick said to Keyes. "If you want to be grateful for anything, be grateful Barney Gallagher is the wing C.O., not some pedantic by-the-book fast-burner." Nick said this, looking across the tent at Gallagher, who was chatting with Colonel Fred Walters, the Chief Flight Surgeon. Gallagher stood in front of the TV, partially obscuring the screen and Christine Campbell's face. The gold-lettered crawl on the bottom of the screen read: BAGHDAD, IRAQ—WCN, LIVE. Chris was talking into a hand-held microphone. The din drowned out her voice.

". . . drink up," Keyes was saying. He popped open a can of Coors and slapped it into Nick's hand.

"Cheers," said Nick, clicking his can against Keyes's and drinking. He would have much preferred gin to beer. But they were fortunate to even have beer, which was smuggled in on the weekly mail flights by some enterprising MAC crewmen. In Dhahran, with its genuine and truly luxurious officers' club, you settled for Perrier or any of a dozen different fruit punches. No alcohol, period. But here at Al Kalir, in the boondocks, there was little danger of offending the Saudis. There were no Saudis here.

". . . can't wait to get a crack at the bad guys," Keyes was saying.

"Another crack at them, you mean," Nick said.

Keyes was unfazed. "Yes, sir, that is exactly what I mean. Another crack at them."

Nick was relieved to see Barney Gallagher coming over to join them. Keyes's ingratiating manner was making him uneasy. Gallagher, Nick, and Keyes bantered politely a few minutes, and then Keyes excused himself and started away.

Nick called after him, "By the way, *Out of Africa* worked like a charm."

Keyes grinned, flipped Nick a crisp salute, and left. Gallagher said to Nick, "*Out of Africa . . . ?*"

"Private joke," Nick said. They remained in the club another half hour. Nick filled Gallagher in on his experiences of the past six weeks: the Shab al-Bir raid, Zvi Sharok's death, Kowalski. Gallagher, in turn, gave Nick a full report on the 358th: accidents, promotions, training, transfers, new and/or modified equipment. The wing was in top form, ready for anything.

But Gallagher's mind was clearly elsewhere. "Nick, let's take a walk," he said.

Leaving the club, they passed the big TV set near the entrance. WCN's "Gulf Watch" was still on. Chris Campbell in Baghdad had just switched back to Don Blakely, the Washington anchor. The screen was split between Blakely and a retired air force general, WCN's military expert for this week. The general was explaining the probable game plan of the USAF if the Allies did attack.

"He's so full of shit," Gallagher whispered to Nick. "I remember him from 'Nam, when he was a light colonel. They had him in Saigon at Divisional HQ. All he ever did was send memos advising all combat units not to be lulled into overconfidence. We're losing three aircraft a day to SAMS and triple-A, and this idiot is telling us not to be overconfident. Hey, but that is one hell of a good-looking woman!"

On the screen, Chris had just come back into the picture. She thanked Blakely and the military expert for the enlightening information and stared sternly into the camera and said, "This is Christine Campbell in Baghdad."

"A bitch on wheels," Nick said. "I met her once. I had a drink with her, in fact."

Gallagher was impressed. "She as good-looking in the flesh?" He opened the door for Nick. Nick gestured the colonel to go first.

"If you like the type, I suppose," said Nick. "I don't."

Outside, a light but steady mist was sweeping in across the desert. They walked along the asphalt pathway to the nearby BOQ, hands plunged into their pockets against the early evening cold. Nick went on to describe his brief encounter with Christine Campbell.

"I flew out to Nellis right after that," Nick continued. "And the damnedest thing, I took a ride into town when I got there. Don't ask me why, but I had this crazy notion to see my ex. It was a class-A disaster."

Even as he spoke, Nick wondered what had impelled him to mention Jean in the first place. Barney Gallagher knew little of Nick's marriage and, rightly, cared less.

". . . have to get back to the office," Gallagher was saying. "I'll see you at breakfast." He took a step toward his personal humvee that was parked outside the building, then stopped. He faced Nick. From long experience, Nick knew something heavy was on Gallagher's mind.

"All right, Barney, spill it."

Gallagher smiled nervously. "There's a problem with a couple of our female airmen. They caught them in the kip—"

"—together?"

"Yeah, a radar tech and an armorer. Nice-looking

girls, too. Maybe all of twenty years old, both of them. Jesus, Nick, these women—what the hell are they doing in our air force? And some of the female pilots, they're not satisfied with flying transports or even tankers—they're screaming for combat duty! Over my dead body that'll happen, at least not in any outfit I'm running! Jesus to Jesus! Nick, maybe you can handle this thing with the radar tech for me. . . ." Gallagher's voice trailed off. He peered, embarrassed, at Nick, then past him to the runway where a C-130 was taking off.

The airplane's landing lights, opaque against the swirling fog, resembled a pair of solid white lines arcing into the air. Gallagher's rambling, almost agitated monologue had told Nick that the sexual preferences of certain female airmen in his command was not what concerned the C.O. It was something else, something far more important.

Nick was right. The white lines of the departing C-130 abruptly vanished as the lights were switched off. Gallagher turned to Nick and said, "Ed Iverson is getting the 358th."

Nick said nothing. The news did not surprise him. It was like hearing the results of a test that you knew you had failed.

"I'm sorry, Nick. The decision was out of my hands."

Nick knew Gallagher wanted him to say that it was okay, that he understood. Nick understood, all right, but it was definitely not okay. And he did not want to make it easy for Gallagher, who could have and should have gone to bat for Nick. Gallagher had long ago made an unspoken promise that Nick would get a chance to run the 358th. Gallagher should have made an issue of it, but had not, and Nick knew why.

"It's called not rocking the boat, Barney. Or don't stick your neck out—especially if it might cost you a star."

Even in the shadows of the BOQ porch light, Nick saw Gallagher's face tighten. "That's not fair, Nick."

"No, maybe not," said Nick. "But it's true."

"Ed will need your help, Nick."

"Oh, now you're telling me not to be a sore loser," Nick said. "Not only should I let them piss on me, I should open my mouth for it. Thanks, Barney. And thanks for standing up for me, too."

"I'll say it again—the decision was out of my hands."

"But you didn't question the decision, did you? You accepted it, you made no protest."

Gallagher said nothing. Nick, grudgingly, admired the man's honesty. Gallagher could have easily claimed that he had in fact stood up for Nick, fought for him.

Nick said, "I'm surprised you're not giving me lecture number three slash A-two: 'Nick, you rubbed too many noses the wrong way. You told too many people to fuck off. You dug your own grave, Nick.' "

"Do I have to say it?"

"When does it happen?"

"When does Iverson take over? Any day now."

"Does he know I'm here?"

"I'm sure he does, yes."

"Yeah," Nick said. "His first official act will probably be to appoint me director of social activities. No," he added dryly, "*deputy* director."

"Want me to get you a transfer?"

Nick could not repress a tight little laugh of irony. "To where, Barney? What outfit would have me, a passed-over light colonel with an OPR stuffed with traffic tickets?"

"Then stay here," Gallagher said. "Where you belong, and where you can work yourself back up."

"Yeah, that's right, Ed Iverson needs my help."

"He does, Nick."

"Ah, yes, Barney. Do it for king and country. Okay, what else?"

For a moment, with no aircraft landing or taking off, it was so quiet that even over the rumble of the generators, the cackle of the chickens was clearly heard. These chickens did not provide eggs or food. Living in coops randomly placed around the airfield perimeter, they functioned like canaries in coal mines. In a chemical attack, as a backup system for the gas-monitoring sensors, the chickens would signal the alarm by dropping dead.

State of the art.

Gallagher reached out to clap Nick on the shoulder but thought better of it. "I'll talk to you in the morning," he said, and wheeled around and strode to the humvee.

Nick watched the ungainly vehicle lumber off in a cloud of desert sand. Ed Iverson, he thought, picturing him in his mind. Edward Morgan Iverson, Jr., West Point '71, whose father, one of the original Tuskegee Airmen, won the Silver Star as a World War II P-51 pilot in Italy. Iverson Jr., in Vietnam, had flown F-4s. Forty-three combat missions, a relatively unimpressive number, but forty-three more than Nick could claim.

Nick had heard more than one woman gushingly comment on Ed Iverson's striking resemblance to the actor Sidney Poitier. A young Poitier, of course, Poitier in his prime. To Nick, Ed Iverson bore more of a resemblance to the late white actor, Walter Huston. In the film where Huston played the devil.

Nick's problems with Ed Iverson dated back to 1985 when Nick, then a major, serving a brief tour at George AFB as a check pilot, busted a young lieutenant. The lieutenant happened to be Iverson's brother-in-law.

At Iverson's personal request, Nick gave the young man a second chance, and then a third. Perhaps, as Iverson claimed, Nick's standards were unreasonably high. Ultimately, Nick refused to revise or even soften the evaluation, and it resulted in the lieutenant's permanent grounding. Iverson never forgave Nick, and although never overtly accusing Nick of racism, the implication was clear. Indeed, there were those who did make that assertion. Over the years Nick and Iverson occasionally ran into each other, always civil enough, but always like boxers probing for a weakness.

And now, irony of ironies, not only had Nick been passed over for promotion to 358th wing C.O., he would be serving under Ed Iverson, who needed Nick's help to run the organization. It was like being asked to command the firing squad at your own execution.

Nick could not sleep. His mind was in turmoil, focused on the disappointing spin of his career and on Ed Iverson. He lay awake for hours, listening to the sounds of jets. All through the night, every four or five minutes, an airplane landed or took off. He began counting them, like sheep, and remembered reaching seventeen.

He fell asleep but woke not long afterward, unsure for a moment where he was. He looked around the tiny room, and through the one small window at the dark gray sky. The weather had been bad all week, with more heavy cloud cover forecast. No bomber's moon, which was good news: Decreased visibility made it difficult for antiaircraft gunners to track you optically.

He felt wide awake. Adrenaline, he thought, the excitement of being back where he belonged. Of course, "belonging" might soon be questionable now that he was working for Ed Iverson. He lay gazing up at the ceiling, listening to the roar of the turbine generators and the rumble of a truck driving past outside. The shrill scream of two jets taking off in afterburner suddenly shook the walls and rattled the window panes. The sound receded rapidly, a hollow echo in the distance, then was gone.

Now, suddenly, he remembered he had dreamed about Jean. He struggled to reconstruct the dream. A dream obviously triggered by his remark to Barney Gallagher about the unhappy visit with Jean. He thought he knew now what had prompted him to mention it to Barney. Guilt, probably, a form of confession. Supposedly good for the soul. Well, he had confessed to Elaine and now to Barney. Good for the soul. He did not believe it, not for a minute.

EIGHT

Achmed Ben Sallah thought that the Hebrew code name for the new Israeli operation was rather imaginative, albeit fanciful. Loosely translated into English as "Presto," the code name was intended to convey the idea of the huge Iraqi radar defense installation at Rutba being here today, gone tomorrow. Vanished from the face of the earth, presto, magic.

Frank Kowalski did not consider Presto fanciful. It was the main topic of discussion—indeed, the only topic —with Achmed Ben Sallah over lunch in the dining room of the Taba Hotel on the Egyptian side of Eilat. The Taba was an ideal meeting place since it enabled Ben Sallah, a Jordanian, to avoid the Israeli checkpoint simply by riding the ferry over from 'Aqaba. Kowalski had driven down from Tel Aviv. The diplomatic license plates on the embassy car allowed him to pass freely through the checkpoint into Egypt.

Achmed Ben Sallah and Frank Kowalski had known each other since 1980, the year Kowalski received his M.B.A. from Harvard. Ben Sallah, twenty years Kowalski's senior, with a doctorate in political science from the University of London, had through the years spent an occasional semester as a Harvard guest lecturer in Middle East geopolitics.

Kowalski, who audited the course, had written Ben Sallah a four-page letter criticizing the lecturer for ignoring the genocidal design of Israeli expansionism. The letter intrigued Ben Sallah. Although not a Palestinian

—he was a fifth-generation Jordanian, one of five sons of an enormously wealthy and landed Hashemite family —Ben Sallah ardently supported a Palestinian homeland. Ironically, if he had not been such a champion of the Palestinian cause, he might not have ever made that first visit to Harvard. It was in 1970, the year King Hussein drove the PLO from Jordan. Out of concern for his own health and longevity, Ben Sallah decided to enjoy a few months of travel.

Now, of course, all was forgiven. Ben Sallah was a respected writer and journalist, the proprietor, publisher, and editor of a weekly English-language newspaper, *The Observer.* Important people both in and out of the Jordanian government regularly sought his advice and counsel.

The previous evening, when Frank Kowalski had phoned to request the meeting, it was obvious to Ben Sallah that he had more in mind than a pleasant afternoon with a former professor. Particularly when Ben Sallah reminded Kowalski that he, Kowalski, would almost surely be under Mossad surveillance.

Kowalski had laughed humorlessly and said, "They might know *where* I am, Doctor, but if you're careful they'll never know *who* I'm with. So please be careful."

Ben Sallah had been very careful. He was certain no one knew of his presence in Taba. And now, only ten minutes after they sat down, he understood why Kowalski felt the need for such secrecy.

Operation Presto.

Kowalski wanted Ben Sallah to deliver the Israeli plans to his contacts in the Iraqi government. Ben Sallah was understandably circumspect. Kowalski's anti-Israeli sentiments notwithstanding, Ben Sallah questioned Kowalski's motive. Before he passed the information on, he wanted to be sure this was not part of some larger, more elaborate scheme. He did not intend to be played for the fool. In a word, he did not trust Kowalski.

Kowalski read the Jordanian's thoughts. "I'm acting on my own, Doctor," he said. "And I'm stepping way out on a limb doing it."

Ben Sallah removed a silk handkerchief from his shirt pocket and dabbed his perspiring forehead. The air-conditioning in the big dining room was only partially working. Here on the Gulf of 'Aqaba, less than two hundred miles from the winter weather of Amman, it was like midsummer. He preferred the colder climate; he believed that the technological and social backwardness of the so-called Third World was a direct product of its intemperate weather.

"I'm also probably risking my own personal safety," Kowalski continued. "That's how strongly I feel about all this."

"Then I must ask you, Frank, why are you taking such a risk?" Ben Sallah said. "What is your reason for doing it?"

"Are you questioning my sincerity?"

"Only your motive."

Kowalski sighed quietly, as though surprised that Ben Sallah required an explanation. "My motive, Doctor, is to prevent a war. A war that Israel is desperate to see started, because Israel is the only nation that can benefit from it. Kuwait is already destroyed. A prolonged war will devastate Iraq, and probably Saudi Arabia. And your country may be dragged into it. So who wins?"

"In your scenario, only Israel."

"Look, Doctor, whether you believe it or not—and I'm sure it's of no difference to you, anyway—I am not anti-Israeli. I'm not even anti-Zionist. I'm interested solely in the welfare of the United States. If we go to war, Americans will bear the brunt of it. When I hear Saddam Hussein talk about ten thousand American dead, my blood runs cold."

"I never knew you to be so eloquent, Frank. All right, I accept your explanation." Ben Sallah rattled the ice in his tall glass of tea and drank some. "But I fail to understand how an Israeli debacle will somehow deter the Americans and their allies from an attack."

"Doctor, the Israelis have already made one incursion into Iraq—" Kowalski paused as Ben Sallah's brushlike gray eyebrows narrowed in mild surprise. "You didn't know?"

"When did this happen?"

Kowalski told him about Shab al-Bir. The gray eyebrows rose now, impressed, which annoyed Kowalski. "They carried out the raid in absolute disregard of our instructions—"

"—your government's instructions, you mean?"

"Yes."

"But you just made a point of telling me that Washington has approved the new Israeli operation. If I understand you correctly, then, this time *you* are disregarding your government's instructions."

"My government is wrong," Kowalski said. "Our policy toward Israel is weak and vacillating. *What* policy?" he added. "We have none. Look, Doctor, if the Israelis take unacceptable casualties at Rutba—which they will if the Iraqis are there waiting for them—it will certainly go a long way toward discouraging any further Israeli adventure. That in itself might damn well prevent the war."

The logic escaped Ben Sallah but convinced him that Kowalski really was acting independently and, equally important, believed that his conduct was correct and justified. However misguided, distorted, or even naive Kowalski might be, it was of no moment to Ben Sallah. He would pass the information on to Baghdad. He left Taba shortly afterward and within three hours was back in Amman. By six the following morning, January 14, the details of Operation Presto were on the desk of the director general of the Baath Party in Baghdad.

The Mossad, contrary to Frank Kowalski's belief, did become aware of his meeting with Achmed Ben Sallah. Neither man realized that Israeli and Egyptian customs officers—attempting to thwart the smuggling of drugs and other contraband—routinely exchanged lists of names of people entering and exiting their respective countries. It would be several days before the information was properly correlated, and several more before any special importance was attached to it.

And, certainly, no one in Israel knew that later that
same morning of January 14, a special courier from the
Defense Ministry in Baghdad delivered a hand-written,
"eyes only" message to Major General Abdullah Talaq,
commander of the 8th Special Forces Brigade in Kuwait. The message ordered General Talaq to fly three
full companies of commandos and their vehicles to a
location near the Jordanian border, twenty miles west of
Rutba. The purpose of the mission was to surprise, surround, and destroy a small motorized Israeli force that
would enter Iraq from Jordan at a yet-unspecified time
and date.

The courier, who followed his instructions to the letter and placed the message directly into General Talaq's
hand, was Second Lieutenant Amir Badran.

2

Talk about pouring salt into the wounds. Bad enough
that while his transfer applicaton to 8th Special Forces
Brigade was being processed, Amir had been consigned
to duty as a General Staff courier. Courier, spelled errand boy. And they were really rubbing his nose in it:
His very first assignment was the delivery of an "eyes
only" dispatch to the commanding officer of that same
8th SFB.

Which was humiliating in and of itself, but not nearly
as much as running into an Academy classmate, Salim
Aflaq, on the marble steps of the veranda of the seaside
villa that General Talaq had requisitioned for his headquarters. Aflaq was wearing camouflage fatigues and
full combat gear, with an AK-47 slung ostentatiously
over his shoulder.

"Hey, Badran," Aflaq yelled. "What the hell are you
doing here? You look like a toy soldier!"

Amir was wearing his dress uniform, complete with
scarlet beret. His fatigues had been filthy with road
dust; he had changed into the Class A's just before
reaching the villa. Now you might think he was about to
march in a garrison parade.

"What the hell do you think I'm doing here?" he replied. Amir did not know Aflaq well but remembered him as a braggart and loudmouth, and was damned if he'd admit to not having been immediately accepted into the 8th. "I'm reporting for duty."

Aflaq glanced at the dispatch case manacled to Amir's wrist. "Since when are transfer orders classified?"

"I was coming down here anyway, so they had me deliver some dispatches," Amir said. He nodded at his driver, Corporal Ralli, seated in the jeep parked in the driveway. Ralli had been listening interestedly to the conversation. "Right, Corporal?"

"Right, sir," said Ralli, who was a regular and knew when to corroborate a superior's lie.

"Well, welcome aboard," Aflaq said uncertainly. "See you at dinner, then."

"Keep a place for me," Amir said.

Since he was to see General Talaq personally, Amir intended to use the opportunity to request the general's assistance in expediting the transfer. He saluted, placed the dispatch case on the general's desk, presented the manacle keys, waited for the general to remove the case, and prepared to make his statement.

Before Amir could speak, the general picked up his telephone and punched a button on the pedestal. "Rashad," he said into the phone, "this officer who brought me the dispatch will escort the Russians." He hung up, and while unlocking the dispatch case, said to Amir, "See my aide for further orders."

"Excuse me, sir, but did you say something about me 'escorting Russians'?"

General Talaq, who was in the process of removing the envelope from the case, stopped long enough to peer coldly at Amir and at the single star on his epaulets. "I said, Lieutenant, that my aide—who is a colonel and sits at the larger of the three desks in the outer office—has instructions for you. Thank you."

Amir stood a numb instant, then saluted, about-faced, and left. In the outer office the aide, a somber, officious man, beckoned Amir to his desk. "Two Russian naval officers require transportation to Shuwaikh," the aide-colonel said brusquely. "They are engineers. You will drive them to the port so that they may inspect the damage there, and then take them wherever they wish. Following that, you are to return here. I will have dispatches for you to carry back to Baghdad. Thank you very much." He picked up a sheaf of papers and began reading.

"Sir . . ." Amir began.

The colonel's eyes flicked angrily up to Amir.

"Respectfully, sir, I thought all the Soviet military advisors had left months ago."

"Admiral Spugarin is here in Kuwait—"

"—I've met the admiral—"

"—to recommend a program for repair of the harbor," the colonel continued. "The two engineers have just arrived from Syria to assist him. Now does that answer all your questions, Lieutenant?" The colonel immediately resumed reading. After a moment he realized Amir had not moved.

"Yes, Lieutenant . . . ?"

"Sir, I'm assuming the harbor is at Shuwaikh?"

"That is correct, Lieutenant. The harbor is at Shuwaikh."

"I don't know where Shuwaikh is. . . ."

"Find it!" said the colonel.

Finding Shuwaikh, only a few miles from the city center, was easy. Dealing with the two Russians was not. Commander Igor Grushenko and Lieutenant Commander Vitaly Rossevitch were two of the most arrogant and overbearing individuals Amir had ever encountered. His first mistake was not thinking fast enough when the Russians, who did not speak a word of Arabic, asked if Amir spoke English. Which he did, as he foolishly informed them, and invited them into the rear seat of the jeep.

Grushenko had immediately barked, "Lieutenant, weren't you ever taught to salute?"

"Forgive me, sir, I wasn't thinking," Amir said, and snapped off a smart salute.

The other Russian, Rossevitch, said, "That's the trouble with you Iraqis. You never think. You couldn't tie your own shoes if we didn't show you how!"

"I'm aware of that, sir," Amir said. He motioned Corporal Ralli to start the jeep. Ralli drove off, deliberately dragging the clutch, jerking the passengers back and forth. Amir turned to the Russians with a lame smile. "Sorry about this, sir, but the corporal is not very mechanically inclined. As you said, we are a backward people."

The next few hours were pure hell. The Russians insisted on examining every foot of the entire quay. They jotted notes and argued with each other, while sipping from a canteen they shared, which Amir suspected contained vodka. It lent an even more surreal feeling to the sight of the appalling destruction.

The time was not all wasted. Amir had brought along his drawing pad and managed to pencil-sketch some scenes of the pier and waterfront. Although not a single ship was docked at the pier, the wrecks of dhows and other small boats were strewn about the harbor and one small freighter lay half submerged a quarter mile out in the bay. Oil oozed blackly across the water from two bombed-out tankers anchored near the mouth of the bay. The roadways were littered with burnt-out tractors, forklifts, trucks, automobiles. Huge construction cranes lay toppled on their sides like wantonly smashed toys.

The line of corrugated iron-roofed warehouses that stretched for a mile along the quay appeared intact except for some jagged holes from shellfire. The interiors were empty, the concrete floors bare, swept clean but for bits and pieces of cardboard and other debris.

Grushenko and Rossevitch, apparently amused that Amir considered the carnage worthy of sketching, exchanged a few jocular remarks in Russian. Amir grasped the meaning: The Iraqis, they were saying, had looted the place. Stolen everything not nailed down, and then everything that was nailed down.

Amir felt a rush of anger, and then shame. He knew the Russians spoke the truth. Today in Baghdad, in any shop in Saadun Street or in the Shurjah market, you could find everything from French paté to Japanese VCRs, all "liberated" from Kuwait. Well, the Kuwaitis had asked for it, hadn't they? What the hell did they expect from years of stealing oil, slant well drilling the Rumaila fields. They were getting what they deserved.

But what disturbed Amir, and what he knew as true— there were too many similar stories and from too many different sources—were the reports of the outrageous behavior of some Iraqi soldiers in the early days of the invasion.

Raping young girls and torturing old men. Of course, more than a few of the guilty soldiers, those animals, had been stood up against a wall and shot. But the world, as always so ready to condemn Iraq and the president, believed that one rotten apple spoiled the whole barrel.

And now these Russian idiots were getting an eyeful and would no doubt go home to spread more lies and exaggerations. Who the hell needed them? Amir put away the sketch pad. Somehow, he endured another hour of the harbor inspection. But when it was over and they were leaving Shuwaikh, he made yet another mistake. He asked the Russians where they would like to go now.

"Someplace for a decent meal," said Grushenko, a thin, almost cadaverous-looking man in his mid-thirties. "Your officers' mess is a sad excuse for a restaurant. No, it is *no* excuse," he added, and laughed, pleased. He considered the remark so clever he repeated it in Russian to Rossevitch, whose English was not as fluent. Rossevitch also laughed.

Amir translated the remark for Ralli and said to the corporal in Arabic, "Let's see if we can find them a restaurant that's open. Maybe they'll get ptomaine."

They had come back into the city, driving along Hilalli Street, where burned-out automobiles lined both sides of the boulevard and every shop was either shuttered or its display windows boarded up. But the street was crowded with civilians—mostly older women and children—and Iraqi soldiers. On Abu Bakr Street a few shops were open, and some sidewalk stalls. Merchants conducted a brisk business, offering their Iraqi customers an entire spectrum of goods, from Japanese wristwatches to American cigarettes.

On the corner of Hilalli and Abu Bakr, next door to the empty shell of the Kuwaiti Airways office, a crowd of soldiers milled about the lobby of a glass-fronted ten-story office building. The lobby had been converted into a theater. Chairs of various sizes and shapes were arranged in a semicircle around a makeshift stage in front of the elevator bank. There were no elevators: The cars had been removed, and the wiring, the cables, even the electronic floor signaling display. All that remained were five gaping holes in the wall.

In the "theater," the audience of soldiers was enthusiastically applauding a chubby dark-haired belly dancer. The appropriate music, provided by a cassette player, blared out into Abu Bakr Street. As Corporal Ralli drove past the building, Rossevitch caught a glimpse of the belly dancer's sequined skirt flashing in the sunlight.

"What's that?" he shouted.

"Entertainment for the boys," Amir explained. He assumed that this was one of the unofficial R and R facilities that had been set up to service the occupation troops. The girls were usually Palestinian or Egyptian residents of Kuwait.

Rossevitch and Grushenko exchanged glances of interest. Rossevitch said, "Let's have a look."

"I don't believe you'll find any food in there, sir," Amir said.

Grushenko leaned over the front seat and gripped Amir's elbow. "Not only don't you Iraqis think, you don't *hear!* Stop the jeep!"

Amir motioned Ralli to stop. The Russians' view of the dancer was obscured by the audience of soldiers. Rossevitch and Grushenko climbed out of the jeep and started toward the building.

"Wait right there," Rossevitch said to Amir.

"Yes, sir," Amir said.

The Russians strode across the street and joined the crowd in the building lobby. The music blared louder. Just as Amir decided to follow the Russians into the building, he noticed a well-dressed woman several doors away. She looked vaguely familiar, a stout but handsome fair-haired woman in her middle years, probably European. She was haggling with an elderly Kuwaiti over a set of handwoven dining table place mats. She turned slightly, providing Amir a clear view of her profile. Now he recognized her. He gazed thoughtfully at her a moment and then at the soldiers enjoying the belly dancer's performance. And he knew what to do.

He said to Ralli, "I'll be right back." He got out of the jeep and walked into the lobby, into the midst of the cheering and applauding soldiers. Rossevitch and Grushenko stood in the front row, clearly intrigued with the belly dancer. Intrigued, more accurately, with her gyrating navel and hips and large firm breasts whose nipples glowed redly through her gossamer-thin costume.

Amir sidled up to Grushenko and whispered into his ear. "She's available, sir, strictly for officers."

Grushenko said, "For money, I suppose?"

"Yes, sir, I'm afraid so," said Amir. "We Iraqis are a very commercial people, you know."

Grushenko relayed Amir's information to Rossevitch. The two studied the dancer more intently now. Even in the chill of the unheated lobby, little beads of sweat glistened on her upper lip. The same sweat began forming on Grushenko's forehead.

Amir said, "You have to arrange it with the madam. She's outside." He started away. The Russians immediately followed him.

On the street the well-dressed European woman was just then walking away in dissatisfaction from the Kuwaiti merchant. Amir pointed to her. "She speaks Russian," he said. "She'll understand you. Just tell her you want to do business with the dancer."

"How much does she charge?" Grushenko asked.

"I really wouldn't know, sir," Amir said. Across the street the European woman had stopped at another sidewalk stall. "You'd better make the arrangements before someone else does."

Rossevitch opened the canteen cap and took a long swallow. He handed the canteen to Grushenko, who also drank. Grushenko capped the canteen and tucked it under his arm. He said to Amir, "For an Iraqi, Lieutenant, you're not a bad sort."

"Thank you very much, sir," Amir said, and continued in Arabic, "You Russians would fuck a camel."

"What are you saying?" Rossevitch asked.

"An ancient Bedouin proverb, sir," said Amir. " 'He who is unafraid to express his passion will forever be blessed with hardness.' "

"Indeed," said Grushenko, pleased. "She speaks Russian, you say?" He indicated the European woman.

"Yes, sir, fluently," Amir said.

Grushenko clapped Amir fondly on the shoulder and he and Rossevitch started across the street. Amir stepped into the doorway of a boarded-up store as the Russians approached the European woman. From here, Amir could see and hear but not be seen. And, again, he understood the gist of their conversation in Russian.

Grushenko grasped the European woman's arm and swung her around to face him. "We want to do business with the dancer," he said.

"What are you talking about?" the woman asked.

"We want to fuck her," Rossevitch said. "What the hell do you think we're talking about?"

The woman stared at him, shocked.

"How much?" Grushenko asked.

The woman could not seem to find her voice. Grushenko turned to Rossevitch and said, "What's the matter with these people?" He did not wait for a reply and did not notice that Rossevitch all at once seemed paralyzed.

"Come on, lady, we don't have all goddamn day!" Grushenko said to her. Then he noticed Rossevitch's expression of utter horror and disbelief. He whirled around to see what Rossevitch was looking at.

It was the Russian admiral, Spugarin, whom Amir had last seen at the Military Academy reception. The woman whispered tersely into the admiral's ear. With each word the woman spoke, the admiral's face turned redder. She was still talking when he marched past her to Grushenko and Rossevitch. Both snapped to rigid attention.

"You, both of you!" Spugarin said. The words crackled like rifle shots. "Are-you-both-insane?"

Amir did not wait to hear their reply. He returned to the jeep and got in beside Ralli. Now, out of Amir's hearing, Grushenko and Rossevitch stood ramrod stiff in front of the admiral, who was obviously giving them hell. The European lady listened, nodding in indignant approval.

Amir said to Ralli, "For a lady her age, the admiral's wife is quite attractive, don't you think, Corporal?"

"A beauty, sir," said Ralli. "A true beauty."

At the time Amir had good reason to think of the amusing little incident with the admiral's wife as an incredible stroke of good luck. It certainly seemed so, for it led directly to Amir receiving his long-sought appointment to the 8th Special Forces Brigade.

It was a case of being in the right place at the right time. With his escort duties abruptly canceled, instead of reporting to General Talaq's HQ late in the afternoon as scheduled, Amir returned hours earlier. Just in time to be ordered to rush a sealed envelope to Major Gamal Othman at the airport.

Except for three IL-76MD transports parked near the terminal, Kuwait International Airport was quiet. There was some helicopter activity and an occasional civilian transport landing or taking off, a 737 and an AB-240, formerly of Kuwaiti Airways but now bearing the green-starred black, white and red Iraqi flag. The airport's runways and taxiways had suffered little or no damage, nor had the hangars, or the multistoried glass-walled terminal.

Not until his jeep drove along the circular driveway to the terminal entrance did Amir realize that the cathedrallike terminal interior contained not a single stick of furniture. Everything, from mosaic tiles in the floor to the pay telephones and the lavatory urinals, had been removed. The vastness of the empty building amplified the hollow echo of the voices of the three hundred commandos gathered in the center of the terminal.

The soldiers, all fully armed and equipped, were to board the IL-76s for a brief flight north. As the unit's sergeant major informed Amir, they were embarking on a top-secret combat operation. Rumor had it that an Israeli invasion was expected. There wasn't a man among them who wasn't eager to give the Israelis a lesson in real soldiering. Amir envied their coolness and professionalism. He envied them, period.

The sergeant major directed Amir to an outside loading ramp at the rear of the terminal, where he would find Major Othman. "Watch out for him, though," the sergeant major warned Amir. "He's in a foul mood. He couldn't move the men into the planes until you brought that dispatch with the radio codes. He's been waiting over an hour for it. And that's not the worst of it."

Thirty seconds later Amir learned what the worst of it was, and that it had multiplied Major Gamal Othman's foul mood by ten. Gamal and some other commandos were at the foot of the ramp near a weapons carrier that had obviously flipped over. The men grimly watched an ambulance drive away.

"What happened?" Amir asked a captain, a slender young man who looked more like a bank clerk than a commando.

"One of our heroes decided he was a Grand Prix driver," said the captain. He indicated the wrecked weapons carrier. "His three passengers got pretty banged up. An officer and two enlisted men. Our very first casualties," he added wryly.

Just then Gamal spotted Amir. "You're the courier?"

"Yes, sir."

"It's about goddamn time!" Gamal snatched the envelope from Amir's hand. "Sign for it," he told the captain and shouted to the others, "All right, let's move!"

The captain signed the receipt as Gamal started into the terminal. Far down the roadway, Amir saw the ambulance containing the injured commandos race past a hangar and out of sight. "Major!" he called, and hurried after Gamal. "Sir, I'm a trained commando. I could replace that officer!"

Amir had no way of knowing that Major Othman was Adnan's friend, the man responsible for delaying his transfer application. For that matter, Amir never suspected any deliberate conspiracy in the delay, let alone that Adnan was behind it. On his part, Gamal did not know Amir; he had never seen him.

Before Gamal could respond, the captain said to Amir, "Too much paperwork involved, Lieutenant. But thanks anyway."

"Fuck the paperwork, we need a replacement!" Gamal said. He jabbed a finger at Amir, "What's your name?"

"Badran, sir. Amir Badran."

Gamal almost asked Amir to repeat the name but knew, to his dismay, he had heard correctly. "Badran? Your sister is Adnan Dulaimi's fiancée?"

"Yes," Amir said. "Do you know Adnan?"

Gamal glanced at the sergeant-major who had just appeared. "Razi, find this officer a combat uniform and some weapons!" Gamal turned to Amir. "Yeah, I know Adnan," he said glumly.

3

The cat was thin and scrawny. Christ only knew what it was doing in the middle of the Iraqi desert. It was hungry, that was for sure, and scratching at the canvas tarpaulin that concealed the trench. Ciafrelli had spotted the cat through the periscope and reached out to pull it inside but the animal darted away. Ciafrelli followed it through the scope and saw the little girl.

From twenty yards, the view was sharp and clear. The little girl, not more than six or seven, had long jet-black hair and large black eyes. Ciafrelli thought she looked remarkably like a child who lived next door to his parents in New Orleans.

She was in the middle of the road, calling to the cat, too far from the trench for Ciafrelli to clearly hear her voice. He nudged Knox and gestured him to the periscope.

Knox looked and said, "Damn!"

The third man, Staff Sergeant Jaime Valdez, also took a turn at the periscope. "Jesus!" he said. He was sitting on the floor of the narrow trench, his back propped against the dirt wall. "She's coming straight at us!"

Knox slid his Beretta service pistol from its holster and drew back the breechblock. In the cramped confines of the trench it sounded like a clanging door.

Valdez whirled around to Knox. "What the fuck you think you need that for?" He flattened his hand on Knox's wrist, pointing the loaded gun downward.

Knox, a sergeant first class and the team leader—and six inches taller and thirty pounds heavier than Valdez—pushed Valdez's hand away. "I hope I *won't* need it," he said quietly. His calm manner and articulate speech annoyed Valdez, who resented Knox's college education even more than he resented being under the command of a black man.

"What's that mean, Doug?" Ciafrelli asked. "You 'hope' you won't need it?"

"It means if she happens to stumble in here, we can't let her go," Knox said.

"You'd kill a kid?" Valdez asked. "A *kid!*"

"Would you prefer that she ran back and told the Iraqi army about the three GIs she just said hello to?" Knox said. "Pull the scope in."

Valdez stared obstinately at Knox a moment, then lowered the periscope into the trench. Outside, the girl was closer. They could hear her shoes scuffling in the sand, and her shrill voice.

"*Quot!*" she called, and then the cat purred. Obviously, the girl had picked him up. "*Quot,*" she said again, pleased.

"*Quot!*" Ciafrelli said. "Cat!" Part of the six-week desert orientation program back at Fort Irwin was a crash course in Arabic. He remembered that much of it, basic words like man, woman, hot, cold—and where is the bathroom?—and cat. "That's the fucking cat's name, 'cat'!"

The three U.S. Army sergeants were members of a Green Beret unit attached to the 3rd Special Forces Group. Their team, code-named "Courtyard," was one of six similar Desert Shield intelligence teams operating in northern and western Iraq since last November.

Courtyard had positioned itself near the two-lane asphalt highway that ran straight through the desert from Baghdad to Amman. They were deep inside Iraq, thirty-two miles east of the Jordanian border and twelve miles west of the town of Rutba. Their mission was to monitor military vehicular traffic to and from Jordan, map the immediate area, and obtain samples of the terrain. A PRC-119 radio kept them in constant communication with the command center in Dhahran via an AWACS aircraft regularly orbiting over Saudi Arabia.

This was Courtyard's second full day at this site. A canvas tarpaulin covered with brambles and tumbleweed concealed the grave-sized hole they lived in. The well-camouflaged trench was ten feet back from the road, obscured by mounds of drifting sand.

Food was strictly MREs, meals-ready-to-eat (sometimes referred to as Meals Rejected by Ethiopians), and the plumbing strictly outdoor. Which meant not going out during the day to piss and controlling your bowels. If you couldn't wait for dark to go outside, then you used the little plastic disposal pouches. But all that, as Staff Sergeant Victor Ciafrelli said, was what they were trained for.

The little girl had been riding in her father's battered

old Renault truck, accompanying him on his weekly delivery of rice and flour to Rutba. Returning home to Jordan, the father had pulled the truck off the road to cool the overheated engine. The little girl's cat scurried away. She went out to look for him.

"Okay, she's got the cat but she's still fucking around out there," Valdez whispered, listening, his ear pressed to the aperture between the canvas tarpaulin and the ground. "Hey, I think she's taking off!"

The three listened. The little girl's footsteps were fading. Valdez lifted the tarpaulin just enough for a glimpse outside. Yes, cat in her arms, the girl was walking away.

Knox raised the periscope and peered through the viewfinder. "That was close," he said. He breathed a sigh of relief and sat back as Valdez moved to the periscope.

"Oh, shit!" Valdez said. "She just turned around and looked back. I think she saw the scope!"

The crunch of footsteps through the sand was suddenly very loud. Pebbles and sand, kicked by the girl's shoes, spilled through the slit in the tarpaulin and into the trench. An instant later a small flap of the canvas was rolled back and the whole trench was bright with sunlight. The girl, cat cradled in her arms, stood at the edge of the trench staring down at the three men. Her eyes were fixed almost hypnotically on the Beretta in Knox's hand, on the muzzle pointed straight at her.

For Douglas Knox, time stopped. A thousand different scenes replayed in his memory, each one in separate, exquisite detail. He saw himself explaining to his parents his decision to drop out of North Carolina State University to enlist in the U.S. Army. The service was the only place you could genuinely feel equal to a white man, if not superior. The only place a black could get a fair shake. Besides—and this he never admitted to his parents—college bored him. He wanted excitement, action, and travel.

He loved the army. It was his home, his family, his life's work. Although he had already been accepted for warrant officer school, he intended to wangle himself into OCS and a full commission. He had enough college credit to qualify. It made him smile whenever he thought of someone like Jimmy Valdez having to salute and address him as sir.

The little girl wore a white print dress and tattered red tennis shoes. Her face was smudged with dirt. *"You'd kill a kid? A* kid!" Valdez's words echoed through Knox's head. He actually saw his own image reflected in her eyes. A twenty-seven-year-old black man with distinctively Negroid features and a white man's articulation, a 9mm Beretta service pistol gripped in his right hand, the barrel trained on the girl's face.

"You'd kill a kid? A kid!"

Yes, he would. He had to. It was her or the three of them. If she told the Iraqis about them, they were dead. Sure as hell, dead. Or, if captured, worse. They would not be POWs. There was no war, they were spies. Spies are shot. He wondered what Valdez and Ciafrelli were thinking and wanted to ask. But their opinions made no difference. The decision was his, and he had already made it.

He felt his finger tightening on the trigger. The muzzle pip was positioned on the little cleft above the girl's nose, directly between the eyes. My God, but she had heavy eyebrows for so young a child. At this point blank range the bullet would probably sever her head from her body. He hoped the blood and brains and slivers of bone did not stain their uniforms. But the cat, he thought crazily, would be unhurt.

Yes, it had to be done. Take no chances. But wait, wait just a second. Suppose she said nothing? It was not impossible. For all they knew, the kid might even be mute. Or retarded. She might go back to wherever she came from and never say a word. And suppose she thought Knox and the others were Iraqis? She must have seen hundreds of soldiers. She wouldn't know an American from a Martian.

To Knox, it seemed hours that he sat there in a half crouch, the gun leveled at the little girl. In truth, exactly five seconds had passed between the time he had pointed the gun at her and the time he all at once realized she was not there, and he was pointing the gun at the empty blue sky.

He was vaguely aware that he had waved the gun barrel at her and cried in English, "Go! Get out of here! Go!"

It seemed another hour before his heart stopped pounding and the roaring in his ears subsided and, as Valdez replaced the tarpaulin, the bright light of the sun shining into the trench became dim and diffused. It was like an impressionist painting suddenly come to life.

Knox said to Valdez, "Call the plane and tell them we have a 'Jigsaw.'" Jigsaw was the code word indicating that the team's location had been compromised.

"You did right, Doug," Ciafrelli said. "I'm glad you didn't hurt the kid. You did right."

"Did right, shit!" Valdez said. "You should have wasted her!"

"*You're* the one who was so horrified about it!" Knox said to him. "Now shut up, you fucking moron, and do what I tell you! Make the call!"

Valdez smiled to himself. It was the first time he had ever heard Knox swear. It made him feel good.

Valdez had no sooner punched the telephone button than the trench began rumbling. For a dreamlike instant Knox thought that Valdez had stupidly closed some electrical circuit that had blown the cadmium batteries. Ciafrelli had the answer.

"Jesus H. Christ!" he shouted, peering through the periscope. "An armored column! Looks like a whole fucking regiment!"

Knox shouldered Ciafrelli aside and took the periscope. It was not a regiment or even a battalion, but it was a heavily armed force of substantial size. Knox counted nineteen vehicles: APCs, Land-Rovers, and East German Robor trucks, all fully loaded with combat troops, all bearing the red triangle emblem of the Republican Guard.

Even as he heard Valdez yelling that the little girl had reported them, Knox knew that was impossible. She had walked away to the west. The Iraqi convoy came from the east.

The column sped past. The road was quiet again. Knox raised the tarpaulin and glanced out. Clouds of brown dust hovered in the air. Knox crawled out of the trench and scanned the area with binoculars. The Iraqis were headed toward Jordan. But why? He dropped back into the trench and closed the tarpaulin.

". . . I gave them the 'Jigsaw,' and then I had to transmit in the clear to tell them about the heavy stuff moving west," Valdez was saying. "They came back with a 'McDonald' and a 'Goldmine.' 'Goldmine,' that means extraction—they'll try to send somebody in to pull us out. Jesus, I sure hope so!" He fumbled with the spiral-bound codebook, searching for the "McDonald" code word.

Knox did not need the book to decipher McDonald. " 'Proceed at team leader's discretion,' " he said, his decision already made. "Okay, destroy the radio and the codebook, but we'll stay put awhile until we can figure out what the hell that troop movement is all about."

"That troop movement has just about caught up with the kid," Ciafrelli said. "I lay ten to one that right now, this very fucking minute, she's telling them all about us."

Ciafrelli would have lost the bet, but only by twelve minutes. After the little girl had returned to the truck, her father immediately resumed driving. The Renault continued to overheat, so he again pulled over to the roadside. The Iraqi column—Major Gamal Othman's 8th Special Forces commandos who had been airlifted in from Kuwait to ambush the anticipated Israeli raid on Rutba—rolled past the disabled truck.

The driver of a supply vehicle in the rear noticed the little girl cuddling the cat. He stopped to assist. He donated a jerrican of water for the truck, some fruit-flavored rock candy for the little girl, and a cup of water from his canteen for the cat. The little girl, pleased with the attention, told the driver how the cat had discovered three of his friends playing hide-and-seek.

The driver knew she was telling the truth. The details of her story were too vivid and concise. He only hoped his three "friends" were not deserters. Orders were clear: deserters to be summarily executed.

He radioed the information to Major Othman. The major ordered Amir Badran to reconnoiter the area. Amir and four commandos drove out in a Land-Rover mounted with a .50 caliber machine gun. The melted, smoking remains of Courtyard's radio lay fifty yards from the trench. The air was heavy with the acrid odor of charred magnesium from the small thermite bomb that Valdez had used to vaporize the radio and codebook.

Knox had spotted the approaching Land-Rover long before it arrived. He knew that whatever his decision, he could not win. There was no place to run, and if he chose to fight, even if they killed all five Iraqis, they would be overwhelmed by the others. But he felt it only fair to consult his men.

"Okay, what do you want to do?" he asked Ciafrelli.

Ciafrelli, always the comedian, said, "I want to be twelve years old, locked up in my bathroom, reading *Penthouse.* You decide, for Christ's sake."

"Jimmy?" Knox did not recall ever previously addressing Valdez by his first name. Guilt, he thought, fully expecting Valdez to blame him for their dilemma. And correctly so: It was his weakness, his cowardice, in not killing the little girl that had brought all this down on them.

But Valdez only shrugged and said, "There ain't much choice, is there?"

As much as he disliked Valdez, Knox could not help admiring his coolness. Maybe he wasn't such a hardcase, after all. "No," Knox said, "there ain't much choice."

Valdez said, "Like Vic says, you decide."

"Whatever I decide is okay?" Knox asked.

"Yeah," said Valdez. "But do it fast, before they shove a couple of grenades up our asses."

No one was more surprised than Amir to see a brown T-shirt poked up out of the trench. The shirt was attached to the barrel of an M-16A2 rifle. A moment later, even more surprising, he saw a black man stand up in the trench. The black man tossed the rifle onto the sand and then his leather-holstered Beretta and ammo belt. Then, arms raised in surrender, he climbed out of the trench. He was a large, husky man whom Amir judged to be in his late twenties or early thirties. He wore desert fatigues, similar to Amir's own but lighter in color. Behind him, their arms also raised in surrender, came two more men, white.

"My name is Douglas T. Knox," the black man said. "I am a sergeant first class in the United States Army. My serial number is 553-14-2689."

NINE

When Barney Gallagher told Nick Harmon that Ed Iverson would be taking over soon, he meant immediately. Colonel Iverson officially assumed command of the 358th Tactical Fighter Wing on the evening of 15 January. An unforgettable date, although no one honestly expected the Allied attack to commence on that exact day. Saddam would be given a short grace period, long enough for him to sweat a little. Or a lot.

Ed Iverson had inherited men and aircraft honed to razor sharpness. He had no intention of tampering with the wing's combat effectiveness. But he did plan to make certain administrative changes, the first of which was to replace his Admin. NCO, Master Sergeant Carlisi, whom he suspected of being a dyke. Not that he cared one way or the other about the lady's sexual preferences—or anyone else's for that matter—he simply did not like her.

For one thing he resented her proprietary attitude. He had not sat in Barney Gallagher's chair ten seconds when Carlisli entered, without knocking. "Sir, I thought you might like to be briefed on our office routine here."

"What's to be briefed about?" he asked.

"It was General Gallagher's suggestion, sir."

" 'General' Gallagher? Has his promotion already come through?"

"As of 0700 tomorrow. If ever a man deserved a star, sir, it's him."

"That's for sure, Sergeant," Iverson said. "All right,

so why does Barney . . . General Gallagher—why does he think I have to be briefed about office routine?"

Carlisi stepped closer. For a moment Iverson thought she intended to sit down for a friendly little chat. A man-to-man chat, he thought wryly. But Carlisi remained standing. "I've established kind of a different system than you might be accustomed to, sir. But you'll catch on fast enough." She nodded gravely. "All my colonels do."

All my colonels do, Iverson thought, and wanted to say *I* am not one of your colonels. But he held his tongue, although he decided then and there to get rid of her. Crackerjack secretary or not, she had to go.

"Tell you what, Sergeant, we'll go over the routine some other time. When we have time. Right now, I'd appreciate it if you'd schedule a meeting at 0900 hours tomorrow with all squadron commanders and group support commanders."

"Yes, sir."

"And I want to see Colonel Harmon ASAP."

"I'll notify him, sir."

"And please bring me the OPRs of all field grade officers."

"Right away, Colonel."

It was not five minutes later that the call came in from George Hamil, CENTAF deputy director of Ops. Hamil said, "Ed, how's it feel to be a Big Gear?"

"I haven't been at it long enough, George."

"You'll find out." Hamil's voice rose an octave as he parodied his own southern drawl. "Purty soon y'awl be sayin', 'I cain't send them kids up in no more of them daith traps!' Ed, put me on the scrambler," he continued in a normal and now serious tone. Iverson punched the button that secured the phone line.

Hamil went on, "Here's the situation: There's a three-man SOF team inside Iraq that SOCCENT believes has been compromised. They've sent in a UH-60 to extract them."

"I'm not in the extraction business, George," Iverson said, but he said it good-naturedly: He thought Hamil's call was a request for the 358th to cap the rescue chopper. The idea pleased him. He might even take on the job personally.

But Iverson's pleasure was short-lived. Hamil said, "You're right, Ed, you aren't in the extraction business. I'm calling to tell you that if the retrieval is successful, and if medical attention is required, we may bring the chopper into Al Kalir. You're the closest facility to the area of operations."

"I'll alert my people," Iverson said. "What's the UH-60's call sign?"

"Broadway Five. It's a 153rd Aviation Regiment bird."

"Broadway Five," Iverson repeated. He put on his reading glasses and jotted the call sign and unit on a legal pad. "And the pilot's name?"

"Mason," said Hamil. "Major Mason."

"Mason," Iverson said. He scribbled the name on the pad. "I'll take care of it."

Iverson instructed Ops to prepare for the possible arrival of the UH-60 and to have the pilot report immediately to him. He had no sooner hung up, when Nick Harmon entered the office.

Nick snapped off a crisp salute. "Lieutenant Colonel Harmon reporting as requested, sir."

"Please, Nick, don't do this to me," Iverson said. "The last thing I need from you is military formality." He rose from the desk and shook Nick's hand. "Sit down."

Nick sat down. "All right, Ed, what is it that you *do* need from me?"

Iverson said, "By the way, I want to congratulate you on the MiG. Must have been a hell of a charge." In the same breath, he continued, "What do I need from you? For openers, cooperation."

"Okay," Nick said, after a moment.

"Look, Nick, I realize you aren't jumping for joy that I'm sitting here—"

"—I said it was okay, Ed. Drop it."

"I want you to stay on as my D.O. I'll try my damnedest to get you an eagle. Christ knows you deserve it."

Christ and everyone else, Nick thought, including Gene Gordon back at the Pentagon, but not the selection review boards. But Iverson sounded sincere; maybe it would all work out. He said, "If that's what you want, sure. I'll stay on."

"Good," said Iverson, and it was then that Nick noticed "Major Mason" jotted on Iverson's notepad. He asked Iverson about it. Iverson related his conversation with George Hamil.

Nick said, "Major Mason's first name is Elaine."

"A woman?"

"Unless there's a male major named Elaine in the 153rd Aviation Regiment," Nick said, and went on to say that he knew Elaine, and had seen her only last month. "And they're sending her on a retrieval mission?" Nick continued. "What the hell is wrong with those people? Are they crazy? Or just plain stupid?" He reached for the phone. "Let me talk to Hamil."

Iverson clamped his hand down on Nick's. "The retrieval order didn't come from Hamil. Besides, this"—he glanced at the notepad—"this Major Mason will stay on this side of the border until she makes contact with the SOF guys. No contact, she does a one-eighty and goes home. Now relax."

Nick withdrew his hand from the telephone. He felt foolish. He had all but told Iverson that it went much further than merely knowing Elaine. The smug little expression on Iverson's face confirmed it.

Iverson peered at Nick over the top of his half-frame reading glasses. "I kind of hope she does come our way," he said. "I'm curious to see what this lady looks like."

Nick hardly heard. He was studying the wall clock and in his mind computing times and distances. If George Hamil's information was correct, Elaine was only minutes away from entering Iraq, which was bad news, although it would happen only if she made contact with the SOF team. Not going in meant no contact with the

SOF team, which was also bad news. Either way, then, it was bad news.

Nick was wrong on several counts. Elaine had already entered Iraq and been there for the past seven and one half minutes. She had decided to go in despite not making contact. What the hell, she came this far, and she knew the SOF team's location. She had requested, and received, permission from AWACS to go in for a closer look.

For more than five minutes now, the only sound in the cockpit had been the smooth steady hum of the turbojet engines and the eggbeater drone of the big main rotor blade. Elaine touched the intercom button on the cyclic control stick and spoke into her headset microphone.

"Tim, try them again."

To her right, in the copilot's seat, fuzzy-cheeked young CW2 Tim Henderson immediately spoke into his microphone. "Zero seven alpha tango, this is Broadway Five, do you copy? Go ahead." Zero seven alpha tango was the SOF team's radio call sign. Henderson repeated the call three times. No response. He tapped a fingernail on the fuel gauge and looked glumly at Elaine. "Major, fuel level is at the turnaround point. We ought to start back."

Yes, we certainly should, Elaine thought, but did not say it. They should have been able to raise the SOF team, Courtyard. They were in the right place. Downtown, the AWACS controlling the sector, had vectored them to the precise coordinates. Courtyard, compromised, would have destroyed its beacons and emergency signal strobes, leaving radio the only means of communication.

Through the UH-60's picture-window windowscreen the black shroud of the desert extended endlessly. They were some twenty miles inside Iraq, flying in CFM—contour flight mode—at two hundred feet, under heavy cloud cover and below Iraqi radar.

Tim Henderson's choirboy voice sounded strained

over the intercom. "What do you say, Major? Don't you think we better start drag-assing out of here?"

"Come on, Tim, how many chances do we get to see Iraq?" Elaine said. "Think how lucky you are."

"Yeah," said the young copilot, "I only wish somebody else was this lucky. Anybody else."

I agree, Elaine thought, thinking of the so-called luck that had brought them here in the first place. A fluke, wrong place at the wrong time, which in this instance was Duwayd, a crossroads outpost in northwestern Saudi Arabia, twelve miles from the Iraqi border. Elaine and her crew had been hauling "Ash and Trash"—mail and supplies—to outlying bases and small encampments. At Duwayd, she was informed that an SOF team operating inside Iraq had been compromised. The closest SOF rescue unit was at least three hours away. The closest asset to the scene was Army 3059, call sign Broadway Five, Elaine's Black Hawk.

The mission was strictly voluntary. Army 3059 had no night vision gear or heavy ordnance but did have sufficient fuel. Elaine never hesitated. Nor did her crew, Tim Henderson and the crew chief, Sergeant Wilbert Feeney of Paris, Maine, who was even younger than Henderson. And so here they were, inside enemy lines. An enemy not yet officially an enemy. What a story for your grandchildren. If you ever had any.

"Zero seven alpha tango, zero seven alpha tango, this is Broadway Five. Go ahead." Tim Henderson's voice echoed in Elaine's earphones. The only response was the hollow crackle of static.

"They've had it, Major," Henderson said to Elaine. "We've got to get out of here."

"Another couple of minutes, Tim," she said. She had just then seen a distant glow of light. The village of Rutba, she was sure, and confirmed it with a glance at the terrain overlay on the CMS-80 display screen.

At that instant a line of yellow tracers arced up out of the darkness. "They're shooting at us!" Feeney said into the intercom. "Mother of Christ!"

The left engine fire warning light flashed on.

"We're hit!" Henderson shouted.

"Number one power control and fuel levers off!" Elaine called out. "Emergency shut-down on number one engine!"

Henderson retracted the power control and fuel levers, pulled the fire extinguisher T-Handle, and cycled the number one fire extinguisher switch. The other engine, absorbing the load of the damaged one, quickly stabilized the big helicopter. But they had lost so much power they were down to fifty feet. The radar altimeter low altitude warning light was flashing. Elaine nosed the Black Hawk into a shallow climb. The helicopter vibrated from tail rotor to cockpit as she gained altitude and decelerated below 130 knots.

"Number two temperature in the red!" Henderson said. "She's bumping up into TGT limitations!"

"I'm watching it," Elaine said. They were at two hundred feet, and she had already wheeled the helicopter around to a heading of 180, southward, out of Iraq.

Behind, the tracers from the machine guns that had hit them still arced yellow through the sky, but harmlessly now. In her earphones she heard Tim Henderson and Wilbert Feeney chattering excitedly. She listened and idly understood their words, but her mind was focused on what had just happened.

She had ventured into hostile territory and been fired upon. Her aircraft was hit. She had dealt with the emergency calmly, coolly, and efficiently. She was proud of herself. But then what the hell was there to be proud of? This was what she had been trained to do. She was a pro.

FIRST U.S. SERVICEWOMAN IN COMBAT!

What a feature story that would make for Chris Campbell. A thousand times more interesting than U.S. Army women being forced to wear *abayahs*. Who gave a damn about *abayahs*? But combat, now that meant something.

"Downtown, this is Broadway Five," she heard her own voice in her earphones.

"Broadway Five, this is Downtown, go ahead."

"Downtown, we have encountered hostile fire and have taken damage," Elaine said into the microphone. Her voice was as calm and steady as though announcing a routine course change. "One engine is out. Please vector us to the nearest airbase or emergency station."

"Roger, Broadway Five. Stand by, please."

"Broadway Five standing by."

It reminded her of watching a movie at home on a VCR. You could stop the tape, go about your business —bathroom, kitchen, telephone, whatever—then return and continue the movie. Same thing here: Reviewing her behavior, congratulating herself on her proficiency and professionalism, she stops in the middle of this cerebral self-serving exercise to communicate with the AWACS. All right, while awaiting the AWACS response, she would resume the movie.

Where was she? Oh, yes, she was a pro. Which of course was why she had decided to leave her husband. End the marriage, start a whole new life. All well and good, except that she had neglected to inform the husband of this minor detail. Oh, to be sure, she had intended to inform him. No guts, eh, lady? No, no guts, she conceded. But for all that, she had performed admirably a few minutes ago. And it certainly required guts. So she did have guts. For certain things.

"Broadway Five, this is Downtown."

She glanced at the instrument panel digital clock. The numbers shone dully green in the dark cockpit. Twenty seconds had passed since Downtown asked her to stand by. Since she had resumed the movie. The story of a woman's life. Make a great daytime soap. "Nights of our Lives."

"Go ahead, Downtown."

"Advise you proceed to Al Kalir. Repeat, Al Kalir. Here are the coordinates. . . ." Again, it was all automatic, reflexive. The AWACS controller droned out the coordinates, Elaine punched the numbers into the inertial navigation computer. Again, she was vaguely aware of Henderson's and Feeney's voices. She was responsible for their well-being. Their lives depended upon her ability. She remembered once asking her father, the old airborne soldier, if the pilot of his airplane was a good pilot.

A good pilot, he had replied, is one who gets you there, and gets you back. Well, she was a good pilot because she had gotten them there, and would get them back.

"Do you copy, Broadway Five?"

"Copy you loud and clear, Downtown," she said into the mike. "I am proceeding to Al Kalir."

Al Kalir, she thought. Al Kalir was Nick Harmon's station before his TDY assignment to Israel. Good old Nick. By now he should be back at Al Kalir on line duty. Well, she'd soon know. If they could make Al Kalir on one engine.

". . . sure wish we could have found those SOF guys," Henderson was saying. "If they were nailed by the Iraqis, they're in for a rough go."

"Hey, be thankful it wasn't *us!*" Feeney said. "Right, Major?"

"Right, Sergeant," Elaine said. Her voice sounded strange. Heart in your throat, she thought, and wondered how fast it was beating. Thumping, more accurately. Fear. A few moments ago she had been too busy to think about fear. Now she was drowning in it.

"We're less than an hour from Al Kalir," she said into the intercom. "We'll make it."

"On one engine?" Feeney asked.

"Even if we have to land, Downtown knows our location," Elaine said. "And we're in friendly territory. We're okay now no matter what happens."

"Stop worrying, kid," Henderson said, addressing Feeney. "This thing flies fine on one engine."

"I think I'll say a little prayer for it," said Feeney, who was a devout Catholic.

"Why not?" Henderson said. "It can't hurt. Right, Major?"

Before Elaine could reply, a new radio voice boomed over the cabin loudspeaker. "Broadway Five, this is Shepherd Leader. Do you copy?"

"Loud and clear, Shepherd Lead."

"We're capping you, Broadway Five. We'll see you to your destination," the voice said.

Elaine peered up into the overcast at the unseen fighters AWACS had sent as an escort. "Thank you, Shepherd Lead," she said into the mike. "That's quite an appropriate call sign, by the way."

"Roger that," the CAP pilot replied, and clicked his mike button to sign off.

"We're being taken care of very nicely," Elaine said into the intercom. She turned and looked at Feeney in the rear. "Say a prayer for Courtyard," she said. "They're the ones who need it."

"You think they were captured, then?" Feeney asked.

"Maybe not," Elaine said. "Anything could have happened. Their radios might be out. They might be okay."

"Amen to that," Feeney said.

"Even if they are captured, they can deal with it," Henderson said. "They're trained especially for that. They're ready for whatever happens."

"You bet," Elaine said absently. She was thinking about Feeney's remark on being thankful it was the SOF team that had been captured, and not them, and how genuinely thankful she was. And she felt no guilt whatever for the thought.

2

The appearance of the helicopter did not surprise Major Gamal Othman. He had anticipated an after-dark rescue attempt. These were not the first Americans to be captured, and certainly not the last. American SOF teams were scattered all over Iraq. Gamal knew of at least half a dozen Americans killed in firefights. The American Central Command listed them as victims of automobile accidents. It was almost funny, the number of U.S. servicemen killed in "automobile accidents."

Gamal had not yet notified 8th SFB HQ of the capture of the three Green Berets. He knew General Talaq would order the prisoners immediately brought to Kuwait and placed under his personal supervision. Not while Gamal had anything to say about it; not while the prisoners could be used as bait for the retrieval helicopter. A helicopter and its crew, plus three Green Berets, now that was a real prize. And Gamal was not about to allow anyone to steal it from him, not even his own C.O. No, Gamal knew how to play the game.

The presence of an American SOF team in the general area of the expected Israeli attack on Rutba was entirely coincidental, and for Gamal an unforeseen bonus. There was no way he could fail. He outnumbered the Israelis at least three-to-one and had the advantage of surprise. He knew the exact location of the enemy's entry into Iraq. He would allow them to proceed along the highway toward Rutba, into an ingeniously conceived trap.

To lure the rescue helicopter into landing, Gamal needed the radio authentication codes. He had turned the prisoners over to Captain Takriti. Takriti knew how to obtain the information.

"How much leeway do I have?" Takriti had asked.

"You mean, how far can you go?"

"Yes, sir, that is what I mean."

Gamal had glanced at the three Americans. Blindfolded, hands bound behind them, they were seated on the ground near the Soviet ZIL-151 steel-bodied van that served as Gamal's command vehicle. Lieutenant Badran stood outside the van, breezily chatting with a couple of other officers. Gamal was amused. The young lieutenant acted as though he had captured Schwarzkopf himself.

"Get me the information, Captain," Gamal said. "I don't care how you do it, just get it."

Although not an academy graduate, Shihab al-Takriti was a Baathist and had served with a Republican Guard mechanized division during the Iran-Iraq War. He was twenty-eight, a skilled and experienced intelligence of-

ficer, and highly ambitious, which was why he had volunteered for a commando brigade. It was the road
either to quick promotion or quick death. The death
part held no fear for him, he was no coward. The cowards were those swine known as "brother Arabs." The
Saudis, who licked the toes of the Americans, and
the Egyptians, who had surrendered their honor to the
Jews. And the Syrians, and the ass-kissing Emirates and
Bahrainis, and all the others who had betrayed Iraq.

Using Amir Badran as an interpreter, Takriti proceeded to interrogate the three Americans. In truth, he
expected no immediate answers; these were trained,
seasoned soldiers. The initial questions were therefore
deliberately innocuous, but enlightening for Takriti. It
helped him decide which one of the prisoners might
bend faster under intense examination.

With the black man, Knox, some type of physical
pressure might be necessary. Of the other two, Ciafrelli
and Valdez, Takriti believed the Hispanic to be the
weaker. But Takriti knew it would not be easy. On the
surface at least, all three Americans were calm and
composed.

"Very well then, let's begin again," Takriti said, and
Amir translated. "I would like to know the exact purpose of your mission here."

He had addressed the question to Valdez, who said to
Amir, "He talking to me?"

"Yes, Sergeant, to you," Amir said. "And please don't
keep boring us with name, rank, and serial number."

"Yeah, well that's the best you'll get from me," Valdez
said. "Hey, how about a cigarette?"

Amir lit a cigarette and placed it between Valdez's
lips. They were inside the ZIL now. The three Americans sat on the steel floor, jackets buttoned tightly
against the cold, gloved hands still tied behind them.
The blindfolds had been removed, but in the diffused
light of the single naked bulb in the ceiling it was impossible for them to clearly see each other's faces, to read
each other's expressions, to gauge feelings.

Now Valdez, smoking, inhaled deeply and then suddenly, almost violently, coughed. The force of the cough propelled the cigarette from Valdez's mouth onto the floor.

"Jesus!" Valdez said. "What the hell kind of cigarette is that?"

"A *Gitane*," Amir said. "French."

"Jesus," Valdez said again.

"Too strong, eh?" Amir said.

"Tastes like rolled dogshit," Valdez said. He grinned, pleased with the simile.

Amir crushed the smoldering butt out on the floor with the heel of his boot and tossed it through one of the partially open steel louvers of the observation windows on the port side. "Sorry we don't have any American tobacco," he said. "When you're in Kuwait, you'll be able to find some."

"Marlboros," Ciafrelli said. "That's my brand. Except I gave it up last year, so I don't miss it a bit. Filthy habit, anyway. Hey, you said Kuwait? We're going to Kuwait?"

In Arabic, Takriti said to Amir, "They think they're clever, evading the question, rambling with pointless conversation." He spoke quietly, almost amused.

Amir said to Takriti, "That's what they're trained to do, Captain."

"Ask them for the radio codes," Takriti said.

"Yes, sir." Amir said. He felt like a veteran. At gunpoint he had captured enemy soldiers, commandos like himself. And now he was their interrogator. He only wished Adnan were here. Adnan would have been proud of the way Amir was conducting himself.

"What'd he say?" Valdez asked, indicating Takriti.

"He said he thinks you're all very bright, but he wants you to answer our questions," Amir said. *Our* questions, he thought. He liked the way it sounded. He decided to focus on the black man, the team leader.

"Sergeant, I understand—and I respect—your reason for not answering our questions," Amir said to Knox. "But we want answers, and we also want to know how you contact anyone who might be sent in to rescue you."

Knox laughed. "Are you kidding?"

Captain Takriti understood the gist of Knox's words easily enough. "The other one," he said to Amir, nodding at Valdez. "He'll give us the information."

"I'll ask you the same question, then," Amir said to Valdez.

"And I'll give you the same answer," Valdez said.

"Blindfold them again, Lieutenant," Takriti said to Amir. He waited patiently for Amir to replace the blindfolds, juggling a heavy flashlight from one hand to the other.

Knox said, "I remind you that we are POWs, sir, and you are obliged to observe the rules of the Geneva convention."

Amir translated Knox's statement for Takriti and translated the captain's reply. "You are spies. The Geneva convention does not apply to spies. In any event, we treat our prisoners humanely, even spies."

"I'll bet," said Ciafrelli.

Ciafrelli never completed the last word. Takriti had drawn back his hand and smashed him flush in the mouth with the flashlight. Ciafrelli uttered a cry of pain. His head fell back against the van's steel wall with a dull thud and then, like a ball attached to a rubber band, snapped forward. Blood spurted from his lips, and a white fragment of a tooth bounced off the toe of his boot and skittered across the vehicle floor.

"What the hell are you people doing?" Knox shouted.

In the same motion that he struck Ciafrelli, Takriti had yanked Valdez's blindfold off. "Jesus!" Valdez cried, peering at Ciafrelli. "You killed him!"

"Goddamn you, what've you done?" Knox shouted. He struggled to rise. Takriti planted the heel of his boot into Knox's chest and shoved him back.

Takriti said to Amir, "Now tell this one"— he pointed the flashlight at Valdez—"that unless he answers my questions, the same will happen to him."

Before Amir could speak, Ciafrelli moaned. He tried to raise his head. Blood pouring down from his mouth soaked the front of his jacket and began pooling in a viscous puddle on the floor between his legs.

"Drowning in their own blood, as the president said," Takriti said quietly, and without warning, in a single, swift, smooth motion, he smashed the flashlight across the side of Ciafrelli's head. This time Ciafrelli did not utter a sound. He slumped sideways.

"Oh, my God!" Valdez said. "Oh, shit! Dear Mother in Heaven, they killed him! Knox, do you hear me? Do you understand what I'm saying? These cocksucking animals have killed Ciafrelli!"

Knox said nothing. He was leaning forward, as though straining to see through the blindfold. Drops of blood suddenly stained his mouth. He had bitten down on his lips so hard he punctured the skin.

Takriti trained the flashlight on Valdez again, and in the same quiet voice said to Amir, "Please repeat my statement to this man."

Amir was staring at Ciafrelli, at Ciafrelli's open, unseeing eyes. In Arabic, he said to Takriti, "His friend is right. He's dead."

"I don't know my own strength," Takriti said. "Lieutenant, kindly obey my orders."

Amir's throat felt suddenly so tight that he thought he might choke. His head began pounding. He heard Takriti speaking again, that same calm, quiet voice. This could not be happening. A Republican Guard officer murders an enemy soldier, a prisoner, and shows less emotion than swatting a fly.

Enemy soldier, he thought. Yes, of course, that was the answer. These were enemies. They had to be treated as such. You could not coddle them. If the positions were reversed, they would do the same. Everyone knew how "humanely" the Iranians had treated the captured enemy. War is cruel.

". . . if this is too difficult for you, Lieutenant, I'll excuse you," Takriti was saying. "I'm sure someone else in the battalion speaks English."

Amir said nothing a moment. He was looking at the blindfolded black man, Knox. Amir admired him. The man realized what lay in store for him and was unafraid. Courage, Amir thought, wondering how he might behave in the same situation. Badly, he thought. Very badly.

He said to Valdez, "For God's sake, Sergeant, answer the Captain's questions." And then, as though another person were speaking, Amir heard himself continuing in English, "He's mad, this captain. He'll kill you, too. Listen to me, please."

Unexpectedly, Valdez laughed. "The 'good cop, bad cop' routine. Fuck you, Saddam. You understand me? Fuck you!"

Amir did not comprehend "good cop, bad cop," but certainly understood the rest of it. "You must cooperate," he said to Valdez. The words sounded silly, but he did not know what else to say.

"Fuck you," Valdez said again. He was looking at Ciafrelli. He had never seen a dead person before, only his uncle when the old man lay in a coffin at the wake. He had never particularly liked Ciafrelli and had never treated him as a friend. Now he wished he could make up for all that. But he knew it was too late. Too late, probably for all of them.

It was right at that instant they heard the helicopter.

"The light!" said Captain Takriti. Amir reached up and switched off the overhead lamp. Takriti hurled open the van door. The drone of the helicopter's rotors was louder, closer.

The shadowed outline of a man appeared in the van doorway. It was Gamal Othman. "Did you learn anything?" he asked Takriti.

"Not yet."

"Damn your soul, Takriti, get them to talk!" Gamal said. He left. Other than the helicopter's whirling blades, the only sound was the crunch of boots in the sand as men raced to the gun emplacements and stripped the camouflage netting from two 12.7mm heavy machine guns.

Takriti closed the van door. He cupped his hand over the flashlight and turned it on. The flashlight was pointed at Ciafrelli. Ciafrelli's open, dead eyes gleamed like those of an animal staring into automobile head-

lights. Takriti swung the flashlight over to Knox. He held
the beam on Knox a moment, then trained it on Valdez.

"Tell him," Takriti said to Amir, "that he has ten seconds to give us what we want. Ten!" And he began
counting off the seconds, *"Waehid, itnen, taelae-
trae . . ."*

The helicopter was directly overhead. The drumming
of its rotors drowned out Takriti's monotone voice but
he had already counted to *khaemsae,* five, by the time
Amir translated the ultimatum.

"Fuck you!" Valdez shouted.

"Saebae," Takriti continued. *"Taemaanyae."*

The sound of the helicopter's engines receded slightly
as the aircraft passed over the camp and headed deeper
into Iraq, east toward Rutba. Amir knew the helicopter
would not venture too close to Rutba and would turn
and fly back over them. A minute, he estimated, two at
most.

"Tisaa," Takriti said, nine.

Amir switched on the overhead lamp. Takriti was
crouched over Valdez, flashlight in one hand, a pearl-
handled Tokarev 7.62mm in the other. The Tokarev's
muzzle was inches away from Valdez's ear. Even in the
dim light Amir could see that the gun was cocked.

"Captain!" Amir shouted. "The helicopter will be
back! Give him a little more time!" In English, in the
same breath, he said to Valdez, "Please. Tell him what
he wants to know!"

Takriti's mouth formed the word *ashara,* ten, but he
did not utter it. Instead, he stood erect and shut off the
overhead lamp. Again, the only light came from the
flashlight. He said to Amir, "This is his last chance."

Amir said, "Sir, you are wasting your time. These
men are not afraid."

Takriti swung the flashlight around into Amir's face.
"You sound as though you admire them."

"I do, sir," said Amir. His own words surprised him;
he had never intended articulating them.

"You're a fool," Takriti said, and trained the flashlight
on Valdez again and then on Knox. The pistol in

Takriti's hand was leveled at Knox's head. He addressed
Valdez in Arabic. "Unless you reveal the radio code I
will shoot this man."

Amir translated for Valdez, who said, "You're crazy!
All of you, you're crazy!" He turned to Knox. "Doug, he
says unless I give him the recognition code, he'll waste
you! Christ, man, what'll I do?"

"Nothing," said Knox. "You do nothing."

"He ain't kidding, Doug. He means it!"

"I said you do nothing," Knox said. "You understand,
soldier? Nothing!" Takriti pressed the gun muzzle into
Knox's forehead. "Fuck you, you Iraqi prick!" Knox
said.

All Valdez could think of was that this was only the
second time in his life he had ever heard Knox swear,
and that this time it did not give him any satisfaction.
Now he wanted to somehow make up for the bad feelings between them. He wanted them to be friends. And
one way was to save the man's life. The recognition
code was Biker.

Biker, a simple word that would save his friend's life.

He heard the young English-speaking Iraqi talking to
him, but the words did not register. Biker. But that
would let them capture the helicopter. Yes, but then
nobody would be killed. Poor Ciafrelli. And if he,
Valdez, did not give them the code word he, too, was a
dead man.

He heard the helicopter. Louder, louder, closer. And
then he heard the gunshot. It sounded like a dull pop,
which was almost impossible. In the enclosed steel-
walled van, the sound should have reverberated like a
clanging bell. And then he realized why the sound was
so muffled.

It was not Knox who had been shot, it was the young
Iraqi. Valdez had watched it all happen and for a moment thought he was imagining it. The young Iraqi had
tried to stop the other one from shooting Knox. The
young Iraqi had grasped the gun. The two had scuffled.
The flashlight fell to the floor, plunging everything into

darkness. When the gun discharged, the young Iraqi's body muffled the sound.

The captain had picked up the flashlight now. Valdez could see clearer. The young Iraqi lay on his back on the floor. The captain said something, then opened the van door and rushed out. A moment later, Valdez heard the heavy caliber antiaircraft machine guns firing.

Firing at the helicopter, Valdez knew, which meant they had given up trying for the code. Good. Fuck them. In the darkened van, he heard a moan of pain from the young Iraqi and then Knox's voice.

"What's happening for God's sake?" Knox cried. "What's going on?"

"It's all crazy, Doug!" Valdez said. "These fucking bastards are all crazy!"

Outside, the guns stopped firing. The van door opened, and the Iraqi captain returned. He closed the door and switched on the overhead light. Now Valdez saw everything as though on an illuminated stage.

Ciafrelli, still slumped sideways, open eyes staring sightlessly. Knox seated, blindfolded. The young Iraqi lying on the floor, peering up at the captain. A little rivulet of blood seeped out from under the back of the young Iraqi's neck and blackened the collar of his desert fatigues. The captain, pistol still gripped in his hand, spoke to the young Iraqi, whose lips moved soundlessly.

"No! No! No!" the words were Valdez's, screamed, as the captain raised the pistol, placed the muzzle against Knox's cheek, and fired. A small hole appeared in Knox's cheek and then the opposite side of his face disintegrated. The sound of the gunshot reverberated through the van, as flesh, bone, and blood flew across the interior of the vehicles and splattered against the wall.

It was next to the last thing Valdez ever saw. The last sight was the gun pointed at him and a bright, blinding flash. He felt nothing, which surprised him, as did the sense of endless time. He wanted to express his thanks to the young Iraqi. He wasn't such a bad dude. He had tried to stop the other Iraqi from shooting Knox. And

what did the kid get for his trouble? A bullet. But he
wasn't dead, which pleased Valdez. Maybe he wasn't seriously hurt, either. That would be nice. Yeah, the kid
was okay. Lots of guts.

Valdez was already dead when the sound of the gunshot reached his ears. Amir, of course, did hear it.
Amir's mind was clear, and he was aware of all that was
happening, even that the bullet had hit him in the
throat, somewhere between his chin and neck. But he
felt no pain. He felt nothing, only a sense of heaviness,
as though he weighed a thousand pounds or was pinned
down by a thousand-pound weight. He could not flex his
toes or move his fingers. But he could move his lips, and
he could talk.

"Captain," he said. "Help me. . . ."

And he could move his head. He saw that Takriti was
not in the truck. The door was open. Outside, he heard
the excited voices of men. Of course, they were talking
about the helicopter. The helicopter, yes.

"Help me!" he said. "Please! Help me!"

And then he screamed. He had tried to move his
hands once more, and could not, not even his fingers.
And he realized why. He was paralyzed. From the neck
down, dead. If his hands were useless, he could not
paint. Painting was his life. His life. He screamed again.

Later, after the medic had bandaged the wound and
they were waiting for the ambulance, Gamal Othman
said to him, "Badran, it would be helpful if we kept all
this between ourselves."

Amir said nothing.

"Do you understand, Badran?"

Amir nodded.

"It was an accident."

Amir nodded again.

"You'll be back on your feet in no time," Gamal said.

Amir did not have the strength to tell the major that
he had overheard the medic say the bullet had severed
his spinal cord.

"You'll be all right," Gamal said. "You'll be fine."

Amir tried to smile, but felt a warm wetness on his face. Blood, he thought. But where the hell did it come from? No, not blood, tears. He was weeping. The tears ran down his cheeks and into his mouth. They tasted bitter and very salty.

3

When Elaine settled the crippled UH-60 squarely in the bull's-eye of the floodlit landing pad in front of the Al Kalir control tower, the first person she saw was Nick Harmon. He stood with another officer, a full colonel, an incredibly handsome black man. Both wore coveralls and leather A-2 flying jackets, and both looked grim. The colonel spoke to Nick, then moved off to join some mechanics examining the helicopter's damaged engine.

Elaine's copilot, CW2 Tim Henderson, and the crew chief, Sergeant Feeney, were already out on the hardstand with the mechanics. Elaine remained in the cockpit an extra moment, trying to compose herself. She had time for only a fast glimpse of her face in the rearview mirror. She looked like hell. Nick opened the cabin door and beckoned her out.

She climbed down to the hardstand and faced him. "History repeats," she said. "This is how we first met, isn't it? Are you going to give me hell again for landing at your base?" Then, as though remembering, she saluted smartly. "Major Mason, sir."

Nick ignored the salute. "I ought to say, 'Thank God, you're okay.' Instead, all I can say is that you're crazy."

"I'm also famished," she said. "And I know my crew is. Can you rustle some chow for us?"

"What the hell were you trying to do? Win a medal?"

Elaine had no chance to reply. The handsome black colonel stepped over to them just then. Elaine saluted. "Major Mason, sir."

Iverson returned the salute. "Colonel Iverson," he said. "I'm base C.O. Sorry your mission failed, Major, but happy you all came back in one piece. There's an

SOF intelligence officer on his way to debrief you. So you'll be our guest for awhile."

"Thank you, sir. Sir, would it be possible for my crew and me to get something to eat?"

"Nick, take the major over to the mess tent and see what you can do for her." Iverson's eyes swept appraisingly over Elaine. "I understand you and Colonel Harmon are old friends?"

Elaine glanced narrowly at Nick, then said to Iverson, "We know each other, yes sir."

"Good, then I'm sure Nick will see that you have everything you need." Iverson wheeled around and walked off to his staff car.

" 'Nick will see that you have everything you need,' " Elaine said, watching Iverson drive off. "I noticed he didn't say a word about accommodations. Maybe he thinks that since we're old friends, we'll bunk together. What did you tell him about me?"

"Only that I knew you," Nick said. "And you won't have to bunk with me, don't worry. There's a couple of empty rooms in the BOQ. Come on, I'll feed you."

Nick got the mess sergeant to prepare some French toast and a pot of strong coffee for Elaine and the two crewmen. It was after eleven by the time Nick and Elaine arrived at the BOQ. He found a vacant room for her not far from his. Like all the Al Kalir BOQ rooms, the furniture consisted of a canvas cot, a small chest of drawers and mirrored dressing table, a writing table and goose-necked lamp. And two chairs, a straight-backed aluminum one and a vinyl-upholstered armchair. Nick switched on the lamp, bending the metal lampshade downward almost to the table's surface to shadow the glare of the bulb.

"It's not the Plaza," he said. "But then it's not a pup tent in the desert, either."

Elaine said, "Are you kidding? Compared to Dhahran, this is positively luxurious. Two other girls and I share what's no bigger than an unheated closet in a renovated hangar. Not to mention what is laughingly referred to as 'the facilities.' "

"All right, get some sleep, and I'll see you in the morning," Nick said, and moved to leave.

"I'm too charged up to sleep," she said. "Besides, you never finished your little lecture about whether I was trying to win a medal."

"Feel like a drink? I've got a fifth of Rémy I smuggled in from Israel."

"I hate brandy."

"It'll go good with the lecture."

"What'll the neighbors say?"

"They're all very discreet," he said.

"Go get the brandy," she said.

He went to his room for the bottle and brought it back, along with two plastic water cups and his battery-powered Panasonic AM-FM radio. With proper atmospherics you could occasionally pick up stations as far away as Athens and sometimes even Paris, otherwise it was DSR, Desert Shield Radio, ninety percent rock 'n' roll.

He was relieved not to run into any "neighbors," the BOQ's other occupants, male and female. By morning, everyone would have known the identity of the officer whom the acting director of Operations had visited the previous evening. With a bottle of brandy.

Elaine, under the blanket and sheets, was sitting up in bed, her back propped against the wall. She had removed her bulky Nomex flight suit and draped another blanket shawllike over her shoulders. Nick knew that all she wore was cotton underwear. Not too comfortable, but very practical for flying: In a fire, synthetic fabrics melted and adhered to the skin.

"This is not a seduction scene," she said. "I had to get out of that goddamn suit." She smiled dryly. "And I'm sure you know what my lingerie, you should excuse the expression, consists of. Now fix me a drink."

Nick filled each plastic cup halfway. He touched his cup to hers, and they drank. She said, "I wasn't very nice to you in Monterey. I'm sorry."

"Forget it."

"I had a lot on my mind."

"We both did."

She drank her remaining brandy and held the cup out for a refill. Her hand was trembling. She had to grasp the cup with both hands to steady it. "You're in great shape," he said.

"I'm pretty shook up after that flight, Nick." She sipped some of the brandy, then placed the cup carefully on the floor. "It took a lot out of me."

"You shouldn't have flown the mission."

Her eyes narrowed in annoyance. "You never change: not a single question about how it was, or that you're happy I didn't burn up in the desert, or a pat on the back for getting out of there alive. Even that fast-burner colonel of yours said he was glad we were all in one piece. From you, though, not even the proverbial 'You okay?' No, what I get from you is a lecture."

"You need a lecture," he said. "It was a goddamn fool thing to do."

"They asked me to do it," she said. "I was the nearest asset."

"They had no business asking you, and you could have turned it down. Nobody would have blamed you. It was too dangerous—"

"—too dangerous for *me,* you mean. Why? Because I don't have a pair of balls I can clank around? Come on, Nick, this is the twentieth century!"

He had looked away to pour himself another drink. When he turned to her again, she had masked her face with her hands. Her shoulders were shaking, her body seemed to be in spasm. Now she lowered her hands. She was crying.

"I guess I'm not the stalwart soldier I thought I was," she said. She wiped her eyes with the corner of the bed sheet. "Those poor guys out there. If only I could have found them!"

Nick said nothing. It had just dawned on him that Elaine's flight into Iraq was near the site of the big Iraqi radar air defense installation at Rutba. Rutba, the target —with U.S. knowledge and approval—of the next Israeli raid. It reminded him of Frank Kowalski.

". . . they're dead or captured," she was saying. "I don't know which is worse. Shit!"

Nick said, "What do you want? A pep talk? About how you did your best, and there was nothing else you could have done after they shot up your airplane?"

"Helicopter," she said.

"Excuse me," he said.

"I'm ashamed of myself, Nick. When I was there, and it was happening, I wasn't thinking about them. I was too busy being scared. So now I'm a wreck and feeling sorry for myself." She wiped her eyes with the bed sheet again and reached down to the floor for the plastic cup. She finished the brandy in a single swallow. "I hate to fail, Nick. That's the problem."

"You're still looking for a pep talk," Nick said. "See the chaplain."

"You bastard! I'm the one who needs the shoulder to cry on now. You're turning away from me!"

He drew her into his arms and held her close. He inhaled the fragrance of her hair and her body, and he felt the smoothness of her skin. He had forgotten all of that, and what it had meant to him, but he remembered it now.

". . . need a shower," she was murmuring into his ear. "I stink of gasoline and oil and sweat—"

He silenced her with his lips. They kissed, gently at first and then with more passion, and he remembered how it had always been like this with her. The nectar-sweet taste of her mouth. The warm wetness of her tongue flitting in and around his. The firm roundness of her breasts as they swelled under his caress.

She shrugged the blanket from her shoulders and removed her cotton T-shirt. She pulled his face down to her breasts. The nipples were already hard as he kissed one, then the other, and then back to the first. They were lying side by side on the cot, clasped in each other's arms. He wanted to move, to plunge himself into her, and at the same time he did not want to let go of her.

They remained in that embrace a few more moments,

silent, hardly breathing. It was as though words or sounds might break the spell. He did not want this ever to end, yet knew it would end, it had to end. The end was something unspoken between them but understood and accepted. He felt sure that on her part what had led to this moment was a desperate need for release. On his part, need, period. Need, he thought, as he felt himself slide effortlessly into her and her muscles contract and close around him—and he did not know how all this had happened, for he did not remember shifting positions or removing clothes—a mutual need fulfilled.

". . . don't stop!" she whispered. "Don't stop, don't stop, don't stop!" She dug her nails into his shoulders and arched her back and cried. "Yes! Yes! Yes!"

The same phrases, the same sounds, the rhapsodic moaning and joyous groaning. He floated away now on the exquisite pleasure of it and at the same time cursed himself for all the years without her. The wasted, empty years. They had been his for the asking, and he stupidly had thrown them away.

But no, nothing had been thrown away. He was here with her now, wasn't he? They were together again, weren't they? And it could go on now. He would not repeat his mistakes of the past.

I love you, he told her in his mind, and then heard himself saying it. "I love you."

"I know."

"I mean it."

"I know that, too," she said.

TEN

In Avi Posner's opinion, for the defense minister to compare himself with Winston Churchill was, to say the least, more than a little pretentious. But then no one had ever accused the D.M. of humility, so Avi was never surprised at what came out of his boss's mouth.

"Coventry," the D.M. had said. "That's what it's like, and that's the decision facing me. The same dilemma Churchill faced."

The D.M. was of course referring to World War II, when Churchill deliberately allowed the Luftwaffe to destroy the English city of Coventry. The British, having broken the German radio codes, knew that Coventry was targeted for a massive air attack. Evacuating, or even alerting the population would have revealed the British secret. In Churchill's view, Coventry was therefore expendable.

"And President Roosevelt, they say, was faced with a similar dilemma at Pearl Harbor," the D.M. went on. "He knew beforehand of the Japanese attack. But he was determined to bring America into the war. A surprise attack would rally the American people as nothing else could."

"So they say," Posner said in Hebrew. The D.M.'s remarks on Churchill and Roosevelt had been in English, as though that was the only language appropriate for the subject.

"Well, we're faced with the same situation, aren't we?" the D.M. asked, returning to Hebrew now.

Posner did not immediately reply. He glanced out the window at the hazy twilight sky. They were in the D.M.'s spacious office on the sixth floor of the Defense Ministry building, where the windows faced west and you could see all the way across the city to the ocean. The weather during the day had been sunny but now at dusk was clouding up. Ideal for Operation Presto, scheduled to commence at 2100, in four hours.

At the big Negev airbase of Hazorim, Colonel Ben Sklar's men and equipment were already loaded into the C-130s, awaiting the final word to go. As a reward for his brilliant success at Shab al-Bir, Sklar had been given command of Presto.

Some reward, Posner thought glumly, glancing again at the red-bordered message on the D.M.'s desk. Red for Most Urgent. "Yes, Minister," he said. "I suppose our situation is similar."

"And the decisions are as agonizing," said the D.M. He tapped his finger delicately on the red-bordered paper that Posner had brought into the office thirty minutes before.

The paper contained a verbatim transcript of a telephone conversation on the newly established Washington–Tel Aviv secure line: A U.S. Army intelligence team operating inside Iraq had reported the presence of a sizable force of Republican Guard commandos in the Rutba area.

Rutba, the target of Operation Presto.

Common sense—not to mention basic military strategy—demanded the cancellation of the Israeli mission. But this would nullify Israel's basic objective. Namely, to so infuriate Saddam Hussein and cause him to lose so much face, he would defy a thousand UN ultimatums.

Thereby leaving the Allies no choice but to proceed with their offensive, which once and for all would eliminate the Iraqi threat to Israel, restore the region's balance of power, and assure Israeli security.

Operation Presto, to paraphrase the defense minister, was a political exigency.

A question of survival.

Thirty minutes ago, after receiving the message, the D.M. had dismissed Posner and immediately contacted the prime minister, the chief of staff, and several other cabinet members. He had then summoned Posner back.

". . . the prime minister has left the decision to me," the D.M. was saying now. "If we cancel Presto, Bush might damn well sit and do nothing for weeks. For months or, who knows, never." He picked up the paper. He dangled it a moment, then let it fall from his fingers and flutter down to the desktop. "If we don't cancel. . . ."

"Then we knowingly send our people into a trap," Posner said. "The casualties might be unacceptable."

"Should my reply to that be that *any* casualties are unacceptable?"

"I would consider that a proper reply."

"A proper reply for a politician, you mean?"

"Even for a soldier, Minister."

"And your recommendation, Avi? Should we or should we not cancel Presto?" Before Posner could answer, the D.M. continued. "The Americans have very cleverly refrained from comment. I have a feeling they might be quite pleased to see us execute the operation. I think they would like to get the war started, get it over with, and get themselves back home."

"I think that I, too, should refrain from comment, sir," Posner said. He was sure the D.M. had already reached a decision. "I am in no position to deal with the broader aspects of this matter."

"You're evading the issue, General!"

"Yes, Minister, I am."

"You have answered my question, then."

Posner said nothing.

The D.M. brushed his fingertips along the paper's red borders. The gesture reminded Posner of a story related by one of the D.M.'s aides. On a recent visit to Dimona, the D.M. had placed his arms around a 40-kiloton nuclear bomb. An embrace, as the aide described it. The D.M. had literally, and lovingly, hugged the bomb. The bomb, said the D.M., represented Israel's salvation.

". . . all right, Avi, thank you," the D.M. was saying. "I'll let you know."

Posner rose to leave. "If we're to stand down, we should inform Sklar as soon as possible."

"What makes you think we'll stand down?"

"I can't believe that you would sacrifice a single one of our kids for political exigencies." Posner instantly regretted the words. The D.M.'s face tightened with anger. Posner said, "That was not intended as criticism, sir."

"The hell it wasn't," said the D.M., but with an indulgent smile. The smile immediately faded. "But suppose the 'sacrifice' saves hundreds of thousands of lives? How do we know the Iraqis aren't seeking some face-saving way of backing down? So they can all parade back to Baghdad in one piece and concentrate on developing their chemical weapons, and probably nukes as well. And one of these mornings we wake up to find Tel Aviv exactly what it was eighty years ago: one big mound of sand!"

"That, Minister, is why you are a politician and I am a soldier," Posner said. "I'll wait to hear from you."

Posner had already opened the door when the D.M. called to him. "Cancel it, Avi. Cancel Presto."

Posner could not repress a smile of relief as he hurried away. He was halfway into the corridor when the D.M. called to him again. The D.M. stood in the outer office doorway. "Is it possible someone in Washington leaked Presto to the Iraqis?"

"We think it came from Jordan."

"Who in Jordan?"

"Achmed Ben Sallah."

"The newspaper publisher?"

"Yes."

"And where," said the D.M., "do you think he got the information?"

"I expect to know all that shortly," Posner said. "I'll keep you advised."

General Posner had not been entirely forthright with the defense minister. The D.M. suspected as much but had no intention of pressing the issue. The Americans had coined a phrase for it: plausible deniability. It meant that what you do not know cannot hurt you. More specifically, in the broadest executive sense, you cannot be held responsible for actions of which you were unaware.

Posner knew the source of Ben Sallah's information. Not only had he decided how and where to deal with the matter, he had already set the machinery in motion.

2

The phone call had come at five that morning. Adnan could still hear Gamal Othman's voice. First, apologizing for awakening Adnan at such an ungodly hour, and then, "Look, Adnan, I have some bad news."

At first, still sluggish with sleep, Adnan could not imagine why Gamal Othman would call him with any bad news. They had little in common and traveled in different social circles. Indeed, they had not spoken in nearly two years until Adnan asked Gamal to quash Amir's request for transfer into a commando unit. "Bad news." Then it had to be bad news about Amir, Adnan thought, as Gamal's voice echoed the name.

". . . it's young Badran, Adnan," Gamal continued. "He's been hurt—"

"—where the hell are you, anyway?"

"I'm in Rutba. Adnan, it was an accident."

"Accident? What accident?" Now Adnan was wide awake. He sat up in bed and clamped the telephone to his ear. "You're talking about *Amir* Badran?"

"Yes, Adnan, your fiancée's brother."

"No, no, Gamal, you must be mistaken. Amir is on courier duty right here at the Defense Ministry. And if you're in Rutba, how do you know about any accident?"

"Adnan, he was with me when it happened. In Rutba, Adnan. He's hurt badly. A spinal cord injury." Gamal paused, expecting a barrage of questions, but Adnan had remained silent. "Adnan. . . . ?"

"Yes, I hear you," Adnan said. He had been trying to

digest all this and also focus on how Amir came to be with Gamal's commando unit in Rutba. "How badly is he hurt?"

Gamal was silent a moment. Adnan had a sudden urge to hang up. He did not want to hear what he knew was coming. "He's paralyzed," Gamal said. "From the neck down. They don't know how permanent it is, or if it is. He should be arriving at Muadham anytime now." Muadham, part of Medical City in central Baghdad, was a medical facility maintained exclusively for the Republican Guard and their families. "I arranged for a special plane to fly him in. Adnan. . . . ?"

"Yes, Gamal, I hear you," Adnan said. He had been wondering how to break the news to Hana. He would not tell her anything until he knew more himself. He was pleased at his own clear thinking and calmness.

". . . no one's fault, really," Gamal was saying. "We captured some American Special Forces people. One of them managed to break loose. My intelligence officer, Takriti, shot the fellow. Unfortunately, in the confusion, Lieutenant Badran got in the way. He took the bullet. Adnan, I can't tell you how sorry I am."

"Gamal, what in the hell was he doing in Rutba anyway?" Adnan asked. "Never mind, you'll tell me later. I'll get over to Muadham right now. Thanks."

Adnan sat a moment in bed, gripping the dead phone. Outside, through the latticed window, a sliver of light whitened the early morning sky. The smooth plastic of the telephone handset was wet and slippery under Adnan's fingers. The back of his pajamas stuck wetly to his skin. He was soaked with sweat. The room was freezing, and he was sweating.

It was after ten that same morning by the time Adnan received permission to see Amir, and it had required a phone call to Major General Hassan Marwaan to achieve that. Although far too early for any comprehensive diagnosis or prognosis, the bright young Western-educated colonel who served as chief neurologist wasted no words.

The bullet had severed Amir's spinal cord, leaving him unable to use his limbs. Quadriplegic, in medical terminology. Although the wound was in the upper quadrant, luckily—if "luck" is the correct phrase, the doctor added wryly—the injury did not impair the patient's respiratory function.

Adnan was unsure what the doctor meant by "luck" not being the correct phrase. Amir could breathe on his own, which spelled luck. And, best of all, he had survived. And then Adnan realized that this was what the doctor meant: Amir was alive. Perhaps, being alive, he was not so lucky after all.

Lucky.

Amir's third-floor room, which was quite spacious and contained only a single bed, smelled of disinfectant and flatulence. Asleep, heavily sedated, he seemed childlike and frail in the bed. A network of tubes and catheters protruded from all parts of his body. His sallow skin looked parchment-thin, his breathing was slow and labored. Adnan stood over him, staring at the motionless, rigid hands. Those delicate fingers that had held the brush that painted the pictures. Had, past tense, Adnan thought. Gazing at him, a crazy notion seized Adnan. He could place a pillow over Amir's face and hold it there until the breathing stopped. An act of mercy.

Adnan finally left. He walked blindly through the corridor, all the way to the end, to the sun porch. Three men in wheelchairs sat reading magazines or newspapers. One, a stout balding man with a thick black mustache, wore silk pajamas under his blue flannel hospital robe. An officer, obviously. Adnan wondered what rank he held and what "accident" had brought him here to the neurological-wound department.

Although the three men had paid no attention to Adnan, he felt obliged to explain his presence. "A friend of mine had an accident," he said, addressing the older man. "Spinal cord injury," Adnan continued, now to a younger man, the youngest of the three. He was reading a newspaper, *Al-Qadissiya*, the official military journal.

The younger man's eyes flicked away from his newspaper to Adnan, then back to the newspaper. Adnan felt foolish. No one had asked his business in the hospital. No one gave a damn. He stood awkwardly, gazing at the front page of the younger man's newspaper, at the Arabic headline.

BLESSED IRAQ AWAITS THE ONSLAUGHT!

Adnan knew that the text consisted of a rambling patriotic discourse, a compilation of handouts from the Information Ministry. The same stuff heard on the radio and television, all day, every day. The gallant soldiers of Iraq bravely awaited the start of the Mother of All Battles. The Americans and their cowardly allies were attempting to create a new dark age. The infidels would be hurled back and sent home in defeat and disgrace. Anyone who believed otherwise was a traitor and coward.

Traitor and coward, which certainly did not apply to the three men here on the sun porch. However their obscene injuries were incurred, it most assuredly was in an honorable fashion. Otherwise, they would not be in this hospital.

Yes, and he could hear himself mouthing those banalities to Hana. Your brother, my darling, behaved with great honor to earn the privilege of admission to this hospital. This hospital, which treats only the brave and honorable.

Adnan was so engrossed in his own reverie that he did not at first hear his name being called. Then, louder, "Major? Adnan . . . ?"

It was Hassan Marwaan. The general, in civilian clothes—a black Homburg hat and gray Savile Row pinstriped suit—stood in the sun porch doorway. He beckoned Adnan into the corridor.

"I've just seen him." Hassan shook his head sadly. "He's quadriplegic, all right. Thank God his father isn't alive to see this. How is Hana taking it?"

"I haven't told her yet," Adnan said.

"Would you like me to do it?"

"It's better that she hears it from me. But thank you."

"I read Major Othman's report of the incident," Hassan said. He shook his head again. "Tragic, really tragic."

"What did the report say?" Adnan asked.

Hassan related the substance of Gamal's brief written statement. It matched Gamal's account to Adnan earlier that day.

"No details about *how* Amir got in the way of the bullet?" Adnan asked. "Or why he did?"

"Not that I recall," Hassan said. "Does it matter?"

"No, I suppose not," Adnan said. He started walking down the rubber-tiled corridor toward the elevators. Hassan kept pace with him. They walked silently until they passed the open door of Amir's room. Adnan stopped and started to go in, then thought better of it. He faced Hassan. "You look tired, General."

"I am." Hassan glanced around to make sure no one could overhear. The corridor was empty and quiet. Some fifty feet away at the nurse's station, two nurses chatted animatedly. Hassan said, "He is not going to withdraw, Adnan, you realize that?"

"Who is not going to withdraw?" Adnan asked, knowing full well to whom and what Hassan referred, and immediately feeling foolish for wasting time playing word games. "He made it quite clear there would be no withdrawal. Why are you so surprised?"

"It's a mistake, Adnan. A terrible, tragic mistake. You said so yourself. 'Little or no chance of winning,' you said. Your exact words, Adnan."

A white-frocked male technician strode past. He nodded respectfully at Hassan, and then at Adnan. Adnan waited until the technician was out of earshot. "What do you want me to do about it, General? What *can* I do? What can anyone do?"

"The ultimatum has already expired," Hassan said. "This country will be destroyed. Is that what you want? Your motherland destroyed? Is that your definition of patriotism?"

Adnan studied Hassan a long moment. The liver-spotted skin under the general's bloodshot eyes was wrinkled and puffy, like twin pouches of dappled leather. The starched collar of his immaculate white shirt seemed much too large for his neck, which appeared almost scrawny. He looked years older than his age, fifty-eight. Retirement age. Which was what Adnan wished Major General Hassan Marwaan would do: retire. What he should do, retire, he and his coconspirators, whoever and wherever they might be. Retire with their good names and reputations intact, not to mention their good health.

Adnan said, "I've got to go now, sir. I have to tell Hana about her brother. You'll excuse me." Without another word, he turned and strode toward the elevators. He could feel Hassan's eyes on him. The general, Adnan realized, had sought him out not to discuss Amir's condition, but to talk to him.

About patriotism.

A word, in Hassan Marwaan's vocabulary, synonymous with treason. More accurately, with stupidity. For all that, Adnan could not help admiring the man. At least Hassan had the courage of his convictions, which was more than Adnan could say for himself.

Adnan did not go directly to see Hana. Already late for one meeting at the Defense Ministry, he had four other urgent conferences scheduled. For this reason—and because he dreaded facing Hana—he convinced himself that it was best to delay informing her until Amir was more stabilized and the doctors knew more. A few hours delay at most. Yes, sparing Hana the terrible pain, even for a few hours, was an act of compassion.

An act of cowardice, more accurately, of which he was well aware but at least allowed him to concentrate on the business at hand. The second meeting that day was held in the ornate conference room of the new presidential palace, presided over by Saddam Hussein himself. Some dozen generals and their aides attended, including the commanders of the 4th, 6th, and 7th Army

Corps, the 1st Presidential Guard Corps, and the commander and deputy commander of the air force. Adnan, in his capacity as Defense Ministry liaison to the Foreign Ministry, was the lowest-ranking officer present.

The hour-long meeting consisted mainly of a reprise of intelligence data gathered to date. Most importantly, the size of coalition forces arrayed against Iraq. As of tomorrow, January 17, enemy ground forces were estimated at more than 450,000, with 2,200 tanks. There were 245,000 U.S. Army, infantry and armored troops plus 75,000 U.S. Marines, 35,000 Egyptians, 25,000 British, 20,000 Saudis, 10,000 French, and 25,000 from Syria and several Gulf states. Allied airplanes numbered 2,000, which included the combat squadrons of six U.S. Navy carriers. Plus two missile-firing U.S. Navy battleships, the *Wisconsin* and *Missouri*.

"Formidable," said the air force deputy commander, who had delivered the report.

The word seemed to intrigue Saddam. He repeated it aloud several times, then posed it as a question to the air force deputy commander. " 'Formidable,' General? We have one million men and forty-five hundred tanks. We outnumber the enemy two-to-one. I hardly consider them . . . formidable."

Saddam's obvious displeasure did not appear to worry the deputy commander, a husky clean-shaven young major general named Abbas al-Sadi. Like his superior, the air force commander, Sadi was a distant cousin of Saddam's. Unlike his superior, Sadi was an experienced fighter pilot whose men respected him.

He addressed Saddam coolly. "What is formidable, sir—and what I referred to—is the Allied air strength. Our nine hundred aircraft against their two thousand. Two thousand, sir. To me, that is formidable."

Saddam said, "I agree that in the air the Allies are formidable. Indeed, yes. But that really poses us no serious threat. And do you know why?"

The question, as all knew, was rhetorical. Saddam continued, "Our *cause* is the great difference. We fight for justice. We fight for survival and for honor. What do they fight for? Oil! Oil, and the Emir's seventeen-year-old whores, and King Fahd's Rolls-Royces. No, gentlemen, we have nothing to fear. We will prevail, I promise you. I honestly doubt that it will be necessary to commit our air force. The Allied planes will fall like stricken sparrows under the withering fire of our superb aerial defense system. Believe me, my brothers, the Americans and their Arab puppets will be taught an unforgettable lesson!"

Listening to the shrill reedy voice, watching the fixed, almost trancelike gaze, Adnan imagined himself jumping up and firmly contradicting the president. This often happened to Adnan in these meetings. The scene in his imagination was always the same: Excuse me, sir, he would say, and go on to explain that as His Excellency was well aware, he, Adnan Dulaimi, had spent considerable time in the United States. He knew the Americans. His Excellency was taking too lightly the American resolve.

History, Adnan would say, was the best teacher. Ask the Japanese about American resolve. Ask the Germans. The experience in Vietnam should be discounted, for those mistakes would not be repeated. This time the Americans would not fight an inhibited war. This time, for a thousand different reasons—not the least of which was the collapse of the Soviet Union—the Americans would mount a massive and merciless campaign.

Adnan was hardly aware that he was standing, facing Saddam, who was surrounded by three or four generals. The meeting was over. ". . . well, Dulaimi, how are you feeling?" Saddam was asking.

"Fine, thank you, sir, top-notch," said Adnan.

Saddam punched Adnan's shoulder playfully. "That American woman you want me to talk to, the one on WCN—" He snapped his fingers to recall the name, then pointed a finger at Latif Jassim, his information minister.

"Christine Campbell," Jassim said.

Saddam turned to Adnan again, now with a knowing smile. "Yes, I've seen her on the television. Very attractive. You like that type, eh, Dulaimi? Tall, well-built blondes?" Saddam's smile broadened. "You have good taste, my boy. Yes, good taste!"

Adnan hardly heard him. Again, in his mind, he was berating the president. This time regarding Amir. Second Lieutenant Amir Badran, whose father was Jamal Badran, whom you murdered. So you see, sir, not only have you killed the father, you have also killed the son. At least he might as well be dead. And I am sure he would prefer death.

". . . Sunday the twentieth," Latif Jassim was saying. "Ten o'clock in the morning, for no longer than one hour. Cameramen, technicians, and all equipment will be provided by Iraqi TV." He wheeled around and joined Saddam, who had already left the room.

Now Adnan realized what Jassim had said. Saddam had agreed to a one-hour WCN interview with Chris Campbell four days from today, January 20 at 10:00 A.M. Adnan left a message for Chris with the concierge at her hotel, then attended his other scheduled meetings, and finally set about the unhappy task of telling Hana about her brother.

As a third-year medical student, Hana had been pressed into service as a physician's aide at the new hospital in the fashionable suburb of Amiriyah. When Adnan found her that evening, she was at a class in infant nutrition. The UN sanctions had created critical food shortages. As the hospital's chief obstetrician had sourly remarked, all patriotic citizens were expected to make sacrifices, babies included.

Not two minutes after Adnan arrived, an air-raid drill was announced. The limited space of the hospital's shelter required students and temporary personnel to use the shelter in a nearby abandoned villa. With several dozen others, Hana and Adnan trooped down the tree-lined street to this shelter, which was furnished like a clubroom, with television, a library, even a kitchen. The bunker had been built during the war with Iran, mainly to accommodate Baath Party officials and their families residing in the area.

The drill was over, and they had returned to the hospital and were having tea in the cafeteria when Adnan finally told Hana about Amir. She did not react at all as Adnan anticipated. She listened quietly, closing her eyes now and then as though to block out the anguish, and then asked Adnan to take her to him. Even then, in Amir's room at the hospital in Muadham, watching him sleep and not a muscle below the neck twitching, she seemed almost serene.

She stood at the foot of the bed for a long time, gazing at her brother with an eerie calm, and then all at once she turned away and said to Adnan, "Take me home, please."

Not once did Hana express the slightest curiosity about the accident, nor Amir's presence in a commando unit. Adnan had fully expected a bitter reminder of his assurance that Amir would not be transferred into the commandos. But then he realized that those questions were important only to him. To Hana, nothing could change what had happened. Nothing would bring Amir's arms and legs back to life. How or why it happened made no difference.

Moreover, Hana seemed indifferent to the possibility of war. That, too, to her, was now unimportant. After all, before the war had even started—if, indeed, it would start—it had cost her two of the people closest to her, her father and her brother. Leaving only Adnan. The man she loved, the man she planned to marry. It was as though by not recognizing the imminence of war, or pretending not to, she could no longer be affected by it. Nothing else could hurt her.

All this occurred to Adnan hours after he had taken her home, returned to the ministry to deal with the interminable paperwork, and finally gone to his flat. It was early morning, before dawn. He had been unable to sleep. Bundled in a heavy wool cardigan sweater and a sleeveless ski jacket, he sat on the terrace and smoked one of Jamal's *Fior de Rafael Gonzales*. He rationed the cigars, no more than one per day, usually after breakfast. The five boxes would last at least four months.

In the distance, following the downstream curve of the river, the city lights glowed brightly. An inviting sight for attacking planes. Yes, right this way, please, follow the arrow. But he knew that Saddam's description of Baghdad's aerial defense system as "superb" was no exaggeration. The early warning radar would provide more than adequate time for the interceptors to scramble. The attackers who evaded the interceptors would then face the lethal gauntlet of the city's outer ring of SAM missiles and radar-controlled antiaircraft.

Lethal gauntlet, Adnan thought. God help me, I am beginning to sound like him, like Saddam. Next, I will be addressing conscripts, assuring them that it is an honor to die for your country and your President. Yes, your President, who defies the strongest nation on earth and promises the enemy the most humiliating of defeats.

It reminded Adnan of the last line in a World War II film he admired, *The Bridge on the River Kwai*. "Madness!" the character, a British medical officer, had cried. "Madness!"

3

As a gag gift for his thirty-eighth birthday, Lieutenant Colonel Leonard Dozier's fifteen-year-old niece in Laguna Niguel, California, had sent him an oversized calendar. The pages for each month were newspaper-sized, each day of the week enclosed in a block of white space for use as a memo pad. The calendar was propped on an aluminum easel behind Dozier's desk in his office at Dhahran International Airport. A plastic model of a UH-60 Black Hawk helicopter emblazoned with the silver crown and wing insignia of the 153rd Aviation Regiment, the Sky Kings, was perched atop the easel's three-legged frame.

Dozier, C.O. of the 153rd's 6th Battalion, had red-penciled tomorrow's date, Thursday, January 17, 1991, the second day of the expiration of the UN ultimatum. Dozier had made a bet with himself that the Allied attack on Iraq would not commence within a week of the designated day. Now, on the day after the deadline, he was beginning to change his mind.

For one thing, in the last twenty-four hours every serviceable UH-60 had been hauling fuel to various forward area refueling points. Enough fuel was already stockpiled at these FARPs to keep the attack helicopters in continuous operation for weeks.

The increased level of activity here at Dhahran, Dozier knew, was being duplicated at every base throughout Saudi Arabia and the Emirates. The two U.S. Navy carriers in the Persian Gulf, the *Midway* and the *Ranger*, were steaming north, closer to Iraq and Kuwait. Four other U.S. carriers were in the Red Sea on full alert, their aircraft armed and ready for launch. Here, every time you looked around, a flight of F-15s or A-10s was landing or taking off on one of the parallel runways. Or KC-10 tankers, or Wild Weasel F-4Gs with full loads of HARMs and Sparrows. Yes, something big was about to happen, you could smell it.

Whenever it started, tomorrow or a week from tomorrow, Len Dozier's battalion would conduct itself like the professional fighting machine that it was. Dozier, who had graduated tenth in his class of 1974 at West Point, had built, bullied, and fine-tuned his people into the smoothest, best-run, and most elite unit in the regiment. A team, each element integrated almost imperceptibly into the other. There was no room for aces or prima donnas.

He intended to stamp this fact indelibly into the psyche of the officer standing at attention before him, Major Elaine Mason. He had sent word to her at Al Kalir that he wanted her back in Dhahran no later than noon today, the sixteenth, and he didn't give a damn how she got there. Swim, for all he cared. Thirty seconds before, at 11:59 on the minute, she had walked into his office, saluted crisply, and said, "Major Mason reporting as ordered, sir."

An Al Kalir Ops officer whom Mason said was an old friend had arranged for her to fly down in a courier plane. She had come directly to the office after landing and was still in her flight suit. But she looked quite calm and composed, almost relaxed, which annoyed Dozier. And she had taken time to comb her hair and apply makeup, which further annoyed him.

"Where is your crew?" he asked.

"At Al Kalir, sir," Elaine said. "Waiting for the helicopter to be repaired. We lost an engine—"

"—you took an unarmed helicopter into a hostile environment. You jeopardized your own safety and that of your crew. I would like you to tell me, Major, why in the name of all that is sensible—tell me why you undertook that mission in the first place?"

The question did not surprise Elaine. As she had remarked to Nick Harmon that morning at breakfast at Al Kalir, this would be Dozier's first comment. Nick said he didn't see how Dozier could find fault with Elaine's decision to try to extricate the SOF team. She had done her job and done it well. In Nick's opinion, Dozier had nothing to complain about.

Yes, but Nick didn't know Lieutenant Colonel Leonard Francis Dozier. The 6th Aviation Battalion C.O., Elaine said, hated women. Which hardly made him unique in the U.S. Army, but at least the other sexist bigots made a semblance of civility toward their female colleagues. Not Len Dozier. To him, the only women privileged to wear uniforms were nurses. For Dozier, as Elaine said, to be saddled with women pilots—one of them a major, no less—was like having a bone lodged in his throat.

Now, true to her prediction, Dozier went on, "You placed yourself in a position that left you entirely at the mercy of the enemy. My God, is that what you call leadership?"

"Excuse me, Colonel, but you know the genesis of that mission as well as I do," Elaine said. "I was the closest asset, I was asked to go in. I really had no choice."

"The hell you didn't! You were instructed *not* to proceed into Iraq if you failed to make contact with the

SOF team. You failed to make contact, but you went on in anyway. Why?"

"Colonel, sir, I asked for, and received, permission from AWACS to go in."

"Why, Major? Why did you go in?"

"I should think the explanation is obvious," she said.

"It certainly is," Dozier said. "It's called grandstanding."

"Excuse me?"

"You heard me, Mason. Grandstanding."

Elaine knew Dozier was correct in one respect: She should never have entered Iraqi airspace, not without an escort, and certainly not in an unarmed helicopter.

FIRST U.S. SERVICEWOMAN IN COMBAT!

Maybe Dozier called it right, she thought, maybe she really was trying to draw attention to herself. But she could not help smiling inwardly, thinking now of Nick. After all, if she had not "grandstanded," she would not have had to make an emergency landing at Al Kalir and for sure would not have ended up in bed with Nick Harmon. All of which was something she had to deal with, and soon, but did not want to think about now.

She said, "Colonel, you can believe whatever you like, whatever makes you happy. All I know is that I was there, I was asked to go in, and I didn't think twice about it."

"Just like you didn't think even *once* about making yourself a big television star," Dozier said.

Yes, of course, Elaine thought, that's what it was all about: her little two-minute WCN "Gulf Watch" segment with Christine Campbell. She relaxed. "You really got your nose out of joint with that one, didn't you, Len?"

"Yes, Elaine, I did, and so did a lot of other people around here. We all work hard, together, and it's not pleasant when somebody presents himself as *the* hero. Herself, I mean."

"Heroine, you also mean," Elaine said.

"Yeah," he said, thinking that he had never realized what a wise-ass she was, and how sad to see what the U.S. Army had come to, giving a cunt like this a pair of oak leaves. And if that wasn't bad enough, making a slot for her in the regular army. PR, he thought, public relations. The army labored under the false assumption that it had to please its critics, mainly a few female members of Congress and some loudmouth feminists.

But that did not mean that he, Len Dozier, should pander to it. In the 6th Battalion you pulled your own weight, or you got out. From pilot to pastry cook, you attained and maintained Len Dozier's standards. That was what made the 6th the best and would keep it the best. And it did not matter if you were a man, woman, or elephant. He had heard all that garbage about him resenting reservists, especially if they were women. Pure, unadulterated bullshit.

He continued to Elaine now, "Major, I told you when you came into this outfit, it is a team operation. T-e-a-m. No aces, no prima donnas. You don't want to be on the team, apply for a transfer. I'll approve it."

"Very gracious of you, Len. Especially when you know there aren't any open slots for a major in another outfit. Len, can I sit down?" she asked, and added, "Colonel, sir."

"No, Major, you may not sit down," Dozier said. "And I'm glad you mentioned your rank. As a field grade officer, you should be doing less flying and more administrative work. And I happen to have—"

"—less flying? That's how you're going to punish me, isn't it?"

"I happen to have," Dozier said, completing his interrupted sentence, "the perfect . . . administrative . . . assignment for you."

"I did a job that attracted a little attention because I'm a woman, and you're penalizing me for it." Elaine sank into the armchair in front of Dozier's desk. To hell with him and his military protocol. "Why?"

"I do not consider it penalizing to ask an officer to assume duties commensurate with his rank. Excuse me, *her* rank," Dozier said. Speaking, he had pulled a green file folder out from under a stack of correspondence and slid it across the desk to Elaine. It was a 201 personnel file. The name on the plastic folder tab read *Griggs, Cynthia*.

Dozier said, "Corporal Griggs is an engine mechanic, a very good one, as you'll see from her various endorsements and evaluations."

"I know her," Elaine said, not opening the folder, and picturing Cynthia Griggs: young, not unattractive, almost demure as Elaine recalled her. "What's she done?"

"How do you know she's 'done' something?"

"Come on, Len, you're not putting on this whole production because she's been named Soldier-of-the-Month. What's she done?"

"She claims a man in HHC raped her."

Elaine knew Dozier expected some display of emotion but she was damned if she'd give him the satisfaction. "Did he?" she asked.

"I don't know," Dozier said. "His name is Robert Lefcourt. He's a sergeant in supply."

Robert Lefcourt, Headquarters and Headquarters Company, Elaine thought, unable to place the man immediately. She opened Cynthia Griggs's folder. An ID photograph was stapled to the inside cover, the pixie face and pageboy chestnut hair. Date of birth, 5 Dec '68, a 1986 Vernon, Texas, high school graduate. She planned to make the army a career and had already submitted her reenlistment papers, this time for a six-year hitch.

An image materialized in Elaine's mind of Robert Lefcourt raping the girl. Lefcourt, whom she envisioned as brutish, thoughtfully pillowing Griggs's head with a rolled-up towel, clamping one hand over her mouth to stifle her screams, spreading her legs with the other hand and his knee, and plunging himself into her.

". . . want you to talk to her and convince her to drop the charges," Dozier was saying.

His voice fragmented the scene Elaine had so vividly conjured up. "Drop the charges?" she asked.

"Drop the charges," Dozier said. "Otherwise, it means a regimental investigation. I'd prefer to handle the matter on strictly a company level. In other words, Major, it stays in the family."

Elaine closed the folder and placed it on her lap. "What you mean, Len, is you want it quashed."

Dozier said coolly, "What I mean, Elaine, is that it's a bad rap for this battalion. How many times do I have to say it?"

"Suppose Corporal Griggs doesn't see it your way?"

"I want you to make sure that she does."

"Now how am I supposed to do that?"

"By talking sense to her. Woman-to-woman, you know."

"No, Len, I don't know. Explain it to me."

Dozier sighed, exasperated. "I already did. The honor of the battalion. Our good name."

Your good name, you mean, Elaine thought. She said, "Suppose the guy is guilty?"

"He'll be disciplined."

"How can he be disciplined if she drops the charges?"

"Believe me, Elaine, if he's guilty, he'll pay for it."

"How? With company punishment? You'll restrict him to base? If he's guilty, they should string him up by his testicles, damn it!"

The corner's of Dozier's mouth crinkled with the hint of a self-righteous smile. It was as though he had finessed Elaine into making a point, his point: To a woman, the mere accusation of rape was automatic proof of the accused man's guilt. He said, "Suppose the girl is lying?"

"Why should she lie about something as serious as that?"

The smile reappeared, he had scored again. "Are you suggesting that that's never happened? A woman concocting a story to get a man in trouble? Revenge, jealousy, who knows?" The smile vanished. "Convince her not to push it, Elaine. That's all I ask."

Elaine said nothing but was tempted to tell him to do his own dirty work. He seemed to read her mind. "It's the same thing we're doing with your"— he paused, searching for the right word or phrase—"case," he said delicately. "Your case."

"My case?" she asked, but knew that he meant her hazardous flight into Iraq. More accurately, her foolish flight.

"Yeah, your case," he said. "I've convinced CENTCOM that you displayed great initiative and courage. Frankly, I think you should have your ass kicked."

"But that would be a black mark on the battalion's reputation," Elaine said. "Excuse me, *your* reputation."

"Not only that, Major, but I'd bet five dollars to a dime that somebody, either at regiment or CENTCOM, would decide you'd be more useful—in your rank—in a staff job."

"A staff job," Elaine repeated dryly, knowingly. "So what you're saying . . . *sir,* is that it's only because of your generosity and understanding that I'm flying? Otherwise, I'd be in regimental HQ, maybe in Plans and Operations, or maybe even running the mess-hall?"

"You got it, lady."

Elaine rose. "So unless I cooperate with you, and somehow talk Corporal Griggs into cooperating with me, I end up pushing a pencil somewhere?"

"Glad we understand each other."

Elaine pointed to the calendar on the aluminum easel, the reddened January 17 block. "Don't you think the fact that we may be fighting a war is a little more important than your problem with Corporal Griggs?"

"One thing has nothing to do with the other, Major."

"Sure thing, Colonel," Elaine said, after a moment.

PART TWO
STORM

ELEVEN

Chris knew it was a dream and struggled to wake up out of it. The woman in the gossamer dress, whose face Chris could not see, stood near an open window. The woman held a kerosene lamp. The lamp flame, flickering brightly in the night breeze, cast the woman's shadow on the wall. The shadow swayed drunkenly.

Words of admonition sprang to Chris's lips, "For God's sake, Mom, can't you go a single day without drinking?" But she did not say them and said instead, "Mom, watch out for the fire." She watched silently now as the breeze whipped the hem of her mother's dress onto the open end of the kerosene lamp's globular glass shade. The dress burst into flame.

"Christine!" her mother screamed. "Christine!"

Chris watched the flames consume her mother. The lamp fell to the floor. The glass shade shattered. The lamp exploded with a dull, distant boom that shook the room.

Immediately, also from a distance, came another muffled boom, and then another, and still another. Chris sat upright in bed and opened her eyes. The curtains of the partially open window across the room slapped gently against the window casing. Outside, lightning whitened the dark sky. More muffled claps of thunder. Chris looked at the green-glowing LED figures of the clock radio on the night table.

2:38 A.M.

She turned to the window again. Now the sky was

bright with little orange and white balls floating upward in a series of graceful arcs. More distant booms, which she now realized were not thunder, and the bursts of light were not lightning.

She got off the bed, slipped into her robe and slippers, and hurried from the room. The corridor echoed with excited voices and heavy footfalls on the carpeted floor. Joe Daley, the AP stringer, raced past her.

"What the hell is going on?" Chris asked.

"The war! The fucking war's started!" came another voice, Diane McCaffrey's. Diane, of the *Los Angeles Times*, was following Joe Daley.

Chris's attention was momentarily focused on the top-coat Diane wore over her nightgown, and the sports jacket over Joe's pajamas, and the interesting fact that both had emerged from Diane's room. And then the words made sense. The war had started.

"Where are you going?" Chris called out to them.

"Downstairs!" Joe said. He pulled open the fire exit door. Diane, directly behind him, stopped.

"Chris, that phone line they put in for WCN," Diane said. "Can we use it?"

"It's not working. Something's wrong with it," Chris lied, pleased at thinking so fast. She'd be crazy to allow someone else to use it.

"You're a real sport, Chris. Thanks," Diane said, and hurried down the fire stairs. The heavy door slammed shut behind her. An instant later it opened. Leila, the chambermaid-Mukhabarat agent, stepped into the corridor. She looked bewildered, her hair askew, the top buttons of her maid's uniform unbuttoned. She saw Chris and stepped hastily back into the stairway. Chris wanted to laugh. Leila was certainly devoted to her work.

Chris moved toward the fire exit herself, then stopped. She returned to her room. She switched on the overhead light and glanced at herself in the dresser mirror. She ran a comb through her hair and dabbed on some lipstick, started out again, and again returned. She pulled her camel's hair coat from the closet and threw it over her shoulders and left the room. If the camera was rolling, not only would she have gone on the air shivering from the freezing cold, but she'd be wearing only her goddamn pajamas.

Climbing to the roof, she rehearsed her opening remarks. "I'm up here on the roof of the Al-Rashid Hotel, an eyewitness to an air raid. As you can see . . ." No, too corny. Outside, the explosions were louder, closer. She could feel the reverberations in her fingers on the stairway's metal banister and in her legs through the thin soles of her slippers. "This is Chris Campbell, and WCN is bringing you . . ." No, that was even worse. The hell with it, she'd simply describe what she saw. The words would flow naturally.

By the time she reached the roof, Ramon Sandoval had already set up the camera. Tom Layton, bundled in a goosedown ski jacket, was talking into a hand-held microphone. Behind him, the night sky seemed filled with the arcing red and white balls and the incessant crump-crump-crump of antiaircraft artillery. The horizon was bright with flashes of white, followed immediately by the dull rumble of explosions.

". . . well, as you can see, this is it, the war has started," Tom was saying, gesturing Chris to join him. "Here's Chris Campbell. Chris, I think we're seeing history made . . ." He handed Chris the microphone.

Ramon Sandoval backed the camera away for a broader background view. For a moment, Chris was speechless. For the first time, watching the spectacle in the sky, she felt fear. When it had started, her only thought was to get on the air with the story. But those were real guns firing. Real planes dropping real bombs. And at the same time, deep in her mind, was the knowledge that her Minder, Salim al-Sadr, was absent. She did not have to worry about censorship.

". . . trying to collect my thoughts," she heard herself saying. "As Tom told you, we're on the roof of the Al-Rashid Hotel in the center of Baghdad. You can see the flashes of light, and you can hear the bombs. At least I think they're bombs—I've yet to hear any

planes." She glanced at Tom Layton for confirmation
but he had moved off camera and was scanning the sky
with binoculars.

". . . it's like a Fourth of July celebration back
home," Chris continued. "Except that what we're seeing
is certainly not fireworks! We can't tell yet exactly what's
happening—oh! Ramon, can you pick that up?"

Behind them, not far off, an enormous blaze of white
had erupted. ". . . the presidential palace!" Tom Layton was shouting. "I think the palace was hit!"

"Tom!" Chris called. "Tom Layton! Can you hear any
planes?" She stepped over to him with the microphone.

Sandoval swung the camera on Tom. "No, Chris, no
planes. But they're up there, that's for sure!" He
pointed into the distance miles to the north, at the spotlights shining on the golden dome and the four minarets
of the Kadhimiya mosque. "The city lights are still on,
which seems strange. Every darn light is still on. Oh,
hold it! There's a whole section that just went dark.
Over there, to the west. They've just blacked it out! And
there's another street gone dark, and another! They're
blacking the city out now, all right!"

"Yes!" Chris said into the microphone. "Listen!" She
held the microphone in the air. The shrill wailing of air
raid sirens drowned out all other sound.

Chris held the microphone above her head another
moment, then backed away from Tom. Ramon Sandoval
tracked her with the camera as she returned to her original position. Behind her was what had become her signature background for "Gulf Watch" telecasts: the
illuminated domes of the two minarets in downtown
Baghdad. The domes were dark now, as was the bridge
and the entire city.

But the sky was bright with the red and white tracers
of antiaircraft and flashes of light, not only on the horizon but nearby as well, all accompanied by the constant
crunch of exploding bombs.

Chris remained on the air most of that morning,
much of the time on audio only—the satellite television
link was broken—as WCN's transmission switched back

and forth between world capitals for other reactions. Salim al-Sadr had finally shown up but seemed almost too dazed to even monitor Chris's off-camera conversations with Larry Hill in Washington. Larry repeatedly exhorted her to just stay with it.

"You're good, Chris!" he said. "You're great! It's a world beat, kid. It's just us and CNN! We're clobbering the networks!"

A world beat.

Later, she remembered how Larry's words had thrilled her. Tens of millions of people were seeing her face on a television screen, listening to her voice. Her name, she remembered thinking, would now be a household term. Her face, an icon. It was what she had worked for, what she wanted more than anything else. Not to mention Larry meeting her demand for a $50,000 bump in salary, up from her present $250,000. Only later did it occur to her that she had achieved all this only because a city was being destroyed, people were dying and maimed. Men, women, children.

A world beat.

The telecommunications center on Rashid Street, not far from the Al-Rashid Hotel, was the first target hit. A Tomahawk missile launched from a U.S. Navy cruiser, the *San Jacinto,* seven hundred miles away in the Red Sea, smashed into the side of the building with a 1,000-pound high-explosive warhead. Another Tomahawk, from the battleship *Wisconsin* anchored in the Persian Gulf, scored a direct hit on the presidential palace. Four other Tomahawks followed, all fired from U.S. naval vessels hundreds of miles away. Three of these four struck their preprogrammed targets.

Then, led by two F-117A Stealths, the first wave of aircraft arrived. One F-117A dropped a 2,000-pound GBU-27 laser-guided bomb squarely into the air shaft on the roof of the air force headquarters building. In all, in this initial attack on Baghdad, eighty-four coalition airplanes struck predetermined targets, including the Parliament building, the Ministry of Defense, the Infor-

mation Ministry, all the major telephone exchanges, and
Al-Mutana airport.

Simultaneously, 150 other Allied aircraft attacked
strategic targets throughout the southern part of the
country, and in Kuwait: airfields, radar defense sites,
electrical stations, nuclear facilities, and all communications
and command installations.

"An attack of such massive size and ferocity has not
been mounted since World War Two," so said the BBC,
which Adnan Dulaimi had no reason to disbelieve. He
was awake when it started. Since midnight he had been
at his desk in the living room of his Zahra apartment,
preparing condensations of Defense Ministry dispatches
for the daily 10:00 A.M. Foreign Ministry staff meeting.

He heard the first bombs drop and thought it was
distant thunder. Then he heard the chainsaw rattle of
light antiaircraft. He listened carefully. Yes, gunfire. He
shut off the desk lamp and went out to the terrace. The
city was brightly lighted, cars moved along the boulevards
and across the bridges. A barge chugged south
down the river.

And then, in the distance, he saw the bursts of blinding
white light and heard the muffled echo of the detonations,
and felt the rumbling of the earth. A moment
later the whole sky erupted. Red and yellow tracers
crisscrossed in the air, blobs of white from heavier antiaircraft
fire streaked up from the ground.

Off to the right now, following a thunderous explosion,
flames leaped into the air. The airport, he thought.
They were bombing Al-Mutana. They were bombing everywhere.
He knew the Americans. When they said no
Vietnam, they meant that this time they would overwhelm
their enemy from the very start, not nibble away.

But why did he hear no planes? The answer came to
him with the question. A missile attack. No, not entirely;
the antiaircraft fire was at too high an altitude for
missiles. It had to be planes. But how did they penetrate
the air defenses? The finest air defense system in the
Arab world. And the air force, where the hell was it? If
the Americans were bombing Baghdad—and probably

the rest of the country as well—and if they had somehow managed to jam or otherwise interfere with the air defense system, why hadn't the Iraqi Air Force intercepted and destroyed them?

Abruptly, the antiaircraft fire and the thud of exploding bombs stopped. The lights of the city had all gone out. The only lights visible were the headlights of automobiles and trucks. The vehicles, two on the bridge and one on the boulevard directly below, moved slowly, almost disdainfully. In the sudden silence the darkness seemed thick and impenetrable, a black cloud enveloping the city. The only sound to break the silence was the shriek of a lone ambulance siren and a ringing telephone.

The ringing continued. Adnan realized it was his own telephone. He hurried back into the living room, closed the terrace door and shuttered the venetian blinds, and groped in the dark for the phone on the desk. He picked it up and switched on the lamp.

"Yes . . . ?"

It was Hana. "It's started, hasn't it?"

"Yes, I'm afraid so," he said.

"You're all right?"

"Yes. Are you?"

"I'm fine." She forced a little laugh. "I'm scared to death, but I'm fine. It's Amir I'm worried about. Lying helpless in that hospital bed—"

"They're not hitting hospitals, I'm sure of that," Adnan said, although he was not sure of anything. "Now listen, don't leave the house." He felt like a fool saying it but did not know what else to say. What *could* he say: Don't worry, darling, everything will be all right . . . ? Well, everything would not be all right. It would never be all right again. An image of the Hebrew biblical figure of Samson popped into his mind. Samson, pulling the temple down around his head. Samson, Saddam, an unfortunate similarity of names.

"Adnan—"

"Don't leave the house," he said again. "Stay where you are."

After a few moments, when she did not answer, he realized the phone was dead. Either a relay station or the central communications building had been hit. Yes, of course, they must have targeted the whole communications system.

He placed the receiver gently into the cradle. It was as though he feared damaging the instrument, causing the system additional harm. Outside, the bombing had resumed. Now it was continuous and almost rhythmic, and he knew that it came from airplanes. It was the second wave of the attack.

2

Eight 358th TFW F-16s participated in the second wave. Ed Iverson commanded the eight-airplane strike package, whose objective was a Scud missile assembly facility ten miles south of Baghdad. The eight 358th Falcons were to proceed in pairs to four separate initial points around the target complex, turn inbound and, from different directions and staggered altitudes, make near-simultaneous bomb runs.

Iverson led the first element of four, Viper Flight. Nick Harmon led the second flight, Gateway. Each airplane carried a full ordnance load, including two 2,000-pound MK-84 free-fall bombs. The eight F-16s had refueled shortly after takeoff and climbed to 25,000 feet for the first leg of the flight, then dropped down to 15,000 for their approach. The heavy overcast extended as far as the eye could see. From forty miles out, it resembled an opaque blanket, flashing silver and white with the explosions on the ground.

Nick, half listening to the babble of excited radio chatter from Wild Weasel and F-15s engaged in clearing Iraqi air defenses, watched the inferno that was downtown Baghdad grow larger and larger in his windscreen. Gateway's target was a warhead storage building. Nick and his wingman, thirty-two-year-old Major Kenneth Taft, would hold their 15,000-foot altitude—above most of the AAA—and fly point-to-point to their target via preselected checkpoints stored in the F-16's navigational computer. From a run-in distance of seventeen miles, they would proceed to the target on radar. The CCIP—continuously computed impact point—would determine the correct release point. And, at the precise moment, send the bomb to its destination, the storage building's L-shaped roof.

Off to his left, slightly behind him, Nick thought he could make out the ghostly silhouette of Gateway Two. In the dark, the wingman maintained position on the leader through radar. Nick felt suddenly alone, isolated in this plastic and metal cocoon. The adrenaline that only an instant before had been pumping through his body seemed to have stopped. It was almost peaceful.

I am going crazy, he thought. I am in an airplane, on a bomb run, moments away from the release point, and I feel as though I am floating on a soft cloud. Every nerve in my body should be screaming, I should be screaming. For another moment he wondered if perhaps he had not been hit, blown to atoms by a SAM, and this was why he felt so disembodied.

Passing the IP, Nick turned the F-16 toward the target and reconfigured the aircraft for bomb release. On the radar map on the right side MFD screen, the computer-generated crosshairs were fixed over the target. The waypoint indicator figures on the HUD read eleven miles from release point.

The ghostly green radar image sharpened as the target came closer. The L-shaped building materialized on the screen. The "in-range" indicator began flashing. Nick pushed the bomb release button on the control stick. For a moment nothing happened. On the HUD, the time delay cue flashed: The CCIP computer was not ready to release. One second, two, three. Then the letters R E L appeared on the screen: the computer had released the bombs. The F-16, free of the 4,000-pound burden, surged momentarily upward. Nick nudged the sidestick control forward and to the left. The airplane rolled smoothly away.

He transferred the radar image of the target to the

left MFD. The L-shaped building was defined with almost television resolution. If the MK-84s had been
equipped with nose cameras, on the MFD screen the
building would have grown larger and larger and more
detailed as the bombs hurtled toward it. The picture of
the building would have quickly encompassed the entire
viewing screen. And then, all at once, like a station on a
home television set that had just gone off the air, the
screen would display a mass of snow.

But even without a television camera, the effect was
almost the same. The radar image of the L-shaped
factory momentarily vanished from the MFD screen.
". . . got it, Nick!" Ken Taft shouted. "We both did!"

"Roger that," Nick said into his microphone. He
eased the throttle forward and began climbing. "Proceed to the rejoin point," he said into the microphone,
and continued climbing to 25,000 feet. The other two
airplanes of his flight, Gateway Three, and Four, reported successful drops and had climbed away to head
for the rejoin point.

The rejoin point was thirty-five miles away. It took
Nick nearly five minutes to get there. Again, one part of
him was an interested listener to the constant radio
voices, the brief, cryptic exchange of information and
orders. The other part of him remained at the run-in,
just before he released the bomb. The eerie sense of
being a third, omniscient entity, an observer. Detached,
disembodied. And now, uneasily, wondering about the
people inside the L-shaped factory. Waiting for their
lives to end. An eternity in and of itself.

You mean, he asked himself, this has only just now
occurred to you? It never entered your head before?

I did not allow it to, he answered himself.

So why now, now after it's done? And you sure as hell
weren't bothered a few months ago when you blew that
MiG out of the sky. In fact, if you remember, you were
proud of it. No, excuse me, elated. You were elated.

That was different. He was trying to kill me.

You are getting old.

No, I am getting a conscience.

Hey, come on, you had a job to do, and you did it.

Sure, that's what they all say.

He pondered all this a few more minutes, then forgot it. By the time he had landed at Al Kalir, been debriefed, celebrated with the other pilots, and agonized over the loss of one 358th F-16, he had satisfied himself that while it was indeed a matter of conscience, it was also something over which he had no control.

Something he had to live with.

3

They were almost too clumsy, too bumbling, which was what at first had confused Kowalski. For nearly that whole day, Sunday, January 20, wherever he went in Tel Aviv—to the supermarket, lunch at the Sheraton, the gasoline station, and now at Josie's—the same man and woman were there, driving the same car, a late model white Ford Escort sedan. The woman, wearing a gray nylon windbreaker and khaki skirt; the man, a camel's hair sports jacket and denim slacks. She, young, dark-haired, not particularly attractive; he, also young, medium height, thin, somewhat scruffy. So nondescript you would never give them a second glance. Unless you knew they were following you.

Josie's was a discotheque on the ground floor of a three-story building on Allenby Road in a once-fashionable and thriving area, now run-down and cramped with cheap bars and fast-turnover hotels. Like the neighborhood, Josie's had seen better times. The club's clientele now consisted of soldiers on leave, blue-collar workers, a few adventurous tourists, and civilian-clad U.S. Navy servicemen from the carriers and support vessels that visited Haifa.

Kowalski had been here only once, four or five weeks ago. He and Nick Harmon had wandered into the place one evening with Nick's friend, Zvi Sharok. They did not stay long, not with the blaring rock music and the eye-smarting strobe lights. Tonight, Kowalski had come here only to see if the man and the woman followed.

They sat at a table at the far end of the room. Kowalski, who was with Nadia, sat at the bar.

He ordered a glass of white wine for Nadia and a beer for himself. "The couple near the door," he said to her. "Do you know them?"

She was unable to hear him clearly over the music and the buzz of voices. He repeated the question into her ear. She glanced at the man and the woman at the table. She could not make out their faces through the blinking red and green strobe lights and the blue haze of tobacco smoke.

She shrugged. "I don't think so."

Kowalski said, "Go to the ladies' room and take a look at them."

"You're interested in the woman, is that it?"

"No, I am not interested in the woman."

"Then what do you care who they are?"

"Will you please do as I ask?"

Nadia shrugged again. She got off the barstool and walked across the room. Kowalski watched the man and the woman as Nadia strolled past their table. They paid no attention to her. She continued into the ladies' room.

"I asked for Amstel," Kowalski said to the barman who was just then serving the drinks. He had given Kowalski a bottle of Maccabee, a local brand.

"All we have tonight," said the barman.

"Why didn't you tell me?" Kowalski said, but he snatched the bottle and drank straight from it. His throat was very dry. The dryness of fear. All week, it had been clinging to him like a heavy hand on his shoulder, from the time Avi Posner notified him of the cancellation of Operation Presto. An American Special Forces team in Rutba had spotted the presence of Iraqi commandos. Satellite reconnaissance had completely missed them. What a piece of incredible luck, Posner said. Perhaps there was a God after all.

Nadia slid onto the barstool beside Kowalski. "I never saw them before," she said. She half smiled. "They look like cops."

Kowalski said nothing. He drank more of the beer

and stared at her. Nadia read his expression as skepticism. "I can smell them, my dear," she said. "And the woman is not very pretty, anyway." Nadia peered over her shoulder at the woman. "No tits."

Five years ago when she arrived in Israel, Nadia did not speak a word of English. Now, heavy Russian accent and all, she was more proficient in that language than in Hebrew. She was a fair-haired, firm-bodied woman with classic Slav features, the wide-set eyes and high-boned cheeks. Even wearing sandals, she towered over Kowalski.

A university graduate and kindergarten teacher, Nadia worked now as a waitress in a sidewalk café on the Esplanade near the Tel Aviv Sheraton. Kowalski had met her on a previous visit to Israel last year. What initially had attracted him was her remarkable resemblance to a woman he had known as a child.

". . . why are you so worried about those people?" Nadia was asking. She pinched his cheek playfully. "Have you been naughty?"

An hour before, when he picked Nadia up at her apartment, he had momentarily forgotten the man and the woman. Nadia was foremost in his thoughts. Just thinking about her excited him to erection. But now, sitting in the same room with the people who were following him and knowing they were watching him, a session with Nadia was the farthest thing from his mind.

He paid the bar bill and got off the stool. "Let's go," he said.

"I haven't finished my wine," Nadia said.

But he was already halfway toward the door. Nadia took her time finishing the wine and then left. She deliberately went out of her way to walk past the man and the woman at the table. They had just been served fresh drinks and apparently had no intention of leaving. The woman regarded Nadia appraisingly, but said nothing. The man again paid no attention.

Kowalski was waiting in the car. He had started the engine and switched on the headlights. He threw open the passenger door for Nadia. She got in and closed the door. "I still say they're cops," she said.

He said nothing. He drove off. He swung around the traffic circle and headed south down Allenby. He knew Nadia thought they were going to Jaffa, to the hotel, but he had already decided to drop her off at her flat. He would return to the embassy and make some phone calls. The digital numbers on the dashboard clock read 7:12. Still too early in Washington; on Sunday no one reported for work before noon.

Well, he could always call the right people at their homes. He had the private numbers. But no, that would look as though he was panicking. Especially when he demanded that they instruct the Israeli government to call off their surveillance. That would sound crazy, paranoid. Why make a fool of himself? He'd wait, play it cool.

Play it cool.

It was like a voice from above. A divine revelation. Playing it cool was precisely what the people who had followed him all day did *not* want him to do. That was why they were so obvious, so comically obvious. To test him.

No, not test him, give him a message. Yes, for sure, a message. And he knew the author of the message: Avi Posner. Yes, of course, and he should have realized it the moment Posner told him about Presto. Posner knew that Kowalski was the one who had informed the Iraqis of Presto. Posner was so casual about it. Posner's message was that they were on to him. Or believed they were.

And that was why the man and the woman were not following him now. They knew the message had been delivered. How seriously to take it was up to him.

How Posner learned of Kowalski's role in Presto was unimportant. Kowalski had acted so amateurishly he might as well have sent Posner a telegram. That clumsy, impulsive trip to Eilat. And it was not impossible that Achmed Ben Sallah was working both sides. No, that made no sense. Ben Sallah was an idealist, a man passionately devoted to his cause.

No, Posner had no hard evidence. His suspicions of Kowalski were no more than that, suspicions. But for all that, Kowalski knew that his days in Israel were over. He made a mental bet with himself: Within the next forty-eight hours the Israelis would quietly order him out of the country.

Vaguely, he heard Nadia's voice. Something about wine and spending the night with her. Her hand rested on his thigh, her fingers stroking him through his fly. Then he felt his fly being unzipped, and then her hair grazing his face as she bent her head down to him.

Her mouth enveloped him, warm and wet. He instantly grew hard. She enjoyed doing it while he was driving. A little piece of kinky business. My Bolshevik Depravee, he had nicknamed her after their first session.

"Mmm, so tasty!" she said, twisting her head around and smiling up at him, then immediately turning and swallowing him into her mouth again. But for only an instant. She knew exactly how far to bring him. She pushed herself away from him and zipped up his fly. She sat up. "Now stop and get me the wine, and then let's see how much you have learned from your last lesson. I intend to give you a test," she added sternly.

"Written or oral?" he asked, now all at once swept back into the delicious fantasy.

"Oral, of course," she said.

Frank Kowalski had first seen Nadia Volvovsky on the beach in front of the Dan Hotel. He jogged there daily, immediately before lunch, from the Dan up to the Hilton and back down to the Ambassador Hotel at the foot of the Esplanade.

She indulged herself with an hour in the sun every day before reporting for work. She relaxed on the sand with a folding plastic lawn chair, a bottle of Evian, a radio, and a book. The day they met he had just finished his run and she was packing her things to leave. They innocently happened to look at each other.

She saw it all in his eyes, she said. It was like watching a movie. She knew exactly what he wanted and how he wanted it. In truth, what she saw in his eyes was his own fantasy of being hurled back in time to a woman named Dana.

On the day of Kowalski's twelfth birthday, Dana, the twenty-eight-year-old daughter of a distant cousin of Kowalski's mother, came to live with the Kowalski family in Lynn, Massachusetts. Dana fascinated Frank, especially her strapping, robust figure. Often, when they were alone, she drew him to her in a playful embrace. The top of his head reached her breasts, which excited him and immediately produced a juvenile erection, which excited her.

One Sunday, his parents drove to Cape Cod for the wedding of one of Dr. Kowalski's patients. Dana decided to teach twelve-year-old Frank a game she called "slave." The boy proved an apt and eager pupil who obeyed the teacher's instructions to the letter. Not long afterward, the elder Kowalskis returned home earlier than expected from a Boston theater. Attracted by sounds of moaning from Frank's room, the parents found their son on his knees, straddled by the woman who stood over him, legs spread wide, ordering him to sink his face deeper into her pubis.

A moment before bursting into the room, Kowalski's mother had placed her ear to the door and heard the conversation between her son and the woman. To her dying day, Mrs. Kowalski recalled those words:

". . . am I doing it right, Dana?" Kowalski had asked in his pubescent soprano. "Am I doing good?"

"You're doing fine," Dana had replied. "Just fine. Oh, yeah! Yeah! Right there! Keep your tongue right there where I showed you. That's what they call The Man in the Boat. . . . Oh, yes! That's so beautiful! Isn't that beautiful, darling?"

The Man in the Boat.

Kowalski's parents immediately sent Dana back to

Wisconsin and young Frank to a psychiatrist. In the intervening years he managed, albeit infrequently, to find women who physically resembled Dana. Nadia was the first not only to comprehend the fantasy totally but also act it out with him.

Totally.

He was thinking about this now, lying naked on the comforter on the bed. In the top-floor room of the little beachfront hotel in Jaffa, the window was open. The night was unusually warm for January, almost balmy. The sound of the surf crashing up on the sand blended musically with the sound of water splattering into the porcelain bathtub in the bathroom. Nadia was taking a shower.

She had exhausted him, forcing him to work on her for nearly two hours. But it was the most gratifying and satisfying session yet. When she came, he thought the whole goddamn ceiling would fall on them. Or people in adjoining rooms would call the police. From all the screaming and moaning and thrashing about, it sounded like a murder was being committed.

As always, it began with her seated on the edge of the bed, ordering him to remove his clothes.

"Everything?" he asked.

"Everything," she said.

Naked, he stood before her. She fondled his testicles in the palm of one hand and with the other hand stroked his penis. This produced an immediate and enormous erection. But she pushed him away. She got up then, turning her back to him, the signal for him to unbutton her blouse. When he finished, he unhooked her brassiere. Slowly, garment by garment, he undressed her. Now she turned to face him, cupping her breasts, one in each hand. Immediately, he leaned forward and kissed one nipple, then the other. Then she lay on the bed on her back, pulling him down with her and placing his head between her thighs.

"Do you know what to do now?" she asked.

He gazed up at her, past the mound of her belly and the space between her breasts. "I think so," he said.

"That's not good enough."

"Then tell me," he said, and lowered his head deeper between her thighs, and his face into her groin. "Teach me what to do."

"What you do," she said, "is take it all in your mouth. With your tongue, you find The Man in the Boat. And do it right, or I'll spank you! Do you understand?"

He nodded, yes.

"You damn well better understand," she said, and to make the point slapped him hard on the buttocks. "You want more of that?"

He shook his head, no.

"Then do a good job."

As always, as he proceeded and Nadia's little climaxes grew lengthier and more intense, she changed positions, rolling him over and climbing on top of him, facing him, her thighs imprisoning his face. As she approached what she called the Big One, she began writhing furiously, pressing herself into his mouth, moving back and forth, up and down. And then, all at once, she clamped her hands around his head and held him against her and he could feel her muscles contracting. Then, in her orgasm, she screamed. The scream, this time, he was sure had continued a full five or ten seconds.

Then, gasping, she fell back on the bed, pulling him down on top of her. The final act of the game. She opened her legs and closed her fist around him, but before allowing him to enter, she said, "You will have to clean me out, you know that."

"Yes!" he said. "Yes! I will! I will!"

"Do you promise?"

"Yes! Please! I can't hold it!"

And with that she guided him into her. "Oooh!" he cried. "Oh, Jesus! Jesus Christ!" Everything inside him was exploding. She held him, arching her back so that he was deep inside her. "Oooh!" he groaned. "Christ! Christ! Christ!"

For a moment then, with him still inside her, their naked bodies slippery with sweat, they lay still. Then, slowly and gently, she eased him out of her and pushed his head down toward her belly.

"Do I have to?" he asked.

"You promised," she said.

"Don't make me do it, Nadia. Please don't."

"You promised."

"Next time," he said. "I swear I'll do it next time."

She regarded him coldly a moment and then all at once smiled. She drew him back up to her and kissed him. "All right, next time," she said.

"Do you forgive me?" he asked.

"I forgive you, this time," she said, which was what she always said.

So now, afterward, with Nadia in the shower, Kowalski lay atop the comforter, his mind focused once more on reality. Reality, meaning Avi Posner. Realistically, the worst that could happen was an Israeli demand for his recall. The only regret on that score was having to leave Nadia. Well, nothing is forever. And then again, maybe he'd damn well bring her to the States. Why not? He could swing a green card for her. Something to think about. Sure, put her up in her own place in Washington, get her a job. Something to think about, all right.

The bathroom door opened. He turned his head lazily to gaze at Nadia. She stood framed in the doorway, naked except for a towel she held almost primly in front of her. The towel covered her belly and thighs.

"I guess we'd better get dressed and get out of here," Kowalski said. The last two words were unspoken, frozen on his tongue as Nadia dropped the towel and he saw, gripped in both of her hands, a small pistol. A silencer was attached to the muzzle. A million words came to his lips, a million thoughts raced through his head. He had no time to speak the words, although the thoughts, each single one, were very clear.

The first bullet struck him just below the rib cage. It tore through his abdomen and shattered his kidneys and severed a main artery. The second bullet was slightly higher and straight into his heart, killing him instantly.

For him, the milliseconds between his life and death stretched on endlessly, quite literally an eternity.

During that eternity, one thought remained prominent and more disturbing than any of the others. It was the memory of Nadia's face when she shot him. Her face bore absolutely no expression. No emotion, which he found both astonishing and disappointing, because he had always believed she really cared for him.

Less than four minutes after Nadia fired the first shot, she was outside on the street, fully dressed, walking past the hotel toward a parked car. A late model white Ford Escort sedan. A man and a woman sat in the car, the woman behind the wheel, the man beside her. Nadia opened the rear door, tossed her gas mask and purse onto the seat, and got in. The woman started the engine and drove off.

"It's done," Nadia said, as the man twisted around in his seat to face her.

"One less enemy to worry about," the man said.

"For sure," Nadia said.

The woman looked at Nadia in the rear mirror. "You're being reassigned to Madrid."

The man smiled blandly. "You'll have to brush up on your Spanish, Nadia," he said. He started to say something else, then apparently thought better of it. He peered at her a moment, then turned to the front. Nadia knew the man well and knew that what he had decided not to say would have been some tasteless remark. A wisecrack, probably about the job turning out to be more enjoyable than she had expected.

"What was so strange about it—" she started to say, and stopped abruptly. The sky in front of them had erupted in a blaze of light, followed an instant later by the rumble of the Scud's explosion.

"I think it landed in the ocean," the woman said. She looked at Nadia in the rearview mirror. "You were saying that something was strange about it?"

"Oh," said Nadia, after a moment, remembering. "He said I reminded him of some other woman. I think he said her name was Dana."

TWELVE

"Victory is near! Forty-eight more enemy planes have been shot down, bringing the total for the three days to one hundred and seventy. The president has stated that those responsible for the cowardly attacks—"

The somber voice of the man reading the 2:00 P.M. news on Baghdad Radio halted in mid-sentence. Adnan jiggled the car radio's volume control knob, but the only sound from the Chrysler's WrapAround Sound speakers was the hollow rush of empty air. A power failure at the radio station, a routine occurrence since the air raids started.

Adnan smiled wryly to himself. It was as though some Supreme Being was punishing Baghdad Radio for its irresponsible reports of countless enemy planes shot down. He had just swung into Al-Adham Street and pulled up in front of the Defense Ministry headquarters. More accurately, in front of where the building had been, past tense. Now the nine-story structure consisted only of an empty shell supported by four partially crumbled walls and, incongruously, an almost intact roof. The buildings on either side—a ten-story insurance company building and the seven story Bank of Iraq's main office—were undamaged. Directly across the street, also undamaged, was the Abasid Museum.

It was this surgical thoroughness that Adnan found both frightening and intriguing. American technological capability permitted a strike precisely on whatever target was desired. And whenever desired: The vaunted

Iraqi air defense system seemed a figment of someone's imagination. In fairness, however, there had been complaints of computer software malfunction. Sabotage was suspected.

"Sabotage," Adnan said aloud. Sabotage, that perennial, reliable scapegoat. He got out of the car and stood gazing at the still-smoldering remains of the building.

The rays of the late afternoon sun filtered through the jagged hole in the roof and shone rainbowlike into the gutted interior of the building. The bomb had plunged through the roof and the ceilings of the top five floors, and into the fourth floor where it exploded. More accurately, *im*ploded. The steel-reinforced concrete exterior walls had contained the force of the detonation and directed the energy inward. What remained of the building's interior was little more than a mound of rubble composed of pulverized furniture, smashed pipes and shredded electrical wire, chunks of plaster and lengths of metal lath dangling from the walls like broken sticks of black spaghetti.

Normally, the area in front of the Defense Ministry headquarters was cordoned off, although the street itself—especially at this time of day—would be crowded with pedestrians and vehicular traffic.

Normally.

Today the street was virtually deserted. And everything so silent, as though the black and white pall of smoke hovering over the city had muffled all sound except the thunderous explosions of the missiles. Which explained the empty streets: air raid in progress. During the day, all day, Tomahawk missiles from the battleships sped at rooftop height through the city, each one programmed for a specific target. Electrical generating stations, water purification plants, communications centers, fuel storage facilities.

At night the planes came. Wave after wave of bombers and fighters. From dusk to dawn, horizon to horizon, the yellow and red balls of the arcing tracers of the antiaircraft batteries filled the sky. The night echoed with the constant hammering of the guns.

"Sabotage," Adnan said again, aloud, as he picked his way through the debris to a blast-proof door. The door opened onto a metal stairway that descended five floors into a series of bunkers. Each bunker was a self-contained unit consisting of a large central room, a few cubicles for high-ranking officers, and a dormitory living quarters for enlisted personnel.

Adnan's "office" was a makeshift desk jammed in with a dozen similar desks in the central room. In addition to his regular duties as liaison officer to the Foreign Ministry, he had been temporarily assigned to the Defense Ministry's intelligence section to help correlate damage reports. Yesterday's reports were so negative as to be almost unbelievable. Today's reports were worse.

The bunker was noisy with ringing telephones, the clack of teleprinters, excited voices. Some enlisted men were clustered in a corner, listening to Baghdad Radio, which had just come back on the air with a revised count of downed Allied planes. As of noon today, one hundred and seventy-six. The Allies had been warned, said the announcer. Blame no one but George Bush and his cowardly Arab stooges for the tragic deaths of these misguided soldiers.

And, for good measure, Tel Aviv and Haifa were burning. Iraqi missiles were at this moment raining death and destruction upon the Zionists, whose air force had been completely destroyed.

". . . and I heard that half of the pilots we've captured are Israelis," a young sergeant was saying to a second lieutenant wearing earphones and monitoring a command radio frequency. "The treacherous bastards are flying planes with American markings!"

"That's fine, but we're still getting the shit blasted out of us," the second lieutenant said. He noticed Adnan and pointed to a glass door behind him. "The Old Man wants to see you."

Adnan and the Old Man, a full colonel whose name was Taher Ayel and who was forty-four years old, were longtime friends. Taher Ayel, like Adnan, was a graduate of both the Military Academy and the higher military studies school at Al Bakr, and a decorated veteran of the Iran-Iraq War.

Adnan knocked once and entered the tiny fiberboard-walled office. Taher, a short man with rich black curly hair and an impeccably trimmed black mustache, motioned him to sit. The only extra chair in the room was a canvas camp chair in front of the bridge table that served as the colonel's desk. The table was extraordinarily neat except for a large cut-crystal ashtray filled with cigarette butts, and Taher had just lit a fresh one. He offered the open pack, English Player's. Adnan declined.

"What word of the air force?" Taher asked.

"Didn't you hear the two o'clock news? They're knocking down Allied planes left and right," Adnan said, and briefly described his visit a few hours ago to air force HQ at Al-Mutana airfield. The complex of air force buildings and the airport's runways simply did not exist. Gone, vanished from the face of the earth.

Taher said, "It's probably the same at every other goddamn airbase. We can't get a plane into the air. No wonder they're grinding us up! What are they saying about it at general staff?"

"A better question is what they're *not* saying about it," Adnan said. He winced as the walls of the bunker all at once reverberated and the glass door rattled. "Tomahawk," he said. "They have a distinct sound, a kind of dull whump." He smiled sourly. "I'm getting pretty good at recognizing it."

Adnan waited a moment, listening for another missile, then went on, "What the General Staff is not saying, Taher, is that every time we launch an interceptor—from the bases with runways that are still functioning—it's shot down. I mean, these people are having a field day. Turkey shoot is what the Americans call it. It means all you do is aim, fire, and you can't miss hitting something."

"Turkey shoot," Taher said in English, the language Adnan had used for the phrase. "You make them sound like supermen, and us like some helpless natives."

"No, they're not supermen," Adnan said. "But this just didn't happen accidentally or coincidentally. The Americans didn't manage that incredible buildup without preparation. They've planned it for years. We knew it but made no protest. They were our friends. They were on our side, remember? We just sat by and watched them store supplies and ammunition—tanks, trucks, you name it—at sites close to Saudi Arabia, and some on ships that always sailed in nearby waters. So it didn't take them long, sometimes only a few days, to build airbases in the desert. I mean, bases with everything. From concrete runways to water purification plants to heated latrines."

"I hope no one else hears you make that speech," Taher said.

"Why? Am I saying something that's not true, or is a secret?" Adnan waited for Taher's reply, but Taher only shrugged. Adnan said, "What did you want to see me about?"

"I've been hearing rumors," Taher said after a moment. "Rumors about high-level officers getting themselves stood up against a wall." He lit a fresh cigarette from the butt of the old one. "Treason is what I heard. Know anything about it?"

"Not a thing," Adnan said. "Where was all this supposed to have happened?"

"I don't know. I thought you might."

"I don't believe it," Adnan said, thinking of Hassan Marwaan and wondering if Hassan and his people had made their move. No, Adnan would have heard. "The rumors you're talking about are just that, rumors."

"That's good to know," Taher said blandly. "All right, get back to work."

"That's what you wanted to see me about?"

"Yes." Taher's face remained expressionless. "I always find it's a good idea to know who we're taking orders from."

Adnan spent the next two hours preparing and typing up himself—the computer printers were not operating

—a summary of bomb damage in the Baghdad area. He would deliver the report to the Ministry of Industry and Military Production. The ministry's buildings, on the eastern edge of Al-Mutana airfield, had been hit but not seriously.

It was four-thirty by the time he completed the report, had it endorsed by Taher, and was back on the street, driving. He turned on the radio and immediately switched it off. Baghdad Radio was the only station operating. More glorious victories. Another dozen Allied planes shot down.

Just as he swung into the Rasafi Square traffic circle, the air raid sirens sounded. He continued around the circle, and onto Amin Street toward Shuhada Bridge. In forty minutes, it would be dark. Tonight's wave of Allied bombers must be well on their way, refueled from the tankers, eager to commence the evening's sport.

A fencelike metal barrier blocked the entrance to Shuhada Bridge. Adnan cursed himself for not remembering. More accurately, not wanting to remember: The damned bridge was closed, unsafe for traffic. It had been hit the first night. Although the bridge roadway appeared intact, you could clearly see huge gouges in the ornate masonry of the two center arches.

He turned around and headed back to Rashid Street. He would pick up the Jumhuriya Bridge, which had not been hit. Not hit yet, he thought, and again found himself admiring the exquisite thoroughness of the Allied attack. Only two bridges had been bombed so far, Shuhada and the 14th of July Bridge. The others could easily have been knocked out, all of them, which made the situation even more ominous. It was as though the Allies were demonstrating that, at will, they could cut one side of the city completely off from the other. The result would be utter chaos.

Now, in the distance, the dull rumble of another explosion. The macadam road surface trembled. Madness, Adnan thought. True madness. Here he was, driving blithely through a city in the midst of an air raid. Other vehicles traveled the streets, army trucks, a few civilian automobiles, even some taxis. Not to mention an occasional pedestrian standing on the corner, interestedly observing the sky. And all this, like some surreal opera, to the music of air raid sirens.

The Mother of All Battles, he thought, as he proceeded along the nearly deserted boulevard and onto the Jumhuriya Bridge. He drove across the bridge at eighty-five kilometers an hour, a speed that only a few days ago would have brought a speeding citation. Well, if nothing else the air raids were solving Baghdad's horrendous traffic jams.

Leaving the bridge, turning onto Yafa Street, he pulled the sun visor down to block the glare of the sun. The sun, setting, flashed against the top windows of the Al-Rashid Hotel. He had been so busy the past three days that he had not seen or talked with Chris Campbell. Her January 20 appointment with Saddam Hussein had been canceled. Obviously, she would want to arrange a new date. Perhaps he should swing by the hotel and talk with her about it. The idea pleased him. The thought of seeing her pleased him. He could spare a few minutes before continuing on to Al-Mutana. He turned into the Al-Rashid's driveway.

A large tourist bus was parked under the porticoed hotel entrance. Several dozen men and women, lined up outside the bus, impatiently waited for an army officer and a sergeant to check names off a list. Two other soldiers and the bus driver packed valises and trunks into the bus's luggage compartment. Adnan recognized the people as journalists he had seen in and around the hotel.

He pulled up behind the bus and got out. The journalists were angrily discussing the situation. ". . . those arrogant bastards!" one man, a stocky, white-goateed American network television producer was saying. "We're reporters, for Christ's sake, not spies!"

"Come on, Ted, you're not that sorry to get out of here, don't shit *me*," another American replied, a younger man wearing a Boston Red Sox baseball cap.

The cap's visor was pulled down low over his eyes as though to conceal his identity.

The white-goateed man unexpectedly grinned. "You're not all that wrong, Freddie," he said. "Staying here and getting bombed by your own people every night, well, that ain't my idea of a choice assignment!"

The army officer, a middle-aged captain wearing a regular army black beret and divisional staff aiguillette, glanced at Adnan but continued examining passports and checking off names on his list.

Adnan called, "Captain. . . ."

The captain did not attempt to conceal his impatience and did not salute. "Yes, sir?"

"What's going on?"

"They're leaving the country. Their visas are canceled."

"By whose order?"

"Ministry of Information," said the captain. "Major, you'll have to excuse me." He stepped past Adnan and resumed his work.

Adnan scanned the crowd for Chris. When he was certain she was not there, he went into the hotel. In contrast to the clamor outside, the atrium-style lobby was quiet. In the adjoining tea lounge, not a single table was occupied. The frosted-glass double doors of the Scheherazade Room were open; the lone customer at the bar was an Asian. Adnan's heels echoed hollowly on the marble floor as he crossed the lobby to the house telephones. He asked the operator to ring Chris's room. There was no answer. Adnan went to the desk now and asked the concierge if Miss Campbell had checked out.

"She is one of the people staying," the concierge immediately replied. "She was not asked to leave, nor was Mr. Layton," he went on, obviously eager to provide information to a Republican Guard officer.

The interview with Saddam, Adnan thought. That was why they allowed Chris to stay. Christine Campbell would tell the American public the truth about what was happening in Iraq. The truth, he thought, returning to the house telephones and again asking for Chris's room.

Again, no answer. He waited for the operator to come back on the line so he could leave a message. But when the phone went dead in his hands, he decided to waste no more time and left.

Outside, the bus was now almost loaded. Adnan wondered where the people were being taken. Out of the country, but to where? Iran? Syria? And what the hell difference did it make? He got into the Chrysler and drove away, still thinking about the "truth" that Chris would tell her audience.

The truth.

Which was that Iraq was being systematically destroyed. "Surgically," as the Americans enjoyed saying. Bombed back into the Stone Age, as they also enjoyed saying, this of course referring to Vietnam. But the Vietnamese had prevailed. Adnan wondered if Iraq could.

When Adnan phoned, Chris was in her room and had heard the telephone but did not bother answering it. She was too engrossed watching a television program.

No, not a program, a show. An exhibition. A spectacular.

On Iraqi TV.

The interrogation of three Allied pilots, two Americans and an Englishman. All three were very young, frightened, and reading their bruised and lacerated faces, apparently willing to cooperate.

Each, in a tight subdued voice, gave his name, rank, and serial number. The off-camera English-speaking interrogator then asked for a statement. The first POW, a U.S. Navy pilot, said he regretted bombing helpless civilians but that he was following the orders of his superiors. The second American identified himself as a marine pilot and repeated essentially the navy pilot's statement. The RAF pilot said that he hoped the good people of Iraq would forgive him for the crimes he had committed.

Chris at first thought it somewhat amusing, and certainly naive, for the Iraqis to believe a Western audience would swallow the performance. A five-year-old could see that the pilots had been subjected to some form of coercion. And you could literally read their minds: What the hell, say anything, no one will hold it against you. Nor are you revealing any national secrets. She was sorry for the pilots, although a different sorrow than she felt for the people of Baghdad, the hundreds, if not thousands, of innocent civilians killed in these first three days and nights of bombing.

Not long after the telephone stopped ringing, just as the air raid sirens came on again, someone knocked on the door. Chris got up and opened the door. It was Tom Layton. He strode past her into the room and went to the window overlooking the hotel driveway.

"You have anything to do with that?" Tom indicated the journalists' bus. Before Chris could reply, the floor trembled with the hollow thud of a distant explosion. A cloud of black smoke mushroomed up on the horizon behind the Baghdad skyline.

Tom said, "This morning, I looked out the window of my room and, so help me Hannah, one of those Tomahawk missiles zipped past! Honest to God, the thing was so close I could almost touch it. Looks like a telephone pole with little tiny wings. And, dammit, we had no camera."

"You asked me if I had anything to do with everybody getting kicked out," Chris said. "Are you crazy?"

Tom removed his glasses and pointed them downward, at the bus. "Let me put it this way: Do I have you to thank for us, you and me, not getting kicked out with the rest of our colleagues?"

"You're free to leave with them," Chris said. "And by the way, a good number of our so-called colleagues are damned happy to be kicked out. They're scared to death —and so am I—at the thought of bombs dropping on them."

"Come on, Chris, answer the question."

"It's a stupid question. But no, I had nothing to do with it. Next case, please."

"Maybe you did have something to do with it, but don't realize it."

"Now what the hell does that mean?"

"It means you have some influence," Tom said. He slipped the glasses into the breast pocket of his jacket. "Hey, don't get me wrong—I think it's great. Except for CNN, we're the only American outfit here. Talk about exclusivity!"

Chris wanted to laugh in his face. He was so stupidly obvious. He believed that her friendship with Adnan Dulaimi—"influence," as he called it—was the reason for WCN remaining in Baghdad. Chris was sure Larry Hill was responsible. Larry had pulled whatever strings were necessary, or called in whatever markers were owed him, or bribed whoever he had to. But maybe Tom Layton was right. Maybe it had been through Adnan. The possibility pleased her.

"All right, so what are you complaining about?" she asked, and told herself, To hell with him, play his game. If he wants to believe I'm sleeping with Adnan, let him believe it. Besides, it wasn't so unpleasant a notion.

"Who's complaining?" Tom moved away from the window and nodded at the television set. The POW show was being replayed. "Doesn't that make your blood boil? The goddamn Viet Cong did that, too, you know. The Geneva Convention's a joke."

"I suppose it's never occurred to you that several hundred civilians were killed?"

"It's called collateral damage," Tom said. He touched the television tube, circling the tip of his finger over the face of the English pilot. "I've already fed that to Washington," he said. "They're running it every hour."

"That should be good for at least a thirty share," Chris said dryly.

"Speaking of thirty shares, I heard a story today that could get us a *fifty*!" Tom said. He smiled, pleased with both the story and the prospect of a fifty share. "Listen to this: Every Saturday morning at ten-thirty A.M., war or peace, His Excellency, Wasfi al-Barak, the deputy interior minister, goes to a certain address in a new tract out in Ishbillya. Seems two sisters living there provide old Wasfi with some very special services. And these ladies, by the way, are no beauty contest winners. In fact, they're both pushing fifty, probably more. Maybe I better not tell you, it's almost too raunchy even for my pornographic mind."

Tom paused for Chris to respond. She folded her arms impatiently and waited for him to continue. "Shall I?" he asked. "I mean, are you ready?"

"Tom, I'm really too busy."

"Barak, you know, really functions as a kind of public morals watchdog. He's like a censor. Movies, books, magazines. He's big with the Fundamentalists, which is why Saddam keeps him around."

Again, Tom paused, and again Chris did not react. She had no intention of playing straight man for him. He continued, "Okay, Barak walks into the house, strips naked, gets into the bathtub—the water's already been run and the tub is half full—and then the first sister comes in. She lifts up her skirt, sits on the edge of the tub with her ass hanging over the water, and relieves herself. She exits, and the other sister comes in and does the same. I mean, they're dumping all their bodily fluids and wastes, everything, on the guy. Not a word is spoken, total silence. After an hour or so—with him playing in the water like a kid with rubber ducks—he climbs out of the tub, cleans himself off, gets dressed, and slips an envelope with three U.S. one hundred dollar bills into the mail slot. Now what do you think of that?"

"I think you enjoy telling me about it, that's what I think," Chris said. "Okay, what's really on your mind?"

Tom sank comfortably into the room's only lounge chair. "Your interview with Saddam," he said. "Since we're still here, it must still be on."

We, Chris thought, and shut off the television. The ghostly form of the bruised and swollen RAF pilot's face faded from the tube. Chris said, "You mean the interview that never was?"

"The interview that will be," he said. "The interview I expect to be in on."

Chris walked over to the window. The bus was driving away. She watched a moment. "I'm glad you told me,

Tom. I had no idea you were interested in joining me on the interview."

Tom smiled sourly but said nothing. He seemed quite calm and unperturbed. Too calm, Chris thought. She said, "At the moment, it's all academic. He canceled the first date for obvious reasons: He is too busy with the war. I'm hoping that when things settle down, if they ever do, he'll remember his public."

Tom pushed himself up out of the chair. The same little smile reappeared. "I hope so, too, Chris." He walked to the door. "See you downstairs," he said, meaning the hotel patio, for their regular mid-afternoon "Gulf Watch" transmission to Washington. The patio had replaced the exposed roof as the signature set for the telecasts.

See me downstairs, she thought, as he left. She knew him well by now, and all his little games. He was warning her that unless she shared the interview with him, there would be no interview. How he planned to interfere, she had no idea, but she did not put anything past him, any dirty trick. And, she was sure, it would concern Major Adnan Dulaimi. A juicy piece of gossip, for example, about an important and influential army officer involved in an affair with an American newswoman.

She turned the television back on. On the screen now, a man sat at a news desk reading from a script. He was quite dapper in his blue double-breasted suit, starched white shirt, and polka-dotted red tie. "Well, Christine, my girl," she said aloud, and paused an instant to listen to the air raid sirens. She waited for the sound of an explosion but heard only the television announcer's Arabic voice. "We'll have to do something about Mr. Tom Layton, won't we?" She went on, finishing her sentence.

Outside, the air raid sirens continued, and the dapper announcer continued his recitation. Chris, whose grasp of Arabic could not even be described as elementary, had no idea that the man was reading an order from the Revolutionary Command Council. The Allied POWs— war criminals by any definition of the term, said the announcer—were to be moved to various strategic sites in and around Baghdad to serve as human shields.

2

It was the first reasonably clear day in the five days since the war started. Substantial cloud cover still extended inland from the Gulf but not enough to obscure the target, the electrical generating station at Yathrib, a small city on the western bank of the Tigris, sixty-three miles north of Baghdad.

The Allied strike package consisted of four USAF F-4G Wild Weasels from Sheik Isa air base in Bahrain and eight F-16s from Al Kalir. The ATO—air tasking order—called for the F-4s to go in first to eliminate Yathrib's radar-controlled AAA batteries and SAM sites. The F-4s did a thorough job. All that remained of the sophisticated defenses were a few manually operated 100mm guns.

The eight 358th TFW F-16s, in two flights of four, approached the area at 26,000 feet. The first element, Cadillac Flight, was led by Colonel Ed Iverson with First Lieutenant Ralph Keyes flying his wing. Cadillac would descend to 16,000 feet for the attack, while the second element, Pontiac Flight, led by Nick Harmon, remained at altitude. Pontiac was to go in, if necessary, for a follow-on bomb run and to also fly cover for Cadillac.

En route, AWACS relayed a message from a J-STARS aircraft patrolling the area. J-STARS—joint surveillance target attack radar system, which monitored ground activity—had sighted an enemy motorized column moving south along the main highway, twenty kilometers west of Yathrib. If Nick's Pontiac Flight was not needed to assist with the generator station, it would be deployed against the motorized column.

No follow-on attack was required. Cadillac's four F-16s hit every building within the complex. The smoke and flames from the rubble rose high into the air in a billowing, greasy yellow and black cloud.

Ed Iverson had just pickled his last 500-pound bomb

and was proceeding to the rejoin point when Cadillac Two, Keyes, called a Mayday. Keyes strained to keep his voice calm and businesslike. "Two, southbound on the egress, I've taken a hit."

"Two, what's your status?" Iverson asked.

"I've got engine caution and fire warning lights," Keyes replied.

Iverson throttled back and moved in on Keyes, who was several miles behind and slightly below. A thin streamer of white smoke trailed from the F-16's right side. The centerline fuel tank, bomb ejector racks, ECM pod, and both Sidewinders floated past as Keyes jettisoned his external stores.

"Are you hurt?" Iverson asked.

"Negative," said Keyes.

Iverson rolled in a little closer, close enough now for a clear view of Keyes's airplane. The rear of the F-16 looked as though it was gouged open by a giant crowbar. The engine nozzle had been blown apart and most of the afterburner eyelid petals were gone. Chunks of aluminum and stringy black composite fibers trailed in the slipstream.

"You've got major aft-section damage," Iverson said to Keyes. "But I don't see any fire. We'll get you back okay." Iverson did not wait for Keyes to reply but immediately called the AWACS. "Yukon, Cadillac Two needs an SAR chopper in here *now!*"

Yukon acknowledged the message, and then relayed a series of advisories: The Iraqis had launched two MiG-29s from their base at Mileh Tharthar, but both aircraft were turning back. No indication of additional hostile aerial activity.

Twenty miles west of Yathrib, with the smoke from the burning buildings of the generator station still visible, Keyes radioed, "I'm not getting any thrust . . ."

"Can you make it to the border?" Iverson asked.

"Maybe," Keyes replied, ". . . if I get out and push."

Five miles away, 10,000 feet above, Nick listened. *If I get out and push.* Nick liked that. It would make great bar conversation.

He said into his microphone, "Cadillac Lead, do you need us down there for backup?"

Iverson replied, "We're okay—" he paused. "Two o'clock low!" he said. "Just over the crest of the highway—"

"—rog, Lead, I see it!" Cadillac Three said.

What they saw was the column reported by J-STARS. A troop convoy, a line of trucks stretching more than half a mile. A battalion, at least.

Fish in a barrel, Iverson thought, cursing himself for using all his air-to-ground ordnance on the generator station. But Nick's flight was still fully armed. And the three remaining Cadillac airplanes had their cannons.

Iverson decided to have Cadillac Three and Four make the first hit on the convoy. Nick's flight would then follow. He, Iverson, would stay with Keyes. He had just touched his mike button to call Cadillac Three and Four, when Keyes's voice blasted into his earphones.

"Two's on fire!" The bravado was gone from the boy's voice. "I'm getting out!"

Flame and engine debris belched from Keyes's tailpipe. The airplane nosed over into a cloud of light cirrus, reappeared, then immediately was enveloped in another, heavier cloud formation.

Iverson said into his mike, "Cad Two, eject! Do you copy? Eject! Eject!"

There was no reply, and the F-16 had still not emerged from the clouds. "Two," Iverson called. "Do you read?"

No reply.

Nick, listening, waited a moment and then instructed his three Pontiac Flight wingmen to maintain their positions and await further orders. He rolled his F-16 over and snapped the control stick forward. "Cad Lead, I'm coming down," he called to Iverson.

"He's out!" Cadillac Three radioed.

Cadillac Four said, "He's got a good chute!"

"Listen for him on Guard," Iverson said.

"Been monitoring Guard," said Three. "Nothing so far. No beeper, either."

At 16,000 feet, Nick leveled out on Iverson's left wing. Iverson, sun visor up, was peering at the ground. Off to the right, through a film of brown road dust, the Iraqi column moved along the two-lane concrete highway that paralleled railway tracks and patches of irrigated farmland.

Cadillac Four called to Iverson, "That's some delicious-looking stuff down there."

"Let's first find out where Keyes is," Nick cut in.

"Rog," Iverson agreed, and then paused abruptly. Below in the near distance he had glimpsed a flash of yellow and a coil of thick black smoke. Keyes's F-16 had crashed. Iverson gazed at it a long moment, then continued his radio transmission. "Cadillac, hold your positions and cap us."

Nick and Iverson, wing to wing, descended through the light overcast. At 8,000 feet, directly beneath them, was the big orange and white parachute. Both F-16s, throttling back with speedboards fully extended, flew past Keyes. He was conscious and appeared uninjured.

"I can't see if he's got his Prick-ninety," Iverson said. Prick-90 was the all-too-befitting nickname for the PRC-90, the infamously unreliable emergency radio carried by all pilots.

"Rog," said Nick. "It either wasn't working or he just forgot to use it."

Just then, AWACS checked in with an SAR—search and rescue—status: "Cadillac, Yukon. Chopper airborne, thirty out, estimate on scene in one-four minutes."

Nick radioed to Iverson, "Lot of bad guys down there, Ed."

"We'll cover him," Iverson said, and then in the same breath added, "Oh, shit!"

Nick saw it at the same time. Despite his desperate efforts to change direction, Keyes's parachute was floating straight toward the Iraqi troop convoy.

Iverson rammed his throttle into military power and put the F-16 into a climbing turn. He rolled out, dove

down, and sped over the armored column. He chandel-
led up and radioed to Nick.

"Follow me in, Nick!"

"Ed, what the hell are you doing?" Nick asked, knowing the answer full well. To cover Keyes until the rescue
helicopter arrived, Iverson intended to strafe the Iraqi
troops. He was 3,000 feet above Nick now and banking
over, nose down in an attack configuration.

"No, Ed, no!" Nick said. "Keyes is right in the middle
of the whole fucking Iraqi army! No way a chopper can
get to him! All we'll do is piss them off, and they'll take
it out on the kid!"

Iverson was already down on the deck, commencing
his run. He opened fire. The muzzle flashes from the
F-16's Vulcan cannon resembled bright little flares. The
Vulcan's shells chewed up the road just ahead of the
Iraqi vehicles and then, abruptly, Iverson ceased firing.
He pulled the F-16's nose up almost vertically and
climbed away. He leveled out at 6,000 feet, off Nick's
right wing.

"Nick . . ."

"Go ahead, Ed."

"I guess I got a little carried away."

"Yeah, Ed, a little," Nick said.

Nick watched Keyes's parachute billow and then collapse. Keyes had landed near the railway tracks, less
than a mile from the Iraqi convoy. Two jeeps and a
flatbed truck were racing along the road toward Keyes.
Nick came down to 1,000 feet and jinked over the vehicles. By the time he had turned and reversed course,
Keyes was in the truck. Nick caught a glimpse of him,
seated on the floor in the rear of the truck, hands
clasped behind his neck. Two soldiers sat facing Keyes,
their rifles pointed at his chest.

Master Sergeant Carlisi carried two mugs of coffee
into Colonel Iverson's office. "One half teaspoon of
sugar for you, sir," she said, placing one mug on the
Miller High Life cardboard coaster on Iverson's desk.

"And black for you, Colonel Harmon." Carlisi set the second mug on the bare wood desktop in front of Nick.

"Thank you, Sergeant," Iverson said.

At that moment both coffee mugs began rattling loudly on the desktop as the walls reverberated with the roar of an airplane taking off. Through the window, Nick saw it was a tanker, a KC-135 that had landed earlier in the day for repairs and now was returning to its home base at King Khalid Military City.

Carlisi, leaving, suddenly wheeled around and strode back to Iverson's desk. Shaking her head in exasperation, she straightened a batch of papers and file folders scattered about the desk. "It must be me," she said, arranging the papers in a single neat stack. "Colonel Gallagher's desk was always like that, too." She finished the sentence as though muttering to herself. "Like a tornado hit it."

Iverson waited in silence for Carlisi to leave. "She's a pain in the ass," he said, when the door closed behind her.

Nick said nothing. He sipped the coffee, hot and strong as he liked it, maybe a little too strong. But after five hours in the air and the shock of seeing Keyes taken prisoner, Nick—and everyone else in the wing—needed something strong.

Iverson had asked Nick to come to the office as soon as they finished debriefing. A personal matter he wanted to discuss. Nick thought he knew what it was: some kind of self-serving explanation for his near-bonehead act of attacking Keyes's captors. To Nick's surprise, far from defending himself, Iverson was apologetic.

"I want to thank you for stopping me from clobbering that Iraqi column. You were right, of course, They would have punished poor Keyes for it. Shame we had to let the bastards get away, though."

"No choice, Ed."

"Tell me about it." Iverson drank his coffee now. He made a face. "Tastes like piss! That woman can't even fix a drinkable cup of instant coffee! I have to get rid of her, Nick."

Nick wanted to say, So do it, for Christ's sake, and stop complaining. But just then Iverson's whole face wrinkled in pain. He clamped his hand to his forehead. ". . . fucking headache!" he muttered.

"Why don't you let Fred give you something for it?" Nick said. Fred was Colonel Fred Walters, the flight surgeon.

"I'm all right," Iverson said. He sat back in his chair and sighed with relief as the spasm passed.

Now Nick noticed the circles under Iverson's eyes and his haggard, taut expression. "You've led every mission we've flown," Nick said. "That means that in the past five days you haven't had ten hours of sleep. No wonder your head aches."

"You're my Ops director, Nick, not my mother," Iverson said. But he said it with a self-effacing smile. "Oh, speaking of operations, I want you—" He plucked an E-mail message from the folder on the desk. "This meeting tomorrow in Dhahran of all 14th Air Division wing commanders, I want you to go in my place. As my representative."

"Tracy should be your representative, not me," Nick said. Colonel Tracy Hart was the 358th vice wing commander.

"Tracy's just marking time until he retires," Iverson said. "Everybody knows that you're the real vice. You're my right arm, Nick," He smiled thinly. "And left hand."

Nick felt a surge of anger. He thought Iverson was needling him with a not-so-subtle reminder that he, Ed Iverson, was the boss. But then he realized Iverson was quite serious. And Nick knew why.

Nick said, "The reason you're not going to that meeting tomorrow is because you plan on flying another mission."

"That's right, Nick, I'll be flying," Iverson said. He lowered the palm of his hand onto the stack of papers that Sergeant Carlisi had so neatly arranged. "Be grateful it's Tracy, not you, who'll have to deal with this batch of a hundred and one chicken-shit little details!"

Which Nick thought—as a pair of F-16s on BARCAP shrieked down the runway and hurtled into the air—truly are one hundred and one chicken-shit little details. But each single one, from disciplinary matters to mess hall menus, was, in its own way, important. Ed Iverson's problem could be summed up in a single word, insecurity. The 358th's C.O. feared that attending the Dhahran meeting, and thereby leaving wing operations in Nick's hands, might make him look bad. Or, putting it another way, make Nick look good. The safest way was not to leave anything in Nick's hands.

Nick said, "My guess is that the purpose of the meeting is to evaluate the past week's operations. A lot of tactics and old ideas have to be reexamined. Among other things, how to deal with this lousy weather. You need to be there, Ed."

Iverson seemed not to have heard. From the stack of correspondence he had plucked a maintenance squadron morning report. "Complaints about the mail delivery. Such goddamn trivia, why can't they handle it on a squadron level?" He pulled another paper from the pile and started to read aloud from it, then changed his mind. He pointed a finger at Nick. "Oh, before I forget: I'm shutting off the beer at the club."

Nick wanted to say, Say again? But he knew he had heard correctly. ". . . matter of discipline," Iverson was continuing. "No, excuse me, not discipline, respect. Respect, goddammit! We're insulting the Saudis by allowing alcohol on the base. They don't allow it in Dhahran or Riyadh or Dammam, do they? Well, neither will we."

Nick said, "We're not in Dhahran or Riyadh or Dammam. We're in the middle of nowhere. Nobody gives a care what we're doing here, only that we get our airplanes up when we're supposed to and handle the job we're assigned. And we're doing it, and damn well. So all you accomplish is to alienate a bunch of guys who are breaking their asses for you. It's a no-win situation."

Iverson did not seem at all annoyed or offended. Indeed, he acted as though he felt sorry for Nick, as though Nick was incapable of comprehending. "That's your trouble," Iverson said mildly. "You're a chronic rule-violator. You're neurotic about it. With you, it's almost axiomatic: Somebody says yes, you'll say no. Black, white. Come on, fella, get with it!"

Nick glanced at the clock with the propeller-shaped hour and minute hands. Barney Gallagher's clock, which Barney for some reason had left behind. Iverson had moved it from its original place above the door. Thank you, Barney, Nick thought. Thank you for Ed Iverson. He drank some of the coffee and rose.

"Ed, I've got a million things to do. Let's talk about my neuroses later. But I'd like you to hold off on that beer thing. Let's first get a consensus from some of the squadron commanders."

Iverson studied Nick with that same indulgent expression. "These people are soldiers. We're in a war. They take orders, I take orders." He started rummaging through another stack of papers in an aluminum tray stanchioned to the desk edge. "You want to hear the actual 'no alcohol' Defense Department directive?"

Nick placed his hand gently on the papers. "It's okay, Ed, I've seen it." He moved to leave. "You need me, I'll be over at Ops. Tomorrow's ATO should be in by now."

"Tomorrow, you'll be in Dhahran," Iverson said.

Iverson's handsome ebony face was not so handsome now, the thick jet-black eyebrows furrowed in headache pain, the square jaw clenched tight. Nick looked at him and suddenly understood that Iverson had no ideas on new tactics, no grasp of grand strategy, and no interest in the mundane but imperative details of command. He was interested only in flying the lead airplane on as many missions as possible. More accurately, flying seemed all he was capable of.

"All right, Ed, if that's how you want it," Nick said.

"That's right, Nick, that's how I want it."

3

Hana had promised herself to act normal. Yes, of course, your brother lies in a hospital, paralyzed from the neck down, and you are expected to behave as if he is suffering nothing worse than a bad cold. Smile, and assure him that he'll soon be home, playing tennis, chasing girls, painting.

Painting.

In her mind she saw Amir seated at his easel, working on one of the abstracts he was so proud of. No more. Not unless, like the photograph of an artist she once saw in an Italian news magazine, he held the paintbrush in his teeth. Immediately, for allowing herself to think of Amir in this manner, she cringed with shame. But she understood the basis of those thoughts, which made her no less ashamed: She was angry—no, enraged—that Amir had done this to himself.

Yes, done it to himself. He had insisted on playing the hero. Insisted on commando duty. And so now he was a hero. He would probably be decorated. Yes, when they presented him with the medal they would place it in his mouth. He could clench the ribbon in his teeth. Just as with the paintbrush.

Amir was wide awake. His eyes followed her as she entered the room and stood at the foot of his bed. It was early evening now and already dark outside. The room's lights were on. The cold glow of the fluorescent ceiling lamps colored Amir's complexion waxy white.

Extinction pallor, Hana thought, and felt tears welling in her eyes because she did not know if she wanted him this way, or dead. You do not want those you love to suffer. She remembered the time in their childhood when their dog was run over by an automobile. She especially loved that dog, a terrier of uncertain ancestry. As her father explained, the dog had to be put to sleep to spare him from suffering.

She smiled cheerily now and said to Amir, "Well, you don't look half as bad as I thought you would. No, not half as bad."

"That's good," he said. His voice was remarkably strong and clear.

She bent down and kissed his cheek, ashamed of her unprofessional revulsion at the rank odors wafting up from him and from the tubes attached to his body that were connected to the plastic bags under the bed. She knew the exact purpose of each tube. She saw a dozen similar cases every day at the hospital in Amiriyah.

She should have handled this with the same professionalism. But my God, this was a brother, her dear brother, her only living relative. Her mother had been taken from her, and her father, and now Amir.

This was only her second visit to the Muadham hospital. She had followed Hassan Marwaan's advice not to see Amir again until his condition stabilized. Now, on the seventh day of the war, eight days after the accident, he was stable.

A stable quadriplegic.

". . . stop crying!" Amir was saying. "If you're going to do that, get out. Please."

She had not realized she was crying. She was glad she wore no makeup, only lipstick. "I'm sorry," she said.

"As a matter of fact, I'd like you to leave anyway," Amir said. "I don't feel like talking."

"Amir, I won't cry." She pulled a tissue from an aluminum dispenser on the night table and dabbed her eyes. She smiled again. "There, is that better?"

"Did you come here with Adnan?"

"He's waiting outside."

"I want to see him."

"They say you're doing very well," she said. "They're planning to give you some solid food. That's a very good sign, you know."

"Tell Adnan to come in."

"Aren't you pleased that you're making progress?"

"I want to see Adnan."

Just then, the air raid sirens sounded outside. Hana whirled around to the window. Over the rooftops in the distance the yellow dots of the antiaircraft tracers floated upward. The pop-pop-pop of gunfire sounded far off.

"They're at it again," she said, turning to Amir, angry that he could not be properly protected during an air raid. At the hospital in Amiriyah you took for granted the impossibility of moving several hundred ill and injured people into the cellar each night. But now, here, with her own brother helpless, the thought terrified her.

He lay gazing up at the ceiling, his face relaxed and calm. He seemed almost pleased, certainly unafraid. And Hana understood why. The nightly attacks meant nothing to him. The war meant nothing. His own existence meant nothing.

"Will you please get Adnan?"

"Just talk to me a minute longer," she said.

"I have something to tell him! Get him!"

Adnan was at the nurses' station, holding a telephone and futilely slamming the cradle up and down. "The whole damn system is out," he said to Hana. He hung up the phone and nodded at Amir's door. "How did it go?"

"He's very bitter," she said.

"Can you blame him?"

"No, of course not. He wants to talk to you."

Adnan placed an arm around Hana and drew her to him. He held her close a moment. Her shoulders were shaking, her whole body was trembling. "He's a brave boy," Adnan said. "He'll learn to accept it."

"He might, *I* can't," she said, hating herself once again for even thinking it, let alone saying it. She closed her eyes and rested her head on Adnan's shoulder. With his arms around her, she felt protected. "What are we going to do, Adnan?" she asked. "What will we do?"

He could only shake his head helplessly. A dozen answers had rushed to his lips, all banal and meaningless. The truth of it was that he did not know what they would do. They would do what they had to. But he did not say this to her, either; it was all the more banal and meaningless.

As they walked to Amir's room, a nearby antiaircraft

battery fired a few brief bursts. Adnan stopped to listen.
Hana stopped with him. The guns abruptly fell silent.
"Firing without the slightest idea of what the hell
they're shooting at," Adnan said, and continued on to
the room.

Amir said to Adnan, "Has Major Othman sent in a
report yet on my 'accident'?"

"I think so," said Adnan. "I haven't seen it, though."

"Whatever he says, it will be a lie."

Hana, standing on the other side of the bed, gasped.
"A lie? What kind of lie?"

Amir half turned his head toward her. The effort
seemed to exhaust him. He closed his eyes and drew a
deep breath. He opened his eyes and addressed Adnan
again.

"Let me tell you about the 'accident,'" he said, and
tersely related how he had been shot trying to prevent
the cold-blooded murder of the American prisoners.

Hana turned to the window. She did not want to believe Amir's story, but knew it was true. "Dear God,
how can this happen?" she said. "It's so unfair. He tries
to do something good, and it destroys his life!"

She heard Amir laugh quietly. "I have to eat, she says.
She says it's the only way I'll regain my strength." He
paused to draw in a breath. "Strength for what?" he
went on. "So I can wipe my ass after I shit? I can't wipe
my ass, Hana. It has to be done for me." His lips twisted
in a cruel little smile. "That'll be your job, my darling
sister," he said. "You'll wipe my ass for me, won't you?
Sure, you'll take care of me. You'll do all that for me."

Hana had begun crying again, and this time could not
stop. She sank down into the room's only chair, a stainless-steel armchair, and buried her face in her hands.
She thought she heard Amir laughing.

THIRTEEN

It was actually funny, Ralph Keyes told himself. If you could take a joke. If, after two days as a POW, you still had a sense of humor. And if you could laugh, which Keyes could not. What he found so unlaughably funny was his recollection of the three-week survival course back at Fairchild AFB and the simulated POW interrogations. The men playing the interrogator roles were tough. They took their jobs very seriously, and so did you, but you knew it was a game.

He was seated on the dank linoleum floor of the tiny room, his back against the wall, his arms wrapped tightly around his chest for warmth. He wore only his flight suit, and they had not given him even a blanket. The room was bright with light from the electric bulb in the wire-meshed metal lamp shade in the ceiling. The bulb remained on all day and all night, although day and night were the same in this windowless room. They blindfolded him whenever they took him out of the room, bringing him each time to a larger room, an office. There, with a 300-watt bulb shining in his eyes, the same man asked the same questions.

Location of squadron, types of aircraft flown, name of commanding officer, targets assigned. His replies, like the questions, were always the same: "My name is Ralph C. Keyes. I am a first lieutenant in the United States Air Force. My serial number is 479-14-0621."

At the first session they had seemed to accept his answers. They returned him to his cell. A few hours later—he had no concept of time; the soldiers who captured him had taken his wristwatch—they brought him back for more questioning.

"My name is Ralph C. Keyes. I am a—"

The words had ended in a cry of pain. A man standing behind him had punched him in the side. The blow toppled him to the floor. He was picked up, propped back on the chair, and punched again, this time in the stomach. He remembered screaming with the pain, gasping for breath and feeling as though his eyes had exploded out of his head.

They were smart, the Iraqis. Instead of repeating the questions, they immediately returned him to the cell. Let him think about it awhile, let him wonder how long before they came back for him.

Well, he would fool them. He would not wonder and worry about his fate. Instead, he would concentrate on something pleasant. Yes, start with home, Des Moines, 1983, Grover Cleveland High School, senior year. Kim McMasters, Kim short for Kimberly, the little brunette originally from Savannah, Georgia. Kim spoke with a drawl everyone said was exaggerated, but it was music to Keyes's ears. Especially that night in the backseat of his father's Lincoln, their second date. When she unzipped Keyes's fly, and in that syrupy drawl said, ". . . this li'l ole dickie-wickie ain't gonna object if I nibble on him some, will he?" No, for sure, the little old dickie-wickie did not object at all. No way. You sure wouldn't need *Out of Africa* music for little old Kim.

He hadn't thought of her in years. They lost touch after he entered the Academy and she went off to school in Vermont. He heard that she married a psychologist and moved to Oregon. A psychologist.

"A shrink," Keyes said aloud now. "Good for you, Kim. I bet you nibble plenty on *his* li'l ole dickie-wickie!" He smiled to himself as he rolled over on his stomach and crawled toward the door. On the floor near the door was an aluminum mess-kit dish and a canteen cup. The dish contained a piece of pita bread, the canteen cup a few ounces of watery broth. Although he had not eaten in the day and a half since his capture, and was not hungry, Keyes knew he had to keep up his strength. He wanted to be able to deal with them when they came back.

He had seen those American and British pilots on Iraqi TV, and sworn never to give in as they did. Mouthing ludicrous statements and confessing to war crimes. Of course, no one believed what was said and no one criticized their behavior. My God, you only needed to look at their faces. Battered, bruised, bleeding.

The food had been deliberately placed next to the incongruously new and shiny tin pail that served as a toilet bowl. Nonflushing type. Although a quarter full now, they had not yet emptied it. No matter, the stink no longer bothered him. The least of his worries.

He sat up and sipped the broth. It tasted like greasy warm water. But all at once he wanted more. He was suddenly famished. He soaked the pita bread in the broth and chewed it slowly. Quickly, much too quickly, it was gone.

He thought again about those POWs on Iraqi TV. The robotic voice of the navy pilot who looked as though he'd just gone ten rounds with Mike Tyson. Keyes and a hundred other officers of the 358th had watched the show on the big television screen in the club at Al Kalir. Although not for an instant did anyone doubt that the statements had been coerced, there was some question as to whether the men were actually beaten. Doc Walters said that facial lacerations were entirely consistent with ejection trauma.

That was another reason why Ralph Keyes wanted to laugh. He had survived the ejection without a scratch. His face was unmarked. The bastard ragheads had not touched his face, only his body. And what a job they'd done: He could hardly stand straight, and he was pissing blood. But to look at him, you'd think he just walked out of Matteo's Trattoria after polishing off one of Matty's genuine Hoboken anchovy-and-pepperoni pizzas. What did somebody once call him? Oh, yes: The Boy from Iowa, the Recruiting Poster Kid.

He was very hungry now and briefly considered banging on the door and asking for more food. No, forget it, fuck the Saddamizers—Saddamizers, he liked that—why even give them the satisfaction? He licked the mess-kit dish clean and placed it carefully on the floor near the door.

Now, in the distance, Keyes heard air raid sirens. So it was probably after dark, the nightly parade of F-117s and F-111s dumping their heavy stuff on the city. It reminded Keyes of a World War II movie, something about a CIA agent—no, an OSS agent, in those days they were OSS—who was captured by the Gestapo. During interrogation the 8th Air Force bombed the Gestapo prison. It was all preplanned. If, within a certain time, the OSS hero failed to report, it meant he was in enemy hands and being tortured. To prevent him from talking, the prison would be destroyed.

The hero—it was Gregory Peck, or James Cagney, or maybe John Wayne—began laughing when the bombs started falling. He knew the bombs would kill him, but he also knew the Germans would never learn the secret.

The door was flung open by two Iraqi soldiers. Keyes had never seen these two and caught only a glimpse of their faces before they bound and blindfolded him. Both were big and brawny, young, with shaggy black mustaches. Their khaki uniforms bore no insignia, nor did their red berets. Not a word was spoken as they escorted him from the cell and across what he knew—from the metallic echo of cleated heels on the concrete floor—was a large hall or enclosed courtyard.

But Keyes quickly realized he was not being taken to the same place. In the previous two sessions it was only a short walk and up one flight of stairs to the interrogation room. Now he was taken *down* a stairway and into another large area. A garage: he felt a brief wave of nausea from the odor of engine exhaust fumes and gasoline. Then he was pushed into an automobile, squeezed between two soldiers in the rear seat.

It was cold in the automobile—the driver kept fiddling with the heater buttons but could not turn the fan on—but Keyes began perspiring. From discomfort or fear. More likely, from both. This, he sensed, would be no routine interrogation.

After a short drive the car stopped. The soldiers led him into another building. Into a lobby, more echoing footsteps on a stone floor. Then, stairs. One flight, two, four, six. A high-rise building, and they were climbing the stairs. The soldiers muttered in Arabic, obviously complaining about no elevators. One jabbed his fist hard into the back of Keyes's neck. He knew they were blaming him for the bombing that had knocked out the city's electrical generating stations. It gave him a sense of achievement, the first time in three days he felt good about anything.

They stopped at the seventh landing. The floor under Keyes's shoes felt smooth and soft, a carpet. The blindfold was removed. A blaze of white light stabbed deep into his eyes. He closed his eyes until the glare subsided. He was in a large room with acoustically paneled walls and an array of powerful spotlights trained on a long picnic table in the center of the room. Seated in straight-backed wood chairs near the table were two Allied airmen, Saudis. Both wore flight suits. Both, faces bruised and puffy, looked dazed.

As Keyes's vision cleared, he saw that only one of the two was a Saudi, a captain. The other man, balding, slightly older, wore the insignia of a Kuwaiti major and silver pilot's wings.

A nattily dressed Iraqi civilian adjusted a video camera mounted on a dolly, while another civilian manipulated the controls of a sound recorder. Several other civilians chatted jovially in Arabic. The man at the video camera shouted at them. Immediately, everyone fell silent. The two soldiers seized Keyes's arms and led him around the table and into a chair. A microphone dangled from a boom above his head.

The man at the camera glanced at a piece of notepaper and then in perfect English addressed Keyes. "Your name, please?"

"My name is Ralph Keyes. I am—"

"Louder, please," said the man. He gestured to someone behind Keyes. The microphone was lowered a few inches. "Start over," he said.

"My name is Ralph Keyes. I am a first lieutenant in the United States Air—"

"Yes, yes, that's fine," said the man. "Now let me explain what you are to do." He snapped his fingers at a man holding a briefcase. The man removed a sheet of paper from the briefcase and placed it in front of Keyes.

The nattily dressed man said to Keyes, "Please read this statement, memorize it, and then recite it into the camera."

Keyes pushed the paper away without reading it. He looked straight into the nattily dressed man's eyes and said, "So tell me, dude, how is your li'l ole dickie-wickie?"

The Iraqi stared at him. "I beg your pardon?"

"I said," said Keyes, "how is your little old dickie-wickie?"

It was the expression of total bewilderment on the Iraqi's face that made Keyes laugh. He glanced at the two other POWs, the Saudi and the Kuwaiti. They either did not understand or were too confused to respond. Or, Keyes thought, drugged. They sat limply, their eyes vacant.

The Iraqi was no fool, and no one to be made a fool of. He said to Keyes, "I will give you one last chance to cooperate."

Keyes started to repeat his name, rank, and serial number, then decided to hell with it. He sat back in the chair and folded his arms. It was too much of an effort to say anything. To do anything. All right, so now they'd go to work on him. This time, for sure, on his face.

The gunshot sounded like a crack of thunder. He thought his eardrums had burst. The bastards, trying to frighten him, had fired a gun inches away from his head. His ears rang. The burning, bitter odor of cordite stung his nostrils. It wouldn't work, he promised himself, as he turned to the nattily dressed Iraqi, determined to stare him down.

The Iraqi's attention, like everyone else's, was focused on the end of the table. Keyes twisted his head lazily around to see what was so interesting. First, he saw the Saudi pilot, his eyes wide with fear, his chunky face frozen in an expression of utter disbelief. And then he saw the Iraqi civilian who had fired the gun. The revolver hung loosely in his hand, his finger was still curled around the trigger.

Then Keyes saw the Kuwaiti pilot. He was sprawled on the floor, on top of the chair, which had tipped over. He had no head. All that remained above his neck was a clump of shredded flesh and bone. It resembled a watermelon that had been smashed open.

Keyes felt the bile surging up from his stomach. He could taste it in his throat. Crazily, he thought it was lucky he had eaten only the piece of pita and the watery soup. If he vomited, it would not make too much of a mess. He watched the Iraqi who had shot the Kuwaiti pilot lay the muzzle of the revolver against the Saudi pilot's forehead.

". . . we will waste no more time," the nattily dressed man was saying. "If you do not cooperate, this officer will be executed. You will be responsible for his death. The decision is yours."

The Saudi's eyes were closed tightly, but his clenched lips moved in silent prayer. Keyes looked at him, then at the Iraqi holding the gun, then at the dead Kuwaiti. The reflection of the photographic lights shimmered redly in the puddle of blood on the floor.

Keyes looked once more at the Saudi. He had stopped praying. His eyes, open now, were surprisingly clear, almost defiant. He seemed unafraid. Keyes was sure that if the gun had been pointed at him, he would beg for mercy.

"Give me the paper," he said to the nattily dressed Iraqi. "I'll have to read it over a few times to memorize it."

2

Nick saw the show—and that is precisely what it was, a "show"—on the giant-sized television screen in the bar of the 1st Tactical Fighter Wing officers' club at Dhahran International Airport. The club occupied the entire premises of a new wood-framed two-story building that the Royal Saudi Air Force had turned over to the USAF. Nick just happened to be there with Barney Gallagher, at the bar, after dinner.

Gallagher and Nick—and the three dozen other wing commanders and senior officers from bases throughout Saudi Arabia and the Emirates—had spent most of the day in conferences. Staff and planning meetings, reprising bomb damage assessment and overall operations of the past eight days. Twelve thousand sorties in those eight days. Forty-one enemy aircraft destroyed at a cost of ten Allied airplanes. Of sixty-six major Iraqi airfields, no more than five were operational. In the past thirty-six hours alone, no Iraqi aircraft had been detected. It was a rout.

But no rout for the familiar face on the TV screen, a face Nick had seen less than forty-eight hours before, six thousand feet in the air near the city of Yathrib in central Iraq, descending in a parachute. On the TV screen Ralph Keyes's boyish features were surprisingly unmarred. His voice was clear and articulate.

"I am First Lieutenant Ralph C. Keyes of the United States Air Force. I do not understand why we have attacked the peace-loving nation of Iraq. I truly believe—" he paused, glancing questioningly over his shoulder.

An off-camera, Arabic-accented voice said in English, "The question was, 'Do you believe what your leaders have told you about why they sent you to attack the people of Iraq?'"

Keyes looked straight into the camera again. "No, I do not believe what they have told me. I have never believed their lies and misstatements. In my opinion, we have committed a grievous crime and whatever punishment is meted out . . . is well deserved."

The off-camera voice asked, "Then you consider yourself a war criminal?"

Keyes's eyes fell downward an instant, then back into the camera. "I regret to say that all of us who have participated in these terrible deeds are war criminals. I condemn the aggression of my countrymen."

Keyes vanished from the screen, replaced immediately by a shot of Don Blakely, WCN's Washington anchor. Behind Blakely was a photographic panorama of the city of Washington. Superimposed at the bottom right of the picture, in letters composed of lightning bolts, was the W C N logo.

". . . so there you have it, a replay of the tape received a few hours ago via satellite," Blakely was saying. "Please bear in mind that what you saw was a report from Iraqi government tele—"

The screen went blank as the head barman, a Saudi in a white *galabiyya,* switched off the set in response to a flurry of catcalls and jeers from the Americans assembled in and around the bar, the gist of which was, "Turn off that fucking shit!"

There were no expressions of rage or promises of revenge. None was needed. It was all unsaid, implicit. The fact that Keyes had not been obviously beaten and appeared very alert served only to further indict the Iraqis for their barbarous treatment of the POWs. Clearly, Keyes had been drugged, or hypnotized, or otherwise coerced.

The instant the television screen went blank, activity at the club returned to normal. A Whitney Houston song blared from the CD player. The bridge and poker games resumed, glasses were refilled with "Saudi champagne"—grape juice and Perrier—or Coke, coffee, tea, or any of the dozen fruit juices. It was as though everyone refused to lend dignity to the absurdity of what they had just seen.

Indeed, Barney Gallagher seemed more disturbed about Ed Iverson than about Ralph Keyes. More accu-

rately, the knowledge that Iverson was continually flying
missions. But what truly disturbed Gallagher was that
this had been brought to his attention by Nick. Tales out
of school, as far as Gallagher was concerned, and he did
not conceal his displeasure.

They had left the officers' club and were just entering
the lobby of the Dhahran International Hotel, where
both were staying for the night. The cavernous lobby
bustled with people coming and going. The five-star International, on the civilian side of the airport, the only
real hotel in the city and therefore home to dozens of
newsmen and newswomen, was fully booked.

"All right, so Iverson is flying too much," Gallagher
said. "What other complaints do you have?"

"Barney—excuse me, General—you asked how the
outfit was doing."

"The outfit, yes, not your personal assessment of the
commanding officer."

"The outfit is doing fine, it's doing its job," Nick said.
"I mentioned the other thing because it's a situation I
think you should be aware of."

"Bullshit," Gallagher said. He stopped and faced
Nick. He was several inches taller, which made Nick feel
like an errant child about to be lectured. "You're still
pissed off that it's him sitting in my chair, not you."

Yeah, and you're probably wishing I *was* sitting in that
chair and not Ed, Nick thought, and almost said it. Instead, he said, "Ed is pushing himself. He's an accident
waiting to happen. Wing commanders shouldn't be flying combat missions, period, let alone every day."

"Don't you think he knows that?"

"He should," Nick said. "He knows every other rule
in the book." He was tempted to tell Gallagher how
Iverson had almost shot up the Iraqi soldiers capturing
Keyes. But he felt foolish enough for having gone this
far. Bad enough that Gallagher had to accuse him of
badmouthing a superior. Bad enough that the accusation was true.

". . . you want to go on record with this?" Gallagher
was saying.

"No, of course not."

"Then for once in your goddamn life, try to accept the fact that you are a member of a huge and sometimes unwieldy organization known as the United States Air Force. You are only one member, however, and the organization does not—repeat, does not—revolve around you!"

"Now what the hell does all that mean?" Nick said, and hastily added, "Sir."

Gallagher drew in his breath angrily but then clamped his mouth shut. It was as though he had decided to count to ten. He ran his fingers through his close-cropped graying hair. He said, "I asked you to stay with the 358th to help Ed. Now I'm wondering if it wasn't a mistake. . . ." The last word trailed off as Gallagher noticed someone coming toward them. "I think your friend is here."

Elaine Mason was striding across the lobby. Overcoat draped over her arm, she looked very handsome in her green class-A blouse and skirt and black beret. Nick had phoned her from Al Kalir and arranged to meet at eight-thirty here at the International. It was exactly eight-thirty.

"Talk about the Seventh Cavalry charging to the rescue," he wisecracked to Gallagher, and introduced Elaine.

"I've heard a lot about you, General," Elaine said as they shook hands.

"All bad, of course," said Gallagher.

"On the contrary, sir," Elaine said. "All good. Very good."

"Not from Nick, I'll bet," Gallagher said dryly.

"Absolutely, sir, from him," she said. "Honest."

"Well, see that you keep it that way, Nick." Gallagher touched the bill of his cap, smiled politely, and walked off.

"What did I rescue you from?" Elaine asked Nick.

"You feel like a drink?"

"A real one?"

"One hundred and ten proof."

"Don't tell me you brought the rest of that brandy?"

"Bourbon," he said. "One of my crew chiefs inherited a case of Jack Daniel's. He owed me a favor."

"And, naturally, it's in your room."

"And a very nice room, too," he said. "A hundred and fifty bucks a night, but we're paying USAF per diem rates, and the room's a hell of a lot more comfortable than the BOQ back at Al Kalir. Not to mention with its own bathroom," he added.

"The bathroom sold me," she said.

They made love. They drank Jack Daniel's over ice and listened to music on the room radio from DSR, Desert Storm Radio, and made love. They sweated out two air raid alerts. Through the window of the room, as they lay in bed, they watched the sky flash white when the Patriots intercepted the Scuds.

It reminded Nick of Shab al-Bir. And of Frank Kowalski, and Zvi. The American air offensive would have pleased Zvi, although he certainly would have expected more success in finding and destroying the Scud launch sites. They were really pasting Tel Aviv. Those video shots of children wearing gas masks were frightening. Zvi was right: The U.S. should have let the Israelis come in. The Israelis would have eliminated the launchers. As for Kowalski, Nick wondered what had become of him. Probably still in Tel Aviv, still playing Oliver North.

Elaine brought him back to the present. ". . . so now tell me what I rescued you from?" she was asking. "When I interrupted whatever you and General Gallagher were talking about."

"What you rescued me from was my worst enemy, *me*," he said, and described how he had made an ass of himself with Gallagher. Gallagher was relying on Nick to keep Iverson in line, so what does Nick do? He badmouths the guy.

He paused abruptly. "Now I'm crying on your shoulder again," he said. "No, not crying. What was it you said I did instead of crying? Oh, yeah, pouring, that was it. Pouring my heart out. I've been thinking about that. I don't think there's much difference between crying and pouring."

"Maybe you're right," she said. "Maybe there isn't much difference. Whatever it is, I don't mind. We're friends. That's what friends are for."

They had been lying side by side in the darkened room, naked under the sheets and comforter, but now he propped himself up on an elbow and looked at her. "Is that all we are, friends?"

"No, and we should talk about it." She peered at the illuminated face of her wristwatch. "It's a little after midnight. What time are you leaving?"

"Zero six hundred," he said. "Can you stay until then?"

"I can't, but I will," she said. "I work for a son of a bitch who makes your new C.O.—what's his name? Johnson?"

"Iverson."

"My guy—Lieutenant Colonel Leonard Francis Dozier, West Point '74—makes your Iverson look like a Salvation Army tambourine player. We have a girl, an enlisted person, who's been raped. Len Dozier is pressuring her not to bring charges because it's a 'stain on the battalion's honor.' And—oh, shit, forget it!" Elaine turned away. She did not want Nick to see her tears of frustration and anger. "God help me: Now *I'm* crying on *your* shoulder!"

"That's what friends are for," he said.

Now, letting the sheet fall away from her breasts, she sat up and faced him. "Nick, I'm leaving my husband."

He said nothing.

"I haven't told him yet," she said. "And I don't quite know how. But I want you to know that it has nothing to do with you—"

"That's not very flattering."

"I made the decision before"—she searched for the phrase—"well, before all this."

"All this?" Nick asked, knowing perfectly well what she meant but wanting to hear it.

"Us," she said. "You and me." She lay back against

the pillow and pulled the sheet up over her breasts.
"But don't worry about it. I told you: We're friends."

"And I told you," he said, "I love you."

She laughed again, now with pleasure, and turned her
head to him. "That's the second time you've said that. I
mean, the second time in all the years we've known each
other."

"Maybe I'm not such an emotional cripple, then."

"You're improving, that's for sure."

He drew her into his arms. He did not especially want
to make love to her. He wanted only to hold her, to feel
her close to him, and the warmth of her body against
his. They lay like that, quietly, contentedly, for a long
time, until the air raid siren sounded again.

They waited silently, listening. Again a Patriot
knocked down the Scud. This time the interception was
closer. The whole building rocked with the explosion. In
his arms, she trembled with fear.

"Hey, relax, it's all over," he said.

"I'm some soldier," she said. "I fly into Iraq and get
shot at, and hardly blink an eye. But I shake like a leaf
at a little old missile."

He said nothing. All he knew was that he wanted to
protect her, and that he was protecting her and always
would. He wanted the moment and the feeling never to
end.

3

If not for the incredibly clumsy POW "confessions,"
Chris might have believed that the factory really did
manufacture powdered baby food formula and not, as
the Allies claimed, bacteriological weapons. In truth, of
course, Chris would not know a bacteriological weapons
factory from a 7-Eleven market. But the shot of herself
standing ankle-deep in rubble, framed against the crumbled shell of the building, was just too good to pass up.

Not to mention a shot of the cardboard sign propped
against the scorched remnants of the factory gate, the

already famous sign with the sloppily hand-painted English letters reading: BABY MILK PLANT.

But the more Chris thought about it the more she wondered if the Iraqis might not be telling the truth after all. That cardboard sign was so ponderously naive that it almost had to be genuine.

Indeed, the more she thought about it, the more the pathetic little sign came to represent Iraq. Each day another block of buildings was obliterated, another neighborhood hammered into dust, more children killed or crippled, more parents weeping. And all this devastation and personal tragedy with the war only in its tenth day, and Baghdad Radio proclaiming ever more glorious victories.

Baby Milk Plant.

So she narrated the segment with just enough of an intonation in her voice to suggest that, this time at least, the Allies had selected the wrong target.

It was after midnight when Larry Hill got through to her on the satellite private wire. She had just fallen asleep after tossing and turning for hours, watching the sky flash white from the bomb bursts and feeling the room rock with each explosion. The staccato crack of the antiaircraft batteries no longer frightened her. On the contrary, she listened carefully for the guns: She had learned that when they stopped it meant at least an hour's respite from the bombing. An hour to sleep.

She had promised herself not to spend another night in the claustrophobia of the Al-Rashid Hotel's basement shelter. The place stank of body odor and stale tobacco smoke and liquor. Not to mention the toilets, which sometimes did not flush for lack of water. To hell with it. You had a better chance of winning an Ed McMahon lottery than the Al-Rashid being hit by a bomb. Even Adnan Dulaimi agreed. The Americans, Adnan said, would never target a hotel occupied by Western journalists. He had phoned her earlier to say that she could expect word any day now on the rescheduling of the Saddam Hussein interview.

"Yes, Larry, of course you woke me," she said into

the telephone, the image of Adnan tantalizing her memory. She had not seen him all week, which seemed to only sharpen her interest in him. No, her curiosity. No, not that, either, call it like it is: excitement. "Larry, don't you realize that it's almost one o'clock in the morning here?"

"Sorry, kid," Larry said. "Listen, I'm really taking a lot of heat about that erstwhile baby milk plant. Can you talk?" he added.

"Are you referring to the phone being tapped, Larry, or that I might be sleeping with someone?" A brief crackle of static fragmented the sentence, but Larry had understood.

"*Are* you?" he asked.

She wanted to laugh. It was so typically Larry: wasting valuable satellite wire time with his fantasies. "No, Larry, I am not sleeping with anybody. Yes, I can talk."

"Well, look, I've been doing a lot of thinking about it, and I've decided to pull you out of there."

Chris sat straight up in bed. "Say again, please?"

"I'm bringing you back to Washington."

Chris said nothing. Her throat suddenly felt as though stuffed with cotton. Her stomach was turning over.

"Chris . . . ?"

"Are you closing the bureau here?" she asked.

"No, Tom will stay on."

"He'll stay on, but I leave?"

"That's right."

"Would you mind telling me why?"

"It's getting too dangerous—"

"—that's a lot of bullshit, Larry, and you know it! It's the baby milk factory story, isn't it? Because of the heat you say you're taking on it? Who's putting the pressure on you? Those little fascists in the Pentagon? And since when can't you handle them? No, Larry, I'm staying here. I've been promised that interview with Saddam. My God, isn't that why you sent me to Baghdad?"

"Chris, I've spoken to people who just came back. The horror stories about what's going on there. . . ."

Larry went on talking, something about the bombing

and the very real possibility of the Iraqis holding all the remaining Western newspeople as hostages. Chris only half listened. She knew Larry's concern was genuine, but also knew how desperately he wanted the exclusive Saddam Hussein interview.

Yes, of course, that was what it was all about. They were cutting her out of the interview. Since she had already set it up, anyone could come in and do it. And since they knew it would be no handout interview such as the one Saddam gave CNN, Larry had probably hired some heavyweight name. Cronkite, or Kissinger, or Liz Taylor, for all that it mattered.

No, not Cronkite or Kissinger.

Tom Layton.

Hardly a heavyweight, not even a middleweight, but he had somehow convinced Larry to let him do the interview. Yes, it had to be Tom. You couldn't be sure of getting anyone else into Baghdad, let alone anyone *wanting* to come here. Who the hell would *want* to come here? To watch the Cruise missiles cruise past your window and listen for the lethal whistle of falling bombs. Beautiful downtown Baghdad.

She realized she had been sitting in the dark. She turned on the night table lamp and caught a glimpse of herself in the mirror. Her hair was wild, all over her face. But her mouth was set firmly and her eyes were cold. It reflected her mood, all right.

She said into the telephone, "You're trying to sell me down the river, Larry!"

"What I'm trying to do is to save your pretty little ass," he said. "Now I want you out of there, Chris. Fast!"

"You're wasting your breath, Larry, I'm staying right where I am. At least until I have the interview."

"Screw the interview!" he said, which was exactly what she had expected him to say, and which proved that he was indeed selling her out. Larry knew that who conducted the interview made no difference to Saddam. All Saddam cared about was WCN's worldwide audience.

Well, Mr. Lawrence Hill was about to be taught a
lesson. "Larry, darling," she said quietly, "I arranged
the interview, and I can unarrange it. Do you read me?
A word from me, my sweet, and whoever you're thinking of giving that assignment to will end up holding his
popo in his hand. No," she corrected, "in *your* hand!"

"You're crazy, Chris."

"I'm glad we understand each other, Larry."

For a long while after she hung up, Chris remained in
bed, sitting with the telephone on her lap. She had won
the round, but she knew Larry would think about it—
brood about it, more accurately. No matter how fond of
Chris he might be, or how anxious for the interview, in
the end he would simply order her to leave Baghdad. If
she refused, he would fire her.

And give the interview to Tom Layton. But maybe
not. If Tom was not in Baghdad, then he could not do
the interview. Simple enough. So let's get rid of Tom.
But how?

The chambermaid, Leila, knocked on the door and
asked if Chris wished the room made up. At *two* in the
morning? Chris thought; good God, didn't these people
ever give up?

"Not right now, thank you, I'm trying to work," Chris
called out, which was true. She had to find a solution to
the Tom Layton problem, and soon. The more she
thought about it the more she was sure that Larry Hill
might at any moment actually come to believe that she
was blackmailing him. And then it would be all over for
her.

Blackmail, she thought, recalling Tom's description of
the Deputy Interior Minister Wasfi al-Barak's Saturday
morning sessions with the micturating sisters. If only she
had something like that on Tom. Photos, for example.
Maybe he liked little boys and enjoyed taking Polaroid
snapshots of himself in action with them. Or little girls.
No, he wasn't the type. He liked big girls.

". . . are you all right, miss?" Leila was saying
through the door. "Do you need anything?"

"I'm fine, Leila, thank you," Chris said, and all at

once she knew exactly what to do about Tom Layton. Tom himself had provided the answer. More specifically, Tom's big mouth had provided it, his penchant for gossip. Yes, the answer lay with Tom, and with the chambermaid, Leila. Leila, the Mukhabarat agent, she of the legendary blow jobs. And it was all so marvelously obvious and simple.

Chris lay back against the pillows now, pulled the comforter up over her, and closed her eyes. She fell asleep almost instantly. It is always easy to sleep when you have solved a difficult problem. Hours later, at dawn, the air raid siren woke her. Through the window the sky was gray-white with low hanging clouds. Another cold and gloomy day. She listened for the sound of explosions but heard none and fell back to sleep. This time, as she drifted off, she concentrated on forming seven numerals in her mind: 541-8634.

Adnan Dulaimi's telephone number. He, after all, was the key to it. She knew he was working hard to arrange the interview. And she knew damn well his motives were not entirely patriotic. She saw it in his eyes when he looked at her. A message, loud and clear. On the other hand, she thought, what she saw might well be only a reflection of the message in her own eyes.

Chris happened to be entirely wrong about Larry Hill's motive for wanting her out of Baghdad. He really was concerned for her safety, and with good reason. Eight hours earlier he had attended a Joint Chiefs' briefing at the Pentagon. Driving out of the Pentagon's underground parking garage, Larry's Lincoln Mark VII nearly collided with another car, an Oldsmobile sedan with diplomatic license plates. Larry recognized one of the two occupants in the rear seat.

A ranking Israeli diplomat, he had been cabinet minister, and was now a world-renowned figure functioning as a special envoy and roving ambassador.

What the hell was he doing at the Pentagon?

When White House press aide Charlie Donnelly denied any knowledge of the ambassador's presence,

Larry knew something big was up. It took several hours
and several telephone calls to learn that the ambassador
was in town for a meeting with top U.S. Defense Department officials.

Larry's sources identified the man accompanying the
ambassador as an Israeli Army general named Avi Posner. Posner was the defense minister's personal assistant, an antiterrorist specialist and notorious hard-liner.
Larry had heard of Avi Posner, whom everyone said
would someday be Chief of Staff and who, it was also
said, made Ariel Sharon look like a Nobel Peace laure-
ate.

To Larry, Avi Posner's presence revealed the exact
nature and purpose of the meeting. Unless someone
presented a most forceful argument against it—and in
this case it might require George Bush himself—Israel
did not intend to passively endure further Scud attacks.
Israel would retaliate.

This was why Larry wanted Chris to leave Baghdad.

As usual, Larry's instinct was good. The visit to the
Pentagon by the Israelis did indeed concern Israeli re-
taliation. But Larry did not know the half of it, nor did
he know that Avi Posner and the Israeli special envoy
were meeting with a DOD assistant secretary, a State
Department undersecretary, and two general officers,
one of whom was Lieutenant General Gene Gordon.
The DOD assistant secretary was standing in for Secretary Cheney, who had been called away to the White
House.

Gordon had met Posner some years before when Posner, as a young major, visited the USAF Academy and,
later, attended the U.S. Army Staff and Command War
College at Fort Leavenworth, Kansas. Gordon really
came to know him in 1987 when the Israeli, then a colonel, spent a year in Washington as military attaché.
Gordon was therefore not surprised at Avi Posner's
bluntness, nor did he take it personally.

The meeting was held in a walnut-paneled VIP conference room on the third floor of the Pentagon.
Gordon, seated opposite Posner at the small circular

table, had talked for some thirty minutes. Gordon's "talk" was more accurately an apology, an admission of the Allied failure to locate all the Iraqi missile launchers. Posner had listened with increasing impatience and finally, tapping a ballpoint pen against a stainless-steel water pitcher, said, "Gentlemen, we're wasting time."

He clipped the pen into his shirt pocket and continued, "The prime minister has authorized me to state that, in the event of an Iraqi chemical attack, Israel will immediately retaliate—"

"—not without our approval, sir," said the State Department undersecretary, Arthur Wingreen, who seemed much too young and handsome for a high-ranking statesman. "And I sincerely doubt such approval will be forthcoming."

"—with nuclear weapons," Posner finished.

The word "nuclear" hovered in the air like an Alpine echo. For a long moment no one spoke. It was as though everyone wanted to pretend the word, the unmentionable, had never been uttered. As though articulating it would awaken some long-dormant monster.

Posner went on now, "We are not seeking approval or disapproval. We are stating a fact."

After another moment of grim silence, Gene Gordon spoke. "I think I can say with some honesty that while we all expected this to happen, we had hoped it wouldn't. I don't have to spell out the unimaginable ramifications of such an act."

"Well, that's begging the question," said the DOD assistant secretary, Burton Fowler, a prim, stern man of fifty. "The United States will never allow it to happen."

"I think General Posner has made it quite clear that whether or not the United States allows it, is a moot point," said the other U.S. general, a white-haired army two-star who represented the Joint Chiefs. "What we have to do now is decide exactly how to deal with this situation."

"Mr. Wingreen?" Gordon said.

Wingreen ignored Gordon and Posner. He addressed the Israeli ambassador directly. "What makes you believe they'll use chemical weapons? They haven't up to now."

"Up to now," the ambassador repeated, with a wry glance at Posner, and continued to Wingreen, "As you know, for forty years the policy of my government has been to instantly respond, twice over, to acts of terrorism. Now, out of deference to the existing . . . political exigencies . . . we have refrained from doing so."

The ambassador, born and educated in England and a decorated World War II British naval officer, paused to glance at Posner again. "With your permission, General, I will elaborate on your remark." His exquisitely Oxfordian voice grew cold. "Frankly, we are disappointed with the American air force's inability to locate and neutralize all the missile launchers. Therefore, unless this situation improves, we will have no choice but take matters into our own hands. And if that requires the use of nuclear weapons, then so be it."

"Sir, are you suggesting that Israel might employ a nuclear option even if the Iraqis do *not* attack with chemical weapons?" Wingreen asked.

"Yes," said the ambassador.

For another long, tense moment no one spoke. The only sound in the room was someone's muffled cough and someone else clearing his throat. Finally, Burton Fowler, the Defense Department assistant secretary, said, "I have to assume that your government arrived at this decision only with a consensus of the cabinet?"

"That is correct, Mr. Fowler," the ambassador said.

Fowler's bald head shone dully under the room's fluorescent ceiling fixture. His face was ashen. "I'll relay this to Mr. Cheney," he said. He walked quickly to the door and left. The army two-star followed immediately behind him.

Again, briefly, the room was silent. Posner and the ambassador regarded each other, and then Posner turned to the window. It was a clear, crisp day. You could see the bumper-to-bumper traffic on the George Mason Bridge and all the way across the river to the patches of ice on the Mall.

"The city looks beautiful," Posner said.

Arthur Wingreen said to the ambassador, "You're giving us an ultimatum."

"Not at all," said the ambassador. "I am merely stating facts."

Wingreen opened his mouth to continue but then thought better of it. There was nothing more for him to say. Gordon said to Posner, "How do you plan to carry out the attack?"

"With aircraft," said Posner. "A missile would be too unreliable."

"Some of our people might react nervously when they spot unidentified aircraft coming in from the west," Gordon said. "They're quite liable to consider you hostile."

The ambassador said, "Then give us the IFF codes."

Gordon looked at Wingreen, who said, "That's a decision for the president."

The ambassador said, "Yes, and while he's deciding, please remind him that had it not been for our 1981 raid on the Baghdad reactor—for which we were universally vilified—if not for that 'outrageous act,' you and your Allies would almost certainly now be facing Iraqi tactical nuclear weapons. And remind him, also, that had the United States not provided Saddam Hussein with a no-questions-asked flow of money and munitions, Israel might not be in this present, terrible predicament. Yes, talk about chickens coming to roost?" He shrugged. "Well, at least we've put you on notice." He rose. Posner rose with him. The ambassador said to Wingreen, "I trust you'll convey all this to the president as soon as possible."

A faint smile creased Wingreen's thin lips. "I wouldn't be at all surprised if that's not being done as we speak. I'm sure Mr. Cheney has already heard from Burt Fowler. I'm also sure, sir, that there will be a few unhappy people in the White House tonight."

"In Riyadh, too, no doubt," said the ambassador.

"No doubt," said Wingreen. "I'm sure you realize

that if you do this, it will surely change the whole complexion of the war."

"It will bring it to a conclusion much sooner," the ambassador said. "That's hardly an undesirable scenario."

"The political ramifications, as General Gordon said, are also undesirable," Wingreen said. "No, excuse me, 'unimaginable' was the phrase he used. Unimaginable."

"What is unimaginable, young man," the ambassador said, "is for the United States to ask us to stand by and do nothing while our cities are assaulted! And we are not even involved in Desert Storm. We are the proverbial innocent bystanders, but each night that madman sends his terror weapons to our country. And with each successive attack, you ask us not to strike back. Where in the hell—you'll pardon my French—is the logic to any of that? We ask for IFF codes, you ignore the request. We ask for more Patriot batteries, you claim you have none, yet you repeatedly deny us the means of defending ourselves. My God, is there no common sense?"

"Sir," Wingreen said carefully, "I don't believe that what you are threatening can be called common sense, either."

"Then find and destroy the Scud launchers," Posner said.

"We're trying," Gene Gordon said. He spoke quietly, as if he were thinking aloud, and with a certain cynicism. Almost deliberately so, Avi Posner noted, as though tacitly approving the Israeli "ultimatum."

But Gordon had something else on his mind. He invited Avi Posner to dinner that evening, at Gordon's home on Mitchell Drive at Bolling Field. It was the first night in the nearly two weeks since the war started that Gordon had been at home earlier than midnight. After dinner, Mary Louise Gordon served coffee and brandy in the library. She excused herself to make a telephone call to their only granddaughter, celebrating her fifth birthday today. Posner did not believe her for an instant: He sensed it had been preplanned so that Gene Gordon could speak privately.

Posner was right. Gordon said, "Tell me what happened to Frank Kowalski. What *really* happened."

"Tell *me* who he really was."

"National Security Agency," Gordon said, after a moment.

"That, we've always known. But why with his own agenda?"

Gordon sighed heavily. Although he had anticipated Posner's questions and had decided to answer them, now he regretted having opened the issue at all. He felt foolish, no, embarrassed. He said, "Mr. Kowalski's mission was to observe. Observe and report. Period, end. As to what you call his own agenda, I cannot speak to that. If he had a private agenda, we were unaware of it. We were aware, however, of some of his, well, his extreme views. We thought it might provide some . . . balance."

Posner seized the word like a shark biting into a chunk of meat. "Balance? The man is literally an Arab agent, and to you that is balance?"

" 'Arab agent' is a little too strong, don't you think? We knew him to favor the Arabs, but—"

"Why not say it as it is—anti-Israeli."

"Yes," Gordon conceded. "All right, so now please answer my question. What really happened to him?"

"You received the embassy's report."

"Please, Avi, no games."

Harry Fleet, the CIA Tel Aviv station chief, had submitted a detailed memorandum on Kowalski's death. Fleet's report was nothing more than an embellished version of the Tel Aviv police investigation: Kowalski was the victim of a mugging, lured to the hotel by a prostitute. To spare Kowalski's family, the account released to the public made no mention of the prostitute.

"Very well, no games," Posner said, and told Gordon how Kowalski had betrayed Operation Presto to the Iraqis, and about the Mossad operative who did the actual killing. "It was a punishment befitting the crime, General."

"It was not a punishment," Gordon said. "It was an execution."

"We do what we have to do," Posner said.

We do what we have to do, Gordon thought. So succinct, so guileless, so effective. He was tempted to ask Posner if the Israelis intended to apply that same credo to their nuclear weapons. He should pose the question not-so-hypothetically: Would Israel, aware that a nuclear attack might result in a direct and unbelievably dangerous confrontation with the United States, "do what they had to do"?

Gordon decided not to ask the question. He already knew the answer.

FOURTEEN

"The cruel and inhumane bombing of our cities will be avenged! And soon, my brothers, soon! When the real war starts, the massive losses we will inflict upon the criminal 'Allies' are only a small sample of what lies in store for them. These invaders, these traitors, these imperialists!"

Vintage Saddam, Adnan was thinking. Tired and haggard as he looked, Saddam Hussein was as animated and forceful as Adnan had ever seen him. He commanded the undivided attention of the seventeen other men in the room. It was the daily Revolutionary Command Council briefing, convened this morning of February 2 in Saddam's personal command bunker, six stories beneath the bomb-shattered presidential palace. Adnan had been summoned to the meeting as a replacement for Taher Ayel, who two days before had suffered a major heart attack.

"They talk of our secret weapons," Saddam continued. "They are too stupid to understand that our most terrifying secret weapon is our people! The people of Iraq! Yes, our people will make whatever sacrifices are required, and Iraq will triumph. It is God's will! The will of God," he said, and raised his hands in a gesture of supplication.

Everyone applauded politely. Saddam then introduced Yusif Allawi, a solemn, graying major general as the new Deputy Commander of the air force. The former deputy, the outspoken Abbas al-Sadi, had been reassigned.

General Allawi sounded almost apologetic. He said that no matter how superb its training or how great the skill and courage of its pilots, no air force could prevail against an adversary's overwhelmingly superior numbers. For that reason, and that reason only, it had been decided to temporarily deploy twelve squadrons of firstline fighter aircraft to Iran, one hundred and eighty airplanes.

"Let's call it preventive attrition," he said.

Attrition, Adnan thought wryly, otherwise known as sending our best fighters out of harm's way. Overwhelmingly superior numbers. Almost the very words used by Allawi's predecessor, General Sadi. Formidable, Adnan remembered, was what Sadi had said. The Allied air strength was formidable. So formidable, apparently, that it resulted in Sadi's reassignment.

Reassignment, an all-purpose euphemism. Reassigned to hell. Rumor had it that Sadi had been shot. Punishment for the air force's dismal performance. Poor Sadi. The Americans had an expression for that—fall guy.

Saddam was speaking again. ". . . but despite the incredibly adverse circumstances, our brave pilots have shot down, as of today"—Saddam glanced at a yellow notepad—"two hundred and seventeen planes. Unhappily, as General Allawi points out, this amounts to only a fraction of their total. But we have some good news." He nodded at the Assistant Director General of the Information Ministry, Assad Hashim.

Hashim rose. A robust man of forty, he was a former news reader in Baghdad Radio's foreign section who had recently married the youngest daughter of the director general of Iraqi television. He spoke slowly and clearly, with no change of expression, as though addressing a radio audience.

"Today an element of the First Armored Division of the Republican Guard entered the Saudi Arabian city of Al Khafji. Several battalions of American marines were brought in to reinforce the Saudi National Guard units defending the city. Our troops routed them."

Hashim rambled on. His monotoned voice made Adnan drowsy. Adnan did not recall when he had last enjoyed a complete night's sleep, which hardly made him unique. Few Baghdadis, if any, slept through a night.

Never mind Baghdad, he thought, what about those poor bastards in Kuwait? The B-52s were bombing them now. Carpet bombing. Someone described it as a combination of hell and a continuous replay of the end of the world. Adnan had himself submitted a two-page summary of a dozen such reports from Kuwait. Why wasn't Hashim mentioning it?

And as for the two hundred and seventeen Allied planes shot down, this was a fantasy all unto itself. Yesterday at Al-Mutana airport, Adnan had run into Abdul Mahti, an air force colonel and former commander of Al-Mutana's military section. "Former" commander because of the first night's debacle that had completely destroyed the air base. Colonel Mahti had been transferred to a transport group. Which, as he grimly pointed out to Adnan, was certainly preferable to a "reassignment" such as the one received by General Sadi.

When Adnan asked about the two hundred and seventeen Allied planes shot down, Mahti had laughed crazily. "Surely, Dulaimi, you aren't swallowing that shit?"

No, Adnan thought now, no I am not swallowing that shit and never have. No more than the shit about the exemplary behavior of the troops in Kuwait. No more than most of the other shit, either. He was thinking all this as he pushed back his chair, rose, and in a loud clear voice said to Saddam, "Sir, I'm curious to know why my report on Kuwait hasn't been mentioned."

Hearing his own voice, for a moment Adnan thought he was indulging himself in his recurring fantasy of confronting Saddam Hussein with the truth. The startled faces of the generals and council ministers who turned to see the fool who had opened his mouth told him it was no fantasy.

"What report is that, Major?" Saddam asked.

"I wrote a report on conditions in Kuwait, sir," Adnan said, marveling at the steadiness of his voice. The realization that he had found the courage to face Saddam filled him with confidence. "That is, as the conditions were relayed to me. Those men might be relatively safe in their positions, but they are being driven mad from the constant bombing. And with the supply lines continually disrupted, there is a serious water shortage. The net result, sir, is a virtual epidemic of malingering, and from the figures I've seen, outright desertion—"

"Why haven't I seen the major's report?" Saddam interrupted, addressing no one in particular and immediately continuing to Adnan, "Where did you obtain this information?"

"It comes in daily to me, sir. I've correlated most of it from intelligence service reports."

"But not firsthand knowledge?"

"No, sir," Adnan said.

Saddam turned to his chief of staff, Lieutenant General Achmed Janabi, a man who but for his short stature might have been Saddam's twin brother. " 'Men driven mad from the bombing'? Do you know anything about that?"

Janabi forced a thin smile. "I should be very surprised if now and then a few people weren't pushed over the edge."

Saddam said, "But if I understand the major correctly, much more than a few."

"I'll look into it," Janabi said.

"And these desertions?" Saddam asked. "Is there truth to that?"

Janabi sighed heavily. "There is a decided increase of unauthorized leave and absence from station. I assure you, sir, we are taking the sternest measures to control it."

"Control it?" Saddam's voice was icy. His eyelids flickered almost as though he were in a trance, a sure signal of impending anger. His gaze was directed at Janabi, who glanced away. Adnan had heard it said that if Saddam, when angry, looked you in the eye, you were dead. "Control it?" he repeated. "I want it *stopped.* The next ten men charged with desertion are to be shot. As a group, and at once!"

Saddam turned to Adnan and continued, "Dulaimi, tomorrow morning you will proceed to Kuwait. You will assess the situation and report back to me personally. I expect a complete account within five days!"

Without pausing for breath, Saddam went on to another topic: the war criminal, U.S. President George Bush. That lackey of the Zionists would roast in the fires of the damned through all eternity. God willing, all in this room today would live to see it happen.

God willing.

Adnan wondered whose side God was on.

Hana also questioned God's allegiance. She could not comprehend why He had seemingly singled her out. Her mother taken from her, then her father, and now this awful punishment meted out to her brother. What terrified her now was the very real possibility of more loss, namely Adnan. They were sending him to Kuwait. An inspection trip, he said. She did not believe him. She knew him: He had volunteered for some dangerous mission.

"Why are you driving there?" she asked. "It's at least five hours. Why don't you fly?"

"Whatever we put into the air is instantly shot down," Adnan said. "Night or day. They have absolute control of the air."

"I see," she said, and decided to change the subject. She was beginning to sound like a nagging wife. "I saw Amir this morning." Hana glanced across the table at Khalid Sadoon. "Khalid thinks Amir is doing quite well," she said.

"He is," said Khalid, Amir's friend and tennis buddy, and Hana's medical colleague. "I've seen him only once, last week, but from what Hana tells me it sounds like genuine progress."

Except for his attitude, Hana thought. But then, what kind of attitude would you expect from a boy whose life was destroyed? Yes, of course, he was depressed and resentful. How could it be otherwise?

"I'll fix some coffee," she said. She stepped to the stove and placed the coffeepot on the still-glowing coals of the hibachi that rested atop the griddle area of the stove.

The three of them—Adnan, Khalid, and Hana—were in the kitchen of Hana's house, where they had just devoured a delicious dinner of lamb chops. Six large meaty loin chops, provided by Khalid and grilled to perfection on the hibachi. The chops were a gift from the father of one of Khalid's pediatric patients at the Amiriyah hospital. The father, a wealthy textile manufacturer, had supervised the selection and removal of weaving machinery from a Kuwait City factory. Among the other items he "liberated" from Kuwait were fifty pounds of frozen lamb.

At Khalid's insistence, Hana had taken an evening off from her twelve-to-fourteen hour shifts at the hospital and made dinner for Khalid and Adnan. With no cooking gas, Hana had to rely on the hibachi, which was probably why the chops turned out so well. It was an almost romantic setting, dinner by candlelight, although in the kitchen, not the dining room, and everyone wearing overcoats. Also aiding digestion was the fact that nearly three hours passed without an air raid.

The chops, kept adequately frozen by dry ice, tasted as though fresh from the supermarket meat rack. Pita, canned string beans, and a salad of tomatoes, cucumbers, and onions accompanied the meal, along with an excellent merlot from Jamal Badran's cellar.

"Believe me, even Mr. George Bush would have appreciated this meal," Adnan said, as Hana served the coffee.

"Thank Khalid," Hana said.

"Khalid, I thank you," Adnan said. He lit a cigar.

Khalid, only half joking, said, "My idea was for an intimate dinner with Hana. But when she said she'd have to check with her fiancé first, I told her to go ahead and invite him, too."

Hana laughed. "It happens, Khalid, that lamb is Adnan's favorite."

"Sure, my luck," Khalid said. He winked at Adnan. "Next time, believe me, I'll make sure it's something you don't like. Sweetbreads, maybe. Or liver. Yes, liver."

Khalid had a habit of speaking fast, the words tumbling from his mouth. It reminded Adnan of the Baghdad Radio announcer he had listened to in the car earlier that evening. More enemy planes shot down. No specific number, just *more*, a phrase used with increasing frequency. Tel Aviv in flames. More Israeli pilots captured.

More bullshit.

What puzzled Adnan was why Saddam recited those false facts and figures to his own staff, people who knew better. But then Saddam himself surely knew better. Or did he? Perhaps his advisors concealed the truth from him. Tell him what he wants to hear. No one wanted, no one dared, to tell the president the truth. Kill the messenger.

No, that was not it. For all his megalomania, Saddam's eyesight was unimpaired. He had merely to peer into the sky or walk down a rubbled street. Or visit one of his ruined airfields. No, if Saddam were unaware of the truth, he would not have approved sending one hundred and eighty fighter planes to Iran. He knew what was happening.

The Mother of All Battles.

Yes, that was the answer. Saddam had convinced himself that the ground war would bring victory. Or, at worst, a stalemate, which in itself could quite logically be claimed a victory.

"Adnan!" It was Hana, her voice tinged with annoyance. "Come back to the land of the living."

"If that's what you can call our beautiful country these days," Khalid said wryly.

Hana stood at the sink, stacking the dirty dishes. The sink was filled with dishes and silverware. Water, like electricity, was available only sporadically. You did not wash dishes after each meal but allowed them to accumulate for several days.

"Second time today I've dozed off," Adnan said. He looked at his cigar. There was very little ash, and the tip still glowed. If he had fallen asleep, it was only for a few seconds. He rose and smiled apologetically at Hana. "I'm going home. I must get some sleep."

"Stay here," she said. She glanced, embarrassed, at Khalid. "I mean, why risk getting caught in another raid?"

Khalid, teasing, said, "Naturally, the invitation includes me?"

"Absolutely," said Hana, who knew Khalid was due back at the hospital within the hour. "But you're on duty tonight, aren't you?"

Khalid grinned ruefully. "My luck," he said.

At that instant a familiar voice boomed through the room, a woman's voice: ". . . no, Linda, at the moment we are not under attack."

Chris Campbell's voice, from the black-and-white television set on the kitchen counter. The electricity, momentarily restored, flooded the room with sudden bright light from the overhead fluorescents. The television screen was split, Chris on the left, Linda Gould on the right.

Chris, swimming pool in the background, stood in the patio of the Al-Rashid Hotel. Linda, WCN's Tel Aviv correspondent, was inside the cramped WCN newsroom. Linda wore a gas mask, as did two women and a man standing behind her. An air raid siren was clearly audible.

". . . we *are* under attack here, Chris. At least that's what we've been told," Linda was saying. "We haven't yet heard any antiaircraft, nor any explosions. But I'm sure you can hear the air raid sirens."

"Yes, I hear them," Chris said. She pointed at the dark sky. "Here, as you see, it's quiet and has been for the past several hours. I notice you're all wearing masks. Is there some indication of a chemical attack?"

The Tel Aviv cameraman moved back for a wider angle. Linda looked like some buxom creature from outer space. Through the gas mask her Bronx-accented voice was hollow and fuzzy. "Standard procedure, Chris. They've threatened chemicals, so we take them seriously. If there's time this segment, I'll roll some tape showing small children wearing masks, and even infants."

Hana glanced at Adnan and said, "I can see why you think she's so attractive."

"Who?" Adnan asked, knowing full well.

"Maybe I should tint my hair blonde," Hana said. "Khalid, would you like me as a blonde?"

Adnan said to Hana, "Look, I hardly know the woman. I see her occasionally—"

"—in the line of duty," Hana said. "Yes, yes, I know."

"Well, dammit, it's true!" Adnan said, and immediately felt foolish. Hana had touched a nerve, the guilt button. He had been thinking about Chris, that fantasy again. Kissing her, making love to her, waking up in the morning with her in his arms. He was sure Hana had read his mind.

But Hana's interest was directed to the television screen, where Chris was saying, ". . . yes, I think it's starting. Yes, listen . . ." she held the microphone in the air. The sound of an air raid siren was loud and clear. "So don't feel alone—" The screen went blank. The overhead lights went out. The electricity had failed again. Outside, like a delayed echo from the television set, the air raid sirens sounded.

Hana said, "Here we go again. We attack them, they attack us. But those gas masks—" she shook her head sadly.

"They asked for it," Khalid said.

"But *chemicals?*" Hana said.

"We're not using chemicals," Adnan said. "And I doubt we ever will. That's just their propaganda. 'Infants with gas masks.' That should be worth another couple of billion in American aid."

Khalid said, "Maybe we damn well should use chemicals. Maybe then, they'll realize what they're doing to us."

Adnan had never disliked Khalid but never particularly liked him, either. More accurately, Adnan never paid much attention to him. Khalid was Amir and Hana's friend, obviously sweet on her, which both amused and flattered Adnan. But now Khalid suddenly reminded Adnan of Saddam's crowd of ass-kissing yesmen.

Adnan said to him, "Do you understand what would happen if we used chemicals?"

"I certainly do," Khalid said. "The Israelis would be on TV again showing infants with gas masks. You should come over to Amiriyah and take a look at *our* infants! Tell him, Hana. Tell him about the pediatric ward. Tell him how it feels to see a two-year-old girl with her face half torn away. Or the five-year-old boy they brought in the other night with both his legs blown off! Cute little bugger, remember? And that's nothing compared to the ones who are dying of malnutrition. Tell him, Hana!"

"It's true," Hana said. "And we've used up almost all our antibiotics and anesthetic supplies. What are we going to do for surgery?"

"And you ask what would happen if we used chemicals? What could happen worse than what's already happening?" Khalid said, and as though to emphasize the point, the whole house suddenly rocked with the shock waves of a distant explosion.

"This is only a small sample of what they can do," Adnan said, and paused. He had momentarily lost his train of thought. He was so tired. "When the Americans were fighting in Vietnam, one of their politicians said they would bomb Hanoi back into the Stone Age. That's what they'll do here. Bomb us back into the Stone Age. Doesn't anyone understand this?"

"You know what I understand, Adnan?" Khalid said. "I understand that they attacked us. I understand that they'll do anything to crush us. But what I *don't* understand is, why?"

"We defied them," Adnan said, wondering why he was indulging Khalid in these banalities, and at the same time marveling at the simplicity of the answer. We defied them.

Khalid was talking, but Adnan was not listening. Adnan wanted to hear no more, to argue no more, to explain no more. He said to Hana, "I think I will stay here. If the invitation is still open."

She smiled. "What do you think?"

Adnan said to Khalid, "Good night, Khalid."

"Talk about hints!" Khalid said. He rose, kissed Hana on the cheek, and shook hands with Adnan.

Hana walked Khalid to the door. When she returned to the kitchen, Adnan was slumped on the table, his head cradled in his arms. He was asleep. She shook him lightly.

"Adnan . . ."

He did not move. Hana wanted to get him up and into bed. She had planned to put him in Amir's room, but now decided she wanted him in her own bedroom, in her own bed.

"Adnan, darling, come on, help me." She shook him again, this time more forcefully. He sat up, immediately awake. He stared blurrily at her. "What's wrong? What time is it?"

"Don't worry about the time," she said. She pulled him toward her and nestled his head against her breasts. "We have all the time in the world."

"Don't let me oversleep," he said. "I have to be on the road no later than six."

She ran her fingers through his hair and then caressed his face. Tomorrow, he would go to Kuwait. He had already told her of the terrible conditions there, the incessant bombing. He might be killed. She would lose the only other important person in her life, the most important person.

"Adnan, I love you," she whispered, and felt herself blush. "Make love to me."

He said nothing. His eyes were closed. He was sound asleep again. She held him for a few more moments, then carefully lowered his head back onto the table. She went into Amir's room for a comforter and a pillow. She wrapped the comforter around Adnan's shoulders and placed the pillow under his head. He did not stir, not once, not even when another distant explosion rattled the windows, and another, and yet another.

The sound was muffled, like a series of dull thuds, and far to the south and west. Too far away for the injured to be brought to the Amiriyah hospital. So tomorrow when Hana reported for duty, no new patients would be crowding the wards and lying on mattresses on the corridor floors. That at least was something to look forward to.

2

Ed Iverson's reaction genuinely surprised Nick. At the very least, Nick expected a grudging acknowledgment of a job well done. He should have known better. Iverson had regarded him with those frosty condescending eyes and said, "I okayed an ATO frag for your flight to attack the nuclear facility at Al Quman. You never came close to Al Quman."

"We had no ordnance left for Al Quman."

"No, because you expended everything you had before you even got near the place."

They were in Iverson's office in the Al Kalir operations building. Nick had landed only a few minutes before and was still in his flight gear. He felt clammy and chilled from the dampness of the perspiration that had soaked his whole body. He had hardly taxied into his revetment when his crew chief informed him that he was to report immediately to Colonel Iverson. Iverson had proceeded to immediately give Nick hell for diverting from the primary target, an industrial complex at Al Quman, thirty miles north of Basra on the Iranian border.

Halfway to the target, Nick had spotted a large mechanized column moving south on the four-lane highway from Baghdad. He went down to five thousand feet for a closer look. The line of APCs, trucks, and cars stretched for miles.

Nick advised Yukon, the AWACS controlling that sector, of the column. Yukon said they would call a nearby A-10 flight for a strike. Nick had started climbing back to rejoin his flight when he realized that in a few minutes it would be dark. The A-10s were at least ten minutes away.

Nick still had the advantage of daylight. He decided to hit the convoy himself. He notified Yukon of his intent, requested cover, and ordered the other five F-16s of his element to join him in the attack. As one pilot later remarked, it was like playing a video arcade game.

In the initial sweep the six F-16s concentrated their fire on vehicles at the front and rear of the convoy. The wrecked vehicles blocked escape in either direction. The column was trapped. One by one, the F-16s swooped down with 500-pound iron bombs and Maverick missiles. And then, as though for an encore, each airplane came back to strafe whatever still moved with cannon fire. Within minutes every vehicle of the convoy was burning or immobilized. The highway and surrounding desert were littered with bodies.

Fish in a barrel.

Nick said to Iverson now, "Ed, you're chewing me out for doing something you yourself would have done in a flash. You're not thinking clearly. You're too tired. You've led the troops on at least two sorties a day. Every day, for eighteen days. What the hell are you trying to prove?"

"Watch your mouth, Nick. I'm still running this operation."

Mouth, Nick thought, as in foot-in-the. Harmon's Disease. He said, "Sir, can we put this discussion on hold for a second? I have to go down the hall to pee."

Iverson had just then swiveled his chair around to close the window blind. It was after six and the heavy overcast made the night even darker, which amplified the brightness of the portable halogen street lamps outside. In the harsh flat light, Iverson's skin looked loose

and sallow, lifeless. The outline of his oxygen mask was
still stamped on the lower half of his face.

Iverson closed the blind. He swiveled the chair
around again and, pointedly ignoring Nick, began reading some papers on his desk. The desk was crowded
with reports, directives, telexes, ATOs, correspondence,
all stacked in small neat piles. Master Sergeant Carlisi
selected only the mandatory daily paperwork for the
wing commander's attention. Iverson no longer spoke of
transferring her. Now he spoke of being unable to get
along without her.

Nick said, "I'll be back in a second."

Iverson glanced up from the papers. "Don't bother,
Nick. I've said my piece. Go on to debriefing and then
get some chow. Tomorrow, no matter what the ATO is,
you're to stand down."

"What the hell does that mean, Ed? I'm grounded?"

"It means I'm giving you a day off." Iverson waved his
hand at the stack of papers on the desk. "I want you to
handle some of this crap for me," he said, and resumed
reading.

"But *you'll* fly tomorrow?"

Iverson did not look up. "That's all, Nick."

"Do I have to call to your attention any single one of
a dozen directives and memos that restrict wing commanders to minimal combat duty?"

Again, Iverson did not look up. "You're dismissed,
Colonel."

Nick left the office, walked through Carlisi's cubicle,
into the larger outer office occupied by the 358th's enlisted administrative personnel: two female sergeants
and a staff sergeant and two male staff sergeants. The
room was noisy with conversation and ringing telephones and the raspy drone of a dot-matrix high-speed
printer.

Carlisi, a mug of coffee in each hand, had just entered
the outer office from the corridor. Nick said, "How're
you doing, Joanie?"

"I'm fine, sir," she said. "Which is more than I can
say for Colonel Iverson."

Nick continued out, then stopped. Carlisi's words and cold, almost rude tone had suddenly penetrated. He called to her, "Sergeant . . ."

She was at the door of her cubicle. She had placed one mug atop a file cabinet to free her hand for opening the door. She opened the door, then turned to Nick. "Sir?"

"Would you mind explaining that, please?"

"Explain what, sir?"

"What you just said." Nick walked back across the office to Carlisi's doorway. "About Colonel Iverson."

Carlisi's lips were pursed tightly, and her small narrow-set eyes glittered defiantly. "I don't think it needs any explanation, sir."

"The hell it doesn't," Nick said.

Carlisi set one coffee mug on her desk. She moved toward Iverson's office with the other mug. "You're pushing him too hard, Colonel," she said. She started to open the door.

Nick stepped past her and blocked the door. "*I'm* pushing him too hard?"

"Yes sir. Straight into a nervous breakdown."

"Joanie, *what* are you talking about?"

Carlisi drew in her breath to reply, then thought better of it. "Nothing, sir," she said quietly. "I was out of line. I'm sorry." She held up the coffee mug. "The colonel hates cold coffee. Excuse me, please." She brushed past Nick and went into the C.O.'s office.

Nick stifled an urge to laugh. It was funny, in a sad way. That look of exasperation on Carlisi's jowly face. He had known her nearly three years now and never known her to be rude or disrespectful. No, protective, that was it, she was being protective. Protective of her boss.

Nick was "pushing" him. Pushing him how? The answer came to Nick a few minutes later in the men's room. He had splashed cold water over his head and face and was regarding himself in the mirror. The mirror began vibrating with the shriek of jet engines outside. Two flights of the 32nd TAC Fighter Squadron, heading up into the Rutba area on a Scud hunt.

The answer to the question was as clear as the roar of the jets. The same one-word answer it had always been: insecurity, Ed Iverson's insecurity. Iverson was being "pushed" by Nick because he did not dare to relax, for fear Nick would show him up. Which Nick was doing, and which of course made Nick the villain.

And also the victim.

Victim of Ed Iverson's insecurity.

Okay, Nick said to the weary, hollow-eyed man in the mirror, so if you have the name, why not play the game?

Meaning what?

Meaning why not let old bird colonel Edward Morgan Iverson, Jr., run himself right into the ground? Or, as old soldier Sergeant Joan Carlisi suggested, straight into a nervous breakdown.

Oh, I get it, the man in the mirror said. Old Ed takes a tumble, so command of the 358th does not go to the vice wing commander, Colonel Tracy Hart, but to a more deserving candidate.

Now who could this more deserving candidate possibly be?

Let me guess.

Yeah, right, your hero and mine: Lieutenant Colonel Nicholas Harmon, the man who really runs the outfit.

Running, an interesting word. As in—if you agree with Carlisi's theory—Iverson running himself into the ground and/or nervous breakdown. Whichever occurs first.

She said we are pushing him into it.

Come on, we aren't pushing poor old Ed into anything. We don't have a fucking thing to do with it. He's doing it because he wants to. He thinks he *has* to.

That is precisely Carlisi's point.

I suppose the next thing you'll tell me is that's the reason I went after the convoy instead of waiting for the A-10s? To put pressure on Ed? Make him work even harder to stay one-up on me? Make him come apart in a thousand little pieces?

Look, friend, Ed Iverson's problem is not rivalry with me, but compensation for Vietnam. Iverson is attempting to redress his conspicuously undistinguished combat record.

Very eloquent, and very familiar. Compensation for Vietnam is something you're an expert in. A guilt monkey you've carried on your back for a long time.

You're talking about Chu-Bai, but I have to remind you that I've already paid that marker. Right here in Iraq. At a place called Shab al-Bir, remember?

If you say so.

You don't believe it?

Hey, believe whatever makes you happy.

"Sir! Colonel, sir!"

Nick whirled around to confront a baby-faced buck sergeant, a man he knew worked in communications but whose name he did not recall.

"You're not ill, are you, sir?" the sergeant asked.

Nick leaned slightly forward to read the sergeant's nameplate. "I feel fine, Rattner," he said. "Why do you ask?"

"You were staring into the mirror like you were in some kind of trance."

"You're kidding?"

"No, sir. That's exactly what it looked like."

Nick forced a self-conscious smile. "I guess I was imagining myself back in the States, or maybe Paris or London, a gorgeous redhead on each arm, drinking up a storm."

Rattner grinned. "Sounds good to me, sir."

"You know it." Nick patted Rattner's shoulder and hurried away. He felt foolish, like a schoolboy caught peeking into the girls' locker room.

The possibility that he actually was pushing Iverson nagged him the rest of the evening and into the night, and cost him nearly fifty dollars in a poker game, because he could not concentrate on the cards. Later, in bed, he tossed and turned for hours. Even his usual trick of counting departing and arriving jets did not help.

Finally he gave up. He got up and dressed and went

over to the club. He sat with Jack Leewood, 54th TFS Squadron C.O., and discussed the 358th's ATO frags. More electrical generating stations and Scud hunting. When Jack left, Nick remained at the table for a third cup of coffee. The big TV set was on, tuned to WCN.

Chris Campbell's face filled the screen. She was speaking into a hand-held microphone. The volume was too low for Nick to clearly hear, and a crawl line across the bottom of the screen read RECORDED 2/07/91.

February 7. Yesterday.

Nick watched, momentarily fascinated with Chris's soundless, moving lips. Whenever he saw her, he was reminded of their Washington meeting last winter. And how she had angered him. All the fatuous talk about American soldiers dying for oil—a four-letter word, he remembered her saying—and to keep the sheiks in their palaces and Rolls-Royces.

Now, after three weeks of a war that was ninety percent American, he was beginning to wonder if perhaps Chris Campbell did not have a point. A pretty fair case could be made of it, from the Saudis with their religious fanaticism and feudal society to those wealthy Kuwaiti families sweating out the occupation in penthouse suites in Saudi resort hotels.

Fighting to the last drop of American blood.

Thankfully, up to now at least, very little American blood. And unless the ground war went unexpectedly sour, the casualties would continue light. In that context, it was beginning to look like Panama all over again.

Overkill.

Nick had actually E-mailed Barney Gallagher a note, questioning the efficacy of continually bombing Iraqi electrical generating stations when the military recipients of the electricity no longer existed. The ministry buildings, the airports, the communications facilities. Why create more hardship for civilians by depriving them of desperately needed electricity?

He poured himself a half-cup more coffee, swallowed it down, and left. On his way out of the club, passing the

TV set, he was able to hear Chris clearly, that husky voice everyone admired.

". . . my colleague Tom Layton is leaving Baghdad. He'll still be on 'Gulf Watch,' although now from Amman. Tom has accepted a new position as bureau chief in that city. So, Tom, if you're listening, I just want to say how great it was working with you and how much you taught me. Good luck and bon voyage. . . ."

Outside, Nick started away. Just as the club door swung closed behind him, he caught a glimpse of the TV screen. Chris was still on. Nick smiled to himself. He had just recalled something Barney Gallagher said. A crying shame, Barney said, that a woman as good-looking as Chris Campbell was a liberal.

3

When Chris Campbell paid tribute to her colleague Tom Layton, she discreetly refrained from mentioning that Tom's departure from Baghdad was not voluntary. In point of fact, his departure was at the specific request of the Iraqi government. More specifically, the request of Wasfi al-Barak, deputy minister of the Interior.

In a word, kicked out.

It had happened the day before, Wednesday, February 6, the twenty-first day of the war. Chris and Tom had just finished lunch, chicken club sandwiches that for a change tasted like fresh chicken and not the usual frozen Kuwaiti brand. Everything was going well that day. The electricity was on, the elevators were operating. Chris and Tom did not have to climb the nine flights from the coffee shop back to their rooms. Another good omen, the weather. The day was pleasant, partly sunny and not cold. Even better, for nearly twelve hours, no air raids.

At lunch they discussed the day's "Gulf Watch" Baghdad segment. Tom wanted to interview the Soviet ambassador about Gorbachev's reported criticism of U.S. bombing of Baghdad residential areas. Chris thought she had a more interesting story in rumors of internal dissension in the Iraqi Air Force. The rumors went so far as to claim that defecting Iraqi pilots had attempted to bomb Saddam Hussein's country home. Tom said the story would never slip past the Minder.

Finally, Chris agreed to the Soviet ambassador interview. They returned to the ninth floor so that Tom could phone Washington to alert the network and prepare a promo. The satellite phone was in Chris's room. They walked quietly down the carpeted corridor toward her room.

"By the way, I'm still waiting to hear how you made out yesterday with the handsome Major Dulaimi," Tom said.

"If I 'made out' with him, Tom, you'd be the last to know."

"You said he promised you an answer on our date with Saddam."

" 'Our' date, I love that," Chris said sourly. "I didn't see the major yesterday. He's out of town. I think he's in Kuwait."

"Jesus, not for good?"

"He said he'd be back in a few days."

They turned the corridor corner and started past Tom's room. The door was open. The room was a shambles: bed and mattress ripped apart; clothes, shoes, papers strewn about. Tom's laptop computer lay on the floor, the cover pried open. In the center of the room, two grim young men were carefully removing the frames from the still-life lithographs that had been hanging on the wall. Observing all this, arms folded tightly across her chest, was the chambermaid, Leila.

The two men, black hair slicked back, heavy-mustached, dressed neatly in business suits, could have been brothers. Tom's Nikon camera was slung over the shorter man's shoulder.

Tom shouted, "Hey, what the hell's going on here?"

In Arabic, Leila said to the young men, "This is Mr. Layton."

Both men glanced blandly at Tom, then ignored him. Tom reached for the shorter man's shoulder, obviously to retrieve the Nikon. Chris said, "For Christ's sake, Tom, can't you see they're police?"

Tom's hand froze in midair. The men, paying him no attention, continued examining the lithographs, poking into the protective paper behind the frames to see if anything was hidden there.

Chris asked Leila, "What are they looking for?"

"Photos," Leila said.

"Photos of *what?*" Tom shouted, and in the same breath said, "Hey! That's my passport!" He had just noticed the blue edge of a U.S. passport protruding from the breast pocket of the taller young man's jacket.

"It will be returned to you," the man said in Arabic.

The shorter young man tossed the empty picture frame onto the bed. "Nothing here," he said in Arabic.

Tom was too flustered to speak coherently in Arabic. In English, he said, "Godammit, what are you trying to find?"

The taller man replied in Arabic and instructed Leila to translate. "Your entry visa into Iraq has been canceled," she said to Tom. "You are to leave the country as soon as you can make arrangements for transportation, but no longer than thirty-six hours. Your belongings and your person will be thoroughly searched for contraband."

"Contraband?" Tom said. "What fucking contraband? Are you all crazy?"

"Excuse me," the taller man said politely in Arabic, and brushed past Tom and left. The shorter one, carrying Tom's camera, followed.

"I'll try to phone Larry and see what can be done!" Chris said. She hurried to her room, closed and locked the door. She plucked the INMARSAT telephone out from the tangle of plastic wiring and relay boxes on the floor behind the desk. Immediately, she put the receiver down. Plenty of time to call Larry, tomorrow would do fine.

Someone was at the door. Tom, she knew, and called out, "I'll be right there." She wanted to laugh. She was remembering the utterly stupefied expression on poor

Tom's face when he saw the two policemen searching his room.

Not so funny for Tom, but not harmful to him, either. He'd have to leave Baghdad, yes, but he wouldn't be in any genuinely serious trouble. So it was all working out nicely: Tom out of Baghdad, but not in trouble. It made her feel better.

"Yes, I'm coming," she called out to the door. "Be right there." She wanted an extra moment to think. She knew Tom would ask her to seek Adnan Dulaimi's help in getting the expulsion order rescinded. Well, the only way to handle that was straight on: Sorry, Tom, I can't do it. No, I *won't* do it. So he'd call her a selfish bitch, so big deal.

"Come on in, Tom," she said, and opened the door.

It was not Tom, it was Leila.

Chris gestured her in and relocked the door. Leila said, "I still cannot believe that Mr. Layton would even *consider* such an outrageous act."

"I don't know what got into him," Chris said. "I suppose he thought it would make a good story."

"Thanks be to God, he never took the photos."

"Luckily for him, he never got the chance," Chris said.

"Lucky, Miss Campbell, is not the word. He would have definitely been arrested," Leila said. "And charged with much more than simply spreading malicious gossip."

"Malicious gossip is bad enough," Chris said.

"Yes, and there is a very strict law against it, and reasonable grounds for deporting him," Leila said. Automatically, in her chambermaid's role, she had begun straightening Chris's unmade bed. She pulled off the top sheet and ran the palms of her hands over the bottom sheet to smooth it out. "I keep thinking about the minister visiting those two women every week. And doing those terrible things with them!"

"Leila, the minister is an adult," Chris said, "What he does is his private business."

Leila thought about this a moment, then nodded

gravely. "Yes, and without photos, Mr. Layton can never prove the story, thanks be to God. It could have caused the minister much embarrassment."

"*I'm* embarrassed to think that it was a colleague of mine," Chris said. "By the way, you were careful not to tell anyone how you learned of all this?"

"Your name was never mentioned, Miss Campbell."

"That's good, Leila. I want you to have all the credit."

FIFTEEN

Chris's poignant farewell tribute to Tom Layton had left at least two of her viewers unmoved. One was Larry Hill. Knowing Chris and recalling her adamant refusal to give up the Saddam interview, Larry would have bet the company that Tom's expulsion was no mere coincidence.

The other astute viewer was Tom Layton himself. He was sure that Chris engineered it. He had no idea how she did it, nor did he care. Her motive was obvious enough: It made Christine Campbell WCN's sole Baghdad correspondent. The charges against him—"spreading gossip detrimental to the welfare of the state"—were of course sheer bullshit.

He saw the replay of Chris's February 7 "Gulf Watch" segment on a brand-new Sony TV set in the dingy office of a small gas station and automobile repair shop a hundred miles south of Baghdad. The Interior Ministry had supplied a Land-Rover, proper transit papers, and an army chauffeur for the long trip to Amman. They were that anxious to get rid of him.

With all but two of Baghdad's bridges destroyed, to reach Highway 1 and head west you had to detour south around the city. The army chauffeur, Mustafa, a draftee, was a friendly man in his late twenties whose hometown was Al Qurnah, supposedly the site of the Garden of Eden. Unfamiliar with the highway network, instead of Highway 1, Mustafa took Highway 6, which continued south. Not until they reached Ctesiphon, the ancient

Parthian city thirty miles south of Baghdad, did he realize his mistake. Highway 6 was the road to Basra.

To Tom, the word "Basra" was sudden magic. It was like reading a horoscope that promised you an unexpected career opportunity. Basra. What the hell, Basra was only down the road a piece. Tom told Mustafa to keep going. Maybe they'd be allowed into the city. Tom had his passport and his press credentials. It was doubtful that anyone in authority outside Baghdad knew he'd been kicked out of the country. From Basra, he could contact the WCN Baghdad production staff or even Chris herself. She'd have no objection to patching him in on her daily report. She'd have no excuse *not* to.

Tom Layton reporting live from Basra.

Mustafa was nervous about a constant rattling from the motor. It sounded like a loose tappet. He pulled in at a garage just outside the village of Aziziya. The problem turned out to be a nearly empty oil reservoir. The elderly garage proprietor had no oil in stock but sent his ten-year-old grandson to the house of a man who owned three taxis and would sell five quarts of oil. At fifty dollars, American.

The proprietor offered Tom a glass of tea and invited him into the tiny office at the rear of the garage. The room's one window was thick with dust and cobwebs, and the floor ankle-deep in empty oil cans and discarded belts and hoses and an assortment of other debris. Incongruously, on a battered work bench, was a brand-new remote-controlled 24-inch Sony television set.

The Sony was a gift from the proprietor's son-in-law, a lieutenant in the Hammurabi Division, the first Iraqi unit to enter Kuwait City. The Sony had been in the display window of a Hilalli Street electronics store. The son-in-law ordered his men to smash the window and help themselves. The automobile repair shop proprietor said that he considered the TV—and whatever else had been removed from Kuwait—a goodwill gesture from the people of Kuwait. A modest first installment of the money Kuwait owed Iraq.

It was on this same Sony TV that Tom Layton saw Chris Campbell's "Gulf Watch" segment. ". . . so, Tom, if you're listening, I just want to say how great it was working with you and how much you taught me. Good luck and bon voyage. . . ."

"Fuck you, you miserable cunt," Tom said quietly to the television screen. He aimed the remote unit at the screen and flicked the off button, erasing Christine Campbell. What a surprise in store for her. He'd telephone her his first report from Basra no later than noon tomorrow. And she, the treacherous bitch, would be obliged to relay it.

Basra, he had heard, was practically bombed out of existence. No other Western newsmen were there. He would have it all to himself. Little bites from people on the street, a pretty girl, a distraught housewife, a mourning parent. Ordinary people, reliving the nightmare of the death and destruction they had already lived through in the eight-year war with Iran.

This is Basra, Tom Layton reporting.

Maybe, by stabbing him in the back, the cunt did him a favor.

The next three hours of the trip were uneventful, almost relaxing. The weather had continued to be good, the day clear, the winter sun comfortably warm. The highway was uncrowded. Heavy military traffic was being rerouted onto side roads and minor highways. Although Tom's transit papers specified Highway 1 as the route of passage, at some checkpoints he was not even asked for papers. The soldiers were probably too distracted by the constant presence of Allied airplanes. Or they simply didn't give a damn.

In An Nasiriyah, ninety miles from Basra, Tom ordered Mustafa to stop at a restaurant near the bombed-out railway station. An unlighted neon sign in the window advertised AMERICAN BAR. The woman managing the restaurant said no food was available. The war, you know. A twenty-dollar bill produced an acceptable meal of roast lamb and salad, an item that Mustafa said was on the menu at three dinars: seventy-five cents at the going black market rate. And two bottles of local beer cost an additional ten bucks. The war, you know.

Outside An Nasiriyah a huge brown triangle loomed up out of the desert, the Ziggurat of Ur. The entry road to the ruins of the four-thousand-year-old terraced pyramid was blocked by a military gatehouse. A high stone wall topped with razor wire encircled the entire area. Protruding up over the top of the wall were the rudders of several jet fighters.

Tom could not help laughing aloud. In English, he said, "The sneaky son of a bitch is hiding his airplanes here! In plain sight, too. He knows damn good and well the Allies would never hit the place. It'd be like bombing the Sphinx."

Mustafa caught the gist of Tom's words and nodded in agreement. Pointing at the pyramid, touching his forehead in a mock gesture of veneration, he cried, "Saddam! Saddam!"

It was Saddam, all right, a thirty-foot-high portrait of him mounted on a white horse, garbed in the flowing robes of a Babylonian warrior. From the highway, the portrait resembled a gigantic picture postcard propped against the base of the Ziggurat.

They drove on. The desert turned gradually to grassy sand. They were in the marshlands now, approaching Shuyukh, a town on the shore of a large freshwater lake. A Nissan pickup truck and a jeep were parked hood to hood across the road. A half dozen soldiers with AK-47's manned the checkpoint. One soldier waved the Land-Rover to a stop.

The soldier, a sergeant, young and hard-looking, wore the red triangular sleeve patch and scarlet beret of the Republican Guard. Mustafa stopped the car. As at previous checkpoints, he smiled congenially and said in Arabic, "Special mission from the Interior Ministry. Want to see our papers?"

"Out of the car!" the sergeant said. "Raise your hands!" Two other soldiers joined him, weapons leveled. Like the sergeant, they were young and hard-looking.

Mustafa said, "Hey, come on, we want to get to Basra before dar—"

He never completed the last word. The sergeant had flung open the door, seized Mustafa's jacket lapel, and hauled him from the car. Another soldier pulled Tom out and then propelled him forward with such force that Tom fell face down on the road. The rocks and sharp pebbles of the road surface scraped deep into his skin.

He felt the buttons of his sheepskin coat torn open, and a hand groping in his inside jacket pocket. Letters, papers, and his passport were removed. Then, abruptly, he was flipped over on his back. He lay looking up into the cold brown eyes of the young sergeant.

"American!" the sergeant said disgustedly in Arabic. He grasped Tom's coat lapels, yanked Tom to his feet, and herded him around to the front of the Land-Rover. Mustafa was there, standing unsteadily, supported by a soldier on each side. Mustafa's face was blood-caked. His nose was flattened. Blood flowed from one nostril down onto the front of his khaki battle jacket.

"What the hell are you people doing?" Tom shouted.

In Arabic, the sergeant said to one of the soldiers, "Drive their car to the command post. Tell the captain it's a present from me. You," he said to Mustafa. "What outfit did you desert from?"

"No, you have it all wrong!" Mustafa said. "I am not a deserter!"

"Then what is your business here?" the sergeant asked.

"I told you, I am driving the American to Basra."

"You're a deserter!"

"No!" Mustafa's eyes widened in terror as the sergeant nodded to a soldier. "No, please!" Mustafa screamed. The soldier prodded the AK-47's barrel into Mustafa's stomach, pushing him backward across the road, and off the road into the sandy grass.

"You goddamn fools, what the hell are you doing?" Tom cried. In his mind, he stepped forward toward Mustafa but it was like running into a wall as, in his mind, the sergeant slammed the butt of an AK-47 across his chest. Tom actually felt the blow, although he knew it was all in his imagination. What he should be doing but lacked the courage to do. At the same time, Tom knew he could not stop whatever was about to happen.

In the pale light of the late afternoon sun it was like watching a silent movie, the characters silhouetted herky-jerky against the horizon. The soldier gripped the back of Mustafa's neck, forcing him to his knees, and in the same motion stepped back and raised the rifle slightly so that the muzzle was just below Mustafa's ear, and fired.

The sound of the shot echoed in Tom Layton's ears. He thought he might be imagining it, just as a moment ago he had imagined the sergeant preventing him from helping Mustafa. Mustafa's body toppled forward onto the sand. A wisp of white smoke curled from the AK-47 muzzle. No, not imagining it, it was all too vivid for imagination. It was a dream, one of those terror dreams where you know you are in a dream and struggle to wake up from it but cannot. All right, in a few seconds he would wake.

Even for a dream, it was incredibly real. He wanted to scream from the pain in his wrists as they were tied behind him by what felt like piano wire. His pulse was pounding in his forehead like a jackhammer, and a sharp pain seared his lower back as he was prodded at gunpoint. Now he was in the front seat of the jeep, the sergeant at the wheel, another soldier in the rear seat.

For a dream, it was also surprisingly complete, not in choppy bits and pieces like ordinary dreams. Especially when they drove past Mustafa's body lying face down in the sand. Mustafa's arms were spread wide as though in some final gesture of entreaty, and the sand beside his head and neck was black with a pool of viscous liquid that shone dully in the setting sun.

In the dream now, Tom closed his eyes. Yes, sleep, so you can wake up out of it. But sleeping, he heard the whirring sound of the tires on the pavement and the rush of wind against the windshield. He opened his eyes. He was still in the front seat of the jeep. Ahead, the

road stretched out as far as he could see. The sergeant
had just then removed one hand from the wheel and
reached blindly behind him to take a lighted cigarette
from the soldier in the rear.

In Arabic, Tom said to the sergeant, *"Saegaeyir?"*

The sergeant shouted over his shoulder to the soldier,
"He wants a cigarette!"

The soldier leaned forward and placed his own half-
smoked cigarette into Tom's mouth. The butt was soggy
with the soldier's saliva. Tom spit the cigarette out. It
dropped onto his lap and then onto the jeep's floor but
it left a smoldering burn mark on the knee of his wool
slacks, and he knew then it was no dream.

2

At Khorramshahr, during the war with Iran, they said
the shells came down like hailstones in a summer storm.
It was not untrue. Adnan recalled it well, the unending
hours of Iranian artillery fire, the utter, abject, unceas-
ing terror. Dead and dying Iraqi soldiers everywhere, in
the city streets and on the beaches. Twice each day, precisely at eleven in the morning and four in the afternoon, the bulldozer shoveled the bodies into a mass
grave in the garden behind the rubbled remains of the
Akhavan Hotel. The hotel overlooked the harbor, which
like some mythical sea of missing ships was clogged
from one end to the other with capsized or half-sunken
freighters.

If Khorramshahr was hell, then Kuwait was hell twice
over, three times, living death. Iraqi positions in Kuwait
were now being bombed by B-52s, carpet-bombed. The
bombers flew too high to be seen or heard. All you saw
was mile after mile of the desert erupting in enormous
geysers of sand. At night the sky was translucent with
the flashes of light from the explosions. Day and night,
the air was charged with the crackling thunder of detonations that rocked the ground like an endless chain of
earthquakes. All day, all night.

Most of the men took shelter in the network of tunnels and trenches that zigzagged across the entire length of the Saudi-Kuwaiti border. The tank crews, not so lucky, sat in their Soviet-built T-72s and T-62s buried turret-deep in the desert. They stuffed cotton in their ears, which blocked the sound but not the rumbling of the earth under the steel floors of the tanks, and certainly did not relieve the sense of utter helplessness. Or the knowledge that each B-52 carried thirty-one 750-pound bombs, and that each B-52 dropped those thirty-one 750 pound bombs into its own individual target "box," which was one mile long and one half mile wide. And that on each raid there were no fewer than twelve B-52s.

There was no respite. When the B-52s were not overhead, the A-10s attacked, and the F-15s, the F-16s, and the RAF Tornados and the Saudi Tornados. The A-10s and Tornados flew close-in, low-level, so you could at least see them and have an opportunity to fight back. At least, when you saw your adversary, it was not so terrifying.

The first forward position Adnan visited, a battalion command post, was commanded by a man he served with at Khorramshahr, Lieutenant Colonel Naji Sadoon. Adnan had arrived early in the morning of a typically gray, hazy day—in the midst of a B-52 raid— and Naji Sadoon's greeting was what had brought the Khorramshahr comparison to mind.

"Kind of makes Khorramshahr seem like a picnic, doesn't it?" Although the area under attack was more than fifteen miles to the north, Naji had to raise his voice to be heard clearly over the thunderous crump of the bombs.

They were in Naji's personal quarters, a small house-trailer a thousand yards to the rear of the third line of three defense lines of T-72 tanks. Naji sat on the edge of his canvas cot, chain-smoking, while Adnan tried to be comfortable in a rickety camp chair.

The plywood floor of the trailer throbbed constantly with the tremors of the distant bombing. The trailer, wheels removed, was surrounded by ten-foot-high sand berms and covered with desert-camouflage netting. A series of similarly camouflaged trenches and tunnels extended in both directions from the trailer. From the air, the site blended indiscernibly into the desert.

"It shouldn't last much longer," Naji said. He looked at his watch. "Ten minutes more. They'll give us a three-hour rest, then start again. You can keep time on it."

In response to Adnan's skeptical glance, Naji reached out to his cluttered desk and picked up a single piece of paper. He handed the paper to Adnan. "They've become quite sporting about it," he said.

The paper, resembling a glossy magazine page, was a propaganda leaflet. It looked like a timetable, which in truth it was, written in classic Arabic.

ALLIED FORCES CENTRAL COMMAND

This announcement has been delivered to you by one of the aircraft that is attacking your positions with high explosive ordnance.

Please be aware that, as of 1400, 12 February, until further notice, you may expect "visits" from B-52 bombers approximately every three hours on the hour.

> Arr 1400, dep 1430–1445
> Arr 1700, dep 1730–1745
> Arr 2000, dep 2030–2045
> Arr 2300, dep 2330–2345

13 February

> Arr 0200, dep 0230–0245
> Arr 0500, dep 0530–0545
> Arr 0800, dep 0830–0845
> Arr 1100, dep 1130–1145
> Arr 1400, dep 1430–1445
> Arr 1700, dep 1730–1745

Arr 2000, dep 2030–2045
Arr 2300, dep 2330–2345

Allied Central Command promises to maintain
and, if possible, improve the above schedule.

"Arrogant slime, aren't they?" Naji said. "And clever,
I have to admit. You'd think knowing when they're coming might give you some chance to prepare. It works just
the opposite. My people are scared shitless. So am I,"
he added.

The floor of the trailer shook with another series of
muffled explosions. "How is your supply situation?" Adnan asked.

Naji Sadoon was a compact man of forty. His bushy
black mustache somehow complemented his bald head.
A jagged scar, souvenir of Iranian shrapnel, ran from
the corner of his mouth all the way up to his eye. The
scar seemed to suddenly redden.

"Adnan, you're a fucking comedian." Naji mashed his
cigarette into the remains of rice and beans on a paper
plate on the floor under the cot. "We're short of water,
food, medicine, gasoline and diesel fuel, and butane gas
for cooking, and even toilet paper. All we're heavy on is
ammo, but so far there's nothing to use it on." He lit a
fresh cigarette. "Not a day goes by that I don't lose two,
three, sometimes four people—"

"—dead?"

The scar grew even redder. "The dead are up ahead,
in the first and second lines. They're really taking casualties up there. Back here, though, the most serious
wound is a dose of clap one of my gunners caught when
he was on leave last month." The scar curled to accommodate a tight, grim smile. "From his wife, yet." The
smile vanished. "I lose them, Adnan, from desertions.
They just walk away. And these are regular army, veter-
ans most of them."

"That's why I'm here," Adnan said. "Saddam himself
sent me. He doesn't believe it's happening."

"Well, you can tell him for me that it's happening,"

Naji said. He waved the B-52 "schedule" leaflet in Adnan's face. "Don't for a minute kid yourself that this isn't effective. When you know *when* they're coming and you don't have any place to hide—and you're thirsty and hungry and freezing your balls off—you'll just pick up and run like hell. As far and as fast as you can."

"What's your recommendation?" Adnan asked, and immediately wanted the words back. Talk about stupid questions! Naji laughed, genuinely amused, which made Adnan feel even more foolish.

"My recommendation, Adnan, is that we shoot the B-52s down," Naji said. "Every last fucking one of them."

"Forget I asked the question," Adnan said. He rose to leave. Naji did not rise with him. "I'll try to do something about the supplies."

Adnan was at the door when Naji called to him. "Adnan, do you think he *really* knows what's going on here?"

"If he doesn't, he will when I get back."

"Will he believe you?"

Adnan groped for a reply, but all at once the trailer floor stopped vibrating. The thunder in the distance also stopped. He looked at his watch. "Four minutes early," he said. "They stopped four minutes before you said they would."

"Maybe they're running low on bombs," Naji said.

"Maybe they're just bored."

"Yes, it would get tiresome, wouldn't it?" Naji said. "Day after day, blasting the shit out of the enemy, and no opposition. Boring as hell."

Adnan spent most of the morning and well into the afternoon at other forward posts. Some commanders were not as forthcoming as Naji Sadoon and, obviously mistrusting Adnan, denied any morale problems. To a man, however, all complained bitterly about supply. By the time Adnan was finished and on his way back to Kuwait City, he had composed half the report. It would be succinct and to the point.

Twice, a marauding American A-10 swooped down out of the greasy-black clouds to rake Adnan's white Mercedes sedan with cannon fire. Adnan's driver veered safely onto the road shoulder each time. Strangely, Adnan felt more humiliation than fear. The very sight of the aircraft, so disdainful in their unchallenged presence, filled him with shame.

This, then, should be made clear in his report. Iraq must face reality. To maintain the illusion that the Allied coalition could be defeated or even maneuvered into a stalemate was nothing short of suicide. But as fast as the thought came to him, he drove it away. Not from shame now, but the certainty that Saddam would never accept it. If, indeed, the report actually ever reached Saddam. Despite his order that Adnan report to him personally, a dozen different people with a dozen different motives would shield him from the truth.

No, what they wanted was a glowing account of conditions in Kuwait. Morale high, troops trained to razor-sharpness. Eager to fight, prepared to die. Adnan knew that such a report would guarantee him the single star and eagle of a lieutenant colonel, maybe even the two stars and eagle of a full colonel.

It was something to think about, especially when he saw the star and eagle on Gamal Othman's shoulder boards. Before returning to Baghdad, Adnan had stopped at 8th Special Forces Brigade HQ in Kuwait City to visit Gamal. He wanted Gamal's version of Amir's so-called accident. Not that it made any difference or that anything could or should be done about it, simply a matter of knowing, of closing the book on an unhappy chapter.

Gamal was disconcertingly frank. Yes, it had happened exactly as Amir described. If anyone was at fault, it was Gamal himself. He was not unaware of Captain Takriti's brutality, but he had demanded results. In Gamal's judgment, a true account of the incident would have served no purpose. In any event, it was now all quite academic. Two weeks ago, while strolling on Hilalli Street in Kuwait, Captain Takriti had been shot and killed by a sniper.

"It almost makes me believe in God," Gamal said. "Poetic justice, I suppose."

"That's of no comfort to Amir," Adnan said.

"Nor are apologies or regrets from me," Gamal said.

"For sure," Adnan said.

Although anxious to return to Baghdad, Adnan accepted Gamal's invitation for dinner and overnight accommodations. Traveling at night, ironically, was more dangerous than in daytime. During the day the roads were safer, obscured by smoke from the burning oil wells and the warmth of the desert sand that distorted the infrared sensors of Allied fighters. At night, the desert cooled rapidly. The heat of an automobile motor showed up on an IFR display screen like the glow of a firefly in the dark. At night, there was no place to hide.

They dined with some of the 8th's staff officers in the ornate dining room of the requisitioned seaside villa that served as the Brigade's HQ. One of the officers was a dignified white-haired, white-mustached provost marshal colonel, Husain Hakim. Colonel Hakim had arrived in Kuwait only a few days before to expedite the apprehension and punishment of army deserters and to take charge of POW interrogation.

"*What* POWs?" someone asked. "The ones we took at the Great Battle of Al Khafji?"

Everyone except Hakim chuckled at the sardonic reference to Al Khafji, the Saudi border town whose capture had been so gloatingly announced. The Allies had reoccupied the city within twelve hours, inflicting heavy losses in the process.

"Don't worry, we'll be taking prisoners," Hakim said, unsmiling. "Speaking of prisoners, I may have a CIA agent on my hands. An American, claims to be a television newsman who was driving to Amman. Driving, mind you, as though on a weekend holiday. But his driver made a mistake, he says, and instead of heading west, all at once they found themselves going south, on the road to Basra."

Gamal Othman, winking at Adnan, said to Hakim, "Sounds reasonable to me, Colonel."

Again, Hakim was the only one not to laugh. He said, "I'm trying to check his identity with Baghdad, but I don't have to tell you how it's almost impossible to get through."

Adnan said, "I know some American television people. What's this fellow's name?"

Hakim withdrew a spiral-bound notebook from his tunic breast pocket, and a pair of tortoise-shell half-frame reading glasses. He opened the notebook to the correct page. "Layton," he said. "Thomas H. Layton."

"I know Tom Layton," Adnan said.

3

The noise woke him. A man's scream of terror and then a gunshot. All from a distance, like a shrill echo. He opened his eyes. He fully expected to see Mustafa's body toppling forward into the sand and the wisp of white smoke from the soldier's rifle muzzle. The goddamn dream repeated, except that this time it was him, Tom Layton, who had been shot. Yes, he felt a slight pressure on his forehead and a sensation of moisture. Blood, he thought. His own blood.

The moist pressure on his forehead was a wet rag, applied by a man kneeling beside him. A dark-complexioned man whose heavily bearded face was puffy with blue-black bruises and whose nose and mouth were swollen to twice their normal size. He wore a fraying red wool cardigan sweater over a blood-spattered white shirt and blue denim trousers. His tennis shoes were mud-encrusted and had no laces. He was speaking to Tom in English, but with a thick Arabic accent.

". . . you will feel better soon."

Tom was sitting on a damp concrete floor, his back propped against a wall, both legs outstretched. He placed his hand on the floor and started to push himself up. He gasped with pain. It was as though a jolt of electricity had surged through every nerve in his body. He slumped back against the wall.

"Try not to move," said the man. "You have been beaten quite badly."

"Where the hell am I?" Tom said.

"You are in Kuwait," the man said.

"Kuwait," Tom repeated, for some reason not at all surprised. "Was that a shot, or was I dreaming?"

"Yes, you heard a shot," said the man. "It was an execution. The first of the morning." One side of his swollen face twisted in a wry smile. "Welcome to our beautiful country."

Now Tom realized there were others in the room. He could make out a blanket-wrapped form huddled on the floor nearby, and seated next to that one was another. Two others lay on canvas cots near a thick firewall door. A few feet from the door was an ironstone laundry sink with a single spigot. The metal drain grille under the sink had been removed. A man stood at the open hole, urinating into it.

It was all coming back to him now. Basra, where the streets oozed with mud from the tens of thousands of sandbags that had been piled against the walls of buildings and had burst open. The room in the Basra Sheraton Hotel where they questioned him. Beating him nearly to unconsciousness, then reviving him. Beating him again. Fists into the stomach and kidneys, rubber truncheons on the buttocks and soles of the feet and, occasionally, on the testicles.

It seemed to have gone on for hours. Each time he denied being a CIA agent, they beat him. He begged them to call Baghdad to verify his identity. Once, to stop the beating, he started to confess. But then he realized that this would almost surely put a bullet into the back of his head. And all the time, outside, he could hear the antiaircraft guns, and the bombs falling, and the whole building shaking. Each explosion only seemed to further infuriate and frustrate his Iraqi captors.

Yes, and now he remembered one of them, a middle-aged major or colonel with wavy white hair like a shampoo ad and a mustache with waxed upturned ends that resembled the tips of white antler horns. The white-haired major-or-colonel was attached to a special GHQ Security Force that had just received orders transferring it to Kuwait. Since their "discussions" had thus far proved inconclusive, and because he considered it imperative not to interrupt the continuity of the "discussions," the white-haired major-or-colonel took Tom with him to Kuwait.

"What day is this?" Tom asked the man.

"Monday."

"Monday," Tom repeated, struggling to mentally compute the date. If Saturday was the ninth, Sunday was the tenth. "Today is the eleventh, February eleventh," he said. "My name is Layton, Tom Layton. I'm a journalist. I work for an American television news network."

The man lowered himself down to the floor beside Tom. "My name is Ali Hamadan."

The name sounded vaguely familiar. Yes, of course, the Resistance. Ali Hamadan was a leader of the Resistance, a symbol. A legend. Tom thought he recalled Chris Campbell once mentioning having met Ali Hamadan.

Chris, that bitch, he thought, and began composing a letter to her. Dear Bitch: You sure did an A-1 good job getting rid of me. But wait, he told himself, be fair. Chris isn't responsible for you being here. You were on your way to Amman. If you hadn't decided to smart-ass your way into Basra, you'd probably be in Amman right now, drinking a powder-dry Beefeater martini at the bar of the Amman Hilton.

Ali Hamadan continued talking but Tom was still thinking about the powder-dry Beefeater martini at the Amman Hilton, and about the gunshot of a few minutes before. An execution, Ali Hamadan said. The first of the morning. It was unreal, just as the past three days were unreal, and now this. Locked up in a cellar with a dozen condemned men.

"How long have you been here?" Tom asked.

"A week," said Ali. "I was arrested a week ago."
Again, his mouth twisted in the hint of a smile, a smile
of pride. "It took them five months to find me."

"And you've already had a trial?"

"The Iraqis do not waste time on trials."

Tom said nothing. His mind was racing ahead to the
story he would write of this encounter. The brave Resistance leader stoically facing death.

". . . but no matter what happens to me," Ali was
saying, "I know that I have helped create a new Kuwait,
an entirely new nation. You will see. After the war, you
will see it happen."

But you won't, because you'll be dead, Tom thought,
and said, "I hope the Emir agrees."

"The Emir is a realist," Ali said. "He sends us guns
and ammunition, knowing that someday those same
guns and ammunition can be turned against him. He
understands the political implications of the Resistance
movement."

Tom envisioned the lead paragraph of his exclusive
story about Ali Hamadan, hero of the Resistance. The
terrible, bloody price paid for a democratic Kuwait. In
Ali's own words, only minutes before facing an Iraqi
firing squad. It could run as a week-long series of three-
to five-minute "Gulf Watch" segments. Not to mention
a marvelous chapter in the book that at that instant Tom
had decided to write. He even had a title: *Gulf Watch
Diary*.

Thank you, Christine Campbell. For the book, which
I should dedicate to you, along with thanks for my balls
that are as big as grapefruit and feel as though they're
clanking against my ankles, and for the blood I'm pissing. But then he had a dedication just as good: "To
Chris Campbell, Who Made It All Possible." And he,
Tom Layton, would make sure everybody understood
the delicious inside joke.

It all sounded fine, except that Tom had no proof Ali
Hamadan was who he claimed. How did Tom know Ali
wasn't an Iraqi agent, planted here for God knew what
purpose? To ingratiate himself with the other prisoners

for information about the Resistance, or to obtain evidence, false or otherwise. Yes, and look how talkative the man had become. And that speech about bringing democracy to Kuwait.

Ali could have been reading Tom's thoughts. He said, "Are you truly a journalist, or . . . something else?"

"Something else?" Tom said. "Such as what? They've accused me of being a CIA agent. Is that what you're getting at? No, I am *not* with the CIA."

At that instant, as though on cue, three red-bereted soldiers appeared in the doorway. One remained in the corridor, a pump-action riot gun cradled in his arms. The other two strode into the room, straight to Tom and Ali Hamadan. Tom knew they had come for him. He wanted to scream in terror and curl himself up into a ball. He wanted to plead with them not to beat him anymore. He wanted to explain that he was not a young man and honestly did not fear death, but did fear permanent injury. Kill me, but please don't leave me crippled.

He closed his eyes and waited. He knew they would seize his arms and pull him to his feet. He could already feel the excruciating pain, like a hundred crazy bones everywhere in his body. He opened his eyes to see two pairs of dusty black combat boots on the floor in front of him. They reminded him of the white-haired major-or-colonel's boots, which were reddish brown. Yes, of course, officers wore reddish-brown boots. Enlisted men's boots were black.

My God, suppose they had not come to take him for more questioning, but to shoot him? No, no, now just wait one second. Your country is a signatory to the Geneva Convention. You can't find me guilty without a trial. Now, look, goddamn you, I am no fucking CIA agent! You have to believe me! You have to give me a chance to prove it!

The soldiers had not come for him, but for Ali Hamadan, and were dragging him off to be shot. Tom felt bad for Ali Hamadan, but also for himself. Now he would never write Ali's story. He tried to put it out of his mind, and for a few minutes he did. Tom had just begun to feel sleepy and, also, hungry—when the hell was feeding time in this hotel?—when he heard the rifle shots. A moment later, a single shot, this one sharper, a pistol. The *coup de grâce*.

Well, that answered one question. Ali was no Iraqi agent. Even while Ali was being dragged away, Tom had wondered if that too might be some kind of charade. But no, because if Ali was a plant, he would have asked Tom pertinent questions and certainly spent much more time with him. Developing a relationship, earning Tom's trust. No, Ali was no Iraqi spy. That final pistol shot was the ultimate proof.

Across the room, at the open drain, another man was relieving himself. He had been there throughout Ali's execution and had continued urinating without pause. He had not even flinched.

SIXTEEN

Nine days before, on February 2, the day U.S. Marines recaptured the Saudi Arabian city of Al Khafji, a representative of the Emir of Kuwait and two other men met in New York City. The meeting took place in a suite at the Belgravia, a small residential hotel on East 71st Street, not too far from the UN.

The suite was booked in the name of Maryland Systems Enterprises, and guaranteed with an American Express corporate card. The card was genuine, the company was not. Maryland Systems Enterprises existed in name only, one of a number of similar mail-drop organizations financed and operated by various agencies of the United States government.

The Kuwaiti had traveled nearly six thousand miles, all the way from the Emir's temporary residence at the Al-Hada Sheraton Hotel in the Saudi Arabian resort city of Taif. The second man, an American, had flown in from Washington, D.C.

The third man had walked to the hotel from his home, an apartment on East River Drive. The apartment, which he shared with his wife and two teenage daughters, was five blocks from his office at the UN and his job as special assistant to the Iraqi ambassador to the United Nations. He was the ambassador's consultant on military affairs. He was also a member of the Baath Party and a third cousin to Saddam Hussein.

A meeting between an important Iraqi and a highly placed Kuwaiti—in the presence of an American—obviously demanded utmost privacy. The hotel's uptown location and noncommercial environment was ideal for the purpose. The men arrived separately and went immediately to the sixth-floor suite. Befittingly, as wartime adversaries, the three were diplomatically aloof, although neither the Kuwaiti nor the Iraqi made any attempt to conceal their thorough, mutual contempt.

For his part, the American disliked both men. At the moment, however, he held an even greater dislike for his White House superiors. They had sent him to the meeting as an observer. "Observer," a euphemism for bestowing the imprimatur of the United States upon the meeting.

The American, Charles Donnelly, was an assistant press secretary and in no sense of the word a diplomat. But he happened to be the only mid-level administration staffer available. Equally important, he could be trusted.

The sixth-floor Belgravia hotel suite overlooked Franklin Roosevelt Drive and the East River. In contrast to the previous day when four inches of snow had fallen, the weather was warm and sunny. From the living room, you could see all the way across the river to Astoria and the squat skyline of low-rise factory buildings outlined against the smoggy horizon. Not an especially inspiring view, a perfect reflection of Charlie Donnelly's mood.

Donnelly, wearing sunglasses against the glare of the late morning sun on the melting snow, stood at the window listening to the two men behind him. More accurately, listening to the silence. Not a word had passed between them since the Iraqi, the last to arrive, entered the room three minutes earlier. Indeed, except for an exchange of sullen glances, the two had hardly acknowledged each other.

Donnelly turned from the window now. He slipped his glasses into his jacket breast pocket and faced the two men. "Gentlemen, I know you both speak English, so I would ask that you please use that language."

The Kuwaiti, a slight, balding man of thirty-eight said, "I am not sure Mr. Assiri is sufficiently fluent."

The Iraqi, Sayid Assiri, in an almost flawless Oxford accent, said, "Well, we can always use sign language." He was a solidly built man whose thick black hair and angular face gave him a certain youthful appearance. Although he looked younger than the Kuwaiti, he was at least ten years older.

Donnelly walked to the divan and sat down. On the coffee table were several bottles of Canada Dry club soda and ginger ale, a bucket of ice, and some glasses. No liquor, not even beer. Some idiotic State Department protocol clerk had probably decided that the presence of alcohol might offend the two Muslims. Donnelly started to pour himself a glass of soda, then changed his mind. To hell with it, he'd have a drink at La Guardia on his way back. Hopefully, within a few hours.

"This meeting is at your request, Mr. Mazin," he said to the Kuwaiti. "Let's get started."

Rami Mazin resembled a shopkeeper or civil servant more than a career soldier, a full colonel of the Kuwaiti National Guard, no less. And you would surely never see him as the main liaison between the Kuwaiti government-in-exile and the Resistance movement inside the Iraqi-occupied nation.

"I am here to share certain information with Mr. Assiri," Mazin said. He had addressed Donnelly, as though expecting Donnelly to relay the statement to Assiri. "For months now, the Iraqis have sought to arrest the leader of the Kuwaiti Resistance movement, the man known as Ali Hamadan. Sometime in the next three days, in the hours between one and four in the morning, Ali Hamadan will be found at an apartment house in the Salwa section of Kuwait City. Number 112 Messilah Street, just off Sixth Ring Road. He will be there—accompanied by several of his men, I am sure—to receive a shipment of explosives and electronic timing devices."

Sayid Assiri's face was impassive, but his eyes betrayed him. The eyes, deep and black, danced with excitement. And now for the first time he faced Mazin directly.

"I shall ask the obvious question: why? Why are you offering me such information?" He glanced at Donnelly. "The Americans have a phrase for it: 'What's the catch?' "

"The Americans also have a phrase, 'Never look a gift horse in the mouth,' " Mazin said. "We have our reasons."

Assiri thought about this a moment. "How can I be sure Ali Hamadan will be at that address?"

"Because that is where I arranged for the material to be delivered," Mazin said.

"That hardly guarantees his presence," Assiri said.

"He will be there," Mazin said. "The people making the delivery will not turn over the material unless it is to him personally."

Donnelly did not believe what he was hearing. He had been told only that the purpose of the meeting was to arrange some kind of quid pro quo. He had assumed it concerned an exchange of prisoners. Never could he have envisioned anything like this: a Kuwaiti sellout of its own people. No, sellout was too benign a description. It was a betrayal. Cold, calculating, for reasons that were uncomfortably clear.

Ali Hamadan was Kuwait's most revered hero. As the leader of an undeniably effective Resistance movement, Ali Hamadan had earned the Emir's respect and gratitude. And assurance from the Emir that Parliament would be reestablished and government censorship of the media ended. The promise of democratic reforms had driven Ali Hamadan and his followers to ever more daring feats of bravery. Each day, every day, Iraqi soldiers were shot by snipers in the streets, or shredded by car bombs, or knifed in back alleys. The Resistance was making life so miserable for the Iraqis that the reward for Ali Hamadan's capture had quadrupled to $100,000.

That, for the Kuwaiti government-in-exile, was the good news. The bad news was that Ali Hamadan had evolved into a potent political force. He had become a symbol for freedom and clearly intended to convert that symbolism into postwar fact. If Ali Hamadan could so successfully inspire the people to fight against oppressive odds, he could inspire them to demand change. Drastic change. Revolutionary change.

". . . the Emir must be a very frightened man," Assiri was saying. The corners of his mouth curved suddenly upward in an ironic smile. "Well, I suspect this to be true of the whole Sabah clan."

"Believe what you will," Mazin said. "And do what you will. You have the information."

Assiri's smile widened. He looked like a man who had all at once understood the punch line of a racy joke. "The heroic Kuwaitis, who fled in panic at the first sight of our tanks, consider one of their own people a greater threat to their survival than the Iraqi Army. And, unable to do their own dirty work, ask the hated enemy to do it for them. This should someday make an intriguing historical footnote."

Which was precisely what Donnelly was thinking. He turned away again, to the window. Behind him he heard Mazin's voice, in Arabic now, and Assiri replying. Discussing details, probably. Donnelly felt not the slightest interest or curiosity. In truth, he felt nothing, only a vague sense of shame, tempered with anger.

The Kuwaitis even in their clumsiness were clever. Clever enough not to have embarked upon this piece of treachery without the approval, tacit or otherwise, of the United States. Cleverer still, to notarize that approval by insisting upon the presence of a representative of the U.S. government as witness to the perfidy. Thereby obviating any U.S. interference or objection, should the restored Kuwaiti regime find it necessary to suppress certain "subversive" elements within the populace.

Donnelly knew all the White House and Pentagon answers, all the catchwords: geopolitics, larger aims, long-term interests. He could just imagine the conversations that had preceded his journey here. A half dozen men sitting around the Oval Office discussing the

Emir's plan for dealing with a postwar popular uprising.
It was in the U.S. national interests—spelled o-i-l—for
the present Kuwaiti government to remain intact. Moreover, this was an explicit promise made to the Sabah
family by the Bush administration.

And talk about pragmatism! Whoever selected him,
Charlie Donnelly, as the observer, certainly knew their
customer. Knew that his own personal ambitions pre-
cluded him from ever breathing a word of what had
transpired here. But then anyone, from the White
House doorman up, who served as observer would remain silent. It was all simply too absurd for belief. A
claim of having been abducted by spacemen would be
taken more seriously.

Kuwaitgate.

". . . then, we have nothing further to discuss," he
heard Mazin saying, in English now.

"Nothing," Assiri said.

Mazin and Assiri were facing each other. Donnelly
wanted to laugh. A crazy picture had just entered his
mind. The men would shake hands, and then each
would place a revolver to the other's head and shoot.
But they did not shake hands, and they did not draw
revolvers. Each merely nodded coldly. Assiri stepped
past Mazin and went to the door.

At the door Assiri stopped. The ironic little smile
reappeared. He said to Mazin, "The reward for Ali Hamadan," he said to Mazin. "Shall I have the check sent
to you? Or to the Emir?"

Mazin's dark-skinned face was taut with anger. His
black eyes narrowed with indignation and humiliation.
Donnelly wanted to applaud. Mazin deserved to be put
down. The whole goddamn treacherous Sabah family
deserved it.

Assiri addressed Donnelly now. "Or perhaps Mr.
George Bush should receive the reward," he said. "In
silver, perhaps? Thirty pieces?"

2

It was Tom Layton's first decent meal in three days, his first *meal*, period. Roast chicken, nicely prepared and served with an excellent Tavel. The chicken courtesy of the 8th Special Forces Brigade's mess officer, who had "liberated" twenty-six hundred pounds of chicken from the frozen food lockers of a Kuwait City wholesaler. The wine, one of the few remaining bottles, from the cellar of the villa presently serving as 8th SFB headquarters. Courtesy of the villa's former occupant, the owner of a chain of large and profitable jewelry stores.

The fact that Tom ate this decent meal as the guest of the Iraqi Army and in the company of two Republican Guard officers made the food no less enjoyable. Not even the presence of the white-haired colonel who only a day before had beaten him senseless marred the pleasure. Especially knowing there would be no further "interrogation" or, worse, summary execution.

Thanks to Adnan Dulaimi.

Which was rather ironic because Adnan knew Tom Layton only through Chris Campbell. Chris—not all that indirectly, either—was responsible for Tom's predicament in the first place. What goes around comes around.

Colonel Hakim offered no apologies for his harsh treatment. He had a job to do, and he did it. Until a few minutes ago when Adnan Dulaimi confirmed Tom's identity, as far as Hakim was concerned, Tom Layton had been an American spy.

". . . but I would appreciate your answering a few more questions," Hakim was saying to Tom in Arabic, which Adnan—not entirely confident of Tom's fluency—translated. "You became acquainted with a man who called himself Ali Hamadan—"

"—the poor son of a bitch you stood up against a wall and shot," Tom said in English. He had just bitten off a huge chunk of a chicken leg and stuffed it into his mouth, talking and chewing all at the same time.

The three—Tom, Hakim, and Adnan—were in the

8th SFB's dining room at the villa, at the same table where only an hour earlier Adnan had learned of Tom's arrest. Colonel Hakim had immediately ordered Tom brought to the villa. Tom's unshaven face was bruised and battered, his hair blood-matted, his clothes torn and stinking of his own dried vomit and urine. A medic cleaned him up and outfitted him with a fresh wardrobe from the closets of the villa's former proprietor. The jewelry merchant's quality garments had long since been "requisitioned," but the medic found some odd pieces of old clothing. A plaid flannel sports shirt, a pinstriped suit jacket that hung like a tent on Tom, and white polyester trousers that fit only slightly better. But he was presentable and smelled better.

Hakim seemed almost amused at Tom's description of Ali Hamadan as a "poor son of a bitch." When Adnan finished translating, Hakim said, "The fact of the matter is that his execution was premature. It was a mistake."

"Mistake?" Adnan said. "That's some mistake!"

"We weren't at all satisfied with his interrogation," Hakim said. "I know I could have gotten more out of him. The prison guards responsible for the error have been punished."

"I bet that goes down as another 'mistake,'" Tom said to Adnan in English.

"Mr. Layton wants to know if you have any further questions," Adnan said blandly to Hakim.

"Does he recall Ali Hamadan mentioning any names?" Hakim asked. "Friends, associates, women?"

Tom shook his head, no. He drank almost half the glass of wine, then wiped his plate clean with a piece of pita. "I owe you, Major," he said to Adnan. He jerked a thumb at Hakim and continued, "This butcher was all ready to slap me up against the same wall."

"I don't think I'll translate that one, either," Adnan said dryly, and immediately continued in Arabic to Hakim, "Mr. Layton says he's grateful to you for sparing his life."

Hakim's face remained impassive. He spoke to Tom in Arabic. Tom understood, but Adnan translated anyway. "Colonel Hakim wonders if you might try very hard to remember your conversations with Ali Hamadan."

"Conversation, singular," Tom said. "I only saw him that once, and then only for a few minutes. We didn't talk about anything important. At least nothing that sounded important. Mostly about democratic reforms in Kuwait after the war."

Hakim again seemed amused when Adnan translated. He then spoke at length to Adnan, this time too rapidly for Tom to fully follow. As he listened, Adnan's eyebrows narrowed with skepticism. When Hakim finished, Tom said to Adnan, "Whatever he just told you, it couldn't have been very good."

"He says that Ali Hamadan was betrayed by a Kuwaiti government official," Adnan said. "One of the royal family, in fact."

Tom said, "Run that by me again, please."

Colonel Hakim caught Tom's meaning. He spoke impatiently to Adnan. Adnan said to Tom, "Ali Hamadan's betrayal had approval from the highest Kuwaiti level, possibly the Emir himself. It was a political decision."

"The Kuwaitis themselves turned him over to the Iraqis?" Tom said. "That's pretty farfetched."

"No," said Adnan. "And the more I think about it, the more it makes sense."

It began to make sense to Tom, too. Hakim was far too unimaginative to concoct such a story, nor had he any reason to. Yes, it made sense. Ali Hamadan's very existence posed a threat to the ruling Sabah family. The threat, thanks to Colonel Hakim, was now eliminated.

Tom Layton knew he had stumbled onto one of the war's biggest stories. No, to hell with the newsbeat, and with WCN. And Larry Hill. Save the betrayal of Ali Hamadan for the book, *Gulf Watch Diary*.

But then again, it was too hot a story to hold. Besides, the book was at least a year away. All right, incorporate the story into the book in the fully detailed fleshed-out form it deserved, but break it now on TV. Yes, break it now. And watch the ratings go through the roof.

Exclusive to WCN, by Tom Layton.

Yes, and thank you, Chris.

Talk about retribution. Chris had finessed herself into a Saddam Hussein interview that might damn well never happen, while the colleague she aced out—correction: *thought* she aced out—walked away with a sure Pulitzer.

Thank you Chris.

". . . and you will be escorted under armed guard to the border crossing at Al Kasib," Adnan was saying.

Adnan's words slowly began registering. It was like a delayed tape. Adnan had been telling Tom that he would be given transit papers for safe passage to Iran.

". . . should you ever return to this country, you will be considered a spy and dealt with accordingly," Adnan continued. "We are at war. You are an enemy."

"I understand," Tom said. He stood and extended his hand toward Hakim. The colonel also rose but ignored the outstretched hand. He turned and strode from the room. Tom lowered his hand and sat down again. He looked at Adnan. "Can you tell me why I wanted to shake that man's hand?"

"It's a foolish question, Mr. Layton." Adnan pushed back his chair and got up. "I'll have the sergeant-major see to your transportation. Help yourself to more wine."

Tom watched Adnan walk to the door. Adnan stopped, turned to Tom and touched his brow in a mock salute, then left. Tom poured himself half a glass of wine. He drank it down in a single swallow and reached for the bottle to pour another half glass. The bottle was empty. Adnan was right, he thought. It really was a foolish question.

3

If you needed a reason to throw a party—if the war itself wasn't reason enough—the officers and men, and the women, of the 358th Tactical Fighter Wing certainly had one. The wing had been ordered to stand down for one entire day. The hiatus allowed the C.O., Ed Iverson, to fly to Riyadh for a staff meeting.

In the C.O.'s absence, the Al Kalir's officers' club experienced a sudden and unexpected reappearance of a number of cases of Coors and a limited selection of stronger spirits. Since Colonel Iverson's order banning alcohol on the base was still in effect, senior officers avoided the club entirely. Not being present, they could not bear witness to the beer cans and wine and whiskey bottles and therefore knew nothing of it, nor had any need to know.

Nick Harmon had his own reason to celebrate, which he did in the privacy of his own quarters with his guests, Major Elaine Mason of the United States Army and Major Mudar Taleb and Captain Zahir Mamhud of the Royal Saudi Air Force.

Elaine's C.O., Len Dozier, had surprised her by okaying her request for a day off. She hitched a ride to Al Kalir with a CENTAF mail courier. The same courier would pick her up on his way back to Dhahran in the morning.

The two Saudis had real cause to celebrate. They had made a safe and near-miraculous emergency landing at Al Kalir. They had brought their Tornado in with half its left wing gone, sliced away by a .37mm AA shell in a low-level attack on the Iraqi air base at As Salman.

The Tornado's safe landing at Al Kalir turned out to be a reunion. Nick knew Zahir Mamhud from Nellis. Zahir, fresh from Saudi flight training, had been sent to the USAF gunnery school. Nick gave him his first F-4 check ride. He liked Zahir, not because Zahir was the only Saudi in the contingent not of royal blood or excessive wealth—Zahir's father owned and operated a popular restaurant in Riyadh—but because Zahir was a fine pilot, a natural. He was good.

Mudar Taleb was Zahir's backseater, the weapons systems officer. Like Zahir, he had been educated in England and was comfortably fluent in the language. Although younger and with less service time, he outranked Zahir. His rapid advancement was understandable. As a nephew of one of the king's brothers-in-law, he was considered a member of the royal family.

Equally important, Mudar's mother was the daughter of a man who owned a fleet of oil tankers.

But Zahir said, and with no sarcasm, that Mudar was an okay guy. Nick had no reason to disagree. The young WSO was friendly enough, although he seemed uneasy at Elaine's presence. Not once, not since they were introduced, had Mudar looked straight at her or directly addressed her.

The two Saudis, their faces shadowed in the muted light of the gooseneck desk lamp, sat in folding chairs Nick had borrowed from neighboring rooms. Nick sat on the bed, while Elaine curled up at the foot. On the floor beside her was an aluminum roasting pan that served as an ice bucket. Lined neatly on the dressing table were cans of beer and soda, plastic cups, and one crystal water tumbler. Nick's Panasonic, volume turned low, was tuned to DSR, Desert Storm Radio, playing a Bonnie Raitt album.

They had been chatting about the war and flying. Whenever Elaine spoke or asked a question, Mudar pointedly ignored her. Elaine hardly noticed. She was relaxing, a luxury she had not known for days, weeks. Relaxing: a twelve-hour furlough from having to deal with Len Dozier, or with quashing rape charges of female corporals, or thinking about how and when to inform her husband that their marriage was over.

She debated whether or not to drink some of Nick's Jack Daniel's. She decided to save it for later. She poured the remainder of the last can of beer into a plastic cup and tried to concentrate on the discussion.

". . . let's first win the war, Zahir, before we start worrying about what happens to our country afterward," Mudar was saying.

"The war is already won," Zahir said. "We should be thinking about the profound social changes that are certain to be created by the presence of a half million foreigners."

"It's already happening," Mudar said. He waved his hand at the beer cans and the bourbon bottle. "Look what we tolerate."

Nick took him seriously. "Are you offended?"

"Suppose I were?" said Mudar. "What could I do about it? Bomb the place?"

Zahir said, "He's not offended. Don't worry about it."

"That's a relief," Elaine said dryly. "Otherwise, he might report us to the Mutawa."

For the first time, Mudar appeared to acknowledge her. "Oh, you've had an experience with the Mutawa?" he asked. The suggestion that she might have encountered the morals police obviously pleased him.

"Yes, Major, I have," Elaine said, and addressed Zahir. "When you make those social changes, first on the agenda should be abolishment of the Mutawa."

"That might not be so easy," Zahir said.

"More than 'not so easy,'" Mudar said. "I doubt it will ever happen." He was a slender, self-confident young man whose carefully trimmed black mustache did not, as he hoped, make him look older than his twenty-six years. His pilot, Zahir, also wore a mustache, but thick and scraggly, almost as though to compensate for his near-baldness. Zahir was thirty-two, short and solid, considerably swarthier than Mudar, with the angular features and hawk nose of his Bedouin forebears.

Mudar addressed Nick. "You see, Colonel, how in coming to our 'rescue,' you have also corrupted us? Social changes!"

"The social changes, Mudar, will come not as a result of any corruption, but from our own need for change," Zahir said. "This is the twentieth century, my friend. Excuse me, soon the twenty-first!"

The twenty-first century, Elaine was thinking, as she listened lazily and inattentively to the men. Yes, in nine years, the turn of the century. *Fin de siècle* in the original French. How many of the four in this room would be alive at that time? She certainly would, or at least certainly planned to be. And she would make damn certain Nick Harmon also celebrated the year 2000. Celebrated it with her, that is. They'd go to Times Square and watch the ball drop. And count the last ten seconds. And be grateful for their luck.

". . . yes, of course, we appreciate America's help," Mudar was saying to Nick. "But that gives you no right to criticize our customs or our society."

"Who's criticizing?" Nick asked.

Mudar's face wrinkled. "Come on, Colonel—"

"You can call me Nick," Nick said.

"Read your newspapers," Mudar said. "And your magazines, and your radio and TV. They are either complaining about no pornographic material being allowed into this country, or suggesting we need a change of government."

Elaine said, "Hey, Mudar, how about spicing up your drink?" She reached for the Jack Daniel's bottle. Mudar had been drinking plain club soda from a plastic cup.

"No thank you," he said politely, not looking at her.

Elaine said, "Don't mind if I do," and poured some Jack Daniel's into her beer cup. She swallowed it down. "You'll never know what you're missing, Major," she said.

She gazed defiantly at Nick, whose eyes were signaling her to stop needling the Saudi. She felt a little drunk, although she knew she was not. But she did feel loose and uninhibited, and she genuinely disliked the two Saudis, especially the younger, arrogant one, Mudar. Well, she disliked *all* Saudis and, dammit, did not care who knew it.

She said to Mudar, "I'm glad to see you're a man of principle, at least. No alcohol for you, right?"

"Yes, right, whatever you say," Mudar said.

She said to Zahir, who was also drinking soda water, "Haven't you ever had alcohol?"

"Many times," he said. "But not here at home."

"Isn't that a little hypocritical?" she said.

"Absolutely," said Zahir. He smiled at her.

Elaine smiled back. She liked him suddenly. He was honest. Not like the other one. She put the bottle back on the the table and tapped Mudar's shoulder. "Hey, Mudar, can I ask you a question?"

"Yes, of course," Mudar said, reluctantly, again not facing her.

Elaine said, "Is it true that you Saudis refuse to admit that American women have been sent over here to help you?"

Mudar now turned to her. Even in the shadows of the desk lamp, his face was red. "Excuse me?" he said.

"You heard me."

Zahir and Nick looked at each other. Zahir was struggling not to laugh. Nick did not find it so humorous. He said quietly to Elaine, "Lay off, please."

Screw you, Nick, she told him in her mind and said to Mudar, "Is it true that your government doesn't want its people to know that American women have been sent to help defend Saudi Arabia against Iraq?" Before Mudar could reply, Elaine went on, "Yes, it's true, and the newspapers call us 'males with female features.' Right?"

Nick knew he should step in and prevent Elaine from further insulting the Saudis. But he saw that Zahir was not offended, and he shared Elaine's dislike for Mudar. To hell with Mudar's sensibilities. Besides, Elaine was right on target.

It was Zahir who replied to Elaine. "Well, technically, you happen to be correct: That particular phrase about American women did appear in a Riyadh newspaper. Believe me, the majority of us don't feel that way."

"Speak for yourself, Zahir, damn you!" Mudar said. But immediately, as though apologizing, he continued in a gentler voice, "There will be changes, but it won't happen overnight."

"By the turn of the century, maybe?" Elaine asked. "I mean the *next* century, the twenty-second."

"That might be a little *too* soon," Mudar said, returning the needle, and went on to Zahir, "It all depends on how much trouble is caused by 'revolutionaries' like you." Although Mudar punched Zahir playfully on the shoulder to show he was kidding, his voice contained no humor.

Comrades-in-arms, Elaine was thinking, again not concentrating on the talk. The three men were discuss-

ing flying again, almost eagerly, as though relieved to
have changed the subject. She smiled to herself: Needling Mudar was so enjoyable that she nearly told him
she was married to a Jew. She wondered how he would
have handled that.

No, how would Nick have handled it? She had promised him she would write the "Dear Marc" letter. Get it
over with. And she fully intended to. It just seemed so
cruel in a letter from six thousand miles away. Marc
deserved better. But that was like asking if a firing
squad was preferable to lethal injection.

She closed her eyes and tried to compose the letter.
Dear Marc, I know this will come as a shock. No, too
abrupt and impersonal. *Darling Marc, I hope you're sitting down.* Somewhere, far in the distance, she heard the
murmur of voices and a door closing. And a familiar
voice:

"You really made a hit with those boys."

She opened her eyes. It was Nick. The two Saudis
were gone. She and Nick were alone. He sat on the floor
beside her, reaching blindly up behind him to the
dresser table for the Jack Daniel's. He opened the bottle and freshened their drinks.

"Did I embarrass you?" she asked.

"Christ, no," he said. "You made that stiff-necked little bastard squirm, that Mudar. It's good for him. Listen, I almost came out with my pet theory: The world
wouldn't be in this mess if back in '73 the U.S. had acted
like a superpower instead of some banana republic. Remember how the Saudis decided to shut off the oil? We
should have just walked in and taken over those goddamn oil fields. Instead, we listened to Mr. Kissinger—
who as a Jew should have known better—and we let the
Saudis squeeze us dry."

"That's quite a theory, Colonel."

"You don't agree?"

Elaine sipped the bourbon. "If the world wasn't in
this mess you'd have no war to fight."

"That was my point."

"Colonel, with no war to fight—well, have you ever

considered what a really dull place the world would be? The writers would have nothing to write about. The aircraft factories wouldn't have planes to make. The tank factories would shut down. The restaurants would close. Talk about Domino Effect! And what about people like us, you and me, what happens to us? What are we supposed to do?"

"Don't worry, there'll always be a war somewhere," Nick said. "This species's been at it ever since one guy banged another over the head with a rock. It's part of our evolution, it's in the genes."

Elaine was engrossed in her no-more-war scenario. "You'd have to get a job making French fries in some fast-food joint," she said. "And I'd have to go back to my traffic helicopter."

Nick finished the bourbon in his glass. "And back to your husband, too," he said.

"I'm not going back, Nick. I told you."

"You haven't told *him*."

"I will."

Nick looked at her and nodded slowly. "You don't *want* to tell him."

"I don't want to hurt him."

Nick nodded again. "Makes sense."

She twisted around and drew his face down to hers. They kissed, a long, languid, tongue-grappling kiss. She pushed him away finally and snuggled her head in the hollow of his shoulder.

"What are we going to do, Nick?" she asked.

"You and me?" he said. "You're talking about the future?"

"The future, yes."

"What do you want to do?"

She swiveled around so that she lay with her head resting on his chest. She focused her eyes on the amber glow of light from the towel-covered lampshade. A candle in the window, she thought. A light at the end of the tunnel.

"These service relationships—notice, Nick, I did not say marriages—never seem to work out," she said.

"You'll be stationed back at MacDill, I suppose, while they'll probably send me to Pope."

"Pope's not so far from MacDill," he said. "Well, maybe it is, a thousand miles, maybe. Why *didn't* you say marriage?"

"I don't think you're ready for it."

"*You* are?"

She said nothing a moment. Then, "On that one, I'll take the fifth."

He said nothing. She felt him rustle around while he reached for the bourbon again and poured some into his glass. He aimed the bottle neck at her plastic cup. She finished what remained in the cup and held it under the bottle for him to add more. It was the last few drops. He tossed the empty bottle up onto the bed.

"How long have we been here?" she asked. "In the room?"

"Hour, hour and a half."

"Not a single airplane has landed or taken off in all that time."

"The hell they haven't," he said. "I heard at least three fighters land. And a couple of heavies take off, turboprops, C-130s. You just weren't listening."

"You're always listening, aren't you?"

"It's called a third ear."

"It's called 'never relaxing.' "

"Come on, it's my job," he said. "There's a war on, you know."

"Yes, I know," She clicked her plastic cup against his glass. "I know."

SEVENTEEN

The girl emerged from Amir's room. She closed the door behind her and for a moment stood staring meditatively down at the rubber-tiled hospital floor. She was quite attractive, small, slim, dark hair in a feather cut. From her manner and clothing—tailored leather jacket, white corduroy slacks, high-heeled suede boots, designer canvas tote bag—Hana at first took her for a Westerner. French or German, perhaps even British. But no, not with that fine olive skin and black eyes and classic Grecian nose. She was Iraqi. A Red Crescent volunteer, Hana thought, come to cheer up the wounded soldiers.

Hana watched from the far end of the corridor as the girl reached into the tote bag and removed a single cigarette and a gold butane lighter. Her hand was shaking. She had to steady the lighter with both hands to light the cigarette. She leaned back against the closed door and inhaled, a long deep drag.

Hana walked over to her now and introduced herself. The girl's name was Aida Yasin. She was a graduate student at Saddam University's college of law and politics, studying for her master's degree in political science. As she explained to Hana, she had met Amir only once, at the Saadun Street art gallery where his paintings were on display.

Aida paused as a leathery-faced nurse approached. The nurse shook an admonishing finger at the cigarette, but continued briskly on her way. Aida ignored her. "I

was at the gallery yesterday," she went on to Hana.
"They told me about Amir."

"It was very nice of you to visit him," Hana said.

"He didn't think so."

Hana could almost hear Amir shouting at the poor
girl, insulting her, probably accusing her of coming here
only to see the crippled freak. Ordering her to leave.
Poor Amir.

"Don't be offended," Hana said. "He treats me the
same way."

"I can understand," Aida said. "I feel so sorry for
him."

"That's exactly why he doesn't want to see anybody,"
Hana said. "Or anybody to see him."

"He's being very silly," Aida said.

Not to mention very bitter, Hana thought, although
certainly with good reason. And I, she thought wryly,
also have good reason for bitterness: My brother will
probably never attend my wedding nor I, to be sure, his.
She was envisioning Aida as a bride in a white satin
gown. A Christian or civil ceremony. Yes, Hana would
bet that this girl was no Muslim. But who cared? Hana
and Amir were brought up by their parents in religious
freedom. Believe in whatever or whoever you wish,
God, Allah, Jesus, the Moon, whatever works for you.
Better yet, believe only in yourself.

She is such a darling girl, my new sister-in-law, Hana
imagined herself saying to the distinguished guests at
the wedding reception. She and Amir make a handsome
couple, don't you think? And you'll never believe how
they met, it was so romantic!

Yes, yes, I know, she told herself. I know it can never
happen, not anymore. She said to Aida, "Why don't you
come back into the room with me? Perhaps he'll behave
better if I'm there."

"It might be better for him not to see me again," Aida
said. "I'm sure he still remembers what he said that time
we met, and how foolish he probably feels about it
now."

"How foolish he feels? What did he say that would make him feel so foolish?"

"It was before the war started. He was so anxious to get into it. All that patriotic drivel—"

"Drivel?" Hana's hand froze on the doorknob. "He sacrifices himself for his country, and to you that's drivel?"

Hana's brusqueness did not faze Aida. "That happens to be precisely what it is, drivel, pure and unadulterated. I can still hear him: 'A just war is glorious!' His exact words. Well, I guarantee you he no longer believes that."

I do not know *what* he no longer believes in, or if he believes in anything at all, Hana told Aida in her mind. She resented what she considered the girl's cruelty; it made her feel empty and defenseless. "Why on earth did you come to see him?" she asked. "To remind him of his foolishness and his patriotic drivel?"

"He doesn't need to be reminded that it's drivel. He knows it, and so do you."

Words of denial died on Hana's lips. The girl spoke the truth, a truth visible not only in Amir's hospital room, but even through the windows across the corridor. The windows overlooked the river and Sarafiya Bridge. More accurately, what remained of the bridge after last night's bombing. The concrete roadway was broken neatly into two pieces at the middle, both pieces sloping downward into the water.

You could also smell the truth. The closed windows did not block out the unbearable stench enveloping the whole city. With much of the electrical system destroyed, the sewage treatment plants were inoperative. This hospital at Muadham, like Hana's hospital at Amiriyah, relied on emergency gasoline generators for power. Now the question was how long would the present stocks of gasoline last?

Never mind gasoline, Hana thought. What about such basics as analgesics? At Amiriyah, a civilian hospital, surgeons operated with minimal anesthesia and nothing stronger than aspirin for postsurgical pain. Even bandages were in short supply. But here in this military facility they apparently lacked nothing. Business as usual, the corridors quiet and clean. White-coated doctors casually making rounds. Technicians toting full trays of drugs, orderlies wheeling food carts. Everything looked so efficient, everybody behaved so professionally.

Patriotic drivel, Hana thought, and opened the door. She and Aida entered Amir's room. The head of his bed, elevated, faced the door. He greeted them with a harsh laugh. "She didn't like my painting," he said to Hana, his eyes on Aida. "She hated it."

"I never 'hated' it," Aida said.

"Then why didn't you buy it?" Amir asked.

"I told you—I couldn't afford it."

"Five hundred dinars, for God's sake!" Amir said. "It's like stealing. 'The last known work of the talented young artist, Amir Badran.' Worth a fortune someday. You're a fool, and a bad businessman. All right, I'll give it to you. You can have it for nothing. Hana, see that Nadhim gives it to her. So what else?" he said to Aida. "What the hell else do you want?"

"Amir, please," Hana said.

"He's feeling sorry for himself," Aida said. "You got what you wanted," she said to Amir. " 'War is glorious,' isn't that what you said? You couldn't wait to get into battle. You got exactly what you asked for, so why are you complaining?"

"I didn't ask for *this*, you idiot!"

"But it happened," the girl said. "Now you have to deal with it."

Once more Amir laughed that harsh, bitter little laugh. "The next thing I know, you'll be telling me how I don't have the courage, the guts, to face my infirmity. I'm afraid to face what's in store for me. Please, spare me the psychological bullshit. I don't need any pep talks. I need a new spinal cord." He paused for breath; it was a long speech and had demanded all his strength. "Sure, you want to do something for me, that's what to do: Find me a new spinal cord."

Amir continued talking, but Hana willed herself not to listen. Instead, she saw herself standing over a hospital bed; Adnan was in the bed, and dead. A premonition, she thought. A page from the book of the future. Adnan would be taken from her, too.

But if the war stopped that could not happen. Yes, of course, if the war stopped, the bombing would stop. And the killing. No more shattered spines, no more maimed children. Yes, the war had to be stopped.

". . . hope to see you again sometime," Aida was saying. She was at the door, leaving. "I left my phone number," she said, pointing to a slip of paper on Amir's tray table. She opened the door and left.

Hana's mind was still focused on the war. And on loyalty. By wanting the war stopped, was she being disloyal? She had to discuss this with Adnan. Absently, aloud, she said, ". . . the fact that I believe what I believe doesn't make me disloyal."

Amir said, "What are you mumbling about?"

"I was thinking out loud."

"It sounded like 'loyalty,' " Amir said. "What were you trying to say about loyalty?"

"I don't remember," said Hana. "It couldn't have been very important."

It preyed on her mind the rest of the day and into the evening, long after she had reported for duty at the hospital. Earlier, after leaving Amir, she had spoken with Adnan on the telephone. She wanted to see him, she said. It was very important, something that could not be discussed on the phone. She would be off duty at seven in the morning. She asked him to meet her for breakfast.

"Meet you for breakfast?" he had repeated wryly. "We don't know how much of the city will still be standing at seven in the morning, and you're talking about meeting for breakfast!" He was honestly amused. "We don't even know if we'll still be alive. All right, where?"

"Here at the hospital," she said. "The cafeteria still makes drinkable coffee."

"I have to ring off," Adnan said. "I love you. What is it you want to talk about that's so important?"

"I'll tell you when I see you. I love you, too."

Adnan did not know, nor could he ever have guessed, that the important matter Hana wanted to discuss was the identical problem troubling him. Not in the same context, to be sure, but to the same end.

Loyalty.

Contrary to his prediction, Adnan's report on the adverse conditions in Kuwait had been delivered to and read by Saddam Hussein. Saddam had sent Adnan a handwritten note of thanks. The willingness of his soldiers to endure those conditions, wrote Saddam, was further proof of their devotion and bravery and only strengthened his conviction that the ground war would bring victory. God was on Iraq's side. God would see Iraq triumph.

Adnan had phoned Hana from the hospital at Muadham. He had arrived there, quite coincidentally, shortly after she left. But Adnan had not come to Muadham to visit Amir. He went there to see Hassan Marwaan, Major General Hassan Marwaan, chief surgeon of the Iraqi Army medical corps.

Hassan had been in surgery since eight that morning, nine consecutive hours. He had supervised no fewer than seven major procedures: three limb amputations, two craniotomies, and two laparotomies. The laparotomies—a perforated viscus and a liver fracture—both proved terminal, as did one of the cranial injuries. Not a good day, but typical.

Adnan waited for Hassan in the general's office on the hospital ground floor. It was a large comfortable room with leather furniture, a refrigerator, and a big-screen television, power provided by the hospital's emergency generators. In the hour and a half Adnan waited—through two separate air raids—he occupied himself watching WCN. A constant stream of reports of Allied successes. Plus a replay of a brief telephone conversation between WCN's Washington anchor and Tom Layton in Tehran. Layton said only that after a series of hair-raising adventures he was now safe in Iran. He expected to be in Amman shortly, at which time he would have much more to say.

Very much more, Adnan thought, no doubt including a complete and gory account of his relationship with Colonel Husain Hakim. More grist for the Allied propaganda mill. Adnan had not yet found time to see Chris Campbell and tell her of his encounter with Layton. A good excuse to see her, of course. Not that any excuse was needed. She had left several messages for him to call her. To remind him, he knew, of his promise to try to arrange a new time for her interview with Saddam.

Saddam, whose handwritten personal note of thanks lay in Adnan's left breast tunic pocket like a thousand-pound chunk of shrapnel. No, like the Strela missile that had shredded Jamal Badran's body. The finger that pulled the trigger of the launcher might as well have been Saddam's own.

God was on Iraq's side. God would see Iraq triumph. God looked favorably upon Saddam.

God was blind.

It was after ten when Hassan finally returned to his office. His white smock was blood-splattered. Blotches of dried blood stained his forehead and cheeks. Adnan wondered why he had not washed his face, let alone not removed the smock. But Hassan's bloodshot eyes and waxy complexion answered that. The man was utterly exhausted.

"Adnan," he said quietly; it was both a greeting and a question as to the purpose of the visit. Absently, he switched the television off. He plucked a cigarette from a leather-covered humidor on the desk and sank wearily into a lounge chair. He lit the cigarette.

Adnan resisted a crazy impulse to chide Hassan, a physician, for smoking. Cigarettes could kill you. So could treason. He said, "General, is your office secure?"

"Is my office secure?" Hassan repeated, and then understood. "Is it safe for us to speak, you mean? Yes, I think so."

"I've changed my mind," Adnan said. Hassan's forehead wrinkled in perplexity. "About what we discussed recently," Adnan said.

Hassan seemed even more perplexed. Adnan at first thought the old general only pretended to be confused, an act of caution. But then he realized that Hassan was simply too weary, physically and mentally, for clear thinking.

"About the . . . dissatisfaction . . . of certain high-ranking officers," Adnan said.

Hassan's hand, bringing the cigarette to his mouth, froze in midair. "Oh, yes, that." He mashed the cigarette into a cut-glass ashtray on the chair's armrest. "You say you've changed your mind? Why have you changed your mind?" And in the same breath he continued, "No, don't bother explaining. It's of no matter."

"My reasons, General, are obvious," Adnan said. He began describing his experience yesterday in Kuwait.

Hassan gestured Adnan to stop talking. "I'll have to consult with some of my"—he groped for the proper word—"my associates."

Adnan said nothing, nor for a moment did Hassan. In the abrupt silence the bland voice of the public-address system's paging operator floated into the room, and the ringing of telephones in other offices, and the relentless siren of an approaching ambulance and, far in the distance, the muffled thud of an explosion.

Hassan said, "I'll contact you." He reached to the desk for another cigarette but seemed not to have the strength to lean forward. He fell back against the leather backrest. "Yes, I'll contact you."

"When?"

"Soon."

"General, if this is to happen, it has to happen immediately. Now! Each day you delay costs hundreds of lives and more destruction. Each hour."

"Please, Adnan, I can give you no further information."

"Dammit, sir, then who can?"

The instant he spoke, Adnan realized how foolish he sounded. Asking for names of people plotting treason.

He might as well have demanded details, their plans for seizing the telecommunications systems, the power stations, the post offices. The timetable for the tanks to surround the presidential palace. The strategy for neutralizing the Republican Guard.

But in the same instant he also realized that Hassan Marwaan's reticence was not from caution. It was from ignorance. There was no plot. No organized, meticulously conceived plan for a coup. Otherwise, it would have occurred long before this, long before the country had been ravaged. Now it was too late, now the nation had no choice but to rally behind Saddam. A matter of pride, of patriotism. Which may well have been Saddam's cunning motive for embarking on this suicidal adventure in the first place.

Yes, discontent existed in certain quarters. But at best —and probably over a bridge game or at the horse races —it consisted of a few generals and disillusioned colonels criticizing Saddam's leadership. And probably, because of mutual mistrust, only in the vaguest of innuendo.

Bumblers. Dreamers.

Adnan said, "I'm sorry, General. I shouldn't have asked that question." He rose. "I'll wait to hear from you."

Hassan nodded slowly, then reached into the humidor for another cigarette. Adnan lit the cigarette for him. The match dropped from Adnan's fingers the first time. He struck another match and, steadying his hands, lit Hassan's cigarette.

Hassan seemed almost amused. "You're nervous, eh, Adnan?"

"Yes, sir," Adnan said, thinking that it is not every day you confide, to someone so clearly inept in such affairs, a desire to participate in a plot to overthrow your government. "I have reason to be nervous, I think."

Hassan drew on the cigarette and exhaled. "Yes," he said. "Yes, I would say so."

2

The air raids that evening started shortly before eleven and continued for three hours. After a forty-minute pause, a second wave of bombing followed, more violent and directed at military installations in the western and southern suburbs of the city.

The Amiriyah shelter was located under the basement of the vacant two-story Mediterranean-style villa near Hana's hospital. The bunker's three large rooms, illuminated by low-wattage, battery-operated night lamps, could comfortably accommodate as many as one hundred people. Tonight, as in each night since the start of the war, more than four hundred crowded in, most of them women and children.

It reminded Hana of pictures of London subways during World War II. It was almost impossible to walk from one room to the other without stepping on someone. The women, wrapped in blankets with children huddled beside them, slept on the floor or sat propped against the wall. For all that—and the heavy odors of perspiring bodies—everyone tonight seemed unusually relaxed and untroubled, and with reason: the bombing was clearly concentrated on areas far from Amiriyah.

Hana had spent each entire night of the past week in the shelter, reading to the children, helping feed them, playing games. It kept her so busy that it eased her own fear and suppressed her guilt and confusion about "disloyalty." Disloyalty, meaning her disapproval of the war and what had brought the war, the invasion of Kuwait.

Tonight Hana had mislaid her book of fairy tales and nursery rhymes. She composed some stories that seemed to please the children, except for one little boy who became bored and demanded to speak with his father, a tank commander in Kuwait.

When Hana said that this was impossible, the little boy began crying, which awakened his mother. "Why can't I talk to him?" the child asked.

"There are no telephones down here," the mother said, rolling her eyes helplessly at Hana: There actually were dozens of telephones, but all were disconnected. The shelter, with its ten-foot-thick reinforced-concrete roof, had been built for Baath Party officials during the Iran war, and at the time contained an array of communications equipment. All that remained now were the useless telephones and empty cable outlets in the walls and floor.

Hana and the boy's mother tried to explain why the telephones did not work. After five minutes of this, his head on Hana's lap, the boy fell unexpectedly asleep. Hana covered him with a blanket. Seated on the floor, her back supported by the wall, she had almost dozed off when the little boy's mother spoke to her.

". . . wish those phones really did work," the woman was saying. Her name was Shadha Saadawi. Her husband, a captain, had been in Kuwait since August.

"I'm sure he'd like to hear from you as well," Hana said. "It's not much fun for him out there in the desert."

"Oh, it's not my husband I want to talk to," Shadha said. "It's the president, Saddam."

"Really?" It was all Hana could think of to say.

"Yes, I believe he needs to hear from some of us."

I agree, Hana thought, but did not say it. She wondered what she would say to the president. If she ever had the opportunity. Stop the war, Your Excellency. Before all of us are killed, stop it.

"He needs to know that we're all behind him," Shadha said. "We should tell him that we'll see the war to its finish, and we'll win!"

"No matter what sacrifices we must make," Hana said, slightly rephrasing one of the president's favorite themes. She had intended it as sarcasm, but the words came out flat.

Shadha smiled approvingly. "That's what I would say to him. That's what he needs to hear: 'Mr. President, we look to you for guidance and inspiration. Lead us, and we gladly and gratefully follow.'"

Yes, Hana thought, listening to Shadha's confident voice but not allowing it to register. More accurately, pushing it from her memory. The girl who visited Amir, Aida Yasin, had a name for it: "patriotic drivel."

On Hana's lap the little boy stirred in his sleep. She touched his face; his skin was soft and smooth. She imagined that he was her son, hers and Adnan's. No military school for this lad, believe me. One professional soldier in the family is quite enough, thank you. One too many.

"Two," she said aloud, thinking aloud. "Two too many. I forgot Amir."

"Excuse me?" Shadha said.

"I was talking to myself," Hana said. "I'm sorry."

"If this keeps up, we'll all be talking to ourselves," Shadha said. She waved her hand around the room at the dozens of sleeping figures.

"Sacrifices," Hana said. "This is only a small part of the sacrifices we must make."

Shadha was not listening. She was peering into the shadows of the dimly lighted room, at the low-ceilinged entry alcove. Standing there, scanning the crowd, was Khalid Sadoon.

"Your doctor friend is here," Shadha said to Hana. She leaned back against her wool coat that was padded up behind her head as a pillow. "A nice-looking man."

Your doctor friend is here, Hana thought. A nice-looking man. Talk about sarcasm! Shadha knew very well that Hana was engaged to an army officer. But Shadha enjoyed teasing Hana. That young doctor is certainly sweet on you, Shadha would say. It's written all over him.

Khalid, like Hana, worked the late-night shift, "graveyard" shift as the Americans called it: Khalid had attended a postgraduate seminar in magnetic resonance imaging at Boston University Medical School. Khalid dropped in at the shelter to see Hana at least once each night. To bring her a thermos of tea, or a soft drink, or something to eat.

Yes, Hana knew Khalid was "sweet" on her. He made no pretense of it. Even thinking about it, watching him approach, she felt herself redden. What amazed her—

and, in truth, also annoyed her—was that it never bothered Adnan. He even joked about Khalid's "dishonorable" intentions.

Meaning what? That Adnan took her too much for granted? Possible, since they had been practically brought up together. Adnan treated her like a kid sister. And if Adnan did take her for granted, so what? She knew he loved her. She smiled now—as she always did with the memory—remembering her twelfth birthday and making him promise to marry her in five years, when she was seventeen. Well, he was a little late, only six years. All right, so they'd be married then, on her twenty-third birthday, September 4. The finest of birthday presents.

". . . it's fairly quiet tonight," Khalid was saying, as he squeezed in beside Hana and two young girls, sisters, sleeping with their arms entwined around each other. "Not a single new blast injury. The only emergency so far is a strangulated hernia, a seventy-six-year-old man."

"How cold is it outside?" Hana asked. In the shelter, even with no heat, it was uncomfortably warm. The body heat of some four hundred people. Hana was perspiring under her flannel shirt and blue jeans. The little boy sleeping on her lap wore only his T-shirt and shorts. His mother, like many of the younger women, wore a thin cotton print dress. Many of the older women stubbornly continued to wear their heavy black *abayahs*, complete with head shawls.

Khalid, in reply to Hana's question, said it was very cold outside. And inside the hospital, too. No oil for the furnaces. They chatted a few minutes, and Khalid left. He climbed the four flights to the street, buttoned his coat against a sudden blast of icy wind, and hurried toward the hospital.

He was halfway up the concrete ramp to the ambulance entrance when he felt himself propelled forward. It was as if some invisible force had struck him from behind. He fell. His forehead struck the concrete. He knew it was the shock wave from a bomb. He also knew the bomb had not hit the hospital because he would have been enveloped in the flash. The bomb had impacted behind him.

Behind him, a hundred yards away, at the shelter.

Khalid did not know that there were two bombs, each with a 2,000-pound warhead, each laser-guided, dropped from an American Stealth fighter from an altitude of 18,000 feet, at a distance of two miles. The first bomb had impacted squarely on the tiled exterior roof of the villa and smashed into the basement, penetrating the shelter's concrete roof and driving through the entire ten feet of thickness before detonating. The second, three seconds later, plunged directly into the aperture created by the first and, exquisitely fused, did not explode until it reached the ceiling of the center room of the three rooms.

Neither Hana nor any of the other 423 people in the shelter—196 children, 207 women, and 20 men—knew that the shelter had been targeted in the belief that it contained a control and command center. Most of the people were asleep. Hana was one of the few awake. She had just lifted the little boy from her lap and placed him down beside his sleeping mother. She leaned back against the wall, shifted about to find a comfortable position, and closed her eyes.

Immediately, feeling the wall tremble, she opened her eyes. She heard a loud pop, almost like a champagne cork, and then a whistling sound, louder and louder. Then, abruptly, the noise stopped. The ceiling became a blinding sheet of white. She felt as though her whole body was expanding and that the air was being sucked out of her lungs. The walls of the room were collapsing, and the ceiling was caving in. But it was all happening so slowly. And so silently. And now, although it was like looking at the transparencies of a photographic negative, she could see everything and everybody clearly.

She watched the little boy float up from the floor, his body tumbling over and over like a limp rag doll. In every direction, other bodies tumbled through the room. Everyone's hair glowed with fire and their clothes crinkled up in red and orange fragments that quickly turned black and, like paper burning in a fireplace, vanished in a burst of sparks. She, too, was in the air, and her clothes were burning. She knew all this and knew she should be screaming with pain but felt none. She felt nothing. And then she was enveloped in blackness. She heard nothing. She saw nothing.

Adnan let the telephone ring. He knew that if he answered he would not fall back to sleep, and at the same time he was impressed at how rapidly the service had been restored. Only a few hours ago all the lines in the northern and eastern parts of the city were out. Shielding his eyes against the early morning sun streaming into the room, he peered at the bedtable clock. The backlighted digital figures read 6:43.

The phone continued ringing. He picked it up. It was Khalid Sadoon. Adnan heard Khalid's voice only through a roaring in his ears. ". . . shelter . . . hit . . . everybody dead . . . Hana . . . horrible . . . hundreds dead . . . *hundreds!* . . . dead . . . DEAD!"

Dead.

The next hour passed in a blur. When he arrived at Amiriyah, it was like a scene from some surrealistic nightmare. The lovely tree-lined street leading to the villa was clogged with ambulances and fire trucks. The villa itself appeared intact until, closer, you realized that only the walls were standing. The interior was a charred, rubble-strewn shell. Wisps of white smoke streamed up from under the rubble.

The immediate area was cordoned off by parade fences. Hundreds of people stood behind the fences, all silently watching helmeted rescue workers carry objects, one by one, from the villa. Wrapped in shiny dark plastic bags, the objects were placed in neat rows on the sidewalk and up onto the lawn of an adjoining house. After a moment Adnan realized that the blackened and withered sticks of wood protruding rigidly from many of the objects were human limbs. Arms, legs, bent at grotesque angles like rough-plastered appendages of a statue.

The collective, grief-stricken wailing grew louder with each dead body. Men and women, weeping, beating their breasts, tearing at their clothes. Adnan caught snatches of conversation from the firemen and policemen: ". . . don't know how many there were, couple of hundred maybe." ". . . so hot down there, can't get near one of the rooms." ". . . like pieces of burnt meat."

Adnan spotted an army major helping the rescue workers. Major, he asked him in his mind, are there any survivors? A reasonable question, but pointless. It had already been determined that a bomb or bombs of considerable size had detonated inside the bunker. Those not killed outright by the blast would have burned to death or died of asphyxiation. The only blessing, as Adnan overheard a fireman saying, was that they all died instantly. Never knew what hit them.

A blessing.

3

". . . stacked like cordwood" was what Chris wanted to say. She caught herself in time and said instead, "There really is no adequate way to describe this . . . this horror, this carnage."

Ramon Sandoval moved the camera back for a wider view. He framed Chris, microphone in hand, standing at the tailgate of a truck whose open bed was lined one end to the other with the shiny plastic bags. Sandoval pulled back another few feet to include a shot of the rubbled villa.

". . . there is no official count of the dead, but it will run into the hundreds. As you can see"—Chris stepped aside and gestured Sandoval to pan around to the other trucks and the rows of body bags on the lawn—"many of the victims are children, many only infants." She hoped Sandoval was focusing in on the small bags. "The search for bodies has gone on throughout the day and will undoubtedly continue well into the night. The Information Ministry claims that this air raid shelter was and always had been used exclusively by civilians. The sight of these body bags, especially the small ones, speaks for itself."

She walked about now, silently, the camera following her. The pictures required no narration. These were *million*-word pictures. The very innocuousness of the villa, the jagged hole in the tiled roof where the bombs had entered, the charred interior, the rubble. The mourning parents and relatives and friends. The procession of trucks with body bags.

The report was going out live to the satellite, for re-broadcast on the next hourly feed, and the next, and probably throughout the night in Europe and the States. She wore minimal makeup and her hair was uncombed. Her nylon windbreaker and baggy denims would win no fashion awards. And she didn't give a damn. Her real concern was that she might break down and begin weeping.

She held together. Whenever she felt herself welling up with tears, she thought of Adnan. As she had seen him a few hours ago when, in answer to the urgent banging on her hotel room door, she opened the door and found him standing there. He had phoned late last night, just before the phones went dead, to tell her of his meeting with Tom Layton, and that he looked forward to seeing her soon. Little had he imagined how soon it would be.

His face was streaked with what looked like ash or charred embers. His uniform was coated with the same material. But his eyes conveyed the message, eyes glazed with pain. As a child, she remembered seeing a cat whose back legs had been crushed, a beautiful Burmese. The same plea for help in its eyes.

"Get dressed and gather your camera crew and come with me," he said. "I'll wait downstairs."

He brought her to Amiriyah, and the plastic body bags. "Let your American audience see what their heroic pilots accomplished today," he said. "Let Mr. Bush and Mr. Cheney and General Powell see it. Let them see what they did to a shelter in the center of a residential area, near a hospital. Let them see what 'collateral damage' really means!"

Not until hours later, long after Adnan had left the scene, did she learn that in one of those plastic bags were the charred remains of the woman he had planned to marry. She wanted desperately to see him, to talk to him. To apologize. In the name of every American, apologize. And we, she thought, we were so goddamn outraged at the Iraqi atrocities in Kuwait.

She, personally, was outraged. She, Christine Campbell, who would never forget the sight of her friend Entessar al-Azimi lying naked in that courtyard in Kuwait City. Entessar, dead, her body so unspeakably violated. Chris had castigated the Iraqi "monsters" responsible. In her broadcasts she had made reference, albeit oblique, to Iraqi barbarity. She had editorialized, sometimes not so obliquely, about Iraq's harsh treatment of POWs. And now her own countrymen had proven themselves no less barbaric. She felt betrayed.

Yes, if the bombs were dropped by mistake, she might not have felt such shame. But there had been no mistake, not with two bombs so flawlessly delivered. The Pentagon claimed the shelter was an Iraqi army command and control center. American technical knowhow.

No mistake.

She did not know how long she remained there, walking aimlessly through the debris, instructing Sandoval to close in on weeping women and the grief-contorted faces of men carrying their own dead children in their arms. A full shot of a truck packed with corpses. Stay with the truck as it pulls away from the scene and proceeds down the street. Hold on the truck as it fades into the distance.

She remembered little of her narration, except that the words seemed to flow endlessly, almost eloquently. She made no attempt at dispassion, at professional objectivity. The women and children in the Amiriyah bomb shelter had been slaughtered. She wanted the whole world to see what she had seen. She ordered

Sandoval to film the horror, all of it, until he ran out of tape. Inside the newsvan—the big multi-antennaed Toyota, all white except for the black W C Ns on the roof and sides—she replayed much of the footage. She stared at the images until her eyes, already swollen and wet from weeping, blurred her vision completely.

Finally, late in the afternoon, she returned to the Al-Rashid. The first person she saw when she entered the candle-lit lobby was Adnan Dulaimi. And to make matters worse, at that instant the air raid warning sounded. Both Chris and Adnan appeared oblivious of the sirens and of the people hurrying across the lobby's marble floor toward the basement entrance.

"I saw some of your broadcast on the monitor in the truck," he said. "You told the truth, I'm grateful for that. When will it be shown in the United States?"

She glanced at her watch, 6:15. Washington was eight hours earlier, 10:15 A.M. "They're probably playing it right now," she said. And probably accusing Larry Hill and me and WCN of outright treason, she thought. "I'm sorry about your fiancée."

He said nothing, only nodded.

The hotel seemed suddenly silent. It took Chris a moment to realize that she and Adnan were alone in the lobby. Everyone else had gone into the shelter. It was as though they two, she and Adnan, were deliberately ignoring the raid as a gesture of defiance, as though refusing to lend it dignity.

"Come upstairs and talk to me," she said. She grasped his hand and pulled him with her toward the stairway. The hotel had moved her—and all the cumbersome INMARSAT telephone equipment—from the ninth floor to the third. A smaller room, but at least she did not have to trudge up or down nine flights when the electricity was out and the elevator not operating. Which was all too often.

They climbed the three flights silently, and only when they reached the third-floor landing did she release his hand. He followed her down the corridor to her room, 307. Just as Chris inserted her key, the door opened from the inside. Leila, a flashlight in her hand, stood staring at them.

"There is an air raid," Leila said.

Chris said, "And my room is the safest in the hotel, isn't it?"

"I was making up the room," Leila said.

Chris brushed past Leila into the darkened room. She waited for Adnan, then closed the door in Leila's face. She pressed the switch on the bedtable lamp back and forth a few times, a reflex: You never knew if the electricity worked. She groped for a match and lit the candle that was propped in an empty saucer on the table next to the lamp.

She said to Adnan, "That chambermaid is the one I told you about. She works for the Mukhabarat. She used to be on the ninth floor but, surprise, they transferred her down here to the third. There's no electricity, the toilets don't flush, there isn't any clean linen, but the hotel provides maid service! She's supposed to be a friend of mine, but she goes through my things every day. I don't know what she expects to find."

Adnan listened politely. He knew Chris was chattering away out of nervousness. He walked to the window. It was dark outside, the air raid still in progress, but the windows of buildings across the boulevard were lighted—obviously, in that area, there was electricity— and the street lights were on. In the distance, on this side of the river near the Haifa Street film studios, flames were visible. But these were probably from the dozens of small fires deliberately set in hopes of deceiving the bombers.

"It doesn't matter anymore, I suppose," Adnan said quietly, thinking aloud.

"It never did matter," Chris said. She had understood what he meant. Whether the targets were blacked out or lighted, the bombers unerringly found their mark. American technical know-how.

She removed her windbreaker and stepped over to him and placed her hands on his shoulders to help him off with his coat. He turned around to face her. She drew him to her. She felt his heart beating against hers and then felt a moistness on the side of her face. She touched his cheek. He was weeping.

She pulled him down onto the couch with her and lowered his head onto her shoulder and held him close. She ran her fingers through his hair and stroked the back of his head. She wanted to say, It's all right, It's all right, I'm here with you. But she knew the words were unnecessary.

She was vaguely aware of the muffled thud of far-off explosions. The sky, through the window across the room, occasionally brightened with the yellow glow of antiaircraft tracers. But it was strangely silent, no staccato barking of the guns. Miles away, she thought. Tonight they were not attacking the city itself. Another "command and control center," she thought. "Hey, hey, hey, Georgie Boy, how many little kids did you kill today?" It did not rhyme.

She knew that for five minutes now, perhaps longer, not a single word had passed between them, and yet she was in his arms, and they were kissing. Chris did not know how it had started; she knew only that she enjoyed the feel of his lips on hers, and his tongue probing hers, and the solidity of his body. No, more important, she enjoyed knowing that he needed her.

No one had ever needed her this way. Her mother needed her for money, Larry Hill needed her for his worldwide WCN audiences, her colleagues needed her for their own power trips, sexual and otherwise. But Adnan Dulaimi, her Iraqi "enemy," needed her for herself. Whatever needing-her-for-herself really meant.

Don't analyze it, she told herself. Enjoy it. Yes, enjoy it, she repeated to herself, smiling to herself realizing that although they both were still more than partially clothed, miraculously—and with not the slightest awkwardness, hardly any fumbling with zippers and buttons —they were making love. It was so natural, so perfect.

Yes, and better yet, this act of love was precisely that, love. An act of love and of discovery. The discovery of trust. Mutual trust and self-honesty. He could weep in her arms with honesty and without embarrassment and make love to her with the same honesty.

It was not intense, and she did not expect it to be or want it to be. Later, yes, for sure. Later, there would be passion and shameless lovemaking. Now he required gentleness and kindness and the security of knowing that she was there for him.

She felt him inside her now, and a flush of warmth in her belly that spread quickly throughout her body. So nice, so nice. Especially a moment later, as he relaxed and they lay side by side in each other's arms, and he kissed her mouth, her nose, her eyes, her forehead. She returned each kiss. She felt giddy, like a schoolgirl in love for the first time.

"I knew this would happen," he said.

"So did I," she said. "From the moment we first met. In Washington, at Larry Hill's. Do you remember?"

"Very clearly. You were anxious to know how fast I could arrange an interview with the president—"

Chris placed her fingers on Adnan's lips to silence him. Her heart had begun racing, from fear now. Fear and humiliation. My God, did he believe she had done this for an *interview*? Nothing could be further from the truth. But then why was she denying it to herself now? Why did denial seem so important to her? Oh, no, she thought. No.

She said, "That's not why I . . . why we . . ."

"Of course not," he said. "I know that."

She said nothing. She knew she still lay in his embrace but she felt unreal, disembodied. The candle flame cast flickering shadows across the wall and up to the ceiling. She was staring at the ceiling, which resembled a motion picture screen. Her whole life was projected onto the screen. Her mother, and her "hero" father, and the socially acceptable background she had fabricated for herself. Her driving ambition and its morality: Do unto others before they can do unto you.

Interview.

The word printed itself in huge, black block letters across the stuccoed ceiling. Interview, the key to all the riches of the Western world. And the eastern, northern, and southern. Only yesterday, she and Larry Hill had discussed the interview. She was working on it, she told him. And she expected a very generous bonus for her trouble. How much, he had asked jocularly, a million? A nice round figure, she had replied. Yes, a million will do nicely.

". . . have to leave," Adnan was saying. He had gently disentangled himself from her and was on his feet, his clothes already straightened. "There's a war on, you know."

"And you're my 'enemy,' " she said, but smiled with the word. She held out her hand to him. He pulled her up to face him. She kissed him lightly on the lips. "A beautiful enemy."

"Do you regret it?"

"It was beautiful," she said. "Why would I regret it?"

"For one thing, I wasn't very—"

Again, she silenced him with a touch of her fingers. "We made love," she said. "I loved it. The earth doesn't have to move—" she broke off, thinking he would not understand.

But he did understand. "It moved for me," he said. He kissed the tips of her fingers. "Thank you," he said. "For everything."

My pleasure, she thought, but did not say it.

After he left, she walked to the window. She stood gazing out at the yellow dots of antiaircraft tracers arcing through the sky. Now and then the horizon flashed white with a distant explosion.

Interview.

Now she saw it written in the sky in letters of fire. She tried to blot the letters from her vision, but they only grew larger and more fiery. What am I supposed to do if he arranges it for me, turn it down? she asked herself.

Nobody suggested that, she answered herself.

Then are you suggesting that there may be something about it that is, let's say, "dishonest"? I am referring, of course, to the sudden new direction of your relationship with Adnan Dulaimi.

Dishonest is your word, not mine. But, hey, if it fits, wear it.

Thanks, for nothing.

"And what the hell difference does it make?" she said aloud, and turned from the window. She walked to the couch and sat down. The cushions were still indented with the imprint of their bodies. It occurred to her just then that the word did fit, after all.

Dishonest.

She had not been entirely honest with Adnan about the earth not moving. It had moved.

EIGHTEEN

Since Corporal Cynthia Griggs was unmarried, it was not surprising that the corporal's 201 file contained no mention of Tiffany. Tiffany Griggs, age four and a half, born three months after her mother's graduation from high school in 1986 and three days before the mother's nineteenth birthday. Curly-haired little Tiffany, a happy and healthy child—in the Polaroid photo at least—lived with Griggs's parents in Vernon, Texas. In point of fact, Tiffany had lived with her grandparents since birth.

Tiffany's father was a trucker from Fort Worth who stopped overnight in Vernon a few days after Christmas, 1985, when his Cummins-Kenworth eighteen-wheeler blew a fuel pump. He pulled in at Rossen's Garage & Truck Stop on Interstate 287 just outside town. Cynthia, working afternoons and weekends, was the mechanic on duty. At age eighteen, Cynthia could take apart and rebuild any diesel ever made. Old man Rossen was lucky to have such a talented mechanic, and a girl at that. You paid a woman half what you paid a man.

Cynthia could pinpoint the date of Tiffany's conception because it was two days after Ricky Nelson died in a plane crash. Cynthia loved Ricky's music, especially "I'm Walkin'" and "Hello Mary Lou." The trucker, himself a Ricky Nelson fan, understood Cynthia's grief and comforted her. He even bought an album of Ricky's which they listened to on his portable CD player in the truck cab. In the back, where he had a bed. Norman Sharpe was his name, and he certainly lived up to it. He turned out to be married, with four young children. He told Cynthia to get lost.

She was five months pregnant when, hit by the recession spreading through the whole state, Rossen's Garage & Truck Stop went bankrupt. Even the best mechanics were on unemployment. After nearly two years of unreliable part-time waitressing, the week before Tiffany's second birthday, Cynthia enlisted in the U.S. Army. It was the most practical way to contribute something substantial to the child's support.

". . . yes, ma'am, she's a real nice little kid," Griggs was saying. "She knows I'm her real mother, but she calls her grandmother 'Mommy.' I guess maybe she thinks she has two moms. Well, in a way, I guess that's true."

"Why isn't it in your 201?" Elaine asked.

"The army doesn't take single mothers, ma'am."

Elaine felt foolish. She should have known that herself. "Why didn't you tell me all this before?"

"Well, you and I, we only first talked about it that one time, the other day, and only for a few minutes. Like I said then, Major Mason, it makes me feel awful good to know you're on my side. And can I say something else?"

Elaine gestured her to continue. Griggs went on, "You probably don't know this, but you're a big reason why I'm staying in the army. Last month, right after you came into the outfit, I applied for one of those army college programs. I mean to get me a commission some day. I want to be like you, ma'am." A timid little smile brightened Griggs's face. "I guess you're what they call a 'role model.' "

Role model, Elaine thought, God help us.

". . . didn't say anything about Tiffany because it didn't seem important," Griggs was saying. "Besides, it might get me in trouble. When I signed the enlistment papers, I said I didn't have any dependents. I'm telling you about it now because I want to be real honest with you. But it sure doesn't have anything to do with the guy raping me."

Elaine wanted to think about that a moment. "It might have a bearing on your—your veracity."

"Excuse me?"

"Whether or not people believe you're telling the truth."

Griggs's angular face wrinkled up in a bemused frown. "Why would anybody not believe me?"

Elaine said nothing a moment. Her task—convincing Griggs to drop charges of rape against Sergeant Robert Lefcourt—would be more difficult than she had anticipated, more complicated. Elaine did not have the patience for all this or, in truth, the tolerance.

"If you were untruthful about one thing, it could mean you were untruthful about something else," Elaine explained.

"Oh," said Griggs. "Oh, I see. Oh."

They were strolling along the hedgerowed sidewalk behind the 153rd's maintenance hangars at Dhahran International. It was a gloomy gray afternoon, chilly and damp from rain that had fallen all morning and only just now stopped. Sandstorms and torrential rains had curtailed nearly all USAF tactical operations. The previous evening, February 17, for the first time since the war began, not a single Allied sortie was flown over Baghdad.

The 153rd Aviation Regiment, the Sky Kings, had spent a busy week. Three hundred and twelve sorties, from fuel delivery to rescue missions. So busy, that not once did Lieutenant Colonel Dozier mention Corporal Griggs to Elaine. Griggs's statement accusing Sergeant Lefcourt of rape still lay locked in Dozier's middle desk drawer. But time was running out. Dozier would soon have to forward the statement on to regimental CIC for an Article 31 criminal investigation.

So that morning, taking advantage of the weather-created standdown, Dozier had sent for Elaine and ordered her to get cracking on the "Griggs thing." Charges of sexual harassment and rape: horseshit, all of it, and not to be dignified. "Get Griggs to drop the charges. The girl is a slut," Dozier said. "She's screwed half the battalion!"

He sounded so indignant that Elaine was tempted to ask if this was the first time he had ever considered the possibility, or probability, of sexual involvement between men and women in the U.S. Army. It would not surprise her if Dozier denied the existence of any drug problems in his squeaky-clean battalion or of covert racism. It reminded her of the famous scene in the movie, *Casablanca,* when the police chief was "shocked" to learn of gambling in Humphrey Bogart's café.

Elaine had no intention of querying Corporal Griggs regarding numbers, and it turned out to be academic anyway. Griggs volunteered the information. Confessed, more accurately. Griggs had not, as Dozier accused, screwed half the battalion, nor even half a dozen, only two. And the second one only after breaking up with the first. She was not at all reticent to admit that she needed and enjoyed the relationships. She liked sex, dammit. She'd lost her virginity at age fourteen and never looked back. Certainly, no crime. It was in this context that Griggs had revealed the existence of her daughter, Tiffany.

". . . but I'm right, aren't I, ma'am?" she was saying now. "There's no connection between Tiffany . . . and this rape thing?"

"*Alleged* rape," Elaine said.

Griggs came to an abrupt halt and faced Elaine. "Nothing alleged about it, ma'am. He did it. Bobby Lefcourt raped me. The more I said no, the more pissed off he got. Finally, he wrestled me down on the cot, pulled down my trousers and ripped my undies apart, and rammed his thing in. It hurt like anything, too! It felt like it was wrapped in sandpaper. But I told you all that."

"Yes, you did tell me all that, didn't you?" Elaine said. She resumed walking. Griggs fell into step beside her. "You asked about a connection between this and your little girl. I think the connection to worry about is . . ." Elaine paused. She would have liked to say,

The connection of concern is not your illegitimate child but the fact that you are fucking some of your male coworkers. Connection, she thought. Male prong plugged into female receptacle. She went on, "Does Lefcourt know about . . . the others?"

Even as she posed the question, "connection" was still on Elaine's mind. Male prong, female receptacle. Nick Harmon, Elaine Mason. She had spent an anxious day yesterday. A Navy rescue chopper from the *Midway* went down in the Gulf in a vain attempt to save an F-16 pilot. She relaxed only after learning that the F-16 came from Bahrain, from the 363rd TFW. In fact, Nick hadn't flown at all that day.

Nick, she thought. Nick, with whom she was carrying on a little affair—no, call it like it is—Nick, whom she was fucking. Cynthia Griggs had fucked two men. Elaine had fucked only one. Where, other than numbers, was the difference? But there was a difference, and quite significant: Cynthia Griggs was not cheating on a husband.

". . . the others?" Griggs was saying. "Does Lefcourt know about them?" And then she understood. "Oh, I guess he does, yes. Not that my . . . friends . . . did any bragging, but it's no special secret. I mean, the close-together way we live it's really hard to keep that kind of stuff secret, you know."

"I'm sure," Elaine said, wondering if Nick bragged. But then, who would he brag to? Certainly not his C.O., Iverson, whom he loathed. To some close friends, then. She didn't think Nick had any truly close friends. He never mentioned any. That said something about the man, didn't it? No close friends. The United States Air Force was his close friend. She, Elaine, was also a close friend. Friends and lovers.

". . . here's the barracks," Griggs was saying. The two-story brick building, at one time a Royal Saudi Air Force cadet classroom, had been renovated into two floors of comfortable dormitories. Ironically, this enlisted women's barracks was far more comfortable than Elaine's BOQ.

Griggs's voice was lost in the screech of two F-15s taking off on the parallel east-west runways. The concrete sidewalk under their feet throbbed as the jets, in afterburner, shot into the air. Elaine, facing Griggs, watching the girl's lips, suddenly understood the words.

". . . have this feeling, ma'am, you don't believe me," Griggs was saying. "And all because I've been honest with you."

Elaine felt herself cringe. She cringed every time she recalled the wide adoring eyes and pert little mouth uttering the words "role model." It was like being befriended by someone who continually embarrassed you.

"I'm glad you trust me enough to be honest," Elaine said, hating the sound of the word, because Griggs was right, Elaine definitely did not believe her. And how the hell could Griggs expect anything different? She conceals the existence of her illegitimate child to enlist in the army, is sent overseas where she unblushingly services one male colleague after another—and then suddenly screams "rape!" Come on, girl, Elaine told her in her mind, Give me a break.

Elaine said, "All right, now let's talk about what you plan to do about these rape charges."

"What I plan to do?" Griggs repeated. "I want this guy to get what's coming to him. Don't you, ma'am?"

The question momentarily startled Elaine. What the hell difference did it make what *she* wanted? Griggs read the annoyance on Elaine's face and went on, "You're wondering why I'm willing to go through with all this, aren't you, ma'am?"

"I know *why* you're doing it," Elaine said. "What I don't know is what you hope to gain. Under these circumstances," she added quickly. "A case that might be hard to prove."

"My word against his, is that what you mean?"

"That makes a very weak case, Cynthia."

"What I hope to gain is . . ." Griggs groped for the word. "Respect," she said after a moment. "That's why I'm doing it. For my own self-respect!"

Elaine said, "Look, let me talk to Sergeant Lefcourt.

Let me hear what he has to say." Her mind raced far ahead of her mouth. She was envisioning the trial. Griggs's lovers, plural, testifying under oath, detailing their sexual encounters with the lady. "I'll talk to Lefcourt, and we'll go on from there."

Griggs laughed bitterly. "You don't think he'll admit anything, do you?"

"Let me talk to him," Elaine said. She gave Griggs no chance to reply. She smiled a little automatic smile, turned, and walked quickly away. She went to the flight line. Her Black Hawk, 3059, was parked at the very end of the hardstand. She climbed up into the cockpit, closed the door, and settled down in the left seat.

None of the mechanics and crew chiefs working on other helicopters paid her any attention. She loved sitting perched high off the ground in the spacious cockpit, enveloped in the aroma of leather and oil and jet fuel, gazing through the greenhouse-like windscreen at the runways and the airplanes. Here, she could think. She needed to think.

Elaine resented Cynthia Griggs, not only for the uninvited responsibility of "role model," but for the girl's naiveté, those ingenuous admissions of sexual favors so freely granted. Little wonder Len Dozier considered servicewomen no better than camp followers in uniform. An opinion, Elaine knew, shared by probably ninety percent of the officers and men of the U.S. armed forces.

But what Elaine resented most was her own disappointment. She had hoped to defy Lieutenant Colonel Dozier and urge Griggs *not* to drop the charges. It was high time to put some of these abusive macho males in their place, and she wanted to help Griggs do it. Yes, and she and Griggs would take the goddamn case all the way to the goddamn Supreme Court if need be. But today's conversation with the alleged victim had destroyed all those laudable notions. Today's conversation had provided Elaine a lesson in reality. Reality in the form of a United States Army enlisted woman readily admitting having had multiple sex partners. No, worse, admitting having *enjoyed* it! In a military court, Corporal Griggs stood less chance of proving rape than Saddam Hussein had of marching triumphantly up Pennsylvania Avenue.

So Corporal Griggs's commanding officer, albeit for the wrong reasons, was perhaps right in wanting the matter quashed. Which was a shame. Elaine would have enjoyed telling Leonard Dozier to fuck off.

2

Nick Harmon was thinking that Saddam Hussein's latest withdrawal offer, which George Bush had termed a "cruel hoax," was not the war's only cruel hoax. I am looking at another one, he told himself, in the person of Colonel Edward Iverson, Jr.

The Cruel Hoax, seated just to the right of Lieutenant General Gene Gordon at the C.O.'s table in the Al Kalir mess tent, was chatting with Brigadier General Barney Gallagher, who sat on Iverson's left. They had just finished dinner and were awaiting coffee and dessert. Ice cream and strawberries, which the 358th TFW's enterprising mess officer, Captain Dan Strone, had scrounged for the occasion.

Some dozen of the 358th's senior officers had been invited to dine with the two visiting generals. This was Gordon's first trip to Saudi Arabia, to "look around," as he explained. Al Kalir was, of course, only one stop on his "look-around" agenda. He would visit six other Saudi and Bahraini bases before returning to Washington.

Gordon and Gallagher had shown up unannounced shortly before Iverson returned from a successful SEAD —suppression of enemy air defenses—mission at Tallil in northern Iraq. It was the 358th's first operational sortie in thirty-six hours, the first halfway decent weather in all that time. As far as Iverson was concerned, the appearance of the two generals could not have been more timely.

Iverson had downed an Iraqi F-1 Mirage.

A memorable achievement, in that it was the first air-to-air victory credited not only to the 358th, but to any USAF F-16 pilot. Officially credited, that is: Nick Harmon's MiG kill had never been acknowledged and probably never would be. Iverson's kill was confirmed by both AWACS and the colonel's wingman, Captain Keith Brancati.

So there he was, the colonel, holding court. The "ace" telling how he did it, describing the maneuvers. It reminded Nick of a World War II movie, the brash young fighter pilot at the club bar acting out the dogfight, his hands simulating the opposing airplanes. To be fair, however, Iverson's feat—in a purely aviation context at least—was truly outstanding.

The battle had occurred after the attack on the Iraqi airbase at Tallil. Four of Iverson's six-airplane flight, outbound now, were running low on fuel. Iverson sent these four on to the tankers while he and Brancati dropped down to 10,000 feet, searching for Scuds. Suddenly, above and behind, two Mirages appeared. Obviously tracking the F-16s, the Mirages had flown at ground level to evade AWACS, and then climbed almost vertically for the interception. By the time AWACS spotted them and notified the two F-16s, it was too late.

Brancati received sufficient warning to begin maneuvering, but the Mirage closest to Iverson had already locked on and launched a missile. With brilliant airmanship and deft deployment of chaff and flares, Iverson evaded that missile and the one that immediately followed. A moment later he completely reversed the situation. He was behind the Mirage now and locked on. The "ready-to-fire" diamond symbol in the F-16's HUD target-designator box flashed invitingly. The Mirage was dead meat, but so close—less than three miles—that Iverson could not resist canceling the missile shot in favor of a cannon kill. He moved in to within a mile.

The Iraqi, momentarily reprieved, reacted precisely as Iverson anticipated. He dove away. Iverson followed him down, forcing him lower and lower, and now decided to forgo the cannon as well. He would finesse the

Mirage pilot into the ground. With Iverson literally on his back, the hapless Iraqi abruptly ran out of sky. The Mirage slammed into a hill and disintegrated in a gigantic orange and black fireball.

The second Mirage, although still enjoying an advantage over Brancati, immediately broke off and sped east. The F-16s were now too fuel-critical for pursuit, and in any event AWACS had already summoned a CAP flight of four F-15s. The F-15s intercepted and brought down the fleeing Mirage just inside the Iraqi border.

Ed Iverson's flying prowess came as no surprise to Nick. No one had ever disputed the colonel's skill as an aviator. But there was another side to the story. There is always another side.

A few hours before dinner, Nick had gone to his room at the BOQ to rest. Not only had he been up since five, he felt a cold coming on. It called for a massive dose of Vitamin C and a brief nap. He arranged to meet General Gordon before dinner for a drink, checked tomorrow's ATO, then headed for his room. He had hardly closed his eyes when Keith Brancati knocked on the door.

"Colonel, I need to talk to you."

Brancati, twenty-nine, who had entered flight training through AFROTC, was built like a linebacker. Indeed, he had played nose tackle with the University of Miami's 1983 national champions. In his nearly two years with the 358th, his record was exemplary. Nick considered him a more than competent pilot.

Nick told him to come in and close the door. Brancati wasted no words. "I have to tell you what really happened up there today," he said.

Nick sat up in bed. He felt as though someone had doused him in ice water. It was as if a dozen different warning lights were flashing all at once. The urge for a cigarette was so strong that he almost asked Brancati if he smoked. "What do you mean, 'what really happened'?"

Brancati twirled the rickety aluminum bridge chair

around so the seat faced backward. He straddled it and sat down. "Nick, I know I shouldn't—" he drew in a deep breath.

Nick read his mind. "If you think this is something you shouldn't say, then maybe you'd better reconsider."

Brancati peered at Nick for a troubled moment. Then, deciding, he said, "Okay, this is how it went down." He hesitated again. "Okay, Colonel Iverson didn't splash the Mirage when he had him locked. Instead, he puts on this flashy airshow exhibition."

"We know all that," Nick said impatiently. It was as though he had hoped to discourage Brancati from continuing. As though he sensed what was coming and preferred not to be involved.

"What you don't know, sir, is that while he's having all this fun with his Iraqi, I'm in trouble. The other Mirage is locked on to me, and I'm not so sure I can break the lock."

"Did Ed know that?" Nick asked, although he already knew the answer.

"Twice, I called him to come over and get the guy off my back. He can finish off his man in one cannon burst, but instead he keeps toying with him like a cat with a mouse."

"He might not have heard you," Nick said, which technically might have been the case. Iverson might have been so intent on running the Mirage into the ground that he blocked out everything else: target fixation. It happens, not often, but more than anyone cared to admit.

"He heard me," Brancati said. "At least the second time, he did. He called back that he was on his way."

"Did AWACS pick up the transmission?"

"I doubt it. There's a lot of noise and clutter, and a lot of back and forth talk between the AWACS and an F-15 CAP patrol they're vectoring in to help us. But by then it doesn't matter: My guy, seeing what happens to the other Mirage, gets scared and—thankfully, I have to say—runs for the hills. To AWACS, it all looks legit."

"All right, so what?" Nick said. "You got home okay. What's your point?"

Brancati seemed almost disgusted. "Come on, Colonel, I could have been a piece of barbecued meat, just like the poor slob in the Mirage. Our esteemed wing commander was so engrossed in making a spectacular kill that he forgot all about protecting his wingman. He left me hanging out there to dry."

"I'll ask you again: What's the point?"

"I thought somebody should know about it."

Nick reached under the bed for the aluminum roasting pan–ice tray. He brought out two cans of Pepsi. He tossed one to Brancati. Brancati palmed the can but did not open it. Nick opened his and drank half in a single swallow.

"Okay, so what else?" he asked.

"Here's the part that to me is really scary: I don't think Colonel Iverson has the slightest notion of what he did. Or didn't do, I mean." Brancati popped open his Pepsi now and drank some. "You asked 'what else?' That's enough, isn't it, sir?"

"Yeah," Nick had said. "Yeah, I guess it is."

Nick never did nap that day. The conversation with Brancati left him wide awake. His first instinct was to tell Barney Gallagher of the incident. Tales out of school, as Barney might say. Correction: as Barney *would* say. So Nick decided he could do nothing about it, other than watch his ass when flying with Iverson. Better yet, avoid flying with Iverson, period.

He briefly considered discussing the problem with Gene Gordon. It would accomplish nothing and definitely irk the general. And, as it happened—although he never made Nick privy to the fact—Gordon was irked enough. His "look-around" trip was not as innocent as it appeared. The trip was a cover for an entirely different purpose. En route, Gordon had stopped in Israel and met with the defense minister. To dangle a little carrot. No, a *large* carrot: In return for Israel's continued "cooperation"—not entering the war or otherwise antagonizing the U.S.'s Arab allies—Israel's request for

$10 billion in American loan guarantees would be granted.

A job for a diplomat, not a soldier, made more disagreeable by the fact that Gordon had been selected to deliver the message because the Israelis trusted him. It reminded him too uncomfortably of the errand he had sent Nick on back in November. And, to be sure, of Frank Kowalski.

Nick and Gordon had their predinner private drink and chat in the special BOQ "suite" for transient VIPs. Suite, meaning that the prefabricated wall of an adjoining cubicle had been removed to create a larger room.

Gordon brought Nick a gift, a bottle of Beefeater, a belated Christmas present from Johnny Donovan. They drank it on the rocks from the plastic cups. They discussed the war, in broad terms only, for Nick knew Gordon already had received a bellyful of complaints from Barney Gallagher. Lack of comprehensive intelligence, inadequate bomb damage assessment, smart bombs not so smart, ordnance shortages, interservice rivalry, friction between regulars and reservists. For sure, Gordon had heard it all.

And, when Gordon said he was well aware of Nick's awkward situation here at the 358th but was proud of him for making it work, Nick congratulated himself for not mentioning the Iverson-Brancati incident.

". . . you're doing a great job, so stay with it," Gordon had continued. "In plain English, keep your mouth shut."

"Yes, sir, read you loud and clear," Nick said, and both men laughed, amused.

Not so amusing was Gordon's reply to Nick's query about Frank Kowalski. Dead, said Gordon, rubbed out by the Mossad. Nick was not surprised. Nothing, he thought, surprised him anymore, not even Ed Iverson's display of unforgivable poor leadership. So all through dinner, listening to Iverson's version of the incident, Nick brooded. What made it worse was the realization that Keith Brancati was right: Iverson was totally, wholly, blissfully ignorant of having placed a wingman in jeopardy.

That evening the weather over eastern and southern Iraq closed up again, canceling many of the 358th's ATO frags. After dinner, Tracy Hart escorted the visiting generals around the base. A dog-and-pony show: All units had been alerted and were at their very best.

Nick could not relax. Brancati's words echoed in his ears. He tried to sleep, to read, listen to DSR. Nothing worked. He went over to Brancati's room. He wanted to hear the captain's account once more. Perhaps he had missed something, some salutary detail or nuance. Brancati was not in his room, nor was he at the club. Nick left a message for him at Ops. But Nick knew he had heard Brancati's story correctly, and that it was true.

Five minutes later, Nick brushed past Master Sergeant Carlisi and strode into the C.O.'s office. Iverson, feet propped up on an open desk drawer, sat gazing through the window at two F-16s rolling down the runway. Nick slammed the door on Carlisi, who he knew stood indignantly in the doorway.

Nick said, "Ed, tell me how you got the Mirage."

Nick's hard, cold tone of voice alerted Iverson. His tentative smile faded. "I can see this is no social call."

"No, Ed, no social call."

Iverson dropped his feet to the floor, swiveled the chair around, and sat up straight. "Okay, shoot."

"I asked you how you got the Mirage."

"Sit down, for Christ's sake."

"Just answer the question, please."

"I ran him into the ground, Nick. You want me to go all over it again for you? What the hell is the matter with you, anyway?"

"Brancati was in trouble. You didn't make a move to help him."

Iverson's eyes narrowed. "Are you crazy?"

"You're not even aware of what happened, goddammit!"

Iverson rose. "What I am not aware of, Colonel Harmon, is what in the name of God you're talking about."

"You finked out on your wingman, you bastard!"

"That's enough, Nick. Get out. Before I fucking well throw you out."

Nick never was really sure how it happened. He knew he had stepped around the desk and confronted Iverson. But he did not recall hitting him. He knew only that an electrical pain was shooting up and down his left hand, and that Iverson's chair had toppled over onto the floor. And that Iverson was sprawled atop the chair, blood spurting from his mouth.

And that standing incredulous in the doorway were Barney Gallagher and Gene Gordon.

Fortunately, no one else had witnessed the incident. Gallagher quickly closed and locked the office door. Iverson was already on his feet, several sheets of Kleenex pressed to his mouth. Nick stood at the window, unable to face the two generals. He had to force himself not to massage the bruised knuckles of his left hand.

To the obligatory question, "What's this all about?" Iverson said, "A personal matter, sir. I'd ask you to please forget what you saw."

The question had been asked by Gallagher, who grasped Nick's sleeve and whirled him around. "I think you've finally done it, Nick. You've finally arranged an early retirement for yourself."

Nick glanced at Gordon. The general's face was ashen. Nick said to Gallagher, "What do you want me to say, Barney?"

Iverson spoke before Gallagher could reply. "This is between Nick and me, Barney. Please let it go at that."

Gallagher said to Nick, "Is that your story, too?"

"Yes, sir," Nick said. "A personal matter. We'll settle it between us."

Gordon said, "Am I to understand, Colonel Iverson, that you choose to offer no explanation?"

Iverson peered at the blood-splotched wad of

Kleenex he just then had removed from his mouth. He touched the corner of his mouth gingerly. The bleeding had stopped. He tossed the Kleenex into the wicker wastebasket in the kneehole of the desk.

"Colonel Harmon has accused me of ignoring my wingman's call for assistance," Iverson said, and in one succinct sentence went on to restate Brancati's charge.

Nick actually wanted to laugh, and almost did, watching Gordon's face abruptly change expression. From annoyance to regret. Regret that he had pressed the issue.

Gordon said to Iverson, "Is this true?"

"Certainly not," said Iverson.

"Did Captain Brancati say anything to you about it?" Gallagher asked.

"Not a word," said Iverson.

"But he obviously spoke to Colonel Harmon," Gordon said.

"Obviously," Iverson said.

The room fell heavily silent. Everyone looked at Gordon. Gordon addressed Gallagher, but his eyes were on Nick. "Colonel Harmon and Captain"—Gordon frowned—"what was his name?"

"Brancati," said Gallagher.

"Colonel Harmon and the captain are to be transferred out of this wing," Gordon said. "Come with me," he said to Nick, and walked from the room.

Nick read the relief in Gallagher's face. Gordon's order for Nick to be transferred meant that the squabble —and what had precipitated it—would never be made public. To all intents and purposes, it was over. Finished, forgotten.

Not quite, not for Nick.

Outside the Ops building, Gordon did not wait for Nick but walked rapidly down the graveled sidewalk. Nick caught up with him on the hardstand. A quarter mile away in the transient parking area, harshly bright under the halogen lights, the six-story-tall rudder of a MAC "Desert Express" C-5A loomed up out of the night. The big airplane had flown nonstop to Al Kalir from the Pratt & Whitney factory in Hartford, Connecticut, with six brand new P&W F-100 engines for the F-16s. "Overnight Delivery with Desert Express," as MAC truthfully boasted.

"Sir, I'm sorry about—" Nick started to say.

"Shut up!" Gordon stopped walking and whirled around to confront Nick. His face was a mask of anger. "You're a goddamn fool!"

Gordon resumed walking. He squared his cloth BDU cap, buttoned the collar of his field jacket, and thrust his hands into the pockets. It was cold, with a brisk wind blowing needle-sharp particles of sand. Nick hurried to keep pace with the older man. They strode past one hangar, then another. Nick did not know where Gordon intended to go; clearly, the general did not know himself.

Finally, between the third and fourth hangar, Gordon spotted a smaller prefabricated building, a storage facility. He flung open the door. The interior, illuminated only by a single fluorescent ceiling fixture, was cramped with tools and small engine and aircraft parts. A female staff sergeant bundled in a BDU field jacket sat at a table near the door. She had been studying a tech manual. Immediately, her eyes glued to the three stars on the crown of Gordon's cap, she jumped to her feet.

Gordon said, "Sergeant, are we disturbing you?"

"No, sir," she said.

"Good, then leave us alone."

"Sir?"

"Get out," said Gordon, and added, "Please."

For a few moments after the sergeant left, Gordon remained silent. He unbuttoned his jacket and leaned against the service counter that ran the length of the building. Behind the counter were shelves packed with boxes of replacement parts.

"Why isn't this place busy?" Gordon asked absently.

"It's a backup unit, sir. The main supply structure is much bigger."

"Sit down." Gordon indicated the chair vacated by the sergeant.

Nick sat. Obviously, Gordon intended to read him the

riot act. Nick's behavior was inexcusable, the general would say, grounds for court-martial. How stupid can you be? And Gordon would also say that this time, for the first time, he could not bail him out. Nick would be quietly transferred and quietly retired. A kind of plea bargain: Nick requests retirement, no charges are brought.

"I never thought I'd be saying this, Nick, but now I realize I saw it coming long ago. Perhaps even in the beginning." Gordon paused. He folded his arms across his chest and gazed unseeingly across the room at a calendar. The February days were x-ed out, even tomorrow's date, 21.

"You don't belong in the peacetime military, Nick," Gordon continued now. "You foul up the machine. It's the Iversons who keep the machine running and keep it in working order so that it's ready for you, your kind— the rule-breakers, the chance-takers—when war does come. But that's all you're good for: war."

"Excuse me, sir, I think I understand what you're saying—I don't agree with it—but the fact of the matter is that this is not peacetime."

"The fact of the matter," said Gordon, "is that this is *not* a war. The fact of the matter is that our so-called enemy is a third-rate nation with fourth-rate fighting men. This is no war, it's a training exercise! Iverson can handle it beautifully. It's perfect for him, tailor-made."

For an instant Nick thought he had caught Gordon's point, but now he was confused again. No, more accurately, annoyed. If Gordon wanted to chew Nick out— and Nick was the first to admit he deserved it—then for Christ's sake, why garble it up with a rambling geopolitical lecture?

Nick said, "All due respect, sir, what does this have to do with Iverson?"

"Nick, you're not listening. I said you're an anachronism, a throwback. You're a warrior in a time when there are no more wars. You don't belong."

"I hear what you're saying, sir. You're wrong."

Gordon smiled kindly, the smile of an impatient but

loving parent. "I wish I damn well were wrong. No, son, I'm one hundred and ten percent right. It's happened in every war we've had. The stodgy, unimaginative, by-the-book regular army people somehow keep the establishment afloat. Keep the wheels oiled, as it were. How did I put it before? The machine running, yes. Keep the machine running, so that when the shit hits the fan, the mavericks, the 'screw-you-and-the-rules' guys can come in and throw away the book, and thereby win the wars for us." He smiled again. "Yes, yes, I know you're a professional, a regular, and that's the sad paradox. That's what I'm trying to make you see, that's what I myself have just now realized. You, and the couple of hundred or thousand like you, are valuable only in times of global conflict, when our national security is in dire peril. This, I repeat, is *not* such an instance. As a matter of fact, I doubt there'll be any more global conflicts. Unless we're attacked by Martians."

Nick's head was spinning. He was angry and sad all at the same time. Angry at Gordon for such pompous lecturing, not to mention the most left-handed compliment ever received. He was unfit for peacetime service but was the soldier who could save the nation in wartime. Sad that it came from Gordon, his idol, his hero, his champion.

Nick said, "I'd almost bet we're safe from the Martians, sir."

Gordon's hard but paternal voice turned abruptly cold. He spoke quietly, articulating each word. "You had no right to confront Iverson with such unsubstantiated charges."

"Iverson is a goddamn menace. I know that, you know it and, I assure you, General, his wingman knows it!"

"What makes you believe the wingman?"

"Captain Brancati has no reason to lie, sir."

"Colonel Iverson denies the accusation."

"He's the one who's lying."

"Were you there? Did you see it happen?" Before Nick could reply, Gordon continued, "I'm not trying to defend Iverson, and certainly not attempting to justify his behavior. If, indeed, it happened the way the other fellow claims. It sounds like a judgment call in any event, a matter of perception. But that's not the point."

"Excuse me, sir, but what the hell *is* the point?"

"The point, Nick, is that you are as guilty of placing a man in jeopardy as you claim Iverson to be. I'm referring to Iverson himself. On the flimsiest evidence possible, hearsay no less, you accuse him of the most heinous of offenses. You seem bound and determined to push this man beyond his limits. Why, I don't know, nor do I particularly care to know."

Nick said nothing. He did not know what to say. What *could* he say: General Gordon, thank you for calling my attention to the truth? Sir, you have made me see the light, thank you, sir. Or, sir, you happen to be full of shit, sir. No, he knew Gordon had cut right to the very heart of it. Even Iverson's secretary, Carlisi, had a fix on it. Nick was indeed pushing Iverson.

And why was all too obvious. Nick wanted that eagle on his shoulder and the command that went with it. He was genuinely surprised Gordon had not come straight out and said it. But maybe Gordon decided that labeling Nick a war-lover was enough for one session. By the truth, shall ye be freed. Bullshit.

He said, "About the only offense you haven't accused me of yet, sir, is racism."

Gordon said nothing, but even in the shadowed room Nick saw the general's eyes glitter angrily. Nick said, "A joke, sir. I guess it didn't go down too well."

"No, Nick, it did not."

Nick knew that in that respect, at least, he was innocent. He didn't give a damn if a man was black, white, brown, or candy-striped. All that mattered was the man's ability.

". . . disappointed in you, Nick," Gordon was saying. "I'm sorry to have to say it, but I am."

"That makes two of us, sir," Nick said.

All in all, then, it was not a good day for Nick Harmon. Nor, for that matter, Ed Iverson, Barney Gallagher, and Gene Gordon. Unpleasant as the day was for them, it had been much worse for Major Mudar Taleb and Captain Zahir Mamhud of the Royal Saudi Air Force. They had not returned from a mission in southern Iraq. They were long overdue and presumed lost.

3

Zahir knew they were going down. He felt the Tornado shudder and then, as though striking a wall, almost stop. She started tumbling like a pebble bouncing across water. Both pilots, Zahir in the front seat and Mudar in the back, were whipsawed brutally back and forth against their shoulder harnesses.

Zahir tried to focus his eyes on the instruments. The violent vibrating of the panel made it impossible to read the gauges. But the engines sounded normal and no warning lights were flashing. Zahir realized what had happened even before Mudar's terrified voice boomed into his earphones.

"The rudder, Zahir! They hit the rudder!"

Zahir kicked one rudder pedal, then the other. It was like flattening an automobile brake pedal to the floor. Yes, AAA fire from the battery on the airstrip perimeter had hit them and torn the rudder to pieces. Probably on the climb-out. Their Tornado was one of two that had attacked the airbase at Jalibah in southern Iraq. The other Tornado was first in, diving down out of the overcast, cratering the runway with 500-pound CBUs, and was gone before the gunners had an accurate track. When Zahir and Mudar barreled in, the triple-A guns were waiting for them.

Zahir tried the rudder pedals again. No response. The Tornado was in a flat spin. Zahir marveled at his calmness and the way he was thinking so clearly, even with Mudar's near-hysterical voice blaring into his earphones. He knew there was no time to radio a Mayday, no time for anything except to get the hell out of this airplane.

"Eject!" he said crisply into the interphone and pulled the ejection control handle. This would punch Mudar's backseat out first and, a half second later, Zahir's front seat.

The canopy blew off. The wind ripped away Zahir's helmet and mask and lashed into his unprotected face. The ejector charges ignited. It was like riding the tip of a rocket. Not fast enough to black you out, but with enough Gs to make you feel as though your stomach was falling down to your ankles, and your liver and kidneys and everything else. But for all that, he still remained calm and clearheaded. He knew the parachute beeper would automatically activate. The AWACS control airplane orbiting near the border would pick up the signal and locate the coordinates.

For all the good it would do. Their chances of rescue were remote. Not because they were inside Iraq—ten to twenty miles north of Basra, he estimated—but because of the overcast. No rescue helicopters would find them. No, as the Americans would say, they were screwed.

Fucked.

Without the loving.

Zahir had to smile to himself. He was thinking in English. The international aviation language. He rephrased the Americanism in Arabic. "Fucked without the loving" did not sound quite right. Arabic was too subtle a language.

All this swept with crystal clarity through his brain as his body, hurtling upward, reached its apogee. Then he began falling. The drogue chute popped open, momentarily jerking him upward. The main chute deployed, again jerking him upward, and then he began floating down through the wet gray clouds.

It was like walking through fog. He enjoyed walking in fog. He remembered it once in San Francisco and once in London. London, he'd never forget, the fog swirling thickly around his feet like tufts of dingy cotton. It was late afternoon, and he had just come down on the train from Barnstable after finishing the Tornado transition course. A three-day holiday before returning home to report for duty with the new Tornado squadron at King Khalid Airfield. He met the girl in a bookstore. She was his age, dark hair, wearing a tan jacket and skirt. She said she'd never known anybody from Saudi Arabia, and after they talked awhile she confessed that bookstores were wonderful places to meet gentlemen.

Especially a Saudi. My God, they were all so rich. I'll bet you live in one of those Arabian Nights palaces. She refused to believe he was not wealthy, that he was a commoner, middle class. Yes, he'd been to college and spoke English fluently, but only because he was a captain in the Royal Saudi Air Force. Really, not all Saudis are millionaires. Really.

Mudar was a millionaire. Mudar Taleb, Zahir's backseater, the weapons systems officer. Mudar, a major, was a Saudi prince. Zahir could still hear the panic in Prince Mudar's voice: *"The rudder, Zahir! They hit the rudder!"* Zahir had expected a more professional reaction from Mudar. More dignified. Dignified? How the hell could you be dignified when instead of a rudder, all you saw was a chunk of shredded metal?

You are not being fair to Mudar, Zahir told himself. Excuse me, *Prince* Mudar. You are expecting too much. Which reminded him of their unending discussions of social conditions in Saudi Arabia. Zahir claimed that the emerging middle class would soon demand more representation. Mudar insisted that these were "radical" ideas and dangerous. Dangerous to whom? Zahir had asked. To what?

And where the hell was Mudar? Somewhere in the fog, hopefully. Hopefully uninjured after punching out. Yes, that girl in the Charing Cross Road bookstore would have gone for Mudar. Mudar was a genuine Saudi millionaire. But then he, Zahir, certainly had acted like a millionaire that day. He spent the entire afternoon and evening and night with her, and it cost him his expense allowance plus every cent in his pocket. More than £150. But worth it, worth every damn penny. An unforgettable experience. Although he could see her clearly in his mind, not for the life of him could he remember her name.

The girl in the fog.

The fog enveloped him and chilled him down to the skin, and then he closed his eyes. The next thing he knew, the hard surface of the ground was under his head. He was on the ground, lying on his back.

". . . this one is coming around," said a man's voice, an Iraqi-accented voice.

Zahir opened his eyes. A semicircle of half a dozen Iraqi soldiers stood staring down at him. Zahir started to speak but the words were choked off by a sharp, rib-crushing pain in his left side. He wanted to scream with the pain and thought that he did, but at the same time he could not catch his breath. Immediately, he felt a similar pain on his right side. They were stomping him with their boots. He tried to roll away.

". . . teach the traitor a lesson!"

The whole world exploded. Everything was a glaring, sparkling white. Then it darkened to a dull gray, almost like pulling 7Gs in a turn. No, 8Gs, because everything was going black, and he was falling, falling, falling. The pain stopped.

He thought he was in the airplane. It was still buffeting, but less violently. Now it began swaying, gently, almost rhythmically. Above him the sky was gray but continually obscured by blurred objects. He strained to focus his eyes. The blurred objects were the tops of trees.

He was still on his back, but on the metal floor of a small open-canopied truck. Two Iraqi soldiers sat opposite him, AK-47s slung over their shoulders. One, cupping his hands over a match, was trying to light a cigarette. He struck five successive matches, then gave up in disgust.

The soldier noticed that Zahir was awake and nudged his partner. The two watched interestedly as Zahir struggled to sit and again nearly screamed with pain. He knew his ribs were broken and the mere effort of moving drove another electric jolt of pain through him. Now he became aware of the wetness between his legs. He looked down at the puddle under him and the large, red-blotched stain at his fly. He had pissed himself. With blood. And he had to go again.

He tried to speak, first forming the words in his mind, but they were all jumbled. He wanted to say that he had to piss, and he also wanted to ask about Mudar. His mouth felt like rubber. He tried again.

The first soldier, eyeing Zahir almost clinically, said, "He's pretty smashed up."

The second soldier laughed harshly. He was a stocky man of forty, his scraggly black mustache flecked with varying shades of white. "What's the difference?" he said. "By the time Hakim is finished with him, it won't make any difference. Hey, can you hear me?" he said to Zahir.

Zahir nodded.

"What's your name?" the first soldier asked.

This time by sheer force of will Zahir managed to speak. "My name is Zahir Mamhud. I am a captain in the Royal Saudi Air Force. My identification number is 12817." He repeated it and then repeated it again. The words, clear in his mind, emerged from his mouth as mumbled gibberish.

The second soldier leaned across the truck floor. He reached into Zahir's shirt and pulled out Zahir's dogtags. He read the information aloud. He tucked the dogtags back into Zahir's shirt, sat back again, and in the same motion struck Zahir flush in the mouth with the AK-47 barrel. Zahir felt only the first twinge of pain and the warm, salty moistness of the blood spurting from his mouth and broken teeth. The darkness closed in around him once more.

NINETEEN

Larry Hill's name was high, if not at the very top, on U.S. Representative Eric Metcalfe's enemies list. It was Larry who had christened Metcalfe "Eric the Red," although Larry swore that the nickname was inspired by the young California congressman's luxurious red beard, and not by his almost pathological anticommunism. Oddly enough, Eric Metcalfe did bear a vague resemblance to the legendary Viking.

To be sure, it had taken more than a nickname to earn Larry his position of prominence on Metcalfe's list. Several years ago, WCN's "Capitol Crimes" series had run a three-part special linking Eric Metcalfe to the president of a defunct savings and loan company. The bank officer, convicted of fraud and embezzlement, was now serving a ten-year sentence in a federal prison. The case against Metcalfe was strong but not strong enough for the Justice Department to indict. He insisted that the charges were utterly false and a communist conspiracy—the Cold War had not yet ended—to drive him from office. He won reelection to his third term that year, but by the slimmest of margins. He attributed his close call to WCN's "scandal-mongering series," which happened to have been anchored by Chris Campbell.

Eric the Red had a long memory.

So when Larry was informed that Eric Metcalfe had just entered the WCN building and wished to see him, he knew it was no goodwill visit. Moreover, the congressman was accompanied by another man Larry could hardly call a fan, Charlie Donnelly. Not three minutes before, Larry had watched Donnelly's boss, Marlin Fitzwater, read a statement from the White House press room, George Bush's ultimatum to Saddam Hussein. Withdraw from Kuwait within twenty-four hours or the Allies would commence ground operations. For Donnelly to leave his desk and travel halfway across town at this incredibly busy time spelled trouble.

And with one look at Eric the Red's smug face, Larry knew that the trouble was all his, Larry's. He decided not to waste time on amenities. The ultimatum demanded all his attention. He wanted on-air reaction from every WCN bureau and a live feed from Chris in Baghdad. The INMARSAT line had been out for the past hour. He needed to speak with her. God, if only she could get to Saddam now, right now.

"Gentlemen, I'm honored and flattered," Larry said, waving Metcalfe and Donnelly into the two leather captain's chairs opposite his desk. An antique pewter cup filled with pens and pencils obscured Metcalfe's face. Larry nudged the cup a few inches to the side. "Let's get to the point."

Metcalfe laughed. "You're something else, Larry. You can smell it, can't you?"

"You look happy, Eric," Larry said. "When you're happy, I know it's bad news for someone."

"It's about Tom Layton," Donnelly said.

"Tom's in Iran," Larry said. He glanced at the digital calendar on his desk. "Well, maybe by now he's in Amman. What about him? What the hell has he done?"

"He's filed a story that you're planning to run on 'Gulf Watch' tonight," Donnelly said. "We—I'm speaking for the Administration—consider the information sensitive. Very sensitive."

"Charlie, I'm blessed if I know what you're talking about," Larry said. He knew perfectly well what Donnelly was talking about. What he did not know was who had tipped Donnelly to Tom's story. A source within WCN obviously, any one of a dozen different people.

". . . this ridiculous—no, scurrilous—this scurrilous

fable about the government of Kuwait deliberately betraying a member of the Resistance for political reasons," Donnelly was saying. "I mean, you talk about media distortion! Thankfully, Congressman Metcalfe brought it to our attention."

The leak had been to Metcalfe, then, not Charlie. Which narrowed it. Now you needed to find out who at WCN had a relationship with the congressman. "Is the Administration denying the story?" Larry asked.

Metcalfe replied, "You're damn right they're denying it!"

"What," said Larry to Metcalfe, "is your interest in all this?"

Metcalfe said, "In addition to serving in Congress, Mr. Hill, I also happen to be an American. The vital interests of the United States are inherently involved here."

Larry thought, Oh shit, and said, "Is Layton's story true?"

"Not even in a joke," said Metcalfe. "Somebody's fantasy, no more, no less."

"Then what are you worried about?" Larry asked quietly.

"What I'm worried about, Larry, is your brand of journalism," Metcalfe said. "I know exactly the kind of sensational spin you'll put on this."

"Whatever that means," Larry said. "But if the story isn't true, just issue the usual denial. No harm done."

"If only it were that easy," Charlie Donnelly said. "The suggestion itself will kill us. The peaceniks and isolationists will sink their fangs into it and never let go. We don't need that."

"Especially with the Mother of All Battles about to start, eh?" Larry said. "Unless, of course, Saddam gets smart and withdraws. What's the word on that up on the Hill?"

"Whether he'll withdraw?" Donnelly said. "No chance."

"And nobody wants him to, either," Larry said. "Not until we've found out how well our tanks work. We know the planes work just great, but we're not sure about the ground stuff."

"That's a lot of crap, and you know it," Metcalfe said. "Now listen to what Charlie is saying. You do that story on WCN, you'll have antiwar protests in every city in the country."

"*More* antiwar protests," Larry said.

"Yeah, Larry, and we all know where *you* stand on that," Metcalfe said. "Repeating this Iraqi propaganda is a good example."

Larry had promised himself to play poker-faced all the way. Let them think he was taking them seriously. But he knew they actually believed what they were saying, and he could not help himself. He laughed aloud.

"Let us in on the joke," Donnelly said.

Donnelly's indignant voice instantly sobered Larry. These arrogant asinine jackasses, he thought, and said, "You guys have just corroborated, in every detail, the truth of the story. Not only that, but you've made me realize the Administration is involved in it up to its ass. Go ahead, Charlie, deny it for me."

"The Administration believes that these irresponsible allegations will offend the Kuwaiti government," Donnelly said. "For Christ's sake, can't you understand that?"

" 'Embarrass' is the word you want," Larry said. "The allegations will embarrass the Kuwaitis. They'd be 'offended' if there were no truth in any of it."

"Come on, Larry, do us a favor, do yourself a favor," Donnelly said. "Drop it. Please."

"You do *yourselves* a favor," Larry said. "Stop wasting further time or energy. Listen close, men. Sensitive or not, national interests or not, I am running the story. Don't miss tonight's 'Gulf Watch.' "

"Look, Larry, I'm speaking for the White House itself," Donnelly said. "We'd prefer you to hold the story."

"Now it's 'prefer,' " Larry said. He wanted to laugh again. "The Administration doesn't want their intrepid Kuwaiti allies embarrassed. I'm surprised I haven't gotten a phone call directly from George Bush. Or is that coming?"

Eric Metcalfe slammed his fist on the desk. The pens and pencils rattled in the pewter cup. "We want that Kuwait story canceled!"

"Yes, Eric, I had that impression," Larry said.

Donnelly said, "If you broadcast it, Larry, we'll release a story of our own. And it's a story you ain't gonna like, pal."

Once more Larry wanted to laugh. These people were so clumsy, so lacking in . . . quality. Yes, that was the word, quality. Thirty years ago, even twenty, Charlie Donnelly would not have been allowed on a White House tour, let alone entrusted with an important and responsible job. It reminded Larry of a favorite phrase of the mother of the Massachusetts lady who had bankrolled his first, failed venture into cable television news: *"The fish stinks from the head."*

He said, "That sounds like a threat, Charlie."

"A promise," said Metcalfe. He withdrew a folded sheet of paper from an inside jacket pocket. Ceremoniously, he unfolded the paper and placed it on the desk. "This should look great in *People* magazine," he said. "And it wouldn't surprise me if even *The New York Times* picked it up, and for sure *The Washington Post.*" Metcalfe was enjoying himself now. "Yeah, and I'll read it into the *Congressional Record,* too."

It was a private detective agency's report. *Subject: Christine Campbell.* Larry scanned the contents. Details of Chris's background, the fiction of her Nob Hill upbringing, her father's military career, and his heroic death. The truth, the whole sad truth. No navy pilot, a draft dodger, killed while drunkenly jaywalking on a Toronto street.

Larry flattened the paper on the desk and with the tip of a finger slid it back across the polished oak top to Metcalfe. "Not a bad investigating service," he said. "Maybe I'll hire them to find out who in this office tipped you to the Layton story."

"Kind of makes you feel foolish, doesn't it?" Metcalfe

said. "Certainly makes *her* look foolish, and speaks volumes about the integrity of World Cablenews Network."

"Integrity," Larry repeated. "That's a new word in your vocabulary, Eric." He glanced at Donnelly. "And one that will never be in yours, Charlie."

"Quid pro quo, Larry," Donnelly said. "You asked for it."

Poker, Larry thought. The idiots wanted to play poker. It required every ounce of self-control not to deal a few cards of his own. Locked in the safe on the wall behind the photograph of the original WCN office were a dozen computer disks. Each disk a small bundle of dynamite, especially the one containing a complete account of the Reagan and Bush administration's prewar dealings with Iraq. Billions of dollars of arms sales, including material for the manufacture of nuclear weapons. Not to mention loan guarantees and outright grants.

Talk about hypocrites, hypocrisy.

You want stories, mister, I'll give you stories! But Larry Hill was saving that big story for the right moment. Now, with George Bush a hero of Lincolnesque stature, it would all be wasted. Lost in the ticker tape of the victory parades. And trading an "Iraqgate" for a story of some second-class Kuwaiti double-dealing was poor business.

"Okay," he said. "Quid pro quo."

Donnelly nodded, pleased, but Metcalfe peered narrowly at Larry. Larry read his mind. "Too easy, huh, Eric? I should have negotiated some more, made it a little tougher for you. I must have something up my sleeve, huh?"

"That's right, Larry. That's exactly what I was thinking."

Larry smiled thinly. "Well, you're right, I do have a little something else in mind." He rose. "But it's in the future, so you'll have time to get your spies working on it."

Donnelly rose now, but Metcalfe remained seated.

He said, "Larry, it would be nice if you gave the stop order so I can hear it with my own ears."

"What's the matter, Eric?" Larry smiled the same thin smile again. "You don't trust me?"

Metcalfe returned the smile. "No," he said. "I don't trust you."

"All right, so to indulge you, I'll order the show stopped," Larry said. "And the minute you're out of the place, I call up and rescind the order."

"Indulge me," Metcalfe said.

And may Tom Layton forgive me, Larry thought. It had just then occurred to him that Chris, once again, albeit indirectly and in this case innocently, had screwed Tom. Tom's big story was being sacrificed for Chris's good name. No, not Chris's good name, the company's name, WCN's shining image. But even as Larry thought this, he knew that his motive for shielding Chris was purely subjective and self-serving. He wanted to be her protector. He still enjoyed those fantasies about her. An old man's whimsy.

Larry flipped a button on the telephone's PBX panel. It connected him with Susan Balter, the "Gulf Watch" producer. He told Susan to kill the Tom Layton segment. Political exigencies, Larry explained. He hung up and faced Metcalfe and Donnelly.

"Okay?"

Metcalfe nodded.

Donnelly said, "Okay."

Larry pointed at the piece of white paper on the edge of the desktop. "Don't you want this heroic document?"

"That's your copy, Larry," Metcalfe said.

Larry watched the two men walk across the length of the office to the door. Donnelly opened the door for Metcalfe, then started out himself.

Larry called to him. "Charlie, one question."

Donnelly stopped.

"We both know the story is true: The Kuwaitis really did betray their own man," Larry said. "But *how* did you know?"

"Easy," said Donnelly, "I was there when the arrangements were made. And now let me ask you one question. When we sprang this on you about Chris, you were cool as a cucumber. No surprise. How come?"

"I knew all about it, Charlie. I've always known."

When the door closed behind them, Larry reached across the desk for the detective agency's report. He tore the paper in half, then again, and once again, and one final time. He tossed the fragments into the wastebasket.

2

It was an omen, Elaine thought, a sign of good things to come. Not only did she make telephone contact with Al Kalir on the first try, but she was immediately patched through to Nick. He just happened to be in Ops when the call came in. She needed to talk with him. She needed him, period.

She was in Len Dozier's office. The C.O. had sent for her but was delayed in a staff meeting at regiment HQ. He left a message for her with Sergeant First Class Chambers, the acting battalion NCOIC.

"The Griggs thing," Chambers said. "The colonel said you'd know what he meant."

The wry curl of Chambers's fleshy lips told Elaine that Chambers also knew what the colonel meant: Bury Corporal Griggs. Elaine thanked Chambers, a man she thoroughly detested, and brushed past him into Dozier's empty office. Chambers followed her in and stood vigilantly in the doorway. Like most lifers, he considered the very existence of female officers a personal affront.

"Close the door on your way out, Sergeant," Elaine said, enjoying bullying him, a small victory, but gratifying. She then helped herself to the C.O.'s direct CENTCOM telephone line. The touch of a button connected her to Al Kalir and to Nick.

"You won't believe this, but I've been trying to reach you, too," he said, and the omen of good turned into a portent of doom. "I'm being transferred." Exactly where, he went on to say, he didn't know. Stateside, he suspected. He couldn't go into detail but said it was no promotion. No goddamn promotion, he repeated. She never remembered him sounding so down.

She had hoped for some objective counsel from him. Well, perhaps a sympathetic ear. This damned Cynthia Griggs business, and that damned misogynist bastard Len Dozier for involving Elaine in it. But Nick was no help. He had his own problems.

After she hung up, Elaine sat with her hand still wrapped around the phone, wondering why neither of them had said "I love you," and wondering what in hell Nick had done to get himself sent home. His mouth, she thought. He had probably mouthed off again to the wrong people at the wrong time.

She pushed the telephone away and swiveled the chair around to study Dozier's oversized calendar. Today's date, February 22, was already x-ed out. February 24 was circled heavily in red. The ground war was scheduled to start before dawn on the day after tomorrow. For 48 straight hours the 153rd's Black Hawks had been delivering fuel, ammunition, and supplies to forward positions. A truly awesome performance.

But not so awesome a performance for Major Elaine Mason. She had flown only one sortie in three days. Dozier had found a dozen different administrative tasks for her. He meant what he said about keeping her on the ground if she refused to help with Griggs.

Elaine glanced at her watch, 1840 hours, and checked the time with the wall clock. In twenty minutes, at seven, she was to meet with Sergeant Robert Lefcourt, Cynthia Griggs's alleged rapist. What a distasteful job, made all the worse because she was following Dozier's scenario to the letter.

He wanted Elaine to pressure Griggs into not filing charges. Elaine's conversations with Griggs had all but convinced her that Griggs, if not exactly lying, was twisting the truth. Victim of her own imagination. Rape, what an ugly word. A real four-letter word.

Twenty minutes later, face to face with Robert Lefcourt, Elaine found the ugly four-letter word to be even uglier. Lefcourt, twenty-six, was tall and slender, with blond curly hair and deep blue eyes. It was unlikely that Cynthia Griggs had said no to this gorgeous young man, a point emphasized by Lefcourt himself.

". . . no, Major, the lady is lying," Lefcourt was saying. "Ma'am, can we talk straight out? I mean, say it like it is?"

"By all means, Sergeant." Elaine tried to make a joke of it. "Just think of me as one of the guys."

Lefcourt did not crack a smile. His handsome features remained stonily impassive. This was serious business, after all. "I've never had to fight for it, if you get my meaning," he said. "Never."

They were seated at a small table in the rear of the 153rd's NCO club, a single-story structure that at one time had been a recreation hall for oil company employees. The room echoed with a hundred voices and continual rock music from a jukebox. Twice in the past thirty minutes the air raid sirens had signaled a Scud attack. MPs ordered everyone out of the club and into an adjoining shelter. The first alarm was false but not the second. A Patriot missile intercepted the Scud several miles from the airfield. The debris fell harmlessly into the Gulf.

"So what are you telling me, Sergeant?" Elaine asked. "Yes, you and Corporal Griggs did have a sexual relationship?"

Lefcourt poured the remainder of a can of 7Up into a plastic cup. He drank some. Elaine waited for him to reply. She looked at him, and then past him at a large poster stapled to the wall.

USEFUL PHRASES FOR COMMUNICATING WITH YOUR CAPTORS

AKBAR KHALI-KILI HAFTIR LOTFAN.
Thank you for showing me your marvelous gun.

FEKR BABUL CADAN DAV AT PAEH GUSH DIV AR.

I am delighted to accept your kind invitation to lie down on the floor with arms above my head and my legs apart.

SHOMAEH FEKR TAMOMEH OEH COFTEH BANDE.

I agree with everything you have ever said or thought in your life.

AUTO ARRAREGH DAV ATEMAN MANO SEPAHEH-HAST.

It is exceptionally kind of you to allow me to travel in the trunk of your car.

FASHAL EH-TUPEHMAN NA DEGAT-MANO GOFTAM CHEESHAYEHI MOHEMARA JEBEHKESHVAREHMAN.

If you will do me the kindness of not harming my genital appendages, I will gladly reciprocate by betraying my country in public.

KHREL, JEPAHEH MANEH VA JAYEII AMRIKAHEY.

I will tell you the names and addresses of many American spies traveling as reporters.

BALLI, BALLI, BALLI!

Whatever you say.

MEZ AHLIEH, GHORBAN.

The red blindfold would be lovely, Excellency.

NUNEH BA KHRELLEH BEZORG VA KKHRUBE BOYAST INUM BERERAM.

The water-soaked bread crumbs are delicious, thank you. You must give me the recipe.

"Yes," Lefcourt said. "Yeah, we had sex. But strictly voluntary on her part. You'll forgive me, ma'am, but *more* than voluntary. On her part, if you get my meaning."

"No, Sergeant, I do not get your meaning. Please explain it to me."

Lefcourt sighed heavily. "I mean . . . well, she was all over me. I almost had to fight her off."

"But you didn't," said Elaine.

Lefcourt apparently decided to try a little joke himself. "No, I figured I better lay back and let it happen. Let her, like they say, 'have her way with me.'"

"Letting her 'have her way' must have been quite a sacrifice for you," Elaine said dryly. She wondered if Lefcourt was really as dumb as he appeared. "Incidentally, are you planning to stay in the army?"

"My hitch isn't up for a year and a half," he said. "I haven't given it much thought. Why do you ask, ma'am?"

"Just curious," she said, which was true but not what had prompted the question. It seemed improbable that a man planning to make the army a career would jeopardize it with rape. "What about schooling?" she went on. "How far did you get?"

"High school," he said. "I graduated."

Elaine felt a sudden twinge of guilt. Her questions were all directed at exonerating him, proving him innocent beyond a shadow of a doubt. Talk about a rigged jury. No, worse, a biased judge. Which certainly did not mean she was going out of her way to prove the falsity of Griggs's accusation. No, she was merely confirming her own instinct. But in fairness to Cynthia Griggs, Elaine's investigation had to be thorough.

"How many times did you see Cynthia?" she asked. "I mean, after that first time."

"You mean how many times did we have sex?"

"Yes, Sergeant, that's what I mean."

"Only that once," he said. "I saw her maybe a couple of dozen times after that. I mean, she kept running after me. *She* wanted sex. I wouldn't do it."

"Why not?"

"For one thing, I could see she had wedding bells on her mind. I'm not ready for anything permanent. And she has a kid, you know. Maybe she saw me as a father for the kid."

"Would it surprise you to know that she admits only one . . . one encounter with you?"

"She's right," Lefcourt said. "There was only one."

"The one when she says you raped her."

"The one when I *didn't* rape her."

"Then why do you think she's crying rape?"

Lefcourt said, "I *know* why. She can't stand being turned down. You know, 'a woman scorned,' or however that goes."

A woman scorned, Elaine thought. It made sense.

It made sense to Lieutenant Colonel Dozier, too, later that day when Elaine reported her findings. Dozier beamed happily and shook Elaine's hand and thanked her for being so cooperative. Moreover, he announced he was scheduling her to fly immediately, that very evening, a night operation.

"Hey, Carl," he called to SFC Chambers, who stood at the file cabinet making a pretense of studying some folders. "Tell operations that Major Mason is working tonight. But will Griggs listen to you?" he asked Elaine in the same breath. "Will she follow your advice?"

Elaine did not immediately reply. Chambers was staring scornfully at her. He had overheard the entire conversation, and evidently believed Elaine's return to flight duty to be a payoff for services rendered. She felt momentary anger, then relaxed. To hell with Chambers. Let him believe whatever he liked. Big deal.

"Yes," she said to Dozier. She turned directly to Chambers and said, "Griggs will do as I say."

Chambers slammed shut the file drawer and hurried from the office. Elaine wanted to laugh. She had put the pompous little prig in his place. She faced Dozier again. "I'm sure of it."

3

The room's only window, an open slit in the wall fifteen feet above the floor, was wide enough for Mudar to see dozens of television antennae on the roof of a nearby building. Obviously an apartment house. And he could hear the constant rumble of vehicle motors, so he knew they were in a large town.

The room—a cell, really—stank of urine and feces. Well, what could you expect? No toilet, only an open tin bucket in the corner of the damp concrete floor. The walls were gouged with the graffiti of the names or initials of hundreds of men. And the dates. All the way back to 1975. The tin bucket had probably been here since then.

He heard Zahir moan. The bastards had treated Zahir like an animal. Beating him mercilessly and then denying him any medical care, not even first aid. Zahir and Mudar had landed near each other, and were captured by soldiers of the same unit, but brought separately to this place. Mudar had survived the ejection without a bruise, not even a scratched face, and his captors had not beaten him. He suspected they wanted a clearheaded POW to interrogate.

Zahir moaned again. His face was a mass of purple and black lumps, the skin cold and clammy. Mudar held the rusty tin cup of brackish water to Zahir's lips. It was the only water since morning, and almost all gone.

"Drink, Zahir," Mudar cradled Zahir's head in his arms and tipped the cup into Zahir's mouth. Zahir managed to swallow a few small mouthfuls of water.

"You'll be all right," Mudar said, which made him feel foolish. Zahir would never again be all right, not with all that internal bleeding.

"What time is it?" Zahir whispered.

"I don't know," Mudar said, wondering why Zahir wanted to know the time. "They took our watches." He glanced at the window slit. "Still daylight. Late afternoon, I think."

"Where are we?"

"Basra, I think."

Zahir closed his eyes. Mudar was almost relieved at Zahir's abrupt silence; he had feared Zahir might ask what was going to happen to them. Mudar did not like to think about that.

Zahir opened his eyes. "We hit the target," he said, his voice unexpectedly strong. "We hit it."

"Try to sleep," Mudar said, and closed his own eyes.

He did not know how long he slept but when he woke, the room was dark. He thought he was back at Khalid, in his air-conditioned room at the BOQ. But the sound of labored breathing beside him told him he was not at Khalid. Maybe he was in Paris or New York, with a woman. Or Monaco, where only a few months ago he had spent eight glorious days in a penthouse suite at the Meridien, with two glorious blonde Norwegians. Blondes, plural.

Wait, he was at home, in his own bedroom in the villa outside Riyadh. The lovely, rambling house that his father, the managing director of the country's second largest refinery, had commissioned a Swedish architect to design and an American construction firm to build. House? Palace, more accurately. And Mudar had personally planned his room when the house was built. A room with its own private entrance so he might come and go as he pleased.

The dark sky through the window slit and the stench of the bucket shattered the illusion. He sat up. He touched Zahir's shoulder. Zahir was sleeping. Good, it would give him strength.

Strength for what?

It was as though Mudar had asked the question aloud. The answer came almost instantly. The door burst open in a blaze of blinding white from the corridor lights. The hulking forms of three bereted soldiers were framed in the doorway.

"On your feet, swine!"

Mudar could not find the energy to move. He rubbed his eyes and tried to focus. And then he felt himself being lifted to his feet and pushed from the room. He stood unsteadily outside the door, watching two soldiers drag Zahir into the corridor.

They were in a cavernous building, unmistakably a prison. The cement floor was strewn with rubble. A section of the ceiling sagged precariously. One entire wall was demolished, open to the street where vehicles drove continuously back and forth. Some of the vehicles' headlights were unhooded and briefly illuminated a gigantic junk pile of bricks and twisted metal, the remains of an industrial park.

Soldiers were everywhere, rushing in and out of the place, scurrying about with dispatches. The prison also functioned as some type of headquarters or command post. Mudar wanted to laugh. He had just then recognized the sound of a small motor as a gasoline generator. With all their electrical plants bombed out of action, the bastards had to rely on portable generators for power.

As they walked across the floor, one soldier continually prodded Mudar in the small of the back with the butt of an AK-47. The other two soldiers dragged Zahir between them. All three were big men, and young, and wore Republican Guard insignia. Mudar wanted to ask where they were taking them, and why, but at the same time he did not want to know.

They crossed the main floor and walked along a wide corridor, and halfway down the corridor to a closed office door. One soldier knocked on the door and entered. He spoke to someone inside, then gestured the others to bring Zahir and Mudar into the room.

The room was dark except for a narrow halo of light from a single gooseneck lamp on a planked-wood table. Two straight-backed wood chairs were positioned neatly in front of the table, which was in the center of the room and contained only a telephone, a triangular glass ashtray, and a yellow legal pad and three pencils. An unlighted cigar lay in the groove of the otherwise clean ashtray. A white-haired man sat at the table. The epaulets of his immaculate khaki uniform bore the eagle and two stars of *aquid,* full colonel.

The soldiers shoved Mudar into one of the chairs and propped Zahir in the other. The colonel turned the lamp so that it shone directly on the two Saudis. Mudar tried to shield his eyes from the glare. A soldier slammed the flat of his hand down on Mudar's wrist. In

the blinding light, Mudar could see only the blurred silhouette of the colonel's head, his carefully blow-dried
hair.

"I am Colonel Hakim." He spoke in a cultured, clas-
sical Eastern accent that Mudar found easy to understand and almost pleasant to the ear. "I will ask you
some questions. I hope your reply will be prompt and
true. First, your name and unit?"

"My name is Mudar Taleb," Mudar said. "I am a major of the Royal Saudi Air Force. My identification number is 75831."

"Your unit?" Hakim said quietly.

"My name is Mudar Taleb. I am a major—"

"Yes, yes," Hakim said in the same quiet voice. "I
happen to know that you were ordered to attack civilian
targets. What targets, and where?"

"My name is Mudar Taleb. I—"

"Major, I beg of you, answer the question," Hakim
said, and in the same breath addressed Zahir. "Perhaps,
Captain, you might be kind enough to respond."

Zahir did not have the strength to reply. He shook his
head. Hakim picked the cigar up from the ashtray. He
examined it to make sure the cut met his approval, then
placed it in his mouth, and lit it with a silver Zippo
lighter.

The only sounds in the room were Zahir's scratchy
breathing and the drone of the gasoline generator.
Mudar heard another sound: his heart pounding. To
him it sounded like the banging of a kettledrum. Fear,
he thought, and told himself he must prepare for the
worst. He knew what these people were capable of.

Concentrate, he told himself. The course in survival
techniques. They taught you that the enemy would commit unspeakable atrocities, first on your body, and then
on your mind. Or was it the other way around? Mind
first, then the body. You could resist only so long, but
longer than you believed possible. The trick was will-
power.

Mudar was suddenly aware that Hakim had risen
from the table and stepped toward Zahir, and that two

soldiers had seized Zahir's arms. Now Mudar had a clear view of the white-haired colonel. An unexpectedly handsome man, tall and deceptively lean, he looked to be in his late forties or early fifties. He said nothing as he drew on the cigar until the ash glowed red. He removed the cigar from his mouth, tipped it toward him to study the ash, and in the same motion mashed it into Zahir's cheek. Zahir screamed. A puff of white smoke spewed from his face. The odor of scorched flesh and burnt tobacco filled the room.

"You son of a bitch!" Mudar shouted. He sprang toward the colonel but was instantly restrained by the soldier behind him. A second soldier wrapped a heavy plastic strap around Mudar's chest, pinning him into the chair.

Hakim gazed glumly at the cigar, which had been snuffed out. He placed it back in the ashtray, shaking his head as though saddened at the waste of such fine tobacco. Then he gestured toward the rear of the room. Two men, civilians, appeared. One wore a black nylon ski jacket and white sailcloth trousers, the other a leather jacket and blue denims. Both were young, with thick shiny black hair and bushy mustaches, and bore a remarkable resemblance to each other.

The ski-jacketed man carried a small aluminum suitcase. He put the box on the floor near Zahir's chair, flipped the snap-latches, and opened the cover. Inside were four cadmium batteries and a mass of wires and switches. The man removed two wires. Large metal alligator clips were attached to the wires.

Hakim said to Zahir, "Once more, Captain, your targets?"

Mudar was astonished at the steadiness of Zahir's voice. "We did not hit civilian targets."

"You are lying," Hakim said.

"We did not hit civilian targets," Zahir repeated.

"He's telling the truth, damn you!" Mudar cried.

"You were instructed to murder women and children, were you not?" Hakim said.

"No," said Zahir. "Never."

Hakim nodded at the ski-jacketed man. The man unzipped the fly of Zahir's flight suit. Gripping each end of the open zipper, he tore the fabric apart and then ripped open Zahir's white cotton boxer shorts. Zahir's penis and testicles lay exposed. The ski-jacketed man placed one alligator clip around the tip of Zahir's penis and the other clip to a pole inside the box. He worked very quickly but carefully, clearly an expert in this line of work.

The leather-jacketed man flipped a toggle button in the suitcase. Zahir screamed. His body stiffened in a single uncontrollable spasm, and then he immediately slumped forward. The alligator clip remained firmly clamped.

Hakim cupped Zahir's chin. Zahir peered at Hakim with glazed eyes. Hakim knew that Zahir could hear and understand him.

"Shall we try it again?" Hakim asked.

Zahir said nothing.

Hakim nodded at the leather-jacketed man. The man twirled a rheostat knob a half turn and flipped the toggle. Again, Zahir's body jerked uncontrollably. The veins in his forehead stood out like strands of blue wire. His eyes bulged. His mouth gaped open in a silent scream. Again, he slumped forward.

Hakim said to Mudar, "You are not a very good friend. You can stop this whenever you wish."

"Then stop it," Mudar said. "Please, stop it."

"Tell him to answer the question."

"He has already answered," Mudar said. "We were not ordered to attack civilians."

Hakim appeared to be reconsidering. It gave Mudar a brief moment of hope. Words of bravado rolled through his mind: Question me instead of him! Can't you see that he's sick! You'll kill him! But Mudar never spoke the words. From the corner of his eye, he had been watching the ski-jacketed man don a pair of latex surgical gloves. The man moved toward Zahir. An instant later, Zahir screamed.

The ski-jacketed man had gripped Zahir's penis with

one hand, and with the other hand he had inserted an instrument deep into Zahir's urethra. A screwdriver. A Phillips screwdriver with a yellow and black plastic handle. Only the handle protruded.

Zahir's head snapped back against the top of the chair. His eyelids rolled up and his eyes stared unseeingly. The man removed the screwdriver. A jet of blood spurted onto the man's white trousers. He leaped backward, cursing.

The leather-jacketed man was speaking to Hakim, but Mudar did not understand a word. His concentration was focused on Zahir. On Zahir's open, unseeing eyes.

Now the words made sense.

". . . dead," the leather-jacketed man was saying.

Hakim gazed blandly at Mudar. "I'm sending you back to your cell. We'll have another chat soon. Perhaps you'll feel more cooperative after a few hours' rest."

TWENTY

From 12,000 feet, fifty miles away, the smoke from the burning oil fields rose up like an ominous black wall. A barrier one hundred miles wide and five miles high, impenetrable even to the sun. It was as though the wall had been erected as a warning that entry was forbidden upon pain of death.

Which, Nick thought, might not be that far from the truth. Not for the air force, but for the coalition ground forces preparing to launch the final assault. Allied casualties were expected to be high. The picnic was over.

Nick's eight-airplane package was en route home, back to Al Kalir. They had hit a Republican Guard armored brigade dug in on the east shore of Bubiyan Island, in Kuwait. Although the poor visibility prevented an accurate damage assessment, Nick knew they had killed at least six tanks.

"Detroit Lead, Four."

John Switzer's youthful voice interrupted Nick's musing. He had to smile, picturing Switzer's strained, practiced air of nonchalance. First Lieutenant Johnny Switzer, whom everyone called "The Kid," which described him perfectly. At twenty-three, the 358th's youngest pilot, he still needed to shave only every other day.

"Go ahead, Four," Nick said into his microphone.

"Sir, better check your fuel."

"Say again?"

"You seem to be leaking fuel," Switzer said. He was behind Nick at six o'clock, and slightly below.

"That's affirm, Lead," said another voice, Detroit Two, Captain Hank Bamberger, Nick's wingman. "You must have taken a hit back there."

Coming off the target, Nick had felt something bang into the airplane. But all systems checked out, so he assumed a piece of shrapnel had glanced harmlessly off the wing or fuselage. Bamberger had looked him over and reported nothing amiss. Now he realized he had indeed been hit, either a fuel tank or a feed line. Electric jet or not, the F-16 was not bulletproof.

Nick's fuel-low warning light came on at the same instant Switzer said, "Nick, it's really pouring out of there!"

The main feed line, Nick thought. The fuel gauges indicated sufficient quantity but the gas was not being transferred to the engine. Now the second fuel-low light illuminated.

"Yeah, I got a problem," he said into the microphone. "It's called 'out-of-gas.' "

Ed Iverson's crisp voice boomed into Nick's earphones. ". . . headed your way, Detroit Lead!"

Who the hell needs you? Nick thought, and was tempted to say it. The eight F-16s of Iverson's strike package, some fifty miles northeast of Nick, had just completed an attack on positions of the 3rd Armored Division along a two-mile section of Wadi al-Batin in northern Kuwait. They were outbound, returning home.

"Bishop Lead, I copy," said Nick.

"Stand by One, Nick," Iverson said, and called to his wingman, "Bishop Two, assume Lead and head for home." He addressed Nick again. "Detroit Lead, how you doing?"

"Not good," Nick said, which he thought might be the understatement of the year. He knew he did not have enough fuel to reach Al Kalir and probably not enough for Al Hafir, the nearest friendly strip. Nor for the nearest tanker. He only hoped he had enough to make the Saudi border.

"Detroit, stay with Lead until I release you," Iverson called to Nick's flight. "Acknowledge."

One by one the seven Detroit F-16s acknowledged. Nick was tempted to tell Iverson to please not do him any favors. Correction: any *more* favors. Nick's transfer orders had already come through. He was scheduled to leave Dhahran that evening on a MAC C-141 to Charleston, and Iverson had graciously offered him this final mission. A kind of no-hard-feelings gesture.

". . . believe I have you visual, Nick." Iverson's radio voice was calm and cool. "AWACS has been notified and a rescue chopper is on the way. We'll stay with you."

Nick glanced away from the instrument panel long enough to scan the sky to the north. Sure enough, he could make out an oncoming speck. He wanted to laugh. The incredible irony of it all, his final sortie. Great title for a movie, *The Last Flight.*

The master caution panel resembled a pinball game scoreboard. Every engine warning light was illuminated. Nick keyed his microphone. "Bishop Lead, I'm about to flame out." In the moment of tense silence that followed, Nick almost expected Iverson to apologize for giving him this final mission.

Iverson said, "Then you better punch out, Nick. You'll be okay."

Thanks for a great piece of advice, Ed, Nick told him in his mind, and wrapped his fingers around the ejection seat handles on each side of the seat. He listened absently to Iverson's request for fuel status checks from Nick's flight. All seven were low. Iverson ordered them to proceed to the nearest tankers, then return to provide cover. In the meantime he, Iverson, would stay with Nick.

Nick pulled the ejector handles. He heard the rocket motor ignite, then felt himself hurled upward and the breath being sucked out of him. Everything went gray. A few seconds later, he was descending in the parachute and gazing at the beautiful orange and white canopy billowing above him. He reached into the left pocket of his survival vest for the PRC-90 radio but then decided to wait until he was on the ground. He did not want to risk dropping the radio.

He did not even attempt to guide the chute shroud lines. He had no idea where he was. The black smoke obscured the entire horizon, but through the haze he could see a short distance in all directions, and directly below. The ground was green, interspersed with rolling patches of brown desert. Now, lower, he recognized the green as a complex of date palm groves. An asphalt highway ran through the green area, and another road paralleled the desert.

Overhead was an F-16. The airplane was several thousand feet above him, about a half mile away, too far off to make out the numbers. Nick knew it was Iverson, and no doubt frantically trying to contact Nick on the PRC-90 frequency.

You surprise me, Ed, Nick said to him in his mind, you surprise the hell out of me. You're fuel-critical yourself, but you're hanging around to make sure the rescue chopper reaches me before the bad guys. I appreciate it, goddamn you, I honest to God do.

Yeah, Ed, Nick continued to him in his mind, you son of a bitch, you'll probably get a DFC for this, and a Star to go along with it. Well, you'll have me to thank for it. In more ways than one, maybe; maybe that punch in the mouth knocked some savvy into you. Sobered you up, let's say.

Nick was one hundred feet from the ground when he saw the helicopter. It was so low it seemed to have flown out of the date palm grove. He assumed Iverson and the chopper were in contact. Iverson had come down now to less than 2,000 feet, orbiting tightly at slow speed.

Nick hit the ground, body relaxed and knees flexed to absorb the shock of the impact. A textbook landing, he thought cheerily, as he released the shrouds and watched the collapsing chute skitter along the sandy grass. The helicopter, some thousand yards away and no more than twenty feet off the ground, lumbered toward him.

Now he pulled the radio from his pocket, flipped up

the antenna, and spoke into the mouthpiece. "Bishop Lead, I'm okay, and the chopper is here! Thanks!"

Iverson immediately began climbing. He had not yet spotted the helicopter and also wanted a better overall view to be sure of no ground activity. He leveled out at 6,000 feet. The layers of black oil smoke and a scattering of cirrus obscured his vision. He climbed a little higher. Now, through an opening, he saw the helicopter. It looked like a giant brown centipede crawling across the desert. But where the hell had it come from, and how did it get here so fast? And why hadn't it contacted him? He called the AWACS.

"Yukon, Bishop Lead. The chopper is here, but I can't raise him. What frequency is he working?"

The AWACS controller, a woman, sounded surprised. "Bishop Lead, SAR is en route, but is approximately one zero zero miles west—"

Iverson did not wait to hear more. He rolled the F-16 over on its back, slammed the throttle into afterburner, and dove through the black smoke and light cloud. He emerged in the clear at 4,000 feet.

The helicopter was a quarter mile from Nick, who one instant stood waving his arms and the next instant was running toward the date palm grove. Iverson leveled the F-16 and banked around. He saw flashes of yellow spurting from the helicopter's nose and realized why Nick was running from the helicopter. It was not a UH-60 or a Chinook. It was a Hind, a Soviet-manufactured assault helicopter, an Iraqi gunship.

Nick had recognized the Hind only an instant before the 12.7mm slugs from its four-barreled chin gun began chewing up the dirt in front of him. The radio fell from his hand as he raced for the shelter of the date palms, one hundred yards away. The Hind whizzed past, so close he could see the helmeted faces of the pilot and gunner.

The Hind turned smoothly and came back toward him. The gunner swung the barrel around with the turning helicopter. Nick continued running for the trees.

The Hind's bullets chewed across the ground toward him.

Iverson, banking the F-16, momentarily lost sight of Nick. Then he spotted him, face down on the ground, crawling with agonizing slowness toward the grove of trees. The Hind had once again reversed direction and was heading back to Nick. Iverson knew Nick had been hit and was still alive, but helpless now and dead meat for the Hind gunner.

Iverson also knew he had no time to line up a missile, and that the only way to kill the Hind was with the cannon, and that the cannon demanded a straight-in dive at an altitude and speed leaving him little or no chance to pull out. But even as all this was rushing through his mind, along with its crystal-clear ramifications, he had already slammed the throttle through the stop into afterburner and pointed the F-16's nose straight down at the Hind.

Nick heard the nearly supersonic shriek of the F-16 and managed to turn over on his back. He gasped with pain. He had no idea of the wound's exact location—on his right side, he thought, in the abdominal area—or its seriousness. The fact that he had been hit was serious enough, although academic: The helicopter was moving toward him. He was literally looking straight into the four barrels of the gun.

The F-16 burst into his field of vision, and then the muzzle flashes of the Vulcan cannon as its shells slammed into the Hind. The helicopter continued on an instant, faltered, hovered in midair, and then disintegrated. An explosive fireball of orange and yellow rumbled through the date palm grove.

Debris spewed in all directions, chunks of flaming aluminum bouncing along the ground like pebbles skipping across the surface of a pond, rotor blades still spinning as they flew about like giant directionless boomerangs. The pieces fell all around Nick. He hardly noticed. He was watching the F-16. Iverson had managed to raise the nose slightly and had hurtled past the flaming wreckage of the Hind, on across the date palm grove, and vanished behind the trees.

The whole world exploded. A flash of orange erupted from beyond the date palm grove, then a sheet of yellow flame. A coil of black greasy smoke rose into the air. The smoke blended with the oil-field smoke in a series of thick clouds that darkened the sky.

Nick gingerly touched the right side of his flight suit. The fabric was shredded and wet. He looked at his hand. The tips of the fingers were red with blood. He peered into the sky. Where the hell was the rescue chopper? Why hadn't more fighters arrived to provide cover? Except for the clouds of black smoke drifting lazily across the horizon, the sky was empty.

Now in the near distance he heard approaching vehicles, jeeps or trucks. He wondered if they would blame him for the helicopter crash and punish him for it. Probably, yes. But all they'd get from him was name, rank, serial number. If they expected him to make any guest television appearances, they were in for a rude awakening. Fuck you, mister, absolutely.

He knew he was concentrating on this so as not to think about Iverson. The dumb son of a bitch had knowingly sacrificed himself for Nick. He tried to drive Iverson from his mind but like a target popping up on the moving belt of a carnival shooting gallery, Iverson's face kept reappearing in Nick's memory.

Nick imagined himself in Iverson's place, the thousands of thoughts flashing through the man's head when he committed himself to that terminal dive. Took guts, more than he ever could have mustered. On the other hand, Iverson may have believed he could somehow recover from what must have been a 9G pullout. Nick saw him try to raise the nose. No, no way. Iverson had to realize the inevitability of the airplane's forward velocity. He knew.

The vehicle motors were louder. Nick closed his eyes and waited.

2

That morning, Elaine and her crew had flown two sorties, a fuel and ammo delivery to a FARP near the Kuwaiti border and a Medevac flight. Everywhere you went, everywhere you looked, the desert was filled with vehicles. Tanks, APCs, trucks, humvees, all moving north and east in a gigantic semicircle under a veritable umbrella of aircraft. B-52s, flying so high only their vapor trails were visible. Fighters, transports, tankers, and like deadly birds of prey, swarms of helicopters.

As a WCN military analyst stated yesterday on "Gulf Watch," even if the Iraqis did agree to leave Kuwait, it was too late. The Allied machine had begun rolling; its own momentum prevented it from being stopped.

Elaine had no sooner landed from the Medevac and stepped into Ops for debriefing when Lieutenant Colonel Dozier appeared. His dour face was worth a thousand words. "I want to talk to you," he said. "Privately."

He did not utter another word as they walked to his office. Elaine knew it concerned Corporal Griggs. The stupid girl had changed her mind and decided to file charges against Lefcourt after all. Making a complete fool of Elaine, who had assured Dozier that the case was closed. Now Dozier would insist that Elaine start all over again with Griggs. But Elaine had no intention of complying. She was through. A direct order from Schwarzkopf would not change her mind. No way, José.

Especially not after the agonizing hour spent with Griggs the previous evening. Elaine had literally seen herself through Griggs's eyes. The idol crumbling. Each word from Elaine's mouth seemed to stagger Griggs. Drop the case, Elaine advised. The cruel facts were that Griggs's past would kill her.

Griggs had said, "Ma'am, my past has nothing to do with this! I thought you were my friend!"

"I am," Elaine said.

"Then why are you doing this to me?"

"What I am doing," said Elaine, "is trying to make you understand what is real, and what is not."

"I can't believe you're letting them get away with it," Griggs said, and then came the weeping and the swearing upon her child that she had told the truth. She had been violated, didn't that mean *anything* to another woman?

For a few moments Griggs stubbornly had held her ground, and to hell with Elaine. She, Griggs, would go it alone. She'd damn well talk to the regimental legal officer. Yes, yes, she'd done her homework, she knew what to do and who to see. She wasn't as stupid as everybody thought.

But Elaine prevailed. Griggs caved in. One thing, though, she'd get the hell out of this crummy army as soon as humanly possible. And she knew exactly how to do it: She'd admit falsifying her enlistment papers. They'd climb all over themselves in their hurry to be rid of her.

Elaine asked Griggs to please reconsider so rash a move. The consequences were unpredictable. And what of her plans for the army college program? Wasn't that reason enough to stay in? So please, Cynthia, give it some thought.

Thank you, ma'am. Thank you very much. Thank you for all you've done.

Dozier's voice shattered Elaine's reverie. "I have some bad news for you."

They were in the C.O.'s office, and he had just then gestured SFC Chambers to leave the room. As Chambers closed the door, Elaine caught a glimpse of his heavy-boned face. The sergeant looked angry, the first time Elaine had ever seen him really display any emotion. Elaine almost laughed aloud. If nothing else, Corporal Cynthia Griggs was certainly stirring things up.

"Sit down," Dozier said quietly. He reached for a paper on the desk. He started to hand it to her, then changed his mind. He placed the paper on the blotter in front of him and sat down himself. "Elaine, sit down, please," he said.

She sat, staring at the paper, at the perforated side strips still attached to the edges. Her stomach began falling as she realized this did not concern Griggs, and that it was indeed bad news. From Seattle, about her husband, Marc. Or from San Antonio, where her father had recently undergone a quadruple bypass.

"It just came in," Dozier said. "It's a CENTCOM Operational Advisory. Aircraft losses as of . . ." he stopped reading. He looked at Elaine and paraphrased the message. "The 358th TFW lost two airplanes. The wing commander was killed." Dozier glanced at the paper. "Iverson, Colonel E. M. Iverson."

Dozier paused. Elaine said nothing. She was unable to speak for the viselike tightness in her throat. She knew what was coming.

"Your friend Nick Harmon was hit, too," Dozier continued. "But he's okay. . . ." he paused again as Elaine closed her eyes with relief. "His chute was good and he was seen landing."

Elaine opened her eyes. "You say he's okay?"

"As far as we know," Dozier said. He pushed the paper across the desktop toward her. "He's presumed to be a POW."

Elaine sat motionless. She felt as though she was falling, tumbling through space, her arms and legs clamped to the chair. A thousand pictures, all unrelated, flashed before her eyes. Nick, Marc, Griggs. Herself, at the Black Hawk controls. Herself, running along the beach with Hamlet.

Hamlet cautiously probing a piece of seaweed with one paw, which instantly brought to mind images of the dog and Marc. Marc preparing Hamlet's food, walking him, ordering him off the sofa fully aware that the moment he left the room the dog would bound back up on the cushions. In Marc's last letter he assured Elaine that he took Hamlet out every evening for a long stroll.

Dependable old Marc.

Which reminded Elaine of the letter, the "Dear Marc" letter, still unwritten. Yes, but she simply had to do it. She had to tell him she was leaving him. She was staying in the army. Yes, selfish of her, and cruel perhaps, and she only hoped that one day Marc would understand and forgive. Hamlet, of course, would never understand. Hamlet would be devastated. So would she, Elaine, without him. But Hamlet, living with Marc, would be well cared for. And loved.

Dear Marc:

She had composed the letter over and over in her mind, sharpening it, revising. A literary masterpiece: *Dear Marc, I know this will come as a shock, and I know you won't believe me when I say the last thing in the world I want to do is hurt you, but . . .* The letter faded abruptly in her mind, replaced by an image of Nick's C.O., Colonel Iverson. Iverson's handsome face loomed up in Elaine's memory like a gigantic ebony bust.

". . . you say he was killed?" she heard herself asking. "Iverson was killed?"

"Did you know him?" Dozier asked.

"I met him once," she said. "Nice man. You didn't know him, did you?"

"No, I didn't," Dozier said. "Elaine, why don't you take the rest of the day off? I'll assign somebody to your flight."

Elaine gazed at the paper. She did not want to pick it up to read the text, because then it would all be real. As long as she did not see the printed words, it might not have happened. It might be a mistake.

"Does it say how it happened?" she asked.

"They never give details in these Ops advisories," Dozier said. "I'll try to find out what I can."

"It's a shame," she said. "Colonel Iverson was a good pilot." She wanted to add that Nick, despite his problems with Iverson, never questioned Iverson's ability. But she could not bring herself to utter Nick's name, nor mention the incredible irony of this happening literally hours before his transfer back to stateside duty. That, too, would make it real.

She hardly realized she was on her feet, moving to leave, and that Dozier still sat at his desk watching her. His solicitude, she thought. It sickened her. So phony, so transparent. It was his additional reward to her, a bonus, for obtaining Griggs's cooperation. Still, it was decent of him to inform her of Iverson's accident. She might otherwise not have known for days, weeks.

Iverson's accident? My God, woman, stop playing Pollyanna and face the facts. The bloody facts. Say his name one hundred times. Nick, Nick, Nick, Nick, Nick. "Nick, goddamn your soul!" she whispered aloud, and closed Dozier's door. She had walked all the way to the building's front entrance when someone called to her.

"Major Mason . . . ?"

It was SFC Chambers. She vaguely recalled the way he had looked at her when she left Dozier's outer office, those narrow little angry eyes. And he had said, "I'm sorry, Major." Yes, of course, he knew about her and Nick. Dozier must have told him. A juicy piece of gossip.

". . . could I see you a minute?" he was saying now.

"Thank you, Sergeant, I'm quite all right," she said, and laughed harshly to herself, thinking, Yeah, I'm fine. My whole world just came crashing down around my ears. I'm just fine.

". . . like to talk to you, Major," he was saying.

Something in his voice, a certain note of controlled urgency, brought her completely out of it. Everything came back into sharp focus. Nick was down but apparently alive, hopefully uninjured. All right, they would deal with whatever happened. You are some soldier, she scolded herself. My God, talk about folding under stress!

She was thinking all this as Chambers escorted her a few paces back into the building, to a small room off the main corridor. A storeroom, cramped with reams of paper, blank tapes, computer and printer supplies. Chambers closed the door and switched on the overhead light.

"It's about Corporal Griggs," he said. "About Bob Lefcourt, I mean." He pushed aside two large cartons of fax paper so he could step farther back and not have to awkwardly crane his neck to face Elaine, who was at least two inches taller. "I heard you telling Colonel Dozier yesterday that Corporal Griggs really only imagined the whole thing. That stuff about Lefcourt raping her."

Elaine said nothing. She crinkled her nose at a sour odor that was unpleasantly familiar. It came from Chambers himself, his clothes. Tobacco, stale cigar smoke. Marc had a friend, a stockbroker with whom he sometimes played poker. Elaine always knew. Marc's clothes stank of cigars.

Chambers said, "Well, you were wrong, Major. Lefcourt really did do it."

Elaine was silent another moment, her eyes fixed on a spot of stubble in the cleft of Chambers's chin where he had missed shaving. And why in the hell was a man so patently opposed to servicewomen suddenly defending one of them? Had she misjudged the son of a bitch? No, no way, these women-haters were as recognizable as though wearing badges. He had a motive, this bigmouth, a beef with Lefcourt probably.

"Lefcourt really did do it," she repeated. "How do you know that?"

"I know him, ma'am."

"You know him. And that's how you know he did it? Because you know him?"

Chambers sighed wearily. At least his breath was tolerable. A medicinal mix of mouthwash and toothpaste. Give him points for that. "Let me put it another way," he said. "I know her, Griggs. I know Griggs."

"What does that mean?"

"We were friends. But when she found out I was married, she kissed me off. Not because she wanted to get married or anything like that. Her whole life is the army. No, she just figured she wouldn't want to be my wife back in Fort Lewis, behaving herself while I'm fooling around with somebody else. I respect her for that."

Respect, Cynthia Griggs's magic word. Self-respect. Cynthia confined her sexual relationships to unmarried men, a virtue that Elaine also could claim. Elaine's lover, Nick, was unmarried, which made her only half an adulteress. Allowing her to feel only half guilty, she thought. Poor Marc. Poor Nick.

". . . so what I'm trying to say," Chambers was saying, "is that she wouldn't lie about it. About the rape stuff."

"That's your opinion," Elaine said.

"Look, Major, I know Lefcourt, too. And I can figure out exactly what happened. Cynthia turned him down flat. For sex, I'm talking about. She didn't want any from him. I guess she just didn't like him. So Bobby went ahead and forced her to do it. It's that simple. Then he covers himself by saying the reason she's crying rape now is that he dumped her."

"Would it surprise you to know, Sergeant, that Lefcourt claims *he* turned *her* down?" Elaine said. "And that's why she made the accusation? To get even with him."

"I don't believe him, Major. I believe Griggs. She's telling the truth."

"Again, your opinion, Sergeant."

"It's enough for me, ma'am."

"How well do you know Sergeant Lefcourt?"

"Well enough to know he's a liar."

Bullshit, Elaine thought. She could see Lefcourt so clearly, that handsome face, those sincere eyes. A woman scorned, he said, which made so much sense. Elaine wondered—no, she feared—she feared that it made so much sense because she wanted it to. It was convenient.

Particularly convenient in that it satisfied Lieutenant Colonel Leonard Dozier, thereby putting Major Elaine Mason back in business. Back in her UH-60 Black Hawk, where she belonged, where she wanted to be. No, I am sorry, she told Chambers in her mind, I will have nothing more to do with Corporal Cynthia Griggs's accusations of rape, real or imagined. The case is closed.

But she knew that the case was not closed. The very act of talking to Chambers automatically reopened it. Pandora's box, she thought, and could not help thinking wryly, Correction: Griggs's box. "I'll see what I can do," she said.

She marveled at the clarity of her thinking and at the

same time understood why it was so clear. It was all so
far removed from plane crashes, and unwritten letters
to unsuspecting husbands, and guilt, that it came as a
welcome change. Psychology 101: We will seize any opportunity to avoid an unpleasantness.

". . . she's a good person, Griggs is," Chambers was
saying. "She deserves better than what she's getting."

So do I, Elaine thought. So do you. So do we all. "I'll
see what I can do," she repeated.

Elaine was grateful for one thing: It kept her mind off
Nick. She had gone out to the flight line and climbed up
into the Black Hawk cockpit. She sat there through two
Scud attacks. Patriots intercepted both Scuds, lighting
up the night sky for miles. The debris plummeted down
in long trails of glowing white streamers. Crashing into
the ground, like her career. Something she'd have to
live with. She had decided to tell Dozier that she had
changed her mind and intended to advise Griggs to go
ahead and press the charges.

And damn the consequences, and this said with not
the slightest doubt in her mind that nice guys never win.
Very noble of you, Major, she told herself. Very brave.
Very commendable. Very stupid.

As soon as the second all clear sounded, she left the
flight line and went to operations to see Dozier. He had
gone out on a mission. Elaine was too impatient to wait
for him to return, so she walked over to Griggs's barracks.

Griggs's bunk was on the top floor. Here, as on the
floor below, women lay on their cots reading, chatting in
groups of two or three, listening to transistor radios and
tape players. Four girls, bundled in sweaters or field
jackets, sat around a makeshift table playing bridge.

Griggs, wearing a nonregulation white turtleneck
sweater over her desert fatigues, was sitting on her bunk
listening to a Walkman. The instant she saw Elaine, her
whole face brightened. She knew why Elaine had come.
She tore off her earphones. "You've changed your mind,
haven't you?"

Elaine sank wearily down on the cot beside Griggs. "I want you to know that this will be very hard on you. They'll embarrass and humiliate you. They'll rip you apart."

"I don't care."

"Yes, I've changed my mind," Elaine said.

Griggs's eyes brimmed with tears. "I knew you believed me. Honest to God, I knew it!"

At that instant the air raid siren sounded. For a moment no one moved. It was like a tableau, a stage play, the actors all frozen in place. The tableau sprang to life. The women scrambled to their feet, gathered up their gas masks, and hurried down the stairs. A few women ignored the alarm, and the card players never stopped playing. It reminded Elaine of the time Marc attended a medical convention in Las Vegas. A flash flood hit the city. Marc said that the gamblers remained glued to the tables, totally oblivious of the water swirling around their ankles.

Elaine was more amused than annoyed. "Doesn't anybody ever pay attention to regulations?"

Through the window directly behind Griggs's bunk, a white glow on the horizon was immediately followed by a resounding, thunder-like roar that shook the barrack walls and rattled the windows.

"Bingo!" Elaine said. "But the damn thing was on us almost before they gave the alarm. I bet somebody catches hell for that."

Griggs sat up and swung her legs over the bed. "That siren is still screaming its head off," she said. "I guess there's more on the way. Maybe we should go to the shelter." She pulled on her boots and began hurriedly lacing them. "You go on down, ma'am. I'll be right along."

"It's all right, I'll wait," said Elaine. She turned to the window again. To the north, two white streaks arced across the sky. More Patriots. Another Scud was indeed coming in.

Elaine peered into the dark, waiting for the flash of the Patriot hitting the Scud. But she saw nothing, only

the two white streaks disappearing into the low-hanging
clouds. She listened for the sharp clap of an explosion
but heard nothing.

"They missed!" she said. She peered into the sky another moment, then turned away to speak to Griggs.

The last thing Elaine ever saw was Griggs's face. She
knew that a Scud had hit the barracks, although she
heard no noise, which was not surprising. Dead people
do not hear. She felt a strange sadness knowing what
this would do to Marc. Poor Marc. And Hamlet, poor
Hamlet. And Nick. God, she hoped Nick was okay. And
having been shot down, and a POW, maybe he'd make
general after all. She would certainly never make general, though. For that matter, she'd never make light
colonel. No more promotions this side of the ocean.

No promotions for Cynthia Griggs, either. Poor
Griggs. No college for her. Dead soldiers were not pro-
moted and for sure never went to college. Everyone inside the building was dead. Well, Elaine thought, thank
God for final favors: He had allowed her enough time to
realize that she was dead.

3

Nick opened his eyes. Thick clusters of date palms lined
each side of the road. Through the haze of black oil
smoke and thin clouds, the sun was opaquely outlined
and directly overhead. He sat on the floor of the pickup
truck's open bed, near the cab. The swirling road dust
stabbed into his eyes and nose and mouth; he could
taste the grittiness. He wore his flight suit, as did Mudar
Taleb, who sat opposite him.

Nick wished it was a dream. But a dream would have
included Chu-Bai, and he had beaten that rap. He had
come to terms with himself about Chu-Bai. But no, he
hadn't, otherwise he would not now be thinking about it.
Iverson, he thought. It was Iverson who brought Chu-
Bai back to Nick. Now, instead, of Chu-Bai, he would
dream about Iverson.

What really puzzled Nick was Mudar. Major Mudar

Taleb, the wealthy young Saudi who rode the backseat of a Tornado. Mudar was dead. Everyone knew that Mudar and his pilot, Zahir Mamhud—although officially listed as MIA—were KIA. Killed In Action. But there he was, Mudar, big as life. And so were the two Iraqi soldiers sitting on the truck's tailgate, AK-47s nestled in their arms.

Mudar nodded grimly at him. "How do you feel?"

Nick wanted to say "lousy," but his voice seemed trapped in the parchment dryness of his throat. His right side throbbed constantly. Where the bullet hit him, he remembered now, just above the hip and below the rib cage. He also remembered the medical term for that area, "flank." A gunshot wound to the right flank. Another Purple Heart.

Mudar said, "I heard how you and another F-16 were shot down by a gunship. The other pilot was killed." He had to shout to be heard over the road noise in the open truck. "Is that true? Were two planes hit?"

"Yeah," Nick said. His voice sounded so hoarse, so grating. It was too much of an effort for him to explain the facts. Later, he thought, he'd tell Mudar the whole story later. "Ed Iverson was the other pilot."

"The black colonel?"

Nick nodded.

"I'm sorry to hear that," Mudar said, and then as though to change the subject, went on. "You've been out cold. Do you remember being picked up?"

"All I remember is Iverson going in," Nick said. He touched his right side. It was wet. He looked at it now. From belt down to ankle, the green flight suit was encrusted with a huge black splotch of dried blood. At the waist the fabric appeared scorched, part of it torn away. Underneath, secured by two flimsy strips of paper adhesive tape, was a large dirt- and bloodstained gauze compress.

"They tried to patch you up at the command post," Mudar said. "The bullet went right through the fleshy part of your side. In and out, I heard the medic say. A big chunk of your skin got sliced away. He said you must

have been crawling around in some dirt or goatshit or
something because it's infected. The medic said he
didn't have any antibiotics, not for POWs anyway.
Maybe they'll find a doctor for you in Baghdad. That's
where we're going, Baghdad," he went on.

"Zahir," Nick said. "Where's Zahir?"

Mudar glanced warily at the soldiers. Both, bored,
were gazing at the clouds of brown road dust billowing
behind the truck. Mudar said, "Nick, we happen to have
the misfortune of being under the tender care of a devil
named Hakim." Mudar nodded at the truck cab. "He's
riding in front, Colonel Husain Hakim."

Mudar then told Nick of Zahir's death at Hakim's
hands, and that Nick's capture had probably saved him,
Mudar, from a similar fate. Hakim saw the obvious benefits in presenting his superiors in Baghdad with not one
live war criminal, but two. A pair of aces.

Nick, listening, suddenly realized why Mudar's hands
were bound behind him, while Nick's were free. Nick,
wounded, posed no threat. Well, the Iraqis would soon
find out for themselves what it meant to be a POW.

"We won't be POWs for long," Nick said. "They're
about to start the ground war. It may have already
started."

Mudar was not listening. He was watching the two
Iraqi soldiers. Both were staring in alarm at the road
ahead. Nick swiveled his head around at the same instant he heard the banshee howl of jet engines and a
split instant before he heard the hollow chug-chug-chug
of a cannon.

It was an A-10, on the deck, streaking straight in at
the truck. The airplane was so low that it was almost at
eye level and so close that you could clearly see the
seven barrels of the Vulcan cannon revolving around the
firing hub. The 30mm slugs plowed into the road just
ahead of the truck. It was as though the A-10 pilot had
aimed straight down the center of the truck, as though
he knew that the two men huddled behind the cab were
POWs and that his cannon would hit only the two
soldiers seated on the tailgate. The bullets thudded into

the metal floor, past Nick and Mudar, and into the soldiers. The sledgehammer impact of the 30mm shells, each the size of a small milk bottle, hurled both men high into the air and out of the truck.

Blinded by shards of metal and glass from the smashed hood and windshield, the driver lost control of the vehicle. He careened off the road and into the trees and came to an abrupt stop against a cinderblock retaining wall.

In the sudden silence the quiet hissing of the Toyota's cracked radiator sounded louder than the full-throttled engines of the egressing A-10. Nick sat dazed a few moments, then crawled across the truck floor to Mudar. He helped Mudar to his feet and removed the plastic straps from his wrists.

Behind them in the middle of the road some thirty feet away, one soldier lay sprawled on his back. The whole top of his head was gone. The other soldier, face down in the grassy sand at the roadside, lay in an ever-widening pool of his own blood.

Now another sound broke the silence, the whimpering of a small animal. Mudar and Nick climbed out of the truck and went around to the cab. The driver's head was jammed into the steering wheel. Blood dripped from his open, staring eyes. The whimpering sound came from Colonel Hakim. His body was jackknifed backward through the open door, his legs on the seat, his torso and arms outside. His head rested on the sand.

He was alive and alert, his eyes fixed on Mudar. A razor-sharp fragment of a 30mm shell had sliced into his stomach, through his body, and blown a six-inch-wide hole in his back where it emerged. The vinyl seat upholstery, torn to shreds, was speckled with blood-soaked tufts of padding and pieces of bone and cartilage.

"*Mae*," he whispered in Arabic, which Nick knew meant water. "*Mae, mae . . .*"

Nick said, "There's a canteen on the window shelf." He started to reach in for it.

Mudar blocked Nick's arm. "No water," he said, and then repeated the words in Arabic to Hakim.

"Please . . ." Hakim said.

"Louder," Mudar said to him. "Beg for it louder!"

Now, as Hakim formed the word, blood bubbled from his mouth. "That's how it looked coming out of Zahir," Mudar said to Nick. He spoke almost conversationally, almost clinically, like a physician discussing a patient's condition with a colleague.

"Get him some water, and let's get the hell out of here while we have the chance," Nick said. Again, he reached for the canteen. Again, Mudar stopped him.

"I have something better for his thirst," Mudar said. He scooped up a large handful of dirt. "This should make you feel better, Colonel. Open your mouth, please," he said in Arabic. As Hakim's mouth opened, Mudar's hands widened just enough to create a small funnel. "You'll really enjoy this, Colonel," he said. The powdery soil looked like sand from an hourglass as it flowed into Hakim's waiting mouth. The dirt, mingling with the blood foaming on Hakim's lips, formed a thick red paste that oozed down his chin and onto the pulsing veins of his neck. Mudar scooped up another handful of dirt.

"That's enough!" Nick said.

Mudar was totally oblivious of Nick's voice, of anything but the task before him. He poured the second batch of dirt into Hakim's mouth, then clamped Hakim's jaw closed. Hakim's body heaved convulsively up and down. Mudar patiently watched Hakim gasp for breath. Sand and blood dribbled from the colonel's mouth. Mudar nodded slowly, pleased, and did not look away even when Nick pounded him on the shoulder.

"Cars!" Nick said. "They're bound to stop here!"

Reluctantly, Mudar turned away to peer at the clouds of swirling dust far down the road. He looked at Hakim a final time, then followed Nick into the trees. He had taken only a few steps when he stopped. He looked back at the truck, at Hakim's body. "The pig is dead," he said. "I was hoping he might stay alive to suffer more."

TWENTY-ONE

At fifty-eight, Najid Bishara had gone entirely deaf in one ear and was experiencing early tinnitus in the good ear. For all that, he immediately recognized the soft ring of the desert in the younger soldier's accent, which Najid knew to be uncommon for the Republican Guard. Guardsmen were almost exclusively city boys. Najid, although a civilian, kept up on such matters.

He had spotted the soldiers lurking in the shadows of an abandoned date palm warehouse and stopped to offer them a lift. He had spoken first to the older man, who seemed flustered. The younger soldier answered for his friend. He thanked Najid but said they were returning to their unit, which was nearby.

"In An Nasiriyah?" Najid had asked.

"Yes, An Nasiriyah," the young soldier had replied.

"That's where I'm going," said Najid. He indicated the rig's tandem trailers. "I'm hauling a load of dates to the army supply depot there. It's a good forty miles. Come on, do yourselves a favor and hop in. Do *me* a favor. I have two sons in the army. I wouldn't want them walking along a dark road. Get in."

The younger one again thanked Najid but again declined. Just then, pinpoints of light from the blacked-out headlamps of approaching vehicles dotted the road behind them. It was a small convoy of tank transporters, led by a Land-Rover. As the convoy passed, someone in the Land-Rover trained a flashlight on Najid's rig. Both soldiers hurriedly clambered up into the truck and joined Najid in the cab.

Najid asked no questions, and neither soldier was very talkative; indeed, the older one never spoke. But Najid understood their silence. Their blood-stained uniforms explained everything. The poor bastards looked as though they had been to hell and back. Not to mention smelling as bad. Putting two and two together, along with the fact that they carried no weapons, Najid realized they were either AWOL or outright deserters. He had visions of them hijacking the rig, and a knife to his throat. Or worse. He was a nervous wreck by the time he drove into An Nasiriyah and pulled the big Mercedes diesel to a stop at the railway station.

The station—more accurately, the pile of bombed-out rubble of what had been the station—bustled with activity. Under the harsh glare of battery-operated portable floodlights, dead and wounded from Kuwait were being loaded aboard a train. Najid knew that for the past two weeks this same train had departed at the same time, shortly after midnight, and arrived seven hours later in Baghdad. Departing at night, he also knew, to conceal from public view the enormous number of casualties, and by train because of little danger of Allied air attack. The railway system, so thoroughly destroyed in the war with Iran, was militarily useless.

"Well, here we are," Najid said.

"Oh," said the younger soldier, but made no move to leave.

Najid leaned past them and opened their door. "Good luck," he said.

"Oh, sure," said the younger soldier. "Thanks for the lift."

"Anytime," said Najid. He smiled woodenly as the two climbed down from the cab. He down-shifted into low and drove off. He breathed a heavy sigh of relief. He had always possessed an instinct for trouble. These two were trouble, big trouble.

* * *

Nick felt stronger. Earlier, at the date palm grove, he slept several hours. He and Mudar had waited until dark before starting out on the road in the uniforms "borrowed" from the dead Iraqi guards. Nick had convinced Mudar not to wear Iraqi dog tags. Bad enough to be caught in the uniforms—and with money Mudar had removed from Colonel Hakim's wallet—but carrying Iraqi ID might mean a firing squad, no questions asked. No, keep their own ID and take their chances.

So, with some vague plan of traveling only at night and reaching Kuwait in a few days and linking up with an Allied spearhead, they had set out. And been picked up by the truck driver and dropped off at this railway station in An Nasiriyah. The uniforms were far from a perfect fit—Nick and Mudar were taller and heavier than their Iraqi benefactors—and an Iraqi military installation was the last place they wanted to be.

The hospital train was made up of three ambulance cars, two second-class passenger coaches, and two unmarked boxcars. Stretcher cases rode in the ambulance cars, the less seriously wounded in the coaches, the dead in the boxcars. The air reeked of disinfectant and unwashed bodies and echoed with the shrill cries of men in pain.

A constant stream of traffic, ambulances and other vehicles, drove back and forth through a large square opposite the station. A stone fountain, long since dry, was in the middle of the square, which branched off into several small streets. No streetlights, and the adjacent buildings were all dark and unoccupied. The entire area beyond the square was dark.

Nick and Mudar started across the square. They were already past the dry fountain when someone called, "Hey, you two!"

The voice, with the sound of a snapping whip, was directly behind them. Nick and Mudar continued walking. "Stop, goddammit!" the voice called, this time accompanied by the metallic clack of a cartridge cranked into a rifle chamber. "Yeah, that's right, you two," said the voice, as Mudar and Nick stopped.

It was an MP captain, wearing the dappled apple-green fatigues of the Popular Army. He carried an SKS carbine, holding it in one hand like a handgun. It was leveled directly on Nick.

"Where the hell do you think you're going?" The captain jabbed the rifle muzzle into Nick's chest. "This is no sight-seeing tour! Get back on the train!" His gray-flecked black mustache quivered with indignation. "You too!" he said, swiveling the gun around on Mudar.

"Yes, sir," Mudar said quietly. "We're getting on the train. Right away, sir."

2

The moment he entered the room Adnan knew he should have followed his instinct. He knew he should have contrived some excuse to not attend the meeting. Instinct? A thousand alarm bells in his head going off all at once. To begin with, the site of today's Command Council meeting was a private home at Rashdiyah, thirteen miles from Baghdad. Driving on the highway, you were dead meat for Allied planes. They were hitting anything that moved on the roads outside the cities.

More ominous was the invitation to the meeting itself, and more a summons than an invitation. Issued personally by Colonel Abdel Zaid, commander of the Al-Khassa, otherwise known as the internal security battalion, whose sole function was to protect Saddam Hussein. For Adnan, attending the meeting meant chewing up the better part of a whole day. Every hour of his time was occupied correlating intelligence assessments of the impending Allied ground offensive. If the Council expected any startling information from him, they were in for a disappointment. He could provide no new real-time data, only yesterday's report, which had already been submitted.

He had tried to explain this to Zaid, who listened patiently and had replied, "Major, *I* don't give a damn whether you attend the meeting, the President does.

He's the one that asked for you. A car will pick you up at ten A.M."

Adnan brooded about it each mile of the thirteen miles to Rashdiyah, and each mile intensified his urge to order the army chauffeur to turn back. By the time the white BMW sedan was passed through the last of the three checkpoints to the house—a flat-roofed concrete structure, an Iraqi architect's version of a French Riviera beachhouse—Adnan was certain that coming here had been a huge mistake.

Three minutes later, he was sure of it. Seated on Saddam's immediate left was Major General Hassan Marwaan. To Adnan's knowledge, Hassan had never before attended a Revolutionary Command Council meeting. There could be only one reason for Hassan's presence.

To be denounced as a traitor.

Which surely meant that Adnan had been summoned here for the same reason. His hand fell to his belt, to the butt of the 9mm Tariq tucked snugly into its leather holster. He felt childish. What the hell good would the gun do him? But then he might get a shot or two off before Zaid's security people stopped him.

Killed him, if he were lucky.

Assad Hashim's youthful voice interrupted Adnan's fantasy. ". . . the so-called last-minute peace plan suggested by Mr. Gorbachev contains many positive facets, enough for us to take it under serious consideration, and we have so informed the Soviet government. As to the shameful ultimatum issued yesterday by the president of the United States, well, that is precisely what it is: shameful! The ravings of a desperate man, a madman. I assure you, it will be ignored."

Hashim paused for an approving nod from Saddam. Hashim, the assistant director general of the Information Ministry, opened a leather-bound portfolio and extracted a sheaf of computer printouts. "A large Allied force that attempted to cross the border in central Kuwait early this morning was repulsed. The enemy suffered heavy casualties."

He went on, but Adnan's attention was fixed on Hassan Marwaan, whose eyes followed Saddam's every gesture, every movement. It was as though Hassan had already resigned himself to Saddam's pronouncement of guilt and stoically awaited the sentence.

He did not have long to wait. The Deputy Chief of Staff, Major General Hammad al-Sultan, had begun a report on the anticipated amphibious landing of seventeen thousand U.S. Marines on the beaches south of Kuwait City. Existing defensive positions had been reinforced with an armored brigade of the Republican Guard Medina Division and a brigade of mechanized infantry from the 15th Infantry Division of 7th Corps. Tactically, the situation was well in control.

Saddam stopped him. "Thank you, Hammad," he said quietly. General Sultan sat down. Saddam buttoned the top button of his greatcoat. Despite the presence of ten men in the small unheated room, a basement bomb shelter constructed during the Iran War, it was uncomfortably chilly.

In the same quiet voice, with no warning or preamble, Saddam went on, "A group of conspirators has plotted my assassination. Our intelligence agencies have been unable to identify these people. We don't know if they are one, or a hundred, or a thousand. Does anyone here have knowledge of this conspiracy?"

All nine men at the table remained silent. Saddam looked at each in turn, counterclockwise around the table, to Hassan Marwaan. "General, perhaps *you* might enlighten us?"

Adnan felt his stomach plummet. The charade was so obvious. A little vein on Hassan's temple began pulsing. His face was ash white. He could not seem to find his voice. He moistened his lips, but no words came.

"Excuse me?" Saddam said. "Could you please speak louder?"

Hassan was still unable to speak. He shook his head numbly. Adnan wondered who had betrayed the plot, which one of Hassan's coconspirators. And how had he, Adnan, been implicated? But wait: the so-called plot had never existed. It was an idea that never progressed beyond talk, an idea that existed only in the imagination of a handful of dreamers. Amateurs, bumblers.

"No, of course not, how could you know of plots or conspiracies?" Saddam said mildly. "You are a physician, a healer. How could you possibly be aware of these sinister schemes?"

Hassan said nothing. He looked away. His gaze fell directly on Adnan. Hassan's eyes glittered with contempt, sending a message to Adnan as clear as though embossed on the wall. Hassan believed that Adnan had betrayed him. Adnan's very presence in this room was incontrovertible proof.

In his mind, Adnan screamed, No! No, Hassan, it was not me! Please, please, hear me! Believe me! But even as all this raced through his mind, he wondered how he himself would behave when his turn came. He knew they would question him, and he knew he would tell all.

All, he thought. What did he know? Hassan never revealed any names. "All" was nothing more than Hassan's intimation of a plot. Adnan averted his eyes. He could not bear facing Hassan.

Saddam was saying, ". . . Doctor, I still cannot hear you."

Hassan had turned to Saddam again. "No," Hassan said. His voice was surprisingly strong and distinct. "No, I have no knowledge of any of it."

"And, of course, you are as shocked as I am to hear of such treachery, is that correct?"

Hassan nodded.

"Please, Doctor, repeat what you said." Saddam made an exaggerated gesture of cupping his ear. "Perhaps my hearing is faulty. Perhaps I should undergo a thorough physical. Yes, and you will be the examining physician. Now, you are shocked at my news of a conspiracy, are you not?"

"Yes, I am shocked," Hassan said. "Yes."

"As I knew you would be," Saddam said. His eyes never left Hassan's as in a single smooth motion he drew his pistol, leveled it at Hassan's face, and fired.

The gunshot reverberated deafeningly in the small room, echoed by the sound of Hassan's chair toppling backward to the floor. Hassan lay on his back atop the chair, staring sightlessly up at the cement ceiling. A tiny blue-red hole in the center of his forehead looked as neat and clean as though machine-punched.

No one at the table had moved. Saddam slipped the pistol, muzzle still smoking, into its holster. He glanced blandly across the room to Colonel Zaid standing near the door. Zaid opened the door. Two men in civilian clothes entered the room and strode to the table. Both wore latex gloves and carried large terry-cloth bath towels. One knelt and deftly wiped away a tiny pool of blood that had formed on the floor under Hassan's head. The other wrapped his towel around Hassan's head. The first then gripped Hassan's feet. The men lugged the body from the room. The entire procedure took no longer than thirty seconds.

Which to Adnan was a lifetime, for he fully expected to hear another gunshot and feel the impact of the bullet that would end his life. He watched Saddam fussily slide his chair away from a splotch of red on the floor that the men had missed.

Adnan looked up, directly into Saddam's stony eyes. Now, he thought, now it would happen, and probably from behind. Probably from Zaid. Adnan hated himself for his cowardice. He should be living out the fantasy of at least going down shooting. But he was paralyzed. He could not move a muscle. He did not even breathe.

". . . oh, Dulaimi, I asked you here for a special reason," he heard Saddam saying. The pleasant little smile playing on Saddam's lips enraged Adnan. The sadistic bastard. Again, Adnan saw himself drawing his own pistol and training it on Saddam. Maybe he'd be lucky enough to get in that one shot. But still he was unable to move.

". . . that television woman," Saddam was saying. "The American, the blonde. I can never remember her damned name."

"Christine Campbell," Assad Hashim said.

"Yes, that one," Saddam said. He faced Adnan again. "Hashim informs me that you deserve credit for the very favorable coverage she gave us on the terrible tragedy at Amiriyah—" Saddam paused abruptly. He seemed almost embarrassed. "You lost your fiancée there, didn't you, Major? I never did have a chance to express my condolences. Jamal Badran's daughter, wasn't she?"

Saddam continued talking, but now his words were lost in the roaring in Adnan's ears. Adnan had just then realized that he would not be killed. It would have already happened. Saddam would not waste time playing games with a junior officer. For sure, those involved with Hassan Marwaan were known and probably by now disposed of, but Adnan was not one of them. He was not even under suspicion.

". . . in appreciation of the lady's efforts, I will grant her the meeting we promised," Saddam was saying. "I might have an important statement shortly. All right, let's get on with today's business."

Adnan remembered little of what followed, except for a Council consensus that the Allied ground attack would not immediately follow the expiration of the ultimatum. Saddam was confident that George Bush, to accommodate President Gorbachev, would wait a few days for an official Iraqi reply to the latest Soviet peace plan.

This, Adnan felt certain, was Saddam's "important statement," the decision to accept the Soviet formula for withdrawal from Kuwait. It would save tens of thousands of Iraqi lives as well as the army itself. Saddam had to know now that he could not win the war. He wanted to make the announcement to the whole world in an interview with Chris Campbell.

Adnan was even more certain of it at the conclusion of the meeting. Saddam shook Adnan's hand and said, "So, Dulaimi, what I want you to do is have the lady prepare to meet with me on very short notice."

"Yes, sir," Adnan said, thinking, And for this you brought me all the way out here? You couldn't have had one of your staff tell me? My God, he thought, was it possible that Saddam did know of Adnan's conversations with Hassan after all? And forcing him to witness Hassan's execution was Saddam's way of informing Adnan? A warning? Yes, it was possible. With Saddam Hussein, anything was possible.

Not until hours later, at the end of the afternoon, when Chris opened the door of her hotel room for him, did Adnan finally relax. He had rushed back to the city after the meeting. He wanted to give the news to Chris in person; he wanted to see the expression on her face. He also wanted to be with her. He needed that. He needed her.

3

It was when the train rolled into Baghdad Central that Nick decided he was crazy. Mad as a hatter, completely out of control. Only a crazy man would have boarded an Iraqi troop train, let alone a train to Baghdad. Not to mention wearing an Iraqi uniform. Sightseeing in Baghdad. Our man in Baghdad.

Nick and Mudar had lucked out. They had found an empty compartment, and managed to keep the door locked throughout the trip. The only person who paid them any attention was the MP captain, and he had merely glanced bemusedly into the compartment through the door glass and continued on his way.

Mudar left the compartment just once, to scrounge for a fresh bandage for Nick's wound. He returned not only with a roll of bandages but some dates and a plastic container of orange juice. Compliments of an artillery sergeant, an older man who would not grow any older. As Mudar explained, the sergeant was dying so he helped ease the poor fellow's pain.

The train came to a lurching stop on a siding a half mile from the station. A double-decked bus and three ambulances were parked nearby. "We have to make a decision," Mudar said. "Do we turn ourselves in?"

Nick said nothing. He gazed out the window at the gray, chilly day. The heavy rain that had fallen throughout the night was now a steady drizzle that clung in thick oil-streaked droplets to the outside window glass. Kuwait's revenge. The oil-laden rain was a legacy from the burning oil fields.

Mudar's question had surprised Nick. They had agreed that their best chance lay in reaching a neutral embassy and demanding political asylum. Internment, at worst. They would somehow get off the train, somehow find their way to the embassy. It would all work out.

Mudar, reading Nick's thoughts, said, "You need a doctor, and fast." He pointed at Nick's stomach. The fresh bandage was already soaked with pus.

"We'll find a doctor at the embassy," Nick said. For the past hour, when not chilled, he felt feverish. He knew it would get worse.

". . . what embassy?" Mudar was saying.

"Swiss," Nick said. "Indian, Pakistani, who the hell knows?"

The MP captain walked past. He banged on the door and yelled, "We're disembarking! Move it!"

Nick and Mudar sat quietly. Through the compartment window they watched the stretchers loaded aboard the ambulances and the wounded men shuffle into the bus. The vehicles drove off across the heavily damaged railway yard. Fresh damage—tracks torn up, buildings flattened, locomotives and railway cars strewn about like discarded model trains—further confirmation of the devastating thoroughness of the Allied air attacks. Nick imagined himself describing the scene to a debriefing officer. Firsthand, eyewitness BDA. Give the man another medal.

"We can't stay here forever," Mudar said. "And we have to get out of these uniforms."

Nick said nothing. The reality of it had again overwhelmed him. The madness of it. Like an adventure novel. Or a movie that held your interest, as you tried to anticipate all the twists and turns of the plot, all the time knowing that such things never really happened. Except that it was really happening.

". . . have money, so maybe we can buy some

clothes, and some food," Mudar was saying. He displayed the roll of bills from Colonel Hakim's wallet. "And find you a doctor."

"Okay," Nick said. "Let's try our luck."

The luck was good. They walked off the train and through the yard. They might have been enjoying a winter morning stroll as they forced themselves to walk casually past the work crews repairing wrecked tracks. No one paid them the slightest attention.

The luck held. An affable taxi driver, pleased with a fifty-dinar tip, drove them across the river to a cheap, clean hotel in Wathba Square, where he said no one asked questions. The driver, like Najid Bishara before him, believed he was dealing with a pair of deserters. And he didn't blame them one iota; he'd probably have done the same if he was back in the army.

The traffic was bumper-to-bumper on Jumhuriya Bridge, one of the two bridges still functioning. The driver kept up a constant chatter as they inched their way along. Nick did not understand a word, of course, but recognized the driver's disapproving tone as a litany of complaints. Nick was right. The driver was describing conditions in Baghdad as absolutely chaotic. People rioting in the streets for food. No gas or electricity, no water. Children dying for lack of basic nutrients. Mudar replied appropriately, cursing the Allies and expressing confidence in the ultimate victory. He was sure the taxi driver was testing them.

On the north side of the river a pall of gray and white smoke hovered above the skyline. The dozens of antennae and satellite dishes that once crowded the roof of the telecommunications building now lay twisted and inert, charred tangles of melted wire. The Information Ministry's television tower, toppled half over, hung precariously across the side of the gutted building. On Rashid Street the gleaming glass and metal facades of undamaged high rises towered incongruously above the empty shells of government buildings.

The driver dropped Nick and Mudar in Wathba Square, at the Cleopatra Hotel. If the Cleopatra was not to their liking, said the driver, there were half a dozen nearby hotels where the staff minded their own business. A generous tip of course helped.

Nick felt crazier than ever. Standing in the middle of downtown Baghdad. People—soldiers and civilians—surging back and forth along the sidewalk, none glancing even twice at the two soldiers, not even at the bloodstained uniforms. At any instant he expected an MP or a policeman to demand their ID. It was insane. And why, he wondered, hadn't they ordered the taxi driver to take them directly to the Swiss embassy? There was a reason for not doing it.

Now he remembered. Going straight to the embassy might be too risky. Police were sure to be standing guard at all embassies. As Iraqi soldiers, Nick and Mudar would be arrested on sight. They needed civilian clothes.

The Cleopatra Hotel was all that the taxi driver claimed, no questions asked. Especially after Mudar stuffed a hundred-dinar note into the elderly desk clerk's shirt pocket. Other than the clerk remarking that the city had been bombed an hour earlier—the first daylight raid in nearly two weeks—not a single word was exchanged. No ID was requested, no register presented for signature. The clerk gave Mudar the key to a second-floor room, number 26, and immediately resumed watching what appeared to be a soap opera on the 9-inch black-and-white screen of a battery-operated television set.

A small room overlooking the square, number 26 was shabbily but functionally furnished. Unmatched twin beds, a bureau, one straight-backed wood chair, a writing desk, a mirrored armoire, a sink, and a bidet. The W.C. was two doors away.

To Nick, it looked like a suite at the Plaza. Well, perhaps not the Plaza, but better than a pup tent in the desert. He knew he had read or heard those words somewhere. Yes, his own words, or a reasonable approximation thereof, spoken a hundred years ago to Elaine Mason, referring to his Al Kalir BOQ room. By now she must know that he had gone down. He wished he could get word to her that he was okay.

"Not the Plaza," he said to Mudar, "but better than sleeping on palm leaves. Better than where Zahir is sleeping," he added, and thought, Or Ed Iverson.

"Zahir is sleeping with heroes," Mudar said. "Sit down and let me take a look at your wound."

Nick sat in the chair. He felt drunk and knew it was from the fever. He tried to laugh. "Talk about playing doctor."

"On the bed, Nick," Mudar said. "You'll have to lie down on the bed."

Nick remained in the chair. "How do you know where Zahir is sleeping?" he asked. "Is that some Islamic fable —sleeping with heroes?"

"Valhalla, Nick. It's an Arabic Valhalla."

"And you believe that?"

"Well, perhaps not for Zahir. His Valhalla is a Saudi democracy. One man, one vote, and all that." Mudar smiled sadly. "Zahir really believed that nonsense."

Nick struggled to concentrate. It kept his mind off the throbbing pain in his side. And he knew Mudar was talking about Zahir and Zahir's beliefs for the same reason, to keep Nick occupied. He said, "That nonsense? Don't you believe it?"

"Saudi Arabia is a monarchy, Nick. It will remain a monarchy. We built a great nation. By 'we,' I mean the ruling family. Without us, there would still be camel shit on the unpaved streets of Riyadh. Now, for God's sake, lie down on the bed and let me see what's going on."

Nick got off the chair and sank down on the bed. He closed his eyes. He wanted to sleep. He felt his jacket being unbuttoned and his belt unbuckled and his pants unzipped. He opened his eyes.

"Dammit!" Mudar said, as he removed the gauze compress. "It's leaking like a sieve. It needs a fresh dressing."

Nick pulled up his pants and zipped the fly. He unlaced and kicked off his boots, which were not the dead Iraqi's but his own flying boots. Even in his semidelirium, he now realized that wearing them was incredibly stupid. Iraqi enlisted men were not issued expensive footwear. Mudar, too, wore flying boots. Neither he nor Nick had bothered to try on the Iraqis' shoes; it had never occurred to them. Amateur night in Baghdad.

". . . going out to look for a pharmacy," Mudar was saying. "I'll get some bandages and see what they have for antibiotics." He went to the sink and splashed water on his face.

"Now you're a doctor," Nick joked. "That's what you'll be when you grow up, doctor to the ruling family. Prince Doctor, they'll call you."

Mudar, at the armoire mirror adjusting his beret, said, "Why does that bother you so much?"

"It bothered Zahir," Nick said.

"Zahir has been avenged," Mudar said.

"Yeah, that should make him feel better," Nick said. "No, Mudar, it doesn't bother me. Forget it."

Mudar, annoyed, removed the beret and stuffed it into his pocket. He slicked back his thick brown hair with his fingers. "Well, it does bother you, Nick, and I'm sorry for that. But that's your problem."

Nick said nothing. He lay back on the bed and closed his eyes again. He heard the door close. He rubbed his beard stubble. He had forgotten to ask Mudar to bring back a razor. He felt foolish, needling the poor kid about democracy. Talk about stupidity. Both of them living in a nightmare, and Professor Nick Harmon decides to give a lecture on freedom.

It is the fever, he told himself.

Fever, my ass, he replied to himself. You never liked Mudar. You always considered him a snob, a spoiled rich kid. Sure, remember that night at Al Kalir when you and Elaine ganged up on him? She, with all the bullshit about social changes in Saudi Arabia after the war, and you with—no, no, it was Zahir who did the number about social changes. Elaine was ragging Mudar about women's rights or some such crap.

Crap? You better not let her hear you say that.

Come on, Elaine knows you, and your chronic case of
Harmon's Syndrome, foot-in-the-mouth disease.

Incurable, eh?

Absolutely, and I will bet you twelve dollars to a dime
that Mudar is thinking the same thing right now.

Nick was wrong. Mudar was thinking about infinitely
more important matters. Namely, how to deal with the
two MPs who were eyeing him. He wanted to do a one-
eighty and head the other way, but that would be too
obvious. He had to keep going and hope they might
ignore him. Pray, he thought, and did.

Mudar, following the desk clerk's directions to the
nearest pharmacy, had crossed Wathba Square to the
south side of Al Jamouri Street. The pharmacy was in
the middle of that block. The MPs were on the corner
and had been watching him cross the traffic circle. Both
carried mahogany batons and wore whitewashed
webbed belts with canvas holsters containing large revolvers attached to lanyards, British style.

Closer, Mudar was encouraged to see that they were
regular army, not Republican Guard. They might not
want to tangle with a Guardsman, especially one whose
bloodstained jacket marked him as a combat veteran. To
hell with them. He looked them straight in the eye as he
approached.

The taller of the two, a sergeant, a swarthy man in his
late twenties, raised one hand like a traffic cop.
"Where's your cap?" he asked.

Mudar touched the top of his bare head. "Oh," he
said, and grinned lamely. He pulled the beret from his
pocket and clamped it on his head. "Sorry about that."

The other MP, almost light-skinned compared to his
partner, said, "Better get that uniform cleaned up, soldier." He aimed his baton at Mudar's bloody jacket.

"I will. I just haven't had a chance." Mudar managed
another weak grin, flipped a salute, and started away.
He had not walked two yards when the swarthy MP
stepped up from behind and clamped a hand on his
shoulder.

"Hold it a second."

Mudar stopped. The swarthy MP moved around in front of Mudar, his eyes trained downward. On Mudar's glossy-black flying boots, the unique zipper that extended from the toe halfway to the calf.

"That's pretty fancy footwear," the MP said. "Where'd you get it?"

"I was afraid you might ask me," Mudar said. His own clear, fast thinking amazed him. "They were a gift" —he winked with the word—"from a POW. In Kuwait. I just got back."

The MP thought about it a moment, then nodded. He gestured Mudar to go on his way. Mudar forced himself not to sag with relief. "See you around," he said, and moved to leave.

"Let's have a look at your papers."

Mudar heard the voice and for an instant imagined it was only a reflection of his own fear. He stared at the light-skinned MP, whose lips had formed the words.

"Your papers," said the MP.

"Oh, sure," Mudar said. The fast-thinking of a moment ago had vanished. Now his mind was a total blank. His knees began trembling with panic. His eyes blurred. He groped in one breast pocket, then opened the flap of the other. "Yeah, here they—" he never completed the sentence.

He lowered his head and hurled the full weight of his body into the light-skinned MP. Arms flailing, the MP toppled backward and fell to the sidewalk. The momentum carried Mudar forward, knocking him briefly off balance, but he stumbled to his feet, steadied himself, and began running.

"Stop!"

Mudar zigzagged through the crowded sidewalk, brushing past people, bumping two women off the curb and into the street. Others frantically darted out of his path. Behind him, he could hear the heavy footfalls of the two MPs and their shouted orders to stop. He ran past shops and storefronts and then spied an alley. He cut blindly into the alley and ran straight ahead, frantically looking for a window, an open door.

"Stop or I shoot!"

Now he knew he was dead. They would torture him. He'd seen what they did to Zahir. They would do the same to him. To hell with them. This way was better. He continued running, faster now. Then, only fifty feet ahead, the alley ended. He could see a main street, automobiles and trucks rumbling past. He dimly realized that he had traveled in a circle and would come out back on Wathba Square, near the hotel.

He heard the crack of the revolver. The first bullet chewed into the pavement just behind him and ricocheted off the cobblestones. Reflexively, he grasped his beret to prevent it from flying from his head. He began laughing. He was outrunning the bullets. He was Superman, like the movie he had seen not long ago at an American officers' club on the base in Emerald City. Which reminded him of Nick and how lucky it was that he, Mudar, had left the hotel room key in the room. The Iraqis would be unable to trace Mudar back to the hotel. But of course that left Nick on his own. Mudar felt bad about that.

The second bullet also missed, but not the third. He never felt it strike him. It entered his body one centimeter to the left of the right lung and severed the aorta. He had just reached the end of the alley and actually stepped onto the sidewalk. Yes, he was back on Wathba Square, all right. He remembered peering around for his bearings, thinking that the hotel should be on the left. It was the last thought his brain would ever process. The fourth and fifth bullets smashed into the back of his head and very nearly decapitated him. Both bullets were entirely superfluous.

Nick heard the shots through the closed hotel room window. He thought the first one was an automobile backfiring. The second and third shots sounded closer, and now he knew it was gunfire and thought it might be AAA. An air raid. Killed by your own people, what goddamn irony. But he recognized the last two shots as small-arms fire.

He rolled off the bed and stepped across the room

and flung open the wood window shutters and the window. In the square below, a crowd had gathered around an object on the sidewalk. Two MPs pushed through the crowd. Now Nick had a clear view of the object, a man in a khaki uniform. A soldier, sprawled facedown in a pool of rapidly widening blood. The blood, streaming from his head, flowed past his outstretched left arm and eddied around a red beret clutched in his hand.

Moments later, Nick found himself downstairs in the lobby. He knew he had put on his boots and jacket and beret, but did not recall when he did all this. He knew only that he had to get out of the room, and out of the hotel, and that his life depended on it.

The desk clerk was not behind the counter but the television set was still on. Yes, of course, the man had rushed outside to see about the commotion. To the right of the desk a corridor led to the first-floor rooms. A rear entrance, Nick thought, and started toward it. The picture on the tiny television screen on the table behind the desk caught his attention.

A woman, talking into a microphone. Speaking in English. Christine Campbell. She was standing in the center of what looked to be a patio. Garden furniture and an empty swimming pool were in the background. On the bottom of the screen the crawl read: LIVE FROM BAGHDAD.

". . . I can only tell you that this city is not—I repeat: not—under attack at this time. Although the start of the ground war has been officially confirmed, everything here appears calm and, on the surface at least, normal. Normal, of course, meaning under these wartime conditions. The only official word has been a terse communiqué—" Chris began reading from a small spiral notebook. " 'The enemy offensive has proved a total failure, and the criminal aggressors are crying for help.' " Chris handed the notebook to someone off camera. "This is Christine Campbell at the Al-Rashid Hotel in Baghdad."

Only when Nick was outside, on the sidewalk at the back entrance to the hotel, did Chris's words register.

The ground war had started. Another nail in his coffin. Now they would probably shoot him on sight. He knew that the people on the street recognized him as an impostor; he could read it in their deliberately indifferent expressions. Any second now he expected to feel the cold steel of a gun barrel against his head.

He started walking, eyes averted. Avoid eye contact, he remembered from survival school. He had no idea where he was, or where to go, what to do. And, to boot, he was ill. His face felt cold and clammy, and he was drenched with perspiration. He could not focus his eyes properly. Yes, that was how it would happen, he would collapse right here in the street. The police would take him away. For sure, before the execution, a session with the interrogators. He shuddered, remembering Mudar's account of what they did to Zahir.

Nick realized that someone was talking to him. A woman, wearing a fur hat and a mink or sable coat. Dark-haired, middle-aged, quite attractive, that presence of wealth and confidence. The wife of a government official, Nick thought. Shit! But wait, hold on, maybe she's not what you think. She might be a foreigner, wife of a diplomat, maybe of the Swiss ambassador himself. A miracle. Why not?

No, he couldn't risk it. Whatever he did, he knew he must not respond. He must say nothing. He must get away. He walked off. He glanced back at her. She stood gazing worriedly after him, and now he realized that she had been asking if he was all right. A very nice, motherly lady, concerned about the health of our boys in the trenches.

A very nice lady, he thought, which suddenly reminded him of another woman. Chris Campbell. ". . . *this is Christine Campbell at the Al-Rashid Hotel in Baghdad.*"

Chris Campbell.

Al-Rashid Hotel.

He should have asked the nice lady in the mink or sable coat directions to the Al-Rashid Hotel. He smiled to himself, envisioning the woman's astonishment as he spoke to her in English. Of course, he could have grunted the words, "Al-Rashid Hotel." She'd have understood.

Half the cars on the street were painted the two-toned orange and white of taxis. Sure, that's all he needed: to get into a taxi and ask to be taken to the Al-Rashid. Taxis were not metered, so he'd have to negotiate the fare. He'd die laughing, which is what undoubtedly would happen. Not to mention that he had no money. All the money was in Mudar's pocket.

Al-Rashid Hotel.

Hey, Abdullah, which way to the Al-Rashid?

But wait, he remembered now. In the taxi from the railway station, the driver had pointed out the zoo on their right and then, as they pulled into line to cross the bridge, they passed a large rectangular building on the right. A curving, tree-lined driveway led to a glass-facaded portico. Atop the entire length of the portico, glittering gold letters spelled AL-RASHID HOTEL.

The bridge, he thought, instinctively glancing up at the sun in the overcast sky to orient himself. They had come from the north, so the bridge was south. He turned abruptly and began walking in the opposite direction. If he could find the bridge, he would find the Al-Rashid Hotel and Chris Campbell. Chris, an American, would help him. He had to find her.

TWENTY-TWO

Leila watched Chris and the soldier walk to room 307, Chris's room. Chris seemed unusually tense as she glanced warily up and down the hotel corridor before entering the room. The soldier followed her in. In the darkened corridor Leila could not make out the soldier's face, but he was definitely not the handsome young army officer Chris had lately been entertaining.

Leila hurried to 307. She flattened her ear against the closed door and immediately felt foolish: The doors of the Al-Rashid Hotel were three inches thick, designed for security. And anyway, Leila thought, what could she overhear that might be useful? The fact that Chris was screwing her way through the Iraqi Army would come as no news to the Mukhabarat. All the same, Leila intended to keep an eye on the situation.

What Leila perceived as Chris's tenseness was in truth incredulity, and not at all surprising, not after what had happened on the fire exit stairway. The disheveled, unshaven Iraqi soldier had appeared out of nowhere, gripping Chris's arm and saying, "I'm Nick Harmon."

"Get your goddamn hands off me!" Chris had said.

"I'm Nick Harmon!" he said. "We met last year in Washington."

She pried his fingers loose from her arm and reached into her shoulder tote bag for her halogen penlight. She flashed it directly into his face. She saw a gaunt, mature man with European features. He could be a renegade

American or Canadian working for the Iraqis. He could even be a Russian. For sure, no Arab.

"Please, don't play these stupid games," she said. "Tell the Mukhabarat or al-Amm, or whoever the hell you work for, they're wasting their time!"

He said, "I'm an American, for Christ's sake! Nick Harmon! We had a drink in a hotel near the Pentagon. The Sheraton, I think. It was last year, around Thanksgiving. I'm *American!* Johnny Donovan introduced us. I shot down the MiG. Goddammit, can't you remember?"

"My God!" she said, as she immediately recalled the occasion, even the hotel where they had the drink, the Crowne Royal. Her brain whirled with questions, but his Iraqi uniform answered most of them. It required no great imagination to realize he had been captured and escaped. He was a flyer, he must have been shot down. She felt almost giddy with excitement and intrigue. An American pilot in enemy territory, in an enemy uniform.

Had the circumstances been different, when she opened the door of her room Chris might have uttered the obligatory "Excuse the mess." The glass window louvers—painted black for blackout use—were open, brightening the room with the hazy late afternoon sun. Camera and sound equipment were strewn about, tripods, canisters of tape, audio cassettes. A maze of insulated wire lay uselessly in one corner: all that remained of the INMARSAT telephone that an Iraqi TV official had literally yanked out of the wall yesterday. Chris was now allowed one telecast per day, strictly scheduled for 3:00 P.M., Baghdad time.

She closed the door and flipped the safety bolt and turned to Nick. He was slumped in the leather armchair, his jacket open, his hand inside his shirt. He grimaced with pain and withdrew his hand. His fingers were wet with a viscous, gray fluid. He wiped his hand against the side of his trousers.

"Could I have some of that?" he asked, pointing to a plastic bottle of Evian. It was one of two flasks of Evian, lined neatly on the floor under the bed with cans of Pepsi and 7Up.

"Yes, of course," she said. She felt stupid. She should have offered him something immediately, not pump him for details. She filled a glass and brought it to him. He drank it down in a single swallow. She refilled the glass. He drank that down, too. He was ravenously thirsty.

Briefly, then, he told her about his capture and subsequent escape, the train ride to Baghdad, and Mudar. And how he had walked all the way across the bridge to the Al-Rashid and managed to evade the army sentries seated in pickup trucks at both entrances to the hotel. He had spotted Chris in the patio chatting with her camera crew and followed her up the fire stairs to the third-floor landing.

For Chris, the excitement and intrigue of a few minutes before—a countryman on the run—abruptly vanished. Listening to him, the hoarse, strained voice. Looking at him, the bloodshot eyes, the three-day beard, and lines of fatigue etched deep into his face. She saw the harsh reality, the foul-smelling bandage and his clammy skin and labored breathing. This was no glamorous adventure. The man was ill and in need of immediate medical attention. If the phone was working, she would call downstairs for the house physician, Dr. Thamir, a kind, gentle old man whose office and residence were nearby. He once had treated her for bronchitis.

But Dr. Thamir would report Nick's presence. Nick would be recaptured, and Chris accused of harboring an escaped prisoner. No, worse, in an enemy uniform Nick might be considered a spy. Leading to the very real possibility that Chris herself would come under suspicion as a spy. The Iraqis recently had tried and convicted a British journalist, Farzad Bazoft, of espionage. Chris vividly recalled the photos of his body hanging from the gallows. The Iraqis were paranoid about newspeople. Everyone knew that Bob Simon, the CBS correspondent who had supposedly "disappeared," was in an Iraqi military prison, charged with spying.

A little sliver of guilt nagged at her. She was thinking of herself, not the poor sick guy sitting there gazing vacantly at her. He must have been through hell. But for all that, *he* was the selfish one, coming to her for help. Not for an instant had he thought of the jeopardy he might place her in.

His voice startled her. "How's the war going?"

"According to the Iraqis, the Allies are begging for mercy," she said.

"I don't think so," he said.

Nor do I, she thought, but did not say it. Her Minder, Salim al-Sadr, had advised her to ignore rumors of ten thousand Iraqi desertions. Zionist propaganda. But Salim said it in a quiet and almost sad voice that told Chris the story was true. Chris did not want to waste time discussing the war. The faster Nick went on his way, the better off they both would be.

"Look—" she suddenly went blank on his name. "You can't stay here," she continued, as his name popped back to her. "Mr. Harmon, Nick. If you're found here, they'll slap us both in a military prison. And they won't be too nice about it. So you have to leave."

Nick said nothing. It made her feel even more resentful. "You had no right to come here," she said. "You have to leave."

He gestured to her for the Evian. She handed it to him. He uncapped the top and drank directly from the bottle, then set it on the floor at his feet. "Where do you suggest I go, Miss Campbell? To the local USO?"

"I can't help you," she said. She wanted to explain that too much was at stake, not the least of which was her personal safety, but she was too embarrassed to say it. No, ashamed, too ashamed to say it.

"What do you mean, you can't help me? You *have* to help me!" Exhausted, he struggled for breath. "Just let me rest a little while. Then I'll go. I promise."

Then you'll go, she thought. *Where,* as he himself had just asked, would he go? But that was not her concern. She had to look out for herself. All right, so he was an American, what was she supposed to do about it? He knew what he was doing when he put on the uniform, he knew the risks. He wasn't drafted. Not like her father, drafted into the navy to fight in a war he did not believe in.

Drafted into the navy, she thought. No, no, if he was a fighter pilot, he wouldn't have been drafted. My God, she was becoming ensnared in her own lies. A quicksand of lies. Be careful, girl, she told herself. One of these days you will fall into the quicksand. Yes, and now she remembered telling Nick Harmon about her "hero" father. She almost expected him to remind her of that now.

He looked so helpless, so vulnerable. The Nazi, she thought wryly, remembering their previous meeting. He certainly did not resemble a Nazi now. Well, perhaps he did: those photos of Nazis surrendering in the final days of World War II. Pitiful supermen.

Supermen, she thought, and remembered the air raid shelter at Amiriyah. The smoke-blackened bodies stacked in the trucks. The odor of charred flesh that lingered for days in her nostrils. Compliments of the supermen. She wondered if this superman realized the unbelievable misery he and his fellow supermen had inflicted upon the people of Iraq. The thousands of starving babies, the dead and maimed children.

And to achieve what? To make the world safe for the diamond-studded bidet faucets in the Emir of Kuwait's palace, or for the King of Saudi Arabia's Swiss bank accounts? That, apparently, plus filling the gasoline tanks of American automobiles.

She heard the knock on the door at the same instant that she saw the great story that, literally, had fallen into her lap. An American pilot, shot down over Baghdad, escapes his Iraqi captors and makes contact with WCN's Christine Campbell! She could actually hear Larry Hill smugly boasting about annihilating the networks with this one. Congratulating her. Not to mention sweetening the already promised bonus.

The knock on the door was more insistent. Nick sprang from the chair and looked wildly around for a place to hide. Chris gestured him to sit back down. She had no intention of opening the door. She heard the grating sound of a key turning in the lock. The chambermaid's passkey, Leila. Thank God the door was bolted.

Through the door, Chris heard her name called. Not Leila's voice. A man's voice.

Adnan.

Leila had smiled to herself when the handsome major appeared in the corridor. He asked Leila if Miss Campbell was in her room. The house telephones were not working.

"Oh, yes, she's there, sir," Leila said. "I saw her a few minutes ago."

The major strode to 307 and knocked on the door. As Leila anticipated, Chris did not respond. "I may have been mistaken," Leila said. "Miss Campbell may have gone out, and I just didn't see her." She inserted her passkey into the door lock.

The door was bolted from the inside. Adnan called through the door, "Chris, it's Adnan. I want to talk to you."

Chris realized she could not avoid answering. She went into the alcove to the door. She slid the safety bolt aside and cracked open the door.

"I was taking a nap."

"May I come in?"

"Really, I'm exhausted. Let's meet later." She started to close the door, but he held it open.

"I have some news for you."

"Later, Adnan. Please." She pushed the door closed and bolted it again.

Watching, listening, Leila thought it was like a movie, what the English called a bedroom farce. The major gazed at the closed door a moment. Then, without a word, he turned and started quickly away. Leila headed off in the opposite direction.

Chris's door opened again. She called out to the major. He whirled around and hurried back to 307. Leila wondered what had prompted Chris to change her mind and immediately answered her own question.

A threesome.

Leila found the concept exciting. She had heard of
threesomes, of course, but had never participated. A
woman with two men. She, Leila, with two men. The
possibilities were endless.

What had changed Chris's mind was Adnan himself:
their relationship, hers and Adnan's. They were lovers,
yes, but also friends. She could trust him. He would
know what to do with Nick and how to do it without
involving Chris. Yes, she could trust Adnan. She had to
trust him, she had no other choice.

As she opened the door for him, he kissed her lightly
on the lips. "Can you stand some good news?" he asked.

She nodded numbly.

"The interview is set for the day after tomorrow," he
said. "Forty-five minutes, live. Iraqi technicians only.
You'll be notified of the exact time."

"Adnan, come in," she said. "Come in." She opened
the door wider for him. He walked past her into the
alcove. She closed the door. From the corner of her eye
she saw that Nick's chair was empty. "Adnan!" she
shouted warningly.

Adnan turned, but too late. Nick stepped around the
alcove corner gripping the folded aluminum legs of a
minicam tripod. He aimed the flat metal base of the
tripod at Adnan's head and swung it like a baseball bat.
Adnan had just enough time to raise his arms protectively and deflect the force of the blow onto his elbow.
The impact propelled him forward, and down. Flailing
for balance, he stumbled into the side of the couch and
fell face down on the floor. Before Adnan could rise,
Nick had leaned over and extracted the pistol from his
holster.

"You fool!" Chris said to Nick. "He would have
helped you!" She knelt to Adnan and helped him to his
feet. He peered in bewilderment at Nick, at the pistol in
Nick's hand, and the bloodstained Iraqi uniform. "He's
an American," Chris said, as though that explained it
all.

To Adnan, it did explain everything, and in a strange
way increased his respect for Chris. And made him feel

less the fool. So she had tricked him. She did it to help her countryman. He, Adnan, would have done the same. He sank down in the leather armchair and looked at Nick.

"He was captured and escaped," Chris continued.

The Iraqi uniform spoke for itself, eloquent testimony to the absolute chaos of the past few days, the near-total collapse of Iraq's military communications system. A POW's escape might go unreported for days, indeed might never be reported.

"Do you know this man?" Adnan asked Chris.

Nick replied for her. "We're old friends." He wiped a thin film of perspiration from his forehead. He felt feverish and dizzy. He tried to grin. "She bought me a drink once."

"Is that why you invited me into the room?" Adnan said to Chris. "To introduce me to your friend?"

"Good God, you don't believe I did this deliberately?" she said. "A minute ago he hardly had the strength to talk. I thought you could help him."

"Help him how?" Adnan asked. He rubbed his bruised elbow. "Help him do what?"

"He's been wounded," Chris said. "He needs a doctor."

Adnan started to push himself up from the chair. Nick leveled the gun at him. Adnan sat back. "Does he have a name?" he asked Chris.

Chris said, "His name is Harmon. He's a pilot." The instant the word came from her mouth she wanted it back. She knew Adnan would immediately relate "pilot" to Amiriyah. Nick could have been one of the pilots who bombed the shelter.

But Adnan seemed unperturbed. "I don't know how you got this far," he said to Nick. "But you must realize you can get no farther. The hotel is ringed with troops. There are observation posts on the roof of every adjoining building. And you do need medical attention," he added, as Nick began to sway. The pistol, which Nick gripped in both hands, wobbled unsteadily.

"I'll be fine," Nick said. He wanted to sit down, to close his eyes, to relax. "Do you have a car?"

"Are you planning a sight-seeing tour of the city?" Adnan asked. With Nick so obviously weak, overpowering him and retrieving the pistol would not be difficult. "Yes, I have a car. It's parked outside, a blue Chrysler convertible. Why don't I just give you the keys, and you can go off on your own?"

Nick drew in his breath to speak. No words came. His eyes narrowed with alarm and confusion. Something was happening to him that he could not control. The pistol slipped from his fingers. It bounced off the sofa armrest and onto the carpet. He saw Adnan's hand reach out for the gun.

Nick's knees buckled. He grasped the sofa arm to break his fall, tottered backward, and crumpled to the floor. He lay on his back, eyes closed. Adnan placed his ear against Nick's chest.

"He's alive," Adnan said. He felt Nick's forehead. "But he's burning up. I think he fainted from sheer exhaustion." Adnan buttoned the pistol back into the holster; the safety was on, and the chamber empty. Nick had never been alert enough to load the gun. "See if the phone is working."

"It wasn't a few minutes ago," Chris said.

"Try it now, please," Adnan said.

"Adnan, you know what they'll do to him—"

"—please, Chris. The phone."

"But Adnan, if they find him—" Chris had started to say "here." If they find Nick here, in this room, with her. Meaning that it might cause problems for her. She was too ashamed to say it, to admit her own cowardice. No, not cowardice, selfishness, her own selfishness. "If they find him in that uniform," she finished lamely.

"He'll be treated as a prisoner of war," Adnan said. "Help me get him up on the couch."

Together they hefted Nick onto the couch. Adnan examined Nick's dog tags and searched his pockets. "The phone, Chris," he said. "If it's working, tell the switchboard I want to see the sergeant in charge of the security squad. Tell him to bring two men with him."

"I don't want to do that, Adnan."

Adnan glanced impatiently at her. "You don't have a choice."

"Suppose the situation were reversed. Suppose this all happened, say, in America. And you came to me for help. I ask my friend, him"—she pointed at Nick—"not to turn you over."

"I know how you feel, Chris, and I admire you for it. But the man is an enemy soldier. And he's ill."

"Surely, you know some doctor you can bring him to."

"Instead of an army doctor, you mean?"

"A doctor who will treat him and say nothing about it."

"You're talking nonsense." Adnan brushed past her to the telephone. He picked it up and listened for a dial tone. None. He slammed down the receiver and started into the alcove. "I'll go downstairs and get somebody."

"Adnan, you know what they'll do to him. You yourself admitted that interrogators sometimes lose control."

"He'll be treated fairly." Adnan reached for the doorknob.

"The interview, Adnan. If they find him here, it will kill the interview!"

Adnan said nothing for a moment. It was as though he wanted to pretend that he had heard incorrectly, that he had misinterpreted her words. But there was no misinterpretation, and he knew it.

"The interview," he said. "You're not concerned about him"—he indicated Nick—"you're worried about losing the interview. You intend to have it no matter what the price. Even if it means selling out your own people." He stopped and stared at her.

Chris read the coldness of his eyes as further reproach, and it galled her. To hell with him. She said, "You're right, I don't want to lose the interview. I've worked too hard for it. I'm asking for your help. Your help, not a lecture in morality."

Adnan was only half listening. His own words echoed in his ears: *"Selling out your own people."* Talk about pots calling kettles black. He had been quite prepared to commit the same offense. And as for morality, only a day earlier at a Revolutionary Command Council meeting, he had witnessed a demonstration of morality. Morality, a murdered general.

Adnan glanced over at Nick, whose eyes were open. He was awake but very confused. He reminded Adnan of Amir. Amir, crippled for life, his reward for attempting to prevent the murder of prisoners. And so now Adnan would be responsible for yet another prisoner murdered, for he knew Nick would not be treated fairly. Far from it. And it would be a crime made even more heinous because the end of the war was only weeks away. Days, more likely. The war that had killed the woman Adnan loved, and killed her father, and destroyed the life of her brother.

Saddam's war.

Adnan said to Chris, "I know a doctor . . ."

2

Khalid Sadoon was in a foul mood when he finally arrived at Adnan's apartment. Amiriyah to Zahra, normally a twenty-minute drive, had taken the better part of a grueling two hours. With only two bridges standing, traffic was in near-gridlock, and in the two hours there were four separate air raids.

Adnan was waiting in the open doorway. He nodded at Khalid's leather medical kit. "Were you able to get it?"

"This must be the only section in town with electricity," Khalid said, pointing at the brightly lit hallway chandelier and the living room lamps inside the apartment. "Yeah, I got it." He hefted the medical kit. "Cefoxitime, a very effective antibiotic. From the way you described your friend's wound, just what the doctor ordered."

Adnan ushered Khalid into the living room. "I'll reimburse you for whatever the cost."

"I'll send you a bill," Khalid said. It pleased him to do something for Adnan. He knew how Hana's death had devastated Adnan. Devastated Khalid, too. Besides, although the drug could be obtained only on the black market, it had cost Khalid nothing. The entrepreneur-pharmacist brother of one of Khalid's medical school classmates owed him a favor. "Where's the patient?"

The patient, Adnan thought. An American pilot. How in the hell would he explain *that* to Khalid? He had not given it a moment's consideration; in truth, he had carefully avoided thinking about it. After the distressing confrontation with Chris, Adnan's immediate concern was to get Nick out of the hotel. It proved to be almost laughably easy. While Chris distracted the chambermaid, Adnan and Nick slipped from the room, went downstairs, blithely strolled through the lobby—Nick had mustered enough strength for that—and outside to Adnan's car, and driven off. The Popular Army guards had snapped to attention with brisk salutes.

Adnan realized that not delivering Nick to the army, providing him sanctuary, was an overt act of aiding and abetting the enemy. He suspected that his motive for undertaking this insane venture was more than subtly related to Chris, to his disillusionment with her, her callous selfishness. That, or as he preferred to believe, it was his way of avenging Hassan Marwaan and all the others who had suffered at Saddam's hands. But the motive or motives were unimportant. He had committed himself, and there was no turning back.

Once he and Nick were in the apartment—and thank God the telephone was working—Adnan had reached Khalid at the hospital and spun a fanciful tale of a "soldier-friend" in need of antibiotics. Khalid grasped the situation. He was well aware of the scarcity of drugs, even for the military.

". . . let's get on with it, Adnan," Khalid was saying now. "I must get right back."

"Khalid, I have to ask you something." Adnan took a deep breath. "I want your promise, your word of honor, never to say a word about this."

"About what? Never say a word about what?"

"About coming here . . . to take care of a wounded man."

Khalid shrugged. "Sure, okay. Who would I say anything to, anyway?"

"He's in the bedroom," Adnan said.

In the guest bedroom Khalid saw a man in blood-stained underwear lying uncomfortably atop the quilted bedspread. His sallow face was rigid, his eyes glazed with pain. Khalid did not need to feel the pulse to know it was rapid and thready or even take his temperature to realize that the man was already septic.

Khalid said cheerily, "Good evening."

Adnan said, "He doesn't speak Arabic. He's an American." Adnan paused because Khalid had started to laugh. "An American," Adnan said. "He's an escaped POW." The geniality faded from Khalid's face. "It's a complicated story," Adnan went on. "I'll give you all the details later."

Khalid stared at Nick another moment, then turned to Adnan. "Are you crazy?"

Before Adnan could reply, Nick laughed humorlessly. He said to Adnan, "You just told him who I am, didn't you?"

Khalid, whose English was almost as fluent and idiomatic as Adnan's, said, "Yes, he told me. And I asked him if he were crazy."

"He must be," said Nick, who thought it was not so far from the truth. Although they had talked very little —and Nick was slipping in and out of consciousness— he had twice asked Adnan his reason for doing this. Adnan told him not to ask questions, not to press his luck.

Nick assumed that the answer lay in Chris Campbell, that iron-assed lady who said she wanted no part of him or his problems. Whatever magic she had worked on Adnan to convince him to help Nick, Nick could not even begin to imagine. But then if not for Chris, Nick right now would undoubtedly be locked up in an Iraqi version of a Viet Cong tiger cage. So give the devil her due.

". . . Khalid, please," Adnan was saying. "Take care of him and we'll go over the details later."

"You *are* crazy, Adnan. You belong in an institution," Khalid said in English. But he had already opened his kit and begun removing items. Plastic bags of saline, IV tubes, hypodermics. Within five minutes he had jammed a thermometer into Nick's mouth, cleaned and re-dressed the wound, and jury-rigged the IV and plugged it into Nick's arm. He showed Adnan how to replenish the antibiotic every four hours and how to replace one IV bag with another.

"Good luck," he said to Nick, who had fallen asleep again. "If the drug works, he should make a dramatic recovery," Khalid continued to Adnan. "If not"—he shrugged—"he'll probably go into shock and die." The prospect did not appear to displease him. He removed a small envelope from the kit. The envelope contained some two dozen pills. "Keflex, five hundred milligrams. As soon as the IVs are finished, start him on these, one every six hours. Use all of them."

"How long will the IVs last?"

"Twelve to fifteen hours. He'll be rehydrated by then. If the infection is checked, he'll require another forty-eight to seventy-two hours of bed rest. Continuing with the oral medication, of course."

"I appreciate this, Khalid," Adnan said.

Khalid closed and fastened the kit and left the room. Adnan remained behind a moment, studying the IV and the pills, and memorizing Khalid's instructions. Khalid waited irritably for him in the living room.

"Who is he?" Khalid asked.

"I met him in Washington," Adnan lied. "We became quite friendly. He was captured but escaped, and he came to me. He's an air force colonel—"

"—a pilot?" Khalid fairly spat the word. "A *pilot,* and you help him? You, of all people! And then you have the unbelievable audacity to ask *me* to assist you in this" —he groped for the proper phrase—"disloyalty. Because that's what it is, Adnan—disloyalty!"

Adnan had anticipated the outburst and was prepared. "I asked you to help as a humanitarian."

"A humanitarian," Khalid repeated. He lit a cigarette and tossed the matchstick into the saucer of an empty teacup on the telephone stand. "Ask Hana about humanitarianism!"

"If they behave as barbarians, that doesn't mean we should," Adnan said in the same calm, quiet voice. "You know damn well that as a POW the man would not receive decent medical care. He'd die. Is that what you want?"

Khalid mashed his cigarette into the teacup. "I can't believe we're having this conversation! The question is not whether I should or should not treat him, but why *you* are harboring an enemy of our country."

"I just explained why. And you explained that he needs to continue the medication for three more days."

Khalid lit a fresh cigarette. "And then what?"

Other than convincing himself that Nick would be safe in the apartment until Schwarzkopf marched into Baghdad, Adnan had not thought beyond that, beyond the next seventy-two hours. Adnan said, "When he's better, I'll turn him over to the appropriate authorities."

Khalid dragged deeply on his cigarette and regarded Adnan cynically. "I have to get back to the hospital," he said. He put on his coat and his astrakhan cap, picked up the medical kit, and started to leave. "By tomorrow afternoon, he can be moved," he said. "If he recovers," he added. He nodded tightly at Adnan and left.

Tomorrow afternoon, Adnan thought. It sounded like an ultimatum.

3

What pleased Larry Hill more than the event itself was that the White House would first hear of it on WCN, and straight from the horse's mouth. The horse in this instance, Saddam Hussein himself. The whole world would hear it on "Gulf Watch," live from Baghdad, today at 8:00 A.M., Washington time.

TUESDAY, FEBRUARY 26, 1991,
CHRISTINE CAMPBELL TALKS WITH SADDAM HUSSEIN!

All WCN affiliates would run that one-line promo at every half-hour station break. As Larry exulted to Chris in their telephone conversation, it was the culmination of all their efforts of the past six months. The big payoff.

She had called Larry on a special hookup via Amman, arranged for the occasion by the Iraqi Ministry of Information. The Iraqis wanted to be sure that WCN's audiences received ample advance notice of Saddam Hussein's "Victory Statement." No matter how Saddam's convoluted logic might corrupt its substance, the statement amounted to a humiliating announcement of unconditional surrender. And it was to be made directly and exclusively to Chris.

"You're a marvel, kid," Larry had said to her.

"Put that into dollars, boss," she had replied.

"How does fifty big ones sound?"

"A hundred sounds better."

"Chris, there's a lot of static on the line. I can't hear you too good."

"A hundred and a quarter, Larry! Can you hear *that*?"

Before Larry could respond, the line went dead. Salim al-Sadr, monitoring the conversation, signaled Chris that the Information Ministry censor had broken the connection. They were in the ministry's temporary quarters in the basement of the Melia Hotel, not far from the bombed-out ministry building and only a few blocks from the Al-Rashid.

An hour before, just as the all-clear sounded—the third time in the past four hours—Salim al-Sadr had burst into the Al-Rashid lobby. He spotted Chris as she was leaving the hotel's basement shelter. He had come to inform her that President Saddam Hussein would see her at 4:00 P.M. today. A government car would pick her up at two-thirty. The president, said Salim, was to make a momentous announcement.

"What is the momentous announcement?" Chris had asked.

"A victory statement, of course," Salim had replied.

Now, peering at the dead telephone in her hand, Chris called across the room to Salim, "Why in the hell did they cut us off? I wasn't finished!"

Salim smiled nervously at a well-dressed young Iraqi standing beside him. It was as though Salim felt obliged to apologize for a female's profane mouth. The young man, a ministry official who had been introduced to Chris only as Mr. Fazal, walked over to her. "Your conversation was completed," he said.

Chris decided not to argue the point. Let the pompous little prick throw his weight around. She was not about to risk blowing the interview. And in truth, she had nothing more to say to Larry. Yes, she would have loved to somehow make Larry aware of her encounter with an American pilot. But even if he picked up on it, he could not break the story, not with Nick still in Iraq. For now at least, with Adnan looking after him, Nick was safe.

". . . you will be given a list of questions to ask the president," Fazal was saying.

Chris's mind was still focused on Nick and Adnan. She had not heard from Adnan in a day and a half, but was sure they were all right, and that Adnan had located his doctor friend. Adnan would come to understand her attitude and, in time, forgive her. As for Nick, he too would eventually understand. My God, how could they have expected her to do anything different? She had had no choice. Moreover, it would have been impossible for Adnan to bring a doctor to Chris's hotel room, not with Leila constantly snooping around.

And Adnan did not fool her: He was, like her, looking out for himself. Adnan knew what he was doing. By not turning Nick over, he would ingratiate himself with the Americans. Yes, he knew what he was doing.

She said to Fazal now, "The list of questions, yes, of course. I understand." The so-called questions were no more than cues for Saddam to spout his propaganda. She would play along. She felt confident of inserting an occasional question of her own of a far more probing nature. For example, with thousands of his soldiers captured or having deserted, why did he believe he had achieved a "victory"? Let him smooth-talk his way out of that.

Fazal was still speaking, apparently attempting to charm her. She could see it in his little cocker spaniel eyes. He was coming on to her. She had to force herself not to laugh in his face. Her mind still wandered. Adnan, and Nick, and Adnan's doctor friend.

". . . may I offer you some lunch?" Fazal was saying. "A drink, perhaps?"

"That's very kind of you," she said. "But I want to get back. I have so many things to do." She smiled. "To prepare to meet the president, you know."

"Some other time, then?"

"By all means. I look forward to it."

"I, too."

She smiled again, thinking that on her way back to the hotel she would stop at a public telephone. If it was working, she would call Adnan at the apartment and explain her situation to him. On second thought, not a good idea. Let things take their natural course. It would all work out. She only hoped that Nick was better and that the doctor could be trusted.

Chris's telephone call would have gone unanswered. Adnan and Nick were no longer at the apartment. The doctor's trustworthiness had also concerned Adnan. Accordingly, earlier that morning, after Nick finished the last IV—as Khalid predicted, he had made a dramatic recovery, with a normal temperature and much of his strength regained—Adnan had gotten him on his feet, into civilian clothes, out of the apartment, and into Adnan's car.

They drove to Mansur, to Hana's house. The house was set well back from the street, obscured by trees, and widely separated from neighboring homes. A safe house. Safer at least than Adnan's apartment.

Adnan had not been in the house since the day of Hana's death. He had come here for her birth certificate and other documents required for the issuance of a death certificate. The certificate needed to be endorsed by the next-of-kin. Adnan forged Amir's signature. To this day, Amir was unaware of his sister's death. Adnan simply could not summon the courage to tell him.

Ironically, upon entering the house, Nick's attention was drawn to a framed, charcoaled likeness of Hana. Amir had sketched it more than a year before.

"Very pretty," Nick said of the sketch. "The owner's daughter?"

"The owner herself," said Adnan. "We were engaged."

Nick said nothing. The very tone of Adnan's voice and use of the past tense told Nick that the story did not end happily. Adnan went on, "She was killed. At Amiriyah. Does that name mean anything to you, Amiriyah?"

Nick thought about it a moment. "No," he said. "I can't place it."

"It's the shelter you people targeted as a control center. It took a direct hit. More than four hundred people killed, mostly women and children. Amiriyah, now do you remember?"

Yes, now Nick did remember and, as it happened, he had first heard of Amiriyah from one of Chris Campbell's WCN broadcasts. She had painted the USAF as merciless butchers. At the time Nick believed that the Iraqis had somehow staged it all for propaganda.

He said nothing. He certainly did not want to say,

"I'm sorry," which would have been the height of hypocrisy. He sank wearily down in a kitchen chair. The sketch was hanging on the wall in the alcove between the kitchen and the dining room.

Adnan set about fixing breakfast for them. Cold coffee (Nescafé mixed with Evian water), canned fruit cocktail, and soda crackers. Nick wolfed down every last morsel. As they ate, Adnan for some reason felt obliged to explain to Nick that he had been practically brought up in this house, where his late father was employed as a gardener and general handyman.

". . . so you see that the opportunity for an ordinary person to succeed does exist in this country," Adnan said, realizing he was saying this only to make conversation and wondering why in hell he considered it necessary to make conversation. It was asinine. No, bizarre. Unreal. Yes, unreal. Well, the whole foolish enterprise —providing aid and comfort to an enemy—was unreal. On the other hand, helping Nick was a genuinely humanitarian gesture, nothing less than common decency.

Yes, but that did not oblige them to establish a relationship, Adnan thought, and said, "Look, I have to report to my duty station. And I think I'd better go back to the apartment and make certain we disposed of the" —the word, as it came to his lips, sounded grimly amusing—"the evidence."

He was referring to the IV bags, tubes, and Nick's Iraqi uniform, now at the bottom of a trash dumpster miles from the apartment. Nick now wore Adnan's favorite tweed sports jacket, denim trousers, and a down ski jacket. The clothes hung a little too loosely on him but not enough to arouse suspicion. As a civilian, Nick would attract less attention. He could always pass as a Russian.

Nick said, "And what do I do while you're gone?"

"You rest."

Nick nodded at the portable television set on the kitchen counter. "Too bad there's no electricity. I could watch my friend, Miss Campbell. Your friend, I mean."

Adnan's jaw tightened. He drew in his breath to reply,

then changed his mind and said instead, "If you need them, there are candles and matches. If you're still hungry, open another can of fruit." He turned and started away. He had hardly reached the alcove when he stopped, frozen. The air raid sirens had just sounded and, simultaneously, the hollow thud of a distant explosion. Then another, and another.

Adnan said, "Your ground offensive is under way. The war is practically over, why are they still bombing Baghdad?"

"To knock out any remaining command and control centers," Nick said. He glanced at Hana's sketch and quickly added, "At least what they believe to be command and control centers."

"No, I think it's to try to kill Saddam Hussein."

"That too, probably."

"It would be ironic, don't you think, if *you* were the one killed by the planes," Adnan said. "Your own planes."

"Solve a lot of problems for you."

Adnan's eyebrows rose pensively; he obviously agreed. He said, "I'll be back as soon as I can. Don't forget to take your Keflex tablet." He turned and left. Another bomb exploded, this one closer. It shook the dishes stacked up in the sink and rattled the windows.

Nick listened for more bombs but heard nothing. They were running out of targets, he thought. After a while he got up and opened the can of fruit cocktail Adnan had left on the counter for him. He ate it straight from the can, saving the liquid to wash down the Keflex tablet.

The condemned man ate a hearty meal of pineapple, peaches, and apricots, he thought. He got up and looked into the cupboard. Cans of vegetables, tomatoes, baked beans, string beans, creamed corn, pencil-thin stalks of Japanese asparagus. If Baghdad was starving, the people who had lived in this house were unaware of it.

He sat down again. He had planned to search the house, perhaps find a weapon. But then what the hell would he do with it if he did find one? From where he sat he had a straight-on view of Hana's portrait. A remarkably attractive girl. Which made the whole crazy situation even crazier. Nick, by association at least, had killed the woman Adnan presumably loved. And yet here was Adnan, quite literally risking his own life to save Nick's.

You are racking up a large load of bills, my friend, he told himself. He had just thought of Ed Iverson. Poor, dumb Ed, committing to a maneuver he knew had to end with him augering in. Dumb Ed, that's real gratitude, Nick continued to himself. And Mudar, what about Mudar? Another guy who probably saved your ass. If Mudar had been captured, right now you'd be talking to another Colonel Hakim. In your book, I guess that makes him pretty dumb, too.

Nick closed his eyes, trying to concentrate on something else. His father. By now, Bob must have been notified that Nick was MIA. Nick wished he had seen Bob last year when he had the chance. Instead, he went up to Monterey to visit Elaine. Cry on her shoulder. He opened his eyes. He was looking into the deep, dark eyes of Adnan's fiancée. Correction: Adnan's dead fiancée. But in the sketch the eyes were so alive and vibrant. Elaine's eyes had the same quality. At that instant Nick made up his mind that he would marry Elaine. If she would have him. If he got back.

TWENTY-THREE

The steering wheel continued to vibrate in Adnan's hands. He had pulled the Chrysler over to the curb and switched off the ignition but the engine remained on, dieseling. No, the engine was not dieseling, it was his own hands trembling on the wheel. Trembling with fear. He sat, straining for composure. He felt hot and cold all at the same time. Deep breaths, he told himself, breathe deeply. He rolled down the window and took a deep breath, then another.

He had just come from an hour at his duty station in the bunker beneath the ruins of the Defense Ministry. An hour that was a waking nightmare. Everyone behaved as though the reports of entire divisions surrendering were part of some grand strategy. Lull the enemy into false security, draw him deeper and deeper into the trap.

A fantasy trap. The battle map was ominously clear. The Allies, sweeping north and east in a huge pincer, were already 125 kilometers into Iraq. All the main lines of Iraqi defenses had been breached or bypassed. The entire army in Kuwait was in imminent danger of being cut off. No one wanted to admit the scope of the defeat. No one dared to admit it.

From the ministry he had driven directly here to Zahra to pick up some clothes at the apartment, and a box of cigars. He had nosed the Chrysler up the gentle slope of the tree-lined avenue, then turned into a side street, a shortcut to the apartment building. From here, he had a clear view of the surrounding streets and beyond, to the tangled wreck of the Aimma Bridge and the river. And the cul-de-sac of his own street immediately below, and his apartment building. And the white Mercedes sedan parked in front of the building.

Another white Mercedes sedan was parked at the mouth of the cul-de-sac, blocking entry or exit. The driver of this second car leaned casually against the left front fender, arms folded, an unlighted cigarette dangling from his lips. He wore the dark glasses and black vinyl jacket favored by members of the Mukhabarat.

Adnan sat in the Chrysler and watched. His hands still trembled, but now more in rage than fear. Chris Campbell had betrayed him. No, it wasn't Chris, it would not have been to her advantage, not at all. It was the frumpy chambermaid, the Mukhabarat agent who knew all about him and Chris. She must have seen him leaving the hotel with Nick.

Adnan could not repress a little glow of satisfaction from the knowledge that this also implicated Chris. She was probably being interrogated at that very moment. Poetic justice. Even now he could hear the indignant, almost self-righteous tone of her husky voice: *"The interview, Adnan! It will kill the interview!"*

Adnan knew better. He knew Chris was not being interrogated. He also knew that if the chambermaid were the informer, he and Nick would not have gotten past the Al-Rashid's security guards. They would not even have reached the hotel lobby.

Khalid Sadoon had betrayed him. Khalid, the doctor, Adnan's "friend." Adnan cursed himself for his naïveté. No, not naïveté, stupidity. He was aware of Khalid's fanatic loyalty to the regime but had discounted it, foolishly relying on Khalid's fondness for Amir and Hana and on Khalid's own conscience.

But Adnan had not blindly trusted Khalid—clearly, now, with good reason—and had followed his own instinct and vacated the apartment. And so now the police were waiting for him and probably tearing the place

apart while they were at it. Within hours, every civil and
military policeman in Baghdad would be alerted.

He slipped the Chrysler's gear lever into neutral and
released the emergency brake. He steered the car backward down the hill to the bottom, then started the engine and drove off. Traffic was surprisingly heavy. He
wondered where they found the gasoline. Black market,
of course. You could buy anything on the black market.
Even patriotism.

Patriotism—lack of it, more accurately—was also on
Chris's mind. She had turned her back on a countryman
in need. The chambermaid, Leila—unwittingly, to be
sure—reminded Chris of this.

Chris and Ramon Sandoval were in the hotel coffee
shop for an early lunch, the dishwater the chef un-
ashamedly called minestrone, and rubbery chicken
sandwiches. Chris was awaiting the arrival of an Information Ministry courier with the "questions" she was to
ask Saddam that afternoon.

For the third time in as many minutes, Chris noticed
Leila walking past the coffee shop. Each time she
passed she had glanced inside, her eyes falling on Chris.
After this third time, Chris excused herself and went
into the deserted lobby. Leila was nowhere in sight.
Then Chris saw the glass doors of the Scheherazade
Room swing open. Leila emerged. She walked across
the tiled floor toward the unused elevators. Chris followed her into the elevator bay.

Leila spoke fast. "I should not be telling you this, but
you have been a friend to our government and to our
people." Leila's quick eyes scanned the lobby to make
sure no one was watching them. "Charges are being
brought against your friend Major Dulaimi. If he comes
here, refuse to see him—"

"—what charges?" Chris asked, although the answer
seemed obvious. The Mukhabarat had learned about
Adnan sheltering an enemy soldier. Adnan and Nick
Harmon had been arrested.

"I don't know the charges," Leila said. "I saw his

name on a list this morning. I have no details. Follow my advice, Miss Campbell, it is well given."

Chris said nothing. Her head had begun pounding, and her throat felt sandpaper dry.

"Do you understand me?" Leila said. "Have nothing more to do with him. Avoid him!"

"Where is he now?" Chris asked.

But Leila was already into the lobby, walking away fast. All right, Chris told herself, calm down and think logically. Refuse to see Adnan if he comes here, Leila said. *If* he came, which meant he had not yet been arrested. Still at large, as the saying went. Yes, it all had to do with him helping Nick. Leila saw them and reported it.

No, that made no sense. An entire day had passed since Adnan and Nick left the hotel. If Leila saw them, she would have immediately informed her superiors. So perhaps Adnan's troubles did not involve Nick after all, it was something else. Something in which Chris had no part and therefore bore no responsibility.

She felt relieved and guilty all at once, guilty for feeling relieved. She rejoined Sandoval in the coffee shop. "Why so glum?" he asked as she slid into the booth.

"I'm reflecting," she said. She forced a smile.

"On what?" Ramon asked. "Life?"

"Death," she said. The word startled her; it had simply slipped out.

"Shit, in this place who doesn't think about death?" Ramon said. "If it's not you Americans blowing everybody to pieces, it's the Iraqis themselves. One of the hotel guards said he heard that four generals landed in front of a firing squad yesterday. Seems the poor fucks talked about surrendering."

Chris heard only "firing squad." Any moment now Adnan would be caught. If Nick were with him, it could mean a firing squad for Adnan. For Nick, too. But suppose not? Suppose, for whatever reason, no one had looked for them at Adnan's apartment. Suppose Adnan's address was unknown. Misplaced, the personnel files burned up, lost in the bombing. It was quite possible.

Adnan might be totally unaware of his predicament. Someone should warn him. Someone should telephone him, except that the telephones were probably not working. Then someone should go to his apartment in person. Someone should take a taxi there. No, not a taxi, especially not from the Al-Rashid Hotel. The taxi driver could be a government agent. Most of them were.

Someone should do something.

Chris knew Sandoval was talking but did not hear a word he said. She was gazing at the pool through the coffee shop's picture window, and at the hotel parking lot behind the fenced hedgerow. The sun, just breaking through the morning overcast, shone dully off the retractable camera crane atop the white roof of the WCN newsvan.

"Ramon, give me the keys to the van."

"The keys?"

"Yes, the keys. Give them to me."

"What for?"

"I want to take a ride," she said. She held out her hand. "Give me the goddamn keys!"

Sandoval plucked a set of two keys from his shirt pocket and tossed them across the table to Chris. He looked at his wristwatch. "It's ten after one. The Info Ministry's questions should be here any second now, and the car is coming for you at two-thirty."

"I'll be back in time," she said.

Sandoval could not even begin to imagine where she was going, and something told him not to ask. He watched her sling her topcoat and purse over her shoulder, hurry from the coffee shop into the parking lot, and climb into the van. She drove away. Oddly enough, had he asked where she was going, she might have told him: Adnan Dulaimi's apartment. And the strangest thing was that although she had been there only once, she knew exactly how to get there.

Chris covered the five miles from the hotel to Zahra in eleven minutes. She drove up the hill and turned into the shortcut that overlooked Adnan's street. And she saw what Adnan had seen only a few minutes before, the white Mercedes sedan parked outside the apartment house. And the other Mercedes blocking the cul-de-sac.

Three men, civilians, were just then leaving the building. One man got into the driver's seat of the Mercedes and closed the door. The other two remained outside. After a brief conversation with the man in the car, the two sauntered back into the building. The car drove off, followed by the other Mercedes. From the newsvan, Chris watched both cars speed down the hill, careen onto Muhit Street and out of sight.

For all the rapid beating of her heart, and the fear loosening her stomach, she could not help smiling. Obviously, Adnan had not been in the apartment, nor had Nick. If they had been there, the two policemen would not have gone back inside. Obviously, they were there to wait for Adnan.

But where was he?

He was on his way back to Mansur, on 14th of July Street, weaving around the deep jagged potholes in the asphalt road surface. These were not bomb craters but damage from antiaircraft shell fragments. Baghdad had suffered as much destruction from its own AAA as from enemy bombs. The street near the rubbled wreck of the Baath Party headquarters was virtually impassable. Adnan detoured onto Ramadan Street and continued south. He thought he would be less conspicuous on the well-traveled thoroughfares.

He was held up for nearly twenty-five minutes at Jaafar Square, trapped in a half-mile-long line of cars snaking around the rubble of a bombed building that had collapsed into the middle of the street. But he was right, no one paid him any attention, not even the hard-looking army MPs who had been brought into the city to direct traffic at every major intersection.

Adnan knew that he and his "prisoner" could not remain long in Mansur. It was only a matter of time before the "safe house" was compromised. A half hour later, when he reached the house and parked the car in the garage next to Jamal's 1985 Chevrolet station wagon, Adnan had decided what to do. More accurately, what he and his prisoner would do.

My prisoner, he thought, as he entered the house. Which of us is the prisoner?

Nick was waiting tensely at the kitchen door. "How are you feeling?" Adnan asked, giving Nick no chance to reply as he strode past him through the kitchen to the front of the house. Nick followed Adnan into the foyer.

"Better," Nick said. "I feel better."

"That's good," Adnan said absently. He was rummaging through the foyer clothes closet, removing an overcoat from its hanger, and then a heavy cardigan sweater, and another coat. "Hold these," he said, piling the garments into Nick's arms. "In the garage, there's a station wagon. We'll load it with whatever food and water we can find and get out of here!"

"Get out to where?" Nick asked.

"Muthanna," Adnan said. "In the desert, six hundred kilometers to the south." He brushed past Nick, back to the kitchen. He opened the cupboard and, one by one, removed cans of food and boxes of crackers from the shelves and placed them on the counter. "The Allies are already in Iraq, in Muthanna. They'll roll down into Kuwait from there. We'll drive through the desert and meet them."

"What do you mean, meet them?"

"Meet them," Adnan repeated. "Turn ourselves over to them. Surrender. What the bloody hell do you think I mean?"

Nick said nothing. He knew he had heard correctly but did not really believe it. On the other hand, as he thought about it, it made some sense. Except that it all sounded just a little too easy.

Adnan resented Nick's silence, which he interpreted as judgmental. He owed no one an explanation, least of all this man. He said, "I'm running away, is that what you think? I'm deserting? Jumping ship, as you might call it? Is that what you think?"

"I don't think anything, Major."

"I'm saving my life, and probably yours, too," Adnan said, and quickly told Nick of Khalid Sadoon's betrayal and the Mukhabarat agents at the apartment. "Find something to put these in," he said, indicating the food items. "We'll take the station wagon because I'm sure they'll be looking for my car."

Just then, outside, an automobile braked to a screeching stop. Adnan whirled around to the window. A white van was in the driveway, the WCN newsvan. Chris was behind the wheel.

Adnan met her on the veranda. They stood facing each other for a long, awkward moment. "The chambermaid told me that the Mukhabarat are after you," she said. "I went to your apartment. They're there, waiting for you."

"Is that why you came here?" he said. "To tell me that?"

"To warn you, yes."

"To warn me," he repeated. "You're risking your own neck to warn me. Isn't that slightly out of character?"

"My good deed for the year."

"How did you know I was here?"

"I didn't," she said. Her eyes flashed past Adnan to Nick standing in the doorway. "You're looking a hell of a lot healthier," she said to him, and then continued to Adnan, "But I didn't know where else to look." She smiled wanly. "A good guess, eh?"

"The Mukhabarat will make the same guess," Adnan said. "But by the time they do it, the colonel and I will be in the middle of the desert, sharing lunch with American officers."

"You're dreaming!" Chris said. "You'll be picked up at the first checkpoint."

"We have no other option," Adnan said.

"No," Chris said after a moment. "No, I suppose not." They stood studying each other another moment. "I have to get back," she said. "We're doing that interview today."

"I thank you for coming here," Adnan said. "I won't forget it."

"Story of my life," she said. "I decide to be a heroine and gallop out here to warn you, and you already know about it. Well, good luck. You, too, Colonel," she said to Nick.

Nick nodded.

"Oh, Colonel, talk about stories," she said. "How about promising me an exclusive on yours? How you were shot down, and escaped, the whole incredible saga. I don't want to stray too much out of character, you know."

This, of course, was for Adnan's benefit, but what she wanted was for him to embrace her, to tell her she was not the bitch he believed her to be. She was not selling out her own people. Didn't coming here prove it?

"Good luck," she said again.

"Thank you," Adnan said.

Chris smiled once more, this time a little smile of encouragement. She turned and started for the van. The black letters on the van's door and on the side panel, W C N, seemed suddenly to spring out and hover in the air. Very large, very black. Everyone knew what WCN was, everyone with a television set watched WCN. The appearance of a WCN camera vehicle in a war zone would surprise no one. A crew of American television journalists filming a story, a familiar sight.

She grasped the door handle. She stood a moment, her back to them, then she turned and looked at the two men. Adnan and Nick watched her curiously. For all their physical dissimilarities—Adnan was taller and heavier-framed—they looked astonishingly alike. Yes, of course, cut from the same cloth, soldiers.

Yes, American television people on assignment and, what would lend even more credibility, accompanied by an Iraqi officer. She slapped her hand gently on the letter W on the van's side panel. "That lunch you're planning to have," she said. "How about me joining you?"

other side of the road, headed north. The blacked-out headlights of the Iraqi vehicles did not pick out the van, which was parked just far enough off the road to be invisible.

After dinner, Adnan checked Nick's wound. Clean as a whistle, he said, thanks to Dr. Khalid Sadoon, the man responsible for this predicament. But Adnan defended Khalid.

"He did what he believed was right," Adnan said.

"You almost sound as though you agree with him," Nick said.

"Whether I agree with him or not hardly makes any difference now, does it?" Adnan said, and abruptly returned to the front seat, where he turned on the radio. He listened briefly to Baghdad Radio, then switched it off. "The Allies have been repulsed," he said. "Their offensive has totally failed. The American criminals are pleading for mercy."

"The question," said Chris, "is *where* are these criminals? Where will we find them?"

"I have a better question," Nick said. "How do we find them without gasoline?"

"In the morning," Adnan said. "We'll deal with the gasoline problem in the morning." He knew precisely how he planned to deal with it. He would step into the road and wave down a truck and order the driver to give him three or four jerricans of gasoline. All army vehicles carried spare fuel. "Let's get some sleep," he said. "Tomorrow will be a hard day."

Understandably, no one slept well, if at all. Shortly before dawn, Adnan left the van. He relieved himself, then walked across the desert to the riverbank. He splashed water over his face. Even in the morning chill the water was warm and brackish and smelled of oil. He sat down on the sand, propped his back against a boulder, and lit a cigar. Just before leaving Mansur he had cleaned out the Chrysler's glove compartment and found two cigars. He had slipped them into his overcoat pocket and forgotten all about them until now. The cigar was old and brittle but smokable. He should offer the remaining one to Nick. He liked Nick. Well, more accurately, he respected him. Which was probably more than Nick might say about him, Adnan. A man turning himself over to the enemy hardly inspired respect.

Respect at that instant was the farthest thing from Nick's mind. Not five seconds before, after finally dozing off in a fitful sleep, he had been shocked into consciousness by a blinding blaze of light.

"Do not move!" The words were in Arabic, but their meaning was unmistakable.

Nick sat up. A flashlight was trained directly in his eyes. He shielded his eyes and glanced at Chris. She was staring at the flashlight and at the muzzle of an AK-47.

3

In the gray predawn light Adnan could clearly see the Republican Guard red triangle decaled on the jeep's front bumper. He had walked casually back from the river, enjoying the cigar and the crisp morning air and, luckily, approached the van from the front. Had he approached from the rear, he would not have immediately seen the jeep, which was parked almost hood to hood with the van. Nor would he have seen the soldier standing outside the open door of the van.

Adnan's first thought was to put the cigar down where he could retrieve it later. It was only half smoked, he hated to waste it. But he snuffed it out in the sand and unbuttoned his holster flap. He flicked the Tariq's safety off.

Now, concealed behind a low-rising dune and some scrub, he watched Chris, her hands over her head, emerge from the van. Behind her, hands also raised, came Nick, and then an officer holding a revolver. The officer, short and chunky, wore a paratrooper's field jacket and beret. He was too far away from Adnan to discern his rank.

In Arabic the officer ordered Chris and Nick to line up against the van. "English!" Chris screamed. "Speak English, you moron!"

The officer swung the flashlight over on Nick and re-peated the order in Arabic. Nick shook his head. "We don't speak Ara—"

The soldier at the van door slammed his rifle butt into Nick's stomach. Nick fell to his knees. Chris reached out to help him. The soldier laid the barrel of his AK-47 across Chris's chest, pushing her backward and pinning her to the side of the van. The officer nudged the flash-light under Nick's chin. Nick was still on his knees, gasp-ing for breath.

"Now, goddamn you, who are you?" the officer asked in Arabic.

Nick, not understanding, could only shake his head helplessly. The officer repeated the question. The voice sounded vaguely familiar to Adnan, who now was able to make out the officer's profile, the high forehead and long chin, and his rank insignia, the eagle and single silver star of a lieutenant colonel.

It was Gamal Othman.

"Gamal!" Adnan shouted. He scrambled to his feet and ran toward the van. "Gamal, these are American journalists!"

Gamal spun around, revolver on Adnan. For a mo-ment he did not recognize Adnan. Then his whole face wrinkled in disbelief. "Dulaimi! What the hell—"

"It's all right, Gamal," Adnan said. He pushed Gamal's gun hand gently aside. "They're in my charge. We're on a special mission. We ran out of gas." He managed a little smile of sarcasm. "I forgot my ration stamps. So if you have a few extra gallons, I'll let you fill us up." He gestured to the soldier, a burly middle-aged man with a walrus mustache and the four stripes of a *rais urafa,* master sergeant. "Sergeant, see what you can do for me."

The sergeant glanced uncertainly at Gamal, who him-self was momentarily indecisive but then nodded a curt approval. The sergeant shouldered the AK-47 and walked back toward the jeep. Gamal said to Adnan, "All right, now what is this special mission of yours?"

"All I know is that I'm to provide safe passage for

these people to the COG, Kuwait," Adnan said. "I'm not only their nursemaid, I'm their translator. They don't speak a bloody word of Arabic. And by the way, Gamal, what are *you* doing in these parts?"

Gamal said nothing for a moment. He still gripped the revolver, but loosely now. His eyes were fixed on Nick, who was on his feet, standing unsteadily beside Chris. Gamal's eyes remained on Nick as he said to Adnan, "I'm carrying some eyes-only dispatches to Baghdad. We're getting the shit kicked out of us, if you didn't know. You!" he said to Nick in the same breath, and pointed the revolver at him. "Let me see your papers!"

"He wants to see your papers," Adnan explained to Nick, and said to Gamal, "*I* have their papers! Dammit, Gamal, you're making me look like an idiot!"

Gamal's attention was still focused on Nick. "Those clothes don't fit this man too well. Adnan, what the hell is going on here?"

Adnan said, "For God's sake, how would I know why his clothes don't fit?" He glanced at the jeep, where the sergeant was unstrapping a jerrican from the rear bumper bracket. "Come on, sergeant, get with it!" he shouted.

"I want to see the papers, Adnan," Gamal said. "I want to see them right now."

"They're in my briefcase," Adnan said. He moved toward the van.

"Stay where you are," Gamal said. He cocked the revolver. The gun was aimed at Adnan's heart. "We'll get the briefcase for you." He turned toward the jeep to call to the sergeant. It gave Nick just enough time to clasp his hands together like an anvil and smash them down on Gamal's wrist. The revolver flew from Gamal's grasp and fell to the ground. Gamal clubbed Nick across the throat with the flat of his elbow and dove for the gun. He retrieved it in the same instant Adnan drew his own pistol from its holster. Gamal, from a half crouch, gripped the revolver in both hands and leveled it at Adnan. Adnan fired the Tariq point-blank into the center of Gamal's chest. As Gamal toppled backward into the van, Adnan whirled to the sergeant, who had tossed the jerrican away and reached for his AK-47.

"Don't touch it!" Adnan shouted. It was too late. The sergeant had already aimed the rifle and fired. The bullet smashed into the van's hood. The weapon had been on single-fire. Before the sergeant could flip it to automatic and correct his aim, Adnan shot him. Two rounds. Both 9mm slugs hit the sergeant squarely in the mouth. His face disintegrated into a pulpy mass of blood and shredded bone.

Now for a long moment all was silent. Adnan stared at Gamal's body, propped in a half-sitting position against the van's right rear wheel. His head was slumped forward, the long chin rested inertly on his chest. The only sign of the bullet's entry was a tiny puncture in the nylon fabric of the field jacket just above the left breast pocket.

"He gave you no choice," Nick said.

Adnan looked at Chris. Her eyes were riveted on Gamal's body, her hand clamped over her mouth as though to stifle a scream. "This should make an interesting addition to your story," Adnan said to her.

She lowered her hand. "You knew him, didn't you?"

"Yes, I knew him." Adnan turned to Gamal again and in his mind said to Gamal, I had to do it.

Yes, he imagined Gamal replying, because you are crazy.

I must be crazy, Adnan agreed. I have to be crazy. And as this conversation played through his mind, he was also thinking that at any instant a vehicle might appear on the road. There was enough daylight now for the van to be visible, and the jeep, and the bodies lying on the sand near the jeep.

Traitor! he heard Gamal saying.

The war is over, Adnan told him. You said it yourself: we're getting the shit kicked out of us, you said.

So you run, eh?

No, Gamal, you don't understand. I had no choice.

All I understand, Adnan, is that you are a coward. A

cowardly piece of scum! That's what you are, Adnan, a coward!

"Major!" It was Nick. He was peering glumly down at the Toyota's radiator grille. The four horizontal chrome strips looked as though twisted apart by a crowbar. The AK-47 round had torn into the grille and gouged a fist-sized hole in the honeycomb construction of the radiator. A steady stream of water poured down onto the sand.

Nick and Adnan exchanged knowing glances: The van would not be going anywhere. Just then, from somewhere down the road came the sound of automobile engines. A vehicle appeared in the distance, then another, and a third. The three were approaching from the south, on the opposite side of the road, and now in daylight, moving fast. The vehicles sped past, two army Land-Rovers and a brand-new lime-green Jaguar sedan. The Jag and one of the Land-Rovers pulled trailers packed with furniture and large appliances. They were quickly out of sight. No one had paid the slightest attention to the van and the jeep on the roadside.

"From Kuwait," Chris said.

"The spoils of victory," Adnan said wryly. He rapped his knuckles on the jeep's front fender. "Let's get going."

Five minutes later, with drinking water from the van packed into the jeep—and Gamal Othman's bona-fide travel orders in Adnan's pocket—they were on their way. Adnan, at the wheel, glanced back at the van as he drove past. The water from the punctured radiator had formed a little rivulet that had flowed down to the indentations of the jeep's tire tracks, where it pooled and merged with the blood of the dead sergeant.

Traffic in the opposite direction, heading north, grew heavier. From army eighteen-wheelers to passenger cars bearing Kuwaiti license plates, every vehicle was crammed with civilian goods. TVs, VCRs, stoves and refrigerators, washing machines, personal computers, even brand-new women's dresses still on their store racks. Even the mannequins.

No one seemed to take any unusual notice of the jeep driven by the Republican Guard major, nor of the major's two civilian passengers. To be sure, the blonde woman seated beside the driver aroused some occasional interest, but more from envy than suspicion.

From Babylon, straight through to An Najaf, they did not encounter a single roadblock or checkpoint. The only interference came from Allied airplanes. Time and again, American A-10s or British Tornados screamed down out of the overcast to attack vehicles in convoy. The roadside was littered with burned-out trucks and cars. For all that, the jeep was probably the safest place to be. No pilot would waste a missile on a lone jeep.

Shortly before noon, when An Najaf's minarets rose into view, it was obvious there would be no more checkpoints. The Iraqi army was fleeing north. No one gave a damn who went south. Even if an alert for Adnan's arrest had been issued—or if Chris and the missing newsvan were the object of a search—it was unlikely anyone outside Baghdad knew of it. Moreover, everyone was too preoccupied saving his own skin. Not to mention escaping with the loot from Kuwait.

The streets of An Najaf were clogged with military traffic. Adnan brazenly asked an MP for directions to Ash Shabicha, an oasis town 150 miles into the desert, fifty miles from the Saudi border. The MP obligingly penciled a rough map outlining a route of side streets and alleys to bypass the city and take them onto the desert road. The MP threw Adnan a crisp salute and wished him good luck.

Adnan followed the MP's map into the southern outskirts of An Najaf, maneuvering through narrow dirt streets and alleys, and soon turned onto the Shabicha "highway," a desolate, dust-swirled, partially surfaced two-lane road. They passed a cluster of shabby mud and stone dwellings, including a small coffee house–restaurant. Chris suggested they stop for some food, real food.

Confronted by a Republican Guard officer, the restaurant's grandmotherly proprietor agreed to open the kitchen. A U.S. ten-dollar bill donated by Chris helped convince her. The woman prepared a meal of greasy roast lamb and stale pita bread, which they took with them and devoured in the jeep. They stopped on the roadside to discard the remains and wash their hands. Nick said he thought it was the finest lunch he'd ever eaten, especially at sixty miles per hour.

Chris said, "What I'd really like is a cold bottle of beer, Anchor Steam. Have you ever had Anchor Steam? I think it's made only in San Francisco."

"I've had Anchor Steam," Nick said. "Frankly, I prefer Kirin. Pearl Harbor notwithstanding," he added dryly.

"When we're out of this, I'll send you case of Kirin," Chris said. "No, champagne, a case of champagne. Dom Perignon, how's that?"

"I'll take Kristal instead," Nick said.

"Kristal it is," Chris said.

"Champagne sound okay to you, Major?" Nick said to Adnan. "We deserve it, after all that Evian we've been drinking, wouldn't you say?"

Adnan said, "You weren't so contemptuous about the Evian a few hours ago. You were damned glad to have water—and damned glad to be alive to drink it!"

The unexpected anger in Adnan's voice startled everyone, including Adnan himself. Chris said to him, "Nick was only joking."

"Yes, I know," said Adnan. He turned abruptly and walked back to the jeep.

Nick realized the outburst was not anger, it was resentment. And not about champagne or bottled water. Nick could almost read Adnan's mind. Not only was Adnan a deserter, he had been forced to kill two of his own people, and would soon be a POW. And all of it the result of his impulsive—and, undoubtedly to him, foolish—decision to help an enemy. His military career was finished, for no matter what new government assumed power in Iraq, Adnan's "crime" was unlikely to be forgiven or forgotten. He had made himself a pariah. He had good cause for resentment.

A pariah, Nick thought. They had something in common, then, he and Adnan. Nick, too, had self-destructed a military career. Birds of a feather.

In the meantime, he thought, Chris Campbell would make out like a bandit, spinning out the "incredible saga" on her television show, earning a potful of money. Probably even sell the story to Hollywood. But good luck to her, she had earned it.

". . . he feels lousy enough about himself as it is," she was saying to Nick now. "He doesn't need our wisecracks. He needs our help."

"Our help," Nick repeated. "All right, so when we get to American lines, what do you plan to do for him?"

"I'll pull some strings, believe me. But first, we have to keep him out of a POW camp. You can help with that, with the military."

"I'll do what I can," Nick said. He moved to leave. Chris stopped him.

"Doing what you can isn't good enough, Colonel. You *owe* that man! He saved your lousy life! You better damn well see to it that they don't make him a POW! You do it, Harmon, even if you have to go all the way to Schwarzkopf!"

She brushed past him and returned to the jeep. She got into the front passenger seat. Adnan sat in the back. Nick was to drive the next leg. He gazed at Chris a moment, thinking that even in her grease-stained polo coat and torn-at-the-knee gray flannel slacks, her face without makeup and hair all askew, Chris Campbell was a damn good-looking woman. But iron-assed, all right, and too much like him: Do it my way, or else.

"Okay, I'll do it," Nick said aloud, to himself. "I'll do it," he said again. "I'll go all the way to Schwarzkopf."

For the next forty minutes, he concentrated on that, on pulling strings for Adnan. Yes, if necessary, all the way to Schwarzkopf. But Adnan might automatically receive VIP treatment. The act of bringing two Americans out of Iraq spoke for itself. Gene Gordon could be helpful, too. No, scratch Gordon. Nick was still on the general's shit list. He could still hear Gordon's craggy voice labeling him a war lover.

A few other vehicles were on the road, mostly military, all going in the opposite direction. One, a Land-Rover crammed with rifle-toting soldiers, blinked its headlights at the oncoming jeep. As the Land-Rover passed, several soldiers waved. Nick and Chris waved back. Adnan stared rigidly, almost defiantly, straight ahead.

Twenty minutes later, after not a single vehicle had appeared in either direction, Adnan leaned over the front seat to Nick. "Have you noticed how deserted the road is? That means it's been cut. The road is cut off. Your forward units must be closer than we thought."

Nick nodded absently, his mind elsewhere. He had just realized that this was the first time he had driven a jeep in the twenty-two years since Chu-Bai. No, not "just" realized it. He had known it the moment he sat behind the wheel but forced it out of his memory.

"Pull off the road!"

It was Adnan. He reached over Nick's shoulder and jerked the steering wheel to the right. Nick swerved onto the crest of a gentle rise and braked to a stop in a cloud of dirt and pebbles. Adnan pointed into the distance. Miles away, behind the blowing sand that obscured the horizon like a semitransparent wall, individual puffs of grubby dust rose up out of the desert floor. Adnan pulled a pair of binoculars from the door well and vaulted out of the jeep.

"Tanks!" Adnan said. He had climbed up on the jeep's front bumper and was scanning the area with the binoculars. There were dozens of the churning dust clouds. They looked like little brown beetles crawling through the scrub and rocks of the desert. "They're American," Adnan said. "Abramses, I think." He handed the binoculars to Nick.

"They're firing!" Nick said. He swung the binoculars to the right. A flash of orange light brightened the afternoon horizon, then another, and another. He returned the binoculars to Adnan. "Whatever they're firing at, they're hitting."

"Iraqi armor is what they're hitting," Adnan said. He lowered the glasses and studied the American tanks with his naked eye, then through the glasses again. He turned slightly and trained the binoculars on the road. "I would guess that not twenty miles from here, there are more Allied armored units." He lowered the binoculars once more. "They'll be on this road and moving fast. It might be safer to wait right here for them."

He broke off in mid-sentence. He had glimpsed movement on the road, a trail of dust. He clamped the binoculars to his eyes again. Far in the distance a vehicle materialized out of the dust. After a moment he had a clear view of it.

"An AML," he said to Nick, handing him the glasses. "An armored car."

"Iraqi?" Chris asked. She had been watching it all unfold before her eyes like some panoramic motion picture. If only she had a camera. My kingdom for a camera, she thought.

"Yes, Iraqi," said Adnan. "And it carries a thirty-millimeter cannon."

Nick, watching through the binoculars, said, "Jesus Christ . . . !" The road dust flowing out from behind the AML had all at once become a burst of red and orange light that billowed into a huge cloud of thick black smoke. Flames erupted from the smoke, which cleared away enough to reveal the AML lying on its side, burning.

A dark, silent speck emerged from the smoke, growing larger in the air as it approached and, with the raspy whir of its rotor blades, louder. It resembled some prehistoric flying insect, a gigantic praying mantis. It was the helicopter that had attacked the AML, an Apache, and very plainly lining up on the red-triangle-marked jeep.

"Hey!" Chris screamed at the oncoming chopper. "Hey, we're Americans! Hey!" She began waving her

arms and then removed her coat and waved it like a
flag. The Apache kept coming, straight in at them.

"Run!" Nick shouted at her. "Both of you, get away
from the jeep! Run!"

Nick did not know what impelled him to scramble
into the jeep, turn the vehicle completely around, and
race off. North, back toward Iraq. He knew only that
the missile or rocket that hit the jeep would also deci-
mate anything or anybody within fifty feet. The moving
jeep might tempt the Apache gunner to forgo the missile for an easy cannon shot, an optical. Nick wanted to
put at least three hundred yards between the jeep and
Chris and Adnan on the roadside. Then all he needed
was time enough, a few seconds, to dive out before the
Apache gunner fired.

It worked out almost exactly that way, except that the
Apache gunner was a few seconds ahead of Nick. He
pumped four cannon rounds at the jeep before Nick
could get out. The first two rounds plowed up the road
surface just behind the jeep, but the third and fourth hit
the jeep. The third virtually disintegrated the vehicle,
and Nick with it. The fourth cannon shot actually struck
Nick, but he was already dead.

Two particular thoughts dominated Nick's brain in
the milliseconds before his death. One was the irony of
being killed by his own people, and it could not be
called "friendly fire" because the Apache crew believed
they were gunning down an enemy. The other, more
prominent thought was of Elaine, and it too was tinged
with irony. Now she would never know he had come to
realize that he could place his trust in a woman, in her,
and that he acknowledged his need for her, and that he
totally, selflessly, and honestly loved her.

There was a third thought of some considerable in-
tensity that he managed to suppress. This third thought
was almost religious, which was why he was able to suppress it. He had no intention of wasting his final thinking moments wallowing in religion, which did not alter
the fact that what was happening was Chu-Bai all over
again. The mirror image of Chu-Bai. In this new Chu-

Bai, Nick had been given the opportunity to redeem himself, and he did.

But how had it all happened? The exquisite similarity of circumstances. It seemed almost planned, and that, of course, was what perplexed him. Who or what could have planned it?

He pondered the answer and at the same time realized that he had not suppressed the thought after all. Even more troubling, he knew he would never find the answer. There was not enough time.

The young captain's eyes behind the granny glasses were wide with skepticism. He had received the Apache pilot's radioed report and dispatched a staff sergeant and three troopers to investigate. The staff sergeant's name was Arnold Fetzer. He was twenty-eight years old, serving his second six-year hitch with the 3rd Armored Cav, and was considered Bravo Company's most reliable noncom.

Fetzer drove his humvee across the desert and onto the road, and then up to the ridge where the Apache, rotors idling, was parked. After a three-minute conversation with the Apache crew, Fetzer radioed back to the captain.

"Sir, I think you better come up here and see this for yourself," he said. "You're gonna find it hard to believe, that's for goddamn sure."

So the captain saw for himself, and did indeed find it hard to believe. The chopper had splashed an enemy vehicle, killing the driver. Two other people involved in the incident, an Iraqi army officer and a woman, were uninjured. The woman was an American television celebrity, Christine Campbell. Her story of how she got here was in itself hard to believe, but grew really bizarre with her insistence that the dead jeep driver was an American pilot.

But the young captain, whose name was William Church, Jr., and who was a 1988 West Point graduate, sensed that the story was true. Especially the part about the dead American sacrificing his life to save the others, which the Apache pilot had substantiated. His gunner had already locked a Hellfire onto the jeep. If the vehicle had not suddenly raced off, the missile would have been launched and almost surely killed all three people.

But now Captain Church had to deal with another strange twist, the Iraqi major's request to be released, to be allowed to return to his own lines. The Iraqi, according to Miss Campbell, had risked his own neck to help the American pilot. He deserved a fair shake, she said. What Miss Campbell did not realize was that Captain Church required no sales pitch; he was not at all anxious to be burdened with a POW. Moreover, he knew that POW stockades and enclosures throughout the KTO were bulging with Iraqi prisoners and deserters. The unofficial word had gone out to encourage capitulating Iraqis to simply surrender their weapons and go home.

For Captain Church, then, the decision was not difficult. How the Iraqi major got back to his own lines was not Church's problem. Before he left, the Iraqi asked to speak privately with Chris Campbell. They went off behind Church's humvee to talk.

From here the still smoldering shell of the jeep was clearly visible, and the black plastic body bag. Adnan leaned against the side of the humvee and lit a cigar. The cigar was old; Chris could hear the leaves crackle under Adnan's fingers. "My last one," he said. "I found it in my coat pocket. All right, you asked me why I decided to return—" he broke off. She seemed not to be listening.

She was staring at the body bag, wondering how much remained of Nick and what he looked like. No different, surely, from the corpses at Amiriyah. All burned bodies looked alike.

Now she faced Adnan again. He said, "I overheard the sergeant saying that at eight P.M. today, in four hours, a cease-fire goes into effect. President Bush has ordered Allied forces to halt their advance immediately. This means the Allies will not go to Baghdad. It means Saddam remains in power."

"That's ridiculous!" Chris waved her arm around at

the three humvees and the helicopter. "They're halfway to Baghdad, why would they stop?"

"But they are stopping. And that's why I'm going back."

"That's why you *shouldn't!*"

Adnan shook his head, no. "Whatever reason Bush—or perhaps it is Schwarzkopf—whatever their reason for not finishing Saddam off, I'm sure they intend to provide massive support for anyone opposing him. Munitions, food, propaganda. Yes, this is precisely why they ordered the offensive stopped: to allow the Iraqis themselves to take care of Saddam. Well, at least to let us *try* to do it on our own. Don't you see, Chris? I can help my country more by being there, by not running away."

Chris said nothing for a moment. She was gazing past Adnan's shoulder at the sky. It was getting dark, although still early, not quite four. The wind was blowing in from the south, from the burning Kuwaiti oil fields. The sky was streaked black from the smoke. Not of course as black as in Kuwait, where they said the smoke was so thick it blotted out the sun. Darkness at noon, they said.

She wanted to ask him not to go back, to stay with her. Stay with me. Come live with me, and be my love. Which was crazy and never could work. Never should. She was crazy to even consider it.

"What will you do?" she asked.

"I haven't the slightest idea." He smiled ruefully. "I don't even know *how* I can get back."

"Or if," she said.

"Or if," he agreed.

"Well, that's sounds like a great start," she said. For a moment now they regarded each other silently. "Good luck," she said, and extended her hand.

He pulled her to him. They held each other very close. Finally, gently, he pushed her away. He brushed the tips of his fingers against her cheek, turned, and walked away.

Chris watched as he got into the passenger side of a humvee and an enlisted man came around to the

driver's side. The humvee drove off, north. Captain
Church got into his humvee. He opened the passenger
door for Chris.

"All set?" he asked.

"All set," she said. "Where are they taking the
Iraqi?"

"Oh, up the road a piece," Church said. "They'll drop
him off five or ten miles from here. Then he's on his
own. I had a chance to talk with him. Strangest goddamn thing, I never once thought about him as an enemy."

Neither did I, Chris thought, but did not say it. She
got into the humvee beside Church. He started the engine. "Yeah, he seemed like a nice guy, the Iraqi,"
Church went on. "He said something real interesting.
'Don't be surprised if someday you have to come back,'
he said. I asked him what he meant. 'To finish the job,'
he said."

To finish the job, Chris thought, and said, "My God,
isn't it finished?"

"The guys who give the orders say it is," Church said.
He started to say something else, then thought better of
it. He put the car into gear and started off. "The battalion's set up a command post on an airbase near
Shabicha. I'll drop you there."

Chris had half twisted around to see through the
humvee's rear window. Two soldiers were lugging the
plastic body bag over to Sergeant Fetzer's humvee. They
placed the bag on the floor of the rear seat, got in with
it, and closed the door. The humvee drove away, and at
the same time the Apache began lifting off.

The smoke from the burning jeep still drifted upward.
Chris gazed at the smoke until it became only a wispy
black line in the sky, and then it was out of sight.

Flung wide across miles of sea, the task force moves across its face with ponderous eagerness; and from each ship, above the antennas and signal lines, streams the red-and-white-striped ensign of impending battle. *The landing has begun....*

THE MED

DAVID POYER

"Update *The Caine Mutiny* and *Away All Boats*, move the action to the Mediterranean, throw in some Arab terrorists with American hostages, and you've got *The Med*...a naval thriller at full speed!"   —*St. Louis Post-Dispatch*

"I LOVED IT!"
            —Stephen Coonts, author of *Flight of the Intruder*